Everyman, I will go with thee,
and be thy guide

Anthony Trollope

HE KNEW
HE WAS RIGHT

Edited by
DAVID SKILTON
Professor and Head of School of English Studies,
Journalism & Philosophy
University of Wales, Cardiff

EVERYMAN
J. M. DENT · LONDON
CHARLES E. TUTTLE
RUTLAND, VERMONT

Chronology, introduction, textual editing and endmatter
© J.M. Dent 1993

This edition first published in Everyman by J.M. Dent 1993

Printed in Great Britain by
The Guernsey Press Co. Ltd
Guernsey, C.I.

for
J.M. Dent Ltd
Orion Publishing Group
Orion House
5 Upper St Martin's Lane, London, WC2H 9EA

and
Charles E. Tuttle Co. Inc.
28 South Main Street, Rutland, Vermont,
05701 USA

British Library-Cataloguing-in-Publication Data
is available upon request.

ISBN 0 460 87237 0

CONTENTS

NOTE ON THE AUTHOR AND EDITOR

Born in London in 1817, the fourth surviving child of a failing barrister with a difficult personality and grandiose expectations, Anthony Trollope spent a miserable childhood and youth. Because of his poverty he felt himself an outcast at Harrow and Winchester, where he was a scholastic failure. After his father went bankrupt, his mother supported the family by her writing. Through a family contact, Anthony was found a clerkship in the Post Office, and he was posted to Ireland, where he became a reliable and energetic public servant. He married Rose Heseltine in 1844. Until retiring in 1867 he combined full-time Post Office work, reorganising large parts of the postal service of Great Britain, Ireland and the West Indies, with a huge literary output, and with life in society and on the hunting field. He published his first novel in 1847, but had only just become well-known on his return to London in 1859. He was immensely popular in the 1860s, and made new efforts after 1870 to retain his market position. When he died in 1882 he had written nine volumes of stories and sketches, nine works of non-fiction and forty-seven novels, including two six-volume cycles, the *Chronicles of Barsetshire* and the Palliser novels. He journeyed extensively in Europe, North America, Australia, New Zealand and South Africa, writing fiction and factual books about his travels. His autobiography was published posthumously in 1883.

DAVID SKILTON was educated at King's College, Cambridge and the University of Copenhagen. After holding posts at the Universities of Stockholm and Glasgow and at Lampeter, he is now Professor of English at Cardiff, and Head of the School of English Studies, Communication and Philosophy there. His books include *Anthony Trollope and His Contemporaries* (Longman, 1972), *Defoe to the Victorians* (Penguin, 1985), *The Early and Mid-Victorian Novel* (Routledge, 1993) and editions of numerous Victorian novels.

CHRONOLOGY OF TROLLOPE'S LIFE

Year	Age	Life
1815		Born at Keppel St, Russell Square, London, on Monday 24 April
1817	2	
1818	3	
1819	4	
1820	5	
1821	6	
1823	8	Attends Harrow as a day boy until 1825
1825	10	Attends private school at Sunbury, Middlesex, until 1827
1827	12	Attends Winchester until 1830
1829	14	
1830	15	Returns to Harrow until 1834
1832	17	
1833	18	
1834	19	Family flees creditors to Belgium Enters General Post Office as a clerk
1837	22	
1838	23	
1840	25	Suffers a serious illness
1841	26	Appointed surveyor's clerk in the Central District of Ireland
1842	27	
1843	28	Starts to write *The Macdermots of Ballycloran* (pub. 1847)
1844	29	Marries Rose Heseltine (1821–1917)
1846	31	

CHRONOLOGY OF HIS TIMES

Year	Literary Context	Historical Events
1815	*Emma* [Austen]	Battle of Waterloo
1817	*Biographia Literaria* [Coleridge]	
1818	*The Heart of Midlothian* [Scott]	
	Frankenstein [M. Shelley]	
1819		Peterloo massacre
1820	*Prometheus Unbound* [P. Shelley]	Death of George III
1821	*Defence of Poetry* [P. Shelley]	
1823		
1825		
1827		
1829		Catholic Emancipation Act passed
1830	*Poems, Chiefly Lyrical* [Tennyson]	
	Rural Rides [Cobbett]	
1832		Reform Act passed
1833		Establishment of Oxford Movement
1834		
1837	*Pickwick Papers* [Dickens]	Accession to throne of Victoria
1838	*Sartor Resartus* [Carlyle]	Emergence of Chartism
	Nicholas Nickleby [Dickens]	
1840	*The Old Curiosity Shop* [Dickens]	Introduction of the Penny Post
1841		Peel becomes Prime Minister
1842	*Poems in Two Volumes* [Tennyson]	Collapse of Chartist movement
1843	*Martin Chuzzlewit* [Dickens]	Peel sends troops to Ireland
1844	*Poems* [Barrett]	O'Connell tried for conspiracy
1846		Ireland devastated by famine
		Peel resigns after corn-law repeal

Year	Age	Life
1847	32	
1848	33	*The Kellys and the O'Kellys*
1850	35	*La Vendée*
1851	36	Tours of duty reorganizing the posts in southwest England and Wales until 1852
1852	37	
1855	40	*The Warden*; writes *The New Zealander* (pub. 1872)
1857	42	*Barchester Towers*; *The Three Clerks*
1858	43	Postal mission to Suez; *Doctor Thorne* Reorganizes postal routes in the West Indies
1859	44	*The Bertrams*; becomes Surveyor of the Eastern District of England
1860	45	*Framley Parsonage* April 1860–April 1861; *Castle Richmond*
1861	46	*Orley Farm* March 1861–October 1862; *Brown, Jones and Robinson* August 1861–March 1862; travels to USA
1862	47	*The Small House at Allington* September 1862–April 1864; *North America*
1863	48	*Rachel Ray*
1864	49	*Can You Forgive Her?* January 1864–August 1865
1865	50	*Miss Mackenzie*; *The Belton Estate* May 1865–January 1866
1866	51	*The Claverings* February 1866–May 1867 *Nina Balatka* July 1866–January 1867 *The Last Chronicle of Barset* December 1866–July 1867
1867	52	*Phineas Finn* October 1867–May 1869 *Linda Tressel* October 1867–May 1868 Edits *St Paul's Magazine* until 1870; resigns from Post Office
1868	53	*He Knew He Was Right* October 1868–May 1869 Postal mission to USA
1869	54	*The Vicar of Bullhampton* July 1869–May 1870
1870	55	*Ralph the Heir* January 1870–July 1871 *Sir Harry Hotspur of Humblethwaite* May–Dec 1870
1871	56	*The Eustace Diamonds* July 1871–February 1873 Travels to Australia and New Zealand, May 1871–December 1872

Year	Literary Context	Historical Events
1847	*Vanity Fair* [Thackeray]	
1848	*Wuthering Heights* [E. Bronte]	Revolution sweeps Europe
	History of England [Macaulay]	
	Communist Manifesto [Marx/ Engels]	
1850	*In Memoriam* [Tennyson]	
1851		Opening of Great Exhibition
1852	*The History of Henry Esmond* [Thackeray]	
1855	*Little Dorrit* [Dickens]	Civil Service exams introduced
1857	*Scenes of Clerical Life* [Eliot]	
1858		
1859	*Adam Bede* [Eliot]	
	The Origin of Species [Darwin]	
1860	*Great Expectations* [Dickens]	
	The Mill on the Floss [Eliot]	
1861	*Silas Marner* [Eliot]	American Civil War begins
1862	*Utilitarianism* [Mill]	Unification of Italy
1863	Thackeray dies	
1864	*Dramatis Personae* [Browning]	
1865		American Civil War ends
1866	*Poems and Ballads* [Swinburne]	Hyde Park riot
	Felix Holt, The Radical [Eliot]	
1867	*The English Constitution* [Bagehot]	Second Reform Act passed
	Das Kapital [Marx]	
1868	*The Moonstone* [Collins]	
	The Ring and the Book [Browning]	
1869	*Culture and Anarchy* [Arnold]	
	The Subjection of Women [Mill]	
1870	Dickens dies	Franco-Prussian War
	Poems [D. G. Rossetti]	Start of Irish Home Rule movement
		Married Women's Property Act
1871	*The Descent of Man* [Darwin]	

Year	Age	Life
1872	57	*The Golden Lion of Granpere* January–August
1873	58	*Lady Anna* April 1873–April 1874; *Phineas Redux* July 1873–January 1874; *Australia and New Zealand*; *Harry Heathcote*
1874	59	*The Way We Live Now* February 1874–September 1875
1875	60	*The Prime Minister* November 1875–June 1876 Travels to Australia and USA, March–October Starts *An Autobiography* (compl. 1876, pub. 1883)
1876	61	*The American Senator* May 1876–July 1877
1877	62	*Is He Popenjoy?* October 1877–July 1878 Travels to South Africa
1878	63	*John Caldigate* April 1878–June 1879 *An Eye for an Eye* August 1878–June 1879; *South Africa*
1879	64	*Cousin Henry* March–May *The Duke's Children* October 1879–July 1880 *Thackeray*
1880	65	*Dr Wortle's School* May–December
1881	66	*Ayala's Angel*; *The Fixed Period* October 1881–March 1882 *Marion Fay* December 1881–June 1882
1882	67	*Kept in the Dark* May–December *Mr Scarborough's Family* May 1882–June 1883 *The Landleaguers* November 1882–October 1883 Dies 6 December, at Welbeck Street, Cavendish Square, London
1883		*An Autobiogaphy*
1884		*An Old Man's Love*

Year	Literary Context	Historical Events
1872	*Middlemarch* [Eliot]	
1873		
1874	*Far From the Madding Crowd* [Hardy]	Irish Home Rule movement grows
1875		
1876	*Daniel Deronda* [Eliot]	Victoria made Empress of India
1877		
1878	*Poems and Ballads: second series* [Swinburne]	Congress of Berlin
1879	*Daisy Miller* [James]	Irish National Land League formed
1880	Eliot dies	Charles Parnell tried for conspiracy
1881	*Portrait of a Lady* [James] *Washington Square* [James]	Land League outlawed
1882		
1883		
1884		Third Reform Act passed

INTRODUCTION

After the passing of well over a century, much of Trollope's fiction still looks as though it belongs to the modern world. In part this is because of some obvious features which make the world it presents a recognisably modern place. Trollope's characters travel on the London Underground, for example. (The firm of Civil Engineers which is prominent in *The Claverings* seems to be engaged in designing what is now the Metropolitan Line of London's Underground.) Moreover Trollope's are among the first fictional characters to live lives controlled by rapid and efficient communications. Like their author, they are tireless train travellers in the British Isles and abroad, they expect and exploit the penny post, and as soon as the telegraph is available to supplement the postal service, they, again like their author, are using it for inland and international messages.

Victorian novelists in general were fascinated by new things around them, yet most, like Dickens and Thackeray, preferred to set their novels in the past, and often in the period of their childhood or youth. For her part George Eliot only ventured into the contemporary world in her last novel, *Daniel Deronda* (1876). In contrast Trollope's novels seemed to their contemporary readers as up-to-the-minute as the latest topical cartoon in *Punch*. Only those novelists who specialised in creating sensation by stories of crime and passion, made more sensational by their unexotic setting – writers like Wilkie Collins and Mary E. Braddon – had as close a relation as Trollope's with the world as it was when they were actually writing. As one critic remarked of the more lurid genre of fiction produced by some of Trollope's contemporaries, 'Proximity is . . . one great element of sensation.'[1] It is also one great element in the work of the leading proponent of what came to be called 'realistic' fiction – Anthony Trollope.

Of all Trollope's major novels, none is more firmly placed in a modern setting than *He Knew He Was Right*, with contemporary details of London and Italy in particular lovingly presented. Louis

Trevelyan is one of the first fictional characters to employ a private detective, and he is the first to be seen drinking Chianti – then a new wine. But of course *He Knew He Was Right* is modern in a more important sense than this. Marital breakdown is a new and still relatively shocking theme in the period, when novels more commonly seek to plot the various paths into and not out of marriage. The Divorce Court had been set up under Sir Creswell Creswell a decade before, and 'respectable' readers were by now used to reading the details of marital strife in the daily newspapers. Yet on the whole they did not expect to read them in novels apparently depicting their own way of life. These recognisably modern qualities are reinforced by the impression we gain that for many of Trollope's characters – and for the narrators of his novels too – the world does not just consist of their own parish, county or country, but includes half of Europe, North America and Australia too. The need for the reader of Trollope to adjust to a world without aeroplanes is less demanding than the adaptation of responses required to appreciate Jane Austen's novels, with their prescribed geographical and social limits, restricted as they are to a few families in a few parishes. It comes as no surprise that a book like *He Knew He Was Right* is the fiction of a writer with an outgoing and practical relationship with the world.

Given that Trollope was a novelist, it is easy to see how his life equipped him to write this rather than another kind of fiction. At the time when he wrote *He Knew He Was Right* he had recently taken early retirement from a Civil Service appointment in the Post Office in order to devote himself full-time to his literary labours. (When we learn in Chapter Eight that Miss Stanbury will not trust the new-fangled pillar-boxes, we remember that Trollope himself first proposed the introduction of the pillar-box in this country, and we do well to recognise the close attention he pays to the transit of mail, and hence of information, in most of his novels.) Before his retirement he had not let his writing and his public service interfere with each other. On the contrary, for years he maintained an extraordinarily demanding schedule of work, rising at five to write for three hours before breakfast, going up to Town for a day's work at the General Post Office, hunting three afternoons a week in the season, and habitually playing whist until late at his club. When his routine was broken, as it frequently was, by travel, he continued to write in trains, ships and hotels. By the end of his prodigiously productive life he had written forty-seven novels, five collections of tales, four travel books, four literary and biographical works, an autobiography, and sufficient journalistic sketches and articles to fill several volumes. Meanwhile his Post Office duties had been of the most practical kind, surveying inland postal deliveries, personally tracing out the routes of postmen over major parts of Ireland, south-west England, south Wales, and the Scottish Lowlands, and establishing steamer routes for the posts in the West Indies, negotiating the terms of transit of the Indian mails through Egypt on the Suez railway, and negotiating a major postal treaty with the United States of America.

The knowledge of the world he thus acquired he built into his fiction, and, combined with a down-to-earth moral concern with personal conduct, it made him the darling author of the well-to-do – 'the Apollo of the circulating library', as one contemporary critic put it.[2] Of course not everybody with an extensive knowledge of how politics and administration work becomes a great novelist, and not all novelists with a flair for presenting an apparently working universe have been active public servants. Nevertheless nobody has ever doubted that Trollope put to unique use his unusually extensive experience as a 'man of the world'. Many parts of *He Knew He Was Right* can be compared with 'real-life' experiences of the author: he too crossed Mont Cenis; he knew Florence, where his mother and elder brother lived; he too met self-important American public men, and charming young American women, becoming emotionally attracted to one of the latter; and he, like Trevelyan (we can guess) drank the newly developed wine, Chianti. He also knew Exeter and the Devon countryside extremely well, having spent a formative period there as acting Surveyor of Posts, and if not as intimately acquainted with the back alleys of London as Sam Weller in *Pickwick Papers*, whose knowledge of London 'was extensive and peculiar', he knew it in such a way that every fictional location and every fictional journey within the metropolis has a distinct social and moral significance.

He Knew He Was Right is set in just the places which its author knew best, and is in that sense as rooted in his life as the novels of Dickens are in his. More important still, he knew a great deal about the dynamics of human relationships, and, whether describing courtship, marriage, social life, business or politics, he uses the strategies of interpersonal behaviour as a higher-level language through which to present his fictional worlds. As a critic put it in 1864, 'It is in his command of what we may call the moral "hooks and eyes" of life that Mr Trollope's greatest power lies.' Another review suggested that Trollope was in effect applying a systematic scientific knowledge of human social life: 'Mr Trollope really knows what we may call the *natural history* of every kind of man or

woman he seeks to sketch'.[3] He never neglects the social construction of his characters' personalities, and treats the whole of human
life in terms of individuals' sense of themselves interacting with
those around them, and issuing in personal conduct and group
dynamics. Richard Holt Hutton remarked on the dominance of an
'atmosphere of affairs' in all Trollope's fiction,[4] and this is true not
just in the public and business lives he presents, but in the private
lives as well. It is this that makes his fiction so unsentimental,
whatever its subject, and makes his down-to-earth understanding
of human motivation so uncynical, despite its lack of idealism.
Most of his contemporaries agreed that he was pre-eminently 'a
man of the world' in his fiction.

   Those with a taste for the biographical explanation of literary
phenomena would argue that crucial to the peculiar strength of *He
Knew He Was Right* is the experience of Trollope's childhood and
youth: for a great shadow hung over his vision of the world. He
had not always been so prosperous. Although his parents came
from the professional and landed middle class, money was chroni-
cally short, and they could not keep Anthony in a mode fitting his
genteel birth. Consequently he passed an agonizing boyhood, a
'pariah' among the boys at Harrow and Winchester, he tells us,
unimaginably ignorant and unkempt. His father was a unsuccessful
barrister, who pinned his hopes on inheriting a substantial estate
from an uncle, but whose unpracticality and moodiness were
indistinguishable from insanity, and led the family into bankruptcy.
The shadow darkening Trollope's practical, middle-class view of
the world is that the conditions which determined that someone
'belonged' to the landed and professional class – and was apparently
secure in that class – might be illusory, to be negated in a trice by
one of both of the ills he understood from his own youth:
bankruptcy and insanity. In *The Last Chronicle of Barsit*, written
just before *He Knew He Was Right*, he had examined the case of a
man who remained a gentleman even when sorely afflicted with
poverty, and how his afflications turned his mind until he himself
hardly knew whether he was sane or not. In *He Knew He Was
Right* he takes the case of a man with a handsome income, and
drives him mad from jealousy. The nineteenth-century complex of
thoughts and feelings in terms of which these two novels are to be
read, and which framed the trauma of Trollope's youth, includes
the heroism of the man who saves himself from potential ruin – as
Trollope did most successfully. (In justice the *women* who saved
themselves and their families, as Trollope's mother did, should have
been just as fêted, but they did not belong to the major economic

myths of the period.) Trollope was a socio-economic hero for the middle classes, and he recognised the category to which he belonged by creating a fictional hero of this type in Hugh Stanbury.

If in his fiction and his life Trollope embodied something of the ambition and fears of the male breadwinners of his class, he was no less sensitive to the aspirations of its women. His fiction is full of women who long for a place in public life, and who would clearly fill it better than their menfolk do theirs. One of his contemporaries, Richard Holt Hutton, whom Trollope called 'of all the critics of my work ... the most observant, and generally the most eulogistic',[5] reproached him for supposedly neglecting the 'essence' of his female characters – that element which women possessed by virtue of being women, and which was undetectable from outside, and thus expressing only in lyric utterances, as it were, from within. Hutton's underlying assumption was that there was a fundamental difference between male and female characters, based upon 'natural' differences between men and women in 'the real world'. Whereas educated men's characters were 'naturally in *position*, and ... have a defined bearing on the rest of the world, a characteristic attitude, a personal latitude and longitude on the map of human affairs', women had no such location 'which an intellectual eye can seize and mark out at once', and hence were best presented by 'indefinable essence', which would characterise them as perfume does a flower or birdsong the bird.[6] The ways in which men and women must be created in a literary work differed because men and women were 'naturally' different.

   In their insistence on the total separation of men's natures from those of women, Hutton's views were typical of his age. Trollope's were not: his women characters have a sense of identity as strongly developed as his men's. Although some when young regard their lovers as gods, and many later find fulfilment in domesticity and child-rearing, the best of his women have or crave exactly that 'position' on the map of the world which Hutton attributes to educated men alone. Many, like Alice Vavasor in *He Knew He Was Right?*, Lady Laura Standish in *Phineas Finn*, or the Duchess of Omnium in *The Prime Minister*, want a political role. Trollope is open-minded enough to make one sympathetic women character, Madam Max Goesler in the Palliser novels, a businesswoman, and to allow her to propose to Phineas Finn without loss of authorial approval, while Lady Mason in *Orley Farm* and Lizzie Eustace in *The Eustace Diamonds* are understood from within, and do not become mere sensational criminal types, when in their different ways they take the law into their own hands. Such fictional women certainly needed a social dimension to their characters as strong as that of fictional men in the novels of the period.

It is not that Trollope was out of step with his age: he was simply unusual among male novelists in giving imaginative form to such aspects of women's social and mental life. Yet his deliberate utterances on feminist issues were crass and uncomprehending, and his satires on feminists in *He Knew He Was Right* and *Is He Popenjoy?* rather crude stuff. It is difficult to reconcile these things with the fact that he knew some of the leading feminists of the day, including a number whom he met through his friend, George Eliot, and Victoria Glendinning makes a convincing case for his having a relatively 'advanced' attitude to them, putting forward a plausible psychological explanation of the contrast between his understanding of the feminist position and his heavy-handed defence of male supremacy.[7] It remains, however, one of the unresolved contradictions of his fiction.

The case of *He Knew He Was Right* is temptingly easy to explain from his warm friendship with the young American feminist, Kate Field, whom, with more than just avuncular interest, he constantly advised to give up campaigning and marry a good man. (The powers of social endurance and the reserves of tolerance amongst nineteenth-century feminists seem amazing today.) If we seek biographical parallels, we are bound to come to the conclusion that Kate Field is broken down in *He Knew He Was Right* into two components: Caroline Spalding, the charming, 'feminine' American, who makes an ideal wife for a conservative Englishman; and Wallachia Petrie, 'the Republican Browning', who combines all Kate Field's most provoking opinions with an exterior unalluring enough to warn off any traditionally minded male. Meanwhile the case for women's rights to property within marriage, to custody of their children, and to protection from dangerous husbands – issues widely debated in the press in the eighteen-sixties – is made with great clarity in the Trevelyans' story. Less obviously, the right of women to determine their own lives is an issue in all the other strands of the plot, with a character like Priscilla Stanbury standing for a real option in life, and acting as far more than a mere foil for her marrying sister.

The different the ways the 'woman question' is handled in each strand of the plot should alert us to Trollope's fictional methods. This novel appears at first sight to be one of those vast, shapeless creations which later critics felt they could sneer at, when they compared them with the formal 'perfection' of some later fiction. The Exeter scenes seem to be detachable from the plot concerning Louis and Emily Trevelyan, and Nora's marital prospects serve, it would seem, merely as a sub-plot, to pad out her sister's story. Without such distractions, the argument runs, *He Knew He Was Right* would be an impressive tragedy, but the Victorian novelist was duty bound to provide a love story and a happy ending for at least some of the characters. Yet the fact is that comparison is invited between Emily's entry into an apparently ideal marriage and Priscilla's reluctance to give up her freedom to a man at all, and between the marital difficulties Louis Trevelyan manufactures for himself and the practical sense of Hugh Stanbury. We are manoeuvred into a position where the question has to be asked whether there is any way of assuring acceptable marital relations, and the answer may lead us to doubt the entire institution of marriage.

This may not be a response which was available to earlier readers, who would have found an explanation in Louis Trevelyan's urge to self-torment, and the fact that he had no occupation to keep him busy. As far as the energetic Anthony Trollope was concerned, it was dangerous to leave the mind to dwell on possibilities, instead of dealing with immediate practicalities. The danger posed by an unencumbered income, with no family ties, no profession to pursue and no estates to manage, was enormous. Insanity lay in wait for the unoccupied. Through a whole series of intertextual references Trevelyan is likened to Othello, with Bozzle as his Iago; but the comparison must not be taken too simply. Othello is a man of action, who at his catastrophe can exclaim that his occupation is gone. Trevelyan never has an occupation, and does not fall into jealousy because of a tendency to take things at face value, but because he deliberately makes things seem bad enough to account for his worries about the world. Trevelyan is one of the greatest self-tormentors in English literature, and has in this respect a force and plausibility which even Josiah Crawley lacks in *The Last Chronicle of Barset*. The perverseness of people in destroying what they have is one of Trollope's frequent themes, and nowhere is it better exemplified than in *He Knew He Was Right*.

From the above remarks it will be apparent why Trollope needed to write a very long novel with a number of plots. The available variety of ways of dealing with a certain range of life's problems and possibilities can only be worked out in such terms, and we are fortunate in having discarded the inappropriate aesthetic view of

the early twentieth century which condemned Trollope for his
fictional method. We can still admire just as much the power of the
Trevelyan plot, without wishing it stripped of its fellows. We can
also see a deliberate authorial cunning in the juxtaposition of plots
which close with marriages and conventional 'happy endings', with
a plot that begins like the ending of a 'love-and-marriage' novel,
and then turns to strife, misery, abduction and death. Trollope was,
as many have said of him, very ordinary in the materials he used
for his fiction, but by suggesting a grim continuation of a story in
which a well-off young man proposes to one of nine daughters of
an impoverished colonial governor, he was making exceptional use
of those materials. He was famous in his own day for his pictures
of life as his contemporaries wished to see it, and was particularly
admired for his fictional marriages. *He Knew He Was Right* is not
only a wonderfully controlled and complex novel, but a new light
on the very stuff of the elements of Trollope's fiction which was
responsible for his popularity. Far from succumbing to mid-Victorian
optimism, he posed radical questions about the assumptions by
which he and his contemporaries lived, and he and his novelist
contemporaries mainly wrote. And if some readers have privileged
the sunny above the gloomy in his work, that may reveal as much
about them as about his fiction; and if they discount his darker
vision, based as it is upon the personal inadequacies of his characters, it may be because they themselves are without weakness; or it
may suggest that like Trollope himself they are aware of these
fearful possibilities, but unlike him are afraid to face them. It does
no harm to remember sunlight on a cathedral close, as long as we
also recollect that at any moment everything that constitutes a
happy, conventional life may crumble, and that it can also be part
of life to be mad and alone on a bleak hilltop in Tuscany.

David Skilton, 1993

1 H. L. Mansel [anon] 'Sensation Novels', *Quarterly Review* 113 (april 1862), 488.
2 E. S. Dallas (anon.), 'Anthony Trollope', *The Times*, 23 May 1859, 12.
3 Anonymous reviews of *The Small House at Allington* and *The Golden Lion of Granpere*, *Spectator* 37 (9 April 1864), 421–3 and 45 (18 May 1872), 630–31.
4 'From Miss Austen to Mr Trollope', *Spectator* 55 (16 December 1882), 1609–11.
5 *An Autobiography*, (Oxford: Oxford University Press, 1950), p. 205.
6 R. H. Hutton, *Essays Theological and Literary* 1871, vol 2, pp. 205–6; and review of Trollope's *Sir Harry Hotspur of Humblethwaite*, *Spectator*

43 (26 November 1970), 1415. This review is anonymous, but is entirely consistent in tone and views with the known reviews of Hutton, the *Spectator*'s literary editor.

7 Victoria Glendinning, *Trollope* (Hutchinson, 1992), 323–4.

NOTE ON THE TEXT

By an agreement dated 15 November 1867, Virtue paid £3,200 for the entire copyright of *He Knew He Was Right*. The novel was issued in thirty-two weekly numbers at sixpence each, from 17 October 1868 to 22 May 1869, and in eight monthly parts at two shillings each over the same period. It was published in two volumes in May 1869 at twenty-one shillings. All versions were printed from the same setting, and all contained the sixty-four wood-engraved illustrations by Marcus Stone. In the United States, Harper brought it out in parts during 1869, and in book form in 1870. There was a three-volume edition from Tauchnitz of Leipzig in 1869.[1]

In 1974, Professor P. D. Edwards of the University of Queensland printed a photographic reproduction of the two-volume edition, with textual notes registering significant variations from the manuscript, which is in the Pierpont Morgan Library, New York.[2] The present edition follows the original text in the main, accepting the manuscript readings in cases where there appear to have been misreadings by the compositors' mistaken regularisation of spellings, or bowdlerisation. Alterations presumably made by Trollope to produce the correct length for each part have been accepted. He frequently adjusted length in this way, and equal instalments were part of his normal expectation in publishing a novel. It is in any case difficult to prove which changes arise from a consideration of length, and which from a more general tidying up and improvement.

In the manuscript Trollope was careful to render Bozzle's speech and writing differently, apparently aware of the falsity of the convention whereby imperfectly educated speakers of non-standard English write as they speak. As originally written, Bozzle's letters are ill-spelt, and plausibly the production of an ill-educated pen. As rendered in all printed editions they are more-or-less correctly spelt, with the improbable exception of a few phonetic renderings of the writer's pronunciation, such as his employer's name. The restoration of the manuscript versions of these letters is the largest single emendation to the first edition. A striking example of bowdlerisation is explained in the note to page 163 where the manuscript reading is restored. For the present edition some spellings have been regularised, and a few modernised where confusion might otherwise result. Full-stops have been omitted after 'Mr', 'Mrs', etc.

1 Michael Sadleir, *Trollope: a Bibliograpahy* (London: Dawsons of Pall Mall, 1964, first published 1928), pp. 92–6 and 291.
2 P. D. Edwards (ed.), *He Knew He Was Right* (St Lucia: University of Queensland Press, 1974).

HE KNEW
HE WAS RIGHT

VOLUME I

Showing how Wrath Began

When Louis Trevelyan was twenty-four years old, he had all the world before him where to choose;* and, among other things, he chose to go to the Mandarin Islands, and there fell in love with Emily Rowley, the daughter of Sir Marmaduke, the governor. Sir Marmaduke Rowley, at this period of his life, was a respectable middle-aged public servant, in good repute, who had, however, as yet achieved for himself neither an exalted position nor a large fortune. he had been governor of many islands, and had never lacked employment; and now, at the age of fifty, found himself at the Mandarins, with a salary of £3,000 a year, living in a temperature at which 80° in the shade is considered to be cool, with eight daughters, and not a shilling saved. A governor at the Mandarins who is social by nature and hospitable on principle, cannot save money in the islands even on £3,000 a year when he has eight daughters. And at the Mandarins, though hospitality is a duty, the gentleman who ate Sir Rowley's dinners were not exactly the men whom he or Lady Rowley desired to welcome to their bosoms as sons-in-law. Nor when Mr Trevelyan came that way, desirous of seeing everything in the somewhat indefinite course of his travels, had Emily Rowley, the eldest of the flock, then twenty years of age, seen as yet any Mandariner who exactly came up to her fancy. And, as Louis Trevelyan was a remarkably handsome young man, who was well connected, who had been ninth wrangler at Cambridge, who had already published a volume of poems, and who possessed £3,000 a year of his own, arising from various perfectly secure investments, he was not forced to sigh long in vain. Indeed, the Rowleys, one and all, felt that providence had been very good to them in sending young Trevelyan on his travels in that direction, for he seemed to be a very pearl among men. Both Sir Marmaduke and Lady Rowley felt that there might be objections to such a marriage as that proposed to them, raised by the Trevelyan family. Lady Rowley would not have liked her daughter to go to England, to be received with cold looks by strangers. But it soon appeared that there was no one to make objections. Louis, the lover, had no living relative nearer than cousins. His father, a barrister of repute, had died a widower, and had left the money which he had made to an only child. The head of the family was a first cousin who lived in Cornwall, on a moderate property, – a very good sort of stupid fellow, as Louis said, who would be quite indifferent as to any marriage that his cousin might make. No man could be more independent or more clearly justified in pleasing himself than was this lover. And then he himself proposed that the second daughter, Nora, should come and live with them in London. What a lover to fall suddenly from the heavens into such a dovecote!

'I haven't a penny-piece to give to either of them,' said Sir Rowley.

'It is my idea that girls should not have fortunes,' said Trevelyan. 'At any rate, I am quite sure that men should never look for money. A man must be more comfortable, and, I think, is likely to be more affectionate, when the money has belonged to himself.'

Sir Rowley was high-minded gentleman, who would have liked to have handed over a few thousand pounds on giving up his daughters; but, having no thousands of pounds to hand over, he could not but admire the principles of his proposed son-in-law. As it was about time for him to have his leave of absence, he and sundry of the girls went to England with Mr Trevelyan, and the wedding was celebrated in London by the Rev Oliphant Outhouse, of Saint Diddulph-in-the-East, who had married Sir Rowley's sister. Then a small house was taken and furnished in Curzon Street, Mayfair, and the Rowleys went back to the seat of their government, leaving Nora, the second girl, in charge of her elder sister.

The Rowleys had found, on reaching London, that they had lighted upon a pearl indeed. Louis Trevelyan was a man of whom all people said all good things.* He might have been a fellow of his college had he not been a man of fortune. He might already, – so Sir Rowley was told, – have been in Parliament, had he not thought it to be wiser to wait awhile. Indeed, he was very wise in many things. He had gone out on his travels thus young, – not in search of excitement, to kill beasts, or to encounter he knew not what novelty and amusement, – but that he might see men and know the world. He had been on his travels for more than a year when the winds blew him to the Mandarins. Oh, how blessed were the winds! And, moreover, Sir Rowley found that his son-in-law was well spoken of at the clubs by those who had known him during his university career, as a man popular as well as wise, not a bookworm, or a dry philosopher, or a prig. He could talk on all subjects, was very generous, a man sure to be honoured and respected; and then such a handsome, manly fellow, with short brown hair, a nose divinely chiselled, an Apollo's mouth, six feet high, with shoulders and legs and arms in proportion, – a pearl of pearls! Only, as Lady Rowley was the first to find out, he liked to have his own way.

'But his way is such a good way,' said Sir Marmaduke. 'He will be such a good guide for the girls!'

'But Emily likes her way too,' said Lady Rowley.

Sir Marmaduke argued the matter no further, but thought, no doubt, that such a husband as Louis Trevelyan was entitled to have his own way. He probably had not observed his daughter's temper so accurately as his wife had done. With eight of them coming up around him, how should he have observed their tempers? At any rate, if there was anything amiss with Emily's temper, it would be well that she should find her master in such a husband as Louis Trevelyan.

For nearly two years the little household in Curzon Street went on well, or if anything was the matter no one outside of the little household was aware of it. And there was a baby, a boy, a young Louis, and a baby in such a household is apt to make things go sweetly. The marriage had taken place in July, and after the wedding tour there had been a winter and a spring in London; and then they passed a month or two at the sea-side, after which the baby had been born. And then there came another winter and another spring. Nora Rowley was with them in London, and by this time Mr Trevelyan had begun to think that he should like to have his own way completely. His baby was very nice, and his wife was clever, pretty, and attractive. Nora was all that an unmarried sister should be. But, – but there had come to be trouble and bitter words. Lady Rowley had been right when she said that her daughter Emily also liked to have her own way.

'If I am suspected,' said Mrs Trevelyan to her sister one morning, as they sat together in the little back drawing-room, 'life will not be worth having.'

'How can you talk of being suspected, Emily?'

'What does he mean then by saying that he would rather not have Colonel Osborne here? A man older than my own father, who has known me since I was a baby!'

'He didn't mean anything of that kind, Emily. You know he did not, and you should not say so. It would be too horrible to think of.'

'It was a great deal too horrible to be spoken, I know. If he does not beg my pardon, I shall, – I shall continue to live with him, of course, as a sort of upper servant, because of baby. But he shall know that I think and feel.'

'If I were you I would forget it.'

'How can I forget it? Nothing that I can do pleases him. He is civil and kind to you because he is not your master; but you don't know what things he says to me. Am I to tell Colonel Osborne not to come? Heavens and earth! How should I ever hold up my head

again if I were driven to do that? He will be here to-day I have no
doubt; and Louis will sit there below in the library, and hear his
step, and will not come up.'

'Tell Richard to say you are not at home.'

'Yes; and everybody will understand why. And for what am I to
deny myself in that way to the best and oldest friend I have? If any
such orders are to be given, let him give them and then see what
will come of it.'

Mrs Trevelyan had described Colonel Osborne truly as far as
words went, in saying that he had known her since she was a baby,
and that he was an older man than her father. Colonel Osborne's
age exceeded her father's by about a month, and as he was now
past fifty, he might be considered perhaps, in that respect, to be a
safe friend for a young married woman. But he was in every respect
a man very different from Sir Marmaduke. Sir Marmaduke, blessed
and at the same time burdened as he was with a wife and eight
daughters, and condemned as he had been to pass a large portion
of his life within the tropics, had become at fifty what many people
call quite a middle-aged man. That is to say, he was one from
whom the effervescence and elasticity and salt of youth had
altogether passed away. He was fat and slow, thinking much of his
wife and eight daughters, thinking much also of his dinner. Now
Colonel Osborne was a bachelor, with no burdens but those
imposed upon him by his position as a member of Parliament, – a
man of fortune to whom the world had been very easy. It was not
therefore said so decidedly of him as of Sir Marmaduke, that he
was a middle-aged man, although he had probably already lived
more than two-thirds of his life. And he was a good-looking man
of his age, bald indeed at the top of his head, and with a
considerable sprinkling of grey hair through his bushy beard; but
upright in his carriage, active, and quick in his step, who dressed
well, and was clearly determined to make the most he could of
what remained to him of the advantages of youth. Colonel Osborne
was always so dressed that no one ever observed the nature of his
garments, being no doubt well aware that no man after twenty-five
can afford to call special attention to his coat, his hat, his cravat, or
his trousers; but nevertheless the matter was one to which he paid
much attention, and he was by no means lax in ascertaining what
his tailor did for him. He always rode a pretty horse, and mounted
his groom on one at any rate as pretty. He was known to have an
excellent stud down in the shires, and had the reputation of going
well with hounds. Poor Sir Marmaduke could not have ridden a
hunt to save either his government or his credit. When, therefore,

Mrs Trevelyan declared to her sister that Colonel Osborne was a man whom she was entitled to regard with semi-parental feelings of veneration because he was older than her father, she made a comparison which was more true in the letter than in the spirit. And when she asserted that Colonel Osborne had known her since she was a baby, she fell again into the same mistake. Colonel Osborne had indeed known her when she was a baby, and had in old days been the very intimate friend of her father; but of herself he had seen little or nothing since those baby days, till he had met her just as she was about to become Mrs Trevelyan; and though it was natural that so old a friend should come to her and congratulate her and renew his friendship, nevertheless it was not true that he made his appearance in her husband's house in the guise of the useful old family friend, who gives silver cups to the children and kisses the little girls for the sake of the old affection which he has borne for the parents. We all know the appearance of that old gentleman, how pleasant and dear a fellow he is, how welcome is his face within the gate, how free he makes with our wine, generally abusing it, how he tells our eldest daughter to light his candle for him, how he gave silver cups when the girls were born, and now bestows tea-services as they get married, – a most useful, safe, and charming fellow, not a year younger-looking or more nimble than ourselves, without whom life would be very blank. We all know that man; but such a man was not Colonel Osborne in the house of Mr Trevelyan's young bride.

Emily Rowley, when she was brought home from the Mandarin Islands to be the wife of Louis Trevelyan, was a very handsome young woman, tall, with a bust rather full for her age, with dark eyes – eyes that looked to be dark because her eye-brows and eye-lashes were nearly black, but which were in truth so varying in colour, that you could not tell their hue. Her brown hair was very dark and very soft; and the tint of her complexion was brown also, though the colour of her cheeks was often so bright as to induce her enemies to say falsely of her that she painted them. And she was very strong, as are some girls who come from the tropics, and whom a tropical climate has suited. She could sit on her horse the whole day long, and would never be weary with dancing at the Government House balls. When Colonel Osborne was introduced to her as the baby whom he had known, he thought it would be very pleasant to be intimate with so pleasant a friend, – meaning no harm indeed, as but few men do mean harm on such occasions, – but still, not regarding the beautiful young woman whom he had seen as one of a generation succeeding to that of his own, to whom it would be his duty to make himself useful on account of the old friendship which he bore to her father.

It was, moreover, well known in London, – though not known at all to Mrs Trevelyan, – that this ancient Lothario had before this made himself troublesome in more than one family. He was fond of intimacies with married ladies, and perhaps was not averse to the excitement of marital hostility. It must be remembered, however, that the hostility to which allusion is here made was not the hostility of the pistol or the horsewhip, – nor indeed was it generally the hostility of a word of spoken anger. A young husband may dislike the too-friendly bearing of a friend, and may yet abstain from that outrage on his own dignity and on his wife, which is conveyed by a word of suspicion. Louis Trevelyan having taken a strong dislike to Colonel Osborne, and having failed to make his wife understand that this dislike should have induced her to throw cold water upon the Colonel's friendship, had allowed himself to speak a word which probably he would have willingly recalled as soon as spoken. But words spoken cannot be recalled, and many a man and many a woman who has spoken a word at once regretted, are far too proud to express that regret. So it was with Louis Trevelyan when he told his wife that he did not wish Colonel Osborne to come so often to his house. He had said it with a flashing eye and an angry tone; and though she had seen the eye flash before, and was familiar with the angry tone, she had never before felt herself to be insulted by her husband. As soon as the word had been spoken Trevelyan had left the room and had gone down among his books. But when he was alone he knew that he had insulted his wife. He was quite aware that he should have spoken to her gently, and have explained to her, with his arm round her waist, that it would be better for both of them that this friend's friendship should be limited. There is so much in a turn of the eye and in the tone given to a word when such things have to be said, – so much more of importance than in the words themselves. As Trevelyan thought of this, and remembered what his manner had been, how much anger he had expressed, how far he had been from having his arm round his wife's waist as he spoke to her, he almost made up his mind to go up-stairs and to apologise. But he was one to whose nature the giving of any apology was repulsive. He could not bear to have to own himself to have been wrong. And then his wife had been most provoking in her manner to him. When he had endeavoured to make her understand his wishes by certain disparaging hints which he had thrown out as to Colonel Osborne, saying that he was a dangerous man, one who did not show his true character, a snake in the grass, a man without settled principles, and such like, his wife had taken up the cudgels for her friend, and had openly declared that she did not believe a word of the things that were alleged against him. 'But still for all that it is true,' the husband had said. 'I have no doubt that you think so,' the wife had replied. 'Men do believe evil of one another, very often. But you must excuse me if I say that I think you are mistaken. I have known Colonel Osborne much longer than you have done, Louis, and papa has always had the highest opinion of him.' Then Mr Trevelyan had become very angry, and had spoken those words which he could not recall. As he walked to an fro among his books down-stairs, he almost felt that he ought to beg his wife's pardon. He knew his wife well enough to be sure that she would not forgive him unless he did so. He would do so, he thought, but not exactly now. A moment would come in which it might be easier than at present. He would be able to assure her when he went up to dress for dinner, that he had meant no harm. They were going out to dine at the house of a lady of rank, the Countess Dowager of Milborough, a lady standing high in the world's esteem, of whom his wife stood a little in awe; and he calculated that this feeling, if it did not make his task easy would yet take from it some of its difficulty. Emily would be, not exactly cowed, by the prospect of Lady Milborough's dinner, but perhaps a little reduced from her usual self-assertion. He would say a word to her when he was dressing, assuring her that he had not intended to animadvert in the slightest degree upon her own conduct.

Luncheon was served, and the two ladies went down into the dining-room. Mr Trevelyan did not appear. There was nothing in itself singular in that, as he was accustomed to declare that luncheon was a meal too much in the day, and that a man should eat nothing beyond a biscuit between breakfast and dinner. But he would sometimes come in and eat his biscuit standing on the hearth-rug, and drink what he would call half a quarter of a glass of sherry. It would probably have been well that he should have done so now; but he remained in his library behind the dining-room, and when his wife and his sister-in-law had gone up-stairs, he became anxious to learn whether Colonel Osborne would come on that day, and, if so, whether he would be admitted. He had been told that Nora Rowley was to be called for by another lady, a Mrs Fairfax, to go out and look at pictures. His wife had declined to join Mrs Fairfax's party, having declared that, as she was going to dine out, she would not leave her baby all the afternoon. Louis Trevelyan, though he strove to apply his mind to an article which he was writing for a scientific quarterly review, could not keep himself from anxiety as to this expected visit from Colonel Osborne. He was not in the least jealous. He swore to himself fifty times over that any such feeling on his part would be a monstrous injury to his wife. Nevertheless he knew that he would be gratified if on that special day Colonel Osborne should be informed that his wife was not at home. Whether the man were admitted or not, he would beg his wife's pardon; but he could, he thought, do so with more thorough efficacy and affection if she should have shown a disposition to comply with his wishes on this day.

'Do say a word to Richard,' said Nora to her sister in a whisper as they were going up-stairs after luncheon.

'I will not,' said Mrs Trevelyan.

'May I do it?'

'Certainly not, Nora. I should feel that I were demeaning myself were I to allow what was said to me in such a manner to have any effect on me.'

'I think you are so wrong, Emily. I do indeed.'

'You must allow me to be the best judge what to do in my own house, and with my own husband.'

'Oh, yes; certainly.'

'If he gives me any command I will obey it. Or if he had expressed his wish in any other words I would have complied. But to be told that he would rather not have Colonel Osborne here! If you had seen his manner and heard his words, you would not have been surprised that I should feel it as I do. It was a gross insult, – and it was not the first.'

As she spoke the fire flashed from her eye, and the bright red colour of her cheek told a tale of her anger which her sister well knew how to read. Then there was a knock on the door, and they both knew that Colonel Osborne was there. Louis Trevelyan, sitting in his library, also knew of whose coming that knock gave notice.

2

Colonel Osborne

It has been already said that Colonel Osborne was a bachelor, a man of fortune, a member of Parliament, and one who carried his half century of years lightly on his shoulders. It will only be necessary to say further of him that he was a man popular with those among whom he lived, as a politician, as a sportsman, and as a member of society. He could speak well in the House, though he spoke but seldom, and it was generally thought of him that he might have been something considerable, had it not suited him better to be nothing at all. He was supposed to be a Conservative, and generally voted with the conservative party; but he could boast that he was altogether independent, and on an occasion would take the trouble of proving himself to be so. He was in possession of excellent health; had all that the world could give; was fond of books, pictures, architecture, and china; had various tastes, and the means of indulging them, and was one of those few men on whom it seems that every pleasant thing had been lavished. There was that little slur on his good name to which allusion has been made; but those who knew Colonel Osborne best were generally willing to declare that no harm was intended, and that the evils which arose were always to be attributed to mistaken jealousy. He had, his friends said, a free and pleasant way with women which women like, – a pleasant way of free friendship; that there was no more, and that the harm which had come had always come from false suspicion. But there were certain ladies about the town, – good, motherly, discreet women, – who hated the name of Colonel Osborne, who would not admit him within their doors, who would not bow to him in other people's houses, who would always speak of him as a serpent, an hyena, a kite, or a shark. Old Lady Milborough was one of these, a daughter of a friend of hers having once admitted the serpent to her intimacy.

'Augustus Poole was wise enough to take his wife abroad,' said old Lady Milborough, discussing about this time with a gossip of hers the danger of Mrs Trevelyan's position, 'or there would have been a break-up there; and yet, there never was a better girl in the world than Jane Marriott.'

The reader may be quite certain that Colonel Osborne had no premeditated evil intention when he allowed himself to become the intimate friend of his old friend's daughter. There was nothing fiendish in his nature. He was not a man who boasted of his conquests. He was not a ravening wolf going about seeking whom he might devour, and determined to devour whatever might come in his way; but he liked that which was pleasant; and of all pleasant things the company of a pretty clever woman was to him the pleasantest. At this exact period of life no woman was so pleasantly pretty to him, and so agreeably clever, as Mrs Trevelyan.

When Louis Trevelyan heard on the stairs the step of the dangerous man, he got up from his chair as though he too would have gone into the drawing-room, and it would perhaps have been

well had he done so. Could he have done this, and kept his temper
with the man, he would have paved the way for an easy reconciliation with his wife. But when he reached the door of his room, and
had placed his hand upon the lock, he withdrew again. He told
himself he withdrew because he would not allow himself to be
jealous; but in truth he did so because he knew he could not have
brought himself to be civil to the man he hated. So he sat down,
and took up his pen, and began to cudgel his brain about the
scientific article. He was intent on raising a dispute with some
learned pundit about the waves of sound, – but he could think of
no other sound than that of the light steps of Colonel Osborne as
he had gone up-stairs. He put down his pen, and clenched his fist,
and allowed a black frown to settle upon his brow. What right had
the man to come three, unasked by him, and disturb his happiness?
And then this poor wife of his, who knew so little of English life,
who had lived in the Mandarin Islands almost since she had been a
child, who had lived in one colony or another almost since she had
been born, who had had so few of those advantages for which he
should have looked in marrying a wife, how was the poor girl to
conduct herself properly when subjected to the arts and practised
villanies of this viper? And yet the poor girl was so stiff in her
temper, had picked up such a trick of obstinacy in those tropical
regions, that Louis Trevelyan felt that he did not know how to
manage her. He too had heard how Jane Marriott had been carried
off to Naples after she had become Mrs Poole. Must he to carry off
his wife to Naples in order to place her out of the reach of this
hyena? It was terrible to him to think that he must pack up
everything and run away from such a one as Colonel Osborne. And
even were he to consent to do this, how could he explain it all to
that very wife for whose sake he would do it? If she got a hint of
the reason she would, he did not doubt, refuse to go. As he thought
of it, and as that visit up-stairs prolonged itself, he amost thought it
would be best for him to be round with her! We all know what a
husband means when he resolves to be round with his wife. He
began to think that he would not apologise at all for the words he
had spoken, – but would speak them again somewhat more sharply
than before. She would be very wrathful with him; there would be
a silent enduring indignation, which, as he understood well, would
be infinitely worse than any torrent of words. But was he, a man,
to abstain from doing that which he believed to be his duty because
he was afraid of his wife's anger? Should he be deterred from
saying that which he conceived it would be right that he should say,
because she was stiff-necked? No. He would not apologise, but

would tell her again that it was necessary, both for his happiness and for hers, that all intimacy with Colonel Osborne should be discontinued.

He was brought to this strongly marital resolution by the length of the man's present visit; by that and by the fact that, during the latter portion of it, his wife was alone with Colonel Osborne. Nora had been there when the man came, but Mrs Fairfax had called, not getting out of her carriage, and Nora had been constrained to go down to her. She had hesitated a moment, and Colonel Osborne had observed and partly understood the hesitation. When he saw it, had he been perfectly well-minded in the matter, he would have gone too. But he probably told himself that Nora Rowley was a fool, and that in such matters it was quite enough for a man to know that he did not intend any harm.

'You had better go down, Nora,' said Mrs Trevelyan; 'Mrs Fairfax will be ever so angry if you keep her waiting.'

Then Nora had gone and the two were alone together. Nora had gone, and Trevelyan had heard her as she was going and knew that Colonel Osborne was alone with his wife.

'If you can manage that it will be so nice,' said Mrs Trevelyan, continuing the conversation.

'My dear Emily,' he said, 'you must not talk of my managing it, or you will spoil it all.'

He had called them both Emily and Nora when Sir Marmaduke and Lady Rowley were with them before the marriage, and, taking the liberty of a very old family friend, had continued the practice. Mrs Trevelyan was quite aware that she had been so called by him in the presence of her husband, – and that her husband had not objected. But that was now some months ago, before baby was born; and she was aware also that he had not called her so latterly in presence of her husband. She thoroughly wished that she knew how to ask him not to do so again; but the matter was very difficult, as she could not make such a request without betraying some fear on her husband's part. The subject which they were now discussing was too important to her to allow her to dwell upon this trouble at the moment, and so she permitted him to go on with his speech.

'If I were to manage it, as you call it, – which I can't do at all, – it would be a gross job.'

'That's all nonsense to us, Colonel Osborne. Ladies always like political jobs, and think that they, – and they only, – make politics bearable. But this would not be a job at all. Papa could do it better than anybody else. Think how long he has been at it!'

The matter in discussion was the chance of an order being sent out to Sir Marmaduke to come home from his islands at the public expense, to give evidence, respecting colonial government in general, to a committee of the House of Commons which was about sit on the subject. The committee had been voted, and two governors were to be brought home for the purpose of giving evidence. What arrangement could be so pleasant to a governor living in the Mandarin Islands, who had had a holiday lately, and who could but ill afford to take any holidays at his own expense? Colonel Osborne was on this committee, and, moreover, was on good terms at the Colonial office. There were men in office who would be glad to do Colonel Osborne a service, and then if this were a job, it would be so very little of a job! Perhaps Sir Marmaduke might not be the very best man for the purpose. Perhaps the government of the Mandarins did not afford the best specimen of that colonial lore which it was the business of the committee to master. But then two governors were to come, and it might be as well to have one of the best sort, and one of the second best. No one supposed that excellent old Sir Marmaduke was a paragon of a governor, but then he had a infinity of experience! For over twenty years he had been from island to island, and had at least steered clear of great scrapes.

'We'll try it, at any rate,' said the Colonel.

'Do, Colonel Osborne. Mamma would come with him, of course?'

'We should leave him to manage all that. It's not very likely that he would leave Lady Rowley behind.'

'He never has. I know he thinks more of mamma than he ever does of himself. Fancy having them here in the autumn! I suppose if he came for the end of the session, they wouldn't send him back quite at once?'

'I rather fancy that our foreign and colonial servants know how to stretch a point when they find themselves in England.'

'Of course they do, Colonel Osborne; and why shouldn't they? Think of all that they have to endure out in those horrible places. How would you like to live in the Mandarins?'

'I should prefer London, certainly.'

'Of course you would; and you mustn't begrudge papa a month or two when he comes. I never cared about your being in parliament before, and I shall think so much of you now if you can manage to get papa home.'

There could be nothing more innocent than this, – nothing more innocent at any rate as regarded any offence against Mr Trevelyan.

But just then there came a word which a little startled Mrs Trevelyan, and made her feel afraid that she was doing wrong.

'I must make one stipulation with you, Emily,' said the Colonel.

'What is that?'

'You must not tell your husband.'

'Oh, dear! and why not?'

'I am sure you are sharp enough to see why you should not. A word of this repeated at any club would put an end at once to your project, and would be very damaging to me. And, beyond that, I wouldn't wish him to know that I had meddled with it at all. I am very chary of having my name connected with anything of the kind; and, upon my word, I wouldn't do it for any living human being but yourself. You'll promise me, Emily?'

She gave the promise, but there were two things in the matter, as it stood at present, which she did not at all like. She was very averse to having any secret from her husband with Colonel Osborne; and she was not at all pleased at being told that he was doing for her a favour that he would not have done for any other living human being. Had he said so to her yesterday, before those offensive words had been spoken by her husband, she would not have thought much about it. She would have connected the man's friendship for herself with his very old friendship for her father, and she would have regarded the assurance as made to the Rowleys in general, and not to herself in particular. But now, after what had occurred, it pained her to be told by Colonel Osborne that he would make, specially on her behalf, a sacrifice of his political pride which he would make for no other person living. And then, as he had called her by her Christian name, as he had exacted the promise, there had been a tone of affection in his voice that she had almost felt to be too warm. But she gave the promise; and when he pressed her hand at parting, she pressed his again, in token of gratitude for the kindness to be done to her father and mother.

Immediately afterwards Colonel Osborne went away, and Mrs Trevelyan was left alone in her drawing-room. She knew that her husband was still down-stairs, and listened for a moment to hear whether he would now come up to her. And he, too, had heard the Colonel's step as he went, and for a few moments had doubted whether or no he would at once go to his wife. Though he believed himself to be a man very firm of purpose, his mind had oscillated backwards and forwards within the last quarter of an hour between those two purposes of being round with his wife, and of begging her pardon for the words which he had already spoken. He believed that he would best do his duty by that plan of being round with her; about then it would be so much pleasanter – at any rate, so much easier, to beg her pardon. But of one thing he was quite certain, he must by some means exclude Colonel Osborne from his house. He could not live and continue to endure the feelings which he had suffered while sitting down-stairs at his desk, with the knowledge that Colonel Osborne was closeted with his wife up-stairs. It might be that there as nothing in it. That his wife was innocent he was quite sure. But nevertheless, he was himself so much affected by some feeling which pervaded him in reference to this man, that all his energy was destroyed, and his powers of mind and body were paralysed. He could not, and would not, stand it. Rather than that, he would follow Mr Poole, and take his wife to Naples. So resolving, he put his hat on his head and walked out of the house. He would have the advantage of the afternoon's consideration before he took either the one step or the other.

As soon as he was gone Emily Trevelyan went up-stairs to her baby. She would not stir as long as there had been a chance of his coming to her. She very much wished that he would come, and had made up her mind, in spite of the fierceness of her assertion to her sister, to accept any slightest hint at an apology which her husband might offer to her. To this state of mind she was brought by the consciousness of having a secret from him, and by a sense not of impropriety on her own part, but of conduct which some people might have called improper in her mode of parting from the man against whom her husband had warned her. The warmth of that hand-pressing, and the affectionate tone in which her name had been pronounced, and the promise made to her, softened her heart towards her husband. Had he gone to her now and said a word to her in gentleness all might have been made right. But he did not go to her.

'If he chooses to be cross and sulky, he may be cross and sulky,' said Mrs Trevelyan to herself as she went up to her baby.

'Has Louis been with you?' Nora asked, as soon as Mrs Fairfax had brought her home.

'I have not seen him since you left me,' said Mrs Trevelyan.

'I suppose he went out before Colonel Osborne?'

'No, indeed. He waited till Colonel Osborne had gone, and then he went himself; but he did not come near me. It is for him to judge of his own conduct, but I must say that I think he is very foolish.'

This the young wife said in a tone which clearly indicated that she had judged her husband's conduct, and had found it to be very foolish indeed.

'Do you think that papa and mamma will really come?' said Nora, changing the subject of conversation.

'How can I tell? How am I to know? After all that has passed I am afraid to say a word lest I should be accused of doing wrong. But remember this, Nora, you are not to speak of it to any one.'

'You will tell Louis?'

'No; I will tell no one.'

'Dear, dear Emily; pray do not keep anything secret from him.'

'What do you mean by secret? There isn't any secret. Only in such matters as that, – about politics, – no gentleman likes to have his name talked about!'

A look of great distress came upon Nora's face as she heard this. To her it seemed to be very bad that there should be a secret between her sister and Colonel Osborne to be kept from her brother-in-law.

'I suppose you will suspect me next?' said Mrs Trevelyan, angrily.

'Emily, how can you say anything so cruel?'

'You look as if you did.'

'I only mean that I think it would be wiser to tell all this to Louis.'

'How can I tell him Colonel Osborne's private business, when Colonel Osborne has desired me not to do so. For whose sake is Colonel Osborne doing this? For papa's and mamma's! I suppose Louis won't be – jealous, because I want to have papa and mamma home. It would not be a bit less unreasonable than the other.'

3

Lady Milborough's Dinner Party

Louis Trevelyan went down to his club in Pall Mall, the Acrobats, and there heard a rumour that added to his anger against Colonel Osborne. The Acrobats was a very distinguished club, into which it was now difficult for a young man to find his way, and almost impossible for a man who was no longer young, and therefore known to many. It had been founded some twenty years since with the idea of promoting muscular exercise and gymnastic amusements; but the promoters had become fat and lethargic, and the Acrobats spent their time mostly in playing whist, and in ordering and eating their dinners. There were supposed to be, in some out-of-the-way part of the building, certain poles and sticks and parallel bars with which feats of activity might be practised, but no one ever asked for them now-a-days, and a man, when he became an Acrobat, did so with a view either to the whist or the cook, or possibly to the social excellences of the club. Louis Trevelyan was an Acrobat; – as was also Colonel Osborne.

'So old Rowley is coming home,' said one distinguished Acrobat to another in Trevelyan's hearing.

'How the deuce is he managing that ? He was here a year ago ?'

'Osborne is getting it done. He is to come as a witness for this committee. It must be no end of a lounge for him. It doesn't count as leave, and he has every shilling paid for him, down to his cab-fares when he goes out to dinner. There's nothing like having a friend at court.'

Such was the secrecy of Colonel Osborne's secret ! He had been so chary of having his name mentioned in connection with a political job, that he had found it necessary to impose on his young friend the burden of a secret from her husband, and yet the husband heard the whole story told openly at his club on the same day ! There was nothing in the story to anger Trevelyan had he not immediately felt that there must be some plan in the matter between his wife and Colonel Osborne, of which he had been kept ignorant. Hitherto, indeed, his wife, as the reader knows, could not have told him. He had not seen her since the matter had been discussed between her and her friend. But he was angry because he first learned at his club that which he thought he ought to have learned at home.

As soon as he reached his house he went at once to his wife's room, but her maid was with her, and nothing could be said at that moment. He then dressed himself, intending to go to Emily as soon as the girl had left her ; but the girl remained, – was as he believed, kept in the room purposely by his wife, so that he should have no moment of private conversation. He went down-stairs, therefore, and found Nora standing by the drawing-room fire.

'So you are dressed first to-day ?' he said. 'I thought your turn always came last.'

'Emily sent Jenny to me first to-day because she thought you would be home, and she didn't go up to dress till the last minute.'

This was intended well by Nora, but it did not have the desired effect. Trevelyan, who had no command over his own features, frowned, and showed that he was displeased. He hesitated a moment, thinking whether he would ask Nora any question as to this report about her father and mother ; but, before he had spoken, his wife was in the room.

'We are all late, I fear,' said Emily.

'You, at any rate, are the last,' said her husband.

'About half a minute,' said the wife.

Then they got into the hired brougham which was standing at the door.

Trevelyan, in the sweet days of his early confidence with his wife, had offered to keep a carriage for her, explaining to her that the luxury, though costly, would not be beyond his reach. But she had persuaded him against the carriage, and there had come to be an agreement that instead of the carriage there should always be an autumn tour. 'One learns something from going about; but one learns nothing from keeping a carriage,' Emily had said. Those had been happy days, in which it had been intended that everything should always be rose-coloured. Now he was meditating whether, in lieu of that autumn tour, it would not be necessary to take his wife away to Naples altogether, so that he might be removed from the influence of – of – of; no, not even to himself would he think of Colonel Osborne as his wife's lover. The idea was too horrible! And yet, how dreadful was it that he should have, for any reason, to withdraw her from the influence of any man!

Lady Milborough lived ever so far away, in Eccleston Square, but Trevelyan did not say a single word to either of his companions during the journey. He was cross and vexed, and was conscious that they know that he was cross and vexed. Mrs Trevelyan and her sister talked to each other the whole way, but they did so in that tone which clearly indicates that the conversation is made up, not for any interest attached to the questions asked or the answers given, but because it is expedient that there should not be silence. Nora said something about Marshall and Snellgrove,* and tried to make believe that she was very anxious for her sister's answer. And Emily said something about the opera at Covent Garden, which was intended to show that her mind was quite at ease. But both of them failed altogether, and knew that they failed. Once or twice Trevelyan thought that he would say a word in token, as it were, of repentance. Like the naughty child who knew that he was naughty, he was trying to be good. But he could not do it. The fiend was too strong within him. She must have known that there was a proposition for her father's return through Colonel Osborne's influence. As that man at the club had heard it, how could she not have known it? When they got out at Lady Milborough's door he had spoken to neither of them.

There was a large dull party, made up mostly of old people. Lady Milborough and Trevelyan's mother had been bosom friends, and Lady Milborough had on this account taken upon herself to be much interested in Trevelyan's wife. But Louis Trevelyan himself, in discussing Lady Milborough with Emily, had rather turned his mother's old friend into ridicule, and Emily had, of course, followed her husband's mode of thinking. Lady Milborough had once or twice given her some advice on small matters, telling her that this or that air would be good for her baby, and explaining that a mother during a certain interesting portion of her life, should refresh herself with a certain kind of malt liquor. Of all counsel on such domestic subjects Mrs Trevelyan was impatient, – as indeed it was her nature to be in all matters, and consequently, authorized as she had been by her husband's manner of speaking of his mother's friend, she had taken a habit of quizzing Lady Milborough behind her back, and almost of continuing the practice before the old lady's face. Lady Milborough, who was the most affectionate old soul alive, and good-tempered with her friends to a fault, had never resented this, but had come to fear that Mrs Trevelyan was perhaps a little flighty. She had never as yet allowed herself to say anything worse of her young friend's wife than that. And she would always add that that kind of thing would cure itself as the nursery became full. It must be understood therefore that Mrs Trevelyan was not anticipating much pleasure from Lady Milborough's party, and that she had accepted this invitation as a matter of duty.

There was present among the guests a certain Honourable Charles Glascock, the eldest son of Lord Peterborough, who made the affair more interesting to Nora than it was to her sister. It had been whispered into Nora's ears, by more than one person, – and among others by Lady Milborough, whose own daughters were all married, – that she might if she thought fit become the Honourable Mrs Charles Glascock. Now, whether she might think fit, or whether she might not, the presence of the gentleman under such circumstances, as far as she was concerned, gave an interest to the evening. And as Lady Milborough took care that Mr Glascock should take Nora down to dinner, the interest was very great. Mr Glascock was a good-looking man, just under forty, in Parliament, heir to a peerage, and known to be well off in respect to income. Lady Milborough and Mrs Trevelyan had told Nora Rowley that should encouragement in that direction come in her way, she ought to allow herself to fall in love with Mr Glascock. A certain amount of encouragement had come in her way, but she had not as yet allowed herself to fall in love with Mr Glascock. It seemed to her that Mr Glascock was quite conscious of the advantages of his own position, and that his powers of talking about other matters than those with which he was immediately connected were limited. She did believe that he had in truth paid her the compliment of falling in love with her, and this is a compliment to which few girls are indifferent. Nora might perhaps have tried to fall in love with Mr Glascock, had she not been forced to make comparisons between him and another. This other one had not fallen in love with her, as she well knew; and she certainly had not fallen in love with him. But still the comparison was forced upon her, and it did not result in favour of Mr Glascock. On the present occasion Mr Glascock as he sat next to her almost proposed to her.

'You have never seen Monkhams?' he said. Monkhams was his father's seat, a very grand place in Worcestershire. Of course he knew very well that she had never seen Monkhams. How should she have seen it?'

'I have never been in that part of England at all,' she replied.

'I should so like to show you Monkhams. The oaks there are the finest in the kingdom. Do you like oaks?'

'Who does not like oaks? But we have none in the islands, and nobody as ever seen so few as I have.'

'I'll show you Monkhams some day. Shall I? Indeed I hope that some day I may really show you Monkhams.'

Now when an unmarried man talks to a young lady of really showing her the house in which it will be his destiny to live, he can hardly mean other than to invite her to live there with him. It must at least be his purpose to signify that, if duly encouraged, he will so invite her. But Nora Rowley did not give Mr Glascock much encouragement on this occasion.

'I'm afraid it is not likely that anything will ever take me into that part of the country,' she said. There was something perhaps in her tone which checked Mr Glascock, so that he did not then press the invitation.

When the ladies were up-stairs in the drawing-room, Lady Milborough contrived to seat herself on a couch intended for two persons only, close to Mrs Trevelyan. Emily, thinking that she might perhaps hear some more advice about Guinness's stout, prepared herself to be saucy. But the matter in hand was graver than that. Lady Milborough's mind was uneasy about Colonel Osborne.

'My dear,' said she, 'was not your father very intimate with that Colonel Osborne?'

'He is very intimate with him, Lady Milborough.'

'Ah, yes; I thought I had heard so. That makes it of course natural that you should know him.'

'We have known him all our lives,' said Emily, forgetting

probably that out of the twenty-three years and some months which she had hitherto lived, there had been a consecutive period of more than twenty years in which she had never seen this man whom she had known all her life.

'That makes a difference, of course; and I don't mean to say anything against him.'

'I hope not, Lady Milborough, because we are all especially fond of him.' This was said with so much of purpose, that poor, dear old Lady Milborough was stopped in her good work. She knew well the terrible strait to which Augustus Poole had been brought with his wife, although nobody supposed that Poole's wife had ever entertained a wrong thought in her pretty little heart. Neverthless he had been compelled to break up his establishment, and take his wife to Naples, because this horrid Colonel would make himself at home in Mrs Poole's drawing-room in Knightsbridge. Augustus Poole, with courage enough to take any man by the beard, had taking by the beard been possible, had found it impossible to dislodge the Colonel. He could not do so without making a row which would have been disgraceful to himself and injurious to his wife; and therefore he had taken Mrs Poole to Naples. Lady Milborough knew the whole story, and thought that she foresaw that the same thing was about to happen in the drawing-room in Curzon Street. When she attempted to say a word to the wife, she found herself stopped. She could not go on in that quarter after the reception with which the beginning of her word had been met. But perhaps she might succeed better with the husband. After all, her friendship was with the Trevelyan side, and not with the Rowleys.

'My dear Louis,' she said, 'I want to speak a word to you. Come here.' And then she led him into a distant corner, Mrs Trevelyan watching her all the while, and guessing why her husband was thus carried away. 'I just want to give you a little hint, which I am sure I believe is quite unnecessary,' continued Lady Milborough. Then she paused, but Trevelyan would not speak. She looked into his face, and saw that it was black. But the man was the only child of her dearest friend, and she persevered. 'Do you know I don't quite like that Colonel Osborne coming so much to your house.' The face before her became still blacker, but still the man said nothing. 'I dare say it is a prejudice on my part, but I have always disliked him. I think he is a dangerous friend; — what I call a snake in the grass. And though Emily's high good sense, and love for you, and general feelings on such a subject, are just what a husband must desire — Indeed, I am quite sure that the possibility of anything wrong has never entered into her head. But it is the very purity of her innocence which makes the danger. He is a bad man, and I would just say a word to her, if I were you, to make her understand that his coming to her of a morning is not desirable. Upon my word, I believe there is nothing he likes so much as going about and making mischief between men and their wives.'

Then she delivered herself; and Louis Trevelyan, though he was sore and angry, could not but feel that she had taken the part of a friend. All that she had said had been true; all that she had said to him he had said to himself more than once. He too hated the man. He believed him to be a snake in the grass. But it was intolerably bitter to him that he should be warned about his wife's conduct by any living human being; that he, to whom the world had been so full of good fortune, – that he, who had in truth taught himself to think that he deserved so much good fortune, should be made the subject of care on behalf of his friend, because of danger between himself and his wife! On the spur of the moment he did not know what answer to make. 'He is not a man whom I like myself,' he said.

'Just be careful, Louis, that is all,' said Lady Milborough, and then she was gone.

To be cautioned about his wife's conduct cannot be pleasant to any man, and it was very unpleasant to Louis Trevelyan. He, too, had been asked a question about Sir Marmaduke's expected visit to England after the ladies had left the room. All the town had heard of it except himself. He hardly spoke another word that evening till the brougham was announced; and his wife had observed his silence. When they were seated in the carriage, he together with his wife and Nora Rowley, he immediately asked a question about Sir Marmaduke. 'Emily,' he said, 'is there any truth in a report I hear that your father is coming home?' No answer was made, and for a moment or two there was silence. 'You must have heard of it, then?' he said. 'Perhaps you can tell me, Nora, as Emily will not reply. Have you heard anything of your father's coming?'

'Yes; I have heard of it,' said Nora slowly.

'And why have I not been told?'

'It was to be kept a secret,' said Mrs Trevelyan boldly.

'A secret from me,; and everybody else knows it! And why was it to be a secret?'

'Colonel Osborne did not wish that it should be known,' said Mrs Trevelyan.

'And what has Colonel Osborne to do between you and your father in any matter with which I may not be made acquainted? I will have nothing more between you and Colonel Osborne. You shall not see Colonel Osborne. Do you hear me?'

'Yes, I hear you, Louis.'

'And do you mean to obey me? By G –, you shall obey me. Remember this, that I lay my positive order upon you, that you shall not see Colonel Osborne again. You do not know it, perhaps, but you are already forfeiting your reputation as an honest woman, and bringing disgrace upon me by your familiarity with Colonel Osborne.'

'Oh, Louis, do not say that!' said Nora.

'You had better let him speak it all at once,' said Emily.

'I have said what I have got to say. It is now only necessary that you should give me your solemn assurance that you will obey me.'

'If you have said all that you have to say, perhaps you will listen to me,' said his wife.

'I will listen to nothing till you have given me your promise.'

'Then I certainly shall not give it you.'

'Dear Emily, pray, pray do what he tells you,' said Nora.

'She has yet to learn that it is her duty to do as I tell her,' said Trevelyan. 'And because she is obstinate, and will not learn from those who know better than herself what a woman may do, and what she may not, she will ruin herself, and destroy my happiness.'

'I know that you have destroyed my happiness by your unreasonable jealousy,' said the wife. 'Have you considered what I must feel in having such words addressed to me by my husband? If I am fit to be told that I must promise not to see any man living, I cannot be fit to be any man's wife.' Then she burst out into an hysterical fit of tears, and in this condition she got out of the carriage, entered her house, and hurried up to her own room.

'Indeed, she has not been to blame,' said Nora to Trevelyan on the staircase.

'Why has there been a secret kept from me between her and this man; that too, after I had cautioned her against being intimate with him? I am sorry that she should suffer; but it is better that she should suffer a little now, than that we should both suffer much by-and-by.'

Nora endeavoured to explain to him the truth about the committee, and Colonel Osborne's promised influence, and the reason why there was to be a secret. But she was too much in a hurry to get to her sister to make the matter plain, and he was too much angered to listen to her. He shook his head when she spoke of Colonel Osborne's dislike to have his name mentioned in connection with the matter. 'All the world knows it,' he said with scornful laughter.

It was in vain that Nora endeavoured to explain to him that though all the world might know it, Emily herself had only heard of the proposition as a thing quite unsettled, as to which nothing at present should be spoken openly. It was in vain to endeavour to make peace on that night. Nora hurried up to her sister, and found that the hysterical tears had again given place to anger. She would not see her husband, unless he would beg her pardon; and he would not see her unless she would give the promise he demanded. And the husband and wife did not see each other again on that night.

4
Hugh Stanbury

It has been already stated that Nora Rowley was not quite so well disposed as perhaps she ought to have been, to fall in love with the Honourable Charles Glascock, there having come upon her the habit of comparing him with another gentleman whenever this duty of falling in love with Mr Glascock was exacted from her. That other gentleman was one with whom she knew that it was quite out of the question that she should fall in love, because he had not a shilling in the world; and the other gentleman was equally aware that it was not open to him to fall in love with Nora Rowley – for the same reason. In regard to such matters Nora Rowley had been properly brought up, having been made to understand by the best and most cautious of mothers, that in that matter of falling in love it was absolutely necessary that bread and cheese should be considered. 'Romance is a very pretty thing,' Lady Rowley had been wont to say to her daughters, 'and I don't think life would be worth having without a little of it. I should be very sorry to think that either of my girls would marry a man only because he had money. But you can't even be romantic without something to eat and drink.' Nora thoroughly understood all this, and being well aware that her fortune in the world, if it ever was to be made at all, could only be made by marriage, had laid down for herself certain hard lines, – lines intended to be as fast as they were hard. Let what might come to her in the way of likings and dislikings, let the temptation to her be ever so strong, she would never allow her heart to rest on a man who, if he should ask her to be his wife, would not have the means of supporting her. There were many, she knew, who would condemn such a resolution as cold, selfish, and heartless. She heard people saying so daily. She read in books that it ought to be so regarded. But she declared to herself that she would respect the judgment neither of the people nor of the books. To be poor alone, to have to live without a husband, to look forward to a life in which there would be nothing of a career, almost nothing to do, to await the vacuity of an existence in which she would be useful to no one, was a destiny which she could teach herself to endure, because it might probably be forced upon her by necessity. Were her father to die there would hardly be bread for that female flock to eat. As it was, she was eating the bread of a man in whose house she was no more than a visitor. The lot of a woman, as she often told herself, was wretched, unfortunate, almost degrading. For a woman such as herself there was no path open to her energy, other than that of getting a husband. Nora Rowley thought of all this till she was almost sick of the prospect of her life, – especially sick of it when she was told with much authority by the Lady Milboroughs of her acquaintance, that it was her bounden duty to fall in love with Mr Glascock. As to falling in love with Mr Glascock, she had not as yet quite made up her mind. There was so much to be said on that side of the question, if such falling in love could only be made possible. But she had quite made up her mind that she would never fall in love with a poor man. In spite, however, of all that, she felt herself compelled to make comparisons between Mr Glascock and one Mr Hugh Stanbury, a gentleman who had not a shilling.

Mr Hugh Stanbury had been at college the most intimate friend of Louis Trevelyan, and at Oxford* had been, in spite of Trevelyan's successes, a bigger man than his friend. Stanbury had not taken so high a degree as Trevelyan, – indeed had not gone out in honours at all. He had done little for the credit of his college, and had never put himself in the way of wrapping himself up for life in the scanty lambswool of a fellowship. But he had won for himself reputation as a clever speaker, as a man who had learned much that college tutors do not profess to teach, as a hard-headed, ready-witted fellow, who, having the world as an oyster before him, which it was necessary that he should open, would certainly find either a knife or a sword with which to open it.*

Immediately on leaving college he had come to town, and had entered himself at Lincoln's Inn. Now, at the time of our story, he was a barrister of four years' standing, but had never yet made a guinea. He had never made a guinea by his work as a barrister, and was beginning to doubt of himself whether he ever would do so. Not, as he knew well, that guineas are generally made with ease by barristers of four years' standing, but because, as he said to his friends, he did not see his way to the knack of it. He did not know an attorney in the world, and could not conceive how any attorney should ever be induced to apply to him for legal aid. He had done his work of learning his trade about as well as other young men, but had had no means of distinguishing himself within his reach. He went the Western Circuit because his aunt, old Miss Stanbury, lived at Exeter, but, as he declared of himself, had he had another aunt living at York, he would have had nothing whatsoever to guide him in his choice. He sat idle in the courts, and hated himself for so sitting. So it had been with him for two years without any consolation or additional burden from other employment than that of his profession. After that, by some chance, he had become acquainted with the editor of the Daily Record, and by degrees had taken to the writing of articles. He had been told by all his friends, and especially by Trevelyan, that if he did this, he might as well sell his gown and wig. He declared, in reply, that he had no objection to sell his gown and wig. He did not see how he should ever make more money out of them than he would do by such sale. But for the articles which he wrote, he received instant payment, a process which he found to be most consolatory, most comfortable, and, as he said to Trevelyan, as warm to him as a blanket in winter.

Trevelyan, who was a year younger than Stanbury, had taken upon himself to be very angry. He professed that he did not think much of the trade of a journalist, and told Stanbury that he was sinking from the highest to almost the lowest business by which an educated man and a gentleman could earn his bread. Stanbury had simply replied that he saw some bread on the one side, but none on the other; and that bread from some side was indispensable to him. Then there had come to be that famous war between Great Britain and the republic of Patagonia,* and Hugh Stanbury had been sent out as a special correspondent by the editor and proprietor of the Daily Record. His letters had been much read, and had called up a great deal of newspaper pugnacity. He had made important statements which had been flatly denied, and found to be utterly false; which again had been warmly reasserted and proved to be most remarkably true to the letter. In this way the correspondence, and he as its author, became so much talked about that, on his return to England, he did actually sell his gown and wig and declare to his friends, – and to Trevelyan among the number, – that he intended to look to journalism for his future career.

He had been often at the house in Curzon Street in the earliest happy days of his friend's marriage, and had thus become acquainted, – intimately acquainted, – with Nora Rowley. And now again, since his return from Patagonia, that acquaintance had been renewed. Quite lately, since the actual sale of that wig and gown had been effected, he had not been there so frequently as before, because Trevelyan had expressed his indignation almost too openly.

'That such a man as you should be so faint-hearted,' Trevelyan had said, 'is a thing that I can not understand.'

'Is a man faint-hearted when he finds it impossible that he shall be able to leap his horse over a house.'

'What you had to do, had been done by hundreds before you.'

'What I had to do has never yet been done by any man,' replied Stanbury. 'I had to live upon nothing till the lucky hour should strike.'

'I think you have been cowardly,' said Trevelyan.

Even this had made no quarrel between the two men; but Stanbury had expressed himself annoyed by his friend's language, and partly on that account, and partly perhaps on another, had stayed away from Curzon Street. As Nora Rowley had made comparisons about him, so had he made comparisons about her. He had owned to himself that had it been possible that he should marry, he would willingly entrust his happiness to Miss Rowley. And he had thought once or twice that Trevelyan had wished that such an arrangement might be made at some future day. Trevelyan had always been much more sanguine in expecting success for his friend at the Bar, than Stanbury had been for himself. It might well be that such a man as Trevelyan might think that a clever rising barrister would be an excellent husband for his sister-in-law, but that a man earning a precarious living as a writer for a penny paper would be by no means so desirable a connection. Stanbury, as he thought of this, declared to himself that he would not care two straws for Trevelyan in the matter, if he could see his way without other impediments. But the other impediments were there in such strength and numbers as to make him feel that it could not have been intended by Fate that he should take to himself a wife. Although those letters of his to the Daily Record had been so preeminently successful, he had never yet been able to earn by writing above twenty-five or thirty pounds a month. If that might be continued to him he could live upon it himself; but, even with his moderate views, it would not suffice for himself and family.

He had told Trevelyan that while living as an expectant barrister he had no means of subsistence. In this, as Trevelyan knew, he was not strictly correct. There was an allowance of £100 a year coming to him from the aunt whose residence at Exeter had induced him to devote himself to the Western Circuit. His father had been a clergyman with a small living in Devonshire, and had now been dead some fifteen years. His mother and two sisters were still living in a small cottage in his late father's parish, on the interest of the money arising from a life insurance. Some pittance from sixty to seventy pounds a year was all they had among them. But there was a rich aunt, Miss Stanbury, to whom had come considerable wealth in a manner most romantic, – the little tale shall be told before this larger tale is completed, – and this aunt had undertaken to educate and place out in the world her nephew Hugh. So Hugh had been sent to Harrow, and then to Oxford, – where he had much displeased his aunt by not accomplishing great things, – and then had been set down to make his fortune as a barrister in London, with an allowance of £100 a year, his aunt having paid, moreover, certain fees for entrance, tuition, and the like. The very hour in which Miss Stanbury learned that her nephew was writing for a penny newspaper she sent off a dispatch to tell him that he must give up her or the penny paper. He replied by saying that he felt himself called upon to earn his bread in the only line from which, as it seemed to him, bread would be forthcoming. By return of post he got another letter to say that he might draw for the quarter then becoming due, but that that would be the last. And it was the last.

Stanbury made an ineffectual effort to induce his aunt to make over the allowance, – or at least a part of it, – to his mother and sisters, but the old lady paid no attention whatever to the request. She never had given, and at that moment did not intend to give, a shilling to the widow and daughters of her brother. Nor did she intend, or had she ever intended, to leave a shilling of her money to Hugh Stanbury, – as she had very often told him. The money was, at her death, to go back to the people from whom it had come to her.

When Nora Rowley made those comparisons between Mr Hugh Stanbury and Mr Charles Glascock, they were always wound up very much in favour of the briefless barrister. It was not that he was the handsomer man, for he was by no means handsome, nor was he the bigger man, for Mr Glascock was six feet tall; nor was he better dressed, for Stanbury was untidy rather than otherwise in his outward person. Nor had he any air of fashion or special grace to recommend him, for he was undoubtedly an awkward-mannered man. But there was a glance of sunshine in his eye, and a sweetness in the curl of his mouth when he smiled, which made Nora feel that it would have been all up with her had she not made so very strong a law for her own guidance. Stanbury was a man about five feet ten, with shoulders more than broad in proportion, stout limbed, rather awkward in his gait, with large feet and hands, with soft wavy light hair, with light grey eyes, with a broad, but by no means ugly, nose. His mouth and lips were large, and he rarely showed his teeth. He wore no other beard than whiskers, which he was apt to cut away through heaviness of his hand in shaving, till Nora longed to bid him to be more careful. 'He doesn't care what sort of a guy he makes of himself,' she once said to her sister, almost angrily. 'He is a plain man, and he knows it,' Emily had replied. Mr Trevelyan was doubtless a handsome man, and it was almost on Nora's tongue to say something ill-natured on the subject. Hugh Stanbury was reputed to be somewhat hot in spirit and manner. He would be very sage in argument, pounding down his ideas in politics, religion, or social life with his fist as well as his voice. He was quick, perhaps, at making antipathies, and quick, too, in making friendships; impressionable, demonstrative, eager, rapid in his movements, — sometimes to the great detriment of his shins and knuckles; and he possessed the sweetest temper that was ever given to a man for the blessing of a woman. This was the man between whom and Mr Glascock Nora Rowley found it to be impossible not to make comparisons.

On the very day after Lady Milborough's dinner party Stanbury overtook Trevelyan in the street, and asked his friend where he was going eastward. Trevelyan was on his way to call upon his lawyer, and said so. But he did not say why he was going to his lawyer. He had sent to his wife by Nora that morning to know whether she would make to him the promise he required. The only answer which Nora could draw from her sister was a counter question, demanding whether he would ask her pardon for the injury he had done her. Nora had been most eager, most anxious, most concilia-tory as a messenger; but no good had come of these messages, and Trevelyan had gone forth to tell all his trouble to his family lawyer. Old Mr Bideawhile had been his father's ancient and esteemed friend, and he could tell things to Mr Bideawhile which he could not bring himself to tell to any other living man; and he could generally condescend to accept Mr Bideawhile's advice, knowing that his father before him had been guided by the same.

'But you are out of your way for Lincoln's Inn Fields,' said Stanbury.

'I have to call at Twining's. And where are you going?'

'I have been three times round St James's Park to collect my thoughts,' said Stanbury, 'and now I'm on my way to the Daily R., 250, Fleet Street. It is my custom of an afternoon. I am prepared to instruct the British public of to-morrow on any subject, as per order, from the downfall of a European compact to the price of a London mutton chop.'

'I suppose there is nothing more to be said about it,' said Trevelyan, after a pause.

'Not another word. How should there be? Aunt Jemima has already drawn tight the purse strings, and it would soon be the casual ward in earnest if it were not for the Daily R. God bless the Daily R. Only think what a thing it is to have all subjects open to one, from the destinies of France to the profit proper to a butcher.'

'If you like it!'

'I do like it. It may not be altogether honest. I don't know what is. But it's a deal honester than defending thieves and bamboozling juries. How is your wife?'

'She's pretty well, thank you.'

Stanbury knew at once from the tone of his friend's voice that there was something wrong.

'And Louis the less?' he said, asking after Trevelyan's child.

'He's all right?'

'And Miss Rowley? When one begins one's inquiries one is bound to go through the whole family.'

'Miss Rowley is pretty well,' said Trevelyan.

Previously to his, Trevelyan when speaking of his sister-in-law to Stanbury, had always called her Nora, and had been wont to speak of her as though she were almost as much the friend of one of them as of the other. The change of tone on this occasion was in truth occasioned by the sadness of the man's thoughts in reference to his wife, but Stanbury attributed it to another cause. 'He need not be afraid of me,' he said to himself, 'and at least he should not show me that he is.' Then they parted, Trevelyan going into Twining's bank, and Stanbury passing on towards the office of the Daily R.

Stanbury had in truth been altogether mistaken as to the state of his friend's mind on that morning. Trevelyan, although he had according to his custom, put in a word in condemnation of the newspaper line of life, was at the moment thinking whether he would not tell all his trouble to Hugh Stanbury. He knew that he should not find anywhere, not even in Mr Bideawhile, a more friendly or more trustworthy listener. When Nora Rowley's name had been mentioned, he had not thought of her. He had simply repeated the name with the usual answer. He was at the moment cautioning himself against a confidence which after all might not be necesary, and which on this occasion was not made. When one is in trouble it is a great ease to tell one's trouble to a friend; but then one should always wash one's dirty linen at home. The latter consideration prevailed, and Trevelyan allowed his friend to go on without burdening him with the story of that domestic quarrel. Nor did he on that occasion tell it to Mr Bideawhile; for Mr Bideawhile was not found at his chambers.

5

Showing how the Quarrel Progressed

Trevelyan got back to his own house at about three, and on going into the library, found on his table a letter to him addressed in his wife's handwriting. He opened it quickly, hoping to find that promise which he had demanded, and resolving that if it were made he would at once become affectionate, yielding, and gentle to his wife. But there was not a word written by his wife within the envelope. It contained simply another letter, already opened, addressed to her. This letter had been brought up to her during her husband's absence from the house, and was as follows;

Acrobats, Thursday

Dear Emily,

I have just come from the Colonial Office. It is all settled, and Sir M. has been sent for. Of course, you will tell T. now.

Yours, F. O.

The letter was, of course, from Colonel Osborne, and Mrs Trevelyan, when she received it, had had great doubts whether she would enclose it to her husband opened or unopened. She had hitherto refused to make the promise which her husband exacted, but nevertheless, she was minded to obey him. Had he included in his demand any requirement that she should receive no letter from Colonel Osborne, she would not have opened this one. But nothing had been said about letters, and she would not show herself to be afraid. So she read the note, and then sent it down to be put on Mr Trevelyan's table in an envelope addressed to him.

'If he is not altogether blinded, it will show him how cruelly he has wronged me,' said she to her sister. She was sitting at the time with her boy in her lap, telling herself that the child's features were in all respects the very same as his father's, and that, come what come might, the child should always be taught by her to love and respect his father. And then there came a horrible thought. What if the child should be taken away from her? If this quarrel, out of which she saw no present mode of escape, were to lead to a separation between her and her husband, would not the law, and the judges, and the courts, and all the Lady Milboroughs of their joint acquaintance into the bargain, say that the child should go with his father? The judges, and the courts, and the Lady Milboroughs would, of course, say that she was the sinner. And what could she do without her boy? Would not any humility, any grovelling in the dust be better for her than that? 'It is a very poor thing to be a woman,' she said to her sister.

'It is perhaps better than being a dog,' said Nora; 'but, of course, we can't compare ourselves to men.'

'It would be better to be a dog. One wouldn't be made to suffer so much. When a puppy is taken away from its mother, she is bad enough for a few days, but she gets over it in a week.' There was a pause then for a few moments. Nora knew well which way ran the current of her sister's thoughts, and had nothing at the present moment which she could say on that subject. 'It is very hard for a woman to know what to do,' continued Emily, 'but if she is to marry, I think she had better marry a fool. After all, a fool generally knows that he is a fool, and will trust some one, though he may not trust his wife.'

'I will never wittingly marry a fool,' said Nora.

'You will marry Mr Glascock, of course. I don't say that he is a fool; but I do not think he has that kind of strength which shows itself in perversity.'

'If he asked me, I should not have him; – and he will never ask me.'

'He will ask you, and, of course, you'll take him. Why not? You can't be otherwise than a woman. And you must marry. And this man is a gentleman, and will be a peer. There is nothing on earth against him, except that he does not set the Thames on fire. Louis intends to set the Thames on fire some day, and see what comes of it.'

'All the same, I shall not marry Mr Glascock. A woman can die, at any rate,' said Nora.

'No, she can't. A woman must be decent; and to die of want is very indecent. She can't die, and she mustn't be in want, and she oughtn't to be a burden. I suppose it was thought necessary that every man should have two to chose from; and therefore there are so many more of us than the world wants. I wonder whether you'd mind taking that down-stairs to his table? I don't like to send it by the servant; and I don't want to go myself.'

Then Nora had taken the letter down, and left it where Louis Trevelyan would be sure to find it.

He did find it, and was sorely disappointed when he perceived that it contained no word from his wife to himself. He opened Colonel Osborne's note, and read it, and became, as he did so, almost more angry than before. Who was this man that he should dare to address another man's wife, as 'Dear Emily?' At the moment Trevelyan remembered well enough that he had heard the man so call his wife, that it had been done openly in his presence, and had not given him a thought. But Lady Rowley and Sir Marmaduke had then been present also; and that man on that occasion had been the old friend of the old father, and not the would-be young friend of the young daughter. Trevelyan could hardly reason about it, but felt that whereas the one was not improper, the other was grossly impertinent and even wicked. And then, again, his wife, his Emily, was to show to him, to her husband, or was not to show to him, the letter which she received from this man, the letter in which she was addressed as 'Dear Emily,' according to this man's judgment and wish, and not according to his judgment and wish, – not according to the judgment and wish of him who was her husband, her lord, and her master! 'Of course, you will tell T. now.' This was intolerable to him. It made him feel that he was to be regarded as second, and this man to be regarded as first. And then he began to recapitulate all the good things he had done for his wife, and all the causes which he had given her for gratitude. Had he not taken her to his bosom, and bestowed upon her the half of all that he had, simply for herself, asking for nothing more than her love? He had possessed money, position, a name, – all that makes life worth having. He had found her in a remote corner of the world, with no fortune, with no advantages of family or social standing, – so circumstanced that any friend would have warned him against such a marriage; but he had given her his heart, and his hand, and his house, and had asked for nothing in return but that he should be all in all to her, – that he should be her one god upon earth. And he had done more even than this. 'Bring your sister,' he had said. 'The house shall be big enough for her also, and she shall be my sister as well as yours.' Who had ever done more for a woman, or shown a more absolute confidence? And now what was the return he received? She was not contented with her one god upon earth, but must make to herself other gods, – another god, and that too out of a lump of the basest clay to be found around her. He thought that he could remember to have heard it said in early days, long before he himself had had an idea of marrying, that no man should look for a wife from among the tropics, that women educated amidst the languors of those sunny climes rarely came to possess those high ideas of conjugal duty and feminine truth which a man should regard as the first requisites of a good wife. As he thought of all this, he almost regretted that he had ever visited the Mandarins, or ever heard of the name of Sir Marmaduke Rowley.

He should have nourished no such thoughts in his heart. He had, indeed, been generous to his wife and to his wife's family; but we may almost say that the man who is really generous in such matters in unconscious of his own generosity. The giver who gives the most, gives, and does not know that he gives. And had not she given too? In that matter of giving between a man and his wife, if each gives all, the two are equal, let the things given be what they may! King Cophetua did nothing for his beggar maid,* unless she were to him, after he had married her, as royal a queen as though he had taken her from the oldest stock of reigning families then extant. Trevelyan knew all this himself, – had said so to himself a score of times, though not probably in spoken words or formed sentences. But, that all was equal between himself and the wife of his bosom, had been a thing ascertained by him as a certainty. There was no debt of gratitude from her to him which he did not acknowledge to exist also as from him to her. But yet, in his anger, he could not keep himself from thinking of the gifts he had showered upon her. And he had been, was, would ever be, if she would only allow it, so true to her! He had selected no other friend to take her place in his councils! There was no 'dear Mary' or 'dear Augusta' with whom he had secrets to be kept from his wife. When there arose with him any question of interest, – question of interest such as was this of the return of Sir Marmaduke to her, – he would show it in all its bearings to his wife. He had his secrets too, but his secrets had all been made secrets for her also. There was not a woman in the world in whose company he took special delight in her absence.

And if there had been, how much less would have been her ground of complaint? Let a man have any such friendships, – what friendships he may, – he does not disgrace his wife. He felt himself to be so true of heart that he desired no such friendships; but for a man indulging in such friendships there might be excuse. Even though a man be false, a woman is not shamed and brought unto the dust before all the world. But the slightest rumour on a woman's name is a load of infamy on her husband's shoulders. It was not enough for Cæsar that his wife should be true; it was necessary to

Cæsar that she should not even be suspected. Trevelyan told himself that he suspected his wife of no sin. God forbid that it should ever come to that, both for his sake and for hers; and, above all, for the sake of that boy who was so dear to them both! But there would be the vile whispers, and dirty slanders would be dropped from envious tongues into envious ears, and minds prone to evil would think evil of him and of his. Had not Lady Milborough already cautioned him? Oh, that he should have lived to have been cautioned about his wife; – that he should be told that eyes outside had looked into the sacred shrine of his heart and seen that things there were fatally amiss! And yet Lady Milborough was quite right. Had he not in his hand at this moment a document that proved her to be right? 'Dear Emily!' He took this note and crushed it in his fist and then pulled it into fragments.

But what should he do? There was, first of all considerations, the duty which he owed to his wife, and the love which he bore her. That she was ignorant and innocent he was sure; but then she was so contumacious that he hardly knew how to take a step in the direction of guarding her from the effects of her ignorance, and maintaining for her the advantages of her innocence. He was her master, and she must know that he was her master. But how was he to proceed when she refused to obey the plainest and most necessary command which he laid upon her? Let a man be ever so much his wife's master, he cannot maintain his masterdom by any power which the law places in his hands. He had asked his wife for a promise of obedience, and she would not give it to him! What was he to do next? He could, no doubt, – at least he thought so, – keep the man from her presence. He could order the servant not to admit the man, and the servant would, doubtless, obey him. But to what a condition would he then have been brought! Would not the world then be over for him, – over for him as the husband of a wife whom he could not love unless he respected her? Better that there should be no such world, than call in the aid of a servant to guard the conduct of his wife!

As he thought of it all it seemed to him that if she would not obey him, and give him this promise, they must be separated. He would not live with her, he would not give her the privileges of his wife, if she refused to render to him the obedience which was his privilege. The more he thought of it, the more convinced he was that he ought not to yield to her. Let her once yield to him, and then his tenderness should begin, and there should be no limit to it. But he would not see her till she had yielded. He would not see her; and if he should find that she did see Colonel Osborne, then he would tell her that she could no longer dwell under the same roof with him.

His resolution on these points was very strong, and yet there came over him a feeling that it was his duty to be gentle. There was a feeling also that that privilege of receiving obedience, which was so indubitably his own, could only be maintained by certain wise practices on his part in which gentleness must predominate. Wives are bound to obey their husbands, but obedience cannot be exacted from wives, as it may from servants, by aid of law and with penalties, or as from a horse, by punishments and manger curtailments. A man should be master in his own house, but he should make his mastery palatable, equitable, smooth, soft to the touch, a thing almost unfelt. How was he to do all this now, when he had already given an order to which obedience had been refused unless under certain stipulations, – an agreement with which would be degradation to him? He had pointed out to his wife her duty, and she had said she would do her duty as pointed out, on condition that he would beg her pardon for having pointed it out! This he could not and would not do. Let the heavens fall, – and the falling of the heavens in this case was a separation between him and his wife, – but he would not consent to such injustice as that!*

But what was he to do at this moment, – especially with reference to that note which he had destroyed. At last he resolved to write to his wife, and he consequently did write and send to her the following letter:

May 4

Dearest Emily,

If Colonel Osborne should write to you again, it will be better that you should not open his letter. As you know his handwriting you will have no difficulty in so arranging. Should any further letter come from Colonel Osborne addressed to you, you had better put it under cover to me, and take no notice of it yourself.

I shall dine at the club to-day. We were to have gone to Mrs Peacock's in the evening. You had better write a line to say that we shall not be there. I am very sorry that Nora should lose her evening. Pray think very carefully over what I have asked of you. My request to you is, that you shall give me a promise that you will not willingly see Colonel Osborne again. Of course you will understand that this is not supposed to extend to accidental meetings, as to which, should they occur, – and they would be sure to occur, – you would find that they would be wholly unnoticed by me.

But I must request that you will comply with my wish in this matter. If you will send for me I will go to you instantly, and after one word

from you to the desired effect, you will find that there will be no
recurrence by me to a subject so hateful. As I have done, and am doing
what I think to be right, I cannot stultify myself by saying that I think I
have been wrong.

Yours always, dearest Emily,
With the most thorough love,
Louis Trevelyan.

This letter he himself put on his wife's dressing-room table, and
then he went out to his club.

6

Showing how Reconciliation was made

'Look at that,' said Mrs Trevelyan, when her sister came into her
room about an hour before dinner-time. Nora read the letter, and
then asked her sister what she meant to do. 'I have written to Mrs
Peacock. I don't know what else I can do. It is very hard upon you,
– that you should have been kept at home. But I don't suppose Mr
Glascock would have been at Mrs Peacock's.'

'And what else will you do, Emily?'

'Nothing; – simply live deserted and forlorn till he shall choose
to find his wits again. There is nothing else that a woman can do. If
he chooses to dine at his club every day I can't help it. We must put
off all the engagements, and that will be hard upon you.'

'Don't talk about me. It is too terrible to think that there should
be such a quarrel.'

'What can I do? Have I been wrong?'

'Simply do what he tells you, whether it is wrong or right. If it's
right, it ought to be done, and if it's wrong, it will not be your
fault.'

'That's very easily said, and it sounds logical; but you must know
it's unreasonable.'

'I don't care about reason. He is your husband, and if he wishes
it you should do it. And what will be the harm? You don't mean to
see Colonel Osborne any more. You have already said that he's not
to be admitted.'

'I have said that nobody is to be admitted. Louis has driven me
to that. How can I look the servant in the face and tell him that any
special gentleman is not to be admitted to see me? Oh dear! oh
dear! have I done anything to deserve it? Was ever so monstrous

an accusation made against any woman ! If it were not for my boy,
I would defy him to do his worst.'

On the day following Nora again became a messenger between
the husband and wife, and before dinner-time a reconciliation had
been effected. Of course the wife gave way at last; and of course
she gave way so cunningly that the husband received none of the
gratification which he had expected in her surrender. 'Tell him to
come,' Nora had urged. 'Of course he can come if he pleases,' Emily
had replied. Then Nora had told Louis to come, and Louis had
demanded whether, if he did so, the promise which he exacted
would be given. It is to be feared that Nora perverted the truth a
little; but if ever such perversion may be forgiven, forgiveness was
due to her. If they could only be brought together, she was sure that
there would be a reconciliation. They were brought together, and
there was a reconciliation.

'Dearest Emily, I am so glad to come to you,' said the husband,
walking up to his wife in their bed-room, and taking her in his
arms.

'I have been very unhappy, Louis, for the last two days,' said she,
very gravely, – returning his kiss, but returning it somewhat coldly.

'We have both been unhappy, I am sure,' said he. Then he paused
that the promise might be made to him. He had certainly understood that it was to be made without reserve, – as an act on her
part which she had fully consented to perform. But she stood silent,
with one hand on the dressing table, looking away from him, very
beautiful, and dignified too, in her manner; but not, as far as he
could judge, either repentant or submissive. 'Nora said that you
would make me the promise which I ask from you.'

'I cannot think, Louis, how you can want such a promise from
me.'

'I think it right to ask it; I do indeed.'

'Can you imagine that I shall ever willingly see this gentleman
again after what has occurred ? It will be for you to tell the servant.
I do not know how I can do that. But, as a matter of course, I will
encourage no person to come to your house of whom you disap-
prove. It would be exactly the same of any man or of any woman.'

'That is all that I ask.'

'I am surprised that you should have thought it necessary to make
any formal request in the matter. Your word was quite sufficient.
That you should find cause of complaint in Colonel Osborne's
coming here is of course a different thing.'

'Quite a different thing,' said he.

'I cannot pretend to understand either your motives or your fears.

I do not understand them. My own self-respect prevents me from supposing it to be possible that you have attributed an evil thought to me.'

'Indeed, indeed, I never have,' said the husband.

'That I can assure you I regard as a matter of course,' said the wife.

'But you know, Emily, the way in which the world talks.'

'The world! And do you regard the world, Louis?'

'Lady Milborough, I believe, spoke to yourself.'

'Lady Milborough! No, she did not speak to me. She began to do so, but I was careful to silence her at once. From you, Louis, I am bound to hear whatever you may choose to say to me; but I will not hear from any other lips a single word that may be injurious to your honour.' This she said very quietly, with much dignity, and he felt that he had better not answer her. She had given him the promise which he had demanded, and he begun to fear that if he pushed the matter further she might go back even from that amount of submission. So he kissed her again, and had the boy brought into the room, and by the time that he went to dress for dinner he was able, at any rate, to seem to be well pleased.

'Richard,' he said to the servant, as soon as he was down-stairs, 'when Colonel Osborne calls again, say that your mistress is − not at home.' He gave the order in the most indifferent tone of voice which he could assume; but as he gave it he felt thoroughly ashamed of it. Richard, who, with the other servants, had of course known that there had been a quarrel between his master and mistress for the last two days, no doubt understood all about it.

While they were sitting at dinner on the next day, a Saturday, there came another note from Colonel Osborne. The servant brought it to his mistress, and she, when she had looked at it, put it down by her plate. Trevelyan knew immediately from whom the letter had come, and understood how impossible it was for his wife to give it up in the servant's presence. The letter lay there till the man was out of the room, and then she handed it to Nora. 'Will you give that to Louis?' she said. 'It comes from the man whom he supposes to be my lover.'

'Emily!' said he, jumping from his seat, 'how can you allow words so horrible and so untrue to fall from your mouth?'

'If it be not so, why am I to be placed in such a position as this? The servant knows, of course, from whom the letter comes, and sees that I have been forbidden to open it.' Then the man returned to the room, and the remainder of the dinner passed off almost in silence. It was their custom when they dined without company to leave the dining-room together, but on this evening Trevelyan remained for a few minutes that he might read Colonel Osborne's letter. He waited, standing on the rug with his face to the fire-place, till he was quite alone, and then he opened it. It ran as follows:

House of Commons, Saturday

Dear Emily, – Trevelyan, as he read this, cursed Colonel Osborne between this teeth.

Dear Emily,

I called this afternoon, but you were out. I am afraid you will be disappointed by what I have to tell you, but you should rather be glad of it. They say at the C.O. that Sir Marmaduke would not receive their letter if sent now till the middle of June, and that he could not be in London, let him do what he would, till the end of July. They hope to have the session over by that time, and therefore the committee is to be put off till next session. They mean to have Lord Bowles home from Canada, and they think that Bowles would like to be here in the winter. Sir Marmaduke will be summoned for February next, and will of course stretch his stay over the hot months. All this will, on the whole, be for the best. Lady Rowley could hardly have packed up her things and come away at a day's notice, whatever your father might have done. I'll call to-morrow at luncheon time.

Yours always,
F.O.

There was nothing objectionable in this letter, – excepting always the 'Dear Emily', – nothing which it was not imperative on Colonel Osborne to communicate to the person to whom it was addressed. Trevelyan must now go up-stairs and tell the contents of the letter to his wife. But he felt that he had created for himself a terrible trouble. He must tell his wife what was in the letter, but the very telling of it would be a renewing of the soreness of his wound. And then what was to be done in reference to the threatened visit for the Sunday morning? Trevelyan knew very well that were his wife denied at that hour, Colonel Osborne would understand the whole matter. He had doubtles in his anger intended that Colonel Osborne should understand the whole matter; but he was calmer now than he had been then, and almost wished that the command given by him had not been so definite and imperious. He remained with his arm on the mantel-piece, thinking of it, for some ten minutes, and then went up into the drawing-room. 'Emily,' he said, walking up to the table at which she was sitting, 'you had better read that letter.'

'I would so much rather not,' she replied haughtily.

'Then Nora can read it. It concerns you both equally.'

Nora, with hesitating hand, took the letter and read it. 'They are not to come after all,' said she, 'till next February.'

'And why not?' asked Mrs Trevelyan.

'Something about the session. I don't quite understand.'

'Lord Bowles is to come from Canada,' said Louis, 'and they think he would prefer being here in the winter. I dare say he would.'

'But what has that to do with papa?'

'I suppose they must both be here together,' said Nora.

'I call that very hard indeed,' said Mrs Trevelyan.

'I can't agree with you there,' said her husband. 'His coming at all is so much of a favour that it is almost a job.'*

'I don't see that it is a job at all,' said Mrs Trevelyan. 'Somebody is wanted, and nobody can know more of the service than papa does. But as the other man is a lord I suppose papa must give way. Does he say anything about mamma, Nora?'

'You had better read the letter yourself,' said Trevelyan, who was desirous that his wife should know of the threatened visit.

'No, Louis, I shall not do that. You must not blow hot and cold too. Till the other day I should have thought that Colonel Osborne's letters were as innocent as an old newspaper. As you have supposed them to be poisoned I will have nothing to do with them.'

This speech made him very angry. It seemed that his wife, who had yielded to him, was determined to take out the value of her submission in the most disagreeable words which she could utter. Nora now closed the letter and handed it back to her brother-in-law. He laid it down on the table beside him, and sat for awhile with his eyes fixed upon his book. At last he spoke again. 'Colonel Osborne says that he will call to-morrow at luncheon time. You can admit him, if you please, and thank him for the trouble he has taken in this matter.'

'I shall not remain in the room if he be admitted,' said Mrs Trevelyan.

There was silence again for some minutes, and the cloud upon Trevelyan's brow became blacker than before. Then he rose from his chair and walked round to the sofa on which his wife was sitting. 'I presume,' said he, 'that your wishes and mine in this matter must be the same.'

'I cannot tell what your wishes are,' she replied. 'I never was more in the dark on any subject in my life. My wishes at present are confined to a desire to save you as far as may be possible from the shame which must be attached to your own suspicions.'

'I have never had any suspicions.'

'A husband without suspicions does not intercept his wife's letters. A husband without suspicions does not call in the aid of his servants to guard his wife. A husband without suspicions – '

'Emily,' exclaimed Nora Rowley, 'how can you say such things, – on purpose to provoke him ?'

'Yes ; on purpose to provoke me,' said Trevelyan.

'And have I not been provoked ? Have I not been injured ? You say now that you have not suspected me, and yet in what condition do I find myself ? Because an old woman has chosen to talk scandal about me, I am placed in a position in my own house which is disgraceful to you and insupportable to myself. This man has been in the habit of coming here on Sundays, and will, of course, know that we are at home. You must manage it as you please. If you choose to receive him, I will go up-stairs.'

'Why can't you let him come in and go away, just as usual ?' said Nora.

'Because Louis has made me promise that I will never willingly be in his company again,' said Mrs Trevelyan. 'I would have given the world to avoid a promise so disgraceful to me; but it was exacted, and it shall be kept.' Having so spoken, she swept out of the room, and went up-stairs to the nursery. Trevelyan sat for an hour with his book before him, reading or pretending to read, but his wife did not come down-stairs. Then Nora went up to her, and he descended to his solitude below. So far he had hardly gained much by the enforced obedience of his wife.

On the next morning the three went to church together, and as they were walking home Trevelyan's heart was filled with returning gentleness towards his wife. He could not bear to be at wrath with her after the church service which they had just heard together. But he was softer-hearted than was she, and knowing this, was almost afraid to say anything that would again bring forth from her expressions of scorn. As soon as they were alone with the house he took her by the hand and led her apart. 'Let all this be,' said he, 'as though it had never been.'

'That will hardly be possible, Louis,' she answered. 'I cannot forget that I have been – cautioned ?'

'But cannot you bring yourself to believe that I have meant it all for your good ?'

'I have never doubted it, Louis; – never for a moment. But it has hurt me to find that you should think that such caution was needed for my good.'

It was almost on his tongue to beg her pardon, to acknowledge that he had made a mistake, and to implore her to forget that he had ever made an objection to Colonel Osborne's visit. He remembered at this moment the painful odiousness of that 'Dear Emily;' but he had to reconcile himself even to that, telling himself that, after all, Colonel Osborne was an old man, – a man older even than his wife's father. If she would only have met him with gentleness, he would have withdrawn his command, and have acknowledged that he had been wrong. But she was hard, dignified, obedient, and resentful. 'It will, I think,' he said, 'be better for both of us that he should be asked in to lunch to-day.'

'You must judge of that,' said Emily. 'Perhaps, upon the whole, it will be best. I can only say that I will not be present. I will lunch up-stairs with baby, and you can make what excuse for me you please.' This was all very bad, but it was in this way that things were allowed to arrange themselves. Richard was told that Colonel Osborne was coming to lunch, and when he came something was muttered to him about Mrs Trevelyan being not quite well. It was Nora who told the innocent fib, and though she did not tell it well, she did her very best. She felt that her brother-in-law was very wretched, and she was most anxious to relieve him. Colonel Osborne did not stay long, and then Nora went up-stairs to her sister.

Louis Trevelyan felt that he had disgraced himself. He had meant to have been strong, and he had, as he knew, been very weak. He had meant to have acted in a high-minded, honest, manly manner; but circumstances had been so untoward with him, that on looking at his own conduct, it seemed to him to have been mean, and almost false and cowardly. As the order for the exclusion of this hated man from his house had been given, he should at any rate have stuck to the order. At the moment of his vacillation he had simply intended to make things easy for his wife; but she had taken advantage of his vacillation, and had now clearly conquered him. Perhaps he respected her more than he had done when he was resolving, three or four days since, that he would be the master in his own house; but it may be feared that the tenderness of his love for her had been impaired.

Late in the afternoon his wife and sister-in-law came down dressed for walking, and, finding Trevelyan in the library, they asked him to join them, – it was a custom with them to walk in the park on a Sunday afternoon, – and he at once assented, and went out with them. Emily, who had had her triumph, was very gracious. There should not be a word more said by her about Colonel Osborne. She would avoid that gentleman, never receiving him in Curzon Street, and having as little to say to him as possible elsewhere; but she would not throw his name in her husband's teeth, or make any reference to the injury which had so manifestly been done to her. Unless Louis should be indiscreet, it should be as though it had been forgotten. As they walked by Chesterfield House and Stanhope Street into the park, she began to discuss the sermon they had heard that morning, and when she found that that subject was not alluring, she spoke of a dinner to which they were to go at Mrs Fairfax's house. Louis Trevelyan was quite aware that he was being treated as a naughty boy, who was to be forgiven.

They went across Hyde Park into Kensington Gardens, and still the same thing was going on. Nora found it to be almost impossible to say a word. Trevelyan answered his wife's questions, but was otherwise silent. Emily worked very hard at her mission of forgiveness, and hardly ceased in her efforts at conciliatory conversation. Women can work so much harder in this way than men find it possible to do! She never flagged, but continued to be fluent, conciliatory, and intolerably wearisome. On a sudden they came across two men together, who, as they all knew, were barely acquainted with each other. These were Colonel Osborne and Hugh Stanbury.

'I am glad to find you are able to be out,' said the Colonel.

'Thanks; yes. I think my seclusion just now was almost as much due to baby as to anything else. Mr Stanbury, how is it we never see you now?'

'It is the D. R., Mrs Trevelyan; – nothing else. The D. R. is a most grateful mistress, but somewhat exacting. I am allowed a couple of hours on Sundays, but otherwise my time is wholly passed in Fleet Street.'

'How very unpleasant.'

'Well; yes. The unpleasantness of this world consists chiefly in the fact that when a man wants wages, he must earn them. The Christian philosophers have a theory about it. Don't they call it the primeval fall, original sin, and that kind of thing?'

'Mr Stanbury, I won't have irreligion. I hope that doesn't come from writing for the newspapers.'

'Certainly not with me, Mrs Trevelyan. I have never been put on to take that branch yet. Scruby does that with us, and does it excellently. It was he who touched up the Ritualists, and then the Commission,* and then the Low Church bishops, till he didn't leave one of them a leg to stand upon.'

'What is it, then, that the Daily Record upholds?'

'It upholds the Daily Record. Believe in that and you will surely be saved.' Then he turned to Miss Rowley, and they two were soon walking on together, each manifestly interested in what the other was saying though there was no word of tenderness spoken between them.

Colonel Osborne was now between Mr and Mrs Trevelyan. She would have avoided the position had it been possible for her to do so. While they were falling into their present places, she had made a little mute appeal to her husband to take her away from the spot, to give her his arm and return with her, to save her in some way from remaining in company with the man to whose company for her he had objected; but he took no such step. It had seemed to him that he could take no such step without showing his hostility to Colonel Osborne.

They walked on along the broad path together, and the Colonel was between them.

'I hope you think it satisfactory, – about Sir Rowley,' he said.

'Beggars must not be choosers, you know, Colonel Osborne. I felt a little disappointed when I found that we were not to see them till February next.'

'They will stay longer then, you know, than they could now.'

'I have no doubt when the time comes we shall all believe it to be better.'

'I suppose you think, Emily, that a little pudding to-day is better than much to-morrow.'

Colonel Osborne certainly had a caressing, would-be affectionate mode of talking to women, which, unless it were reciprocated and enjoyed, was likely to make itself disagreeable. No possible words could have been more innocent than those he had now spoken; but he had turned his face down close to her face, and had almost whispered them. And then, too, he had again called her by her Christian name. Trevelyan had not heard the words. He had walked on, making the distance between him and the other man greater than was necessary, anxious to show to his wife that he had no jealousy at such a meeting as this. But his wife was determined that she would put an end to this state of things, let the cost be what it might. She did not say a word to Colonel Osborne, but addressed herself at once to her husband.

'Louis,' she said, 'will you give me your arm? We will go back, if you please.' Then she took her husband's arm, and turned herself and him abruptly away from their companion.

The thing was done in such a manner that it was impossible that Colonel Osborne should not perceive that he had been left in anger. When Trevelyan and his wife had gone back a few yards, he was obliged to return for Nora. He did so, and then rejoined his wife.

'It was quite unnecessary, Emily,' he said, 'that you should behave like that.'

'Your suspicions,' she said, 'have made it almost impossible for me to behave with propriety.'

'You have told him everything now,' said Trevelyan.

'And it was requisite that he should be told,' said his wife. Then they walked home without interchanging another word. When they reached their house, Emily at once went up to her own room, and Trevelyan to his. They parted as though they had no common interest which was worthy of a moment's conversation. And she by her step, and gait, and every movement of her body showed to him that she was not his wife now in any sense that could bring to him a feeling of domestic happiness. Her compliance with his command was of no use to him unless she could be brought to comply in spirit. Unless she would be soft to him he could not be happy. He walked about his room uneasily for half-an-hour, trying to shake off his sorrow, and then he went up to her room. 'Emily,' he said, 'for God's sake let all this pass away.'

'What is to pass away ?'

'This feeling of rancour between you and me. What is the world to us unless we can love one another ? At any rate it will be nothing to me.'

'Do you doubt my love ?' said she.

'No ; certainly not.'

'Nor I yours. Without love, Louis, you and I can not be happy. But love alone will not make us so. There must be trust, and there must also be forbearance. My feeling of annoyance will pass away in time ; and till it does, I will show it as little as may be possible.'

He felt that he had nothing more to say, and then he left her ; but he had gained nothing by the interview. She was still hard and cold, and still assumed a tone which seemed to imply that she had manifestly been the injured person.

Colonel Osborne, when he was left alone, stood for a few moments on the spot, and then with a whistle, a shake of the head, and a little low chuckle of laughter, rejoined the crowd.

7

Miss Jemima Stanbury, of Exeter

Miss Jemima Stanbury, the aunt of our friend Hugh, was a maiden lady, very much respected, indeed, in the city of Exeter. It is to be hoped that no readers of these pages will be so un-English as to be unable to appreciate the difference betwen county society and town society, – the society, that is, of a provincial town, or so ignorant as not to know also that there may be persons so privileged, that although they live distinctly within a provincial town, there is accorded to them, as though by brevet rank, all the merit of living in the county. In reference to persons so privileged, it is considered that they have been made free from the contamination of contiguous bricks and mortar by certain inner gifts, probably of birth, occasionally of profession, possibly of merit. It is very rarely, indeed, that money alone will bestow this acknowledged rank; and in Exeter, which by the stringency and excellence of its well-defined rules on such matters, may perhaps be said to take the lead of all English provincial towns, money alone has never availed. Good blood, especially if it be blood good in Devonshire, is rarely rejected. Clergyman are allowed within the pale, – though by no means as certainly as used to be the case; and, indeed, in these days of literates,* clergymen have to pass harder examinations than those ever imposed upon them by bishops' chaplains, before they are admitted ad eundem* among the chosen ones of the city of Exeter. The wives and daughters of the old prebendaries see well to that. And, as has been said, special merit may prevail. Sir Peter Mancrudy, the great Exeter physician, has won his way in, – not at all by being Sir Peter, which has stood in his way rather than otherwise, – but by the acknowledged excellence of his book about saltzes.* Sir Peter Mancrudy is supposed to have quite a metropolitan, almost a European reputation, – and therefore is acknowledged to belong to the county set, although he never dines out at any house beyond the limits of the city. Now, let it be known that no inhabitant of Exeter ever achieved a clearer right to be regarded as 'county,' in opposition to 'town,' than had Miss Jemima Stanbury. There was not a tradesman in Exeter who was not aware of it, and who did not touch his hat to her accordingly. The men who drove the flies, when summoned to take her out at night, would bring oats with them, knowing how probable it was that they might have to travel far. A distinct apology was made if she was asked to drink tea with people who were simply 'town.' The Noels of Doddiscombe Leigh, the Cliffords of Budleigh Salterton, the Powels of

Haldon, the Cheritons of Alphington, – all county persons, but very frequently in the city, – were greeted by her, and greeted her, on terms of equality. Her most intimate friend was old Mrs MacHugh, the widow of the last dean but two, who could not have stood higher had she been the widow of the last bishop. And then, although Miss Stanbury was intimate with the Frenches of Heavitree, with the Wrights of Northernhay, with the Apjohns of Helion Villa, – a really magnificent house, two miles out of the city on the Crediton Road, and with the Crumbies of Cronstadt House, Saint Ide's, – who would have been county people, if living in the country made the difference; – although she was intimate with all these families, her manner to them was not the same, nor was it expected to be the same, as with those of her own acknowledged set. These things are understood in Exeter so well!

Miss Stanbury belonged to the county set, but she lived in a large brick house, standing in the Close, almost behind the Cathedral. Indeed it was so close to the eastern end of the edifice that a carriage could not be brought quite up to her door. It was a large brick house, very old, with a door in the middle, and five steps ascending to it between high iron rails. On each side of the door there were two windows on the ground floor, and above that there were three tiers of five windows each, and the house was double throughout, having as many windows looking out behind into a gloomy courtyard. But the glory of the house consisted in this, that there was a garden attached to it, a garden with very high walls, over which the boughs of trees might be seen, giving to the otherwise gloomy abode a touch of freshness in the summer, and a look of space in the winter, which no doubt added something to the reputation even of Miss Stanbury. The fact, – for it was a fact, – that there was no gloomier or less attractive spot in the whole city than Miss Stanbury's garden, when seen inside, did not militate against this advantage. There were but half-a-dozen trees, and a few square yards of grass that was never green, and a damp ungravelled path on which no one ever walked. Seen from the inside the garden was not much; but, from the outside, it gave a distinct character to the house, and produced an unexpressed acknowledgment that the owner of it ought to belong to the county set.

The house and all that was in it belonged to Miss Stanbury herself, as did also many other houses in the neighbourhood. She was the owner of the 'Cock and Bottle', a very decent second class inn on the other side of the Close, an inn supposed to have clerical tendencies, which made it quite suitable for a close. The choristers took their beer there, and the landlord was a retired verger. Nearly the whole of one side of a dark passage leading out of the Close towards the High street belonged to her; and though the passage be narrow and the houses dark, the locality is known to be good for trade. And she owned two large houses in the High Street, and a great warehouse at St Thomas's, and had been bought out of land by the Railway at St David's, – much to her own dissatisfaction, as she was wont to express herself, but, undoubtedly, at a very high price. It will be understood therefore, that Miss Stanbury was wealthy, and that she was bound to the city in which she lived by peculiar ties.

But Miss Stanbury had not been born to this wealth, nor can she be said to have inherited from her forefathers any of these high privileges which had been awarded to her. She had achieved them by the romance of her life and the manner in which she had carried herself amidst its vicissitudes. Her father had been vicar of Nun-combe Putney, a parish lying twenty miles west of Exeter, among the moors. And on her father's death, her brother, also now dead, had become vicar of the same parish, – her brother, whose only son, Hugh Stanbury, we already know, working for the 'D. R.' up in London. When Miss Stanbury was twenty-one she became engaged to a certain Mr Brooke Burgess, the eldest son of a banker in Exeter – or, it might, perhaps, be better said, a banker himself; for at the time Mr Brooke Burgess was in the firm. It need not here be told how various misfortunes arose, how Mr Burgess quarrelled with the Stanbury family, how Jemima quarrelled with her own family, how, when her father died, she went out from Nuncombe Putney parsonage, and lived on the smallest pittance in a city lodging, how her lover was untrue to her and did not marry her, and how at last he died and left her every shilling that he possessed.

The Devonshire people, at the time, had been much divided as to the merits of the Stanbury quarrel. There were many who said that the brother could not have acted otherwise than he did; and that Miss Stanbury, though by force of character and force of circum-stances she had weathered the storm, had in truth been very indiscreet. The results, however, were as have been described. At the period of which we treat, Miss Stanbury was a very rich lady, living by herself in Exeter, admitted, without question, to be one of the county set, and still at variance with her brother's family. Except to Hugh, she had never spoken a word to one of them since her brother's death. When the money came into her hands, she at that time being, over forty and her nephew being then just ten years old, she had undertaken to educate him, and to start him in the world.

We know how she had kept her word, and how and why she had withdrawn herself from any further responsibility in the matter.

And in regard to this business of starting the young man she had been careful to let it be known that she would do no more than start him. In the formal document, by means of which she had made the proposal to her brother, she had been careful to let it be understood that simple education was all that she intended to bestow upon him, – 'and that only,' she had added, 'in the event of my surviving till his education be completed.' And to Hugh himself she had declared that any allowance which she made him after he was called to the Bar, was only made in order to give him room for his foot, a spot of ground from whence to make his first leap. We know how he made that leap, infinitely to the disgust of his aunt, who, when he refused obedience to her in the matter of withdrawing from the Daily Record, immediately withdrew from him, not only her patronage and assistance, but even her friendship and acquaintance. This was the letter which she wrote to him –

I don't think that writing radical stuff for a penny newspaper is a respectable occupation for a gentleman, and I will have nothing to do with it. If you choose to do such work, I cannot help it ; but it was not for such that I sent you to Harrow and Oxford, nor yet up to London and paid £100 a year to Mr Lambert. I think you are treating me badly, but that is nothing to your bad treatment of yourself. You need not trouble yourself to answer this, unless you are prepared to say that you will not write any more stuff for that penny newspaper. Only I wish to be understood. I will have no connection that I can help, and no acquaintance at all, with radical scribblers and incendiaries.

Jemima Stanbury

The Close, Exeter, April 15, 186 – .

Hugh Stanbury had answered this, thanking his aunt for past favours, and explaining to her, – or striving to do so, – that he felt it to be his duty to earn his bread, as a means of earning it had come within his reach. He might as well have spared himself the trouble. She simply wrote a few words across his own letter in red ink : 'The bread of unworthiness should never be earned or eaten;' and then sent the letter back under a blank envelope to her nephew.

She was a thorough Tory of the old school. Had Hugh taken to writing for a newspaper that had cost sixpence, or even threepence, for its copies, she might perhaps have forgiven him. At any rate the offence would not have been so flagrant. And had the paper been conservative instead of liberal, she would have had some qualms of conscience before she gave him up. But to live by writing for a newspaper! and for a penny newspaper!! and for a penny radical newspaper!!! It was more than she could endure. Of what nature were the articles which he contributed it was impossible that she should have any idea, for no consideration would have induced her to look at a penny newspaper, or to admit it within her doors. She herself took in the John Bull and the Herald,* and daily groaned deeply at the way in which those once great organs of true British public feeling were becoming demoralised and perverted. Had any reduction been made in the price of either of them, she would at once have stopped her subscription. In the matter of politics she had long since come to think that every thing good was over. She hated the name of Reform so much that she could not bring herself to believe in Mr Disraeli and his bill.* For many years she had believed in Lord Derby.* She would fain believe in him still if she could. It was the great desire of her heart to have some one in whom she believed. In the bishop of her diocese she did believe, and annually sent him some little comforting present from her own hand. And in two or three of the clergymen around her she believed, finding in them a flavour of the unascetic godliness of ancient days which was gratifying to her palate. But in politics there was hardly a name remaining to which she could fix her faith and declare that there should be her guide. For awhile she thought she would cling to Mr Lowe;* but, when she made inquiry, she found that there was no base there of really well-formed conservative granite. The three gentlemen who had dissevered themselves from Mr Disraeli when Mr Disraeli was passing his Reform bill,* were doubtless very good in their way; but they were not big enough to fill her heart. She tried to make herself happy with General Peel,* but General Peel was after all no more than a shade to her. But the untruth of others never made her untrue, and she still talked of the excellence of George III and the glories of the subsequent reign. She had a bust of Lord Eldon,* before which she was accustomed to stand with hands closed and to weep, – or to think that she wept.

She was a little woman, now nearly sixty years of age, with bright grey eyes, and a strong Roman nose, and thin lips, and a sharp-cut chin. She wore a head-gear that almost amounted to a mob-cap, and beneath it her grey hair was always frizzled with the greatest care. Her dress was invariably of black silk, and she had five gowns, – one for church, one for evening parties, one for driving out, and one for evenings at home and one for mornings. The dress when new, always went to church. Nothing, she was wont to say, was too good for the Lord's house. In the days of crinolines she had protested that she had never worn one, – protest, however, which was hardly true; and now, in these later days, her hatred was especially developed in reference to the head-dresses of young women. 'Chignon'* was a word which she had never been heard to pronounce. She would talk of 'those bandboxes which the sluts wear behind their noddles;' for Miss Stanbury allowed herself the use of much strong language. She was very punctilious in all her habits, breakfasting ever at half-past eight, and dining always at six. Half-past five had been her time, till the bishop, who, on an occasion, was to be her guest, once signified to her that such an hour cut up the day and interfered with clerical work. Her lunch was always of bread and cheese, and they who lunched with her either ate that, – or the bread without the cheese. An afternoon 'tea' was a thing horrible to her imagination. Tea and buttered toast at half-past eight in the evening was the great luxury of her life. She was as strong as a horse, and had never hitherto known a day's illness. As a consequence of this, she did not believe in the illness of other people, – especially not in the illness of women. She did not like a girl who could not drink a glass of beer with her bread and cheese in the middle of the day, and she thought that a glass of port after dinner was good for everybody. Indeed, she had a thorough belief in port wine, thinking that it would go far to cure most miseries. But she could not put up with the idea that a woman, young or old, should want the stimulus of a glass of sherry to support her at any odd time of the day. Hot concoctions of strong drink at Christmas she would allow to everybody, and was very strong in recommending such comforts to ladies blessed, or about to be blessed, with babies. She took the sacrament every month, and gave away exactly a tenth of her income to the poor. She believed that there was a special holiness in a tithe of a thing, and attributed the commencement of the downfall of the Church of England to rent charges, and the commutation of clergymen's incomes.* Since Judas, there had never been, to her thinking, a traitor so base, or an apostate so sinful, as Colenso;* and yet, of the nature of Colenso's teaching she was as ignorant as the towers of the cathedral opposite to her.

She believed in Exeter, thinking that there was no other provincial town in England in which a maiden lady could live safely and decently. London to her was an abode of sin; and though, as we have seen, she delighted to call herself one of the county set, she did not love the fields and lanes. And in Exeter the only place for a lady was the Close. Southernhay and Northernhay might be very well, and there was doubtless a respectable neighbourhood on the Heavitree side of the town; but for the new streets, and especially for the surburban villas, she had no endurance. She liked to deal at dear shops; but would leave any shop, either dear or cheap, in regard to which a printed advertisement should reach her eye. She paid all her bills at the end of each six months, and almost took a delight in high prices. She would rejoice that bread should be cheap, and grieve that meat should be dear, because of the poor; but in regard to other matters no reduction in the cost of an article ever pleased her. She had houses as to which she was told by her agent that the rents should be raised; but she would not raise them. She had others which it was difficult to let without lowering the rents, but she would not lower them. All change was to her hateful and unnecessary.

She kept three maid-servants, and a man came in every day to clean the knives and boots. Service with her was well requited, and much labour was never exacted. But it was not every young woman who could live with her. A rigidity as to hours, as to religious exercises, and as to dress, was exacted, under which many poor girls altogther broke down; but they who could stand this rigidity came to know that their places were very valuable. No one belonging to them need want for aught, when once the good opinion of Miss Stanbury had been earned. When once she believed in her servant there was nobody like that servant. There was not a man in Exeter could clean a boot except Giles Hickbody, – and if not in Exeter, then where else? And her own maid Martha, who had lived with her now for twenty years, and who had come with her to the brick house when she first inhabited it, was such a woman that no other servant anywhere was fit to hold a candle to her. But then Martha had great gifts; – was never ill, and really liked having sermons read to her.

Such was Miss Stanbury, who had now discarded her nephew Hugh. She had never been tenderly affectionate to Hugh, or she would hardly have asked him to live in London on a hundred a year. She had never really been kind to him since he was a boy, for although she had paid for him, she had been almost penurious in her manner of doing so, and had repeatedly given him to understand, that in the event of her death not a shilling would be left to him. Indeed, as to that matter of bequeathing her money, it was understood that it was her purpose to let it all go back to the Burgess family. With the Burgess family she had kept up no sustained connection, it being quite understood that she was never to be asked to meet the only one of them now left in Exeter. Nor was it as yet known to any one in what manner the money was to go back, how it was to be divided, or who were to be the recipients.

But she had declared that it should go back, explaining that she had conceived it to be a duty to let her own relations know that they would not inherit her wealth at her death.

About a week after she had sent back poor Hugh's letter with the endorsement on it as to unworthy bread, she summoned Martha to the back parlour in which she was accustomed to write her letters. It was one of the theories of her life that different rooms should be used only for the purposes for which they were intended. She never allowed pens and ink up into the bed-rooms, and had she ever heard that any guest in her house was reading in bed, she would have made an instant personal attack upon that guest, whether male or female, which would have surprised that guest. Poor Hugh would have got on better with her had he not been discovered once smoking in the garden. Nor would she have writing materials in the drawing-room or dining-room. There was a chamber behind the dining-room in which there was an inkbottle, and if there was a letter to be written, let the writer go there and write it. In the writing of many letters, however, she put no confidence, and regarded penny postage as one of the strongest evidences of the coming ruin.

'Martha,' she said, 'I want to speak to you. Sit down. I think I am going to do something.' Martha sat down, but did not speak a word. There had been no question asked of her, and the time for speaking had not come. 'I am writing to Mrs Stanbury, at Nuncombe Putney; and what do you think I am saying to her?'

Now the question had been asked, and it was Martha's duty to reply.

'Writing to Mrs Stanbury, ma'am?'

'Yes, to Mrs Stanbury.'

'It ain't possible for me to say, ma'am, unless it's to put Mr Hugh from going on with the newspapers.'

'When my nephew won't be controlled by me, I shan't go elsewhere to look for control over him; you may be sure of that, Martha. And remember, Martha, I don't want to have his name mentioned again in the house. You will tell them all so, if you please.'

'He was a very nice gentleman, ma'am.'

'Martha, I won't have it; and there's an end of it. I won't have it. Perhaps I know what goes to the making of a nice gentleman as well as you do.'

'Mr Hugh, ma'am, – '

'I won't have it, Martha. And when I say so, let there be an end of it.' As she said this, she got up from her chair, and shook her head, and took a turn about the room. 'If I'm not mistress here, I'm nobody.'

'Of course you're mistress here, ma'am.'

'And if I don't know what's fit to be done, and what's not fit. I'm too old to learn; and, what's more, I won't be taught. I'm not going to have my house crammed with radical incendiary stuff, printed with ink that stinks, on paper made out of straw. If I can't live without penny literature, at any rate I'll die without it. Now listen to me.'

'Yes, ma'am.'

'I have asked Mrs Stanbury to send one of the girls over here.'

'To live, ma'am?' Martha's tone as she asked the question, showed how deeply she felt its importance.

'Yes, Martha; to live.'

'You'll never like it, ma'am.'

'I don't suppose I shall.'

'You'll never get on with it, ma'am; never. The young lady'll be out of the house in a week; or if she ain't, somebody else will.'

'You mean yourself.'

'I'm only a servant, ma'am, and it don't signify about me.'

'You're a fool.'

'That's true, ma'am, I don't doubt.'

'I've sent for her, and we must do the best we can. Perhaps she won't come.'

'She'll come fast enough,' said Martha. 'But whether she'll stay, that's a different thing. I don't see how it's possible she's to stay. I'm told they're feckless, idle young ladies. She'll be so soft, ma'am, and you, – '

'Well; what of me?'

'You'll be so hard, ma'am!'

'I'm not a bit harder than you, Martha; nor yet so hard. I'll do my duty, or at least I'll try. Now you know all about it, and you may go away. There's the letter, and I mean to go out and post it myself.'

8

I Know it Will do

Miss Stanbury carried her letter all the way to the chief post-office in the city, having no faith whatever in those little subsidiary receiving houses which are established in different parts of the city.

As for the iron pillar boxes which had been erected of late years for the receipt of letters,* one of which, – a most hateful thing to her, – stood almost close to her own hall door, she had not the faintest belief that any letter put into one of them would ever reach its destination. She could not understand why people should not walk with their letters to a respectable post-office instead of chucking them into an iron stump, – as she called it, – out in the middle of the street with nobody to look after it. Positive orders had been given that no letter from her house should ever be put into the iron post. Her epistle to her sister-in-law, of whom she never spoke otherwise than as Mrs Stanbury, was as follows:

> The Close, Exeter, 22nd April, 186 –
>
> My Dear Sister Stanbury,
> Your son, Hugh, has taken to courses of which I do not approve, and therefore I have put an end to my connection with him. I shall be happy to entertain your daughter Dorothy in my house if you and she approve of such a plan. Should you agree to this, she will be welcome to receive you or her sister, – *not her brother*, – in my house any Wednesday morning between half-past nine and half-past twelve. I will endeavour to make my house pleasant to her and useful, and will make her an allowance of £25 per annum for her clothes as long as she may remain with me. I shall expect her to be regular at meals, to be constant in going to church, and not to read modern novels.
>
> I intend the arrangement to be permanent, but of course I must retain the power of closing it if, and when, I shall see fit. Its permanence must be contingent on my life. I have no power of providing for any one *after my death*,
>
> Yours truly,
> Jemima Stanbury
>
> I hope the young lady does not have any false hair about her.

When this note was received at Nuncombe Putney the amazement which it occasioned was extreme. Mrs Stanbury, the widow of the late vicar, lived in a little morsel of a cottage on the outskirts of the village, with her two daughters. Priscilla and Dorothy. Their whole income, out of which it was necessary that they should pay rent for their cottage, was less than £70 per annum. During the last few months a five-pound note now and again had found its way to Nuncombe Putney out of the coffers of the 'D. R.,' but the ladies there were most unwilling to be so relieved, thinking that their brother's career was of infinitely more importance than their comforts or even than their living. They were very poor, but they were accustomed to poverty. The elder sister was older than Hugh, but Dorothy, the younger, to whom this strange invitation was now made, was two years younger than her brother, and was now nearly twenty-six. How they had lived, and dressed themselves, and had continued to be called ladies by the inhabitants of the village was, and is, and will be a mystery to those who have had the spending of much larger incomes, but have still been always poor. But they had lived, had gone to church every Sunday in decent apparel, and had kept up friendly relations with the family of the present vicar, and with one or two other neighbours.

When the letter had been read first by the mother, and then aloud, and then by each of them separately, in the little sitting-room in the cottage, there was silence among them, – for neither of them desired to be the first to express an opinion. Nothing could be more natural than the proposed arrangement, had it not been made unnatural by a quarrel existing nearly throughout the whole life of the person most nearly concerned. Priscilla, the elder daughter, was the one of the family who was generally the ruler, and she at last expressed an opinion adverse to the arrangement. 'My dear, you would never be able to bear it,' said Priscilla.

'I suppose not,' said Mrs Stanbury, plaintively.

'I could try,' said Dorothy.

'My dear, you don't know that woman,' said Priscilla.

'Of course I don't know her,' said Dorothy.

'She has always been very good to Hugh,' said Mrs Stanbury.

'I don't think she has been good to him at all,' said Priscilla.

'But think what a saving it would be,' said Dorothy. 'And I could send home half of what Aunt Stanbury says she would give me.'

'You must not think of that,' said Priscilla, 'because she expects you to be dressed.'

'I should like to try,' she said, before the morning was over, – 'if you and mamma don't think it would be wrong.'

The conference that day ended in a written request to Aunt Stanbury that a week might be allowed for consideration, – the letter being written by Priscilla, but signed with her mother's name, – and with a very long epistle to Hugh, in which each of the ladies took a part, and in which advice and decision were demanded. It was very evident to Hugh that his mother and Dorothy were for compliance, and that Priscilla was for refusal. But he never doubted for a moment. 'Of course she will go,' he said in his answer to Priscilla; 'and she must understand that Aunt Stanbury is a most excellent woman, as true as the sun, thoroughly honest, with no fault but this, that she likes her own way. Of course Dolly can go back again if she finds the house too hard for her.' Then he sent another five-pound note, observing that Dolly's journey to Exeter would cost money, and that her wardrobe would want some improvement.

'I'm very glad that it isn't me,' said Priscilla, who, however, did not attempt to oppose the decision of the man of the family. Dorothy was greatly gratified by the excitement of the proposed change in her life, and the following letter, the product of the wisdom of the family, was written by Mrs Stanbury.

Nuncombe Putney, 1st May, 186 –

My Dear Sister Stanbury,
We are all very thankful for the kindness of your offer, which my daughter Dorothy will accept with feelings of affectionate gratitude. I think you will find her docile, good-tempered, and amiable; but a mother, of course, speaks well of her own child. She will endeavour to comply with your wishes in all things reasonable. She, of course, understands that should the arrangement not suit, she will come back home on the expression of your wish that it should be so. And she will, of course, do the same, if she should find that living in Exeter does not suit herself.' (This sentence was inserted at the instance of Priscilla, after much urgent expostulation.) 'Dorothy will be ready to go to you on any day you may fix after the 7th of this month.

Believe me to remain,
Your affectionate sister-in-law,
P. Stanbury

'She's going to come,' said Miss Stanbury to Martha, holding the letter in her hand.

'I never doubted her coming, ma'am,' said Martha.

'And I mean her to stay, unless it's her own fault. She'll have the small room up-stairs, looking out front, next to mine. And you must go and fetch her.'

'Go and fetch her, ma'am?'

'Yes. If you won't, I must.'

'She ain't a child, ma'am. She's twenty-five years old, and surely she can come to Exeter by herself, with a railroad all the way from Lessboro'.'

'There's no place a young woman is insulted in so bad as those railway carriages, and I won't have her come by herself. If she is to live with me, she shall begin decently at any rate.'

Marthua argued the matter, but was of course beaten, and on the day fixed started early in the morning for Nuncombe Putney, and returned in the afternoon to the Close with her charge. By the time that she had reached the house she had in some degree reconciled herself to the dangerous step that her mistress had taken, partly by perceiving that in face Dorothy Stanbury was very like her brother Hugh, and partly, perhaps, by finding that the young woman's manner to herself was both gentle and sprightly. She knew well that gentleness alone, without some back-bone of strength under it, would not long succeed with Miss Stanbury. 'As far as I can judge, ma'am, she's a sweet young lady,' said Martha, when she reported her arrival to her mistress, who had retired up-stairs to her own room, in order that she might thus hear a word of tidings from her lieutenant, before she showed herself on the field of action.

'Sweet! I hate your sweets,' said Miss Stanbury.

'Then why did you send for her, ma'am?'

'Because I was an old fool. But I must go down and receive her, I suppose.'

Then Miss Stanbury went down, almost trembling as she went. The matter to her was one of vital importance. She was going to change the whole tenour of her life for the sake, – as she told herself, – of doing her duty by a relative whom she did not even know. But we may fairly suppose that there had in truth been a feeling beyond that, which taught her to desire to have some one near her to whom she might not only do her duty as guardian, but whom she might also love. She had tried this with her nephew; but her nephew had been too strong for her, too far from her, too unlike to herself. When he came to see her he had smoked a short pipe, – which had been shocking to her, – and he had spoken of Reform, and Trades' Unions, and meetings in the parks,* as though they had not been Devil's ordinances. And he was very shy of going to church, – utterly refusing to be taken there twice on the same Sunday. And he had told his aunt that owing to a peculiar and unfortunate weakness in his constitution he could not listen to the reading of sermons. And then she was almost certain that he had once kissed one of the maids! She had found it impossible to manage him in any way; and when he positively declared himself as permanently devoted to the degrading iniquities of penny news-papers, she had thought it best to cast him off altogether. Now, thus late in life, she was going to make another venture, to try an altogether new mode of living, – in order, as she said to herself, with a further unexpressed hope in her bosom, that the solitude of her life might be relieved by the companionship of some one whom she might love. She had arrayed herself in a clean cap and her evening gown, and she went down-stairs looking sternly, with a full-developed idea that she must initiate her new duties by assuming a mastery at once. But inwardly she trembled, and was intensely anxious as to the first appearance of her niece. Of course there would be a little morsel of a bonnet. She hated those vile patches, – dirty flat daubs of millinery as she called them; but they had become too general for her to refuse admittance for such a thing within her doors. But a chignon, – a bandbox behind the noddle, – she would not endure. And then there were other details of feminine gear, which shall not be specified, as to which she was painfully anxious, – almost forgetting in her anxiety that the dress of this young woman whom she was about to see must have ever been regulated by the closest possible economy.

The first thing she saw on entering the room was a dark straw hat, a straw hat with a strong penthouse flap to it, and her heart was immediately softened.

'My dear,' she said, 'I am glad to see you.'

Dorothy, who, one her part, was trembling also, whose position was one to justify most intense anxiety, murmured some reply.

'Take off your hat,' said the aunt, 'and let me give you a kiss.'

The hat was taken off and the kiss was given. There was certainly no chignon there. Dorothy Stanbury was light haired, with almost flaxen ringlets, worn after the old-fashioned way which we used to think so pretty when we were young. She had very soft grey eyes, which ever seemed to beseech you to do something when they looked at you, and her mouth was a beseeching mouth. There are women who, even amidst their strongest efforts at giving assistance to others, always look as though they were asking aid themselves, and such a one was Dorothy Stanbury. Her complexion was pale, but there was always present in it a tint of pink running here and there, changing with every word she spoke, changing indeed with every pulse of her heart. Nothing ever was softer than her cheek; but her hands were thin and hard, and almost fibrous with the working of the thread upon them. She was rather tall than otherwise, but that extreme look of feminine dependence which always accompanied her, took away something even from the appearance of her height.

'These are all real, at any rate,' said her aunt, taking hold of the curls, 'and won't be hurt by a little cold water.'

Dorothy smiled but said nothing, and was then taken up to her bed-room. Indeed, when the aunt and niece sat down to dinner together Dorothy had hardly spoken. But Miss Stanbury had spoken, and things upon the whole had gone very well.

'I hope you like roast chicken, my dear?' said Miss Stanbury.

'Oh, thank you.'

'And bread sauce? Jane, I do hope the bread sauce is hot.'

If the reader thinks that Miss Stanbury was indifferent to considerations of the table, the reader is altogether ignorant of Miss Stanbury's character. When Miss Stanbury gave her niece the liver-wing, and picked out from the attendant sausages one that had been well browned and properly broken in the frying, she meant to do a real kindness.

'And now, my dear, there are mashed potatoes and bread sauce. As for green vegetables, I don't know what has become of them. They tell me I may have green peas from France at a shilling a quart; but if I can't have English green peas, I won't have any.'

Miss Stanbury was standing up as she said this, – as she always did on such occasions, liking to have a full mastery over the dish.

'I hope you like it, my dear?'

'Everything is so very nice.'

'That's right. I like to see a young woman with an appetite. Remember that God sends the good things for us to eat; and as long as we don't take more than our share, and give away something to those who haven't a fair share of their own, I for one think it quite right to enjoy my victuals. Jane, this bread sauce isn't hot. It never is hot. Don't tell me; I know what hot is!'

Dorothy thought that her aunt was very angry; but Jane knew Miss Stanbury better, and bore the scolding without shaking in her shoes.

'And now, my dear, you must take a glass of port wine. It will do you good after your journey.'

Dorothy attempted to explain that she never did drink any wine, but her aunt talked down her scruples at once.

'One glass of port wine never did anybody any harm, and as there is port wine, it must be intended that somebody should drink it.'

Miss Stanbury, as she sipped hers out very slowly, seemed to enjoy it much. Although May had come, there was a fire in the grate, and she sat with her toes on the fender, and her silk dress folded up above her knees. She sat quite silent in this position for a quarter of an hour, every now and then raising her glass to her lips. Dorothy sat silent also. To her, in the newness of her condition, speech was impossible.

'I think it will do,' said Miss Stanbury at last.

As Dorothy had no idea what would do, she could make no reply to this.

'I'm sure it will do,' said Miss Stanbury, after another short interval. 'You're as like my poor sister as two eggs. You don't have headaches, do you?'

Dorothy said that she was not ordinarily affected in that way.

'When girls have headaches it comes from tight-lacing, and not walking enough, and carrying all manner of nasty smells about with them. I know what headaches mean. How is a woman not to have a headache, when she carries a thing on the back of her poll as big as a gardener's wheel-barrow? Come, it's a fine evening, and we'll go out and look at the towers. You've never even seen them yet, I suppose?'

So they went out, and finding the verger at the Cathedral door, he being a great friend of Miss Stanbury, they walked up and down the aisles, and Dorothy was instructed as to what would be expected from her in regard to the outward forms of religion. She was to go to the Cathedral service on the morning of every week-day, and on Sundays in the afternoon. On Sunday mornings she was to attend the little church of St Margaret. On Sunday evenings it was the practice of Miss Stanbury to read a sermon in the dining-room to all of whom her household consisted. Did Dorothy like daily servies? Dorothy, who was more patient than her brother, and whose life had been much less energetic, said that she had no objection to going to church every day when there was not too much to do.

'There never need be too much to do to attend the Lord's house,' said Miss Stanbury, somewhat angrily.

'Only if you've got to make the beds,' said Dorothy.

'My dear, I beg your pardon,' said Miss Stanbury. 'I beg your pardon, heartily. I'm a thoughtless old woman, I know. Never mind. Now, we'll go in.'

Later in the evening, when she gave her niece a candlestick to go to bed, she repeated what she had said before.

'It'll do very well, my dear. I'm sure it'll do. But if you read in bed either night or morning, I'll never forgive you.'

This last caution was uttered with so much energy, that Dorothy gaved a little jump as she promised obedience.

9

Showing how the Quarrel Progressed again

On one Sunday morning, when the month of May was nearly over, Hugh Stanbury met Colonel Osborne in Curzon Street, not many yards from Trevelyan's door. Colonel Osborne had just come from the house, and Stanbury was going to it. Hugh had not spoken to

Osborne since the day, now a fortnight since, on which both of them had witnessed the scene in the park; but on that occasion they had been left together, and it had been impossible for them not to say a few words about their mutual friends. Osborne had expressed his sorrow that there should be any misunderstanding, and had called Trevelyan a 'confounded fool.' Stanbury had suggested that there was something in it which they two probably did not understand, and that matters would be sure to come all right. 'The truth is Trevelyan bullies her,' said Osborne; 'and if he goes on with that he'll be sure to get the worst of it.' Now, — on this present occasion, — Stanbury asked whether he would find the ladies at home. 'Yes, they are both there,' said Osborne. 'Trevelyan has just gone out in a huff. She'll never be able to go on living with him. Anybody can see that with half an eye.' Then he had passed on, and Hugh Stanbury knocked at the door.

He was shown up into the drawing-room, and found both sisters there; but he could see that Mrs Trevelyan had been in tears. The avowed purpose of his visit, — that is, the purpose which he had avowed to himself, — was to talk about his sister Dorothy. He told Miss Rowley, while walking in the park with her, how Dorothy had been invited over to Exeter by her aunt, and how he had counselled his sister to accept the invitation. Nora had expressed herself very interested as to Dorothy's fate, and had said how much she wished that she knew Dorothy. We all understand how sweet it is, when two such persons as Hugh Stanbury and Nora Rowley cannot speak of their love for each other, to say these tender things in regard to some one else. Nora had been quite anxious to know how Dorothy had been received by that old conservative warrior, as Hugh Stanbury had called his aunt, and Hugh had now come to Curzon Street with a letter from Dorothy in his pocket. But when he saw that there had been some cause for trouble, he hardly knew how to introduced his subject.

'Trevelyan is not at home?' he asked.

'No,' said Emily, with her face turned away. 'He went out and left us a quarter of an hour since. Did you meet Colonel Osborne?'

'I was speaking to him in the street not a moment since.' As he answered he could see that Nora was making some sign to her sister. Nora was most anxious that Emily should not speak of what had just occurred, but her signs were all thrown away. 'Somebody must tell him,' said Mrs Trevelyan, 'and I don't know who can do so better than so old a friend as Mr Stanbury.'

'Tell what, and to whom?' he asked.

'No, no, no,' said Nora.

'Then I must tell him myself,' said she, 'that is all. As for standing this kind of life, it is out of the question. I should either destroy myself or go mad.'

'If I could do any good I should be so happy,' said Stanbury.

'Nobody can do any good between a man and his wife,' said Nora.

Then Mrs Trevelyan began to tell her story, putting aside, with an impatient motion of her hands, the efforts which her sister made to stop her. She was very angry, and as she told it, standing up, all trace of sobbing soon disappeared from her voice. 'The fact is,' she said, 'he does not know his own mind, or what to fear or what not to fear. He told me that I was never to see Colonel Osborne again.'

'What is the use, Emily, of your repeating that to Mr Stanbury?'

'Why should I not repeat it? Colonel Osborne is papa's oldest friend, and mine too. He is a man I like very much, — who is a real friend to me. As he is old enough to be my father, one would have thought that my husband could have found no objection.'

'I don't know much about his age,' said Stanbury.

'It does make a difference. It must make a difference. I should not think of becoming so intimate with a younger man. But, however, when my husband told me that I was to see him no more, — though the insult nearly killed me, I determined to obey him. An order was given that Colonel Osborne should not be admitted. You may imagine how painful it was; but it was given, and I was prepared to bear it.'

'But he had been lunching with you on that Sunday.'

'Yes; that is just it. As soon as it was given Louis would rescind it, because he was ashamed of what he had done. He was so jealous that he did not want me to see the man; and yet he was so afraid that it should be known that he ordered me to see him. He ordered him into the house at last, and I, — I went away up-stairs.'

'That was on the Sunday that we met you in the park?' asked Stanbury.

'What is the use of going back to all that?' said Nora.

'Then I met him by chance in the park,' continued Mrs Trevelyan, 'and because he said a word which I knew would anger my husband, I left him abruptly. Since that my husband has begged that things might go on as they were before. He could not bear that Colonel Osborne himself should think that he was jealous. Well; I gave way, and the man has been here as before. And now there has been a scene which has been disgraceful to us all. I cannot stand it, and I won't. If he does not behave himself with more manliness, — I will leave him.'

'But what can I do?'

'Nothing, Mr Stanbury,' said Nora.

'Yes; you can do this. You can go to him from me, and can tell him that I have chosen you as a messenger because you are his friend. You can tell him that I am willing to obey him in anything. If he chooses, I will consent that Colonel Osborne shall be asked never to come into my presence again. It will be very absurd; but if he chooses, I will consent. Or I will let thing go on as they are, and continue to receive my father's old friend when he comes. But if I do, I will not put up with an imputation on my conduct because he does not like the way in which the gentleman thinks fit to address me. I take upon myself to say that if any man alive spoke to me as he ought not to speak, I should know how to resent it myself. But I cannot fly into a passion with an old gentleman for calling me by my Christian name, when he has done to habitually for years.'

From all this it will appear that the great godsend of a rich marriage, with all manner of attendant comforts, which had come in the way of the Rowley family as they were living at the Mandarins, had not turned out to be an unmixed blessing. In the matter of the quarrel, as it had hitherto progressed, the husband had perhaps been more in the wrong than his wife; but the wife, in spite of all her promises of perfect obedience, had proved herself to be a woman very hard to manage. Had she been earnest in her desire to please her lord and master in this matter of Colonel Osborne's visits, – to please him even after he had so vacillated in his own behests, – she might probably have so received the man as to have quelled all feeling of jealousy in her husband's bosom. But instead of doing so she had told herself that as she was innocent, and as her innocence had been acknowledged, and as she had been specially instructed to receive this man whom she had before been specially instructed not to receive, she would now fall back exactly into her old manner with him. She had told Colonel Osborne never to allude to that meeting in the park, and to ask no question as to what had occasioned her conduct on that Sunday; thus having a mystery with him, which of course he understood as well as she did. And then she had again taken to writing notes to him and receiving notes from him, – none of which she showed to her husband. She was more intimate with him than ever, and yet she hardly ever mentioned his name to her husband. Trevelyan, acknowledging to himself that he had done no good by his former interference, feeling that he had put himself in the wrong on that occasion, and that his wife had got the better of him, had borne with all this, with soreness and a moody savageness of general conduct, but still without further words of anger with reference to the man himself. But now, on this Sunday, when his wife had been closeted with Colonel Osborne in the back drawing-room, leaving him with his sister-in-law, his temper had become too hot for him, and he had suddenly left the house, declaring that he would not walk with the two women on that day. 'Why not, Louis?' his wife had said, coming up to him. 'Never mind why not, but I shall not,' he had answered; and then he left the room.

'What is the matter with him?' Colonel Osborne had asked.

'It is impossible to say what is the matter with him,' Mrs Trevelyan had replied. After that she had at once gone up-stairs to her child, telling herself that she was doing all that the strictest propriety could require in leaving the man's society as soon as her husband was gone. Then there was an awkward minute or two between Nora and Colonel Osborne, and he took his leave.

Stanbury at last promised that he would see Trevelyan, repeating, however, very frequently that often-used assertion, that no task is so hopeless as that of interfering between a man and his wife. Nevertheless he promised, and undertook to look for Trevelyan at the Acrobats on that afternoon. At last he got a moment in which to produce the letter from his sister, and was able to turn the conversation for a few minutes to his own affairs. Dorothy's letter was read and discussed by both the ladies with much zeal. 'It is quite a strange world to me,' said Dorothy, 'but I am beginning to find myself more at my ease than I was at first. Aunt Stanbury is very good-natured, and when I know what she wants, I think I shall be able to please her. What you said of her disposition is not so bad to me, as of course a girl in my position does not expect to have her own way.'

'Why shouldn't she have her share of her own way as well as anybody else?' said Mrs Trevelyan.

'Poor Dorothy would never want to have her own way,' said Hugh.

'She ought to want it,' said Mrs Trevelyan.

She has enough spirit to turn if she'd trodden on,' said Hugh.

'That's more than what most women have,' said Mrs Trevelyan.

Then he went on with the letter. 'She is very generous, and has given me £6 5s. in advance of my allowance. When I said I would send part of it home to mamma, she seemed to be angry, and said that she wanted me always to look nice about my clothes. She told me afterwards to do as I pleased, and that I might try my own way for the first quarter. So I was frightened, and only sent thirty shillings. We went out the other evening to drink tea with Mrs

MacHugh, and old lady whose husband was once dean. I had to go, and it was all very nice. There were a great many clergymen there, but many of them were young men.' 'Poor Dorothy,' exclaimed Nora. 'One of them was the minor canon who chants the service every morning. He is a bachelor – ' 'Then there is a hope for her,' said Nora, – 'and he always talks a little as though he were singing the Litany.' 'That's very bad,' said Nora; 'fancy having a husband to sing the Litany to you always.' 'Better that, perhaps, than having him always singing something else,' said Mrs Trevelyan.

It was decided between them that Dorothy's state might on the whole be considered as flourishing, but that Hugh was bound as a brother to go down to Exeter and look after her. He explained, however, that he was expressly debarred from calling on his sister, even between the hours of half-past nine and half-past twelve on Wednesday mornings, and that he could not see her at all unless he did so surreptitiously.

'If I were you I would see my sister in spite of all the old viragos in Exeter,' said Mrs Trevelyan. 'I have no idea of anybody taking so much upon themselves.'

'You must remember, Mrs Trevelyan, that she has taken upon herself much also in the way of kindness, in doing what perhaps I ought to call charity. I wonder what I should have been doing now if it were not for my Aunt Stanbury.'

He took his leave, and went at once from Curzon Street to Trevelyan's club, and found that Trevelyan had not been there as yet. In another hour he called again, and was about to give it up, when he met the man whom he was seeking on the steps.

'I was looking for you,' he said.

'Well, here I am.'

It was impossible not to see in the look of Trevelyan's face, and not to hear in the tone of his voice, that he was, at the moment, in an angry and unhappy frame of mind. He did not move as though he were willing to accompany his friend, and seemed almost to know beforehand that the approaching interview was to be an unpleasant one.

'I want to speak to you, and perhaps you wouldn't mind taking a turn with me,' said Stanbury.

But Trevelyan objected to this, and led the way into the club waiting-room. A club waiting-room is always a gloomy, unpromising place for a confidential conversation, and so Stanbury felt it to be on the present occasion. But he had no alternative. There they were together, and he must do as he had promised. Trevelyan kept on his hat and did not sit down, and looked very gloomy. Stanbury having to commence without any assistance from outward auxiliaries, almost forgot what it was that he had promised to do.

'I have just come from Curzon Street,' he said.

'Well!'

'At least I was there about two hours ago.'

'It doesn't matter, I suppose, whether it was two hours or two minutes,' said Trevelyan.

'Not in the least. The fact is this; I happened to come upon the two girls there, when they were very unhappy, and your wife asked me to come and say a word or two to you.'

'Was Colonel Osborne there?'

'No; I had met him in the street a minute or two before.'

'Well now; look here, Stanbury. If you'll take my advice, you'll keep your hands out of this. It is not but that I regard you as being as good a friend as I have in the world; but, to own the truth, I cannot put up with interference between myself and my wife.'

'Of course you understand that I only come as a messenger.'

'You had better not be a messenger in such a cause. If she has anything to say she can say it to myself.'

'Am I to understand that you will not listen to me?'

'I had rather not.'

'I think you are wrong,' said Stanbury.

'In that matter you must allow me to judge for myself. I can easily understand that a young woman like her, especially with her sister to back her, should induce such a one as you to take her part.'

'I am taking nobody's part. You wrong your wife, and you especially wrong Miss Rowley.'

'If you please, Stanbury, we will say nothing more about it.' This Trevelyan said holding the door of the room half open in his hand, so that the other was obliged to pass out through it.

'Good evening,' said Stanbury, with much anger.

'Good evening,' said Trevelyan, with an assumption of indifference.

Stanbury went away in absolute wrath, though the trouble which he had had in the interview was much less than he had anticipated, and the result quite as favourable. He had known that no good would come of his visit. And yet he was now full of anger against Trevelyan, and had become a partisan in the matter, – which was exactly that which he had resolutely determined that he would not become. 'I believe that no woman on earth could live with him,' he said to himself as he walked away. 'It was always the same with him, – a desire for mastery, which he did not know how to use when he had obtained it. If it were Nora, instead of the other sister, he would break her sweet heart within a month.'

Trevelyan dined at his club, and hardly spoke a word to any one during the evening. At about eleven he started to walk home, but went by no means straight thither, taking a long turn through St James's Park, and by Pimlico. It was necessary that he should make up his mind as to what he would do. He had sternly refused the interference of a friend, and he must be prepared to act on his own responsibility. He knew well that he could not begin again with his wife on the next day, as though nothing had happened. Stanbury's visit to him, if it had done nothing else, had made this impossible. He determined that he would not go to her room to-night, but would see her as early as possible in the morning; – and would then talk to her with all the wisdom of which he was master.

How many husbands have come to the same resolution ; and how few of them have found the words of wisdom to be efficacious !

10

Hard Words

It is to be feared that men in general do not regret as they should do any temporary ill-feeling, or irritating jealousy between husbands and wives, of which they themselves have been the cause. The author is not speaking now of actual love-makings, of intrigues and devilish villany, either perpetrated or imagined; but rather of those passing gusts of short-lived and unfounded suspicion to which, as to other accidents, very well-regulated families may occasionally be liable. When such suspicion rises in the bosom of a wife, some woman intervening or being believed to intervene between her and the man who is her own, that woman who has intervened or been supposed to intervene, will either glory in her position or bewail it bitterly, according to the circumstances of the case. We will certainly suppose that in a great majority of such instances, she will bewail it. But when such painful jealous doubts annoy the husband, the man who is in the way will almost always feel himself justified in extracting a slightly pleasurable sensation from the transaction. He will say to himself probably, unconsciously indeed, and with no formed words, that the husband is an ass, as ass if he be in a twitter either for that which he has kept or for that which he has been unable to keep, that the lady has shown a good deal of appreciation, and that he himself is – is – is – quite a

Captain bold of Halifax.* All the while he will not have the slightest intention of wronging the husband's honour, and will have received no greater favour from the intimacy accorded to him than the privilege of running on one day to Marshall and Snellgrove's, the haberdashers, and on another to Handcocks', the jewellers. If he be allowed to buy a present or two, or to pay a few shillings here or there, he has achieved much. Terrible things now and again do occur, even here in England; but women, with us, are slow to burn their household gods. It happens, however, occasionally, as we are all aware, that the outward garments of a domestic deity will be a little scorched; and when this occurs, the man who is the interloper, will generally find a gentle consolation in his position, let its interest be ever so flaccid and unreal, and its troubles in running about, and the like, ever so considerable and time-destructive.

It was so certainly with Colonel Osborne when he became aware that his intimacy with Mrs Trevelyan had caused her husband uneasiness. He was not especially a vicious man, and had now, as we know, reached a time of life when such vice as that in question might be supposed to have lost its charm for him. A gentleman over fifty, popular in London, with a seat in Parliament, fond of good dinners, and possessed of everything which the world has to give, could hardly have wished to run away with his neighbour's wife, or to have destroyed the happiness of his old friend's daughter. Such wickedness had never come into his head; but he had a certain pleasure in being the confidential friend of a very pretty woman; and when he heard that that pretty woman's husband was jealous, the pleasure was enhanced rather than otherwise. On that Sunday, as he had left the house in Curzon Street, he had told Stanbury that Trevelyan had just gone off in a huff, which was true enough, and he had walked from then down Clarges Street, and across Piccadilly to St James's Street, with a jauntier step than usual, because he was aware that he himself had been the occasion of that trouble. This was very wrong; but there is reason to believe that many such men as Colonel Osborne, who are bachelors at fifty, are equally malicious.

He thought a good deal about it on that evening, and was still thinking about it on the following morning. He had promised to go up to Curzon Street on the Monday, – really on some most trivial mission, on a matter of business which no man could have taken in hand whose time was of the slightest value to himself or any one else. But now that mission assumed an importance in his eyes, and seemed to require either a special observance or a special excuse. There was no real reason why he should not have stayed away from

Curzon Street for the next fortnight; and had he done so he need have made no excuse to Mrs Trevelyan when he met her. But the opportunity for a little excitement was not to be missed, and instead of going he wrote to her the following note:

Albany, Monday

Dear Emily,

What was it all about yesterday? I was to have come up with the words of that opera, but perhaps it will be better to send it. If it be not wicked, do tell me whether I am to consider myself as a banished man. I thought that our little meetings were so innocent, – and so pleasant! The green-eyed monster is of all monsters the most monstrous, – and the most unreasonable. Pray let me have a line, if it be not forbidden.

Yours always heartily,
F. O.

Putting aside all joking, I beg you to remember that I consider myself always entitled to be regarded by you as your most sincere friend.

When this was brought to Mrs Trevelyan, about twelve o'clock in the day, she had already undergone the infliction of those words of wisdom which her husband had prepared for her, and which were threatened at the close of the last chapter. Her husband had come up to her while she was yet in her bedroom, and had striven hard to prevail against her. But his success had been very doubtful. In regard to the number of words, Mrs Trevelyan certainly had had the best of it. As far as any understanding, one of another, was concerned, the conversation had been useless. She believed herself to be injured and aggrieved, and would continue so to assert, let him implore her to listen to him as loudly as he might. 'Yes; – I will listen, and I will obey you,' she had said, 'but I will not endure such insults without telling you that I feel them.' Then he had left her, fully conscious that he had failed, and went forth out of his house into the City, to his club, to wander about the streets, not knowing what he had best do to bring back that state of tranquillity at home which he felt to be so desirable.

Mrs Trevelyan was alone when Colonel Osborne's note was brought to her, and was at that moment struggling with herself in anger against her husband. If he laid any command upon her, she would execute it; but she would never cease to tell him that he had ill-used her. She would din it into his ears, let him come to her as often as he might with his wise words. Wise words! What was the use of wise words when a man was such a fool in nature? And as for Colonel Osborne, – she would see him if he came to her three times a day, unless her husband gave some clearly intelligible order to the contrary. She was fortifying her mind with this resolution when Colonel Osborne's letter was brought to her. She asked whether any servant was waiting for an answer. No, – the servant, who had left it, had gone at once. She read the note, and sat working, with it before her, for a quarter of an hour; and then walked over to her desk and answered it.

My Dear Colonel Osborne,
It will be best to say nothing whatever about the occurrence of yesterday; and if possible, not to think of it. As far as I am concerned, I wish for no change; – except that people should be more reasonable. You can call of course whenever you please; and I am very grateful for your expression of friendship.

Yours most sincerely,
Emily Trevelyan

Thanks for the words of the opera.

When she had written this, being determined that all should be open and above board, she put a penny stamp on the envelope, and desired that the letter should be posted. But she destroyed that which she had received from Colonel Osborne. In all things she would act as she would have done if her husband had not been so foolish, and there could have been no reason why she should have kept so unimportant a communication.

In the course of the day Trevelyan passed through the hall to the room which he himself was accustomed to occupy behind the parlour, and as he did so saw the note lying ready to be posted, took it up, and read the address. He held it for a moment in his hand, then replaced it on the hall table, and passed on. When he reached his own table he sat down hurriedly, and took up in his hand some Review that was lying ready for him to read. But he was quite unable to fix his mind upon the words before him. He had spoken to his wife on that morning in the strongest language he could use as to the unseemliness of her intimacy with Colonel Osborne; and then, the first thing she had done when his back was turned was to write to this very Colonel Osborne, and tell him, no doubt, what had occurred between her and her husband. He sat thinking of it all for many minutes. He would probably have declared himself that he had thought of it for an hour as he sat there. Then he got up, went up-stairs and walked slowly into the drawing-room. There he found his wife sitting with her sister. 'Nora,' he said, 'I want to speak to Emily. Will you forgive me, if I ask you to leave us for a few minutes?' Nora, with an anxious look at Emily, got up and left the room.

'Why do you send her away?' said Mrs Trevelyan.

'Because I wish to be alone with you for a few minutes. Since what I said to you this morning, you have written to Colonel Osborne.'

'Yes; – I have. I do not know how you have found it out; but I suppose you keep a watch on me.'

'I keep no watch on you. As I came into the house, I saw your letter lying in the hall.'

'Very well. You could have read it if you pleased.'

'Emily, this matter is becoming very serious, and I strongly advise you to be on your guard in what you say. I will bear much for you, and much for our boy; but I will not bear to have my name made a reproach.'

'Sir, if you think your name is shamed by me, we had better part,' said Mrs Trevelyan, rising from her chair, and confronting him with a look before which his own almost quailed.

'It may be that we had better part,' he said slowly. 'But in the first place I wish you to tell me what were the contents of that letter.'

'If it was there when you came in, no doubt it is there still. Go and look at it.'

'That is no answer to me. I have desired you to tell me what are its contents.'

'I shall not tell you. I will not discuss myself by repeating anything so insignificant in my own justification. If you suspect me of writing what I should not write, you will suspect me also of lying to conceal it.'

'Have you heard from Colonel Osborne this morning?'

'I have.'

'And where is his letter?'

'I have destroyed it.'

Again he paused, trying to think what he had better do, trying to be calm. And she stood still opposite to him, confronting him with the scorn of her bright angry eyes. Of course, he was not calm. He was the very reverse of calm. 'And you refuse to tell me what you wrote,' he said.

'The letter is there,' she answered, pointing away towards the door. 'If you want to play the spy, go and look at it for yourself.'

'Do you call me a spy?'

'And what have you called me? Because you are a husband, is the privilege of vituperation to be all on your side?'

'It is impossible that I should put up with this,' he said; – 'quite impossible. This would kill me. Anything is better than this. My present orders to you are not to see Colonel Osborne, not to write to him or have any communication with him, and to put under cover to me, unopened, any letter that may come from him. I shall expect your implicit obedience to these orders.'

'Well; – go on.'

'Have I your promise?'

'No; – no. You have no promise. I will make no promise exacted from me in so disgraceful a manner.'

'You refuse to obey me?'

'I will refuse nothing, and will promise nothing.'

'Then we must part; – that is all. I will take care that you shall hear from me before to-morrow morning.'

So saying, he left the room, and, passing through the hall, saw that the letter had been taken away.

11

Lady Milborough as Ambassador

'Of course, I know you are right,' said Nora to her sister; – 'right as far as Colonel Osborne is concerned; but nevertheless you ought to give way.'

'And be trampled upon?' said Mrs Trevelyan.

'Yes; and be trampled upon, if he should trample on you; – which, however, he is the last man in the world to do.'

'And to endure any insult and any names? You yourself, – you would be a Griselda,* I suppose.'

'I don't want to talk about myself,' said Nora, 'nor about Griselda. But I know that, however unreasonable it may seem, you had better give way to him now and tell him what there was in the note to Colonel Osborne.'

'Never! He has ordered me not to see him or to write to him, or to open his letters, – having, mind you, ordered just the reverse a day or two before; and I will obey him. Absurd as it is, I will obey him. But as for submitting to him, and letting him suppose that I think he is right; – never! I should be lying to him then, and I will never lie to him. He has said that we must part, and I suppose it will be better so. How can a woman live with a man that suspects her? He cannot take my baby from me.'

There were many such conversations as the above between the two sisters before Mrs Trevelyan received from her husband the communication with which she had been threatened. And Nora, acting on her own judgment in the matter, made an attempt to see Mr Trevelyan, writing to him a pretty little note, and beseeching him to be kind to her. But he declined to see her, and the two women sat at home, with the baby between them, holding such pleasant conversations as that above narrated. When such tempests occur in a family, a woman will generally suffer the least during the thick of the tempest. While the hurricane is at the fiercest, she will be sustained by the most thorough conviction that the right is on her side, that she is aggrieved, that there is nothing for her to acknowledge, and no position that she need surrender. Whereas her husband will desire a compromise, even amidst the violence of the storm. But afterwards, when the wind has lulled, but while the heavens around are still all black and murky, then the woman's sufferings begin. When passion gives way to thought and me. ory, she feels the loneliness of her position, – the loneliness, and the possible degradation. It is all very well for a man to talk about his name and his honour; but it is the woman's honour and the woman's name that are, in truth, placed in jeopardy. Let the woman do what she will, the man can, in truth, show his face in the world; – and, after awhile, does show his face. But the woman may be compelled to veil hers, either by her own fault, or by his. Mrs Trevelyan was now told that she was to be separated from her husband, and she did not, at any rate, believe that she had done any harm. But, if such separation did come, where could she live, what could she do, what position in the world would she possess? Would not her face be, in truth, veiled as effectually as though she had disgraced herself and her husband?

And then there was that terrible question about the child. Mrs Trevelyan had said a dozen times to her sister that her husband could not take the boy away from her. Nora, however, had never assented to this, partly from a conviction of her own ignorance, not knowing what might be the power of a husband in such a matter, and partly thinking that any argument would be good and fair by which she could induce her sister to avoid a catastrophe so terrible as that which was now threatened.

'I suppose he could take him, if he chose,' she said at last.

'I don't believe he is wicked like that,' said Mrs Trevelyan. 'He would not wish to kill me.'

'But he will say that he loves baby as well as you do.'

'He will never take my child away from me. He could never be so bad as that.'

'And you will never be so bad as to leave him,' said Nora after a pause. 'I will not believe that it can come to that. You know that he is good at heart, – that nobody on earth loves you as he does.'

So they went on for two days, and on the evening of the second day there came a letter from Trevelyan to his wife. They had neither of them seen him, although he had been in and out of the house. And on the afternoon of the Sunday a new grievance, a very terrible grievance was added to those which Mrs Trevelyan was made to bear. Her husband had told one of the servants in the house that Colonel Osborne was not to be admitted. And the servant to whom he had given this order was the – cook. There is no reason why a cook should be less trustworthy in such a matter than any other servant; and in Mr Trevelyan's household there was a reason why she should be more so, – as she, and she alone, was what we generally call an old family domestic. She had lived with her master's mother, and had known her master when he was a boy. Looking about him, therefore, for some one in his house to whom he could speak, – feeling that he was bound to convey the order through some medium, – he called to him the ancient cook, and imparted to her so much of his trouble as was necessary to make the order intelligible. This he did with various ill-worded assurances to Mrs Prodgers that there really was nothing amiss. But when Trevelyan heard what had been done, – which she did from Mrs Prodgers herself, Mrs Prodgers having been desired by her master to make the communication, – she declared to her sister that everything was now over. She could never again live with a husband who had disgraced his wife by desiring her own cook to keep a guard upon her. Had the footman been instructed not to admit Colonel Osborne, there would have been in such instruction some apparent adherence to the recognised usages of society. If you do not desire either your friend or your enemy to be received into your house, you communicate your desire to the person who has charge of the door. But the cook!

'And now, Nora, if it were you, do you mean to say that you would remain with him?' asked Mrs Trevelyan.

Nora simply replied that anything under circumstances would be better than a separation.

On the morning of the third day there came the following letter:

Wednesday, June 1, 12 midnight

Dearest Emily,

You will readily believe me when I say that I never in my life was so wretched as I have been during the last two days. That you and I should be in the same house together and not able to speak to each other is in itself a misery, but this is terribly enhanced by the dread lest this state of things should be made to continue.

I want you to understand that I do not in the least suspect you of having as yet done anything wrong, – or having even said anything injurious either to my position as your husband, or to your position as my wife. But I cannot but perceive that you are allowing yourself to be entrapped into an intimacy with Colonel Osborne which, if it be not checked, will be destructive to my happiness and your own. After what had passed before, you cannot have thought it right to receive letters from him which I was not to see, or to write letters to him of which I was not to know the contents. It must be manifest to you that such conduct on your part is wrong as judged by any of the rules by which a wife's conduct can be measured. And yet you have refused even to say that this shall be discontinued! I need hardly explain to you that if you persist in this refusal you and I cannot continue to live together as man and wife. All my hopes and prospects in life will be blighted by such a separation. I have not as yet been able to think what I should do in such wretched circumstances. And for you, as also for Nora, such a catastrophe would be most lamentable. Do, therefore, think of it well, and write me such a letter as may bring me back to your side.

There is only one friend in the world to whom I could endure to talk of this great grief, and I have been to her and told her everything. You will know that I mean Lady Milborough. After much difficult conversation I have persuaded her to see you, and she will call in Curzon Street to-morrow about twelve. There can be no kinder-hearted, or more gentle woman in the world than Lady Milborough; nor did any one ever have a warmer friend than both you and I have in her. Let me implore you then to listen to her, and be guided by her advice.

Pray believe, dearest Emily, that I am now, as ever, your most affectionate husband, and that I have no wish so strong as that we should not be compelled to part.

Louis Trevelyan

This epistle was, in many respects, a very injudicious composition. Trevelyan should have trusted either to the eloquence of his own written words, or to that of the ambassador whom he was about to despatch; but by sending both he weakened both. And then there were certain words in the letter which were odious to Mrs Trevelyan, and must have been odious to any young wife. He had said that he did not 'as yet' suspect her of having done anything wrong. And then, when he endeavoured to explain to her that a separation would be very injurious to himself, he had coupled her sister with her, thus seeming to imply that the injury to be avoided was of a material kind. She had better do what he told her, as, otherwise she and her sister would not have a roof over their head!

That was the nature of the threat which his words were supposed to convey.

The matter had become so serious, that Mrs Trevelyan, haughty and stiff-necked as she was, did not dare to abstain from showing the letter to her sister. She had no other counsellor, at any rate, till Lady Milborough came, and the weight of the battle was too great for her own unaided spirit. The letter had been written late at night, as was shown by the precision of the date, and had been brought to her early in the morning. At first she had determined to say nothing about it to Nora, but she was not strong enough to maintain such a purpose. She felt that she needed the poor consolation of discussing her wretchedness. She first declared that she would not see Lady Milborough. 'I hate her, and she knows that I hate her, and she ought not to have thought of coming,' said Mrs Trevelyan.

But she was at last beaten out of this purpose by Nora's argument, that all the world would be against her if she refused to see her husband's old friend. And then, though the letter was an odious letter, as she declared a dozen times, she took some little comfort in the fact that not a word was said in it about the baby. She thought that if she could take her child with her into any separation, she could endure it, and her husband would ultimately be conquered.

'Yes; I'll see her,' she said, as they finished the discussion. 'As he chooses to send her, I suppose I had better see her. But I don't think he does much to mend matters when he sends the woman whom he knows I dislike more than any other in all London.'

Exactly at twelve o'clock Lady Milborough's carriage was at the door. Trevelyan was in the house at the time and heard the knock at the door. During those two or three days of absolute wretchedness, he spent most of his hours under the same roof with his wife and sister-in-law, though he spoke to neither of them. He had had his doubts as to the reception of Lady Milborough, and was, to tell the truth, listening with most anxious ear, when her Ladyship was announced. His wife, however, was not so bitterly contumacious as to refuse admittance to his friend, and he heard the rustle of the ponderous silk as the old woman was shown up-stairs. When Lady Milborough reached the drawing-room, Mrs Trevelyan was alone.

'I had better see her by myself,' she had said to her sister.

Nora had then left her, with one word of prayer that she would be as little defiant as possible.

'That must depend,' Emily had said, with a little shake of her head.

There had been a suggestion that the child should be with her, but the mother herself had rejected this.

'It would be stagey,' she had said, 'and clap-trap. There is nothing I hate so much as that.'

She was sitting, therefore, quite alone, and as stiff as a man in armour, when Lady Milborough was shown up to her.

And Lady Milborough herself was not at all comfortable as she commenced the interview. She had prepared many wise words to be spoken, but was not so little ignorant of the character of the woman with whom she had to deal, as to suppose that the wise words would get themselves spoken with interruption. She had known from the first that Mrs Trevelyan would have much to say for herself, and the feeling that it would be so became stronger than ever as she entered the room. The ordinary feelings between the two ladies were cold and constrained, and then there was silence for a few moments when the Countess had taken her seat. Mrs Trevelyan had quite determined that the enemy should fire the first shot.

'This is a very sad state of things,' said the Countess.

'Yes, indeed, Lady Milborough.'

'The saddest in the world; – and so unnecessary; – is it not?'

'Very unnecessary, indeed, as I think.'

'Yes, my dear, yes. But, of course, we must remember – '

Then Lady Milborough could not clearly bring to her mind what it was that she had to remember.

'The fact is, my dear, that all this kind of thing is too monstrous to be thought of. Goodness, gracious, me; two young people like you and Louis, who thoroughly love each other, and who have got a baby, to think of being separated! Of course it is out of the question.'

'You cannot suppose, Lady Milborough, that I want to be separated from my husband?'

'Of course not. How should it be possible? The very idea is too shocking to be thought of. I declare I haven't slept since Louis was talking to me about it. But, my dear, you must remember, you know, that a husband has a right to expect some – some – some – a sort of – submission from his wife.'

'He has a right to expect obedience, Lady Milborough.'

'Of course; that is all that one wants.'

'And I will obey Mr Trevelyan – in anything reasonable.'

'But, my dear, who is to say what is reasonable? That, you see, is always the difficulty. You must allow that your husband is the person who ought to decide that.'

'Has he told you that I have refused to obey him, Lady Milborough?'

The Countess paused a moment before she replied. 'Well, yes; I think he has,' she said. 'He asked you to do something about a letter, – a letter to that Colonel Osborne, who is a man, my dear, really to be very much afraid of; a man who has done a great deal of harm, – and you declined. Now in a matter of that kind of course the husband – '

'Lady Milborough, I must ask you to listen to me. You have listened to Mr Trevelyan, and I must ask you to listen to me. I am sorry to trouble you, but as you have come here about this unpleasant business, you must forgive me if I insist upon it.'

'Of course I will listen to you, my dear.'

'I have never refused to obey my husband, and I do not refuse now. The gentleman of whom you have been speaking is an old friend of my father's; and has become my friend. Nevertheless, had Mr Trevelyan given me any plain order about him, I should have obeyed him. A wife does not feel that her chances of happiness are increased when she finds that her husband suspects her of being too intimate with another man. It is a thing very hard to bear. But I would have endeavoured to bear it, knowing how important it is for both our sakes, and more especially for our child. I would have made excuses, and would have endeavoured to think that this horrid feeling on his part is nothing more than a short delusion.'

'But, my dear – '

'I must ask you to hear me out, Lady Milborough. But when he tells me first that I am not to meet the man, and so instructs the servants; then tells me that I am to meet him, and go on just as I was going before, and then again tells me that I am not to see him, and again instructs the servants, – and, above all, the cook! – that Colonel Osborne is not to come into the house, then obedience becomes rather difficult.'

'Just say now that you will do what he wants, and then all will be right.'

'I will not say so to you, Lady Milborough. It is not to you that I ought to say it. But as he has chosen to send you here, I will explain to you that I have never disobeyed him. When I was free, in accordance with Mr Trevelyan's wishes, to have what intercourse I pleased with Colonel Osborne, I received a note from that gentleman on a most trivial matter. I answered it as trivially. My husband saw my letter, closed, and questioned me about it. I told him that the letter was still there, and that if he chose to be a spy upon my actions he could open it and read it.'

'My dear, how could you bring yourself to use the word spy to your husband?'

'How could he bring himself to accuse me as he did? If he cares for me let him come and beg my pardon for the insult he has offered me.'

'Oh, Mrs Trevelyan, – '

'Yes; that seems very wrong to you, who have not had to bear it. It is very easy for a stranger to take a husband's part, and help to put down a poor woman who has been ill used. I have done nothing wrong, nothing to be ashamed of; and I will not say that I have. I never have spoken a word to Colonel Osborne that all the world might not hear.'

'Nobody has accused you, my dear.'

'Yes; he has accused me, and you have accused me, and you will make all the world accuse me. He may put me out of his house if he likes, but he shall not make me say I have been wrong, when I know I have been right. He cannot take my child from me.'

'But he will.'

'No,' shouted Mrs Trevelyan, jumping up from her chair, 'no; he shall never do that. I will cling to him so that he cannot separate us. He will never be so wicked, – such a monster as that. I would go about the world saying what a monster he had been to me.' The passion of the interview was becoming too great for Lady Milborough's power of moderating it, and she was beginning to feel herself to be in a difficulty. 'Lady Milborough,' continued Mrs Trevelyan, 'tell him from me that I will bear anything but that. That I will not bear.'

'Dear Mrs Trevelyan, do not let us talk about it.'

'Who wants to talk about it? Why do you come here and threaten me with a thing so horrible? I do not believe you. He would not dare to separate me and my – child.'

'But you have only to say that you will submit yourself to him.'

'I have submitted myself to him, and I will submit no further. What does he want? Why does he send you here? He does not know what he wants. He has made himself miserable by an absurd idea, and he wants everybody to tell him that he has been right. He has been very wrong; and if he desires to be wise now, he will come back to his home, and say nothing further about it. He will gain nothing by sending messengers here.'

Lady Milborough, who had undertaken a most disagreeable task from the purest motives of old friendship, did not like being called a messenger; but the woman before her was so strong in her words, so eager, and so passionate, that she did not know how to resent the injury. And there was coming over her an idea, of which she herself was hardly conscious, that after all, perhaps, the husband was not in the right. She had come there with th general idea that wives, and especially young wives, should be submissive. She had naturally taken the husband's part; and having a preconceived dislike to Colonel Osborne, she had been willing enough to think that precautionary measures were necessary in reference to so eminent, and notorious, and experienced a Lothario. She had never altogether loved Mrs Trevelyan, and had always been a little in dread of her. But she had thought that the authority with which she would be invested on this occasion, the manifest right on her side, and the undeniable truth of her grand argument, that a wife should obey, would carry her, if not easily, still successfully through all difficulties. It was probably the case that Lady Milborough when preparing for her visit, had anticipated a triumph. But when she had been closeted for an hour with Mrs Trevelyan, she found that she was not triumphant. She was told that she was a messenger, and an unwelcome messenger; and she began to feel that she did not know how she was to take herself away.

'I am sure I have done everything for the best,' she said, getting up from her chair.

'The best will be to send him back, and make him feel the truth.'

'The best for you, my dear, will be to consider well what should be the duty of a wife.'

'I have considered, Lady Milborough. It cannot be a wife's duty to acknowledge that she has been wrong in such a matter as this.'

Then Lady Milborough made her curtsey and got herself away in some manner that was sufficiently awkward, and Mrs Trevelyan curseyed also as she rang the bell; and, though she was sore and wretched, and, in truth, sadly frightened, she was not awkward. In that encounter, so far as it had gone, she had been the victor.

As soon as she was alone and the carriage had been driven well away from the door, Mrs Trevelyan left the drawing-room and went up to the nursery. As she entered she clothed her face with her sweetest smile. 'How is his own mother's dearest, dearest, darling duck?' she said, putting out her arms and taking the boy from the nurse. The child was at this time about ten months old, and was a strong, hearty, happy infant, always laughing when he was awake and always sleeping when he did not laugh, because his little limbs were free from pain and his little stomach was not annoyed by internal troubles. He kicked, and crowed, and sputtered, when his mother took him, and put up his little fingers to clutch her hair, and was to her as a young god upon the earth. Nothing in the world had ever been created so beautiful, so joyous, so satisfactory, so divine! And they told her that this apple of her eye was to be taken away from her! No; – that must be impossible. 'I will take him into my own room, nurse, for a little while – you have had him all the morning,' she said; as though the 'having baby' was a privilege over which there might almost be a quarrel. Then she took her boy away with her, and when she was alone with him, went through such a service in baby-worship as most mothers will understand. Divide these two! No; nobody should do that. Sooner than that, she, the mother, would consent to be no more than a servant in her husband's house. Was not her baby all the world to her?

On the evening of that day the husband and wife had an interview together in the library, which, unfortunately, was as unsatisfactory as Lady Milborough's visit. The cause of the failure of them all lay probably in this, – that there was no decided point which, if conceded, would have brought about a reconciliation. Trevelyan asked for general submission, which he regarded as his right, and which in the existing circumstances he thought it necessary to claim, and though Mrs Trevelyan did not refuse to be submissive she would make no promise on the subject. But the truth was that each desired that the other should acknowledge a fault, and that neither of them would make that acknowledgment. Emily Trevelyan felt acutely that she had been ill-used, not only by her husband's suspicion, but by the manner in which he had talked of his suspicion to others, – to Lady Milborough and the cook, and she was quite convinced that she was right herself, because he had been so vacillating in his conduct about Colonel Osborne. But Trevelyan was equally sure that justice was on his side. Emily must have known his real wishes about Colonel Osborne; but when she had found that he had rescinded his verbal orders about the admission of the man to the house, – which he had done to save himself and her from slander and gossip, – she had taken advantage of this and had thrown herself more entirely than ever into the intimacy of which he disapproved! When they met, each was so sore that no approach to terms was made by them.

'If I am to be treated in that way, I would rather not live with you,' said the wife. 'It is impossible to live with a husband who is jealous.'

'All I ask of you is that you promise me to have no further communication with this man.'

'I will make no promise that implies my own disgrace.'

'Then we must part; and if that be so, this house will be given up. You may live where you please, – in the country, not in

London; but I shall take steps that Colonel Osborne does not see you.'

'I will not remain in the room with you to be insulted thus,' said Mrs Trevelyan. And she did not remain, but left the chamber, slamming the door after her as she went.

'It will be better that she should go,' said Trevelyan, when he found himself alone. And so it came to pass that that blessing of a rich marriage, which had as it were fallen upon them at the Mandarins from out of heaven, had become, after an interval of but two short years, anything but an unmixed blessing.

12

Miss Stanbury's Generosity

On one Wednesday morning early in June, great preparations were being made at the brick house in the Close at Exeter for an event which can hardly be said to have required any preparation at all. Mrs Stanbury and her elder daughter were coming into Exeter from Nuncombe Putney to visit Dorothy. The reader may perhaps remember that when Miss Stanbury's invitation was sent to her niece, she was pleased to promise that such visits should be permitted on a Wednesday morning. Such a visit was now to be made, and old Miss Stanbury was quite moved by the occasion. 'I shall not see them, you know, Martha,' she had said, on the afternoon of the preceding day.

'I suppose not, ma'am.'

'Certainly not. Why should I? It would be no good.'

'It is not for me to say, ma'am, of course.'

'No, Martha, it is not. And I am sure that I am right. It's no good going back and undoing in ten minutes what twenty years have done. She's a poor harmless creature, I believe.'

'The most harmless in the world, ma'am.'

'But she was as bad as poison to me when she was young, and what's the good of trying to change it now? If I was to tell her that I loved her, I should only be lying.'

'Then, ma'am, I would not say it.'

'And I don't mean. But you'll take in some wine and cake, you know.'

'I don't think they'll care for wine and cake.'

'Will you do as I tell you? What matters whether they care for it or not. They need not take it. It will look better for Miss Dorothy.

If Dorothy is to remain here I shall choose that she should be respected.' And so the question of the cake and wine had been decided overnight. But when the morning came Miss Stanbury was still in a twitter. Half-past ten had been the hour fixed for the visit, in consequence of there being a train in from Lessboro', due at the Exeter station at ten. As Miss Stanbury breakfasted always at half-past eight, there was no need of hurry on account of the expected visit. But, nevertheless, she was in a fuss all the morning; and spoke of the coming period as one in which she must necessarily put herself into solitary confinement.

'Perhaps your mamma will be cold,' she said, 'and will expect a fire.'

'Oh, dear, no, Aunt Stanbury.'

'It could be lighted of course. It is a pity they should come just so as to prevent you from going to morning service; is it not?'

'I could go with you, aunt, and be back very nearly in time. They won't mind waiting a quarter of an hour.'

'What; and have them here all alone! I wouldn't think of such a thing. I shall go up-stairs. You had better come to me when they are gone. Don't hurry them. I don't want you to hurry them at all; and if your require anything, Martha will wait upon you. I have told the girls to keep out of the way. They are so giddy, there's no knowing what they might be after. Besides, – they've got their work to mind.'

All this was very terrible to poor Dorothy, who had not as yet quite recovered from the original fear with which her aunt had inspired her, – so terrible that she was almost sorry that her mother and sister were coming to her. When the knock was heard at the door, precisely as the cathedral clock was striking half-past ten, – to secure which punctuality, and thereby not to offend the owner of the mansion, Mrs Stanbury and Priscilla had been walking about the Close for the last ten minutes, – Miss Stanbury was still in the parlour.

'There they are!' she exclaimed, jumping up. 'They haven't given a body much time to run away, have they, my dear? Half a minute, Martha, – just half a minute!' Then she gathered up her things as though she had been ill-treated in being driven to make so sudden a retreat, and Martha, as soon as the last hem of her mistress's dress had become invisible on the stairs, opened the front door for the visitors.

'Do you mean to say you like it?' said Priscilla, when they had been there about a quarter of an hour.

'H – u – sh,' whispered Mrs Stanbury.

'I don't suppose she's listening at the door,' said Priscilla.

'Indeed, she's not,' said Dorothy. 'There can't be a truer, honester woman, than Aunt Stanbury.'

'But is she kind to you, Dolly?' asked her mother.

'Very kind; too kind. Only I don't understand her quite, and then she gets angry with me. I know she thinks I'm a fool, and that's the worst of it.'

'Then, if I were you, I would come home,' said Priscilla.

'She'll never forgive you if you do,' said Mrs Stanbury.

'And who need care about her forgiveness?' said Priscilla.

'I don't mean to go home yet, at any rate,' said Dorothy. Then there was a knock at the door, and Martha entered with the cake and wine. 'Miss Stanbury's compliments, ladies, and she hopes you'll take a glass of sherry.' Whereupon she filled out the glasses and carried them round.

'Pray give my compliments and thanks to my sister Stanbury,' said Dorothy's mother. But Priscilla put down the glass of wine without touching it, and looked her sternest at the maid.

Altogether, the visit was not very successful, and poor Dorothy almost felt that if she chose to remain in the Close she must lose her mother and sister, and that without really making a friend of her aunt. There had as yet been no quarrel, – nothing that had been plainly recognised or disagreeable; but there had not as yet come to be any sympathy, or assured signs of comfortable love. Miss Stanbury had declared more than once that it would do, but had not succeeded in showing in what the success consisted. When she was told that the two ladies were gone, she desired that Dorothy might be sent to her, and immediately began to make anxious inquiries.

'Well, my dear, and what do they think of it?'

'I don't know, aunt, that they think very much.'

'And what do they say about it?'

'They didn't say very much, aunt. I was very glad to see mamma and Priscilla. Perhaps I ought to tell you that mamma gave me back the money I sent her.'

'What did she do that for?' asked Miss Stanbury very sharply.

'Because she says that Hugh sends her now what she wants.' Miss Stanbury, when she heard this, looked very sour. 'I thought it best to tell you, you know.'

'It will never come to any good, got in that way, – never.'

' But, Aunt Stanbury, isn't it good of him to send it?'

'I don't know. I suppose it's better than drinking, and smoking, and gambling. But I dare say he gets enough for that too. When a man, born and bred like a gentleman, condescends to let out his talents and education for such purposes, I dare say they are willing enough to pay him. The devil always does pay high wages. But that only makes it so much the worse. One almost comes to doubt whether any one ought to learn to write at all, when it is used for such vile purposes. I've said what I've got to say, and I don't mean to say anything more. What's the use? But it has been hard upon me, – very. It was my money did it, and I feel I've misused it. It's a disgrace to me which I don't deserve.'

For a couple of minutes Dorothy remained quite silent, and Miss Stanbury did not herself say anything further. Nor during that time did she observe her niece, or she would probably have seen that the subject was not to be dropped. Dorothy, though she was silent, was not calm, and was preparing herself for a crusade in her brother's defence.

'Aunt Stanbury, he's my brother, you know.'

'Of course he's your brother. I wish he were not.'

'I think him the best brother in the world, – and the best son.'

'Why does he sell himself to write sedition?'

'He doesn't sell himself to write sedition. I don't see why it should be sedition, or anything wicked, because it's sold for a penny.'

'If you are going to cram him down my throat, Dorothy, you and I had better part.'

'I don't want to say anything about him, only you ought – not – to abuse him – before me.' By this time Dorothy was beginning to sob, but Miss Stanbury's countenance was still very grim and very stern. 'He's coming home to Nuncombe Putney, and I want to – see – see him,' continued Dorothy.

'Hugh Stanbury coming to Exeter! He won't come here.'

'Then I'd rather go home, Aunt Stanbury.'

'Very well, very well,' said Miss Stanbury, and she got up and left the room.

Dorothy was in dismay, and began to think that there was nothing for her to do but to pack up her clothes and prepare for her departure. She was very sorry for what had occurred, being fully alive to the importance of the aid not only to herself, but to her mother and sister, which was afforded by the present arrangement, and she felt very angry with herself, in that she had already driven her aunt to quarrel with her. But she had found it to be impossible to hear her own brother abused without saying a word on his behalf. She did not see her aunt again till dinner-time, and then there was hardly a word uttered. Once or twice Dorothy made a little effort to speak, but these attempts failed utterly. The old woman would hardly reply even by a monosyllable, but simply muttered something, or shook her head when she was addressed. Jane, who waited at table, was very demure and silent, and Martha, who once came into the room during the meal, merely whispered a word into Miss Stanbury's ear. When the cloth was removed, and two glasses of port had been poured out by Miss Stanbury herself, Dorothy felt that she could endure this treatment no longer. How was it possible that she could drink wine under such circumstances?

'Not for me, Aunt Stanbury,' said she, with a deploring tone.

'Why not?'

'I couldn't drink it to-day.'

'Why didn't you say so before it was poured out? And why not to-day? Come, drink it. Do as I bid you.' And she stood over her niece, as a tragedy queen in a play with a bowl of poison. Dorothy took it and sipped it from mere force of obedience. 'You make as many bones about a glass of port wine as though it were senna and salts,' said Miss Stanbury. 'Now I've got something to say to you.' By this time the servant was gone, and the two were seated alone together in the parlour. Dorothy, who had not as yet swallowed above half her wine, at once put the glass down. There was an importance in her aunt's tone which frightened her, and made her feel that some evil was coming. And yet, as she had made up her mind that she must return home, there was no further evil that she need dread. 'You didn't write any of those horrid articles?' said Miss Stanbury.

'No, aunt; I didn't write them. I shouldn't know how.'

'And I hope you'll never learn. They say women are to vote, and become doctors,* and if so, there's no knowing what devil's tricks they mayn't do. But it isn't your fault about that filthy newspaper. How he can let himself down to write stuff that is to be printed on straw is what I can't understand.'

'I don't see how it can make a difference as he writes it.'

'It would make a great deal of difference to me. And I'm told that what they call ink comes off on your fingers like lamp-black. I never touched one, thank God; but they tell me so. All the same; it isn't your fault.'

'I've nothing to do with it, Aunt Stanbury.'

'Of course you've not. And as he is your brother it wouldn't be natural that you should like to throw him off. And, my dear, I like you for taking his part. Only you needn't have been so fierce with an old woman.'

'Indeed – indeed I didn't mean to be – fierce, Aunt Stanbury.'

'I never was taken up so short in my life. But we won't mind that.

There; he shall come and see you. I suppose he won't insist on leaving any of his nastiness about.'

'But is he to come here, Aunt Stanbury?'

'He may if he pleases.'

'Oh, Aunt Stanbury!'

'When he was here last he generally had a pipe in his mouth, and I dare say he never puts it down at all now. Those things grow upon young people so fast. But if he could leave it on the door-step just while he's here I should be obliged to him.'

'But, dear aunt, couldn't I see him in the street?'

'Out in the street! No, my dear. All the world is not to know that he's your brother; and he is dressed in such a rapscallion manner that the people would think you were talking to a house-breaker.' Dorothy's face became again red as she heard this, and the angry words were very nearly spoken. 'The last time I saw him,' continued Miss Stanbury, 'he had on a short, rough jacket, with enormous buttons, and one of those flipperty-flopperty things on his head, that the butcher-boys wear. And, oh, the smell of tobacco! As he had been up in London I suppose he thought Exeter was no better than a village, and he might do just as he pleased. But he knew that if I'm particular about anything, it is about a gentleman's hat in the streets. And he wanted me – me! – to walk with him across to Mrs MacHugh's! We should have been hooted about the Close like a pair of mad dogs; – and so I told him.'

'All the young men seem to dress like that now, Aunt Stanbury.'

'No, they don't. Mr Gibson doesn't dress like that.'

'But he's a clergyman, Aunt Stanbury.'

'Perhaps I'm an old fool. I dare say I am, and of course that's what you mean. At any rate I'm too old to change, and I don't mean to try. I like to see a difference between a gentleman and a house-breaker. For the matter of that I'm told that there is a difference, and that the house-breakers all look like gentlemen now. It may be proper to make us all stand on our heads, with our legs sticking up in the air; but I for one don't like being topsy-turvey, and I won't try it. When is he to reach Exeter?'

'He is coming on Tuesday next, by the last train.'

'Then you can't see him that night. That's out of the question. No doubt he'll sleep at the Nag's Head, as that's the lowest radical public-house in the city. Martha shall try to find him. She knows more about his doings than I do. If he chooses to come here the following morning before he goes down to Nuncombe Putney, well and good. I shall wait up till Martha comes back from the train on Tuesday night, and hear.' Dorothy was of course full of gratitude and thanks; but yet she felt almost disappointed by the result of her aunt's clemency on the matter. She had desired to take her brother's part, and it had seemed to her as though she had done so in a very lukewarm manner. She had listened to an immense number of accusations against him, and had been unable to reply to them because she had been conquered by the promise of a visit. And now it was out of the question that she should speak of going. Her aunt had given way to her, and of course had conquered her.

Late on the Tuesday evening, after ten o'clock, Hugh Stanbury was walking round the Close with his aunt's servant. He had not put up at that dreadfully radical establishment of which Miss Stanbury was so much afraid, but had taken a bedroom at the Railway Inn. From there he had walked up to the Close with Martha, and now was having a few last words with her before he would allow her to return to the house.

'I suppose she'd as soon see the devil as see me,' said Hugh.

'If you speak in that way, Mr Hugh, I won't listen to you.'

'And yet I did everything I could to please her; and I don't think any boy ever loved an old woman better than I did her.'

'That was while she used to send you cakes, and ham, and jam to school, Mr Hugh.'

'Of course it was, and while she sent me flannel waistcoats to Oxford. But when I didn't care any longer for cakes or flannel then she got tired of me. It is much better as it is, if she'll only be good to Dorothy.'

'She never was bad to any body, Mr Hugh. But I don't think an old lady like her ever takes to a young woman as she does to a young man, if only he'll let her have a little more of her own way than you would. It's my belief that you might have had it all for your own some day, if you'd done as you ought.'

'That's nonsense, Martha. She means to leave it all to the Burgesses. I've heard her say so.'

'Say so; yes. People don't always do what they say. If you'd managed rightly you might have it all; – and so you might now.'

'I'll tell you what, old girl; I shan't try. Live for the next twenty years under her apron strings, that I may have the chance at the end of it to of cutting some poor devil out of his money! Do you know the meaning of making a score off your own bat, Martha?'

'No, I don't; and if it's anything you're like to do, I don't think I should be the better for learning, – by all accounts. And now if you please, I'll go in.'

'Good night, Martha. My love to them both, and say I'll be there to-morrow exactly at half-past nine. You'd better take it. It won't turn to slate-stone. It hasn't come from the old gentleman.'

'I don't want anything of that kind, Mr Hugh; – indeed I don't.'

'Nonsense. If you don't take it you'll offend me. I believe you think I'm not much better than a schoolboy still.'

'I don't think you're half so good, Mr Hugh,' said the old servant, sticking the sovereign which Hugh had given her in under her glove as she spoke.

On the next morning that other visit was made at the brick house, and Miss Stanbury was again in a fuss. On this occasion, however, she was in a much better humour than before, and was full of little jokes as to the nature of the visitation. Of course, she was not to see her nephew herself, and no message was to be delivered from her, and none was to be given to her from him. But an accurate report was to be made to her as to his appearance, and Dorothy was to be enabled to answer a variety of questions respecting him after he was gone. 'Of course, I don't want to know anything about his money,' Miss Stanbury said, 'only I should like to know how much these people can afford to pay for their penny trash.' On this occasion she had left the room and gone up-stairs before the knock came at the door, but she managed, by peeping over the balcony, to catch a glimpse of the 'flipperty-flopperty' hat which her nephew certainly had with him on this occasion.

Hugh Stanbury had great news for his sister. The cottage in which Mrs Stanbury lived at Nuncombe Putney, was the tiniest little dwelling in which a lady and her two daughters ever sheltered themselves. There was, indeed, a sitting-room, two bed-rooms, and a kitchen; but they were all so diminutive in size that the cottage was little more than a cabin. But there was a house in the village, not large indeed, but eminently respectable, three stories high, covered with ivy, having a garden behind it, and generally called the Clock House, because there had once been a clock upon it. This house had been lately vacated, and Hugh informed his sister that he was thinking of taking it for his mother's accommodation. Now, the late occupants of the Clock House, at Nuncombe Putney, had been people with five or six hundred a-year. Had other matters been in accordance, the house would almost have entitled them to consider themselves as county people. A gardener had always been kept there, – and a cow!

'The Clock House for mamma!'

'Well, yes. Don't say a word about it as yet to Aunt Stanbury, as she'll think that I've sold myself altogether to the old gentleman.'

'But, Hugh, how can mamma live there?'

'The fact is, Dorothy, there is a secret. I can't tell you quite yet. Of course, you'll know it, and everybody will know it, if the thing comes about. But as you won't talk, I will tell you what most concerns ourselves.'

'And am I to go back?'

'Certainly not, – if you will take my advice. Stick to your aunt. You don't want to smoke pipes, and wear Tom-and-Jerry hats,* and write for the penny newspapers.'

Now Hugh Stanbury's secret was this; – that Louis Trevelyan's wife and sister-in-law were to leave the house in Curzon Street, and come and live at Nuncombe Putney, with Mrs Stanbury and Priscilla. Such, at least, was the plan to be carried out, if Hugh Stanbury should be successful in his present negotiations.

13
The Honourable Mr Glascock

By the end of July Mrs Trevelyan with her sister was established in ths Clock House, at Nuncombe Putney, under the protection of Hugh's mother; but before the reader is made acquainted with any of the circumstances of their life there, a few words must be said of an occurrence which took place before those two ladies left Curzon Street.

As to the quarrel between Trevelyan and his wife things went from bad to worse. Lady Milborough continued to interfere, writing letters to Emily which were full of good sense, but which, as Emily said herself, never really touched the point of dispute. 'Am I, who am altogether unconscious of having done anything amiss, to confess that I have been in the wrong? If it were about a small matter, I would not mind, for the sake of peace. But when it concerns my conduct in reference to another man I would rather die first.' That had been Mrs Trevelyan's line of thought and argument in the matter; but then old Lady Milborough in her letters spoke only of the duty of obedience as promised at the altar. 'But I didn't promise to tell a lie,' said Mrs Trevelyan. And there were interviews between Lady Milborough and Trevelyan, and interviews between Lady Milborough and Nora Rowley. The poor dear old dowager was exceedingly busy and full of groans, prescibing Naples, prescribing a course of extra prayers, prescribing a general course of letting by-gones be by-gones, – to which, however, Trevelyan would by no means assent without some assurance, which he might regard as a guarantee, – prescribing retirement to a small town in the west of France, if Naples would not suffice; but she could effect nothing.

Mrs Trevelyan, indeed, did a thing which was sure of itself to render any steps taken for a reconciliation ineffectual. In the midst of all this turmoil, – while she and her husband were still living in the same house, but apart because of their absurd quarrel respecting Colonel Osborne, she wrote another letter to that gentleman. The argument by which she justified this to herself, and to her sister after it was done, was the real propriety of her own conduct throughout her whole intimacy with Colonel Osborne. 'But that is just what Louis doesn't want you to do,' Nora had said, filled with anger and dismay. 'Then let Louis give me an order to that effect, and behave to me like a husband, and I will obey him,' Emily had answered. And she had gone on to plead that in her present condition she was under no orders from her husband. She was left to judge for herself, and, – judging for herself, – she knew, as she said, that it was best that she should write to Colonel Osborne. Unfortunately there was no ground for hoping that Colonel Osborne was ignorant of this insane jealousy on the part of her husband. It was better, therefore, she said, that she should write to him, – whom on the occasion she took care to name to her sister as 'papa's old friend,' – and explain to him what she would wish him to do, and what not to do. Colonel Osborne answered the letter very quickly, throwing much more of demonstrative affection than he should have done into his 'Dear Emily,' and his 'Dearest Friend.' Of course Mrs Trevelyan had burned this answer, and of course Mr Trevelyan had been told of the correspondence. His wife, indeed, had been especially careful that there should be nothing secret about the matter, – that it should be so known in the house that Mr Trevelyan should be sure to hear of it. And he had heard of it, and been driven almost mad by it. He had flown off to Lady Milborough, and had reduced his old friend to despair by declaring that, after all, he began to fear that his wife was – was – was – infatuated by that d – scoundrel. Lady Milborough forgave the language, but protested that he was wrong in his suspicion. 'To continue to correspond with him after what I have said to her !' exclaimed Trevelyan. 'Take her to Naples at once,' – said Lady Milborough; – 'at once !' 'And have him after me ?' said Trevelyan. Lady Milborough had no answer ready, and not having thought of this looked very blank. 'I should find it harder to deal with her there even than here,' continued Trevelyan. Then it was that Lady Milborough spoke of the small town in the west of France, urging as her reason that such a man as Colonel Osborne would certainly not follow them there; but Trevelyan had become indignant at this, declaring that if his wife's good name could be preserved in no other manner than that, it would not be worth preserving at all. Then Lady Milborough had begun to cry, and had continued crying for a very long time. She was very unhappy, – as unhappy as her nature would allow her to be. She would have made almost any sacrifice to bring the two young people together; – would have willingly given her time, her money, her labour in the cause; – would probably herself have gone to the little town in the west of France, had her going been of any service. But, nevertheless, after her own fashion, she extracted no small enjoyment out of the circumstances of this miserable quarrel. The Lady Milboroughs of the day hate the Colonel Osbornes from the very bottoms of their warm hearts and pure souls; but they respect the Colonel Osbornes almost as much as they hate them, and find it to be an inestimable privilege to be brought into some contact with these roaring lions.

But there arose to dear Lady Milborough a great trouble out of this quarrel, irrespective of the absolute horror of the separation of a young husband from his young wife. And the excess of her trouble on this head was great proof of the real goodness of her heart. For, in this matter, the welfare of Trevelyan himself was not concerned; – but rather that of the Rowley family. Now the Rowleys had not given Lady Milborough any special reason for loving them. When she had first heard that her dear young friend Louis was going to marry a girl from the Mandarins, she had been almost in despair. It was her opinion that had he properly understood his own position, he would have promoted his welfare by falling in love with the daughter of some English country gentleman, – or some English peer, to which honour, with his advantages, Lady Milborough thought that he might have aspired. Nevertheless, when the girl from the Mandarins had been brought home as Mrs Trevelyan, Lady Milborough had received her with open arms, – had received even the sister-in-law with arms partly open. Had either of them shown any tendency to regard her as a mother, she would have showered motherly cares upon them. For Lady Milborough was like an old hen, in her capacity for taking many under her wings. The two sisters had hardly done more than bear with her, – Nora, indeed, bearing with her more graciously than Mrs Trevelyan; and in return, even for this, the old dowager was full of motherly regard. Now she knew well that Mr Glascock was over head and ears in love with Nora Rowley. It only wanted the slightest management and the easiest discretion to bring him on his knees, with an offer of his hand. And, then, how much that hand contained! – how much, indeed, as compared with that other hand, which was to be given in return, and which was, – to speak the truth, – completely empty! Mr Glascock was the heir to a peer, was the heir to a rich peer, was the heir to a very, very old peer. He was in Parliament. The world spoke well of him. He was not, so to say, by any means an old man himself. He was good-tempered, reasonable, easily led, and yet by no means despicable. On all subjects connected with land, he held an opinion that was very much respected, and was supposed to be a thoroughly good specimen of an upper-class Englishman. Here was a suitor! But it was not to be supposed that such a man as Mr Glascock would be so violently in love as to propose to a girl whose nearest known friend and female relation was misbehaving herself?

Only they who have closely watched the maternal uneasinesses of human hens can understand how great was Lady Milborough's anxiety on this occasion. Marriage to her was a thing always delightful to contemplate. Though she had never been sordidly a match-maker, the course of the world around her had taught her to regard men as fish to be caught, and girls as the anglers who ought to catch them. Or, rather, could her mind have been accurately analysed, it would have been found that the girl was regarded as half-angler and half-bait. Any girl that angled visibly with her own hook, with a manifestly expressed desire to catch a fish, was odious to her. And she was very gentle-hearted in regard to the fishes, thinking that every fish in the river should have the hook and bait presented to him in the mildest, pleasantest form. But still, when the trout was well in the basket, her joy was great; and then came across her unlaborious mind some half-formed idea that a great ordinance of nature was being accomplished in the teeth of difficulties. For, – as she well knew, – there is a difficulty in the catching of fish.

Lady Milborough, in her kind anxiety on Nora's behalf, – that the fish should be landed before Nora might be swept away in her sister's ruin, – hardly knew what step she might safely take. Mrs Trevelyan would not see her again, – having already declared that any further interview would be painful and useless. She had spoken to Trevelyan, but Trevelyan had declared that he could do nothing. What was there that he could have done? He could not, as he said, overlook the gross improprieties of his wife's conduct, because his wife's sister had, or might possibly have, a lover. And then as to speaking to Mr Glascock himself, – nobody knew better than Lady Milborough how very apt fish are to be frightened.

But at last Lady Milborough did speak to Mr Glascock, – making no allusion whatever to the hook prepared for himself, but saying a word or two as to the affairs of that other fish, whose circumstances, as he floundered about in the bucket of matrimony, were not as happy as they might have been. The care, the discretion, nay, the wisdom with which she did this were most excellent. She had become aware that Mr Glascock had already heard of the unfortunate affair in Curzon Street. Indeed, every one who knew the Trevelyans had heard of it, and a great many who did not know them. No harm, therefore, could be done by mentioning the circumstance. Lady Milborough did mention it, explaining that the only person really in fault was that odious destroyer of the peace of families, Colonel Osborne, of whom Lady Milborough, on that occasion, said some very severe things indeed. Poor dear Mrs Trevelyan was foolish, obstinate, and self-reliant; – but as innocent as the babe unborn. That things would come right before long no one who knew the affair, – and she knew it from beginning to end, – could for a moment doubt. The real victim would be that sweetest of all girls, Nora Rowley. Mr Glascock innocently asked why Nora Rowley should be a victim. 'Don't you understand, Mr Glascock, how the most remote connection with a thing of that kind tarnishes a young woman's standing in the world?' Mr Glascock was almost angry with the well-pleased Countess as he declared that he could not see that Miss Rowley's standing was at all tarnished; and old Lady Milborough, when he got up and left her, felt that she had done a good morning's work. If Nora could have known it all, Nora ought to have been very grateful, for Mr Glascock got into a cab in Eccleston Square and had himself driven direct to Curzon Street. He himself believed that he was at that moment only doing the thing which he had for some time past resolved that he would do; but we perhaps may be justified in thinking that the actual resolution was first fixed by the discretion of Lady Milborough's communication. At any rate he arrived in Curzon Street with his mind fully resolved, and had spent the minutes in the cab considering how he had better perform the business in hand.

He was at once shown into the drawing-room, where he found the two sisters, and Mrs Trevelyan, as soon as she saw him, understood the purpose of his coming. There was an air of determination about him, a manifest intention of doing something, an absence of that vagueness which almost always flavours a morning visit. This was so strongly marked that Mrs Trevelyan felt that she would have been almost justified in getting up and declaring that, as this visit was paid to her sister, she would retire. But any such declaration on her part was unnecessary, as Mr Glascock had not been in the room three minutes before he asked her to go. By some clever device of his own, he got her into the back room and whispered to her that he wanted to say a few words in private to her sister.

'Oh, certainly,' said Mrs Trevelyan, smiling.

'I dare say you may guess what they are,' said he. 'I don't know what chance I may have?'

'I can tell you nothing about that,' she replied, 'as I know nothing. But you have my good wishes.'

And then she went.

It may be presumed that gradually some idea of Mr Glascock's intention had made its way into Nora's mind by the time that she found herself alone with that gentleman. Why else had he brought into the room with him that manifest air of a purpose? Why else had he taken the very strong step of sending the lady of the house out of her own drawing-room? Nora, beginning to understand this, put herself into an attitude of defence. She had never told herself that she would refuse Mr Glascock. She had never acknowledged to herself that there was another man whom she liked better than she liked Mr Glascock. But had she ever encouraged any wish for such an interview, her feelings at this moment would have been very different from what they were. As it was, she would have given much to postpone it, so that she might have asked herself questions, and have discovered whether she could reconcile herself to do that which, no doubt, all her friends would commend her for doing. Of course, it was clear enough to the mind of the girl that she had her fortune to make, and that her beauty and youth were the capital on which she had to found it. She had not lived so far from all taint of corruption as to feel any actual horror at the idea of a girl giving herself to a man, – not because the man had already, by his own capacities in that direction, forced her heart from her, – but because he was one likely to be at all points a good husband. Had all this affair concerned any other girl, any friend of her own, and had she known all the circumstances of the case, she would have had no hesitation in recommending that other girl to marry Mr Glascock. A girl thrown out upon the world without a shilling must make her hay while the sun shines. But, nevertheless, there was something within her bosom which made her long for a better thing than this. She had dreamed, if she had not thought, of being able to worship a man; but she could hardly worship Mr Glascock. She had dreamed, if she had not thought, of leaning upon a man all through life with her whole weight, as though that man had been specially made to be her staff, her prop, her support, her wall of comfort and protection. She knew that if she were to marry Mr Glascock and become Lady Peterborough, in due course she must stand a good deal by her own strength, and live without that comfortable leaning. Nevertheless, when she found herself alone with the man, she by no means knew whether she would refuse him or not. But she knew that she must pluck up courage for an important moment, and she collected herself, braced her muscles, as it were, for a fight, and threw her mind into an attitude of contest.

Mr Glascock, as soon as the door was shut behind Mrs Trevelyan's back, took a chair and placed it close beside the head of the sofa on which Nora was sitting. 'Miss Rowley,' he said, 'you and I have known each other for some months, and I hope you have learned to regard me as a friend.'

'Oh, yes, indeed,' said Nora, with some spirit.

'It has seemed to me that we have met as friends, and I can most truly say for myself, that I have taken the greatest possible pleasure in your acquaintance. It is not only that I admire you very much,' – he looked straight before him as he said this, and moved about the point of the stick which he was holding in both his hands, – 'it is not only that, – perhaps not chiefly that, though I do admire you very much; but the truth is, that I like everything about you.'

Nora smiled, but she said nothing. It was better, she thought, to let him tell his story; but his mode of telling it was not without its efficacy. It was not the simple praise which made its way with her; but a certain tone in the words which seemed to convince her that they were true. If he had really found her, or fancied her to be what he said, there was a manliness in his telling her so in the plainest words that pleased her much.

'I know,' continued he, 'that this is a very bald way of telling – of pleading – my cause; but I don't know whether a bald way may not be the best, if it can only make itself understood to be true. Of course, Miss Rowley, you know what I mean. As I said before, you have all those things which not only make me love you, but which make me like you also. If you think that you can love me, say so; and, as long as I live, I will do my best to make you happy as my wife.'

There was a clearness of expression in this, and a downright surrender of himself, which so flattered her and so fluttered her that she was almost reduced to the giving of herself up because she could not reply to such an appeal in language less courteous than that of agreement. After a moment or two she found herself remaining silent, with a growing feeling that silence would be taken as conveying consent. There floated quickly across her brain an idea of the hardness of a woman's lot, in that she should be called upon to decide her future fate for life in half a minute. He had had weeks to think of this, – weeks in which it would have been almost unmaidenly in her so to think of it as to have made up her mind to accept the man. Had she so made up her mind, and had he not come to her, where would she have been then? But he had come to her. There he was, still poking about with his stick, waiting for her, and she must answer him. And he was the eldest son of a peer, – an enormous match for her, very proper in all respects; such a man, that if she should accept him, everybody around her would regard her fortune in life as miraculously successful. He was not such a man that anyone would point at her and say, – 'there; see another of them who has sold herself for money and a title!' Mr Glascock was not an Apollo, not an admirable Crichton;* but he was a man whom any girl might have learned to love. Now he had asked her to be his wife, and it was necessary that she should answer him. He sat there waiting for her very patiently, still poking about the point of his stick.

Did she really love him? Though she was so pressed by consideration of time, she did find a moment in which to ask herself the question. With a quick turn of an eye she glanced at him, to see what he was like. Up to this moment, though she knew him well, she could have given no details of his personal appearance. He was a better-looking man than Hugh Stanbury, – so she told herself with a passing thought; but he lacked – he lacked; – what was it that he lacked? Was it youth, or spirit, or strength; or was it some outward sign of an inward gift of mind?* Was it that he was heavy while Hugh was light? Was it that that she could find no fire in his eye, while Hugh's eyes were full of flashing? Or was it that for her, especially for her, Hugh was the appointed staff and appropriate wall of protection? Be all that as it might, she knew at the moment that she did love, not this man, but that other who was writing articles for the Daily Record. She must refuse the offer that was so brilliant, and give up the idea of reigning as queen at Monkhams.

'Oh, Mr Glascock,' she said, 'I ought to answer you more quickly.'

'No, dearest; not more quickly than suits you. Nothing ever in this world can be more important both to you and to me. If you want more time to think of it, take more time.'

'No, Mr Glascock; I do not. I don't know why I should have paused. Is not the truth best?'

'Yes, – certainly the truth is best.'

'I do not – love you. Pray, pray understand me.'

'I understand it too well, Miss Rowley.' The stick was still going, and the eyes more intently fixed than ever on something opposite.

'I do like you; I like you very much. And I am so grateful! I cannot understand why such a man as you should want to make me your wife.'

'Because I love you better than all the others; simply that. That reason, and that only, justifies a man in wanting to marry a girl.' What a good fellow he was, and how flattering were his words! Did he not deserve what he wanted, even though it could not be given without a sacrifice? But yet she did not love him. As she looked at him again she could not there recognise her staff. As she looked at him she was more than ever convinced that that other staff ought to be her staff. 'May I come again, – after a month, say?' he asked, when there had been another short period of silence.

'No, no. Why should you trouble yourself? I am not worth it.'

'It is for me to judge of that, Miss Rowley.'

'All the same, I know that I am not worth it. And I could not tell you to do that.'

'Then I will wait, and come again without your telling me.'

'Oh, Mr Glascock, I did not mean that; indeed I did not. Pray do not think that. Take what I say as final. I like you more than I can say; and I feel a gratitude to you that I cannot express, – which I shall never forget. I have never known any one who has seemed to be so good as you. But – It is just what I said before.' And then she fairly burst into tears.

'Miss Rowley,' he said, very slowly, 'pray do not think that I want to ask any question which it might embarrass you to answer. But my happiness is so greatly at stake; and, if you will allow me to say so, your happiness, too, is so greatly concerned, that it is most important that we should not come to a conclusion too quickly. If I thought that your heart were vacant I would wait patiently. I have been thinking of you as my possible wife for weeks past, – for months past. Of course you have not had such thoughts about me.' As he said this she almost loved him for his considerate goodness. 'It has sometimes seemed to me odd that girls should love men in such a hurry. If your heart be free, I will wait. And if you esteem me, you can see, and try whether you cannot learn to love me.'

'I do esteem you.'

'It depends on that question, then?' he said, slowly.

She sat silent for fully a minute, with her hands clasped; and then she answered him in a whisper. 'I do not know,' she said.

He also was silent for a while before he spoke again. He ceased to poke with his stick, and got up from his chair, and stood a little apart from her, not looking at her even yet.

'I see,' he said at last. 'I understand. Well, Miss Rowley, I quite perceive that I cannot press my suit any further now. But I shall not despair altogether. I know this, that if I might possibly succeed, I should be a very happy man. Good-bye, Miss Rowley.'

She took his offered hand and pressed it so warmly, that had he not been manly and big-hearted, he would have taken such pressure as a sign that she wished him to ask her again. But such was his nature.

'God bless you,' he said, 'and make you happy, whatever you may choose to do.'

Then he left her, and she heard him walk down the stairs with heavy slow steps, and she thought that she could perceive from the sound that he was sad at heart, but that he was resolved not to show his sadness outwardly.

When she was alone she began to think in earnest of what she had done. If the reader were told that she regretted the decision which she had been forced to make so rapidly, a wrong impression would be given of the condition of her thoughts. But there came upon her suddenly a strange capacity for counting up and making a mental inventory of all that might have been hers. She knew, – and where is the girl so placed that does not know? – that it is a great thing to be an English peeress. Now, as she stood there thinking of it all, she was Nora Rowley without a shilling in the world, and without a prospect of a shilling. She had often heard her mother speak fearful words of future possible days, when colonial governing should no longer be within the capacity of Sir Marmaduke. She had been taught from a very early age that all the material prosperity of her life must depend on matrimony. She could never be comfortably disposed of in the world, unless some fitting man who possessed those things of which she was so bare, should wish to make her his wife. Now there had come a man so thoroughly fitting, so marvellously endowed, that no worldly blessing would have been wanting. Mr Glascock had more than once spoken to her of the glories of Monkhams. She thought of Monkhams now more than she had ever thought of the place before. It would have been a great privilege to be the mistress of an old time-honoured mansion, to call oaks and elms her own, to know that acres of gardens were submitted to her caprices, to look at herds of cows and oxen, and be aware that they lowed on her own pastures. And to have been the mother of a future peer of England, to have the nursing, and sweet custody and very making of a future senator, – would not that have been much? And the man himself who would have been her husband was such a one that any woman might have trusted herself to him with perfect confidence. Now that he was gone she almost fancied that she did love him. Then she thought of Hugh Stanbury, sitting as he had described himself, in a little dark closet at the office of the 'D. R.,' in a very old inky shooting-coat, with a tarnished square-cut cloth cap upon his head, with a short pipe in his mouth, writing at midnight for the next morning's impression, this or that article according to the order of his master, 'the tallow-chandler;' – for the editor of the Daily Record was a gentleman whose father happened to be a grocer in the City, and Hugh had been accustomed thus to describe the family trade. And she might certainly have had the peer, and the acres of garden, and the big house, and the senatorial honours; whereas the tallow-chandler's journeyman had never been so outspoken. She told herself from moment to moment that she had done right; that she would do the same a dozen times, if a dozen times the experiment could be repeated; but still, still, there was the remembrance of all that she had lost. How would her mother look at her, her anxious, heavily-laden mother, when the story should be told of all that had been offered to her and all that had been refused?

As she was thinking of this Mrs Trevelyan came into the room. Nora felt that though she might dread to meet her mother, she could be bold enough on such an occasion before her sister. Emily had not done so well with her own affairs, as to enable her to preach with advantage about marriage.

'He has gone?' said Mrs Trevelyan, as she opened the door.

'Yes, he has gone.'

'Well? Do not pretend, Nora, that you will not tell me.'

'There is nothing worth the telling, Emily.'

'What do you mean? I am sure he has proposed. He told me in so many words that it was his intention.'

'Whatever has happened, dear, you may be quite sure that I shall never be Mrs Glascock.'

'Then you have refused him, – because of Hugh Stanbury!'

'I have refused him, Emily, because I did not love him. Pray let that be enough.'

Then she walked out of the room with something of stateliness in her gait, – as might become a girl who had had it in her power to be the future Lady Peterborough; but as soon as she reached the sacredness of her own chamber, she gave way to an agony of tears. It would, indeed, be much to be a Lady Peterborough. And she had, in truth, refused it all because of Hugh Stanbury! Was Hugh Stanbury worth so great a sacrifice?

14

The Clock House at Nuncombe Putney

It was not till a fortnight had passed after the transaction recorded in the last chapter, that Mrs Trevelyan and Nora Rowley first heard the proposition that they should go to live at Nuncombe Putney. From bad to worse the quarrel between the husband and the wife had gone on, till Trevelyan had at last told his friend Lady Milborough that he had made up his mind that they must live apart. 'She is so self-willed, – and perhaps I am the same,' he had said, 'that it is impossible that we should live together.' Lady Milborough had implored and called to witness all testimonies, profane and sacred, against such a step, – had almost gone down on her knees. Go to Naples, – why not Naples? Or to the quiet town in the west of France, which was so dull that a wicked roaring lion, fond of cities and gambling, and eating and drinking, could not live in such a place! Oh, why not go to the quiet town in the west of France? Was not anything better than this flying in the face of God and man? Perhaps Trevelyan did not himself like the idea of the quiet dull French town. Perhaps he thought that the flying in the face of God and man was all done by his wife, not by him; and that it was right that his wife should feel the consequences. After many such entreaties, many such arguments, it was at last decided that the house in Curzon Street should be given up, and that he and his wife live apart.

'And what about Nora Rowley?' asked Lady Milborough, who had become aware by this time of Nora's insane folly in having refused Mr Glascock.

'She will go with her sister, I suppose.'

'And who will maintain her? Dear, dear, dear! It does seem as though some young people were bent upon cutting their own throats, and all their family's.'

Poor Lady Milborough just at this time went as near to disliking the Rowleys as was compatible with her nature. It was not possible to her to hate anybody. She thought that she hated the Colonel Osborne; but even that was a mistake. She was very angry, however, with both Mrs Trevelyan and her sister, and was disposed to speak of them as though they had been born to create trouble and vexation.

Trevelyan had not given any direct answer to that question about Nora Rowley's maintenance, but he was quite prepared to bear all necessary expense in that direction, at any rate till Sir Marmaduke should have arrived. At first there had been an idea that the two sisters should go to the house of their aunt, Mrs Outhouse. Mrs Outhouse was the wife, – as the reader may perhaps remember, – of a clergyman living in the east of London. St Diddulph's-in-the-East was very much in the east indeed. It was a parish outside the City, lying near the river, very populous, very poor, very low in character, and very uncomfortable. There was a rectory-house, queerly situated at the end of a little blind lane, with a gate of its own, and a so-called garden about twenty yards square. But the rectory of St Diddulph's cannot be said to have been a comfortable abode. The neighbourhood was certainly not alluring. Of visiting society within a distance of three or four miles there was none but what was afforded by the families of other East-end clergymen. And then Mr Outhouse himself was a somewhat singular man. He was very religious, devoted to his work, most kind to the poor; but he was unfortunately a strongly-biassed man, and at the same time very obstinate withal. He had never allied himself very cordially with his wife's brother, Sir Marmaduke, allowing himself to be carried away by a prejudice that people living at the West-end, who frequented clubs and were connected in any way with fashion, could not be appropriate companions for himself. The very title which Sir Marmaduke had acquired was repulsive to him, and had induced him to tell his wife more than once that Sir this or Sir that could not be fitting associates for a poor East-end clergyman. Then his wife's niece had married a man of fashion, – a man supposed at St Diddulph's to be very closely allied to fashion; and Mr Outhouse had never been induced even to dine in the house in Curzon Street. When, therefore, he heard that Mr and Mrs Trevelyan were to be separated within two years of their marriage, it could not be expected that he should be very eager to lend to the two sisters the use of his rectory.

There had been interviews between Mr Outhouse and Trevelyan, and between Mrs Outhouse and her niece; and then there was an interview between Mr Outhouse and Emily, in which it was decided that Mrs Trevelyan would not go to the parsonage of St Diddulph's. She had been very outspoken to her uncle, declaring that she by no means intended to carry herself as a disgraced woman. Mr Outhouse had quoted St Paul to her: 'Wives, obey your husbands.'*

Then she had got up and had spoken very angrily. 'I look for support from you,' she said, 'as the man who is the nearest to me, till my father shall come.' 'But I cannot support you in what is wrong,' said the clergyman. Then Mrs Trevelyan had left the room, and would not see her uncle again.

She carried things altogether with a high hand at this time. When old Mr Bideawhile called upon her, her husband's ancient family lawyer, she told that gentleman that if it was her husband's will that they should live apart, it must be so. She could not force him to remain with her. She could not compel him to keep up the house in Curzon Street. She had certain rights, she believed. She spoke then, she said, of pecuniary rights, – not of those other rights which her husband was determined, and was no doubt able, to ignore. She did not really know what those pecuniary rights might be, nor was she careful to learn their exact extent. She would thank Mr Bideawhile to see that things were properly arranged. But of this her husband, and Mr Bideawhile, might be quite sure; – she would take nothing as a favour. She would not go to her uncle's house. She declined to tell Mr Bideawhile why she had so decided; but she had decided. She was ready to listen to any suggestion that her husband might make as to her residence, but she must claim to have some choice in the matter. As to her sister, of course she intended to give Nora a home as long as such a home might be wanted. It would be very sad for Nora, but in existing circumstances such an arrangement would be expedient. She would not go into details as to expense. Her husband was driving her away from him, and it was for him to say what proportion of his income he would choose to give for her maintenance, – for hers and for that of their child. She was not desirous of anything beyond the means of decent living, but of course she must for the present find a home for her sister as well as for herself. When speaking of her baby she had striven hard, so to speak that Mr Bideawhile should find no trace of doubt in the tones of her voice. And yet she had been full of doubt, – full of fear. As Mr Bideawhile had uttered nothing antagonistic to her wishes in this matter, – had seemed to agree that wherever the mother went thither the child would go also, Mrs Trevelyan had considered herself to be successful in this interview.

The idea of a residence at Nuncombe Putney had occurred first to Trevelyan himself, and he had spoken of it to Hugh Stanbury. There had been some difficulty in this, because he had snubbed Stanbury grievously when his friend had attempted to do some work of gentle interference between him and his wife; and when he began the conversation, he took the trouble of stating, in the first instance, that the separation was a thing fixed, – so that nothing might be urged on that subject. 'It is to be. You will understand that,' he said; 'and if you think that your mother would agree to the arrangement, it would be satisfactory to me, and might, I think, be made pleasant to her. Of course, your mother would be made to understand that the only fault with which my wife is charged is that of indomitable disobedience to my wishes.'

'Incompatibility of temper,' suggested Stanbury.

'You may call it that if you please; – though I must say for myself that I do not think that I have displayed any temper to which a woman has a right to object.' Then he had gone on to explain what he was prepared to do about money. He would pay, through Stanbury's hands, so much for maintenance and so much for house rent, on the understanding that the money was not to go into his wife's hands. 'I shall prefer,' he said, 'to make myself, on her behalf, what disbursement may be necessary. I will take care that she receives a proper sum quarterly through Mr Bideawhile for her own clothes, – and for those of our poor boy.' Then Stanbury had told him of the Clock House, and there had been an agreement made between them; – an agreement which was then, of course, subject to the approval of the ladies at Nuncombe Putney. When the suggestion was made to Mrs Trevelyan, – with a proposition that the Clock House should be taken for one year, and that for that year, at least, her boy should remain with her, – she assented to it. She did so with all the calmness that she was able to assume; but, in truth, almost everything seemed to have been gained, when she found that she was not to be separated from her baby. 'I have no objection to living in Devonshire if Mr Trevelyan wishes it,' she said, in her most stately manner; 'and certainly no objection to living with Mr Stanbury's mother.' Then Mr Bideawhile explained to her that Nuncombe Putney was not a large town, – was, in fact, a very small and very remote village. 'That will make no difference whatsoever as far as I am concerned,' she answered; 'and as for my sister, she must put up with it till my father and my mother are here. I believe the scenery at Nuncombe Putney is very pretty.' 'Lovely !' said Mr Bideawhile, who had a general idea that Devonshire is supposed to be a picturesque county. 'With such a life before me as I must lead,' continued Mrs Trevelyan, 'an ugly neighbourhood, one that would itself have had no interest for a stranger, would certainly have been an additional sorrow.' So it had been settled, and by the end of July, Mrs Trevelyan, with her sister and baby, was established at the Clock House, under the protection of Mrs Stanbury. Mrs Trevelyan had brought down her own maid and her own nurse, and had found that the arrangements made by her husband had, in truth, been liberal. The house in Curzon Street had been given up, the furniture had been sent to a warehouse, and Mr Trevelyan had gone into lodgings. 'There never were two young people so insane since the world began,' said Lady Milborough to her old friend, Mrs Fairfax, when the thing was done.

'They will be together again before next April,' Mrs Fairfax had replied. But Mrs Fairfax was a jolly dame who made the best of everything. Lady Milborough raised her hands in despair and shook her head. 'I don't suppose, though, that Mr Glascock will go to Devonshire after his lady love,' said Mrs Fairfax. Lady Milborough again raised her hands, and again shook her head.

Mrs Stanbury had given an easy assent when her son proposed to her this new mode of life, but Priscilla had had her doubts. Like all women, she thought that when a man was to be separated from his wife, the woman must be in the wrong. And though it must be doubtless comfortable to go from the cottage to the Clock House, it would, she said, with much prudence, be very uncomfortable to go back from the Clock House to the cottage. Hugh replied very cavalierly, – generously, that is, rashly, and somewhat imperiously, – that he would guarantee them against any such degradation.

'We don't want to be a burden upon you, my dear,' said the mother.

'You would be a great burden on me,' he replied, 'if you were living uncomfortably while I am able to make you comfortable.'

Mrs Stanbury was soon won over by Mrs Trevelyan, by Nora, and especially by the baby; and even Priscilla, after a week or two, began to feel that she liked their company. Priscilla was a young woman who read a great deal, and even had some gifts of understanding what she read. She borrowed books from the clergy- man, and paid a penny a week to the landlady of the Stag and Antlers for the hire during half a day of the weekly newspaper. But now there came a box of books from Exeter, and a daily paper from London, and, – to improve all this, – both the new comers were able to talk with her about the things she read. She soon declared to her mother that she liked Miss Rowley much the best of the two. Mrs Trevelyan was too fond of having her own way. She began to understand, she would say to her mother, that a man might find it difficult to live with Mrs Trevelyan. 'She hardly ever yields about anything,' said Priscilla. At Miss Priscilla Stanbury was also very fond of having her own way, it was not surprising that she should object to that quality in this lady, who had come to live under the same roof with her.

The country about Nuncombe Putney is perhaps as pretty as any in England. It is beyond the river Teign, between that and Dartmoor, and is so lovely in all its variations of rivers, rivulets, broken ground, hills and dales, old broken, battered, time-worn timber, green knolls, rich pastures, and heathy common, that the wonder is that English lovers of scenery know so little of it. At the Stag and Antlers old Mrs Crocket, than whom no old woman in the public line was ever more generous, more peppery, or more kind, kept two clean bedrooms, and could cook a leg of Dartmoor mutton and make an apple pie against any woman in Devonshire. 'Drat your fish!' she would say, when some self-indulgent and exacting traveller would wish for more than these accustomed viands. 'Cock you up with dainties! If you can't eat your victuals without fish, you must go to Exeter. And then you'll get it stinking mayhap.' Now Priscilla Stanbury and Mrs Crocket were great friends, and there had been times of deep want, in which Mrs Crocket's friendship had been very serviceable to the ladies at the cottage. The three young women had been to the inn one morning to ask after a conveyance from Nuncombe Putney to Princetown, and had found that a four-wheeled open carriage with an old horse and a very young driver could be hired there. 'We have never dreamed of such a thing,' Priscilla Stanbury had said, 'and the only time I was at Princetown I walked there and back.' So they had called at the Stag and Antlers, and Mrs Crocket had told them her mind upon several matters.

'What a dear old woman!' said Nora, as they came away, having made their bargain for the open carriage.

'I think she takes quite enough upon herself, you know,' said Mrs Trevelyan.

'She is a dear old woman,' said Priscilla, not attending at all to the last words that had been spoken. 'She is one of the best friends I have in the world. If I were to say the best out of my own family, perhaps I should not be wrong.'

'But she uses such very odd language for a woman,' said Mrs Trevelyan. Now Mrs Crocket had certainly 'dratted' and 'darned' the boy, who wouldn't come as fast as she had wished, and had laughed at Mrs Trevelyan very contemptuously, when that lady had suggested that the urchin, who was at last brought forth, might not be a safe charioteer down some of the hills.

'I suppose I'm used to it,' said Priscilla. 'At any rate I know I like it. And I like her.'

'I dare say she's a good sort of woman,' said Mrs Trevelyan, 'only – '

'I am not saying anything about her being a good woman now,' said Priscilla, interrupting the other with some vehemence, 'but only that she is my friend.'

'I liked her of all things,' said Nora. 'Has she lived here always?'

'Yes; all her life. The house belonged to her father and to her grandfather before her, and I think she says she has never slept out of it a dozen times in her life. Her husband is dead, and her daughters are married away, and she has the great grief and trouble of a ne'er-do-well son. He's away now, and she's all alone.' Then after a pause, she continued; 'I dare say it seems odd to you, Mrs Trevelyan, that we should speak of the innkeeper as a dear friend; but you must remember that we have been poor among the poorest – and are so indeed now. We only came into our present house to receive you. That is where we used to live,' and she pointed to the tiny cottage, which now that it was dismantled and desolate, looked to be doubly poor. 'There have been times when we should have gone to bed very hungry if it had not been for Mrs Crocket.'

Later in the day Mrs Trevelyan, finding Priscilla alone, had apologized for what she had said about the old woman. 'I was very thoughtless and forgetful, but I hope you will not be angry with me. I will be ever so fond of her if you will forgive me.'

'Very well,' said Priscilla, smiling; 'on those conditions I will forgive you.' And from that time there sprang up something like a feeling of friendship between Priscilla and Mrs Trevelyan. Nevertheless Priscilla was still of opinion that the Clock House arrangement was dangerous, and should never have been made; and Mrs Stanbury, always timid of her own nature, began to fear that it must be so, as soon as she was removed from the influence of her son. She did not see much even of the few neighbours who lived around her, but she fancied that people looked at her in church as though she had done that which she ought not to have done, in taking herself to a big and comfortable house for the sake of lending her protection to a lady who was separated from her husband. It was not that she believed that Mrs Trevelyan had been wrong; but that, knowing herself to be weak, she fancied that she and her daughter would be enveloped in the danger and suspicion which could not but attach themselves to the lady's condition, instead of raising the lady out of the cloud, – as would have been the case had she herself been strong. Mrs Trevelyan, who was sharpsighted and clear-witted, soon saw that it was so, and spoke to Priscilla on the subject before she had been a fortnight in the house. 'I am afraid your mother does not like our being here,' she said.

'How am I to answer that?' Priscilla replied.

'Just tell the truth.'

'The truth is so uncivil. At first I did not like it. I disliked it very much.'

'Why did you give way?'

'I didn't give way. Hugh talked my mother over. Mamma does what I tell her, except when Hugh tells her something else. I was afraid, because, down here, knowing nothing of the world, I didn't wish that we, little people, should be mixed up in the quarrels and disagreements of those who are so much bigger.'

'I don't know who it is that is big in this matter.'

'You are big, – at any rate by comparison. But now it must go on. The house has been taken, and my fears are over as regards you. What you observe in mamma is only the effect, not yet quite worn out, of what I said before you came. You may be quite sure of this, – that we neither of us believe a word against you. Your position is a very unfortunate one; but if it can be remedied by your staying here with us, pray stay with us.'

'It cannot be remedied,' said Emily; 'but we could not be anywhere more comfortable than we are here.'

15

What they said about it in The Close

When Miss Stanbury, in the Close at Exeter, was first told of the arrangement that had been made at Nuncombe Putney, she said some very hard words as to the thing that had been done. She was quite sure that Mrs Trevelyan was no better than she should be. Ladies who were separated from their husbands never were any better than they should be. And what was to be thought of any woman, who, when separated from her husband, would put herself under the protection of such a Paladin as Hugh Stanbury. She heard the tidings of course from Dorothy, and spoke her mind even to Dorothy plainly enough; but it was to Martha that she expressed herself with her fullest vehemence.

'We always knew,' she said, 'that my brother had married an addle-pated, silly woman, one of the most unsuited to be the mistress of a clergyman's house that ever a man set eyes on; but I didn't think she'd allow herself to be led into such a stupid thing as this.'

'I don't suppose the lady has done anything amiss, – any more than combing her husband's hair, and the like of that,' said Martha.

'Don't tell me! Why, by their own story, she has got a lover.'

'But he ain't to come after her down here, I suppose. And as for lovers, ma'am, I'm told that the most of 'em have 'em up in London. But it don't mean much, only just idle talking and gallivanting.'

'When women can't keep themselves from idle talking with strange gentlemen, they are very far gone on the road to the devil. That's my notion. And that was everybody's notion a few years ago. But now, what with divorce bills, and woman's rights, and penny papers, and false hair, and married women being just like giggling girls, and giggling girls knowing just as much as married women, when a woman has been married a year or two she begins to think whether she mayn't have more fun for her money by living apart from her husband.'

'Miss Dorothy says – '

'Oh, bother what Miss Dorothy says! Miss Dorothy only knows what it has suited that scamp, her brother, to tell her. I understand this woman has come away because of a lover; and if that's so, my sister-in-law is very wrong to receive her. The temptation of the Clock House has been too much for her. It's not my doing; that's all.'

That evening Miss Stanbury and Dorothy went out to tea at the house of Mrs MacHugh, and there the matter was very much discussed. The family of the Trevelyans was known by name in these parts, and the fact of Mrs Trevelyan having been sent to live in a Devonshire village, with Devonshire ladies who had a relation in Exeter so well esteemed as Miss Stanbury of the Close, were circumstances of themselves sufficient to ensure a considerable amount of prestige at the city tea-tables for the tidings of this unfortunate family quarrel. Some reticence was of course necessary because of the presence of Miss Stanbury and of Dorothy. To Miss Stanbury herself Mrs MacHugh and Mrs Crumbie, of Cronstadt House, did not scruple to express themselves every plainly, and to whisper a question as to what was to be done should the lover make his appearance at Nuncombe Putney; but they who spoke of the matter before Dorothy, were at first more charitable, or, at least, more forbearing. Mr Gibson, who was one of the minor canons, and the two Miss Frenches from Heavitree, who had the reputation of hunting unmarried clergymen in couples, seemed to have heard all about it. When Mrs MacHugh and Miss Stanbury, with Mr and Mrs Crumbie, had seated themselves at their whist-table, the younger people were able to express their opinions without danger of interruption or of rebuke. It was known to all Exeter by this time, that Dorothy Stanbury's mother had gone to

the Clock House, and that she had done so in order that Mrs
Trevelyan might have a home. But it was not yet known whether
anybody had called upon them. There was Mrs Merton, the wife of
the present parson of Nuncombe, who had known the Stanburys
for the last twenty years; and there was Mrs Ellison of Lessboro',
who lived only four miles from Nuncombe, and who kept a pony-
carriage. It would be a great thing to know how these ladies had
behaved in so difficult and embarrassing a position. Mrs Trevelyan
and her sister had now been at Nuncombe Putney for more than a
fortnight, and something in that matter of calling must have been
done, – or have been left undone. In answer to an ingeniously-
framed question asked by Camilla French, Dorothy at once set the
matter at rest. 'Mrs Merton,' said Camilla French, 'must find it a
great thing to have two new ladies come to the village, especially
now that she has lost you, Miss Stanbury ?'

'Mamma tells me,' said Dorothy, 'that Mrs Trevelyan and Miss
Rowley do not mean to know anybody. They have given it out
quite plainly, so that there should be no mistake.'

'Dear, dear !' said Camilla French.

'I dare say it's for the best,' said Arabella French, who was the
elder, and who looked very meek and soft. Miss French almost
always looked meek and soft.

'I'm afraid it will make it very dull for your mother, – not seeing
her old friends,' said Mr Gibson.

'Mamma won't feel that at all,' said Dorothy.

'Mrs Stanbury, I suppose, will see her own friends at her own
house just the same,' said Camilla.

'There would be great difficulty in that, when there is a lady who
is to remain unknown,' said Arabella. 'Don't you think so, Mr
Gibson ?' Mr Gibson replied that perhaps there might be a difficulty,
but he wasn't sure. The difficulty, he thought, might be got over if
the ladies did not always occupy the same room.

'You have never seen Mrs Trevelyan, have you, Miss Stanbury ?'
asked Camilla.

'Never.'

'She is not an old family friend, then, – or anything of that sort ?'

'Oh, dear, no.'

'Because,' said Arabella, 'it is so odd how different people get
together sometimes.' Then Dorothy explained that Mr Trevelyan
and her brother Hugh had long been friends.

'Oh ! – of Mr Trevelyan,' said Camilla. 'Then it is he that has
sent his wife to Nuncombe, not she that has come there ?'

'I suppose there has been some agreement,' said Dorothy.

'Just so; just so,' said Arabella, the meek. 'I should like to see her. They say that she is very beautiful; don't they?'

'My brother says that she is handsome.'

'Exceedingly lovely, I'm told,' said Camilla. 'I should like to see her, – shouldn't you, Mr Gibson?'

'I always like to see a pretty woman,' said Mr Gibson, with a polite bow, which the sisters shared between them.

'I suppose she'll go to church,' said Camilla.

'Very likely not,' said Arabella. 'Ladies of that sort very often don't go to church. I dare say you'll find that she'll never stir out of the place at all, and that not a soul in Nuncombe will ever see her except the gardener. It is such a thing for a woman to be separated from her husband! Don't you think so, Mr Gibson?'

'Of course it is,' said he, with a shake of his head, which was intended to imply that the censure of the church must of course attend any sundering of those whom the church had bound together; but which implied also by the absence from it of any intense clerical severity, that as the separated wife was allowed to live with so very respectable a lady as Mrs Stanbury, there must probably be some mitigating circumstances attending this special separation.

'I wonder what he is like?' said Camilla, after a pause.

'Who?' asked Arabella.

'The gentleman,' said Camilla.

'What gentleman?' demanded Arabella.

'I don't mean Mr Trevelyan,' said Camilla.

'I don't believe there really is, – eh, – is there?' said Mr Gibson, very timidly.

'Oh dear, yes,' said Arabella.

'I'm afraid there's something of the kind,' said Camilla. 'I've heard that there is, and I've heard his name.' Then she whispered very closely into the ear of Mr Gibson the words, 'Colonel Osborne,' as though her lips were by far too pure to mention aloud any sound so full of iniquity.

'Indeed!' said Mr Gibson.

'But he's quite an old man,' said Dorothy, 'and knew her father intimately before she was born. And, as far as I can understand, her husband does not suspect her in the least. And it's only because there's a misunderstanding between them, and not at all because of the gentleman.'

'Oh!' exclaimed Camilla.

'Ah!' exclaimed Arabella.

'That would make a difference,' said Mr Gibson.

'But for a married woman to have her name mentioned at all with a gentleman, – it is so bad; is it not, Mr Gibson?' And then Arabella also has her whisper into the clergyman's ear, – very closely. 'I'm afraid there's not a doubt about the Colonel. I'm afraid not. I am indeed.'

'Two by honours and the odd, and it's my deal,' said Miss Stanbury, briskly, and the sharp click with which she put the markers down upon the table was heard all through the room. 'I don't want anybody to tell me,' she said, 'that when a young woman is parted from her husband, the chances are ten to one that she has been very foolish.'

'But what's a woman to do, if her husband beats her?' said Mrs Crumbie.

'Beat him again,' said Mrs MacHugh.

'And the husband will be sure to have the worst of it,' said Mr Crumbie. 'Well, I declare, if you haven't turned up an honour again, Miss Stanbury!'

'It was your wife that cut it to me, Mr Crumbie.' Then they were again at once immersed in the play, and the name neither of Trevelyan nor Osborne was heard till Miss Stanbury was marking her double under the candlestick; but during all pauses in the game the conversation went back to the same topic, and when the rubber was over they who had been playing it lost themselves for ten minutes in the allurements of the interesting subject. It was so singular a coincidence that the lady should have gone to Nuncombe Putney of all villages in England, and to the house of Mrs Stanbury of all ladies in England. And then was she innocent, or was she guilty: and if guilty, in what degree? That she had been allowed to bring her baby with her was considered to be a great point in her favour. Mr Crumbie's opinion was that it was 'only a few words.' Mrs Crumbie was afraid that she had been a little light. Mrs MacHugh said that there was never fire without smoke. And Miss Stanbury, as she took her departure, declared that the young women of the present day didn't know what they were after. 'They think that the world should be all frolic and dancing, and they have no more idea of doing their duty and earning their bread than a boy home for the holidays has of doing lessons.'

Then, as she went home with Dorothy across the Close, she spoke a word which she intended to be very serious. 'I don't mean to say anything against your mother for what she has done as yet. Somebody must take the woman in, and perhaps it was natural. But if that Colonel What's-his-name makes his way down to

Nuncombe Putney, your mother must send her packing, if she has any respect either for herself or for Priscilla.'

16

Dartmoor

The well-weighed decision of Miss Stanbury respecting the Stanbury-Trevelyan arrangement at Nuncombe Putney had been communicated to Dorothy as the two walked home at night across the Close from Mrs MacHugh's house, and it was accepted by Dorothy as being wise and proper. It amounted to this. If Mrs Trevelyan should behave herself with propriety in her retirement at the Clock House, no further blame in the matter should be attributed to Mrs Stanbury for receiving her, – at any rate in Dorothy's hearing. The existing scheme, whether wise or foolish, should be regarded as an accepted scheme. But if Mrs Trevelyan should be indiscreet, – if, for instance, Colonel Osborne should show himself at Nuncombe Putney, – then, for the sake of the family, Miss Stanbury would speak out, and would speak out very loudly. All this Dorothy understood, and she could perceive that her aunt had strong suspicion that there would be indiscretion.

'I never knew one like her,' said Miss Stanbury, 'who, when she'd got away from one man, didn't want to have another dangling after her.'

A week had hardly passed after the party at Mrs MacHugh's, and Mrs Trevelyan had hardly been three weeks at Nuncombe Putney, before the tidings which Miss Stanbury almost expected reached her ears.

'The Colonel's been at the Clock House, ma'am,' said Martha.

Now, it was quite understood in the Close by this time that 'the Colonel' meant Colonel Osborne.

'No !'

'I'm told he has though, ma'am, for sure and certain.'

'Who says so ?'

'Giles Hickbody was down at Lessboro', and see'd him hisself, – a portly, middle-aged man, – not one of your young scampish-like lovers.'

'That's the man.'

'Oh, yes. He went over to Nuncombe Putney, as sure as anything; – hired Mrs Clegg's chaise and pair, and asked for Mrs Trevelyan's house as open as anything. When Giles asked in the yard, they told him as how that was the married lady's young man.'

'I'd like to be at his tail, – so I would, – with a mop-handle,' said Miss Stanbury, whose hatred for those sins by which the comfort and respectability of the world are destroyed, was not only sincere, but intense. 'Well; and what then?'

'He came back and slept at Mrs Clegg's that night, – at least, that was what he said he should do.'

Miss Stanbury, however, was not so precipitate or uncharitable as to act strongly upon information such as this. Before she even said a word to Dorothy, she made further inquiry. She made very minute inquiry, writing even to her very old and intimate friend Mrs Ellison, of Lessboro', – writing to that lady a most cautious and guarded letter. At last it became a fact proved to her mind that Colonel Osborne had been at the Clock House, had been received there, and had remained there for hours, – had been allowed access to Mrs Trevelyan, and had slept the night at the inn at Lessboro'. The thing was so terrible to Miss Stanbury's mind, that even false hair, Dr Colenso, and penny newspapers did not account for it.

'I shall begin to believe that the Evil One has been allowed to come among us in person because of our sins,' she said to Martha; – and she meant it.

In the meantime, Mrs Trevelyan, as may be remembered, had hired Mrs Crocket's open carriage, and the three young women, Mrs Trevelyan, Nora, and Priscilla, made a little excursion to Princetown, somewhat after the fashion of a picnic. At Princetown, in the middle of Dartmoor, about nine miles from Nuncombe Putney, is the prison establishment at which are kept convicts undergoing penal servitude. It is regarded by all the country round with great interest, chiefly because the prisoners now and again escape, and then there comes a period of interesting excitement until the escaped felon shall have been again taken. How can you tell where he may be, or whether it may not suit him to find his rest in your own cupboard, or under your own bed? And then, as escape without notice will of course be the felon's object, to attain that he will probably cut your throat, and the throat of everybody belonging to you. All which considerations give an interest to Princetown, and excite in the hearts of the Devonians of these parts a strong affection for the Dartmoor prison. Of those who visit Princetown comparatively few effect an entrance within the walls of the gaol. They look at the gloomy place with a mysterious interest, feeling something akin to envy for the prisoners who have enjoyed the privilege of solving the mysteries of prison life, and who know how men feel when they have their hair cut short, and are free from moral responsibility for their own conduct, and are moved about in gangs, and treated like wild beasts.

But the journey to Princetown, from whatever side it is approached, has the charm of wild and beautiful scenery. The spot itself is ugly enough; but you can go not thither without breathing the sweetest, freshest air, and encountering that delightful sense of romance which moorland scenery always produces. The idea of our three friends was to see the Moor rather than the prison, to learn something of the country around, and to enjoy the excitement of eating a sandwich sitting on a hillock, in exchange for the ordinary comforts of a good dinner with chairs and tables. A bottle of sherry and water and a paper of sandwiches contained their whole banquet; for ladies, though they like good things at picnics, and, indeed, at other times, almost as well as men like them, very seldom prepare dainties for themselves alone. Men are wiser and more thoughtful, and are careful to have the good things, even if they are to be enjoyed without companionship.

Mrs Crocket's boy, though he was only about three feet high, was a miracle of skill and discretion. He used the machine, as the patent drag* is called, in going down the hills with the utmost care. He never forced the beast beyond a walk if there was the slightest rise in the ground; and as there was always a rise, the journey was slow. But the three ladies enjoyed it thoroughly, and Mrs Trevelyan was in better spirits than she herself had thought to be possible for her in her present condition. Most of us have recognised the fact that a dram of spirits will create, – that a so-called nip of brandy will create hilarity, or, at least, alacrity, and that a glass of sherry will often 'pick up' and set in order the prostrate animal and mental faculties of the drinker. But we are not sufficiently alive to the fact that copious draughts of fresh air, – of air fresh and unaccustomed, – will have precisely the same effect. We do know that now and again it is very essential to 'change the air;' but we generally consider that to do that with any chance of advantage, it is necessary to go far afield; and we think also that such change of the air is only needful when sickness of the body has come upon us, or when it threatens to come. We are seldom aware that we may imbibe long potations of pleasure and healthy excitement without perhaps going out of our own county; that such potations are within a day's journey of most of us; and that they are to be had for half-a-crown a head, all expenses told. Mrs Trevelyan probably did not know that the cloud was lifted off her mind, and the load of her sorrow made light to her, by the special vigour of the air of the

Moor; but she did know that she was enjoying herself, and that the world was pleasanter to her than it had been for months past.

When they had sat upon their hillocks, and eaten their sandwiches, – regretting that the basket of provisions had not been bigger, – and had drunk their sherry and water out of the little horn mug which Mrs Crocket had lent them, Nora started off across the moorland alone. The horse had been left to be fed in Princetown, and they had walked back to a bush under which they had rashly left their basket of provender concealed. It happened, however, that on that day there was no escaped felon about to watch what they had done, and the food and the drink had been found secure. Nora had gone off, and as her sister and Priscilla sat leaning against their hillocks with their backs to the road, she could be seen standing now on one little eminence and now on another, thinking, doubtless, as she stood on the one how good it would be to be Lady Peterborough, and, as she stood on the other, how much better to be Mrs Hugh Stanbury. Only, – before she could be Mrs Hugh Stanbury it would be necessary that Mr Hugh Stanbury should share her opinion, – and necessary also that he should be able to maintain a wife. 'I should never do to be a very poor man's wife,' she said to herself; and remembered as she said it, that in reference to the prospect of her being Lady Peterborough, the man who was to be Lord Peterborough was at any rate ready to make her his wife, and on that side there were none of those difficulties about house, and money, and position which stood in the way of the Hugh Stanbury side of the question. She was not, she thought, fit to be the wife of a very poor man; but she conceived of herself that she would do very well as a future Lady Peterborough in the drawing-rooms of Monkhams. She was so far vain as to fancy that she could look, and speak, and move, and have her being after the fashion which is approved for the Lady Peterboroughs of the world. It was not clear to her that Nature had not expressly intended her to be a Lady Peterborough; whereas, as far as she could see, Nature had not intended her to be a Mrs Hugh Stanbury, with a precarious income of perhaps ten guineas a week when journalism was doing well. So she moved on to another little eminence to think of it there. It was clear to her that if she should accept Mr Glascock she would sell herself, and not give herself away; and she had told herself scores of times before this, that a young woman should give herself away, and not sell herself; – should either give herself away, or keep herself to herself as circumstances might so. She had been quite sure that she would never sell herself. But this was a lesson which she had taught herself when she was very young, before she had come to understand the world and its hard necessities. Nothing, she now told herself, could be worse than to hang like a mill-stone round the neck of a poor man. It might be a very good thing to give herself away for love, – but it would not be a good thing to be the means of ruining the man she loved, even if that man were willing to be so ruined. And then she thought that she could also love that other man a little, – could love him sufficiently for comfortable domestic purposes. And it would undoubtedly be very pleasant to have all the troubles of her life settled for her. If she were Mrs Glascock, known to the world as the future Lady Peterborough, would it not be within her power to bring her sister and her sister's husband again together? The tribute of the Monkhams authority and influence to her sister's side of the question would be most salutary. She tried to make herself believe that in this way she would be doing a good deed. Upon the whole, she thought that if Mr Glascock should give her another chance she would accept him. And he had distinctly promised that he would give her another chance. It might be that this unfortunate quarrel in the Trevelyan family would deter him. People do not wish to ally themselves with family quarrels. But if the chance came in her way she would accept it. She had made up her mind to that, when she turned round from off the last knoll on which she had stood, to return to her sister and Priscilla Stanbury.

They two had sat still under the shade of a thorn bush, looking at Nora as she was wandering about, and talking together more freely than they had ever done before on the circumstances that had brought them together. 'How pretty she looks,' Priscilla had said, as Nora was standing with her figure clearly marked by the light.

'Yes; she is very pretty, and has been much admired. This terrible affair of mine is a cruel blow to her.'

'You mean that it is bad for her to come and live here – without society.'

'Not exactly that, – though of course it would be better for her to go out. And I don't know how a girl is ever to get settled in the world unless she goes out. But it is always an injury to be connected in any way with a woman who is separated from her husband. It must be bad for you.'

'It won't hurt me,' said Priscilla. 'Nothing of that kind can hurt me.'

'I mean that people say such ill-natured things.'

'I stand alone, and can take care of myself,' said Priscilla. 'I defy the evil tongues of all the world to hurt me. My personal cares are limited to an old gown and bread and cheese. I like a pair of gloves to go to church with, but that is only the remnant of a prejudice. The world has so very little to give me, that I am pretty nearly sure that it will take nothing away.'

'And you are contented?'

'Well, no; I can't say that I am contented. I hardly think that anybody ought to be contented. Should my mother die and Dorothy remain with my aunt, or get married, I should be utterly alone in the world. Providence, or whatever you call it, has made me a lady after a fashion, so that I can't live with the ploughmen's wives, and at the same time has so used me in other respects, that I can't live with anybody else.'

'Why should not you get married, as well as Dorothy?'

'Who would have me? And if I had a husband I should want a good one, – a man with a head on his shoulders, and a heart. Even if I were young and good-looking, or rich, I doubt whether I could please myself. As it is I am as likely to be taken bodily to heaven, as to become any man's wife.'

'I suppose most women think so of themselves at some time, and yet they are married.'

'I am not fit to marry. I am often cross, and I like my own way, and I have a distaste for men. I never in my life saw a man whom I wished even to make my intimate friend. I should think any man an idiot who began to make soft speeches to me, and I should tell him so.'

'Ah; you might find it different when he went on with it.'

'But I think,' said Priscilla, 'that when a woman is married there is nothing to which she should not submit on behalf of her husband.'

'You mean that for me.'

'Of course I mean it for you. How should I not be thinking of you, living as you are under the same roof with us? And I am thinking of Louey.' Louey was the baby. 'What are you to do when after a year or two his father shall send for him to have him under his own care?'

'Nothing shall separate me from my child,' said Mrs Trevelyan eagerly.

'That is easily said; but I suppose the power of doing as he pleased would be with him.'

'Why should it be with him? I do not at all know that it would be with him. I have not left his house. It is he that has turned me out.'

'There can, I think, be very little doubt what you should do,' said

Priscilla, after a pause, during which she had got up from her seat under the thorn bush.

'What should I do?' asked Mrs Trevelyan.

'Go back to him.'

'I will to-morrow if he will write and ask me. Nay; how could I help myself? I am his creature, and must go or come as he bids me. I am here only because he has sent me.'

'You should write and ask him to take you.'

'Ask him to forgive me because he has ill-treated me?'

'Never mind about that,' said Priscilla, standing over her companion, who was still lying under the bush. 'All that is twopenny-halfpenny pride, which should be thrown to the winds. The more right you have been hitherto the better you can afford to go on being right. What is it that we all live upon but self-esteem? When we want praise it is only because praise enables us to think well of ourselves. Everyone to himself is the centre and pivot of all the world.'

'It's a very poor world that goes round upon my pivot,' said Mrs Trevelyan.

'I don't know how this quarrel came up,' exclaimed Priscilla, 'and I don't care to know. But it seems a trumpery quarrel, – as to who should beg each other's pardon first, and all that kind of thing. Sheer and simple nonsense! Ask him to let it all be forgotten. I suppose he loves you?'

'How can I know? He did once.'

'And you love him?'

'Yes. I love him certainly.'

'I don't see how you can have a doubt. Here is Jack with the carriage, and if we don't mind he'll pass us by without seeing us.'

Then Mrs Trevelyan got up, and when they had succeeded in diverting Jack's attention for a moment from the horse, they called to Nora, who was still moving about from one knoll to another, and who showed no desire to abandon the contemplations in which she had been engaged.

It had been mid-day before they left home in the morning, and they were due to be at home in time for tea, – which is an epoch in the day generally allowed to be more elastic than some others. When Mrs Stanbury lived in the cottage her hour for tea had been six; this had been stretched to half-past seven when she received Mrs Trevelyan at the Clock House; and it was half-past eight before Jack landed them at their door. It was manifest to them all as they entered the house that there was an air of mystery in the face of the girl who had opened the door for them. She did not speak, however, till they were all within the passage. Then she uttered a few words very solemnly. 'There be a gentleman come,' she said.

'A gentleman!' said Mrs Trevelyan, thinking in the first moment of her husband, and in the second of Colonel Osborne.

'He be for you, miss,' said the girl, bobbing her head at Nora.

Upon hearing this Nora sank speechless into the chair which stood in the passage.

17

A Gentleman Comes to Nuncombe Putney

It soon become known to them all as they remained clustered in the hall that Mr Glascock was in the house. Mrs Stanbury came out to them and informed them that he had been at Nuncombe Putney for the last five hours, and that he had asked for Mrs Trevelyan when he called. It became evident as the affairs of the evening went on, that Mrs Stanbury had for a few minutes been thrown into a terrible state of amazement, thinking that 'the Colonel' had appeared. The strange gentleman, however, having obtained admittance, explained who he was, saying that he was very desirous of seeing Mrs Trevelyan, – and Miss Rowley. It may be presumed that a glimmer of light did make its way into Mrs Stanbury's mind on the subject; but up to the moment at which the three travellers arrived, she had been in doubt on the subject. Mr Glascock had declared that he would take a walk, and in the course of the afternoon had expressed high approval of Mrs Crocket's culinary skill. When Mrs Crocket heard that she had entertained the son of a lord, she was very loud in her praise of the manner in which he had eaten two mutton chops and called for a third. He had thought it no disgrace to apply himself to the second half of an apple pie, and had professed himself to be an ardent admirer of Devonshire cream. 'It's them counter-skippers as turns up their little noses at the victuals as is set before them,' said Mrs Crocket.

After his dinner Mr Glascock had returned to the Clock House, and had been sitting there for an hour with Mrs Stanbury, not much to her delight or to his, when the carriage was driven up to the door.

'He is to go back to Lessboro' to-night,' said Mrs Stanbury in a whisper.

'Of course you must see him before he goes?' said Mrs Trevelyan to her sister. There had, as was natural, been very much said between the two sisters about Mr Glascock. Nora had abstained from asserting in any decided way that she disliked the man, and had always absolutely refused to allow Hugh Stanbury's name to be mixed up with the question. Whatever might be her own thoughts about Hugh Stanbury she had kept them even from her sister. When her sister had told her that she had refused Mr Glascock because of Hugh, she had shown herself to be indignant, and had since that said one or two fine things as to her capacity to refuse a brilliant offer simply because the man who made it was indifferent to her. Mrs Trevelyan had learned from her that her suitor had declared his intention to persevere; and here was perseverance with a vengeance! 'Of course you must see him, – at once,' said Mrs Trevelyan. Nora for a few seconds had remained silent, and then had run up to her room. Her sister followed her instantly.

'What is the meaning of it all?' said Priscilla to her mother.

'I suppose he is in love with Miss Rowley,' said Mrs Stanbury.

'But who is he?'

Then Mrs Stanbury told all that she knew. She had seen from his card that he was an Honourable Mr Glascock. She had collected from what he had said that he was an old friend of the two ladies. Her conviction was strong in Mr Glascock's favour, – thinking, as she expressed herself, that everything was right and proper, – but she could hardly explain why she thought so.

'I do wish that they had never come,' said Priscilla, who could not rid herself of an idea that there must be danger in having to do with women who had men running after them.

'Of course I'll see him,' said Nora to her sister. 'I have not refused to see him. Why do you scold me?'

'I have not scolded you, Nora; but I do want you to think how immensely important this is.'

'Of course it is important.'

'And so much the more so because of my misfortunes! Think how good he must be, how strong must be his attachment, when he comes down here after you in this way.'

'But I have to think of my own feelings.'

'You know you like him. You have told me so. And only fancy what mamma will feel? Such a position! And the man so excellent! Everybody says that he hasn't a fault in any way.'

'I hate people without faults.'

'Oh, Nora, Nora, that is foolish! There, there; you must go down. Pray, – pray do not let any absurd fancy stand in your way, and destroy everything. It will never come again, Nora. And, only think; it is all now your own, if you will only whisper one word.'

'Ah! – one word, – and that a falsehood!'

'No, – no. Say you will try to love him, and that will be enough. And you do love him?'

'Do I?'

'Yes, you do. It is only the opposition of your nature that makes you fight against him. Will you go now?'

'Let me be for two minutes by myself,' said Nora, 'and then I'll come down. Tell him that I'm coming.' Mrs Trevelyan stooped over her, kissed her, and then left her.

Nora, as soon as she was alone, stood upright in the middle of the room and held her hands up to her forehead. She had been far from thinking, when she was considering the matter easily among the hillocks, that the necessity for an absolute decision would come upon her so instantaneously. She had told herself only this morning that it would be wise to accept the man, if he should ever ask a second time; – and he had come already. He had been waiting for her in the village while she had been thinking whether he would ever come across her path again. She thought that it would have been easier for her now to have gone down with a 'yes' in her mouth, if her sister had not pressed her so hard to say that 'yes.' The very pressure from her sister seemed to imply that such pressure ought to be resisted. Why should there have been pressure, unless there were reasons against her marrying him? And yet, it she chose to take him, who would have a right to complain of her? Hugh Stanbury had never spoken to her a word that would justify her in even supposing that he would consider himself to be ill-used. All others of her friends would certainly rejoice, would applaud her, pat her on the back, cover her with caresses, and tell her that she had been born under a happy star. And she did like the man. Nay; – she thought she loved him. She withdrew her hands from her brow, assured herself that her lot in life was cast, and with hurrying fingers attempted to smooth her hair and to arrange her ribbons before the glass. She would go to the encounter boldly and accept him honestly. It was her duty to do so. What might she not do for brother and sisters as the wife of Lord Peterborough of Monkhams? She saw that that arrangement before the glass could be of no service, and she stepped quickly to the door. If he did not like her as she was, he need not ask her. Her mind was made up, and she would do it. But as she went down the stairs to the room in which she knew that he was waiting for her, there came over her a cold feeling of self-accusation, – almost of disgrace. 'I do not care,' she said. 'I know that I'm right.' She opened the door quickly, that there might be no further doubt, and found that she was alone with him.

'Miss Rowley,' he said, 'I am afraid you will think that I am persecuting you.'

'I have no right to think that,' she answered.

'I'll tell you why I have come. My dear father, who has always been my best friend, is very ill. He is at Naples, and I must go to him. He is very old, you know, – over eighty; and will never live to come back to England. From what I hear, I think it probable that I may remain with him till everything is over.'

'I did not know that he was so old as that.'

'They say that he can hardly live about a month or two. He will never see my wife, – if I can have a wife; but I should like to tell him, if it were possible, – that, – that – '

'I understand you, Mr Glascock.'

'I told you that I should come to you again, and as I may possibly linger at Naples all the winter, I could not go without seeing you. Miss Rowley, may I hope that you can love me?'

She did not answer him a word, but stood looking away from him with her hands clasped together. Had he asked her whether she would be his wife, it is possible that the answer which she had prepared would have been spoken. But he had put the question in another form. Did she love him? If she could only bring herself to say that she could love him, she might be lady of Monkhams before the next summer had come round.

'Nora,' he said, 'do you think that you can love me?'

'No,' she said, and there was something almost of fierceness in the tone of her voice as she answered him.

'And must that be your final answer to me?'

'Mr Glascock, what can I say?' she replied. 'I will tell you the honest truth; – I will tell you everything. I came into this room determined to accept you. But you are so good, and so kind, and so upright, that I cannot tell you a falsehood. I do not love you. I ought not to take what you offer me. If I did, it would be because you are rich, and a lord; and not because I love you. I love some one else. There; – pray, pray do not tell of me; but I do.' Then she flung away from him and hid her face in a corner of the sofa out of the light.

Her lover stood silent, not knowing how to go on with the conversation, not knowing how to bring it to an end. After what she had now said to him it was impossible that he should press her further. It was almost impossible that he should wish to do so.

When a lady is frank enough to declare that her heart is not her own to give, a man can hardly wish to make further prayer for the gift. 'If so,' he said, 'of course I have nothing to hope.'

She was sobbing, and could not answer him. She was half repentant, partly proud of what she had done, – half repentant in that she had lost what had seemed to her to be so good, and full of remorse in that she had so unnecessarily told her secret.

'Perhaps,' said he, 'I ought to assure you that what you have told me shall never be repeated by my lips.'

She thanked him for this by a motion of her head and hand, not by words; – and then he was gone. How he managed to bid adieu to Mrs Stanbury and her sister, or whether he saw them as he left the house, she never knew. In her corner of the sofa, weeping in the dark, partly proud and partly repentant, she remained till her sister came to her. 'Emily,' she said, jumping up, 'say nothing about it; not a word. It is of no use. The thing is done and over, and let it altogether be forgotten.'

'It is done and over, certainly,' said Mrs Trevelyan.

'Exactly; – and I suppose a girl may do what she likes with herself in that way. If I choose to decline to take anything that is pleasant, and nice, and comfortable, nobody has a right to scold me. And I won't be scolded.'

'But, my child, who is scolding you?'

'You mean to scold me. But it is of no use. The man has gone, and there is an end of it. Nothing that you can say or I can think will bring him back again. I don't want anybody to tell me that it would be better to be Lady Peterborough, with everything that the world has to give, than to live here without a soul to speak to, and to have to go back to those horrible islands next year. You can't think that I am very comfortable.'

'But what did you say to him, Nora?'

'What did I say to him? What could I say to him? Why didn't he ask me to be his wife without saying anything about love? He asked me if I loved him. Of course I don't love him. I would have said I did, but it stuck in my throat. I am willing enough, I believe, to sell myself to the devil, but I don't know how to do it. Never mind. It's done, and now I'll go to bed.'

She did go to bed, and Mrs Trevelyan explained to the two ladies as much as was necessary of what had occurred. When Mrs Stanbury came to understand that the gentleman who had been closeted with her would, probably, in a few months be a lord himself, that he was a very rich man, a member of Parliament, and one of those who are decidedly born with gold spoons in their

mouths, and understood also that Nora Rowley had refused him,
she was lost in amazement. Mr Glascock was about forty years of
age, and appeared to Nora Rowley, who was nearly twenty years
his junior, to be almost an old man. But to Mrs Stanbury, who was
over sixty, Mr Glascock seemed to be quite in the flower of his age.
The bald place at the top of his head simply showed that he had
passed his boyhood, and the grey hairs at the back of his whiskers
were no more than outward signs of manly discretion. She could
not understand why any girl should refuse such an offer, unless the
man were himself bad in morals, or in temper. But Mrs Trevelyan
had told her while Nora and Mr Glascock were closeted together,
that he was believed by them all to be good and gentle. Nevertheless
she felt a considerable increase of respect for a young lady who had
refused the eldest son of a lord. Priscilla, when she heard what had
occurred, expressed to her mother a moderated approval. According
to her views a girl would much more often be right to refuse an
offer of marriage than to accept it, let him who made the offer be
who he might. And the fact of the man having been sent away with
a refusal somewhat softened Priscilla's anger at his coming there at
all.

'I suppose he is a goose,' said she to her mother, 'and I hope there
won't be any more of this kind running after them while they are
with us.'

Nora, when she was alone, wept till her heart was almost broken.
It was done, and the man was gone, and the thing was over. She
had quite sufficient knowledge of the world to realise perfectly the
difference between such a position as that which had been offered
to her, and the position which in all probability she would now be
called upon to fill. She had had her chance, and Fortune had placed
great things at her disposal. It must be said of her also that the great
things which Fortune had offered to her were treasures very
valuable in her eyes. Whether it be right and wise to covet or to
despise wealth and rank, there was no doubt but that she coveted
them. She had been instructed to believe in them, and she did
believe in them. In some mysterious manner of which she herself
knew nothing, taught by some preceptor the nobility of whose
lessons she had not recognised though she had accepted them, she
had learned other things also, – to revere truth and love, and to be
ambitious as regarded herself of conferring the gift of her whole
heart upon some one whom she could worship as a hero. She had
spoken the simple truth when she had told her sister that she had
been willing to sell herself to the devil, but that she had failed in her
attempt to execute the contract. But now as she lay weeping on her

bed, tearing herself with remorse, picturing to herself in the most vivid colours all that she had thrown away, telling herself of all that she might have done and all she might have been, had she not allowed the insane folly of a moment to get the better of her, she received little or no comfort from the reflection that she had been true to her better instincts. She had told the man that she had refused him because she loved Hugh Stanbury; – at least, as far as she could remember what had passed, she had so told him. And how mean it was of her to allow herself to be actuated by an insane passion for a man who had never spoken to her of love, and how silly of her afterwards to confess it! Of what service could such a passion be to her life? Even were it returned, she could not marry such a one as Hugh Stanbury. She knew enough of herself to be quite sure that were he to ask her to do so to-morrow, she would refuse him. Better go and be scorched, and bored to death, and buried at the Mandarins, than attempt to regulate a poor household which, as soon as she made one of its number, would be on the sure road to ruin!

For a moment there came upon her, not a thought, hardly an idea, – something of a waking dream that she would write to Mr Glascock and withdraw all that she had said. Were she to do so he would probably despise her, and tell her that he despised her; – but there might be a chance. It was possible that such a declaration would bring him back to her; – and did it not bring him back to her she would only be where she was, a poor lost, shipwrecked creature, who had flung herself upon the rocks and thrown away her only chance of a prosperous voyage across the ocean of life; her only chance, for she was not like other girls, who at any rate remain on the scene of action, and may refit their spars and still win their way. For there were to be no more seasons in London, no more living in Curzon Street, no renewed power of entering the ball-rooms and crowded staircases in which high-born wealthy lovers can be conquered. A great prospect had been given to her, and she had flung it aside! That letter of retractation was, however, quite out of the question. The reader must not suppose that she had ever thought that she could write it. She thought of nothing but of coming misery and remorse. In her wretchedness she fancied that she had absolutely disclosed to the man who loved her the name of him whom she had been mad enough to say that she loved. But what did it matter? Let it be as it might, she was destroyed.

The next morning she came down to breakfast pale as a ghost; and they who saw her knew at once that she had done that which had made her a wretched woman.

18

The Stanbury Correspondence

Half an hour after the proper time, when the others had finished their tea and bread and butter, Nora Rowley came down among them pale as a ghost. Her sister had gone to her while she was dressing, but she had declared that she would prefer to be alone. She would be down directly, she had said, and had completed her toilet without even the assistance of her maid. She drank her cup of tea and pretended to eat her toast; and then sat herself down, very wretchedly, to think of it all again. It had been all within her grasp, – all of which she had ever dreamed! And now it was gone! Each of her three companions strove from time to time to draw her into conversation, but she seemed to be resolute in her refusal. At first, till her utter prostration had become a fact plainly recognised by them all, she made some little attempt at an answer when a direct question was asked of her; but after a while she only shook her head, and was silent, giving way to absolute despair.

Late in the evening she went out into the garden, and Priscilla followed her. It was now the end of July, and the summer was in its glory. The ladies, during the day, would remain in the drawing-room with the windows open and the blinds down, and would sit in the evening reading and working, or perhaps pretending to read and work, under the shade of a cedar which stood upon the lawn. No retirement could possibly be more secluded than was that of the garden of the Clock House. No stranger could see into it, or hear sounds from out of it. Though it was not extensive, it was so well furnished with those charming garden shrubs which, in congenial soils, became large trees, that one party of wanderers might seem to be lost from another amidst its walls. On this evening Mrs Stanbury and Mrs Trevelyan had gone out as usual, but Priscilla had remained with Nora Rowley. After a while Nora also got up and went through the window all alone. Priscilla having waited for a few minutes, followed her; and caught her in a long green walk that led round the bottom of the orchard.

'What makes you so wretched?' she said.

'Why do you say I am wretched?'

'Because it's so visible. How is one to go on living with you all day and not notice it?'

'I wish you wouldn't notice it. I don't think it kind of you to notice it. If I wanted to talk of it, I would say so.'

'It is better generally to speak of a trouble than to keep it to oneself,' said Priscilla.

'All the same, I would prefer not to speak of mine,' said Nora.

Then they parted, one going one way and one the other, and Priscilla was certainly angry at the reception which had been given to the sympathy which she had proffered. The next day passed almost without a word spoken between the two. Mrs Stanbury had not ventured as yet to mention to her guest the subject of the rejected lover, and had not even said much on the subject to Mrs Trevelyan. Between the two sisters there had been, of course, some discussion on the matter. It was impossible that it should be allowed to pass without it; but such discussions always resulted in an assertion on the part of Nora that she would not be scolded. Mrs Trevelyan was very tender with her, and made no attempt to scold her, – tried, at last, simply to console her; but Nora was so continually at work scolding herself, that every word spoken to her on the subject of Mr Glascock's visit seemed to her to carry with it a rebuke.

But on the second day she herself accosted Priscilla Stanbury. 'Come into the garden,' she said, when they two were for a moment alone together; 'I want to speak to you.' Priscilla, without answering, folded up her work and put on her hat. 'Come down to the green walk,' said Nora. 'I was savage to you last night, and I want to beg your pardon.'

'You were savage,' said Priscilla, smiling, 'and you shall have my pardon. Who would not pardon you any offence, if you asked it?'

'I am so miserable!' she said.

'But why?'

'I don't know. I can't tell. And it is of no use talking about it now, for it is all over. But I ought not to have been cross to you, and I am very sorry.'

'That does not signify a straw; only so far, that when I have been cross, and have begged a person's pardon, – which I don't do as often as I ought, – I always feel that it begets kindness. If I could help you in your trouble I would.'

'You can't fetch him back again.'

'You mean Mr Glascock. Shall I go and try?'

Nora smiled and shook her head. 'I wonder what he would say if you asked him. But if he came, I should do the same thing.'

'I do not in the least know what you have done, my dear. I only see that you mope about, and are more down in the mouth than any one ought to be, unless some great trouble has come.'

'A great trouble has come.'

'I suppose you have had your choice, – either to accept your lover or to reject him.'

'No; I have not had my choice.'

'It seems to me that no one has dictated to you; or, at least, that you have obeyed no dictation.'

'Of course, I can't explain it to you. It is impossible that I should.'

'If you mean that you regret what you have done because you have been false to the man, I can sympathise with you. No one has ever a right to be false, and if you are repenting a falsehood, I will willingly help you to eat your ashes and to wear your sackcloth. But if you are repenting a truth – '

'I am.'

'Then you must eat your ashes by yourself, for me; and I do not think that you will ever be able to digest them.'

'I do not want anybody to help me,' said Nora proudly.

'Nobody can help you, if I understand the matter rightly. You have got to get the better of your own covetousness and evil desires, and you are in the fair way to get the better of them if you have already refused to be this man's wife because you could not bring yourself to commit the sin of marrying him when you did not love him. I suppose that is about the truth of it; and indeed, indeed, I do sympathise with you. If you have done that, though it is no more than the plainest duty, I will love you for it. One finds so few people that will do any duty that taxes their self-indulgence.'

'But he did not ask me to marry him.'

'Then I do not understand anything about it.'

'He asked me to love him.'

'But he meant you to be his wife?'

'Oh yes; – he meant that of course.'

'And what did you say?' asked Priscilla.

'That I didn't love him,' replied Nora.

'And that was the truth?'

'Yes; – it was the truth.'

'And what do you regret? – that you didn't tell him a lie?'

'No; – not that,' said Nora slowly.

'What then? You cannot regret that you have not basely deceived a man who has treated you with a loving generosity?' They walked on silent for a few yards, and then Priscilla repeated her question. 'You cannot mean that you are sorry that you did not persuade yourself to do evil?'

'I don't want to go back to the islands, and to lose myself there, and to be nobody; – that is what I mean. And I might have been so much! Could one step from the very highest rung of the ladder to the very lowest and not feel it?'

'But you have gone up the ladder, – if you only knew it,' said

Priscilla. 'There was a choice given to you between the foulest mire of the clay of the world, and the sun-light of the very God. You have chosen the sun-light, and you are crying after the clay! I cannot pity you; but I can esteem you, and love you, and believe in you. And I do. You'll get yourself right at last, and there's my hand on it, if you'll take it.' Nora took the hand that was offered to her, held it in her own for some seconds, and then walked back to the house and up to her own room in silence.

The post used to come into Nuncombe Putney at about eight in the morning, carried thither by a wooden-legged man who rode a donkey. There is a general understanding that the wooden-legged men in country parishes should be employed as postmen, owing to the great steadiness of demeanour which a wooden leg is generally found to produce. It may be that such men are slower in their operations than would be biped postmen; but as all private employers of labour demand labourers with two legs, it is well that the lame and halt should find a refuge in the less exacting service of the government. The one-legged man who rode his donkey into Nuncombe Putney would reach his post-office not above half an hour after his proper time; but he was very slow in stumping round the village, and seldom reached the Clock House much before ten. On a certain morning two or three days after the conversation just recorded it was past ten when he brought two letters to the door, one for Mrs Trevelyan, and one for Mrs Stanbury. The ladies had finished their breakfast, and were seated together at an open window. As was usual, the letters were given into Priscilla's hands, and the newspaper which accompanied them into those of Mrs Trevelyan, its undoubted owner. When her letter was handed to her, she looked at the address closely and then walked away with it into her own room.

'I think it's from Louis,' said Nora, as soon as the door was closed. 'If so, he is telling her to come back.'

'Mamma, this is for you,' said Priscilla. 'It is from Aunt Stanbury. I know her handwriting.'

'From your aunt? What can she be writing about? There is something wrong with Dorothy.' Mrs Stanbury held the letter but did not open it. 'You had better read it, my dear. If she is ill, pray let her come home.'

But the letter spoke of nothing amiss as regard Dorothy, and did not indeed even mention Dorothy's name. Luckily Priscilla read the letter in silence, for it was an angry letter. 'What is it, Priscilla? Why don't you tell me? Is anything wrong?' said Mrs Stanbury.

'Nothing is wrong, mamma, – except that my aunt is a silly woman.'

'Goodness me ! what is it ?'

'It is a family matter,' said Nora smiling, 'and I will go.'

'What can it be ?' demanded Mrs Stanbury again as soon as Nora had left the room.

'You shall hear what it can be. I will read it you,' said Priscilla. 'It seems to me that of all the women that ever lived my Aunt Stanbury is the most prejudiced, the most unjust, and the most given to evil thinking of her neighbours. This is what she has thought fit to write to you, mamma.' Then Priscilla read her aunt's letter, which was as follows :

The Close, Exeter, July 31, 186 –

Dear Sister Stanbury,

I am informed that the lady who is living with you because she could not continue to live under the same roof with her lawful husband, has received a visit at your house from a gentleman who was named as her lover before she left her own. I am given to understand that it was because of this gentleman's visits to her in London, and because she would not give up seeing him, that her husband would not live with her any longer.

'But the man has never been here at all,' said Mrs Stanbury, in dismay.

'Of course he has not been here. But let me go on.'

I have got nothing to do with your visitors, continued the letter, 'and I should not interfere but for the credit of the family. There ought to be somebody to explain to you that much of the abominable disgrace of the whole proceeding will rest upon you, if you permit such goings on in your house. I suppose it is your house. At any rate you are regarded as the mistress of the establishment, and it is for you to tell the lady that she must go elsewhere. I do hope that you have done so, or at least that you will do now. It is intolerable that the widow of my brother, – a clergyman, – should harbour a lady who is separated from her husband and who receives visits from a gentleman who is reputed to be her lover. I wonder much that your eldest daughter should countenance such a proceeding.

Yours truly,
Jemima
Stanbury.

Mrs Stanbury, when the letter had been read to her, held up both her hands in despair. 'Dear, dear,' she exclaimed. 'Oh, dear !'

'She had such pleasure in writing it,' said Priscilla, 'that one ought hardly to begrudge it her.' The blackest spot in the character of Priscilla Stanbury was her hatred for her aunt in Exeter. She knew that her aunt had high qualities, and yet she hated her aunt. She was well aware that her aunt was regarded as a shining light by very many food people in the country, and yet she hated her aunt. She could not but acknowledge that her aunt had been generous to her brother, and was now very generous to her sister, and yet she hated her aunt. It was now a triumph to her that her aunt had fallen into so terrible a quagmire, and she was by no means disposed to let the sinning old woman easily out of it.

'It is as pretty a specimen,' she said, 'as I ever knew of malice and eaves-dropping combined.'

'Don't use such hard words, my dear.'

'Look at her words to us,' said Priscilla. 'What business has she to talk to you about the credit of the family and abominable disgrace? You have held your head up in poverty, while she has been rolling in money.'

'She has been very good to Hugh, – and now to Dorothy.'

'If I were Dorothy I would have none of her goodness. She likes some one to trample on, – some one of the name to patronise. She shan't trample on you and me, mamma.'

Then there was a discussion as to what should be done; or rather a discourse in which Priscilla explained what she thought fit to do. Nothing, she decided, should be said to Mrs Trevelyan on the subject; but an answer should be sent to Aunt Stanbury. Priscilla herself would write this answer, and herself would sign it. There was some difference of opinion on this point, as Mrs Stanbury thought that if she might be allowed to put her name to it, even though Priscilla should write it, the wording of it would be made, in some degree, mild, – to suit her own character. But her daughter was imperative, and she gave way.

'It shall be mild enough in words,' said Priscilla, 'and very short.'

Then she wrote her letter as follows:

Nuncombe Putney, August 1, 186 –

Dear Aunt Stanbury,

You have found a mare's nest. The gentleman you speak of has never been here at all, and the people who bring you news have probably hoaxed you. I don't think that mamma has ever disgraced the family, and you can have no reason for thinking that she ever will. You should, at any rate, be sure of what you are saying before you make such cruel accusations,

Yours truly,
Priscilla Stanbury.

PS – Another gentleman did call here, – not to see Mrs Trevelyan ; but I suppose mamma's house need not be closed against all visitors.

Poor Dorothy had passed evil hours from the moment in which her aunt had so far certified herself as to Colonel Osborne's visit to Nuncombe as to make her feel it to be incumbent on her to interfere. After much consideration Miss Stanbury had told her niece the dreadful news, and had told also what she intended to do. Dorothy, who was in truth horrified at the iniquity of the fact which was related, and who never dreamed of doubting the truth of her aunt's information, hardly knew how to interpose. 'I am sure mamma won't let there be anything wrong,' she had said.

'And you don't call this wrong ?' said Miss Stanbury, in a tone of indignation.

'But perhaps mamma will tell them to go.'

'I hope she will. I hope she has. But he was allowed to be there for hours. And now three days have passed and there is no sign of anything being done. He came and went and may come again when he pleases.' Still Dorothy pleaded. 'I shall do my duty,' said Miss Stanbury.

'I am quite sure mamma will do nothing wrong,' said Dorothy. But the letter was written and sent, and the answer to the letter reached the house in the Close in due time.

When Miss Stanbury had read and re-read the very short reply which her niece had written, she became at first pale with dismay, and then red with renewed vigour and obstinacy. She had made herself, as she thought, quite certain of her facts before she had acted on her information. There was some equivocation, some most unworthy deceit in Priscilla's letter. Or could it be possible that she herself had been mistaken ? Another gentleman had been there; – not, however, with the object of seeing Mrs Trevelyan ! So said Priscilla. But she had made herself sure that the man in question was a man from London, a middle-aged man from London, who had specially asked for Mrs Trevelyan, and who had at once been known to Mrs Clegg, at the Lessboro' inn, to be Mrs Trevelyan's lover. Miss Stanbury was very unhappy, and at last sent for Giles Hickbody. Giles Hickbody had never pretended to know the name. He had seen the man and had described him, 'Quite a swell, ma'am ; and a Lon'oner, and one as'd be up to anything ; but not a young 'un ; no, not just a young 'un, zartainly.' He was cross-examined again now, and said that all he knew about the man's name was that there was a handle to it. This was ended by Miss Stanbury sending him down to Lessboro' to learn the very name of the gentleman, and by his coming back with that of the Honourable George Glascock written on a piece of paper. 'They say now as he was arter the other young 'ooman,' said Giles Hickbody. Then was the confusion of Miss Stanbury complete.

It was late when Giles returned from Lessboro', and nothing could be done that night. It was too late to write a letter for the next morning's post. Miss Stanbury, who was as proud of her own discrimination as she was just and true, felt that a day of humiliation had indeed come for her. She hated Priscilla almost as vigorously as Priscilla hated her. To Priscilla she would not write to own her fault; but it was incumbent on her to confess it to Mrs Stanbury. It was incumbent on her also to confess it to Dorothy. All that night she did not sleep, and the next morning she went about abashed, wretched, hardly mistress of her own maids. She must confess it also to Martha, and Martha would be very stern to her. Martha had pooh-poohed the whole story of the lover, seeming to think that there could be no reasonable objection to a lover past fifty.

'Dorothy,' she said at last, about noon, 'I have been over hasty about your mother and this man. I am sorry for it, and must – beg – everybody's – pardon.'

'I knew mamma would do nothing wrong,' said Dorothy.

'To do wrong is human, and she, I suppose, is not more free than others; but in this matter I was misinformed. I shall write and beg her pardon; and now I beg your pardon.'

'Not mine, Aunt Stanbury.'

'Yes, yours and your mother's, and the lady's also, – for against her has the fault been most grievous. I shall write to your mother and express my contrition.' She put off the evil hour of writing as long as she could, but before dinner the painful letter had been written, and carried by herself to the post. It was as follows:

The Close, August 3, 186 –

Dear Sister Stanbury,
I have now learned that the information was false on which my former letter was based. I am heartily sorry for any annoyance I may have given you. I can only inform you that my intentions were good and upright. Nevertheless, I humbly beg your pardon.

Yours truly,
Jemima Stanbury

Mrs Stanbury, when she received this, was inclined to let the matter drop. That her sister-in-law should express such abject contrition was to her such a lowering of the great ones of the earth, that the apology conveyed to her more pain than pleasure. She could not hinder herself from sympathising with all that her sister-in-law had felt when she had found herself called upon to humiliate herself. But it was not so with Priscilla. Mrs Stanbury did not observe that her daughter's name was scrupulously avoided in the apology; but Priscilla observed it. She would not let the matter drop, without an attempt at the last word. She therefore wrote back again as follows:

> Nuncombe Putney, August 4, 186 –
>
> Dear Aunt Stanbury,
> I am glad you have satisfied yourself about the gentleman who has so much disquieted you. I do not know that the whole affair would be worth a moment's consideration, were it not that mamma and I, living as we do so secluded a life, are peculiarly apt to feel any attack upon our good name, – which is pretty nearly all that is left to us. If ever there were women who should be free from attack, at any rate from those of their own family, we are such women. We never interfere with you, or with anybody; and I think you might abstain from harassing us by accusations.
> Pray do not write to mamma in such a strain again, unless you are quite sure of your ground.
>
> Yours truly,
> Priscilla Stanbury

'Impudent vixen!' said Miss Stanbury to Martha, when she had read the letter. 'Ill-conditioned, insolent vixen!'

'She was provoked, miss,' said Martha.

'Well; yes; yes; – and I suppose it is right that you should tell me of it. I dare say it is part of what I ought to bear for being an old fool and too cautious about my own flesh and blood. I will bear it. There. I was wrong, and I will say that I have been justly punished. There, – there!'

How very much would Miss Stanbury's tone have been changed had she known that at that very moment Colonel Osborne was eating his breakfast at Mrs Crocket's inn, in Nuncombe Putney!

19

Bozzle, the Ex-Policeman

When Mr Trevelyan had gone through the miserable task of breaking up his establishment in Curzon Street, and had seen all his furniture packed, including his books, his pictures, and his pet

Italian ornaments, it was necessary that he should go and live somewhere. He was very wretched at this time, – so wretched that life was a burden to him. He was a man who loved his wife; – to whom his child was very dear; and he was one too to whom the ordinary comforts of domestic life were attractive and necessary. There are men to whom release from the constraint imposed by family ties will be, at any rate for a time, felt as a release. But he was not such a man. There was no delight to him in being able to dine at his club, and being free to go whither he pleased in the evening. As it was, it pleased him to go no whither in the evenings; and his mornings were equally blank to him. He went so often to Mr Bideawhile, that the poor old lawyer became quite tired of the Trevelyan family quarrel. Even Lady Milborough, with all her power of sympathising, began to feel that she would almost prefer on any morning that her dear young friend, Louis Trevelyan, should not be announced. Nevertheless, she always saw him when he came, and administered comfort according to her lights. Of course he would have his wife back before long. That was the only consolation she was able to offer; and she offered it so often that he began gradually to feel that something might be done towards bringing about so desirable an event. After what had occurred they could not live again in Curzon Street, – nor even in London for awhile; but Naples was open to them. Lady Milborough said so much to him of the advantages which always came in such circumstances from going to Naples, that he began to regard such a trip as almost the natural conclusion of his adventure. But then there came that very difficult question; – what step should be first taken? Lady Milborough proposed that he should go boldly down to Nuncombe Putney, and make the arrangement. 'She will only be too glad to jump into your arms,' said Lady Milborough. Trevelyan thought that if he went to Nuncombe Putney, his wife might perhaps jump into his arms; but what would come after that? How would he stand then in reference to his authority? Would she own that she had been wrong? Would she promise to behave better in future? He did not believe that she was yet sufficiently broken in spirit to make any such promise. And he told himself again and again that it would be absurd in him to allow her to return to him without such subjection, after all that he had gone through in defence of his marital rights. If he were to write to her a long letter, argumentative, affectionate, exhaustive, it might be better. He was inclined to believe of himself that he was good at writing long, affectionate, argumentative, and exhaustive letters. But he would not do even this as yet. He had broken up his house, and scattered all his domestic gods to the winds, because she had behaved badly to him; and the thing done was too important to allow of redress being found so easily.

So he lived on a wretched life in London. He could hardly endure to show himself at his club, fearing that every one would be talking of him as the man who was separated from his wife, – perhaps as the man of whose wife Colonel Osborne was the dear friend. No doubt for a day or two there had been much of such conversation; but it had died away from the club long before his consciousness had become callous. At first he had gone into a lodging in Mayfair; but this had been but for a day or two. After that he had taken a set of furnished chambers in Lincoln's Inn, immediately under those in which Stanbury lived; and thus it came to pass that he and Stanbury were very much thrown together. As Trevelyan would always talk of his wife this was rather a bore; but our friend bore with it, and would even continue to instruct the world through the columns of the D. R. while Trevelyan was descanting on the peculiar cruelty of his own position.

'I wish to be just, and even generous; and I do love her with all my heart,' he said one afternoon, when Hugh was very hard at work.

'"It is all very well for gentlemen to call themselves reformers,"' Hugh was writing, '"but have these gentlemen ever realised to themselves the meaning of that word? We think that they have never done so as long as – " Of course you love her,' said Hugh, with his eyes still on the paper, still leaning on his pen, but finding by the cessation of sound that Trevelyan had paused, and therefore knowing that it was necessary that he should speak.

'As much as ever,' said Trevelyan, with energy.

'"As long as they follow such a leader, in such a cause, into whichever lobby he may choose to take them – " Exactly so, – exactly,' said Stanbury; 'just as much as ever.'

'You are not listening to a word,' said Trevelyan.

'I haven't missed a single expression you have used,' said Stanbury. 'But a fellow has to do two things at a time when he's on the daily press.'

'I beg your pardon for interrupting you,' said Trevelyan, angrily, getting up, taking his hat, and stalking off to the house of Lady Milborough. In this way he became rather a bore to his friends. He could not divest his mind of the injury which had accrued to him from his wife's conduct, nor could he help talking of the grief with which his mind was laden. And he was troubled with sore suspicions, which, as far as they concerned his wife, had certainly not been merited. It had seemed to him that she had persisted in her intimacy with Colonel Osborne in a manner that was not compatible with that wife-like indifference which he regarded as her duty. Why had she written to him and received letters from him when her husband had plainly told her that any such communication was objectionable? She had done so, and as far as Trevelyan could remember her words, had plainly declared that she would continue to do so. He had sent her away, into the most remote retirement he could find for her; but the post was open to her. He had heard much of Mrs Stanbury, and of Priscilla, from his friend Hugh, and thoroughly believed that his wife was in respectable hands. But what was to prevent Colonel Osborne from going after her, if he chose to do so? And if he did so choose, Mrs Stanbury could not prevent their meeting. He was racked with jealousy, and yet he did not cease to declare to himself that he knew his wife too well to believe that she would sin. He could not rid himself of his jealousy, but he tried with all his might to make the man whom he hated the object of it, rather than the woman whom he loved.

He hated Colonel Osborne with all his heart. It was a regret to him that the days of duelling were over, so that he could not shoot the man. And yet, had duelling been possible to him, Colonel Osborne had done nothing that would have justified him in calling his enemy out, or would even have enabled him to do so with any chance of inducing his enemy to fight. Circumstances, he thought, were cruel to him beyond compare, in that he should have been made to suffer so great torment without having any of the satisfaction of revenge. Even Lady Milborough, with all her horror as to the Colonel, could not tell him that the Colonel was amenable to any punishment. He was advised that he must take his wife away and live at Naples because of this man, – that he must banish himself entirely if he chose to repossess himself of his wife and child; – and yet nothing could be done to the unprincipled rascal by whom all his wrongs and sufferings were occasioned! Thinking it very possible that Colonel Osborne would follow his wife, he had a watch set upon the Colonel. He had found a retired policeman, – a most discreet man, as he was assured, – who, for a consideration, undertook the management of interesting jobs of this kind. The man was one Bozzle, who had not lived without a certain reputation in the police courts. In these days of his madness, therefore, he took Mr Bozzle into his pay; and after a while he got a letter from Bozzle with the Exeter post-mark. Colonel Osborne had left London with a ticket for Lessboro'. Bozzle also had taken a place by the same train for that small town. The letter was written in the railway carriage, and, as Bozzle explained, would be posted by him as he passed through Exeter. A further communication should be made by the next day's post, in a letter which Mr Bozzle proposed to address to Z. A., Post-office, Waterloo Place.

On receiving this first letter, Trevelyan was in an agony of doubt, as well as misery. What should he do? Should he go to Lady Milborough, or to Stanbury; or should he at once follow Colonel Osborne and Mr Bozzle to Lessboro'. It ended in his resolving at last to wait for the letter which was to be addressed to Z. A. But he spent an interval of horrible suspense, and of insane rage. Let the laws say what they might, he would have the man's blood, if he found that the man had even attempted to wrong him. Then, at last, the second letter reached him. Colonel Osborne and Mr Bozzle had each of them spent the day in the neighbourhood of Lessboro', not exactly in each other's company, but very near to each other. 'The Colonel' had ordered a gig, on the day after his arrival at Lessboro', for the village of Cockchaffington; and, for all Mr Bozzle knew, the Colonel had gone to Cockchaffington. Mr Bozzle was ultimately inclined to think that the Colonel had really spent his day in going to Cockchaffington. Mr Bozzle himself, knowing the wiles of such men as Colonel Osborne, and thinking at first that that journey to Cockchaffington might only be a deep ruse, had walked over to Nuncombe Putney. There he had a pint of beer and some bread and cheese at Mrs Crocket's house, and had asked various questions, to which he did not receive very satisfactory answers. But he inspected the Clock House very minutely, and came to a decided opinion as to the point at which it would be attacked, if burglary were the object of the assailants. And he observed the iron gates, and the steps, and the shape of the trees, and the old pigeon-house-looking fabric in which the clock used to be placed. There was no knowing when information might be wanted, or what information might not be of use. But he made himself tolerably sure that Colonel Osborne did not visit Nuncombe Putney on that day; and then he walked back to Lessboro'. Having done this, he applied himself to the little memorandum book in which he kept the records of these interesting duties, and entered a claim against his employer for a conveyance to Nuncombe Putney and back, including driver and ostler; and then he wrote his letter. After that he had a hot supper, with three glasses of brandy and water, and went to bed with a thorough conviction that he had earned his bread on that day.

The letter to Z. A. did not give all these particulars, but it did explain that Colonel Osborne had gone off, apparently, to Cock-

chaffington, and that he, – Bozzle, – had himself visited Nuncombe
Putney. 'The hawk hasn't been nigh the dovecot as yet,' said Mr
Bozzle in his letter, meaning to be both mysterious and facetious.

It would be difficult to say whether the wit or the mystery
disgusted Trevelyan the most. He had felt that he was defiling
himself with dirt when he first went to Mr Bozzle. He knew that he
was having recourse to means that were base and low, – which
could not be other than base or low, let the circumstances be what
they might. But Mr Bozzle's conversation had not been quite so bad
as Mr Bozzle's letters; as it may have been that Mr Bozzle's
successful activity was more insupportable than his futile attempts.
But, nevertheless, something must be done. It could not be that
Colonel Osborne should have gone down to the close neighbourhood of Nuncombe Putney without the intention of seeing the lady
whom his obtrusive pertinacity had driven to that seclusion. It was
terrible to Trevelyan that Colonel Osborne should be there, and not
the less terrible because such a one as Mr Bozzle was watching the
Colonel on his behalf. Should he go to Nuncombe Putney himself?
And if so, when he got to Nuncombe Putney what should he do
there? At last, in his suspense and his grief, he resolved that he
would tell the whole to Hugh Stanbury.

'Do you mean,' said Hugh, 'that you have put a policeman on his
track?'

'The man was a policeman once.'

'What we call a private detective. I can't say I think you were
right.'

'But you see that it was necessary,' said Trevelyan.

'I can't say that it was necessary. To speak out, I can't understand
that a wife should be worth watching who requires watching.'

'Is a man to do nothing then? And even now it is not my wife
whom I doubt.'

'As for Colonel Osborne, if he chooses to go to Lessboro', why
shouldn't he? Nothing that you can do, or that Bozzle can do, can
prevent him. He has a perfect right to go to Lessboro'.'

'But he has not a right to go to my wife.'

'And if your wife refuses to see him; or having seen him, – for a
man may force his way in anywhere with a little trouble, – if she
sends him away with a flea in his ear, as I believe she would – '

'She is so frightfully indiscreet.'

'I don't see what Bozzle can do.'

'He has found out at any rate that Osborne is there,' said
Trevelyan. 'I am not more fond of dealing with such fellows than

you are yourself. But I think it is my duty to know what is going on. What ought I to do now?'

'I should do nothing, – except dismiss Bozzle.'

'You know that that is nonsense, Stanbury.'

'Whatever I did I should dismiss Bozzle.' Stanbury was now quite in earnest, and, as he repeated his suggestion for the dismissal of the policeman, pushed his writing things away from him. 'If you ask my opinion, you know, I must tell you what I think. I should get rid of Bozzle as a beginning. If you will only think of it, how can your wife come back to you if she learns that you have set a detective to watch her?'

'But I haven't set the man to watch her.'

'Colonel Osborne is nothing to you, except as he is concerned with her. This man is now down in her neighbourhood; and, if she learns that, how can she help feeling it as a deep insult? Of course the man watches her as a cat watches a mouse.'

'But what am I to do? I can't write to the man and tell him to come away. Osborne is down there, and I must do something. Will you go down to Nuncombe Putney yourself, and let me know the truth?'

After much debating of the subject, Hugh Stanbury said that he would himself go down to Nuncombe Putney alone. There were difficulties about the D. R.; but he would go to the office of the newspaper and overcome them. How far the presence of Nora Rowley at his mother's house may have assisted in bringing him to undertake the journey, perhaps need not be accurately stated. He acknowledged to himself that the claims of friendship were strong upon him; and that as he had loudly disapproved of the Bozzle arrangement, he ought to lend a hand to some other scheme of action. Moreover, having professed his conviction that no improper visiting could possibly take place under his mother's roof, he felt bound to show that he was not afraid to trust to that conviction himself. He declared that he would be ready to proceed to Nuncombe Putney to-morrow; – but only on condition that he might have plenary power to dismiss Bozzle.

'There can be no reason why you should take any notice of the man,' said Trevelyan.

'How can I help noticing him when I find him prowling about the place? Of course I shall know who he is.'

'I don't see that you need know anything about him.'

'My dear Trevelyan, you cannot have two ambassadors engaged in the same service without communication with each other. And any communication with Mr Bozzle, except that of sending him back to London, I will not have.' The controversy was ended by the writing of a letter from Trevelyan to Bozzle, which was confided to Stanbury, in which the ex-policeman was thanked for his activity and requested to return to London for the present. 'As we are now aware that Colonel Osborne is in the neighbourhood,' said the letter, 'my friend Mr Stanbury will know what to do.'

As soon as this was settled Stanbury went to the office of the D. R. and made arrangements as to his work for three days. Jones could do the article on the Irish Church* upon a pinch like this, although he had not given much study to the subject as yet; and Puddlethwaite, who was great in City matters, would try his hand on the present state of society in Rome,* a subject on which it was essential that the D. R. should express itself at once. Having settled these little troubles Stanbury returned to his friend, and in the evening they dined together at a tavern.

'And now, Trevelyan, let me know fairly what it is that you wish,' said Stanbury.

'I wish to have my wife back again.'

'Simply that. If she will agree to come back, you will make no difficulty.'

'No; not quite simply that. I shall desire that she shall be guided by my wishes as to any intimacies she may form.'

'That is all very well; but is she to give any undertaking? Do you intend to exact any promise from her? It is my opinion that she will be willing enough to come back, and that when she is with you there will be no further cause for quarrelling. But I don't think she will bind herself by any exacted promise; and certainly not through a third person.'

'Then say nothing about it. Let her write a letter to me proposing to come, – and she shall come.'

'Very well. So far I understand. And now what about Colonel Osborne? You don't want me to quarrel with him I suppose?'

'I should like to keep that for myself,' said Trevelyan, grimly.

'If you will take my advice you will not trouble yourself about him,' said Stanbury. 'But as far as I am concerned, I am not to meddle or make with him? Of course,' continued Stanbury, after a pause, 'if I find that he is intruding himself in my mother's house, I shall tell him that he must not come there.'

'But if you find him installed in your mother's house as a visitor, – how then?'

'I do not regard that as possible.'

'I don't mean living there,' said Trevelyan, 'but coming backwards and forwards, – going on in habits of intimacy with, –

with, – ?' His voice trembled so as he asked these questions, that he could not pronounce the word which was to complete them.

'With Mrs Trevelyan, you mean.'

'Yes; with my wife. I don't say that it is so; but it may be so. You will be bound to tell me the truth.'

'I will certainly tell you the truth.'

'And the whole truth.'

'Yes; the whole truth.'

'Should it be so I will never see her again, – never. And as for him; – but never mind.' Then there was another short period of silence, during which Stanbury smoked his pipe and sipped his whisky toddy. 'You must see,' continued Trevelyan, 'that it is absolutely necessary that I should do something. It is all very well for you to say that you do not like detectives. Neither do I like them. But what was I to do? When you condemn me you hardly realise the difficulties of my position.'

'It is the deuce of a nuisance certainly,' said Stanbury, through the cloud of smoke, – thinking now not at all of Mrs Trevelyan, but of Mrs Trevelyan's sister.

'It makes a man almost feel that he had better not marry at all,' said Trevelyan.

'I don't see that. Of course there may come troubles. The tiles may fall on your head, you know, as you walk through the streets. As far as I can see, women go straight enough nineteen times out of twenty. But they don't like being, – what I call looked after.'

'And did I look after my wife more than I ought?'

'I don't mean that; but if I were married, – which I never shall be, for I shall never attain to the respectability of a fixed income, – I fancy I shouldn't look after my wife at all. It seems to me that women hate to be told about their duties.'

'But if you saw your wife, quite innocently, falling into an improper intimacy, – taking up with people she ought not to know, – doing that in ignorance, which could not but compromise yourself; – wouldn't you speak a word then?'

'Oh! I might just say, in an off-hand way, that Jones was a rascal, or a liar, or a fool, or anything of that sort. But I would never caution her against Jones. By George, I believe a woman can stand anything better than that.'

'You have never tried it, my friend.'

'And I don't suppose I ever shall. As for me, I believe Aunt Stanbury was right when she said that I was a radical vagabond, I dare say I shall never try the thing myself, and therefore it's very easy to have a theory. But I must be off. Good night, old fellow. I'll do the best I can; and, at any rate, I'll let you know the truth.'

There had been a question during the day as to whether Stanbury should let his sister know by letter that he was expected; but it had been decided that he should appear at Nuncombe without any previous notification of his arrival. Trevelyan had thought that this was very necessary, and when Stanbury had urged that such a measure seemed to imply suspicion, he had declared that in no other way could the truth be obtained. He, Trevelyan, simply wanted to know the facts as they were occurring. It was a fact that Colonel Osborne was down in the neighbourhood of Nuncombe Putney. That, at least, had been ascertained. It might very possibly be the case that he would be refused admittance to the Clock House, – that all the ladies there would combine to keep him out. But, – so Trevelyan urged, – the truth on this point was desired. It was essentially necessary to his happiness that he should know what was being done.

'Your mother and sister,' said he, 'cannot be afraid of your coming suddenly among them.'

Stanbury, so urged, had found it necessary to yield, but yet he had felt that he himself was almost acting like a detective policeman, in purposely falling down upon them without a word of announcement. Had chance circumstances made it necessary that he should go in such a manner he would have thought nothing of it. It would simply have been a pleasant joke to him.

As he went down by the train on the following day, he almost felt ashamed of the part which he had been called upon to perform.

20

Showing how Colonel Osborne Went to Cockchaffington

Together with Miss Stanbury's first letter to her sister-in-law a letter had also been delivered to Mrs Trevelyan. Nora Rowley, as her sister had left the room with this in her hand, had expressed her opinion that it had come from Trevelyan; but it had in truth been written by Colonel Osborne. And when that second letter from Miss Stanbury had been received at the Clock House, – that in which she in plain terms begged pardon for the accusation conveyed in her first letter, – Colonel Osborne had started on his deceitful little journey to Cockchaffington, and Mr Bozzle, the ex-policeman who had him in hand, had already asked his way to Nuncombe Putney.

When Colonel Osborne learned that Louis Trevelyan had broken up his establishment in Curzon Street, and had sent his wife away into a barbarous retirement in Dartmoor, – for such was the nature of the information on the subject which was spread among Trevelyan's friends in London; – and when he was made aware also that all this was done on his account, – because he was so closely intimate with Trevelyan's wife, and because Trevelyan's wife was, and persisted in continuing to be, so closely intimate with him, – his vanity was gratified. Although it might be true, – and no doubt was true, – that he said much to his friends and to himself of the deep sorrow which he felt that such a trouble should befall his old friend and his old friend's daughter; nevertheless, as he curled his grey whiskers before the glass, and made the most of such remnant of hair as was left on the top of his head, as he looked to the padding of his coat, and completed a study of the wrinkles beneath his eyes, so that in conversation they might be as little apparent as possible, he felt more of pleasure than of pain in regard to the whole affair. It was very sad that it should be so, but it was human. Had it been in his power to set the whole matter right by a word, he would probably have spoken that word; but as this was not possible, as Trevelyan had in his opinion made a gross fool of himself, as Emily Trevelyan was very nice, and not the less nice in that she certainly was fond of himself, as great tyranny had been used towards her, and as he himself had still the plea of old family friendship to protect his conscience, – to protect his conscience unless he went so far as to make that plea an additional sting to his conscience, – he thought that, as a man, he must follow up the matter. Here was a young, and fashionable, and very pretty woman banished to the wilds of Dartmoor for his sake. And, as far as he could understand, she would not have been so banished had she consented to say that she would give up her acquaintance with him. In such circumstances as these was it possible that he should do nothing? Various ideas ran through his head. He began to think that if Trevelyan were out of the way, he might, – might perhaps be almost tempted to make this woman his wife. She was so nice that he almost thought that he might be rash enough for that, although he knew well the satisfaction of being a bachelor; – but as the thought suggested itself to him, he was well aware that he was thinking of a thing quite distant from him. The reader is not to suppose that Colonel Osborne meditated any making away with the husband. Our Colonel was certainly not the man for a murder. Nor did he even think of running away with his friend's daughter. Though he told himself that he could dispose of his wrinkles satisfactorily, still he knew himself and his powers sufficiently to be aware that he was no longer fit to be the hero of such a romance as that. He acknowledged to himself that there was much labour to be gone through in running away with another man's wife; and that the results, in respect to personal comfort, are not always happy. But what if Mrs Trevelyan were to divorce herself from her husband on the score of her husband's cruelty? Various horrors were related as to the man's treatment of his wife. By some it was said that she was in the prison on Dartmoor, – or, if not actually in the prison, an arrangement which the prison discipline might perhaps make difficult, – that she was in the custody of one of the prison warders who possessed a prim cottage and a grim wife, just outside the prison walls. Colonel Osborne did not himself believe even so much as this, but he did believe that Mrs Trevelyan had been banished to some inhospitable region, to some dreary comfortless abode, of which, as the wife of a man of fortune, she would have great ground to complain. So thinking, he did not probably declare to himself that a divorce should be obtained, and that, in such event, he would marry the lady, – but ideas came across his mind in that direction. Trevelyan was a cruel Bluebeard; Emily, – as he was studious to call Mrs Trevelyan, – was a dear injured saint. And as for himself, though he acknowledged to himself that the lumbago pinched him now and again, so that he could not rise from his chair with all the alacrity of youth, yet, when he walked along Pall Mall with his coat properly buttoned, he could not be observe that a great many young women looked at him with admiring eyes.

It was thus with no settled scheme that the Colonel went to work, and made inquiries, and ascertained Mrs Trevelyan's address in Devonshire. When he learned it, he thought that he had done much; though, in truth, there had been no secrecy in the matter. Scores of people knew Mrs Trevelyan's address besides the newsvendor who supplied her paper, from whose boy Colonel Osborne's servant obtained the information. But when the information had been obtained, it was expedient that it should be used; and therefore Colonel Osborne wrote the following letter:

Acrobats Club, July 31, 186 –

Dear Emily,

Twice the Colonel wrote Dearest Emily, and twice he tore the sheet on which the words were written. He longed to be ardent, but still it was so necessary to be prudent! He was not quite sure of the lady. Women sometimes tell their husbands, even when they have quarrelled with them. And, although ardent expressions in writing to pretty women are pleasant to male writers, it is not pleasant for a gentleman to be asked what on earth he means by that sort of thing at his time of life. The Colonel gave half an hour to the consideration, and then began the letter, Dear Emily. If prudence be the soul of valour, may it not be considered also the very mainspring, or, perhaps, the pivot of love?

Dear Emily,
I need hardly tell you with what dismay I have heard of all that has taken place in Curzon Street. I fear that you must have suffered much, and that you are suffering now. It is an inexpressible relief to me to hear that you have your child with you, and Nora. But, nevertheless, to have your home taken away from you, to be sent out of London, to be banished from all society! And for what? The manner in which the minds of some men work is quite incomprehensible.

As for myself, I feel that I have lost the company of a friend whom indeed I can very ill spare. I have a thousand things to say to you, and among them one or two which I feel that I must say, – that I ought to say. As it happens, an old schoolfellow of mine is Vicar of Cockchaffington, a village which I find by the map is very near to Nuncombe Putney. I saw him in town last spring, and he then asked me to pay him a visit. There is something in his church which people go to see, and though I don't understand churches much, I shall go and see it. I shall run down on Wednesday, and shall sleep at the inn at Lessboro'. I see that Lessboro' is a market town, and I suppose there is an inn. I shall go over to my friend on the Thursday, but shall return to Lessboro'. Though a man he ever so eager to see a church door-way, he need not sleep at the parsonage. On the following day, I will get over to Nuncombe Putney, and I hope that you will see me. Considering my long friendship with you, and my great attachment to your father and mother, I do not think that the strictest martinet would tell you that you need hesitate in the matter.

I have seen Mr Trevelyan twice at the club, but he has not spoken to me. Under such circumstances I could not of course speak to him. Indeed, I may say that my feelings towards him just at present are of such a nature as to preclude me from doing so with any appearance of cordiality.

> Dear Emily,
> Believe me now, as always, your affectionate friend,
> Frederic Osborne

When he read that letter over to himself a second time he felt quite sure that he had not committed himself. Even if his friend were to send the letter to her husband, it could not do him any harm. He was aware that he might have dilated more on the old friendship between himself and Sir Marmaduke, but he experienced a certain distaste to the mention of things appertaining to years long past. It did not quite suit him in his present frame of mind to speak of his regard in those quasi-paternal terms which he would have used had it satisfied him to represent himself simply as her father's friend. His language therefore had been a little doubtful, so that the lady might, if she were so minded, look upon him in that tender light in which her husband had certainly chosen to regard him.

When the letter was handed to Mrs Trevelyan, she at once took it with her up to her own room, so that she might be alone when she read it. The handwriting was quite familiar to her, and she did not choose that even her sister should see it. She had told herself twenty times over that, while living at Nuncombe Putney, she was not living under the guardianship of Mrs Stanbury. She would consent to live under the guardianship of no one, as her husband did not choose to remain with her and protect her. She had done no wrong, and she would submit to no other authority, than that of her legal lord and master. Nor, according to her views of her own position, was it in his power to depute that authority to others. He had caused the separation, and now she must be the sole judge of her own actions. In itself, a correspondence between her and her father's old friend was in no degree criminal or even faulty. There was no reason, moral, social, or religious, why an old man, over fifty, who had known her all her life, should not write to her. But yet she could not say aloud before Mrs Stanbury, and Priscilla, and her sister, that she had received a letter from Colonel Osborne. She felt that the colour had come to her cheek, and that she could not even walk out of the room as though the letter had been a matter of indifference to her.

And would it have been a matter of indifference had there been nobody there to see her? Mrs Trevelyan was certainly not in love with Colonel Osborne. She was not more so now than she had been when her father's friend, purposely dressed for the occasion, had kissed her in the vestry of the church in which she was married, and had given her a blessing, which was then intended to be semi-paternal, – as from an old man to a young woman. She was not in love with him, – never would be, never could be in love with him. Reader, you may believe in her so far as that. But where is the woman, who, when she is neglected, thrown over, and suspected by the man that she loves, will not feel the desire of some sympathy, some solicitude, some show of regard from another man? This woman's life, too, had not hitherto been of such a nature that the tranquillity of the Clock House at Nuncombe Putney afforded to her all that she desired. She had been there now a month, and was almost sick from the want of excitement. And she was full of wrath against her husband. Why had he sent her there to break her heart in a disgraceful retirement, when she had never wronged him? From morning to night she had no employment, no amusement, nothing to satisfy her cravings. Why was she to be doomed to such an existence? She had declared that as long as she could have her boy with her, she would be happy. She was allowed to have her boy; but she was anything but happy. When she received Colonel Osborne's letter, – while she held it in her hand still unopened, she never for a moment thought that that could make her happy. But there was in it something of excitement. And she painted the man to herself in brighter colours now than she had ever given to him in her former portraits. He cared for her. He was gracious to her. He appreciated her talents, her beauty, and her conduct. He knew that she deserved a treatment very different from that accorded to her by her husband. Why should she reject the sympathy of her father's oldest friend, because her husband was madly jealous about an old man? Her husband had chosen to send her away, and to leave her, so that she must act on her own judgment. Acting on her own judgment, she read Colonel Osborne's letter from first to last. She knew that he was wrong to speak of coming to Nuncombe Putney; but yet she thought that she would see him. She had a dim perception that she was standing on the edge of a precipice, on broken ground which might fall under her without a moment's warning, and yet she would not retreat from the danger. Though Colonel Osborne was wrong, very wrong in coming to see her, yet she liked him for coming. Though she would be half afraid to tell her news to Mrs Stanbury, and more than half afraid to tell Priscilla, yet she liked the excitement of the fear. Nora would scold her; but Nora's scolding she thought she could answer. And then it was not the fact that Colonel Osborne was coming down to Devonshire to see her. He was coming as far as Lessboro' to see his friend at Cockchaffington. And when at Lessboro', was it likely that he should leave the neighbourhood without seeing the daughter of his old ally? And why should he do so? Was he to be unnatural in his conduct, uncivil, and unfriendly, because Mr Trevelyan had been foolish, suspicious, and insane?

So arguing with herself, she answered Colonel Osborne's letter before she had spoken on the subject to any one in the house, – and this was her answer:

My dear Colonel Osborne,

I must leave it to your own judgment to decide whether you will come to Nuncombe Putney or not. There are reasons which would seem to make it expedient that you should stay away, — even though circumstances are bringing you into the immediate neighbourhood. But of these reasons I will leave you to be the judge. I will never let it be said that I myself have had cause to dread the visit of any old friend. Nevertheless, if you stay away, I shall understand why you do so.

Personally, I shall be glad to see you, — as I have always been. It seems odd to me that I cannot write in warmer terms to my father's and mother's oldest friend. Of course, you will understand that thought I shall readily see you if you call, I cannot ask you to stay. In the first place, I am not now living in my own house. I am staying with Mrs Stanbury, and the place is called the Clock House.

Yours very sincerely,
Emily Trevelyan

The Clock House, Nuncombe Putney, Monday.

Soon after she had written it, Nora came into her room, and at once asked concerning the letter which she had seen delivered to her sister that morning.

'It was from Colonel Osborne,' said Mrs Trevelyan.

'From Colonel Osborne! How very wrong!'

'I don't see that it is wrong at all. Becaue Louis is foolish and mad, that cannot make another man wrong for doing the most ordinary thing in the world.'

'I had hoped it had been from Louis,' said Nora.

'Oh dear, no. He is by no means so considerate. I do not suppose I shall hear from him, till he chooses to give some fresh order about myself or my child. He will hardly trouble himself to write to me, unless he takes up some new freak to show me that he is my master.'

'And what does Colonel Osborne say?'

'He is coming here.'

'Coming here?' almost shouted Nora.

'Yes; absolutely here. Does it sound to you as if Lucifer himself were about to show his face. The fact is, he happens to have a friend in the neighbourhood whom he has long promised to visit; and as he must be at Lessboro', he does not choose to go away without the compliment of a call. It will be as much to you as to me.'

'I don't want to see him in the least,' said Nora.

'There is his letter. As you seem to be so suspicious, you had better read it.'

Then Nora read it.

'And there is a copy of my answer,' said Mrs Trevelyan. 'I shall keep both, because I know so well what ill-natured things people will say.'

'Dear Emily, do not send it,' said Nora.

'Indeed I shall. I will not be frightened by bugbears. And I will not be driven to confess to any man on earth that I am afraid to see him. Why should I be afraid of Colonel Osborne? I will not submit to acknowledge that there can be any danger in Colonel Osborne. Were I to do so I should be repeating the insult against myself. If my husband wished to guide me in such matters, why did he not stay with me?'

'Then she went out into the village and posted the letter. Nora meanwhile was thinking whether she would call in the assistance of Priscilla Stanbury; but she did not like to take any such a step in opposition to her sister.

21

Showing how Colonel Osborne went to Nuncombe Putney

Colonel Osborne was expected at Nuncombe Putney on the Friday, and it was Thursday evening before either Mrs Stanbury or Priscilla was told of his coming. Emily had argued the matter with Nora, declaring that she would make the communication herself, and that she would make it when she pleased, and how she pleased. 'If Mrs Stanbury thinks,' said she, 'that I am going to be treated as a prisoner, or that I will not judge myself as to whom I may see, or whom I may not see, she is very much mistaken.' Nora felt that were she to give information to those ladies in opposition to her sister's wishes, she would express suspicion on her own part by doing so; and she was silent. On that same Thursday Priscilla had written her last defiant leter to her aunt, – that letter in which she had cautioned her aunt to make no further accusation without being sure of her facts. To Priscilla's imagination that coming of Lucifer in person, of which Mrs Trevelyan had spoken, would hardly have been worse than the coming of Colonel Osborne. When, therefore, Mrs Trevelyan declared the fact on the Thursday evening, vainly endeavouring to speak of the threatened visit in an ordinary voice, and as of an ordinary circumstance, it was as though a thunderbolt had fallen upon them.

'Colonel Osborne coming here!' said Priscilla mindful of the Stanbury correspondence, – mindful of the evil tongues of the world.

'And why not?' demanded Mrs Trevelyan, who had heard nothing of the Stanbury correspondence.

'Oh dear, oh dear!' ejaculated Mrs Stanbury, who, of course, was aware of all that had passed between the Clock House and the house in the Close, though the letters had been written by her daughter.

Nora was determined to stand up for her sister, whatever might be the circumstances of the case. 'I wish Colonel Osborne were not coming,' said she, 'because it makes a foolish fuss; but I cannot understand how anybody can suppose it to be wrong that Emily should see papa's very oldest friend in the world.'

'But why is he coming?' demanded Priscilla.

'Because he wants to see an acquaintance at Cockchaffington,' said Mrs Trevelyan; 'and there is a wonderful church-door there.'

'A church-fiddlestick!' said Priscilla.

The matter was debated throughout all the evening. At one time there was a great quarrel between the ladies, and then there was a reconciliation. The point on which Mrs Trevelyan stood with the greatest firmness was this, – that it did not become her, as a married woman whose conduct had always been good and who was more careful as to that than she was even of her name, to be ashamed to meet any man. 'Why should I not see Colonel Osborne, or Colonel anybody else who might call here with the same justification for calling which his old friendship gives him?' Priscilla endeavoured to explain to her that her husband's known wishes ought to hinder her from doing so. 'My husband should have remained with me, to express his wishes,' Mrs Trevelyan replied.

Neither could Mrs Stanbury nor could Priscilla bring herself to say that the man should not be admitted into the house. In the course of the debate, in the heat of her anger, Mrs Trevelyan delcared that were any such threat held out to her, she would leave the house and see Colonel Osborne in the street, or at the inn.

'No Emily; no,' said Nora.

'But I will. I will not submit to be treated as a guilty woman, or as a prisoner. They may say what they like, but I won't be shut up.'

'No one has tried to shut you up,' said Priscilla.

'You are afraid of that old woman at Exeter,' said Mrs Trevelyan; for by this time the facts of the Stanbury correspondence had all been elicited in general conversation; 'and yet you know how uncharitable and malicious she is.'

'We are not afraid of her,' said Priscilla. 'We are afraid of nothing but of doing wrong.'

'And will it be wrong to let an old gentleman come into the house,' said Nora, 'who is nearly sixty, and who has known us ever since we were born?'

'If he is nearly sixty, Priscilla,' said Mrs Stanbury, 'that does seem to make a difference.' Mrs Stanbury herself was only just sixty, and she felt herself to be quite an old woman.

'They may be devils at eighty,' said Priscilla.

'Colonel Osborne is not a devil at all,' said Nora.

'But mamma is so foolish,' said Priscilla. 'The man's age does not matter in the least.'

'I beg your pardon, my dear,' said Mrs Stanbury, very humbly.

At that time the quarrel was raging, but afterwards came the reconciliation. Had it not been for the Stanbury correspondence the fact of Colonel Osborne's threatened visit would have been admitted as a thing necessary – as a disagreeable necessity; but how was the visit to be admitted and passed over in the teeth of that correspondence? Priscilla felt very keenly the peculiar cruelty of her position. Of course, Aunt Stanbury would hear of the visit. Indeed, any secrecy in the matter was not compatible with Priscilla's ideas of honesty. Her aunt had apologised humbly for having said that Colonel Osborne had been at Nuncombe. That apology, doubtless, had been due. Colonel Osborne had not been at Nuncombe when the accusation had been made, and the accusation had been unjust and false. But his coming had been spoken of by Priscilla in her own letters as an occurrence which was quite out of the question. Her anger against her aunt had been for saying that the man had come, not for objecting to such a visit. And now the man was coming, and Aunt Stanbury would know all about it. How great, how terrible, how crushing would be Aunt Stanbury's triumph!

'I must write and tell her,' said Priscilla.

'I am sure I shall not object,' said Mrs Trevelyan.

'And Hugh must be told,' said Mrs Stanbury.

'You may tell all the world, if you like,' said Mrs Trevelyan.

In this way it was settled among them that Colonel Osborne was to be received. On the next morning, Friday morning, Colonel Osborne, doubtless having heard something of Mrs Crocket from his friend at Cockchaffington, was up early, and had himself driven over to Nuncombe Putney before breakfast. The ever-watchful Bozzle was, of course, at his heels, – or rather, not at his heels on the first two miles of the journey; for Bozzle, with painful zeal, had made himself aware of all the facts, and had started on the Nuncombe Putney road half an hour before the Colonel's fly was in motion. And when the fly passed him he was lying discreetly hidden behind an old oak. Thd driver, however, had caught a glimpse of him as he was topping a hill, and having seen him about on the previous day, and perceiving that he was dressed in a decent coat and trousers, and that, nevertheless, he was not a gentleman, began to suspect that he was – somebody. There was a great deal said afterwards about Bozzle in Mrs Clegg's yard at Lessboro'; but the Lessboro' mind was never able to satisfy itself altogether respecting Bozzle and his mission. As to Colonel Osborne and his mission, the Lessboro' mind did satisfy itself with much certainty. The horse was hardly taken from out of Colonel Osborne's fly in Mrs Crocket's yard when Bozzle stepped into the village by a path which he had already discovered, and soon busied himself among the tombs in the churchyard. Now, one corner of the churchyard was immediately opposite to the iron gate leading into the Clock House. 'Drat 'un,' said the wooden-legged postman, still sitting on his donkey, to Mrs Crocket's ostler, 'if there be'ant the chap as was here yesterday when I was a starting, and I zeed 'un in Lezbro' street thick very morning.' 'He be'ant arter no good, that 'un,' said the ostler. After that a close watch was kept upon the watcher.

In the meantime, Colonel Osborne had ordered his breakfast at the Stag and Antlers, and had asked questions as to the position of the Clock House. He was altogether ignorant of Mr Bozzle, although Mr Bozzle had been on his track now for two days and two nights. He had determined, as he came on to Nuncombe Putney, that he would not be shame-faced about his visit to Mrs Trevelyan. It is possible that he was not so keen in the matter as he had been when he planned his journey in London; and, it may be, that he really tried to make himself believe that he had come all the way to the confines of Dartmoor to see the porch of Cockchaffington Church. The session in London was over, and it was necessary for such a man as Colonel Osborne that he should do something with himself before he went down to the Scotch grouse. He had long desired to see something of the most picturesque county in England; and now, as he sat eating his breakfast in Mrs Crocket's parlour, he almost looked upon his dear Emily as a subsidiary attraction. 'Oh, that's the Clock House,' he said to Mrs Crocket. 'No, I have not the pleasure of knowing Mrs Stanbury; very respectable lady, so I have heard; widow of a clergyman; ah, yes; son up in London; I know him; – always writing books, is he? Very clever, I dare say. But there's a lady, – indeed, two ladies, –

whom I do know. Mrs Trevelyan is there, I think, – and Miss Rowley.'

'You be'ant Muster Trevelyan, be you?' said Mrs Crocket, looking at him very hard.

'No, I'm not Mr Trevelyan.'

'Nor yet "the Colonel" they doo be talking about?'

'Well, yes, I am a colonel. I don't know why anybody should talk about me. I'll just step out now, however, and see my friends.'

'It's madam's lover,' said Mrs Crocket to herself, 'as sure as eggs is eggs.' As she said so, Colonel Osborne boldly walked across the village and pulled the bell at the iron gate, while Bozzle, crouching among the tombs, saw the handle in his hand. 'There he is,' said Priscilla. Everybody in the Clock House had known that the fly, which they had seen, had brought 'the Colonel' into Nuncombe Putney. Everybody had known that he had breakfasted at the Stag and Antlers. And everybody now knew that he was at the gate ringing the bell. 'Into the drawing-room,' said Mrs Stanbury, with a fearful, tremulous whisper, to the girl who went across the little garden in front to open the iron gate. The girl felt as though Apollyon* were there, and as though she were called upon to admit Apollyon. Mrs Stanbury having uttered her whisper, hurried away up-stairs. Priscilla held her ground in the parlour, determined to be near the scene of action if there might be need. And it must be acknowledged that she peeped from behind the curtain, anxious to catch a glimpse of the terrible man, whose coming to Nuncombe Putney she regarded as so severe a misfortune.

The plan of the campaign had all been arranged. Mrs Trevelyan and Nora together received Colonel Osborne in the drawing-room. It was understood that Nora was to remain there during the whole visit. 'It is horrible to think that such a precaution should be necessary,' Mrs Trevelyan had said, 'but perhaps it may be best. There is no knowing what the malice of people may not invent.'

'My dear girls,' said the Colonel, 'I am delighted to see you,' and he gave a hand to each.

'We are not very cheerful here,' said Mrs Trevelyan, 'as you may imagine.'

'But the scenery is beautiful,' said Nora, 'and the people we are living with are kind and nice.'

'I am very glad of that,' said the Colonel. Then there was a pause, and it seemed, for a moment or two, that none of them knew how to begin a general conversation. Colonel Osborne was quite sure, by this time, that he had come down to Devonshire with the express object of seeing the door of the church at Cockchaffington, and

Mrs Trevelyan was beginning to think that he certainly had not come to see her. 'Have you heard from your father since you have been here?' asked the Colonel.

Then there was an explanation about Sir Marmaduke and Lady Rowley. Mr Trevelyan's name was not mentioned; but Mrs Trevelyan stated that she had explained to her mother all the painful circumstances of her present life. Sir Marmaduke, as Colonel Osborne was aware, was expected to be in England in the spring, and Lady Rowley would, of course, come with him. Nora thought that they might probably now come before that time; but Mrs Trevelyan declared that it was out of the question that they should do so. She was sure that her father could not leave the islands except when he did so in obedience to official orders. The expense of doing so would be ruinous to him. And what good would he do? In this way there was a great deal of family conversation, in which Colonel Osborne was able to take a part; but not a word was said about Mr Trevelyan.

Nor did 'the Colonel' find an opportunity of expressing a spark of that sentiment, for the purpose of expressing which he had made this journey to Devonshire. It is not pleasant to make love in the presence of a third person, even when that love is all fair and above board; but it is quite impracticable to do so to a married lady, when that married lady's sister is present. No more futile visit than this of Colonel Osborne's to the Clock House was ever made. And yet, though not a word was spoken to which Mr Trevelyan himself could have taken the slightest exception, the visit, futile as it was, could not but do an enormous deal of harm. Mrs Crocket had already guessed that the fine gentleman down from London was the lover of the married lady at the Clock House, who was separated from her husband. The wooden-legged postman and the ostler were not long in connecting the man among the tombstones with the visitor to the house. Trevelyan, as we are aware, already knew that Colonel Osborne was in the neighbourhood. And poor Priscilla Stanbury was now exposed to the terrible necessity of owning the truth to her aunt. 'The Colonel,' when he had sat an hour with his young friends, took his leave; and, as he walked back to Mrs Crocket's, and ordered that his fly might be got ready for him, his mind was heavy with the disagreeable feeling that he had made an ass of himself. The whole affair had been a failure; and though he might be able to pass off the porch at Cockchaffington among his friends, he could not but be aware himself that he had spent his time, his trouble, and his money for nothing. He became aware, as he returned to Lessboro', that had he intended to make any pleasant use whatever of his position in reference to Mrs Trevelyan, the tone of his letter and his whole mode of proceeding should have been less patriarchal. And he should have contrived a meeting without the presence of Nora Rowley.

As soon as he had left them, Mrs Trevelyan went to her own room, and Nora at once rejoined Priscilla.

'Is he gone?' asked Priscilla.

'Oh, yes; – he has gone.'

'What would I have given that he had never come!'

'And yet,' said Nora, 'what harm has he done? I wish he had not come, because, of course, people will talk! But nothing was more natural than that he should come over to see us when he was so near us.'

'Nora!'

'What do you mean?'

'You don't believe all that? In the neighbourhood! I believe he came on purpose to see your sister, and I think that it was a dastardly and most ungentleman-like thing to do.'

'I am quite sure you are wrong, then, – altogether wrong,' said Nora.

'Very well. We must have our own opinions. I am glad you can be so charitable. But he should not have come here, – to this house, even though imperative business had brought him into the very village. But men in their vanity never think of the injury they may do to a woman's name. Now I must go and write to my aunt. I am not going to have it said hereafter that I deceived her. And then I shall write to Hugh. Oh dear; oh dear!'

'I am afraid we are a great trouble to you.'

'I will not deceive you, because I like you. This is a great trouble to me. I have meant to be so prudent, and with all my prudence I have not been able to keep clear of rocks. And I have been so indignant with Aunt Stanbury! Now I must go and eat humble-pie.'

Then she eat humble pie, – after the following fashion:

Dear Aunt Stanbury,

After what has passed between us, I think it right to tell you that Colonel Osborne has been at Nuncombe Putney, and that he called at the Clock House this morning. We did not see him. But Mrs Trevelyan and Miss Rowley, together, did see him. He remained here perhaps an hour.

I should not have thought it necessary to mention this to you, the matter being one in which you are not concerned, were it not for our former correspondence. When I last wrote, I had no idea that he was coming, – nor had mamma. And when you first wrote, he was not even expected by Mrs Trevelyan. The man you wrote about, was another gentleman; – as I told you before. All this is most disagreeable, and tiresome; – and would be quite nonsensical, but that circumstances seem to make it necessary.

As for Colonel Osborne, I wish he had not been here; but his coming would do no harm – only that it will be talked about.

I think you will understand how it is that I feel myself constrained to write to you. I do hope that you will spare mamma, who is disturbed and harassed when she gets angry letters. If you have anything to say to myself, I don't mind it.

Yours truly,
Priscilla Stanbury

The Clock House, Friday, August 5

She wrote also to her brother Hugh; but Hugh himself reached Nuncombe Putney before the letter reached him.

Mr Bozzle watched the Colonel out of the house, and watched him out of the village. When the Colonel was fairly started, Mr Bozzle walked back to Lessboro'.

22

Showing how Miss Stanbury Behaved to her Two Nieces

The triumph of Miss Stanbury when she received her niece's letter was certainly very great, – so great that in its first flush she could not restrain herself from exhibiting it to Dorothy. 'Well, – well, – what do you think, Dolly?'

'About what, aunt? I don't know who the letter is from.'

'Nobody writes to me now so constant as your sister Priscilla. The letter is from Priscilla. Colonel Osborne has been at the Clock House, after all. I knew that he would be there. I knew it! I knew it!'

Dorothy, when she heard this, was dumbfounded. She had rested her defence of her mother and sister on the impossibility of any such visit being admitted. According to her lights the coming of Colonel Osborne, after all that had been said, would be like the coming of Lucifer himself. The Colonel was, to her imagination, a horrible roaring lion. She had no idea that the erotic manœuvres of such a beast* might be milder and more innocent than the cooing of any turtle-dove. She would have asked whether the roaring lion had gone away again, and, if so, whether he had taken his prey with him, were it not that she was too much frightened at the moment to ask any question. That her mother and sister should have been wilfully concerned in such iniquity was quite incredible to her, but yet she did not know how to defend them. 'But are you quite sure of it, Aunt Stanbury ? May there not be another mistake ?'

'No mistake this time, I think, my dear. Any way, Priscilla says that he is there.' Now in this there was a mistake. Priscilla had said nothing of the kind.

'You don't mean that he is staying at the Clock House, Aunt Stanbury ?'

'I don't know where he is now. I'm not his keeper. And, I'm glad to say, I'm not the lady's keeper either. Ah, me ! It's a bad business. You can't touch pitch and not be defiled, my dear. If your mother wanted the Clock House, I would sooner have taken it for her my-self than that all this should have happened, – for the family's sake.'

But Miss Stanbury, when she was alone, and when she had read her niece's three letters again and again, began to understand something of Priscilla's honesty, and began also to perceive that there might have been a great difficulty respecting the Colonel, for which neither her niece nor her sister-in-law could fairly be held to be responsible. It was perhaps the plainest characteristic of all the Stanburys that they were never wilfully dishonest. Ignorant, preju-diced, and passionate they might be. In her anger Miss Stanbury, of Exeter, could be almost malicious; and her niece at Nuncombe Putney was very like her aunt. Each could say most cruel things, most unjust things, when actuated by a mistaken consciousness of perfect right on her own side. But neither of them could lie, – even by silence. Let an error be brought home to either of them, – so as to be acknowledged at home, – and the error would be assuredly confessed aloud. And, indeed, with differences in the shades, Hugh and Dorothy were of the same nature. They were possessed of sweeter tempers than their aunt and sister, but they were filled with the same eager readiness to believe themselves to be right, – and to own themselves to others to be wrong, when they had been constrained to make such confession to themselves. The chances of life, and something probably of inner nature, had made Dorothy mild and obedient; whereas, in regard to Hugh, the circumstances of his life and disposition had made him obstinate and self-reliant. But in all was to be found the same belief in self, – which amounted almost to conceit, – the same warmth of affection, and the same love of justice.

When Miss Stanbury had again perused the correspondence, and

had come to see, dimly, how things had gone at Nuncombe Putney,
– when the conviction came upon her mind that Priscilla had
entertained a horror as to the coming of this Colonel equal to that
which she herself had felt, – when her imagination painted to her
all that her niece had suffered, her heart was softened somewhat.
She had declared to Dorothy that pitch, if touched, would certainly
defile; and she had, at first, intended to send the same opinion,
couched in very forcible words, to her correspondents at the Clock
House. They should not continue to go astray for want of being
told that they were going astray. It must be acknowledged, too, that
there was a certain amount of ignoble wrath in the bosom of Miss
Stanbury because her sister-in-law had taken the Clock House. She
had never been told, and had not even condescended to ask
Dorothy, whether the house was taken and paid for by her nephew
on behalf of his mother, or whether it was paid for by Mr Trevelyan
on behalf of his wife. In the latter case, Mrs Stanbury would, she
thought, be little more than an upper servant, or keeper, – as she
expressed it to herself. Such an arrangement appeared to her to be
quite disgraceful in a Stanbury; but yet she believed that such must
be the existing arrangement, as she could not bring herself to
conceive that Hugh Stanbury could keep such an establishment over
his mother's head out of money earned by writing for a penny
newspaper. There would be a triumph of democracy in this which
would vanquish her altogether. She had, therefore, been anxious
enough to trample on Priscilla and upon all the affairs of the Clock
House; but yet she had been unable to ignore the nobility of
Priscilla's truth, and having acknowledged it to herself she found
herself compelled to acknowledge it aloud. She sat down to think
in silence, and it was not till she had fortified herself by her first
draught of beer, and till she had finished her first portion of bread
and cheese, that she spoke. 'I have written to your sister herself, this
time,' she said. 'I don't know that I ever wrote a line to her before
in my life.'

'Poor Priscilla!' Dorothy did not mean to be severe on her aunt,
either in regard to the letters which had not been written, or to the
one letter which now had been written. But Dorothy pitied her
sister, whom she felt to be in trouble.

'Well; I don't know about her being so poor. Priscilla, I'll be
bound, thinks as well of herself as any of us do.'

'She'd cut her fingers off before she'd mean to do wrong,' said
Dorothy.

'But what does that come to? What's the good of that? It isn't
meaning to do right that will save us. For aught I know, the

Radicals may mean to do right. Mr Beales means to do right — perhaps.'*

'But, aunt, — if everybody did the best they could?'

'Tush, my dear! you are getting beyond your depth. There are such things still, thank God! as spiritual pastors and masters. Entrust yourself to them. Do what they think right.' Now if aught were known in Exeter of Miss Stanbury, this was known, — that if any clergyman volunteered to give to her, unasked and uninvited, counsel, either ghostly or bodily, that clergyman would be sent from her presence with a wigging which he would not soon forget. The thing had been tried more than once, and the wigging had been complete. There was no more attentive listener in church than Miss Stanbury; and she would, now and again, appeal to a clergyman on some knotty point. But for the ordinary authority of spiritual pastors and masters she showed more of abstract reverence than of practical obedience.

'I'm sure Priscilla does the best she can,' said Dorothy, going back to the old subject.

'Ah, — well, — yes. What I want to say about Priscilla is this. It is a thousand pities she is so obstinate, so pig-headed, so certain that she can manage everything for herself better than anybody else can for her.' Miss Stanbury was striving to say something good of her niece, but found the task to be difficult and distasteful to her.

'She has managed for mamma ever so many years; and since she took it we have hardly ever been in debt,' said Dorothy.

'She'll do all that, I don't doubt. I don't suppose she cares much for ribbons and false hair for herself.'

'Who? Priscilla! The idea of Priscilla with false hair!'

'I dare say not; — I dare say not. I do not think she'd spend her mother's money on things of that kind.'

'Aunt Stanbury, you don't know her.'

'Ah; very well. Perhaps I don't. But, come, my dear, you are very hard upon me, and very anxious to take your sister's part. And what is it all about? I've just written to her as civil a letter as one women ever wrote to another. And if I had chosen, I could have, — could have, — h — m — m.' Miss Stanbury, as she hesitated for words in which to complete her sentence, revelled in the strength of the vituperation which she could have poured upon her niece's head, had she chosen to write her last letter about Colonel Osborne in her severe strain.

'If you have written kindly to her, I am so much obliged to you,' said Dorothy.

'The truth is, Priscilla has meant to be right. Meaning won't go for much when the account is taken, unless the meaning comes from a proper source. But the poor girl has done as well as she has known how. I believe it is Hugh's fault more than anybody else's.' This accusation was not pleasant to Dorothy, but she was too intent just now on Priscilla's case to defend her brother. 'That man never ought to have been there; and that woman never ought to have been there. There cannot be a doubt about that. If Priscilla were sitting there opposite to me, she would own as much. I am sure she would.' Miss Stanbury was quite right if she meant to assert that Priscilla had owned as much to herself. 'And because I think so, I am willing to forgive her part in the matter. To me, personally, she has always been rude, – most uncourteous, – and, – and unlike a younger woman to an older one, and an aunt, and all that. I suppose it is because she hates me.'

'Oh, no, Aunt Stanbury!'

'My dear, I suppose it is. Why else should she treat me in such a way? But I do believe of her that she would rather eat an honest, dry crust, than dishonest cake and ale.'

'She would rather starve than pick up a crumb that was dishonest,' said Dorothy, fairly bursting out into tears.

'I believe it. I do belive it. There; what more can I say? Clock House, indeed! What matter what house you live in, so that you can pay the rent of it honestly?'

'But the rent is paid – honestly,' said Dorothy, amidst her sobs.

'It's paid, I don't doubt. I dare say the woman's husband and your brother see to that among them. Oh, that my boy, Hugh, as he used to be, should have brought us all to this! But there's no knowing what they won't do among them. Reform indeed! Murder, sacrilege, adultery, treason, atheism; – that's what Reform means; besides every kind of nastiness under the sun.' In which latter category Miss Stanbury intended especially to include bad printer's ink, and paper made of straw.

The reader may as well see the letter which was as civil a letter as ever one woman wrote to another, so that the collection of the Stanbury correspondence may be made perfect.

The Close, August 6, 186 –

My Dear Niece,

Your letter has not astonished me nearly as much as you expected it would. I am an older woman than you, and, though you will not believe it, I have seen more of the world. I knew that the gentleman would come after the lady. Such gentlemen always do go after their ladies. As for yourself, I can see all that you have done, and pretty nearly hear all that you have said, as plain as a pike-staff. I do you the credit of believing that the plan is none of your making. I know who made the plan, and a very bad plan it is.

As to my former letters and the other man, I understand all about it. You were very angry that I should accuse you of having this man at the house; and you were right to be angry. I respect you for having been angry. But what does all that say as to his coming, – now that he has come?

'If you will consent to take an old woman's advice, get rid of the whole boiling of them. I say it in firm love and friendship, for I am, –

> Your affectionate aunt,
> Jemima Stanbury.

The special vaunted courtesy of this letter consisted, no doubt, in the expression of respect which it contained, and in that declaration of affection with which it terminated. The epithet was one which Miss Stanbury would by no means use promiscuously in writing to her nearest relatives. She had not intended to use it when she commenced her letter to Priscilla. But the respect of which she had spoken had glowed, and had warmed itself into something of temporary love; and feeling at the moment that she was an affectionate aunt, Miss Stanbury had so put herself down in her letter. Having done such a deed she felt that Dorothy, though Dorothy knew nothing about it, ought in her gratitude to listen patiently to anything that she might now choose to say against Priscilla.

But Dorothy was in truth very miserable, and in her misery wrote a long letter than afternoon to her mother, – which, however, it will not be necessary to place entire among the Stanbury records, – begging that she might be informed as to the true circumstances of the case. She did not say a word of censure in regard either to her mother or sister; but she expressed an opinion in the mildest words which she could use, that if anything had happened which had compromised their names since their residence at the Clock House, she, Dorothy, had better go home and join them. The meaning of which was that it would not become her to remain in the house in the Close, if the house in the Close would be disgraced by her presence. Poor Dorothy had taught herself to think that the iniquity of roaring lions spread itself very widely.

In the afternoon she made some such proposition to her aunt in ambiguous terms. 'Go home!' said Miss Stanbury. 'Now?'

'If you think it best, Aunt Stanbury.'

'And put yourself in the middle of all this iniquity and abomination! I don't suppose you want to know the woman?'

'No, indeed!'

'Or the man?'

'Oh, Aunt Stanbury!'

'It's my belief that no decent gentleman in Exeter would look at you again if you were to go and live among them at Nuncombe Putney while all this is going on. No, no. Let one of you be saved out of it, at least.'

Aunt Stanbury had more than once made use of expressions which brought the faintest touch of gentle pink up to her niece's cheeks. We must do Dorothy the justice of saying that she had never dreamed of being looked at by any gentleman, whether decent or indecent. Her life at Nuncombe Putney had been of such a nature, that though she knew that other girls were looked at, and even made love to, and that they got married and had children, no dim vision of such a career for herself had ever presented itself to her eyes. She had known very well that her mother and sister and herself were people apart, – ladies, and yet so extremely poor that they could only maintain their rank by the most rigid seclusion. To live, and work unseen, was what the world had ordained for her. Then her call to Exeter had come upon her, and she had conceived that she was henceforth to be the humble companion of a very imperious old aunt. Her aunt, indeed, was imperious, but did not seem to require humility in her companion. All the good things that were eaten and drunk were divided between them with the strictest impartiality. Dorothy's cushion and hassock in the church and in the cathedral were the same as her aunt's. Her bedroom was made very comfortable for her. Her aunt never gave her any orders before company, and always spoke of her before the servants as one whom they were to obey and respect. Gradually Dorothy came to understand the meaning of this; – but her aunt would sometimes say things about young men which she did not quite understand. Could it be that her aunt supposed that any young man would come and wish to marry her, – her, Dorothy Stanbury? She herself had not quite so strong an aversion to men in general as that which Priscilla felt, but she had not as yet found that any of those whom she had seen at Exeter were peculiarly agreeable to her. Before she went to bed that night her aunt said a word to her which startled her more than she had ever been startled before. On that evening Miss Stanbury had a few friends to drink tea with her. There were Mr and Mrs Crumbie, and Mrs MacHugh of course, and the Cheritons from Alphington, and the Miss Apjohns from Helion Villa, and old Mr Powel all the way from Haldon, and two of the Wrights from their house in the Northernhay, and Mr Gibson; – but the Miss

Frenches from Heavitree were not there. 'Why don't you have the Miss Frenches, aunt?' Dorothy had asked.

'Bother the Miss Frenches! I'm not bound to have them every time. There's Camilla has been and got herself a band-box on the back of her head a great deal bigger than the place inside where her brains ought to be.' But the band-box at the back of Camilla French's head was not the sole cause of the omission of the two sisters from the list of Miss Stanbury's visitors on this occasion.

The party went off very much as usual. There were two whist tables, for Miss Stanbury could not bear to cut out. At other houses than her own, when there was cutting out, it was quite understood that Miss Stanbury was to be allowed to keep her place. 'I'll go away, and sit out there by myself, if you like,' she would say. But she was never thus banished; and at her own house she usually contrived that there should be no system of banishment. She would play dummy whist, preferring it to the four-handed game; and, when hard driven, and with a meet opponent, would not even despise double-dummy. It was told of her and of Mrs MacHugh that they had played double-dummy for a whole evening together; and they who were given to calumny had declared that the candles on that evening had been lighted very early. On the present occasion a great many sixpenny points were scored, and much tea and cake were consumed. Mr Gibson never played whist, – nor did Dorothy. That young John Wright and Mary Cheriton should do nothing but talk to each other was a thing of course, as they were to be married in a month or two. There was Ida Cheriton, who could not very well be left at home; and Mr Gibson made himself pleasant to Dorothy and Ida Cheriton, instead of making himself pleasant to the two Miss Frenches. Gentlemen in provincial towns quite understood that, from the nature of social circumstances in the provinces, they should always be ready to be pleasant at least to a pair at a time. At a few minutes before twelve they were all gone, and then came the shock.

'Dolly, my dear, what do you think of Mr Gibson?'

'Think of him, Aunt Stanbury?'

'Yes; think of him; – think of him. I suppose you know how to think?'

'He seems to me always to preach very drawling sermons.'

'Oh, bother his sermons! I don't care anything about his sermons now. He is a very good clergyman, and the Dean thinks very much about him.'

'I am glad of that, Aunt Stanbury.' Then came the shock. 'Don't you think it would be a very good thing if you were to become Mrs Gibson?'

It may be presumed that Miss Stanbury had assured herself that she could not make progress with Dorothy by 'beating about the bush.' There was an inaptitude in her niece to comprehend the advantages of the situations, which made some direct explanation absolutely necessary. Dorothy stood half smiling, half crying, when she heard the proposition, her cheeks suffused with that pink colour, and with her hands extended with surprise.

'I've been thinking about it ever since you've been here,' said Miss Stanbury.

'I think he likes Miss French,' said Dorothy, in a whisper.

'Which of them? I don't believe he likes them at all. Maybe if they go on long enough they may be able to toss up for him. But I don't think it of him. Of course they're after him, but he'll be too wise for them. And he's more of a fool than I take him to be if he don't prefer you to them.' Dorothy remained quite silent. To such an address as this it was impossible that she should reply a word. It was incredible to her that any man should prefer herself to either of the young women in question; but she was too much confounded for the expression even of her humility. 'At any rate you're wholesome, and pleasant and modest,' said Miss Stanbury.

Dorothy did not quite like being told that she was wholesome; but, nevertheless, she was thankful to her aunt.

'I'll tell you what it is,' continued Miss Stanbury; 'I hate all mysteries, especially with those I love. I've saved two thousand pounds, which I've put you down for in my will. Now, if you and he can make it up together, I'll give you the money at once. There's no knowing how often an old woman may alter her will; but when you've got a thing, you've got it. Mr Gibson would know the meaning of a bird in the hand as well as anybody. Now those girls at Heavitree will never have above a few hundreds each, and not that while their mother lives.' Dorothy made one little attempt at squeezing her aunt's hand, wishing to thank her aunt for this affectionate generosity; but she had hardly accomplished the squeeze, when she desisted, feeling strangely averse to any acknowledgment of such a boon as that which had been offered to her. 'And now, good night, my dear. If I did not think you a very sensible young woman, I should not trust you by saying all this.' Then they parted, and Dorothy soon found herself alone in her bedroom.

To have a husband of her own, a perfect gentleman too, and a clergyman; – and to go to him with a fortune! She believed that two thousand pounds represented nearly a hundred a year. It was a large fortune in those parts, – according to her understanding of ladies' fortunes. And that she, the humblest of the humble, should be selected for so honourable a position! She had never quite known, quite understood as yet, whether she had made good her footing in her aunt's house in a manner pleasant to her aunt. More than once or twice she had spoken even of going back to her mother, and things had been said which had almost made her think that her aunt had been angry with her. But now, after a month or two of joint residence, her aunt was offering to her – two thousand pounds and a husband!

But was it within her aunt's power to offer to her the husband? Mr Gibson had always been very civil to her. She had spoken more to Mr Gibson than to any other man in Exeter. But it had never occurred to her for a moment that Mr Gibson had any special liking for her. Was it probable that he would ever entertain any feeling of that kind for her? It certainly had occurred to her before now that Mr Gibson was sometimes bored by the Miss Frenches; – but then gentlemen do get bored by ladies.

And at last she asked herself another question, – had she any special liking for Mr Gibson? As far as she understood such matters everything was blank there. Thinking of that other question, she went to sleep.

23
Colonel Osborne and Mr Bozzle
Return to London

Hugh Stanbury went down on the Saturday, by the early express to Exeter, on his road to Lessboro'. He took his ticket through to Lessboro', not purposing to stay at Exeter; but, from the exigencies of the various trains, it was necessary that he should remain for half an hour at the Exeter Station. This took place on the Saturday, and Colonel Osborne's visit to the Clock House had been made on the Friday. Colonel Osborne had returned to Lessboro', had slept again at Mrs Clegg's house, and returned to London on the Saturday. It so happened that he also was obliged to spend half an hour at the Exeter Station, and that his half-hour, and Hugh Stanbury's half-hour, were one and the same. They met, therefore, as a matter of course, upon the platform. Stanbury was the first to see the other, and he found that he must determine on the spur of the moment what he would say, and what he would do. He had received no direct commission from Trevelyan as to his meeting with Colonel Osborne. Trevelyan had declared that, as to the matter of quarrelling, he meant to retain the privilege of doing that for himself; but Stanbury had quite understood that this was only the vague expression of an angry man. The Colonel had taken a glass of sherry, and had lighted a cigar, and was quite comfortable, – having thrown aside, for a time, that consciousness of the futility of his journey which had perplexed him, – when Stanbury accosted him.

'What! Mr Stanbury, – how do you do? Fine day, isn't it? Are you going up or down?'

'I'm going to see my own people at Nuncombe Putney, a village beyond Lessboro',' said Hugh.

'Ah; – indeed.' Colonel Osborne of course perceived at once that as this man was going to the house at which he had just been visiting, it would be better that he should himself explain what he had done. It he were to allow this mention of Nuncombe Putney to pass without saying that he himself had been there, he would be convicted of at least some purpose of secrecy in what he had been doing. 'Very strange,' said he; 'I was at Nuncombe Putney myself yesterday.'

'I know you were,' said Stanbury.

'And how did you know it?' There had been a tone of anger in Stanbury's voice which Colonel Osborne had at once appreciated, and which made him assure a similar tone. As they spoke there was a man standing in a corner close by the bookstall, with his eye upon them, and that man was Bozzle, the ex-policeman, – who was doing his duty with sedulous activity by seeing 'the Colonel' back to London. Now Bozzle did not know Hugh Stanbury, and was angry with himself that he should be so ignorant. It is the pride of a detective ex-policeman to know everybody that comes in his way.

'Well, I had been so informed. My friend Trevelyan knew that you were there, – or that you were going there.'

'I don't care who knew that I was going there,' said the Colonel.

'I won't pretend to understand how that may be, Colonel Osborne; but I think you must be aware, after what took place in Curzon Street, that it would have been better that you should not have attempted to see Mrs Trevelyan. Whether you have seen her I do not know.'

'What business is it of yours, Mr Stanbury, whether I have seen that lady or not?'

'Unhappily for me, her husband has made it my business.'

'Very unhappily for you, I should say.'

'And the lady is staying at my mother's house.'

'I presume the lady is not a prisoner in your mother's house, and that your mother's hospitality is not so restricted but that her guest may see an old friend under her roof.' This, Colonel Osborne said with an assumed look of almost righteous indignation, which was not at all lost upon Bozzle. They had returned back towards the bookstall, and Bozzle, with his eyes fixed on a copy of the 'D. R.' which he had just bought, was straining his ears to the utmost to catch what was being said.

'You best know whether you have seen her or not.'

'I have seen her.'

'Then I shall take leave to tell you, Colonel Osborne, that you have acted in a most unfriendly way, and have done that which must tend to keep an affectionate husband apart from his wife.'

'Sir, I don't at all understand this kind of thing addressed to me. The father of the lady you are speaking of has been my most intimate friend for thirty years.' After all, the Colonel was a mean man when he could take pride in his youth, and defend himself on the score of his age, in one and the same proceeding.

'I have nothing further to say,' replied Stanbury.

'You have said too much already, Mr Stanbury.'

'I think not, Colonel Osborne. You have, I fear, done an incredible deal of mischief by going to Nuncombe Putney; and, after all that you have heard on the subject, you must have known that it would be mischievous. I cannot understand how you can force yourself about a man's wife against the man's expressed wish.'

'Sir, I didn't force myself upon anybody. Sir, I went down to see an old friend, – and a remarkable piece of antiquity. And, when another old friend was in the neighbourhood, close by, – one of the oldest friends I have in the world, – wasn't I to go and see her? God bless my soul! What business is it of yours? I never heard such impudence in my life!' Let the charitable reader suppose that Colonel Osborne did not know that he was lying, – that he really thought, when he spoke, that he had gone down to Lessboro' to see the remarkable piece of antiquity.

'Good morning,' said Hugh Stanbury, turning on his heels and walking away. Colonel Osborne shook himself, inflated his cheeks, and blew forth the breath out of his mouth, put his thumbs up to the armholes of his waistcoat, and walked about the platform as though he thought it to be incumbent on him to show that he was somebody, – somebody that ought not to be insulted, – somebody, perhaps, whom a very pretty woman might prefer to her own husband, in spite of a small difference in age. He was angry, but not quite so much angry as proud. And he was safe, too. He thought that he was safe. When he should come to account for himself and his actions to his old friend, Sir Marmaduke, he felt that he would be able to show that he had been, in all respects, true to friendship. Sir Marmaduke had unfortunately given his daughter to a jealous, disagreeable fellow, and the fault all lay in that. As for Hugh Stanbury, – he would simply despise Hugh Stanbury, and have done with it.

Mr Bozzle, though he had worked hard in the cause, had heard but a word or two. Eaves-droppers seldom do hear more than that. A porter had already told him who was Hugh Stanbury, – that he was Mr Hugh Stanbury, and that his aunt lived at Exeter. And Bozzle, knowing that the lady about whom he was concerned was living with a Mrs Stanbury at the house he had been watching, put two and two together with his natural cleverness. 'God bless my soul! what business is it of yours?' Those words were nearly all that Bozzle had been able to hear; but even those sufficiently indicated a quarrel. 'The lady' was living with Mrs Stanbury, having been so placed by her husband; and young Stanbury was taking the lady's part! Bozzle began to fear that the husband had not confided in him with that perfect faith which he felt to be essentially necessary to the adequate performance of the duties of his great profession. A sudden thought, however, struck him. Something might be done on the journey up to London. He at once made his way back to the ticket-window and exhanged his ticket, – second-class for first-class. It was a noble deed, the expense falling all upon his own pocket; for, in the natural course of things, he would have charged his employers with the full first-class fare. He had seen Colonel Osborne seat himself in a carriage, and within two minutes he was occupying the opposite place. The Colonel was aware that he had noticed the man's face lately, but did not know where.

'Very fine summer weather, sir,' said Bozzle.

'Very fine,' said the Colonel, burying himself behind a newspaper.

'They is getting up their wheat nicely in these parts, sir.'

The answer to this was no more than a grunt. But Bozzle was not offended. Not to be offended is the special duty of all policemen, in and out of office; and the journey from Exeter to London was long, and was all before him.

'A very nice little secluded village is Nuncombe Putney,' said Bozzle, as the train was leaving the Salisbury Station.

At Salisbury two ladies had left the carriage, no one else had got in, and Bozzle was alone with the Colonel.

'I dare say,' said the Colonel, who by this time had relinquished his shield, and who had begun to compose himself for sleep, or to pretend to compose himself, as soon as he heard Bozzle's voice. He had been looking at Bozzle, and though he had not discovered the man's trade, had told himself that his companion was a thing of dangers, – a thing to be avoided, by one engaged, as had been he himself, on a special and secret mission.

'Saw you there, – calling at the Clock House,' said Bozzle.

'Very likely,' said the Colonel, throwing his head well back into the corner, shutting his eyes, and uttering a slight preliminary snore.

'Very nice family of ladies at the Clock House,' said Bozzle. The Colonel answered him by a more developed snore. 'Particularly Mrs T – ' said Bozzle.

The Colonel could not stand this. He was so closely implicated with Mrs Trevelyan at the present moment that he could not omit to notice an address so made to him. 'What the devil is that to you, sir ?' said he, jumping up and confronting Bozzle in his wrath.

But policemen have always this advantage in their difficulties, that they know to a fraction what the wrath of men is worth, and what it can do. Sometimes it can dismiss a policeman, and sometimes break his head. Sometimes it can give him a long and troublesome job, and sometimes it may be wrath to the death. But in nineteen out of twenty cases it is not a fearful thing, and the policeman knows well when he need not fear it. On the present occasion Bozzle was not at all afraid of Colonel Osborne's wrath.

'Well, sir, not much, indeed, if you come to that. Only you was there, sir.'

'Of course I was there,' said the Colonel.

'And a very nice young gentleman is Mr Stanbury,' said Bozzle.

To this Colonel Osborne made no reply, but again had resort to his newspaper in the most formal manner.

'He's a going down to his family, no doubt,' continued Bozzle.

'He may be going to the devil for what I know,' said the Colonel, who could not restrain himself.

'I suppose they're all friends of Mrs T.'s ?' asked Bozzle.

'Sir,' said the Colonel, 'I believe that you're a spy.'

'No, Colonel, no ; no, no ; I'm no spy. I wouldn't demean myself to be such. A spy is a man as has no profession, and nothing to justify his looking into things. Things must be looked into, Colonel ; or how's a man to know where he is ? or how's a lady to know where she is ? But as for spies, except in the way of evidence, I don't think nothing of 'em.' Soon after this, two more passengers entered the train, and nothing more was said between Bozzle and the Colonel.

The Colonel, as soon as he reached London, went home to his lodgings, and then to his club, and did his best to enjoy himself. On the following Monday he intended to start for Scotland. But he could not quite enjoy himself, – because of Bozzle. He felt that he was being watched; and there is nothing that any man hates so much as that, especially when a lady is concerned. Colonel Osborne knew that his visit to Nuncombe Putney had been very innocent; but he did not like the feeling that even his innocence had been made the subject of observation.

Bozzle went away at once to Trevelyan, whom he found at his chambers. He himself had had no very deep-laid scheme in his addresses to Colonel Osborne. He had begun to think that very little would come of the affair, – especially after Hugh Stanbury had appeared upon the scene, – and had felt that there was nothing to be lost by presenting himself before the eyes of the Colonel. It was necessary that he should make a report to his employer, and the report might be made a little more full after a few words with the man whom he had been 'looking into.' 'Well, Mr Trewillian,' he said, seating himself on a chair close against the wall, and holding his hat between the knees, – 'I've seen the parties, and know pretty much all about it.'

'All I want to know, Mr Bozzle, is, whether Colonel Osborne has been at the Clock House?'

'He has been there, Mr Trewillian. There is no earthly doubt about that. From hour to hour I can tell you pretty nearly where he's been since he left London.' Then Bozzle took out his memorandum-book.

'I don't care about all that,' said Trevelyan.

'I dare say not, sir; but it may be wanted all the same. Any gentleman acting in our way can't be too particular, – can't have too many facts. The smallest little, – tiddly things,' – and Bozzle as he said this seemed to enjoy immensely the flavour of his own epithet, – 'the smallest little "tiddly" things do so often turn up trumps when you get your evidence into court.'

'I'm not going to get any evidence into court.'

'Maybe not, sir. A gentleman and lady is always best out of court as long as things can hang on any way; – but sometimes things won't hang on no way.'

Trevelyan, who was conscious that the employment of Bozzle was discreditable, and whose affairs in Devonshire were now in the hands of, at any rate, a more honourable ally, was at present mainly anxious to get rid of the ex-policeman. 'I have no doubt you've been very careful, Mr Bozzle,' said he.

'There isn't no one in the business could be more so, Mr Trewillian.'

'And you have found out what it was necessary that I should know. Colonel Osborne did go to the Clock House?'

'Was let in at the front door on Friday the 5th by Sarah French, the housemaid, at 10.37 A.M., and was let out again by the same young woman at 11.41 A.M. Perhaps you'd like to have a copy of the entry, Mr Trewillian?'

'No, no, no.'

'It doesn't matter. Of course it'll be with me when it's wanted. Who was with him, exactly, at that time, I can't say. There is things, Mr Trewillian, one can't see. But I don't think as he saw neither Mrs Stanbury, nor Miss Stanbury, – not to speak to. I did just have one word, promiscuous, with Sarah French, after he was gone. Whether the other young lady was with 'em or not, and if so for how long, I – can't – say. There is things, Mr Trewillian, which one can't see.'

How Trevelyan hated the man as he went on with his odious details, – details not one of which possessed the slightest importance. 'It's all right, I dare say, Mr Bozzle. And now about the account.'

'Quite so, Mr Trewillian. But there was one question; – just one question.'

'What question?' said Trevelyan, almost angrily.

'And there's another thing I must tell you, too, Mr Trewillian. I come back to town in the same carriage with the Colonel. I thought it better.'

'You did not tell him who you were?'

'No, Mr Trewillian; I didn't tell him that. I don't think he'd say if you was to ask him that I told him much of anything. No, Mr Trewillian, I didn't tell him nothing. I don't often tell folks much till the time comes. But I thought it better, and I did have a word or two with the gent, – just a word or two. He's not so very downy,* isn't the Colonel; – for one that's been at it so long, Mr Trewillian.'

'I dare say not. But if you could just let me have the account, Mr Bozzle, – '

'The account? Oh, yes; – that is necessary; ain't it? These sort of inquiries do come a little expensive, Mr Trewillian; because time goes for so much; and when one has to be down on a thing, sharp, you know, and sure, so that counsel on the other side can't part you from it, though he shakes you like a dog does a rat, – and one has to get oneself up ready for all that, you know, Mr Trewillian, – as I was saying, one can't count one's shillings when one has such a job as this in hand. Clench your nail; – that's what I say; be it even so. Clench your nail; – that what's you've got to do.'

'I dare say we shan't quarrel about the money, Mr Bozzle.'

'Oh dear no. I find I never has any words about the money. But there's that one question. There's a young Mr Stanbury has gone down, as knows all about it. What's he up to?'

'He's my particular friend,' said Trevelyan.

'Oh – h. He do know all about it, then?'

'We needn't talk about that, if you please, Mr Bozzle.'

'Because there was words between him and the Colonel upon the platform; – and very angry words. The young man went at the Colonel quite open-mouthed, – savage-like. It's not the way such things should be done, Mr Trewillian; and though of course it's not for me to speak; – she's your lady, – still, when you has got a thing of this kind in hand, one head is better than a dozen. As for myself, Mr Trewillian, I never wouldn't look at a case, – not if I knew it, – unless I was to have it all to myself. But of course there was no bargain, and so I says nothing.'

After considerable delay the bill was made out on the spot, Mr Bozzle copying down the figures painfully from his memorandum-book, with his head much inclined on one side. Trevelyan asked him, almost in despair, to name the one sum; but this Bozzle declined to do, saying that right was right. He had a scale of pilfering of his own, to which he had easily reconciled his conscience; and beyond that he prided himself on the honesty of his accounts. At last the bill was made out, was paid, and Bozzle was gone. Trevelyan, when he was alone, threw himself back on a sofa, and almost wept in despair. To what a depth of degradation had he not been reduced!

24

Niddon Park

As Hugh Stanbury went over to Lessboro', and from thence to Nuncombe Putney, he thought more of himself and Nora Rowley than he did of Mr and Mrs Trevelyan. As to Mrs Trevelyan and Colonel Osborne, he felt that he knew everything that it was necessary that he should know. The man had been there, and had seen Mrs Trevelyan. Of that there could be no doubt. That Colonel Osborne had been wickedly indifferent to the evil consequences of such a visit, and that all the women concerned had been most foolish in permitting him to make it, was his present conviction. But he did not for a moment doubt that the visit had in itself been of all things the most innocent. Trevelyan had sworn that if his wife received the man at Nuncombe Putney, he would never see her again. She had seen him, and this oath would be remembered, and there would be increased difficulties. But these difficulties, whatever they might be, must be overcome. When he had told himself this, then he allowed his mind to settle itself on Nora Rowley.

Hitherto he had known Miss Rowley only as a fashionable girl living with the wife of an intimate friend of his own in London. He had never been staying in the same house with her. Circumstances had never given to him the opportunity of assuming the manner of an intimate friend, justifying him in giving advice, and authorising him to assume that semi-paternal tone which is by far the easiest preliminary to love-making. When a man can tell a young lady what she ought to read, what she ought to do, and whom she ought to know, nothing can be easier than to assure her that, of all her duties, her first duty is to prefer himself to all the world. And any young lady who has consented to receive lessons from such a teacher, will generally be willing to receive this special lesson among others. But Stanbury had hitherto had no such opportunities. In London Miss Rowley had been a fashionable young lady, living in Mayfair, and he had been, – well, anything but a fashionable young man. Nevertheless, he had seen her often, had sat by her very frequently, was quite sure that he loved her dearly, and had, perhaps, some self-flattering idea in his mind that had he stuck to his honourable profession as a barrister, and were he possessed of some comfortable little fortune of his own, he might, perhaps, have been able, after due siege operations, to make this charming young woman his own. Things were quite changed now. For the present, Miss Rowley certainly could not be regarded as a fashionable London young lady. The house in which he would see her was, in some sort, his own. He would be sleeping under the same roof with her, and would have all the advantages which such a position could give him. He would have no difficulty now in asking, if he should choose to ask; and he thought that she might be somewhat softer, somewhat more likely to yield at Nuncombe Putney, than she would have been in London. She was at Nuncombe in weak circumstances, to a certain degree friendless; with none of the excitement of society around her, with no elder sons buzzing about her and filling her mind, if not her heart, with the glories of luxurious primogeniture. Hugh Stanbury certainly did not dream that any special elder son had as yet been so attracted as to have made a journey to Nuncombe Putney on Nora's behalf. But should he on this account, – because she would be, as it were, without means of defence from his attack, – should he therefore take advantage of her weakness? She would, of course, go back to her London life after some short absence, and would again, if free, have her chance among the favoured ones of the earth. What had he to offer to her? He had taken the Clock House for his mother, and it would be quite as much as he could do, when Mrs Trevelyan should have left the village, to keep up that establishment and maintain himself in London, – quite as much as he could do, even though the favours of the 'D. R.' should flow upon him with their fullest tides. In such circumstances, would it be honourable in him to ask a girl to love him because he found her defenceless in his mother's house?

'If there bain't another for Nuncombe,' said Mrs Clegg's Ostler to Mrs Clegg's Boots, as Stanbury was driven off in a gig.

'That be young Stanbury, a-going of whome.'

'They be all a-going for the Clock House. Since the old 'ooman took to thick there house, there be folk a comin' and a-goin' every day loike.'

'It's along of the madam that they keeps there, Dick,' said the Boots.

'I didn't care if they'd be madams allays. They're the best as is going for trade anyhow,' said the ostler. What the ostler said was true. When there comes to be a feeling that a woman's character is in any way tarnished, there comes another feeling that everybody on the one side may charge double, and that everybody on the other side must pay double, for everything. Hugh Stanbury could not understand why he was charged a shilling a mile, instead of ninepence, for the gig to Nuncombe Putney. He got no satisfactory answer, and had to pay the shilling. The truth was, that gigs to Nuncombe Putney had gone up, since a lady, separated from her husband, with a colonel running after her, had been taken in at the Clock House.

'Here's Hugh!' said Priscilla, hurrying to the front door. And Mrs Stanbury hurried after her. Her son Hugh was the apple of her eye, the best son that ever lived, generous, noble, a thorough man, – almost a god!

'Dear, dear, oh dear! Who'd have expected it? God bless you, my boy! Why didn't you write? Priscilla, what is there in the house that he can eat?'

'Plenty of bread and cheese,' said Priscilla, laughing, with her hand inside her brother's arm. For though Priscilla hated all other men, she did not hate her brother Hugh. 'If you wanted things nice to eat directly you got here, you ought to have written.'

'I shall want my dinner, like any other Christian, – in due time,' said Hugh. 'And how is Mrs Trevelyan, – and how is Miss Rowley?'

He soon found himself in company with those two ladies, and experienced some immediate difficulty in explaining the cause of his sudden coming. But this was soon put aside by Mrs Trevelyan.

'When did you see my husband?' she asked.

'I saw him yesterday. He was quite well.'

'Colonel Osborne has been here,' she said.

'I know that he has been here. I met him at the station at Exeter. Perhaps I should not say so, but I wish he had remained away.'

'We all wish it,' said Priscilla.

Then Nora spoke. 'But what could we do, Mr Stanbury? It seemed so natural that he should call when he was in the neighbourhood. We have known him so long; and how could we refuse to see him?'

'I will not let any one think that I'm afraid to see any man on earth,' said Mrs Trevelyan. 'If he had ever in his life said a word that he should not have said, a word that would have been an insult, of course it would have been different. But the notion of it is preposterous. Why should I not have seen him?'

'I think he was wrong to come,' said Hugh.

'Of course he was wrong; – wickedly wrong,' said Priscilla.

Stanbury, finding that the subject was openly discussed between them, declared plainly the mission that had brought him to Nuncombe. 'Trevelyan heard that he was coming, and asked me to let him know the truth.'

'Now you can tell him the truth,' said Mrs Trevelyan, with something of indignation in her tone, as though she thought that Stanbury had taken upon himself a task of which he ought to be ashamed.

'But Colonel Osborne came specially to pay a visit to Cockchaffington,' said Nora, 'and not to see us. Louis ought to know that.'

'Nora, how can you demean yourself to care about such trash?' said Mrs Trevelyan. 'Who cares why he came here? His visit to me was a thing of course. If Mr Trevelyan disapproves of it, let him say so, and not send secret messengers.'

'Am I a secret messenger?' said Hugh Stanbury.

'There has been a man here, inquiring of the servants,' said Priscilla. So that odious Bozzle had made his foul mission known to them! Stanbury, however, thought it best to say nothing of Bozzle,

– not to acknowledge that he had ever heard of Bozzle. 'I am sure Mrs Trevelyan does not mean you,' said Priscilla.

'I do not know what I mean,' said Mrs Trevelyan. 'I am so harassed and fevered by these suspicions that I am driven nearly mad.' Then she left the room for a minute and returned with two letters. 'There, Mr Stanbury ; I got that note from Colonel Osborne, and wrote to him that reply. You know all about it now. Can you say that I was wrong to see him ?'

'I am sure that he was wrong to come,' said Hugh.

'Wickedly wrong,' said Priscilla, again.

'You can keep the letters, and show them to my husband,' said Mrs Trevelyan ; 'then he will know all about it.' But Stanbury declined to keep the letters.

He was to remain the Sunday at Nuncombe Putney and return to London on the Monday. There was, therefore, but one day on which he could say what he had to say to Nora Rowley. When he came down to breakfast on the Sunday morning he had almost made up his mind that he had nothing to say to her. As for Nora, she was in a state of mind much less near to any fixed purpose. She had told herself that she loved this man, – had indeed done so in the clearest way, by acknowledging the fact of her love to another suitor, by pleading to that other suitor the fact of her love as an insuperable reason why he should be rejected. There was no longer any doubt about it to her. When Priscilla had declared that Hugh Stanbury was at the door, her heart had gone into her mouth. Involuntarily she had pressed her hands to her sides, and had held her breath. Why had he come there ? Had he come there for her ? Oh ! if he had come there for her, and if she might dare to forget all the future, how sweet, – sweetest of all things in heaven or earth, – might be an August evening with him among the lanes ! But she, too, had endeavoured to be very prudent. She had told herself that she was quite unfit to be the wife of a poor man, – that she would be only a burden round his neck, and not an aid to him. And in so telling herself, she had told herself also that she had been a fool not to accept Mr Glascock. She should have dragged out from her heart the image of this man who had never even whispered a word of love in her ears, and should have constrained herself to receive with affection a man in loving whom there ought to be no difficulty. But when she had been repeating those lessons to herself, Hugh Stanbury had not been in the house. Now he was there ; – and what must be her answer if he should whisper that word of love ? She had an idea that it would be treason in her to disown the love she felt, if questioned concerning her heart by the man to whom it had been given.

They all went to church on the Sunday morning, and up to that time Nora had not been a moment alone with the man she loved. It had been decided that they should dine early, and then ramble out, when the evening would be less hot than the day had been, to a spot called Niddon Park. This was nearly three miles from Nuncombe, and was a beautiful wild slope of ground full of ancient, blighted, blasted, but still half-living oaks, – oaks that still brought forth leaves, – overlooking a bend of the river Teign. Park, in the usual sense of the word, there was none, nor did they who lived round Nuncombe Putney know whether Niddon Park had ever been enclosed. But of all the spots in that lovely neighbourhood, Priscilla Stanbury swore that it was the loveliest; and, as it had never yet been seen by Mrs Trevelyan or her sister, it was determined that they would walk there on this August afternoon. There were four of them, – and, as was natural, they fell into parties of two and two. But Priscilla walked with Nora, and Hugh Stanbury walked with his friend's wife. Nora was talkative, but demure in her manner, and speaking now and again as though she were giving words and not thoughts. She felt that there was something to hide, and was suffering from disappointment that their party should not have been otherwise divided. Had Hugh spoken to her and asked her to be his wife, she could not have accepted him, because she knew that they were both poor, and that she was not fit to keep a poor man's house. She had declared to herself most plainly that that must be her course; – but yet she was disappointed, and talked on with the knowledge that she had something to conceal.

When they were seated beneath an old riven, withered oak, looking down upon the river, they were still divided in the same way. In seating herself she had been very anxious not to disarrange that arrangement, – almost equally anxious not to seem to adhere to it with any special purpose. She was very careful that there should be nothing seen in her manner that was in any way special, – but in the meantime she was suffering an agony of trouble. He did not care for her in the least. She was becoming sure of that. She had given all her love to a man who had none to give her in return. As she thought of this she almost longed for the offer of that which she knew she could not have accepted had it been offered to her. But she talked on about the scenery, about the weather, – descanting on the pleasure of living where such loveliness was within reach. Then there came a pause for a moment. 'Nora,' said Priscilla, 'I do not know what you are thinking about, but it is not of the beauty of Niddon Park.' Then there came a faint sound as of an hysterical sob, and then a gurgle in the throat, and then a pretence at laughter.

'I don't believe I am thinking of anything at all,' said Nora.

After which Hugh insisted on descending to the bank of the river, but, as the necessity of re-climbing the slope was quite manifest, none of the girls would go with him. 'Come, Miss Rowley,' said he, 'will you not show them that a lady can go up and down a hill as well as a man?'

'I had rather not go up and down the hill,' said she.

Then he understood that she was angry with him; and in some sort surmised the cause of her anger. Not that he believed that she loved him; but it seemed possible to him that she resented the absence of his attention. He went down, and scrambled out on the rocks into the bed of the river, while the girls above looked down upon him, watching the leaps that he made. Priscilla and Mrs Trevelyan called to him, bidding him beware; but Nora called not at all. He was whistling as he made his jumps, but still he heard their voices, and knew that he did not hear Nora's voice. He poised himself on the edge of a rock in the middle of the stream, and looked up the river and down the river, turning himself carefully on his narrow foothold; but he was thinking only of Nora. Could there be anything nobler than to struggle on with her, if she only would be willing? But then she was young; and should she yield to such a request from him, she would not know what she was yielding. He turned again, jumping from rock to rock till he reached the bank, and then made his way again up to the withered oak.

'You would not have repented it if you had come down with me,' he said to Nora.

'I am not so sure of that,' she answered.

When they started to return she stepped on gallantly with Priscilla; but Priscilla was stopped by some chance, having some word to say to her brother, having some other word to say to Mrs Trevelyan. Could it be that her austerity had been softened, and that in kindness she contrived that Nora should be left some yards behind them with her brother? Whether it were kindness, or an unkind error, so it was. Nora, when she perceived what destiny was doing for her, would not interfere with destiny. If he chose to speak to her she would hear him and would answer him. She knew very well what answer she would give him. She had her answer quite ready at her fingers' ends. There was no doubt about her answer.

They had walked half a mile together and he had spoken of nothing but the scenery. She had endeavoured to appear to be excited. Oh, yes, the scenery of Devonshire was delightful. She hardly wanted anything more to make her happy. If only this misery respecting her sister could be set right!

'And you, you yourself,' said he, 'do you mean that there is nothing you want in leaving London?'

'Not much, indeed.'

'It sometimes seemed to me that that kind of life was, – was very pleasant to you.'

'What kind of life, Mr Stanbury?'

'The life that you were living, – going out, being admired, and having the rich and dainty all around you.'

'I don't dislike people because they are rich,' she said.

'No; nor do I; and I despise those who affect to dislike them. But all cannot be rich.'

'Nor all dainty, as you choose to call them.'

'But they who have once been dainty, – as I call them, – never like to divest themselves of their daintiness. You have been one of the dainty, Miss Rowley.'

'Have I?'

'Certainly; I doubt whether you would be happy if you thought that your daintiness had departed from you.'

'I hope, Mr Stanbury, that nothing nice and pleasant has departed from me. If I have ever been dainty, dainty I hope I may remain. I will never, at any rate, give it up of my own accord.' Why she said this, she could never explain to herself. She had certainly not intended to rebuff him when she had been saying it. But he spoke not a word to her further as they walked home, either of her mode of life or of his own.

25

Hugh Stanbury Smokes his Pipe

Nora Rowley, when she went to bed, after her walk to Niddon Park in company with Hugh Stanbury, was full of wrath against him. But she could not own her anger to herself, nor could she even confess to herself, – though she was breaking her heart, – that there really existed for her the slightest cause of grief. But why had he been so stern to her? Why had he gone out of his way to be uncivil to her? He had called her 'dainty,' meaning to imply by the epithet that she was one of the butterflies of the day, caring for nothing but sunshine and an opportunity of fluttering her silly wings. She had understood well what he meant. Of course he was right to be cold to her if his heart was cold, but he need not have insulted her by his ill-concealed rebukes. Had he been kind to her, he might have rebuked her as much as he liked. She quite appreciated the delightful intimacy of a loving word of counsel from the man she loved, – how nice it is, as it were, to play at marriage, and to hear beforehand something of the pleasant weight of gentle marital authority. But there had been nothing of that in his manner to her. He had told her that she was dainty, – and had so told it her, as she thought, that she might learn thereby, that under no circumstances would he have any other tale to tell her. If he had no other tale, why had he not been silent? Did he think that she was subject to his rebuke merely because she lived under his mother's roof? She would soon show him that her residence at the Clock House gave him no such authority over her. Then, amidst her wrath and despair, she cried herself asleep.

While she was sobbing in bed, he was sitting, with a short, black pipe stuck in his mouth, on the corner of the churchyard wall opposite. Before he had left the house he and Priscilla had spoken together for some minutes about Mrs Trevelyan. 'Of course she was wrong to see him,' said Priscilla. 'I hesitate to wound her by so saying, because she has been ill-used, – though I did tell her so, when she asked me. She could have lost nothing by declining his visit.'

'The worst of it is that Trevelyan swears that he will never receive her again if she received him.'

'He must unswear it,' said Priscilla, 'that is all. It is out of the question that a man should take a girl from her home, and make her his wife, and then throw her off for so little of an offence as this. She might compel him by law to take her back.'

'What would she get by that?'

'Little enough,' said Priscilla; 'and it was little enough she got by marrying him. She would have had bread, and meat, and raiment without being married, I suppose.'

'But it was a love-match.'

'Yes; – and now she is at Nuncombe Putney, and he is roaming about in London. He has to pay ever so much a year for his love-match, and she is crushed into nothing by it. How long will she have to remain here, Hugh?'

'How can I say? I suppose there is no reason against her remaining as far as you are concerned?'

'For me personally, none. Were she much worse than I think she is, I should not care in the least for myself, if I thought that we were doing her good, – helping to bring her back. She can't hurt me. I am so fixed, and dry, and established, that nothing anybody says will affect me. But mamma doesn't like it.'

'What is it she dislikes?'

'The idea that she is harbouring a married woman, of whom people say, at least, that she has a lover.'

'Is she to be turned out because people are slanderers?'

'Why should mamma suffer because this woman, who is a stranger to her, has been imprudent? If she were your wife, Hugh –'

'God forbid!'

'If we were in any way bound to her, of course we would do our duty. But if it makes mamma unhappy I am sure you will not press it. I think Mrs Merton has spoken to her. And then Aunt Stanbury has written such letters!'

'Who cares for Aunt Jemima?'

'Everybody cares for her, – except you and I. And now this man who has been here asking the servant questions has upset her greatly. Even your coming has done so, knowing, as she does, that you have come, not to see us, but to make inquiries about Mrs Trevelyan. She is so annoyed by it, that she does not sleep.'

'Do you wish her to be taken away at once?' asked Hugh, almost in an angry tone.

'Certainly not. That would be impossible. We have agreed to take her, and must bear with it. And I would not have her moved from this, if I thought that if she stayed awhile it might be arranged that she might return from us direct to her husband.'

'I shall try that, of course; – now.'

'But if he will not have her; – if he be so obstinate, so foolish, and so wicked, do not leave her here longer than you can help.' Then Hugh explained that Sir Marmaduke and Lady Rowley were to be in England in the spring, and that it would be very desirable that the poor woman should not be sent abroad to look for a home before that. 'If it must be so, it must,' said Priscilla. 'But eight months is a long time.'

Hugh went out to smoke his pipe on the church-wall in a moody, unhappy state of mind. He had hoped to have done so well in regard to Mrs Trevelyan! Till he had met Colonel Osborne, he felt sure, almost sure, that she would have refused to see that pernicious troubler of the peace of families. In this he found that he had been disappointed; but he had not expected that Priscilla would have been so much opposed to the arrangement which he had made about the house, and then he had been buoyed up by the antici-pation of some delight in meeting Nora Rowley. There was, at any rate, the excitement of seeing her to keep his spirits from flagging. He had seen her, and had had the opportunity of which he had so long been thinking. He had seen her, and had had every possible advantage on his side. What could any man desire better than the privilege of walking home with the girl he loved through country lanes of a summer evening ? They had been an hour together, – or might have been, had he chosen to prolong the interview. But the words which had been spoken between them had not the slightest interest, – unless it were that they had tended to make the interval between him and her wider than ever. He had asked her, – he thought that he had asked, – whether it would grieve her to abandon that delicate, dainty mode of life to which she had been accustomed; and she had replied, that she would never abandon it of her own accord. Of course she had intended him to take her at her word.

He blew forth quick clouds of heavy smoke, as he attempted to make himself believe that this was all for the best. What would such a one as he was do with a wife ? Or, seeing as he did see, that marriage itself was quite out of the question, how could it be good either for him or her that they should be tied together by a long engagement ? Such a future would not at all suit the purpose of his life. In his life absolute freedom would be needed; – freedom from unnecessary ties, freedom from unnecessary burdens. His income was most precarious, and he certainly would not make it less so by submission to any closer literary thraldom. And he believed himself to be a Bohemian, – too much of a Bohemian to enjoy a domestic fireside with children and slippers. To be free to go where he liked, and when he liked; to think as he pleased; to be driven nowhere by conventional rules ; to use his days, Sundays as well as Mondays, as he pleased to use them; to turn Republican, if his mind should take him that way, – or Quaker, or Mormon, or Red Indian, if he wished it, and in so turning to do no damage to any one but himself; – that was the life which he had planned for himself. His aunt Stanbury had not read his character altogether wrongly, as he thought, when she had once declared that decency and godliness were both distasteful to him. Would it not be destruction to such a one as he was, to fall into an interminable engagement with any girl, let her be ever so sweet ?

But yet, he felt as he sat there filling pipe after pipe, smoking away till past midnight, that though he could not bear the idea of trammels, though he was totally unfit for matrimony, either present or in prospect, – he felt that he had within his breast a double identity, and that that other division of himself would be utterly crushed if it were driven to divest itself of the idea of love. Whence was to come his poetry, the romance of his life, the springs of clear water in which his ignoble thoughts were to be dipped till they should become pure, if love was to be banished altogether from the list of delights that were possible to him? And then he began to speculate on love, – that love of which poets wrote, and of which he found that some sparkle was necessary to give light to his life. Was it not the one particle of divine breath given to man, of which he had heard since he was a boy? And how was this love to be come at, and was it to be a thing of reality, or merely an idea? Was it a pleasure to be attained, or a mystery that charmed by the difficulties of the distance, – a distance that never could be so passed that the thing should really be reached? Was love to be ever a delight, vague as is that feeling of unattainable beauty which far-off mountains give, when you know that you can never place yourself amidst their unseen valleys? And if love could be reached, – the love of which the poets sing, and of which his own heart was ever singing, – what were to be its pleasures? To press a hand, to kiss a lip, to clasp a waist, to hear even the low voice of the vanquished, confessing loved one as she hides her blushing cheek upon your shoulder, – what is it all but to have reached the once mysterious valley of your far-off mountain, and to have found that it is as other valleys, – rocks and stones, with a little grass, and a thin stream of running water? But beyond that pressing of the hand, and that kissing of the lips, – beyond that short-lived pressure of the plumage which is common to birds and men, – what could love do beyond that? There were children with dirty faces, and household bills, and a wife who must, perhaps, always darn the stockings, – and be sometimes cross. Was love to lead only to this, – a dull life, with a woman who had lost the beauty from her cheeks, and the gloss from her hair, and the music from her voice, and the fire from her eye, and the grace from her step, and whose waist an arm should no longer be able to span? Did the love of the poets lead to that, and that only? Then, through the cloud of smoke, there came upon him some dim idea of self-abnegation, – that the mysterious valley among the mountains, the far-off prospect of which was so charming to him, – which made the poetry of his life, was, in fact, the capacity of caring more for other human beings than for himself. The beauty of it all was not so much in the thing loved, as in the loving. 'Were she a cripple, hunchbacked, eyeless,' he said to himself, 'it might be the same. Only, she must be a woman.' Then he blew off a great cloud of smoke, and went into bed lost amidst poetry, philosophy, love, and tobacco.

It had been arranged over-night that he was to start the next morning at half-past seven, and Priscilla had promised to give him his breakfast before he went. Priscilla, of course, kept her word. She was one of those women who would take a grim pleasure in coming down to make the tea at any possible hour, – at five, at four, if it were needed, – and who would never want to go to bed again when the ceremony was performed. But when Nora made her appearance, – Nora, who had been called dainty, – both Priscilla and Hugh were surprised. They could not say why she was there, – nor could Nora tell herself. She had not forgiven him. She had no thought of being gentle and loving to him. She declared to herself that she had no wish of saying good-bye to him once again. But yet she was in the room, waiting for him, when he came down to his breakfast. She had been unable to sleep, and had reasoned with herself as to the absurdity of lying in bed awake, when she preferred to be up and out of the house. It was true that she had not been out of her bed at seven any morning since she had been at Nuncombe Putney; but that was no reason why she should not be more active on this special morning. There was a noise in the house, and she never could sleep when there was a noise. She was quite sure that she was not going down because she wished to see Hugh Stanbury, but she was equally sure that it would be a disgrace to her to be deterred from going down, simply because the man was there. So she descended to the parlour, and was standing near the open window when Stanbury bustled into the room, some quarter of an hour after the proper time. Priscilla was there also, guessing something of the truth, and speculating whether these two young people, should they love each other, would be the better or the worse for such love. There must be marriages, – if only that the world might go on in accordance with the Creator's purpose. But, as far as Priscilla could see, blessed were they who were not called upon to assist in the scheme. To her eyes all days seemed to be days of wrath, and all times, times of tribulation. And it was all mere vanity and vexation of spirit.* To go on and bear it till one was dead, – helping others to bear it, if such help might be of avail, – that was her theory of life. To make it pleasant by eating, and drinking, and dancing, or even by falling in love, was, to her mind, a vain crunching of ashes between the teeth. Not to have ill things said of her and of hers, not to be disgraced, not to be rendered incapable of some human effort, not to have actually to starve, – such was the extent of her ambition in this world. And for the next, – she felt so assured of the goodness of God that she could not bring herself to doubt of happiness in a world that was to be eternal. Her doubt was this, whether it was really the next world which would be eternal. Of eternity she did not doubt; – but might there not be many worlds? These things, however, she kept almost entirely to herself. 'You down!' Priscilla had said.

'Well, yes; I could not sleep when I heard you all moving. And the morning is so fine, and I thought that perhaps you would go out and walk after your brother has gone.' Priscilla promised that she would walk, and then the tea was made.

'Your sister and I are going out for an early walk,' said Nora, when she was greeted by Stanbury. Priscilla said nothing, but thought she understood it all.

'I wish I were going with you,' said Hugh. Nora, remembering how very little he had made of his opportunity on the evening before, did not believe him.

The eggs and fried bacon were eaten in a hurry, and very little was said. Then there came the moment for parting. The brother and sister kissed each other, and Hugh took Nora by the hand. 'I hope you make yourself happy here,' he said.

'Oh, yes; – if it were only for myself I should want nothing.'

'I will do the best I can with Trevelyan.'

'The best will be to make him, and every one, understand that the fault is altogether his, and not Emily's.'

'The best will be to make each think that there has been no real fault,' said Hugh.

'There should be no talking of faults,' said Priscilla. 'Let the husband take his wife back, – as he is bound to do.'

These words occupied hardly a minute in the saying, but during that minute Hugh Stanbury held Nora by the hand. He held it fast. She would not attempt to withdraw it, but neither would she return his pressure by the muscle of a single finger. What right had he to press her hand; or to make any sign of love, any pretence of loving, when he had gone out of his way to tell her that she was not good enough for him? Then he started, and Nora and Priscilla put on their hats and left the house.

'Let us go to Niddon Park,' said Nora.

'To Niddon Park again?'

'Yes; it is so beautiful! And I should like to see it by the morning light. There is plenty of time.'

So they walked to Niddon park in the morning, as they had done on the preceding evening. Their conversation at first regarded Trevelyan and his wife, and the old trouble; but Nora could not keep herself from speaking of Hugh Stanbury.

'He would not have come,' she said, 'unless Louis had sent him.'

'He would not have come now, I think.'

'Of course not; – why should he ? – before Parliament was hardly over, too ? But he won't remain in town now, – will he ?'

'He says somebody must remain, – and I think he will be in London till near Christmas.'

'How disagreeable ! But I suppose he doesn't care. It's all the same to a man like him. They don't shut the clubs up, I dare say. Will he come here at Christmas ?'

'Either then or for the New Year; – just for a day or two.'

'We shall be gone then, I suppose ?' said Nora.

'That must depend on Mr Trevelyan,' said Priscilla.

'What a life for two women to lead; – to depend upon the caprice of a man who must be mad ! Do you think that Mr Trevelyan will care for what your brother says to him ?'

'I do not know Mr Trevelyan.'

'He is very fond of your brother, and I suppose men friends do listen to each other. They never seem to listen to women. Don't you think that, after all, they despise women ? They look on them as dainty, foolish things.'

'Sometimes women despise men,' said Priscilla.

'Not very often; – do they ? And then women are so dependent on men. A woman can get nothing without a man.'

'I manage to get on somehow,' said Priscilla.

'No, you don't, Miss Stanbury, – if you think of it. You want mutton. And who kills the sheep ?'

'But who cooks it ?'

'But the men-cooks are the best,' said Nora ; 'and the men-tailors, and the men to wait at table, and the men-poets, and the men-painters, and the men-nurses. All the things that women do, men do better.'

'There are two things they can't do,' said Priscilla.

'What are they ?'

'They can't suckle babies, and they can't forget themselves.'

'About the babies, of course not. As for forgetting themselves, – I am not quite so sure that I can forget myself. – That is just where your brother went down last night.'

They had at this moment reached the top of the steep slope below which the river ran brawling among the rocks, and Nora seated herself exactly where she had sat on the previous evening.

'I have been down scores of times,' said Priscilla.

'Let us go now.'

'You wouldn't go when Hugh asked you yesterday.'

'I didn't care then. But do come now, – if you don't mind the

climb.' Then they went down the slope and reached the spot from
whence Hugh Stanbury had jumped from rock to rock across the
stream. 'You have never been out there, have you ?' said Nora.

'On the rocks ? Oh, dear, no ! I should be sure to fall.'

'But he went ; just like a goat.'

'That's one of the things that men can do, I suppose,' said
Priscilla. 'But I don't see any great glory in being like a goat.'

'I do. I should like to be able to go, and I think I'll try. It is so
mean to be dainty and weak.'

'I don't think it at all dainty to keep dry feet.'

'But he didn't get his feet wet,' said Nora. 'Or if he did, he didn't
mind. I can see at once that I should be giddy and tumble down if I
tried it.'

'Of course you would.'

'But he didn't tumble down.'

'He has been doing it all his life,' said Priscilla.

'He can't do it up in London. When I think of myself, Miss
Stanbury, I am so ashamed. There is nothing that I can do. I
couldn't write an article for a newspaper.'

'I think I could. But I fear no one would read it.'

'They read his,' said Nora, 'or else he wouldn't be paid for
writing them.' Then they climbed back again up the hill, and during
the climbing there were no words spoken. The slope was not much
of a hill, – was no more than the fall from the low ground of the
valley to the course which the river had cut for itself ; but it was
steep while it lasted ; and both the young women were forced to
pause for a minute before they could proceed upon their journey.
As they walked home Priscilla spoke of the scenery, and of the
country, and of the nature of the life which she and her mother and
sister had passed at Nuncombe Putney. Nora said but little till they
were just entering the village, and then she went back to the subject
of her thoughts. 'I would sooner,' said she, 'write for a newspaper
than do anything else in the world.'

'Why so ?'

'Because it is so noble to teach people everything ! And then a
man who writes for a newspaper must know so many things
himself ! I believe there are women who do it, but very few. One or
two have done it, I know.'

'Go and tell that to Aunt Stanbury, and hear what she will say
about such women.'

'I suppose she is very, – prejudiced.'

'Yes ; she is ; but she is a clever woman. I am inclined to think
women had better not write for newspapers.'

'And why not?' Nora asked.

'My reasons would take me a week to explain, and I doubt whether I have them very clear in my own head. In the first place there is that difficulty about the babies. Most of them must get married, you know.'

'But not all,' said Nora.

'No; thank God; not all.'

'And if you are not married you might write for a newspaper. At any rate, if I were you, I should be very proud of my brother.'

'Aunt Stanbury is not at all proud of her nephew,' said Priscilla, as they entered the house.

26

A Third Party is so Objectionable

Hugh Stanbury went in search of Trevelyan immediately on his return to London, and found his friend at his rooms in Lincoln's Inn.

'I have executed my commission,' said Hugh, endeavouring to speak of what he had done in a cheery voice.

'I am much obliged to you, Stanbury; – very much; – but I do not know that I need trouble you to tell me anything about it.'

'And why not?'

'I have learned it all from that – man.'

'What man?'

'From Bozzle. He has come back, and has been with me, and has learned everything.'

'Look here, Trevelyan; – when you asked me to go down to Devonshire, you promised me that there should be nothing more about Bozzle. I expect you to put that rascal, and all that he has told you, out of your head altogether. You are bound to do so for my sake, and you will be very wise to do so for your own.'

'I was obliged to see him when he came.'

'Yes, and to pay him, I do not doubt. But that is all done, and should be forgotten.'

'I can't forget it. Is it true or untrue that he found that man down there? Is it true or untrue that my wife received Colonel Osborne at your mother's house? Is it true or untrue that Colonel Osborne went down there with the express object of seeing her? Is it true or untrue that they had corresponded? It is nonsense to bid me to forget all this. You might as well ask me to forget that I had desired her neither to write to him, nor to see him.'

'If I understand the matter,' said Trevelyan, 'you are incorrect in one of your assertions.'

'In which?'

'You must excuse me if I am wrong, Trevelyan; but I don't think you ever did tell your wife not to see this man, or not to write to him?'

'I never told her! I don't understand what you mean.'

'Not in so many words. It is my belief that she has endeavoured to obey implicitly every clear instruction that you have given her.'

'You are wrong; — absolutely and altogether wrong. Heaven and earth! Do you mean to tell me now, after all that has taken place, that she did not know my wishes?'

'I have not said that. But you have chosen to place her in such a position, that though your word would go for much with her, she cannot bring herself to respect your wishes.'

'And you call that being dutiful and affectionate!'

'I call it human and reasonable; and I think that it is compatible with duty and affection. Have you consulted her wishes?'

'Always!'

'Consult them now then, and bid her come back to you.'

'No; — never! As far as I can see, I will never do so. The moment she is away from me this man goes to her, and she receives him. She must have known that she was wrong, — and you must know it.'

'I do not think that she is half so wrong as you yourself,' said Stanbury.' To this Trevelyan made no answer, and they both remained silent some minutes. Stanbury had a communication to make before he went, but it was one which he wished to delay as long as there was a chance that his friend's heart might be softened; — one which he need not make if Trevelyan would consent to receive his wife back to his house. There was the day's paper lying on the table, and Stanbury had taken it up and was reading it, — or pretending to read it.

'I will tell you what I propose to do,' said Trevelyan.

'Well.'

'It is best both for her and for me that we should be apart.'

'I cannot understand how you can be so mad as to say so.'

'You don't understand what I feel. Heaven and earth! To have a man coming and going — . But, never mind. You do not see it, and nothing will make you see it. And there is no reason why you should.'

'I certainly do not see it. I do not believe that your wife cares more for Colonel Osborne, except as an old friend of her father's, than she does for the fellow that sweeps the crossing. It is a matter in which I am bound to tell you what I think.'

'Very well. Now, if you have freed your mind, I will tell you my purpose. I am bound to do so, because your people are concerned in it. I shall go abroad.'

'And leave her in England?'

'Certainly. She will be safer here than she can be abroad, – unless she should choose to go back with her father to the islands.'

'And take the boy?'

'No; – I could not permit that. What I intend is this. I will give her £800 a year, as long as I have reason to believe that she has no communication whatever, either by word of mouth or by letter, with that man. If she does, I will put the case immediately into the hands of my lawyer, with instructions to him to ascertain from counsel what severest steps I can take.'

'How I hate that word severe, when applied to a woman.'

'I dare say you do, – when applied to another man's wife. But if I approve of the place in which she lives, as I do at present, – he shall remain with her for nine months in the year till he is six years old. Then he must come to me. And he shall come to me altogether if she sees or hears from that man. I believe that £800 a year will enable her to live with all comfort under your mother's roof.'

'As to that,' said Stanbury, slowly, 'I suppose I had better tell you at once, that the Nuncombe Putney arrangement cannot be considered as permanent.'

'Why not?'

'Because my mother is timid, and nervous, and altogether unused to the world.'

'That unfortunate woman is to be sent away, – even from Nuncombe Putney!'

'Understand me, Trevelyan.'

'I understand you. I understand you most thoroughly. Nor do I wonder at it in the least. Do not suppose that I am angry with your mother, or with you, or with your sister. I have no right to expect that they should keep her after that man has made his way into their house. I can well conceive that no honest, high-minded lady would do so.'

'It is not that at all.'

'But it is that. How can you tell me that it isn't? And yet you would have me believe that I am not disgraced!' As he said this Trevelyan got up, and walked about the room, tearing his hair with his hands. He was in truth a wretched man, from whose mind all expectation of happiness was banished, who regarded his own position as one of incurable ignominy, looking upon himself as one who had been made unfit for society by no fault of his own. What was he to do with the wretched woman who could be kept from the evil of her pernicious vanity by no gentle custody, whom no most distant retirement would make safe from the effects of her own ignorance, folly, and obstinacy? 'When is she to go?' he asked in a low, sepulchral tone, – as though these new tidings that had come upon him had been fatal – laden with doom, and finally subversive of all chance even of tranquillity.

'When you and she may please.'

'That is all very well; – but let me know the truth. I would not have your mother's house – contaminated; but may she remain there for a week?'

Stanbury jumped from his seat with an oath. 'I tell you what it is, Trevelyan; – if you speak of your wife in that way, I will not listen to you. It is unmanly and untrue to say that her presence can – contaminate any house.'

'That is very fine. It may be chivalrous in you to tell me on her behalf that I am a liar, – and that I am not a man.'

'You drive me to it.'

'But what am I to think when you are forced to declare that this unfortunate woman can not be allowed to remain at your mother's house, – a house which has been especially taken with reference to a shelter for her? She has been received, – with the idea that she would be discreet. She has been indiscreet, past belief, and she is to be turned out, – most deservedly. Heaven and earth! Where shall I find a roof for her head?' Trevelyan as he said this was walking about the room with his hands stretched up towards the ceiling; and as his friend was attempting to make him comprehend that there was no intention on the part of any one to banish Mrs Trevelyan from the Clock House, at least for some months to come, – not even till after Christmas unless some satisfactory arrangement could be sooner made, – the door of the room was opened by the boy, who called himself a clerk, and who acted as Trevelyan's servant in the chambers, and a third person was shown into the room. That third person was Mr Bozzle. As no name was given, Stanbury did not at first know Mr Bozzle, but he had not had his eye on Mr Bozzle for half a minute before he recognised the ex-policeman by the outward attributes and signs of his profession. 'Oh; is that you, Mr Bozzle?' said Trevelyan, as soon as the great man had made his bow of salutation. 'Well; – what is it?'

'Mr Hugh Stanbury, I think,' said Bozzle, making another bow to the young barrister.

'That's my name,' said Stanbury.

'Exactly so, Mr S. The identity is one as I could prove on oath in any court in England. You was on the railway platform at Exeter on Saturday when we was waiting for the 12 express hup; – wasn't you now, Mr S. ?'

'What's that to you ?'

'Well; – as it do happen, it is something to me. And, Mr S., if you was asked that question in hany court in England or before even one of the metropolitan bekes, you wouldn't deny it.'

'Why the devil should I deny it ? What's all this about, Trevelyan ?'

'Of course you can't deny it, Mr S. When I'm down on a fact, I am down on it. Nothing else wouldn't do in my profession.'

'Have you anything to say to me, Mr Bozzle ?' asked Trevelyan.

'Well; – I have ; just a word.'

'About your journey to Devonshire ?'

'Well; – in a way it is about my journey to Devonshire. It's all along of the same job, Mr Trewillian.'

'You can speak before my friend here,' said Trevelyan. Bozzle had taken a great dislike to Hugh Stanbury, regarding the barrister with a correct instinct as one who was engaged for the time in the same service with himself, and who was his rival in that service. When thus instigated to make as it were a party of three in this delicate and most confidential matter, and to take his rival into his confidence, he shook his head slowly and looked Trevelyan hard in the face, – 'Mr Stanbury is my particular friend,' said Trevelyan, 'and knows all the circumstances of this unfortunate affair. You can say anything before him.'

Bozzle shook his head again. 'I'd rayther not, Mr Trewillian,' said he. 'Indeed I'd rayther not. It's something very particular.'

'If you take my advice,' said Stanbury, 'you will not hear him yourself.'

'That's your advice, Mr S. ?' asked Mr Bozzle.

'Yes; – that's my advice. I'd never have anything to do with such a fellow as you as long as I could help it.'

'I dare say not, Mr. S.; I dare say not. We're hexpensive, and we're haccurate; – neither of which is much in your line, Mr S., if I understand about it rightly.'

'Mr Bozzle, if you've got anything to tell, tell it,' said Trevelyan, angrily.

'A third party is so objectionable,' pleaded Bozzle.

'Never mind. That is my affair.'

'It is your affair, Mr Trewillian. There's not a doubt of that. The lady is your wife.'

'Damnation!' shouted Trevelyan.

'But the credit, sir,' said Bozzle. 'The credit is mine. And here is Mr S. has been down a interfering with me, and doing no 'varsal good, as I'll undertake to prove by evidence before the affair is over.'

'The affair is over,' said Stanbury.

'That's as you think, Mr S. That's where your information goes to, Mr S. Mine goes a little beyond that, Mr S. I've means as you can know nothing about, Mr S. I've irons in the fire, what you're as ignorant on as the babe as isn't born.'

'No doubt you have, Mr Bozzle,' said Stanbury.

'I has. And now if it be that I must speak before a third party, Mr Trewillian, I'm ready. It ain't that I'm no ways ashamed. I've done my duty, and knows how to do it. And let a counsel be ever so sharp, I never yet was so 'posed but what I could stand up and hold my own. The Colonel, Mr Trewillian, got, – a letter, – from your lady, – this morning.'

'I don't believe it,' said Stanbury, sharply.

'Very likely not, Mr S. It ain't in my power to say anything whatever about you believing or not believing. But Mr T.'s lady has wrote the letter; and the Colonel, – he has received it. You don't look after these things, Mr S. You don't know the ways of 'em. But it's my business. The lady has wrote the letter, and the Colonel, – why, he has received it.' Trevelyan had become white with rage when Bozzle first mentioned this continued correspondence between his wife and Colonel Osborne. It never occured to him to doubt the correctness of the policeman's information, and he regarded Stanbury's assertion of incredulity as being simply of a piece with his general obstinacy in the matter. At this moment he began to regret that he had called in the assistance of his friend, and that he had not left the affair altogether in the hands of that much more satisfactory, but still more painful, agent, Mr Bozzle. He had again seated himself, and for a moment or two remained silent on his chair. 'It ain't my fault, Mr Trewillian,' continued Bozzle, 'if this little matter oughtn't never to have been mentioned before a third party.'

'It is of no moment,' said Trevelyan, in a low voice. 'What does it signify who knows it now?'

'Do not believe it, Trevelyan,' said Stanbury.

'Very well, Mr S. Very well. Just as you like. Don't believe it. Only it's true, and it's my business to find them things out. It's my business, and I finds 'em out. Mr Trewillian can do as he likes about it. If it's right, why, then it is right. It ain't for me to say nothing about that. But there's the fact. The lady, she has wrote another letter; and the Colonel, – why, he has received it. There ain't nothing wrong about the post-office. If I was to say what was inside of that billydou, – why, then I should be proving what I didn't know; and when it came to standing up in court, I shouldn't be able to hold my own. But as for the letter, the lady wrote it, and the Colonel, – he received it.'

'That will do, Mr Bozzle,' said Trevelyan.

'Shall I call again, Mr Trewillian?'

'No; – yes. I'll send to you, when I want you. You shall hear from me.'

'I suppose I'd better be keeping my eyes open about the Colonel's place, Mr Trewillian?'

'For God's sake, Trevelyan, do not have anything more to do with this man!'

'That's all very well for you, Mr S.,' said Bozzle. 'The lady ain't your wife.'

'Can you imagine anything more disgraceful than all this?' said Stanbury.

'Nothing; nothing; nothing!' answered Trevelyan.

'And I'm to keep stirring, and be on the move?' again suggested Bozzle, who prudently required to be fortified by instructions before he devoted his time and talents even to so agreeable a pursuit as that in which he had been engaged.

'You shall hear from me,' said Trevelyan.

'Very well; – very well. I wish you good-day, Mr Trewillian. Mr S., yours most obedient. There was one other point, Mr Trewillian.'

'What point?' asked Trevelyan, angrily.

'If the lady was to join the Colonel –'

'That will do, Mr Bozzle,' said Trevelyan, again jumping up from his chair. 'That will do.' So saying, he opened the door, and Bozzle, with a bow, took his departure. 'What on earth am I to do? How am I to save her?' said the wretched husband, appealing to his friend.

Stanbury endeavoured with all his eloquence to prove that this latter piece of information from the spy must be incorrect. If such a letter had been written by Mrs Trevelyan to Colonel Osborne, it must have been done while he, Stanbury, was staying at the Clock House. This seemed to him to be impossible; but he could hardly explain why it should be impossible. She had written to the man before, and had received him when he came to Nuncombe Putney.

Why was it even improbable that she should have written to him again? Nevertheless, Stanbury felt sure that she had sent no such letter. 'I think I understand her feelings and her mind,' said he; 'and if so, any such correspondence would be incompatible with her previous conduct.' Trevelyan only smiled at this, – or pretended to smile. He would not discuss the question; but believed implicitly what Bozzle had told him in spite of all Stanbury's arguments. 'I can say nothing further,' said Stanbury.

'No, my dear fellow. There is nothing further to be said, except this, that I will have my unfortunate wife removed from the decent protection of your mother's roof with the least possible delay. I feel that I owe Mrs Stanbury the deepest apology for having sent such an inmate to trouble her repose.'

'Nonsense!'

'That is what I feel.'

'And I say that it is nonsense. If you had never sent that wretched blackguard down to fabricate lies at Nuncombe Putney, my mother's repose would have been all right. As it is, Mrs Trevelyan can remain where she is till after Christmas. There is not the least necessity for removing her at once. I only meant to say that the arrangement should not be regarded as altogether permanent. I must go to my work now. Good-bye.'

'Good-bye, Stanbury.'

Stanbury paused at the door, and then once more turned round. 'I suppose it is of no use my saying anything further; but I wish you to understand fully that I regard your wife as a woman much ill-used, and I think you are punishing her, and yourself, too, with a cruel severity for an indiscretion of the very slightest kind.'

27

Mr Trevelyan's Letter to his Wife

Trevelyan, when he was left alone, sat for above a couple of hours contemplating the misery of his position, and endeavouring to teach himself by thinking what ought to be his future conduct. It never occurred to him during these thoughts that it would be well that he should at once take back his wife, either as a matter of duty, or of welfare, for himself or for her. He had taught himself to believe that she had disgraced him; and, though this feeling of disgrace made him so wretched that he wished that he were dead, he would allow himself to make no attempt at questioning the correctness of his conviction. Though he were to be shipwrecked for ever, even that seemed to be preferable to supposing that he had been wrong. Nevertheless, he loved his wife dearly, and, in the white heat of his anger endeavoured to be merciful to her. When Stanbury accused him of severity, he would not condescend to defend himself; but he told himself then of his great mercy. Was he not as fond of his own boy as any other father, and had he not allowed her to take the child because he had felt that a mother's love was more imperious, more craving in its nature, than the love of a father? Had that been severe? And had he not resolved to allow her every comfort which her unfortunate position, – the self-imposed misfortune of her position, – would allow her to enjoy? She had come to him without a shilling; and yet, bad as her treatment of him had been, he was willing to give enough not only to support her, but her sister also, with every comfort. Severe! No; that, at least, was an undeserved accusation. He had been anything but severe. Foolish he might have been, in taking a wife from a home in which she had been unable to learn the discretion of a matron; too trusting he had been, and too generous, – but certainly not severe. But, of course, as he said to himself, a young man like Stanbury would take the part of a woman with whose sister he was in love. Then he turned his thoughts upon Bozzle, and there came over him a crushing feeling of ignominy, shame, moral dirt, and utter degradation, as he reconsidered his dealings with that ingenious gentleman. He was paying a rogue to watch the steps of a man whom he hated, to pry into the home secrets, to read the letters, to bribe the servants, to record the movements of this rival, this successful rival, in his wife's affections! It was a filthy thing, – and yet what could he do? Gentlemen of old, his own grandfather or his father, would have taken such a fellow as Colonel Osborne by the throat and have caned him, and afterwards would have shot him, or have stood to be shot. All that was changed now, – but it was not his fault that it was changed. He was willing enough to risk his life, could any opportunity of risking it in this cause be obtained for him. But were he to cudgel Colonel Osborne, he would be simply arrested, and he would then be told that he had disgraced himself foully by striking a man old enough to be his father!

How was he to have avoided the employment of some such man as Bozzle? He had also employed a gentleman, his friend, Stanbury; and what was the result? The facts were not altered. Even Stanbury did not attempt to deny that there had been a correspondence, and that there had been a visit. But Stanbury was so blind to all impropriety, or pretended such blindness, that he defended that

which all the world agreed in condemning. Of what use had
Stanbury been to him? He had wanted facts, not advice. Stanbury
had found out no facts for him; but Bozzle, either by fair means or
foul, did get at the truth. He did not doubt but that Bozzle was
right about that letter written only yesterday, and received on that
very morning. His wife, who had probably been complaining of her
wrongs to Stanbury, must have retired from that conversation to
her chamber, and immediately have written this letter to her lover!
With such a woman as that what can be done in these days
otherwise than by the aid of such a one as Bozzle? He could not
confine his wife in a dungeon. He could not save himself from the
disgrace of her misconduct, by any rigours of surveillance on his
own part. As wives are managed now-a-days, he could not forbid
to her the use of the post-office, – could not hinder her from seeing
this hypocritical scoundrel, who carried on his wickedness under
the false guise of family friendship. He had given her every chance
to amend her conduct; but, if she were resolved on disobedience,
he had no means of enforcing obedience. The facts, however, it was
necessary that he should know.

And now, what should he do? How should he go to work to
make her understand that she could not write even a letter without
his knowing it; and that if she did either write to the man or see
him he would immediately take the child from her, and provide for
her only in such fashion as the law should demand from him? For
himself, and for his own life, he thought that he had determined
what he would do. It was impossible that he should continue to live
in London. He was ashamed to enter a club. He had hardly a friend
to whom it was not an agony to speak. They who knew him, knew
also of his disgrace, and no longer asked him to their houses. For
days past he had eaten alone, and sat alone, and walked alone. All
study was impossible to him. No pursuit was open to him. He spent
his time in thinking of his wife, and of the disgrace which she had
brought upon him. Such a life as this, he knew, was unmanly and
shameful, and it was absolutely necessary for him that he should in
some way change it. He would go out of England, and would travel,
– if only he could so dispose of his wife that she might be safe from
any possible communication with Colonel Osborne. If that could
be effected, nothing that money could do should be spared for her.
If that could not be effected he would remain at home, – and crush
her.

That night before he went to bed he wrote a letter to his wife,
which was as follows:

Dear Emily,

I have learned, beyond the shadow of a doubt, that you have corresponded with Colonel Osborne since you have been at Nuncombe Putney, and also that you have seen him there. This has been done in direct opposition to my expressed wishes, and I feel myself compelled to tell you that such conduct is disgraceful to you, and disgracing to me. I am quite at a loss to understand how you can reconcile to yourself so flagrant a disobedience of my instructions, and so perverse a disregard to the opinion of the world at large.

But I do not write now for the sake of finding fault with you. It is too late for me to have any hope that I can do so with good effect, either as regards your credit or my happiness. Nevertheless, it is my duty to protect both you and myself from further shame ; and I wish to tell you what are my intentions with that view. In the first place, I warn you that I keep a watch on you. The doing so is very painful to me, but it is absolutely necessary. You cannot see Colonel Osborne, or write to him, without my knowing it. I pledge you my word that in either case, – that is, if you correspond with him or see him, – I will at once take our boy away from you. I will not allow him to remain, even with a mother, who shall so misconduct herself. Should Colonel Osborne address a letter to you, I desire that you will put it under an envelope addressed to me.

If you obey my commands on this head I will leave our boy with you nine months out of every year till he shall be six years old. Such, at least, is my present idea, though I will not positively bind myself to adhere to it. And I will allow you £800 per year for your own maintenance and that of your sister. I am greatly grieved to find from my friend Mr Stanbury that your conduct in reference to Colonel Osborne has been such as to make it necessary that you should leave Mrs Stanbury's house. I do not wonder that it should be so. I shall immediately seek for a future home for you, and when I have found one that is suitable, I will have you conveyed to it.

I must now further explain my purposes, – and I must beg you to remember that I am driven to do so by your direct disobedience to my expressed wishes. Should there be any further communication between you and Colonel Osborne, not only will I take your child away from you, but I will also limit the allowance to be made to you to a bare sustenance. In such case, I shall put the matter into the hands of a lawyer, and shall probably feel myself driven to take steps towards freeing myself from a connection which will be disgraceful to my name.

For myself, I shall live abroad during the greater part of the year. London has become to me uninhabitable, and all English pleasures are distasteful.

Yours affectionately,
Louis Trevelyan

When he had finished this he read it twice, and believed that he had written, if not an affectionate, at any rate a considerate letter. He had no bounds to the pity which he felt for himself in reference to the injury which was being done to him, and he thought that the offers which he was making, both in respect to his child and the money, were such as to entitle him to his wife's warmest gratitude. He hardly recognised the force of the language which he used when he told her that her conduct was disgraceful, and that she had disgraced his name. He was quite unable to look at the whole question between him and his wife from her point of view. He conceived it possible that such a woman as his wife should be told that her conduct would be watched, and that she should be threatened with the Divorce Court, with an effect that should, upon the whole, be salutary. There be men, and not bad men either, and men neither uneducated, or unintelligent, or irrational in ordinary matters, who seem to be absolutely unfitted by nature to have the custody or guardianship of others. A woman in the hands of such a man can hardly save herself or him from endless trouble. It may be that between such a one and his wife, events shall flow on so evenly that no ruling, no constraint is necessary, – that even the giving of advice is never called for by the circumstances of the day. If the man be happily forced to labour daily for his living till he be weary, and the wife be laden with many ordinary cares, the routine of life may run on without storms; – but for such a one, if he be without work, the management of a wife will be a task full of peril. The lesson may be learned at last; he may after years come to perceive how much and how little of guidance the partner of his life requires at his hands; and he may be taught how that guidance should be given; – but in the learning of the lesson there will be sorrow and gnashing of teeth. It was so now with this man. He loved his wife. To a certain extent he still trusted her. He did not believe that she would be faithless to him after the fashion of women who are faithless altogether. But he was jealous of authority, fearful of slights, self-conscious, afraid of the world, and utterly ignorant of the nature of a woman's mind.

He carried the letter with him in his pocket throughout the next morning, and in the course of the day he called upon Lady Milborough. Though he was obstinately bent on acting in accordance with his own views, yet he was morbidly desirous of discussing the grievousness of his position with his friends. He went to Lady Milborough, asking for her advice, but desirous simply of being encouraged by her to do that which he was resolved to do on his own judgment.

'Down, – after her, – to Nuncombe Putney !' said Lady Milborough, holding up both her hands.

'Yes; he has been there. And she has been weak enough to see him.'

'My dear Louis, take her to Naples at once, – at once.'

'It is too late for that now, Lady Milborough.'

'Too late! Oh, no. She has been foolish, indiscreet, disobedient, – what you will of that kind. But, Louis, don't send her away; don't send your young wife away from you. Those whom God has joined together, let no man put asunder.'

'I cannot consent to live with a wife with whom neither my wishes nor my word have the slightest effect. I may believe of her what I please; but, think what the world will believe! I cannot disgrace myself by living with a woman who persists in holding intercourse with a man whom the world speaks of as her lover.'

'Take her to Naples,' said Lady Milborough, with all the energy of which she was capable.

'I can take her nowhere, nor will I see her, till she has given proof that her whole conduct towards me has been altered. I have written a letter to her, and I have brought it. Will you excuse me if I ask you to take the trouble to read it ?'

Then he handed Lady Milborough the letter, which she read very slowly, and with much care.

'I don't think I would – would – would – '

'Would what ?' demanded Trevelyan.

'Don't you think that what you say is a little, – just a little prone to make, – to make the breach perhaps wider ?'

'No, Lady Milborough. In the first place, how can it be wider ?'

'You might take her back, you know; and then if you could only get to Naples !'

'How can I take her back while she is corresponding with this man ?'

'She wouldn't correspond with him at Naples.'

Trevelyan shook his head and became cross. His old friend would not at all do as old friends are expected to do when called upon for advice.

'I think,' said he, 'that what I have proposed is both just and generous.'

'But, Louis, why should there be any separation ?'

'She has forced it upon me. She is headstrong, and will not be ruled.'

'But this about disgracing you. Do you think that you must say that ?'

'I think I must, because it is true. If I do not tell her the truth, who is there that will do so? It may be bitter now, but I think that it is for her welfare.'

'Dear, dear, dear!'

'I want nothing for myself, Lady Milborough.'

'I am sure of that, Louis.'

'My whole happiness was in my home. No man cared less for going out than I did. My child and my wife were everything to me. I don't suppose that I was ever seen at a club in the evening once throughout a season. And she might have had anything that she liked, – anything! It is hard, Lady Milborough; is it not?'

Lady Milborough, who had seen the angry brow, did not dare to suggest Naples again. But yet, if any word might be spoken to prevent this utter wreck of a home, how good a thing it would be! He had got up to leave her, but she stopped him by holding his hand. 'For better, for worse, Louis; remember that.'

'Why has she forgotten it?'

'She is flesh of your flesh, bone of your bone. And for the boy's sake! Think of your boy, Louis. Do not send that letter. Sleep on it, Louis, and think of it.'

'I have slept on it.'

'There is no promise in it of forgiveness after a while. It is written as though you intended that she should never come back to you.'

'That shall be as she behaves herself.'

'But tell her so. Let there be some one bright spot in what you say to her, on which her mind may fix itself. If she be not altogether hardened, that letter will drive her to despair.'

But Trevelyan would not give up the letter, nor indicate by a word that he would reconsider the question of its propriety. He escaped as soon as he could from lady Milborough's room, and almost declared as he did so, that he would never enter her doors again. She had utterly failed to see the matter in the proper light. When she talked of Naples she must surely have been unable to comprehend the extent of the ill-usage to which he, the husband, had been subjected. How was it possible that he would live under the same roof with a wife who claimed to herself the right of receiving visitors of whom he disapproved, – a visitor, – a gentleman, – one whom the world called her lover? He gnashed his teeth and clenched his fist as he thought of his old friend's ignorance of the very first law in a married man's code of laws.

But yet when he was out in the streets he did not post his letter at once; but thought of it throughout the whole day, trying to prove the weight of every phrase that he had used. Once or twice his heart almost relented. Once he had the letter in his hand, that he might tear it. But he did not tear it. He put it back into his pocket, and thought again of his grievance. Surely it was his first duty in such an emergency to be firm!

It was certainly a wretched life that he was leading. In the evening he went all alone to an eating-house for his dinner, and then, sitting with a miserable glass of sherry before him, he again read and re-read the epistle which he had written. Every harsh word that it contained was, in some sort, pleasant to his ear. She had hit him hard, and should he not hit her again? And then, was it not his bounden duty to let her know the truth. Yes; it was his duty to be firm.

So he went out and posted the letter.

28

Great Tribulation*

Trevelyan's letter to his wife fell like a thunderbolt among them at Nuncombe Putney. Mrs Trevelyan was altogether unable to keep it to herself; – indeed she made no attempt at doing so. Her husband had told her that she was to be banished from the Clock House because her present hostess was unable to endure her misconduct, and of course she demanded the reasons of the charge that was thus brought against her. When she first read the letter, which she did in the presence of her sister, she towered in her passion.

'Disgraced him! I have never disgraced him. It is he that has disgraced me. Correspondence! Yes; – he shall see it all. Unjust, ignorant, foolish man! He does not remember that the last instructions he really gave me, were to bid me see Colonel Osborne. Take my boy away! Yes. Of course, I am a woman and must suffer. I will write to Colonel Osborne, and will tell him the truth, and will send my letter to Louis. He shall know how he has ill-treated me! I will not take a penny of his money; – not a penny. Maintain you! I believe he thinks that we are beggars. Leave this house because of my conduct! What can Mrs Stanbury have said? What can any of them have said? I will demand to be told. Free himself from the connection! Oh, Nora, Nora! that it should come to this! – that I should be thus threatened, who have been as innocent as a baby! If it were not for my child, I think that I should destroy myself!'

Nora said what she could to comfort her sister, insisting chiefly on the promise that the child should not be taken away. There was no doubt as to the husband's power in the mind of either of them ; and though, as regarded herself, Mrs Trevelyan would have defied her husband, let his power be what it might, yet she acknowledged to herself that she was in some degree restrained by the fear that she would find herself deprived of her only comfort.

'We must just go where he bids us, – till papa comes,' said Nora.

'And when papa is here, what help will there be then ? He will not let me go back to the islands, – with my boy. For myself I might die, or get out of his way anywhere. I can see that. Priscilla Stanbury is right when she says that no woman should trust herself to any man. Disgraced ! That I should live to be told by my husband that I had disgraced him, – by a lover !'

There was some sort of agreement made between the two sisters as to the manner in which Priscilla should be interrogated respecting the sentence of banishment which had been passed. They both agreed that it would be useless to make inquiry of Mrs Stanbury. If anything had really been said to justify the statement made in Mr Trevelyan's letter, it must have come from Priscilla, and have reached Trevelyan through Priscilla's brother. They, both of them, had sufficiently learned the ways of the house to be sure that Mrs Stanbury had not been the person active in the matter. They went down, therefore, together, and found Priscilla seated at her desk in the parlour. Mrs Stanbury was also in the room, and it had been presumed between the sisters that the interrogation should be made in that lady's absence ; but Mrs Trevelyan was too hot in the matter for restraint, and she at once opened out her budget of grievance.

'I have a letter from my husband,' she said, – and then paused. But Priscilla, seeing from the fire in her eyes that she was much moved, made no reply, but turned to listen to what might further be said. 'I do not know why I should trouble you with his suspicions,' continued Mrs Trevelyan, 'or read to you what he says about – Colonel Osborne.' As she spoke she was holding her husband's letter open in her hands. 'There is nothing in it that you do not know. He says I have corresponded with him. So I have ; – and he shall see the correspondence. He says that Colonel Osborne visited me. He did come to see me and Nora.'

'As any other old man might have done,' said Nora.

'It was not likely that I should openly confess myself to be afraid to see my father's old friend. But the truth is, my husband does not know what a woman is.'

She had begun by declaring that she would not trouble her friend with any statement of her husband's complaints against her ; but now she had made her way to the subject, and could hardly refrain herself. Priscilla understood this, and thought that it would be wise to interrupt her by a word that might bring her back to her original purpose. 'Is there anything,' said she, 'which we can do to help you?'

'To help me? No; – God only can help me. But Louis informs me that I am to be turned out of this house, because you demand that we should go.'

'Who says that?' exclaimed Mrs Stanbury.

'My husband. Listen; this is what he says; – "I am greatly grieved to hear from my friend Mr Stanbury that your conduct in reference to Colonel Osborne has been such as to make it necessary that you should leave Mrs Stanbury's house." Is that true? Is that true?' In her general mode of carrying herself, and of enduring the troubles of her life, Mrs Trevelyan was a strong woman; but now her grief was too much for her, and she burst out into tears. 'I am the most unfortunate woman that ever was born!' she sobbed out through her tears.

'I never said that you were to go,' said Mrs Stanbury.

'But your son has told Mr Trevelyan that we must go,' said Nora, who felt that her sense of injury against Hugh Stanbury was greatly increased by what had taken place. To her mind he was the person most important in the matter. Why had he desired that they should be sent away from the Clock House? She was very angry with him, and declared to herself that she hated him with all her heart. For this man she had sent away that other lover, – a lover who had really loved her! And she had even confessed that it was so!

'There is a misunderstanding about this,' said Priscilla.

'It must be with your brother, then,' said Nora.

'I think not,' said Priscilla. 'I think that it has been with Mr Trevelyan.' Then she went on to explain, with much difficulty, but still with a slow distinctness that was peculiar to her, what had really taken place. 'We have endeavoured,' she said, 'to show you, – my mother and I, – that we have not misjudged you; but it is certainly true that I told my brother that I did not think the arrangement a good one, – quite as a permanence.' It was very difficult, and her cheeks were red as she spoke, and her lips faltered. It was an exquisite pain to her to have to give the pain which her words would convey; but there was no help for it, – as she said to herself more than once at the time, – there was nothing to be done but to tell the truth.

'I never said so,' blurted out Mrs Stanbury, with her usual weakness.

'No, mother. It was my saying. In discussing what was best for us all, with Hugh, I told him, – what I have just now explained.'

'Then of course we must go,' said Mrs Trevelyan, who had gulped down her sobs and was resolved to be firm, – to give way to no more tears, to bear all without sign of womanly weakness.

'You will stay with us till your father comes,' said Priscilla.

'Of course you will,' said Mrs Stanbury, – 'you and Nora. We have got to be such friends, now.'

'No,' said Mrs Trevelyan. 'As to friendship for me, it is out of the question. We must pack up, Nora, and go somewhere. Heaven knows where !'

Nora was now sobbing. 'Why your brother – should want to turn us out, – after he has sent us here – !'

'My brother wants nothing of the kind,' said Priscilla. 'Your sister has no better friend than my brother.'

'It will be better, Nora, to discuss the matter no further,' said Mrs Trevelyan. 'We must go away, – somewhere; and the sooner the better. To be an unwelcome guest is always bad; but to be unwelcome for such a reason as this is terrible.'

'There is no reason,' said Mrs Stanbury; 'indeed there is none.'

'Mrs Trevelyan will understand us better when she is less excited,' said Priscilla. 'I am not surprised that she should be indignant now. I can only say again that we hope you will stay with us till Sir Marmaduke Rowley shall be in England.'

'That is not what your brother means,' said Nora.

'Nor is it what I mean,' said Mrs Trevelyan. 'Nora, we had better go to our own room. I suppose I must write to my husband; indeed, of course I must, that I may send him – the correspondence. I fear I cannot walk out into the street, Mrs Stanbury, and make you quit of me, till I hear from you. And if I were to go to an inn at once, people would speak evil of me; – and I have no money.'

'My dear, how can you think of such a thing !' said Mrs Stanbury.

'But you may be quite sure that we shall be gone within three days, – or four at the furthest. Indeed, I will pledge myself not to remain longer that that, – even though I should have to go to the poor-house. Neither I nor my sister will stay in any family, – to contaminate it. Come, Nora.' And so speaking she sailed out of the room, and her sister followed her.

'Why did you say anything about it ? Oh dear, oh dear ! why did you speak to Hugh ? See what you have done ?'

'I am sorry that I did speak,' replied Priscilla, slowly.

'Sorry ! Of course you are sorry; but what good is that ?'

'But, mother; I do not think that I was wrong. I feel sure that the real fault in all this is with Mr Trevelyan, – as it has been all through. He should not have written to her as he has done.'

'I suppose Hugh did tell him.'

'No doubt; – and I told Hugh; but not after the fashion in which he has told her. I blame myself mostly for this, – that we ever consented to come to this house. We had no business here. Who is to pay the rent?'

'Hugh insisted upon taking it.'

'Yes; – and he will pay the rent; and we shall be a drag upon him, as though he had been fool enough to have a wife and a family of his own. And what good have we done? We had not strength enough to say that that wicked man should not see her when he came; – for he is a wicked man.'

'If we had done that she would have been as bad then as she is now.'

'Mother, we had no business to meddle either with her badness or her goodness. What had we to do with the wife of such a one as Mr Trevelyan, or with any woman who was separated from her husband?'

'It was Hugh who thought we should be of service to them.'

'Yes; – and I do not blame him. He is in a position to be of service to people. He can do work and earn money, and has a right to think and to speak. We have a right to think only for ourselves, and we should not have yielded to him. How are we to get back again out of this house to our cottage?'

'They are pulling the cottage down, Priscilla.'

'To some other cottage, mother. Do you not feel while we are living here that we are pretending to be what we are not? After all, Aunt Stanbury was right, though it was not her business to meddle with us. We should never have come here. That poor woman now regards us as her bitter enemies.'

'I meant to do for the best,' said Mrs Stanbury.

'The fault was mine, mother.'

'But you meant it for the best, my dear.'

'Meaning for the best is trash. I don't know that I did mean it for the best. While we were at the cottage we paid our way and were honest. What is it people say of us now?'

'They can't say any harm.'

'They say that we are paid by the husband to keep his wife, and paid again by the lover to betray the husband.'

'Priscilla!'

'Yes; – it is shocking enough. But that comes of people going out of their proper course. We were too humble and low to have a right to take any part in such a matter. How true it is that while one crouches on the ground, one can never fall.'

The matter was discussed in the Clock House all day, between Mrs Stanbury and Priscilla, and between Mrs Trevelyan and Nora, in their rooms and in the garden; but nothing could come of such discussions. No change could be made till further instructions should have been received from the angry husband; nor could any kind of argument be even invented by Priscilla which might be efficacious in inducing the two ladies to remain at the Clock House, even should Mr Trevelyan allow them to do so. They all felt the intolerable injustice, as it appeared to them, – of their subjection to the caprice of an unreasonable and ill-conditioned man; but to all of them it seemed plain enough that in this matter the husband must exercise his own will, – at any rate, till Sir Marmaduke should be in England. There were many difficulties throughout the day. Mrs Trevelyan would not go down to dinner, sending word that she was ill, and that she would, if she were allowed, have some tea in her own room. And Nora said that she would remain with her sister. Priscilla went to them more than once; and late in the evening they all met in the parlour. But any conversation seemed to be impossible; and Mrs Trevelyan, as she went up to her room at night, again declared that she would rid the house of her presence as soon as possible.

One thing, however, was done on that melancholy day. Mrs Trevelyan wrote to her husband, and enclosed Colonel Osborne's letter to herself, and a copy of her reply. The reader will hardly require to be told that no such further letter had been written by her as that of which Bozzle had given information to her husband. Men whose business it is to detect hidden and secret things, are very apt to detect things which have never been done. What excuse can a detective make even to himself for his own existence if he can detect nothing? Mr Bozzle was an active-minded man, who gloried in detecting, and who, in the special spirit of his trade, had taught himself to believe that all around him were things secret and hidden, which would be within his power of unravelling if only the slightest clue were put in his hand. He lived by the crookednesses of people, and therefore was convinced that straight doings in the world were quite exceptional. Things dark and dishonest, fights fought and races run that they might be lost, plants and crosses, women false to their husbands, sons false to their fathers, daughters to their mothers, servants to their masters, affairs always secret, dark, foul, and fraudulent, were to him the normal condition of life. It was to be presumed that Mrs Trevelyan should continue to correspond with her lover, – that old Mrs Stanbury should betray her trust by conniving at the lover's visit, – that everybody concerned should be steeped to the hips in lies and iniquity. When, therefore, he found at Colonel Osborne's rooms that the Colonel had received a letter with the Lessboro' post-mark, addressed in the handwriting of a woman, he did not scruple to declare that Colonel Osborne had received, on that morning, a letter from Mr Trevelyan's 'lady.' But in sending to her husband what she called with so much bitterness, 'the correspondence,' Mrs Trevelyan had to enclose simply the copy of one short note from herself.

But she now wrote again to Colonel Osborne, and enclosed to her husband, not a copy of what she had written, but the note itself. It was as follows:

Nuncombe Putney, Wednesday, August 10

My dear Colonel Osborne,
My husband has desired me not to see you, or to write to you, or to hear from you again. I must therefore beg you to enable me to obey him, – at any rate, till papa comes to England.

Yours truly,
Emily Trevelyan

And then she wrote to her husband, and in the writing of this letter there was much doubt, much labour, and many changes. We will give it as it was written when completed; –

I have received your letter, and will obey your commands to the best of my power. In order that you may not be displeased by any further unavoidable correspondence between me and Colonel Osborne, I have written to him a note, which I now send to you. I send it that you may forward it. If you do not choose to do so, I cannot be answerable either for his seeing me, or for his writing to me again.

I send also copies of all the correspondence I have had with Colonel Osborne since you turned me out of your house. When he came to call on me, Nora remained with me while he was here. I blush while I write this; – not for myself, but that I should be so suspected as to make such a statement necessary.

You say that I have disgraced you and myself. I have done neither. I am disgraced; – but it is you that have disgraced me. I have never spoken a word or done a thing, as regards you, of which I have cause to be ashamed.

I have told Mrs Stanbury that I and Nora will leave her house as soon as we can be made to know where we are to go. I beg that this may be decided instantly, as else we must walk out into the street without a shelter. After what has been said, I cannot remain here.

My sister bids me say that she will relieve you of all burden respecting herself as soon as possible. She will probably be able to find a home with my aunt, Mrs Outhouse, till papa comes to England. As for myself, I can only say that till he comes, I shall do exactly what you order.

Emily Trevelyan

Nuncombe Putney, August 10

29

Mr and Mrs Outhouse

Both Mr Outhouse and his wife were especially timid in taking upon themselves the cares of other people. Not on that account is it to be supposed that they were bad or selfish. They were both given much to charity, and bestowed both in time and money more than is ordinarily considered necessary even from persons in their position. But what they gave, they gave away from their own quiet hearth. Had money been wanting to the daughters of his wife's brother, Mr Outhouse would have opened such small coffer as he had with a free hand. But he would have much preferred that his benevolence should be used in a way that would bring upon him no further responsibility and no questionings from people whom he did not know and could not understand.

The Rev Oliphant Outhouse had been Rector of St Diddulph's-in-the-East for the last fifteen years, having married the sister of Sir Marmaduke Rowley, – then simply Mr Rowley, with a colonial appointment in Jamaica of £120 per annum, – twelve years before his promotion, while he was a curate in one of the populous borough parishes. He had thus been a London clergyman all his life; but he knew almost as little of London society as though he had held a cure in a Westmoreland valley. He had worked hard, but his work had been altogether among the poor. He had no gift of preaching, and had acquired neither reputation nor popularity. But he could work; – and having been transferred because of that capability to the temporary curacy of St Diddulph's, – out of one diocese into another, – he had received the living from the bishop's hands when it became vacant.

A dreary place was the parsonage of St Diddulph's-in-the-East for the abode of a gentleman. Mr Outhouse had not, in his whole parish, a parishioner with whom he could consort. The greatest men around him were the publicans, and the most numerous were men employed in and around the docks. Dredgers of mud, navvies employed on suburban canals, excavators, loaders and unloaders of cargo, cattle drivers, whose driving, however, was done mostly on board ship, – such and such like were the men who were the fathers of the families of St Diddulph's-in-the-East. And there was there, not far removed from the muddy estuary of a little stream that makes its black way from the Essex marshes among the houses of the poorest of the poor into the Thames, a large commercial establishment for turning the carcasses of horses into manure. Messrs Flowsem and Blurt were in truth the great people of St Diddulph's-in-the-East; but the closeness of their establishment was not an additional attraction to the parsonage. They were liberal, however, with their money, and Mr Outhouse was disposed to think, – custom perhaps having made the establishment less objectionable to him than it was at first, – that St Diddulph's-in-the-East would be more of a Pandemonium than it now was, if by any sanitary law Messrs Flowsem and Blurt were compelled to close their doors. 'Non olet,'* he would say with a grim smile when the charitable cheque of the firm would come punctually to hand on the first Saturday after Christmas.

But such a house as his would be, as he knew, but a poor residence for his wife's nieces. Indeed, without positively saying that he was unwilling to receive them, he had, when he first heard of the breaking up of the house in Curzon Street, shown that he would rather not take upon his shoulders so great a responsibility. He and his wife had discussed the matter between them, and had come to the conclusion that they did not know what kind of things might have been done in Curzon Street. They would think no evil, they said; but the very idea of a married woman with a lover was dreadful to them. It might be that their niece was free from blame. They hoped so. And even though her sin had been of ever so deep a dye, they would take her in, – if it were indeed necessary. But they hoped that such help from them might not be needed. They both knew how to give counsel to a poor woman, how to rebuke a poor man, – how to comfort, encourage, or to upbraid the poor. Practice had told them how far they might go with some hope of doing good; – and at what stage of demoralisation no good from their hands was any longer within the scope of fair expectation. But all this was among the poor. With what words to encourage such a one as their niece Mrs Trevelyan, – to encourage her or to rebuke her, as her conduct might seem to make necessary, – they both felt that they were altogether ignorant. To them Mrs Trevelyan was a fine lady. To Mr Outhouse, Sir Marmaduke had ever been a fine gentleman, given much to worldly things, who cared more for whist and a glass of wine than for anything else, and who thought that he had a good excuse for never going to church in England because he was called upon, as he said, to show himself in the governor's pew always once on Sundays, and frequently twice, when he was at the seat of his government. Sir Marmaduke manifestly looked upon church as a thing in itself notoriously disagreeable. To Mr Outhouse it afforded the great events of the week. And Mrs Outhouse would declare that to hear her husband preach was the greatest joy of her life. It may be understood therefore that though the family connection between the Rowleys and the Outhouses had been kept up with a semblance of affection, it had never blossomed forth into cordial friendship.

When therefore the clergyman of St Diddulph's received a letter from his niece, Nora, begging him to take her into his parsonage till Sir Marmaduke should arrive in the course of the spring, and hinting also a wish that her uncle Oliphant should see Mr Trevelyan and if possible arrange that his other niece should also come to the parsonage, he was very much perturbed in spirit. There was a long consultation between him and his wife before anything could be settled, and it may be doubted whether anything would have been settled, had not Mr Trevelyan himself made his way to the parsonage, on the second day of the family conference. Mr and Mrs Outhouse had both seen the necessity of sleeping upon the matter. They had slept upon it, and the discourse betweem them on the second day was so doubtful in its tone that more sleeping would probably have been necessary had not Mr Trevelyan appeared and compelled them to a decision.

'You must remember that I make no charge against her,' said Trevelyan, after the matter had been discussed for about an hour.

'Then why should she not come back to you?' said Mr Outhouse, timidly.

'Some day she may, – if she will be obedient. But it cannot be now. She has set me at defiance; and even yet it is too clear from the tone of her letter to me that she thinks that she has been right to do so. How could we live together in amity when she addresses me as a cruel tyrant?'

'Why did she go away at first?' asked Mrs Outhouse.

'Because she would compromise my name by an intimacy which I did not approve. But I do not come here to defend myself, Mrs Outhouse. You probably think that I have been wrong. You are her friend; and to you, I will not even say that I have been right. What

I want you to understand is this. She cannot come back to me now. It would not be for my honour that she should do so.'

'But, sir, – would it not be for your welfare, as a Christian?' asked Mr Outhouse.

'You must not be angry with me, if I say that I will not discuss that just now. I did not come here to discuss it.'

'It is very sad for our poor niece,' said Mrs Outhouse.

'It is very sad for me,' said Trevelyan, gloomily; – 'very sad, indeed. My home is destroyed; my life is made solitary; I do not even see my own child. She has her boy with her, and her sister. I have nobody.'

'I can't understand, for the life of me, why you should not live together just like any other people,' said Mrs Outhouse, whose woman's spirit was arising in her bosom. 'When people are married, they must put up with something; – at least, most always.' This she added, lest it might be for a moment imagined that she had had any cause for complaint with her Mr Outhouse.

'Pray excuse me, Mrs Outhouse; but I cannot discuss that. The question between us is this, – can you consent to receive your two nieces till their father's return; – and if so, in what way shall I defray the expense of their living? You will of course understand that I willingly undertake the expense not only of my wife's maintenance and of her sister's also, but that I will cheerfully allow anything that may be required either for their comfort or recreation.'

'I cannot take my nieces into my house as lodgers,' said Mr Outhouse.

'No, not as lodgers; but of course you can understand that it is for me to pay for my own wife. I know I owe you an apology for mentioning it; – but how else could I make my request to you?'

'If Emily and Nora come here they must come as our guests,' said Mrs Outhouse.

'Certainly,' said the clergyman. 'And if I am told they are in want of a home they shall find one here till their father comes. But I am bound to say that as regards the elder I think her home should be elsewhere.'

'Of course it should,' said Mrs Outhouse. 'I don't know anything about the law, but it seems to me very odd that a young woman should be turned out in this way. You say she has done nothing?'

'I will not argue the matter,' said Trevelyan.

'That's all very well, Mr Trevelyan,' said the lady, 'but she's my own niece, and if I don't stand up for her I don't know who will. I never heard such a thing in my life as a wife being sent away after such a fashion as that. We wouldn't treat a cookmaid so; that we wouldn't. As for coming here, she shall come if she pleases, but I shall always say that it's the greatest shame I ever heard of.'

Nothing came of this visit at last. The lady grew in her anger; and Mr Trevelyan, in his own defence, was driven to declare that his wife's obstinate intimacy with Colonel Osborne had almost driven him out of his senses. Before he left the parsonage he was brought even to tears by his own narration of his own misery; — whereby Mr Outhouse was considerably softened, although Mrs Outhouse became more and more stout in the defence of her own sex. But nothing at last came of it. Trevelyan insisted on paying for his wife, wherever she might be placed; and when he found that this would not be permitted to him at the parsonage, he was very anxious to take some small furnished house in the neighbourhood, in which the two sisters might live for the next six months under the wings of their uncle and aunt. But even Mr Outhouse was moved to pleasantry by this suggestion, as he explained the nature of the tenements which were common at St Diddulph's. Two rooms, front and back, they might have for about five-and-sixpence a week in a house with three other families. 'But perhaps that is not exactly what you'd like,' said Mr Outhouse. The interview ended with no result, and Mr Trevelyan took his leave, declaring to himself that he was worse off than the foxes, who have holes in which to lay their heads; — but it must be presumed that his sufferings in this respect were to be by attorney; as it was for his wife, and not for himself, that the necessary hole was now required.

As soon as he was gone Mrs Outhouse answered Nora's letter, and without meaning to be explicit, explained pretty closely what had taken place. The spare bedroom at the parsonage was ready to receive either one or both of the sisters till Sir Marmaduke should be in London, if one or both of them should choose to come. And though there was no nursery at the parsonage, — for Mr and Mrs Outhouse had been blessed with no children, — still room should be made for the little boy. But they must come as visitors, — 'as our own nieces,' said Mrs Outhouse. And she went on to say that she would have nothing to do with the quarrel between Mr Trevelyan and his wife. All such quarrels were very bad, — but as to this quarrel she could take no part either one side or the other. Then she stated that Mr Trevelyan had been at the parsonage, but that no arrangement had been made, because Mr Trevelyan had insisted on paying for their board and lodging.

This letter reached Nuncombe Putney before any reply was received by Mrs Trevelyan from her husband. This was on the

Saturday morning, and Mrs Trevelyan had pledged herself to Mrs Stanbury that she would leave the Clock House on the Monday. Of course, there was no need that she should do so. Both Mrs Stanbury and Priscilla would now have willingly consented to their remaining till Sir Marmaduke should be in England. But Mrs Trevelyan's high spirit revolted against this after all that had been said. She thought that she should hear from her husband on the morrow, but the post on Sunday brought no letter from Trevelyan. On the Saturday they had finished packing up, – so certain was Mrs Trevelyan that some instructions as to her future destiny would be sent to her by her lord.

At last they decided on the Sunday that they would both go at once to St Diddulph's; or perhaps it would be more correct to say that this was the decision of the elder sister. Nora would willingly have yielded to Priscilla's entreaties, and have remained. But Emily declared that she could not, and would not, stay in the house. She had a few pounds, – what would suffice for her journey; and as Mr Trevelyan had not thought proper to send his orders to her, she would go without them. Mrs Outhouse was her aunt, and her nearest relative in England. Upon whom else could she lean in this time of her great affliction? A letter, therefore, was written to Mrs Outhouse, saying that the whole party, including the boy and nurse, would be at St Diddulph's on the Monday evening, and the last cord was put to the boxes.

'I suppose that he is very angry,' Mrs Trevelyan said to her sister, 'but I do not feel that I care about that now. He shall have nothing to complain of in reference to any gaiety on my part. I will see no one. I will have no – correspondence. But I will not remain here after what he has said to me, let him be ever so angry. I declare, as I think of it, it seems to me that no woman was ever so cruelly treated as I have been.' Then she wrote one further line to her husband.

Not having received any orders from you, and having promised Mrs Stanbury that I would leave this house on Monday, I go with Nora to my aunt, Mrs Outhouse, to-morrow.

                                                                    E. T.

On the Sunday evening the four ladies drank tea together, and they all made an effort to be civil, and even affectionate, to each other. Mrs Trevelyan had at last allowed Priscilla to explain how it had come to pass that she had told her brother that it would be better both for her mother and for herself that the existing arrangements should be brought to an end, and there had come to be an agreement between them that they should all part in amity. But the conversation on the Sunday evening was very difficult.

'I am sure we shall always think of you both with the greatest kindness,' said Mrs Stanbury.

'As for me,' said Priscilla, 'your being with us has been a delight that I cannot describe; – only it has been wrong.'

'I know too well,' said Mrs Trevelyan, 'that in our present circumstances we are unable to carry delight with us anywhere.'

'You hardly understand what our life has been,' said Priscilla; 'but the truth is that we had no right to receive you in such a house as this. It has not been our way of living, and it cannot continue to be so. It is not wonderful that people should talk of us. Had it been called your house, it might have been better.'

'And what will you do now?' asked Nora.

'Get out of this place as soon as we can. It is often hard to go back to the right path; but it may always be done, – or at least attempted.'

'It seems to me that I take misery with me wherever I go,' said Mrs Trevelyan.

'My dear, it has not been your fault,' said Mrs Stanbury.

'I do not like to blame my brother,' said Priscilla, 'because he has done his best to be good to us all; – and the punishment will fall heaviest upon him, because he must pay for it.'

'He should not be allowed to pay a shilling,' said Mrs Trevelyan.

Then the morning came, and at seven o'clock the two sisters, with the nurse and child, started for Lessboro' Station in Mrs Crocket's open carriage, the luggage having been sent on in a cart. There were many tears shed, and any one looking at the party would have thought that very dear friends were being torn asunder.

'Mother,' said Priscilla, as soon as the parlour door was shut, and the two were alone together, 'we must take care that we never are brought into such a mistake as that. They who protect the injured should be strong themselves.'

30

Dorothy makes up her Mind

It was true that most ill-natured things had been said at Lessboro' and at Nuncombe Putney about Mrs Stanbury and the visitors at the Clock House, and that these ill-natured things had spread themselves to Exeter. Mrs Ellison of Lessboro', who was not the most good-natured woman in the world, had told Mrs Merton of Nuncombe that she had been told that the Colonel's visit to the lady had been made by express arrangement between the Colonel and Mrs Stanbury. Mrs Merton, who was very good-natured, but not the wisest woman in the world, had declared that any such conduct on the part of Mrs Stanbury was quite impossible. 'What does it matter which it is, – Priscilla or her mother?' Mrs Ellison had said. 'These are the facts. Mrs Trevelyan has been sent there to be out of the way of this Colonel; and the Colonel immediately comes down and sees her at the Clock House. But when people are very poor they do get driven to do almost anything.'

Mrs Merton, not being very wise, had conceived it to be her duty to repeat this to Priscilla; and Mrs Ellison, not being very good-natured, had conceived it to be hers to repeat it to Mrs MacHugh at Exeter. And then Bozzle's coming had become known.

'Yes, Mrs MacHugh, a policeman in mufti down at Nuncombe! I wonder what our friend in the Close here will think about it! I have always said, you know, that if she wanted to keep things straight at Nuncombe, she should have opened her purse-strings.'

From all which it may be understood, that Priscilla Stanbury's desire to go back to their old way of living had not been without reason.

It may be imagined that Miss Stanbury of the Close did not receive with equanimity the reports which reached her. And, of course, when she discussed the matter either with Martha or with Dorothy, she fell back upon her own early appreciation of the folly of the Clock House arrangement. Nevertheless, she had called Mrs Ellison very bad names, when she learned from her friend Mrs MacHugh what reports were being spread by the lady from Lessboro'.

'Mrs Ellison! Yes; we all know Mrs Ellison. The bitterest tongue in Devonshire, and the falsest! There are some people at Lessboro' who would be well pleased if she paid her way there as well as those poor women do at Nuncombe. I don't think much of what Mrs Ellison says.'

'But it is bad about the policeman,' said Mrs MacHugh.

'Of course it's bad. It's all bad. I'm not saying that it's not bad. I'm glad I've got this other young woman out of it. It's all that young man's doing. If I had a son of my own, I'd sooner follow him to the grave than hear him call himself a Radical.'

Then, on a sudden, there came to the Close news that Mrs Trevelyan and her sister were gone. On the very Monday on which they went, Priscilla sent a note on to her sister, in which no special allusion was made to Aunt Stanbury, but which was no doubt written with the intention that the news should be communicated.

'Gone; are they? As it is past wishing that they hadn't come, it's the best thing they could do now. And who is to pay the rent of the house, now they have gone?' As this was a point on which Dorothy was not prepared to trouble herself at present; she made no answer to the question.

Dorothy at this time was in a state of very great perturbation on her own account. The reader may perhaps remember that she had been much startled by a proposition that had been made to her in reference to her future life. Her aunt had suggested to her that she should become – Mrs Gibson. She had not as yet given any answer to that proposition, and had indeed found it to be quite impossible to speak about it at all. But there can be no doubt that the suggestion had opened out to her altogether new views of life. Up to the moment of her aunt's speech to her, the idea of her becoming a married woman had never presented itself to her. In her humility it had not occurred to her that she should be counted as one among the candidates for matrimony. Priscilla had taught her to regard herself, – indeed, they had both so regarded themselves, – as born to eat and drink, as little as might be, and then to die. Now, when she was told that she could, if she pleased, become Mrs Gibson, she was almost lost in a whirl of new and confused ideas. Since her aunt had spoken, Mr Gibson himself had dropped a hint or two which seemed to her to indicate that he also must be in the secret. There had been a party, with a supper, at Mrs Crumbie's, at which both the Miss Frenches had been present. But Mr Gibson had taken her, Dorothy Stanbury, out to supper, leaving both Camilla and Arabella behind him in the drawing-room! During the quarter of an hour afterwards in which the ladies were alone while the gentlemen were eating and drinking, both Camilla and Arabella continued to wreak their vengeance. They asked questions about Mrs Trevelyan, and suggested that Mr Gibson might be sent over to put things right. But Miss Stanbury had heard them, and had fallen upon them with a heavy hand.

'There's a good deal expected of Mr Gibson, my dears,' she said, 'which it seems to me Mr Gibson is not inclined to perform.'

'It is quite indifferent to us what Mr Gibson may be inclined to perform,' said Arabella. 'I'm sure we shan't interfere with Miss Dorothy.'

As this was said quite out loud before all the other ladies, Dorothy was overcome with shame. But her aunt comforted her when they were again at home.

'Laws, my dear; what does it matter? When you're Mrs Gibson, you'll be proud of it all.'

Was it then really written in the book of the Fates that she, Dorothy Stanbury, was to become Mrs Gibson? Poor Dorothy began to feel that she was called upon to exercise an amount of thought and personal decision to which she had not been accustomed. Hitherto, in the things which she had done, or left undone, she had received instructions which she could obey. Had her mother and Priscilla told her positively not to go to her aunt's house, she would have remained at Nuncombe without complaint. Had her aunt since her coming given her orders as to her mode of life, – enjoined, for instance, additional church attendances, or desired her to perform menial services in the house, – she would have obeyed, from custom, without a word. But when she was told that she was to marry Mr Gibson, it did seem to her to be necessary to do something more than obey. Did she love Mr Gibson? She tried hard to teach herself to think that she might learn to love him. He was a nice-looking man enough, with sandy hair, and a head rather bald, with thin lips, and a narrow nose, who certainly did preach drawling sermons; but of whom everybody said that he was a very excellent clergyman. He had a house and an income, and all Exeter had long since decided that he was a man who would certainly marry. He was one of those men of whom it may be said that they have no possible claim to remain unmarried. He was fair game, and unless he surrendered himself to be bagged before long, would subject himself to just and loud complaint. The Miss Frenches had been aware of this, and had thought to make sure of him among them. It was a little hard upon them that the old maid of the Close, as they always called Miss Stanbury, should interfere with them when their booty was almost won. And they felt it to be the harder because Dorothy Stanbury was, as they thought, so poor a creature. That Dorothy herself should have any doubt as to accepting Mr Gibson, was an idea that never occurred to them. But Dorothy had her doubts. When she came to think of it, she remembered that she had never as yet spoken a word to Mr Gibson, beyond such little trifling remarks as are made over a tea-table. She might learn to love him, but she did not think that she loved him as yet.

'I don't suppose all this will make any difference to Mr Gibson,' said Miss Stanbury to her niece, on the morning after the receipt of Priscilla's note stating that the Trevelyan's had left Nuncombe.

Dorothy always blushed when Mr Gibson's name was mentioned, and she blushed now. But she did not at all understand her aunt's allusion. 'I don't know what you mean, aunt,' she said.

'Well, you know, my dear, what they say about Mrs Trevelyan and the Clock House is not very nice. If Mr Gibson were to turn round and say that the connexion wasn't pleasant, no one would have a right to complain.'

The faint customary blush on Dorothy's cheeks which Mr Gibson's name had produced now covered her whole face even up to the roots of her hair. 'If he believes bad of mamma, I'm sure, Aunt Stanbury, I don't want to see him again.'

'That's all very fine, my dear, but a man has to think of himself, you know.'

'Of course he thinks of himself. Why shouldn't he? I dare say he thinks of himself more than I do.'

'Dorothy, don't be a fool. A good husband isn't to be caught every day.'

'Aunt Stanbury, I don't want to catch any man.'

'Dorothy, don't be a fool.'

'I must say it. I don't suppose Mr Gibson thinks of me the least in the world.'

'Psha! I tell you he does.'

'But as for mamma and Priscilla, I never could like anybody for a moment who would be ashamed of them.'

She was most anxious to declare that, as far as she knew herself and her own wishes at present, she entertained no partiality for Mr Gibson, – no feeling which could become partiality even if Mr Gibson was to declare himself willing to accept her mother and her sister with herself. But she did not dare to say so. There was an instinct within her which made it almost impossible to her to express an objection to a suitor before the suitor had declared himself to be one. She could speak out as touching her mother and her sister, – but as to her own feelings she could express neither assent or dissent.

'I should like to have it settled soon,' said Miss Stanbury, in a melancholy voice. Even to this Dorothy could make no reply. What did soon mean? Perhaps in the course of a year or two. 'If it could be arranged by the end of this week, it would be a great comfort to me.' Dorothy almost fell off her chair, and was stricken altogether dumb. 'I told you, I think, that Brooke Burgess is coming here?'

'You said he was to come some day.'

'He is to be here on Monday. I haven't seen him for more than twelve years; and now he's to be here next week! Dear, dear! When I think sometimes of all the hard words that have been spoken, and the harder thoughts that have been in people's minds,

I often regret that the money ever came to me at all. I could have done without it, very well, – very well.'

'But all the unpleasantness is over now, aunt.'

'I don't know about that. Unpleasantness or that kind is apt to rankle long. But I wasn't going to give up my rights. Nobody but a coward does that. They talked of going to law and trying the will, but they wouldn't have got much by that. And then they abused me for two years. When they had done and got sick of it, I told them they should have it all back again as soon as I am dead. It won't be long now. This Burgess is the elder nephew, and he shall have it all.'

'Is not he grateful?'

'No. Why should he be grateful? I don't do it for special love of him. I don't want his gratitude; nor anybody's gratitude. Look at Hugh. I did love him.'

'I am grateful, Aunt Stanbury.'

'Are you, my dear? Then show it by being a good wife to Mr Gibson, and a happy wife. I want to get everything settled while Burgess* is here. If he is to have it, why should I keep him out of it whilst I live? I wonder whether Mr Gibson would mind coming and living here, Dolly?'

The thing was coming so near to her that Dorothy began to feel that she must, in truth, make up her mind, and let her aunt know also how it had been made up. She was sensible enough to perceive that if she did not prepare herself for the occasion she would find herself hampered by an engagement simply because her aunt had presumed that it was out of the question that she should not acquiesce. She would drift into marriage with Mr Gibson against her will. Her greatest difficulty was the fact that her aunt clearly had no doubt on the subject. And as for herself, hitherto her feelings did not, on either side, go beyond doubts. Assuredly it would be a very good thing for her to become Mrs Gibson, if only she could create for herself some attachment for the man. At the present moment her aunt said nothing more about Mr Gibson, having her mind much occupied with the coming of Mr Brooke Burgess.

'I remember him twenty years ago and more; as nice a boy as you would wish to see. His father was the fourth of the brothers. Dear, dear! Three of them are gone; and the only one remaining is old Barty, whom no one ever loved.'

The Burgesses had been great people in Exeter, having been both bankers and brewers there, but the light of the family had paled; and though Bartholomew Burgess, of whom Miss Stanbury declared that no one had ever loved him, still had a share in the bank, it was well understood in the city that the real wealth in the firm of Cropper and Burgess, belonged to the Cropper family. Indeed the most considerable portion of the fortune that had been realised by old Mr Burgess had come into the possession of Miss Stanbury herself. Bartholomew Burgess had never forgiven his brother's will, and between him and Jemima Stanbury the feud was irreconcileable. The next brother, Tom Burgess, had been a solicitor at Liverpool, and had done well there. But Miss Stanbury knew nothing of the Tom Burgesses as she called them. The fourth brother, Harry Burgess, had been a clergyman, and this Brooke Burgess, Junior, who was now coming to the Close, had been left with a widowed mother, the eldest of a large family. It need not now be told at length how there had been ill-blood also between this clergyman and the heiress. There had been attempts at friendship, and at one time Miss Stanbury had received the Rev Harry Burgess and all his family at the Close; – but the attempts had not been successful; and though our old friend had never wavered in her determination to leave the money all back to some one of the Burgess family, and with this view had made a pilgrimage to London some twelve years since, and had renewed her acquaintance with the widow and the children, still there had been no comfortable relations between her and any of the Burgess family. Old Barty Burgess, whom she met in the Close, or saw in the High Street every day of her life, was her great enemy. He had tried his best, – so at least she was convinced, – to drive her out of the pale of society, years upon years ago, by saying evil things of her. She had conquered in that combat. Her victory had been complete, and she had triumphed after a most signal fashion. But this triumph did not silence Barty's tongue, nor soften his heart. When she prayed to be forgiven, as she herself forgave others, she always exempted Barty Burgess from her prayers. There are things which flesh and blood cannot do. She had not liked Harry Burgess' widow, nor, for the matter of that, Harry Burgess himself. When she had last seen the children she had not liked any of them much, and had had her doubts even as to Brooke. But with that branch of the family she was willing to try again. Brooke was now coming to the Close, having received, however, an intimation, that if, during his visit to Exeter, he chose to see his Uncle Barty, any such intercourse must be kept quite in the background. While he remained in Miss Stanbury's house he was to remain there as though there were no such person as Mr Bartholomew Burgess in Exeter.

At this time Brooke Burgess was a man just turned thirty, and was a clerk in the Ecclesiastical Record Office, in Somerset House.

No doubt the peculiar nature and name of the public department to which he was attached had done something to recommend him to Miss Stanbury. Ecclesiastical records were things greatly to be reverenced in her eyes, and she felt that a gentleman who handled them and dealt with them would probably be sedate, gentlemanlike, and conservative. Brooke Burgess, when she had last seen him, was just about to enter upon the duties of the office. Then there had come offence, and she had in truth known nothing of him from that day to this. The visitor was to be at Exeter on the following Monday, and very much was done in preparation of his coming. There was to be a dinner party on that very day, and dinner parties were not common with Miss Stanbury. She had, however, explained to Martha that she intended to put her best foot forward. Martha understood perfectly that Mr Brooke Burgess was to be received as the heir of the property. Sir Peter Mancrudy, the great Devonshire chemist, was coming to dinner, and Mr and Mrs Powel from Haldon, – people of great distinction in that part of the county, – Mrs MacHugh of course; and, equally of course, Mr Gibson. There was a deep discussion between Miss Stanbury and Martha as to asking two of the Cliffords, and Mr and Mrs Noel from Doddis-combeleigh. Martha had been very much in favour of having twelve. Miss Stanbury had declared that with twelve she must have two waiters from the greengrocers, and that two waiters would over-power her own domesticities below stairs. Martha had declared that she didn't care about them any more than if they were puppy dogs. But Miss Stanbury had been quite firm against twelve. She had consented to have ten, – for the sake of artistic arrangement at the table; 'They should be pantaloons and petticoats alternate, you know,' she had said to Martha, – and had therefore asked the Cliffords. But the Cliffords could not come, and then she had declined to make any further attempt. Indeed, a new idea had struck her. Brooke Burgess, her guest, should sit at one end of the table, and Mr Gibson, the clergyman, at the other. In this way the proper alternation would be effected. When Martha heard this, Martha quite understood the extent of the good fortune that was in store for Dorothy. If Mr Gibson was to be welcomed in that way, it could only be in preparation of his becoming one of the family.

And Dorothy herself became aware that she must make up her mind. It was not so declared to her, but she came to understand that it was very probable that something would occur on the coming Monday which would require her to be ready with her answer on that day. And she was greatly tormented by feeling that if she could not bring herself to accept Mr Gibson, – should Mr

Gibson propose to her, as to which she continued to tell herself that the chance of such a thing must be very remote indeed, – but that if he should propose to her, and if she could not accept him, her aunt ought to know that it would be so before the moment came. But yet she could not bring herself to speak to her aunt as though any such proposition were possible.

It happened that during the week, on the Saturday, Priscilla came into Exeter. Dorothy met her sister at the railway station, and then the two walked together two miles and back along the Crediton Road. Aunt Stanbury had consented to Priscilla coming to the Close, even though it was not the day appointed for such visits; but the walk had been preferred, and Dorothy felt that she would be able to ask for counsel from the only human being to whom she could have brought herself to confide the fact that a gentleman was expected to ask her to marry him. But it was not till they had turned upon their walk, that she was able to open her mouth on the subject even to her sister. Priscilla had been very full of their own cares at Nuncombe, and had said much to her determination to leave the Clock House and to return to the retirement of some small cottage. She had already written to Hugh to this effect, and during their walk had said much of her own folly in having consented to so great a change in their mode of life. At last Dorothy struck in with her story.

'Aunt Stanbury wants me to make a change too.'

'What change?' asked Priscilla anxiously.

'It is not my idea, Priscilla, and I don't think that there can be anything in it. Indeed, I'm sure there isn't. I don't see how it's possible that there should be.'

'But what is it, Dolly?'

'I suppose there can't be any harm in my telling you.'

'If it's anything concerning yourself, I should say not. If it concerns Aunt Stanbury, I dare say she'd rather you held your tongue.'

'It concerns me most,' said Dorothy.

'She doesn't want you to leave her, does she?'

'Well; yes; no. By what she said last, – I shouldn't leave her at all in that way. Only I'm sure it's not possible.'

'I am the worst hand in the world, Dolly, at guessing a riddle.'

'You've heard of that Mr Gibson, the clergyman; – haven't you?'

'Of course I have.'

'Well – . Mind, you know, it's only what Aunt Stanbury says. He has never so much as opened his lips to me himself, except to say, "How do you do?" and that kind of thing.'

'Aunt Stanbury wants you to marry him?'

'Yes!'

'Well?'

'Of course it's out of the question,' said Dorothy, sadly.

'I don't see why it should be out of the question,' said Priscilla, proudly. 'Indeed, if Aunt Stanbury has said much about it, I should say that Mr Gibson himself must have spoken to her.'

'Do you think he has?'

'I do not believe that my aunt would raise false hopes,' said Priscilla.

'But I haven't any hopes. That is to say, I had never thought about such a thing.'

'But you think about it now, Dolly?'

'I should never have dreamed about it, only for Aunt Stanbury.'

'But, dearest, you are dreaming of it now, are you not?'

'Only because she says that it is to be so. You don't know how generous she is. She says that if it should be so, she will give me ever so much money; – two thousand pounds!'

'Then I am quite sure that she and Mr Gibson must understand each other.'

'Of course,' said Dorothy, sadly, 'if he were to think of such a thing at all, it would only be because the money would be convenient.'

'Not at all,' said Priscilla, sternly, – with a sternness that was very comfortable to her listener. 'Not at all. Why should not Mr Gibson love you as well as any man ever loved any woman? You are nice-looking,' – Dorothy blushed beneath her hat even at her sister's praise, – 'and good-tempered, and lovable in every way. And I think you are just fitted to make a good wife. And you must not suppose, Dolly, that because Mr Gibson wouldn't perhaps have asked you without the money, that therefore he is mercenary. It so often happens that a gentleman can't marry unless the lady has some money!'

'But he hasn't asked me at all.'

'I suppose he will, dear.'

'I only know what Aunt Stanbury says.'

'You may be sure that he will ask you.'

'And what must I say, Priscilla?'

'What must you say? Nobody can tell you that, dear, but yourself. Do you like him?'

'I don't dislike him.'

'Is that all?'

'I know him so very little, Priscilla. Everybody says he is very good; – and then it's a great thing, isn't it, that he should be a clergyman?'

'I don't know about that.'

'I think it is. If it were possible that I should ever marry any one, I should like a clergyman so much the best.'

'Then you do know what to say to him.'

'No, I don't, Priscilla. I don't know at all.'

'Look here, dearest. What my aunt offers to you is a very great step in life. If you can accept this gentleman I think you would be happy; – and I think, also, which should be of more importance for your consideration, that you would make him happy. It is a brighter prospect, dear Dolly, than to live either with us at Nuncombe, or even with Aunt Stanbury as her niece.'

'But I don't love him, Priscilla?'

'Then give it up, and be as you are, my own own, dearest sister.'

'So I will,' said Dorothy, and at that time her mind was made up.

31

Mr Brooke Burgess

The hour at which Mr Brooke Burgess was to arrive had come round, and Miss Stanbury was in a twitter, partly of expectation, and partly, it must be confessed, of fear. Why there should be any fear she did not herself know, as she had much to give and nothing to expect. But she was afraid, and was conscious of it, and was out of temper because she was ashamed of herself. Although it would be necessary that she should again dress for dinner at six, she had put on a clean cap at four, and appeared at that early hour in one of her gowns which was not customarily in use for home purposes at that early hour. She felt that she was 'an old fool' for her pains, and was consequently cross to poor Dorothy. And there were other reasons for some display of harshness to her niece. Mr Gibson had been at the house that very morning, and Dorothy had given herself airs. At least, so Miss Stanbury thought. And during the last three or four days, whenever Mr Gibson's name had been mentioned, Dorothy had become silent, glum, and almost obstructive. Miss Stanbury had been at the trouble of explaining that she was specially anxious to have that little matter of the engagement settled at once. She knew that she was going to behave with great generosity; – that she was going to sacrifice, not her money only, of which she did not think much, but a considerable portion of her authority, of which she did think a great deal; and that she was about to behave in a manner which demanded much gratitude. But it seemed to her that Dorothy was not in the least grateful. Hugh had proved himself to be 'a mass of ingratitude,' as she was in the habit of saying. None of the Burgesses had ever shown to her any gratitude for promises made to them, or, indeed, for any substantial favours conferred upon them. And now Dorothy, to whom a very seventh heaven of happiness had been opened, – a seventh heaven, as it must be computed in comparison with her low expectations, – now Dorothy was already showing how thankless she could become. Mr Gibson had not yet declared his passion, but he had freely admitted to Miss Stanbury that he was prepared to do so. Priscilla had been quite right in her suggestion that there was a clear understanding between the clergyman and her aunt.

'I don't think he is come after all,' said Miss Stanbury, looking at her watch. Had the train arrived at the moment that it was due, had the expectant visitor jumped out of the railway carriage into a fly, and had the driver galloped up to the Close, it might have been possible that the wheels should have been at the door as Miss Stanbury spoke.

'It's hardly time yet, aunt.'

'Nonsense; it is time. The train comes in at four. I dare say he won't come at all.'

'He is sure to come, aunt.'

'I've no doubt you know all about it better than any one else. You usually do.' Then five minutes were passed in silence. 'Heaven and earth! what shall I do with these people that are coming? And I told them especially that it was to meet this young man! It's the way I am always treated by everybody that I have about me.'

'The train might be ten minutes late, Aunt Stanbury.'

'Yes; – and monkeys might chew tobacco. There; – there's the omnibus at the Cock and Bottle; the omnibus up from the train. Now, of course, he won't come.'

'Perhaps he's walking, Aunt Stanbury.'

'Walking; – with his luggage on his shoulders? Is that your idea of the way in which a London gentleman goes about? And there are two flies, – coming up from the train, of course.' Miss Stanbury was obliged to fix the side of her chair very close to the window in order that she might see that part of the Close in which the vehicles of which she had spoken were able to pass.

'Perhaps they are not coming from the train, Aunt Stanbury.'

'Perhaps a fiddlestick! You have lived here so much longer than I have done that, of course, you must know all about it.' Then there was an interval of another ten minutes, and even Dorothy was beginning to think that Mr Burgess was not coming. 'I've given him up now,' said Miss Stanbury. 'I think I'll send and put them all off.' Just at that moment there came a knock at the door. But there was no cab. Dorothy's conjecture had been right. The London gentleman had walked, and his portmanteau had been carried behind him by a boy. 'How did he get here?' exclaimed Miss Stanbury, as she heard the strange voice speaking to Martha downstairs. But Dorothy knew better than to answer the question.

'Miss Stanbury, I am very glad to see you,' said Mr Brooke Burgess, as he entered the room. Miss Stanbury curtseyed, and then took him by both hands. 'You wouldn't have known me, I dare say,' he continued. 'A black beard and a bald head do make a difference.'

'You are not bald at all,' said Miss Stanbury.

'I am beginning to be thin enough at the top. I am so glad to come to you, and so much obliged to you for having me! How well I remember the old room!'

'This is my niece, Miss Dorothy Stanbury, from Nuncombe Putney.' Dorothy was about to make some formal acknowledgement of the introduction, when Brooke Burgess came up to her, and shook her hand heartily. 'She lives with me,' continued the aunt.

'And what has become of Hugh?' said Brooke.

'We never talk of him,' said Miss Stanbury gravely.

'I hope there's nothing wrong? I hear of him very often in London.'

'My aunt and he don't agree; – that's all,' said Dorothy.

'He has given up his profession as a barrister, – in which he might have lived like a gentleman,' said Miss Stanbury, 'and has taken to writing for a – penny newspaper.'

'Everybody does that now, Miss Stanbury.'

'I hope you don't, Mr Burgess.'

'I! Nobody would print anything that I wrote. I don't write for anything, certainly.'

'I'm very glad to hear it,' said Miss Stanbury.

Brooke Burgess, or Mr Brooke, as he came to be called very shortly by the servants in the house, was a good-looking man, with black whiskers and black hair, which, as he said, was beginning to be thin on the top of his head, and pleasant small bright eyes. Dorothy thought that next to her brother Hugh he was the most good-natured looking man she had ever seen. He was rather below the middle height, and somewhat inclined to be stout. But he would boast that he could still walk his twelve miles in three hours, and would add that as long as he could do that he would never recognise the necessity of putting himself on short commons. He had a well-cut nose, not quite aquiline, but tending that way, a chin with a dimple on it, and as sweet a mouth as ever declared the excellence of a man's temper. Dorothy immediately began to compare him with her brother Hugh, who was to her, of all men, the most godlike. It never occurred to her to make any comparison between Mr Gibson and Mr Burgess. Her brother Hugh was the most godlike of men; but there was something godlike also about the new comer. Mr Gibson, to Dorothy's eyes, was by no means divine.

'I used to call you Aunt Stanbury,' said Brooke Burgess to the old lady; 'am I to go on doing it now?'

'You may call me what you like,' said Miss Stanbury. 'Only, – dear me; – I never did see anybody so much altered.' Before she went up to dress herself for dinner, Miss Stanbury was quite restored to her good humour, as Dorothy could perceive.

The dinner passed off well enough. Mr Gibson, at the head of the table, did, indeed, look very much out of his element, as though he conceived that his position revealed to the outer world those ideas of his in regard to Dorothy, which ought to have been secret for a while longer. There are few men who do not feel ashamed of being paraded before the world as acknowledged suitors, whereas ladies accept the position with something almost of triumph. The lady perhaps regards herself as the successful angler, whereas the gentleman is conscious of some similitude to the unsuccessful fish. Mr Gibson, though he was not yet gasping in the basket, had some presentiment of this feeling, which made his present seat of honour unpleasant to him. Brooke Burgess, at the other end of the table, was as gay as a lark. Mrs MacHugh sat on one side of him, and Miss Stanbury on the other, and he laughed at the two old ladies, reminding them of his former doings in Exeter, – how he had hunted Mrs MacHugh's cat, and had stolen Aunt Stanbury's best apricot jam, till everybody began to perceive that he was quite a success. Even Sir Peter Mancrudy laughed at his jokes, and Mrs Powel, from the other side of Sir Peter, stretched her head forward so that she might become one of the gay party.

'There isn't a word of it true,' said Miss Stanbury. 'It's all pure invention, and a great scandal. I never did such a thing in my life.'

'Didn't you though?' said Brooke Burgess. I remember it as well as if it was yesterday, and old Dr Ball, the prebendary, with the carbuncles on his nose, saw it too!'

'Dr Ball had no carbuncles on his nose,' said Mrs MacHugh. 'You'll say next that I have carbuncles on my nose.'

'He had three. I remember each of them quite well, and so does Sir Peter.'

Then everybody laughed; and Martha, who was in the room, knew that Brooke Burgess was a complete success.

In the meantime Mr Gibson was talking to Dorothy; but Dorothy was endeavouring to listen to the conversation at the other end of the table. 'I found it very dirty on the roads to-day outside the city,' said Mr Gibson.

'Very dirty,' said Dorothy, looking round at Mr Burgess, as she spoke.

'But the pavement in the High Street was dry enough.'

'Quite dry,' said Dorothy. Then there came a peal of laughter from Mrs MacHugh and Sir Peter, and Dorothy wondered whether anybody before had ever made those two steady old people laugh after that fashion.

'I should so like to get a drive with you up to the top of Haldon Hill,' said Mr Gibson. 'When the weather gets fine, that is. Mrs Powel was talking about it.'

'It would be very nice,' said Dorothy.

'You have never seen the view from Haldon Hill yet?' asked Mr Gibson. But to this question Dorothy could make no answer. Miss Stanbury had lifted one of the table-spoons, as though she was going to strike Mr Brooke Burgess with the bowl of it. And this during a dinner party! From that moment Dorothy turned herself round, and became one of the listeners to the fun at the other end of the table. Poor Mr Gibson soon found himself 'nowhere.'

'I never saw a man so much altered in my life,' said Mrs MacHugh, up in the drawing-room. 'I don't remember that he used to be clever.'

'He was a bright boy!' said Miss Stanbury.

'But the Burgesses all used to be such serious, strait-laced people,' said Mrs MacHugh. 'Excellent people,' she added, remembering the source of her friend's wealth; 'but none of them like that.'

'I call him a very handsome man,' said Mrs Powel. 'I suppose he's not married yet?'

'Oh, dear no,' said Miss Stanbury. 'There's time enough for him yet.'

'He'll find plenty here to set their caps at him,' said Mrs MacHugh.

'He's a little old for my girls,' said Mrs Powel, laughing. Mrs Powel was the happy mother of four daughters, of whom the eldest was only twelve.

'There are others who are more forward,' said Mrs MacHugh. 'What a chance it would be for dear Arabella French!'

'Heaven forbid!' said Miss Stanbury.

'And then poor Mr Gibson wouldn't any longer be like the donkey between two bundles of hay,'* said Mrs Powel. Dorothy was quite determined that she would never marry a man who was like a donkey between two bundles of hay.

When the gentlemen came up into the drawing-room Dorothy was seated behind the urn and tea-things at a large table, in such a position as to be approached only at one side. There was one chair at her left hand, but at her right hand there was no room for a seat, – only room for some civil gentleman to take away full cups and bring them back empty. Dorothy was not sufficiently ready-witted to see the danger of this position till Mr Gibson had seated himself in the chair. Then it did seem cruel to her that she should be thus besieged for the rest of the evening as she had been also at dinner. While the tea was being consumed Mr Gibson assisted at the service, asking ladies whether they would have cake or bread and butter; but when all that was over Dorothy was still in her prison, and Mr Gibson was still the jailer at the gate. She soon perceived that everybody else was chatting and laughing, and that Brooke Burgess was the centre of a little circle which had formed itself quite at a distance from her seat. Once, twice, thrice she meditated an escape, but she had not the courage to make the attempt. She did not know how to manage it. She was conscious that her aunt's eye was upon her, and that her aunt would expect her to listen to Mr Gibson. At last she gave up all hope of moving, and was anxious simply that Mr Gibson should confine himself to the dirt of the paths and the noble prospect from Haldon Hill.

'I think we shall have more rain before we have done with it,' he said. Twice before during the evening he had been very eloquent about the rain.

'I dare say we shall,' said Dorothy. And then there came the sound of loud laughter from Sir Peter, and Dorothy could see that he was poking Brooke Burgess in the ribs. There had never been anything so gay before since she had been in Exeter, and now she was hemmed up in that corner, away from it all, by Mr Gibson!

'This Mr Burgess seems to be different from the other Burgesses,' said Mr Gibson.

'I think he must be very clever,' said Dorothy.

'Well; – yes; in a sort of a way. What people call a Merry Andrew.'

'I like people who make me laugh and laugh themselves,' said Dorothy.

'I quite agree with you that laughter is a very good thing, – in its place. I am not at all one of those who would make the world altogether grave. There are serious things, and there must be serious moments.'

'Of course,' said Dorothy.

'And I think that serious conversation upon the whole has more allurements than conversation which when you come to examine it is found to mean nothing. Don't you?'

'I suppose everybody should mean something when he talks.'

'Just so. That is exactly my idea,' said Mr Gibson. 'On all such subjects as that I should be so sorry if you and I did not agree. I really should.' Then he paused, and Dorothy was so confounded by what she conceived to be the dangers of the coming moment that she was unable even to think what she ought to say. She heard Mrs MacHugh's clear, sharp, merry voice, and she heard her aunt's tone of pretended anger, and she heard Sir Peter's continued laughter, and Brooke Burgess as he continued the telling of some story; but her own trouble was too great to allow of her attending to what was going on at the other end of the room. 'There is nothing as to which I am so anxious as that you and I should agree about serious things,' said Mr Gibson.

'I suppose we do agree about going to church,' said Dorothy. She knew that she could have made no speech more stupid, more senseless, more inefficacious; – but what was she to say in answer to such an assurance?

'I hope so,' said Mr Gibson; 'and I think so. Your aunt is a most excellent woman, and her opinion has very great weight with me on all subjects, – even as to matters of church discipline and doctrine, in which, as a clergyman, I am of course presumed to be more at home. But your aunt is a woman among a thousand.'

'Of course I think she is very good.'

'And she is so right about this young man and her property. Don't you think so?'

'Quite right, Mr Gibson.'

'Because, you know, to you, of course, being her near relative, and the one she has singled out as the recipient of her kindness, it might have been cause for some discontent.'

'Discontent to me, Mr Gibson!'

'I am quite sure your feelings are what they ought to be. And for myself, if I ever were, – that is to say, supposing I could be in any way interested – . But perhaps it is premature to make any suggestion on that head at present.'

'I don't at all understand what you mean, Mr Gibson.'

'I thought that perhaps I might take this opportunity of expressing – . But, after all, the levity of the moment is hardly in accordance with the sentiments which I should wish to express.'

'I think that I ought to go to my aunt now, Mr Gibson, as perhaps she might want something.' Then she did push back her chair and stand upon her legs, – and Mr Gibson, after pausing for a moment, allowed her to escape. Soon after that the visitors went, and Brooke Burgess was left in the drawing-room with Miss Stanbury and Dorothy.

'How well I recollect all the people,' said Brooke; 'Sir Peter, and old Mrs MacHugh; and Mrs Powel, who then used to be called the beautiful Miss Noel. And I remember every bit of furniture in the room.'

'Nothing changed except the old woman, Brooke,' said Miss Stanbury.

'Upon my word you are the least changed of all, – except that you don't seem to be so terrible as you were then.'

'Was I very terrible, Brooke?'

'My mother had told me, I fancy, that I was never to make a noise, and be sure not to break any of the china. You were always very good-natured, and when you gave me a silver watch I could hardly believe the extent of my own bliss.'

'You wouldn't care about a watch from an old woman now, Brooke?'

'You try me. But what rakes you are here! It's past eleven o'clock, and I must go and have a smoke.'

'Have a what?' said Miss Stanbury, with a startled air.

'A smoke. You needn't be frightened, I don't mean in the house.'

'No; – I hope you don't mean that.'

'But I may take a turn round the Close with a pipe; – mayn't I?'

'I suppose all young men do smoke now,' said Miss Stanbury, sorrowfully.

'Every one of them; and they tell me that the young women mean to take to it before long.'

'If I saw a young woman smoking, I should blush for my sex; and though she were the nearest and dearest that I had, I would never speak to her; – never. Dorothy, I don't think Mr Gibson smokes.'

'I'm sure I don't know, aunt.'

'I hope he doesn't. I do hope that he does not. I cannot understand what pleasure it is that men take in making chimneys of themselves, and going about smelling so that no one can bear to come near them.'

Brooke merely laughed at this, and went his way, and smoked his pipe out in the Close, while Martha sat up to let him in when he had finished it. Then Dorothy escaped at once to her room, fearful of being questioned by her aunt about Mr Gibson. She had, she thought now, quite made up her mind. There was nothing in Mr Gibson that she liked. She was by no means so sure as she had been when she was talking to her sister, that she would prefer a clergyman to any one else. She had formed no strong ideas on the subject of love-making, but she did think that any man who really cared for her, would find some other way of expressing his love than that which Mr Gibson had adopted. And then Mr Gibson had spoken to her about her aunt's money in a way that was distasteful to her. She thought that she was quite sure that if he should ask her, she would not accept him.

She was nearly undressed, nearly safe for the night, when there came a knock at the door, and her aunt entered the room. 'He has come in,' said Mrs Stanbury.

'I suppose he has had his pipe, then.'

'I wish he didn't smoke. I do wish he didn't smoke. But I suppose an old woman like me is only making herself a fool to care about such things. If they all do it I can't prevent them. He seems to be a very nice young man – in other things; does he not, Dolly?'

'Very nice indeed, Aunt Stanbury.'

'And he has done very well in his office. And as for his saying that he must smoke, I like that a great deal better than doing it on the sly.'

'I don't think Mr Burgess would do anything on the sly, aunt.'

'No, no; I don't think he would. Dear me; he's not at all like what I fancied.'

'Everybody seemed to like him very much.'

'Didn't they? I never saw Sir Peter so much taken. And there was quite a flirtation between him and Mrs MacHugh. And now, my dear, tell me about Mr Gibson.'

'There is nothing to tell, Aunt Stanbury.'

'Isn't there? From what I saw going on, I thought there would be something to tell. He was talking to you the whole evening.'

'As it happened he was sitting next to me, – of course.'

'Indeed he was sitting next to you; – so much so that I thought everything would be settled.'

'If I tell you something, Aunt Stanbury, you mustn't be angry with me.'

'Tell me what? What is it you have to tell me?'

'I don't think I shall ever care for Mr Gibson; – not in that way.'

'Why not, Dorothy?'

'I'm sure he doesn't care for me. And I don't think he means it.'

'I tell you he does mean it. Mean it! Why, I tell you it has all been settled between us. Since I first spoke to you I have explained to him exactly what I intend to do. He knows that he can give up his house and come and live here. I am sure he must have said something about it to you to-night.'

'Not a word, Aunt Stanbury.'

'Then he will.'

'Dear aunt, I do so wish you would prevent it. I don't like him. I don't indeed.'

'Not like him!'

'No; – I don't care for him a bit, and I never shall. I can't help it, Aunt Stanbury. I thought I would try, but I find it would be impossible. You can't want me to marry a man if I don't love him.'

'I never heard of such a thing in my life. Not love him! And why shouldn't you love him? He's a gentleman. Everybody respects him. He'll have plenty to make you comfortable all your life! And then why didn't you tell me before?'

'I didn't know, Aunt Stanbury. I thought that perhaps – '

'Perhaps what?'

'I could not say all at once that I didn't care for him, when I had never so much as thought about it for a moment before.'

'You haven't told him this?'

'No, I have not told him. I couldn't begin by telling him, you know.'

'Then I must pray that you will think about it again. Have you imagined what a great thing for you it would be to be established for life, – so that you should never have any more trouble again about a home, or about money, or anything? Don't answer me now, Dorothy, but think of it. It seemed to me that I was doing such an excellent thing for both of you.' So saying Miss Stanbury left the room, and Dorothy was enabled to obey her, at any rate, in one matter. She did think of it. She laid awake thinking of it almost all the night. But the more she thought of it, the less able was she to realise to herself any future comfort or happiness in the idea of becoming Mrs Gibson.

32

The 'Full Moon' at St Diddulph's

The receipt of Mrs Trevelyan's letter on that Monday morning was a great surprise both to Mr and Mrs Outhouse. There was no time for any consideration, no opportunity for delaying their arrival till they should have again referred the matter to Mr Trevelyan. Their two nieces were to be with them on that evening, and even the telegraph wires, if employed with such purpose, would not be quick enough to stop their coming. The party, as they knew, would have left Nuncombe Putney before the arrival of the letter at the parsonage of St Diddulph's. There would have been nothing in this to have caused vexation, had it not been decided between Trevelyan and Mr Outhouse that Mrs Trevelyan was not to find a home at the parsonage. Mr Outhouse was greatly afraid of being so entangled in the matter as to be driven to take the part of the wife against the husband; and Mrs Outhouse, though she was full of indignation against Trevelyan, was at the same time not free from anger in regard to her own niece. She more than once repeated that most unjust of all proverbs, which declares that there is never smoke without fire, and asserted broadly that she did not like to be with people who could not live at home, husbands with wives, and wives with husbands, in a decent, respectable manner. Nevertheless the preparations went on busily, and when the party arrived at seven o'clock in the evening, two rooms had been prepared close to each other, one for the two sisters, and the other for the child and nurse, although poor Mr Outhouse himself was turned out of his own little chamber in order that the accommodation might be given. They were all very hot, very tired, and very dusty, when the cab reached the parsonage. There had been the preliminary drive from Nuncombe Putney to Lessboro'. Then the railway journey from thence to the Waterloo Bridge Station* had been long. And it had seemed to them that the distance from the station to St Diddulph's had been endless. When the cabman was told whither he was to go, he looked doubtingly at his poor old horse, and then at the luggage which he was required to pack on the top of his cab, and laid himself out for his work with a full understanding that it would not be accomplished without considerable difficulty. The cabman made it twelve miles from Waterloo Bridge to St Diddulph's, and suggested that extra passengers and parcels would make the fare up to ten and six. Had he named double as much Mrs Trevelyan would have assented. So great was the fatigue, and so wretched the occasion, that there was sobbing and crying in the cab, and when at last the parsonage was reached, even the nurse was hardly able to turn her hand to anything. The poor wanderers were made welcome on that evening without a word of discussion as to the cause of their coming. 'I hope you are not angry with us, Uncle Oliphant,' Emily Trevelyan had said, with tears in her eyes. 'Angry with you, my dear; – for coming to our house! How could I be angry with you?' Then the travellers were hurried up-stairs by Mrs Outhouse, and the master of the parsonage was left alone for a while. He certainly was not angry, but he was ill at ease, and unhappy. His guests would probably remain with him for six or seven months. He had resolutely refused all payment from Mr Trevelyan, but, nevertheless, he was a poor man. It is impossible to conceive that a clergyman in such a parish as St Diddulph's, without a private income, should not be a poor man. It was but a hand-to-mouth existence which he lived, paying his way as his money came to him, and sharing the proceeds of his parish with the poor. He was always more or less in debt. That was quite understood among the tradesmen. And the butcher who trusted him, though he was a bad churchman, did not look upon the parson's account as he did on other debts. He would often hint to Mr Outhouse that a little money ought to be paid, and then a little money would be paid. But it was never expected that the parsonage bill should be settled. In such a household the arrival of four guests, who were expected to remain for an almost indefinite number of months, could not be regarded without dismay. On that first evening, Emily and Nora did come down to tea, but they went up again to their rooms almost immediately afterwards; and Mr Outhouse found that many hours of solitary meditation were allowed to him on the occasion. 'I suppose your brother has been told all about it,' he said to his wife, as soon as they were together on that evening.

'Yes; – he has been told. She did not write to her mother till after she had got to Nuncombe Putney. She did not like to speak about her troubles while there was a hope that things might be made smooth.'

'You can't blame her for that, my dear.'

'But there was a month lost, or nearly. Letters go only once a month. And now they can't hear from Marmaduke or Bessy,' – Lady Rowley's name was Bessy, – 'till the beginning of September.'

'That will be in a fortnight.'

'But what can my brother say to them? He will suppose that they are still down in Devonshire.'

'You don't think he will come at once?'

'How can he, my dear? He can't come without leave, and the

expense would be ruinous. They would stop his pay, and there would be all manner of evils. He is to come in the spring, and they must stay here till he comes.' The parson of St Diddulph's sighed and groaned. Would it not have been almost better that he should have put his pride in his pocket, and have consented to take Mr Trevelyan's money?

On the second morning Hugh Stanbury called at the parsonage, and was closeted for a while with the parson. Nora had heard his voice in the passage, and every one in the house knew who it was that was talking to Mr Outhouse, in the little back parlour that was called a study. Nora was full of anxiety. Would he ask to see them, – to see her? And why was he there so long? 'No doubt he has brought a message from Mr Trevelyan,' said her sister. 'I dare say he will send word that I ought not to have come to my uncle's house.' Then, at last, both Mr Outhouse and Hugh Stanbury came into the room in which they were all sitting. The greetings were cold and unsatisfactory, and Nora barely allowed Hugh to touch the tip of her fingers. She was very angry with him, and yet she knew that her anger was altogether unreasonable. That he had caused her to refuse a marriage that had so much to attract her was not his sin; – not that; but that, having thus overpowered her by his influence, he should then have stopped. And yet Nora had told herself twenty times that it was quite impossible that she should become Hugh Stanbury's wife; – and that, were Hugh Stanbury to ask her, it would become her to be indignant with him, for daring to make a proposition so outrageous. And now she was sick at heart, because he did not speak to her!

He had, of course, come to St Diddulph's with a message from Trevelyan, and his secret was soon told to them all. Trevelyan himself was up-stairs in the sanded parlour of the Full Moon public-house, round the corner. Mrs Trevelyan, when she heard this, clasped her hands and bit her lips. What was he there for? If he wanted to see her, why did he not come boldly to the parsonage? But it soon appeared that he had no desire to see his wife. 'I am to take Louey to him,' said Hugh Stanbury, 'if you will allow me.'

'What; – to be taken away from me!' exclaimed the mother. But Hugh assured her that no such idea had been formed; that he would have concerned himself in no such stratagem, and that he would himself undertake to bring the boy back again within an hour. Emily was, of course, anxious to be informed what other message was to be conveyed to her; but there was no other message – no message either of love or of instruction.

'Mr Stanbury,' said the parson, 'has left something in my hands for you.' This 'something' was given over to her as soon as Stanbury had left the house, and consisted of cheques for various small sums, amounting in all to £200. 'And he hasn't said what I am to do with it?' Emily asked of her uncle. Mr Outhouse declared that the cheques had been given to him without any instructions on that head. Mr Trevelyan had simply expressed his satisfaction that his wife should be with her uncle and aunt, had sent the money, and had desired to see the child.

The boy was got ready, and Hugh walked with him in his arms round the corner, to the Full Moon. He had to pass by the bar, and the barmaid and the potboy looked at him very hard. 'There's a young 'ooman has to do with that ere little game,' said the potboy. 'And it's two to one the young 'ooman has the worst of it,' said the barmaid. 'They mostly does,' said the potboy, not without some feeling of pride in the immunities of his sex. 'Here he is,' said Hugh, as he entered the parlour. 'My boy, there's papa.' The child at this time was more than a year old, and could crawl about and use his own legs with the assistance of a finger to his little hand, and could utter a sound which the fond mother interpreted to mean papa; for with all her hot anger against her husband, the mother was above all things anxious that her child should be taught to love his father's name. She would talk of her separation from her husband as though it must be permanent; she would declare to her sister how impossible it was that they should ever again live together; she would repeat to herself over and over the tale of the injustice that had been done to her, assuring herself that it was out of the question that she should ever pardon the man; but yet, at the bottom of her heart, there was a hope that the quarrel should be healed before her boy would be old enough to understand the nature of quarrelling. Trevelyan took the child on to his knee, and kissed him; but the poor little fellow, startled by his transference from one male set of arms to another, confused by the strangeness of the room, and by the absence of things familiar to his sight, burst out into loud tears. He had stood the journey round the corner in Hugh's arms manfully, and, though he had looked about him with very serious eyes, as he passed through the bar, he had borne that, and his carriage up the stairs; but when he was transferred to his father, whose air, as he took the boy, was melancholy and lugubrious in the extreme, the poor little fellow could endure no longer a mode of treatment so unusual, and, with a grimace which for a moment or two threatened the coming storm, burst out with an infantile howl. 'That's how he has been taught,' said Trevelyan.

'Nonsense,' said Stanbury. 'He's not been taught at all. It's Nature.'

'Nature that he should be afraid of his own father! He did not cry when he was with you.'

'No; – as it happened, he did not. I played with him when I was at Nuncombe; but, of course, one can't tell when a child will cry, and when it won't.'

'My darling, my dearest, my own son!' said Trevelyan, caressing the child, and trying to comfort him; but the poor little fellow only cried the louder. It was now nearly two months since he had seen his father, and, when age is counted by months only, almost everything may be forgotten in six weeks. 'I suppose you must take him back again,' said Trevelyan, sadly.

'Of course, I must take him back again. Come along, Louey, my boy.'

'It is cruel; – very cruel,' said Trevelyan. 'No man living could love his child better than I love mine; – or, for the matter of that, his wife. It is very cruel.'

'The remedy is in your own hands, Trevelyan,' said Stanbury, as he marched off with the boy in his arms.

Trevelyan had now become so accustomed to being told by everybody that he was wrong, and was at the same time so convinced that he was right, that he regarded the perversity of his friends as a part of the persecution to which he was subjected. Even Lady Milborough, who objected to Colonel Osborne quite as strongly as did Trevelyan himself, even she blamed him now, telling him that he had done wrong to separate himself from his wife. Mr Bideawhile, the old family lawyer, was of the same opinion. Trevelyan had spoken to Mr Bideawhile as to the expediency of making some lasting arrangement for a permanent maintenance for his wife; but the attorney had told him that nothing of the kind could be held to be lasting. It was clearly the husband's duty to look forward to a reconciliation, and Mr Bideawhile became quite severe in the tone of rebuke which he assumed. Stanbury treated him almost as though he were a madman. And as for his wife herself, – when she wrote to him she would not even pretend to express any feeling of affection. And yet, as he thought, no man had ever done more for a wife. When Stanbury had gone with the child, he sat waiting for him in the parlour of the public-house, as miserable a man as one could find. He had promised himself something that should be akin to pleasure in seeing his boy; – but it had been all disappointment and pain. What was it that they expected him to do? What was it that they desired? His wife had behaved with such indiscretion as almost to have compromised his honour; and in return for that he was to beg her pardon, confess himself to have done wrong, and allow her to return in triumph! That was the light in which he regarded his own position; but he promised to himself that let his own misery be what it might he would never so degrade him. The only person who had been true to him was Bozzle. Let them all look to it. If there were any further intercourse between his wife and Colonel Osborne, he would take the matter into open court, and put her away publicly, let Mr Bideawhile say what he might. Bozzle should see to that; — and as to himself, he would take himself out of England and hide himself abroad. Bozzle should know his address, but he would give it to no one else. Nothing on earth should make him yield to a woman who had ill-treated him, — nothing but confession and promise of amendment on her part. If she would acknowledge and promise, then he would forgive all, and the events of the last four months should never again be mentioned by him. So resolving he sat and waited till Stanbury should return to him.

When Stanbury got back to the parsonage with the boy he had nothing to do but to take his leave. He would fain have asked permission to come again, could he have invented any reason for doing so. But the child was taken from him at once by its mother, and he was left alone with Mr Outhouse. Nora Rowley did not even show herself, and he hardly knew how to express sympathy and friendship for the guests at the parsonage, without seeming to be untrue to his friend Trevelyan. 'I hope all this may come to an end soon,' he said.

'I hope it may, Mr Stanbury,' said the clergyman; 'but to tell you the truth, it seems to me that Mr Trevelyan is so unreasonable a man, so much like a madman indeed, that I hardly know how to look forward to any future happiness for my niece.' This was spoken with the utmost severity that Mr Outhouse could assume.

'And yet no man loves his wife more tenderly.'

'Tender love should show itself by tender conduct, Mr Stanbury. What has he done to his wife? He has blackened her name among all his friends and hers, he has turned her out of his house, he has reviled her, — and then thinks to prove how good he is by sending her money. The only possible excuse is that he must be mad.'

Stanbury went back to the Full Moon, and retraced his steps with his friend towards Lincoln's Inn. Two minutes took him from the parsonage to the public-house, but during these two minutes he resolved that he would speak his mind roundly to Trevelyan as they returned home. Trevelyan should either take his wife back again at once, or else he, Stanbury, would have no more to do with him. He said nothing till they had threaded together the maze of streets which led them from the neighbourhood of the church of St Diddulph's into the straight way of the Commercial Road. Then he began. 'Trevelyan,' said he, 'you are wrong in all this from beginning to end.'

'What do you mean?'

'Just what I say. If there was anything in what your wife did to offend you, a soft word from you would have put it all right.'

'A soft word! How do you know what soft words I used?'

'A soft word now would do it. You have only to bid her come back to you, and let bygones be bygones, and all would be right. Can't you be man enough to remember that you are a man?'

'Stanbury, I believe you want to quarrel with me.'

'I tell you fairly that I think that you are wrong.'

'They have talked you over to their side.'

'I know nothing about sides. I only know that you are wrong.'

'And what would you have me do?'

'Go and travel together for six months.' Here was Lady Milborough's receipt again! 'Travel together for a year if you will. Then come back and live where you please. People will have forgotten it; – or if they remember it, what matters? No sane person can advise you to go on as you are doing now.'

But it was of no avail. Before they had reached the Bank the two friends had quarrelled and had parted. Then Trevelyan felt that there was indeed no one left to him but Bozzle. On the following morning he saw Bozzle, and on the evening of the next day he was in Paris.

33

Hugh Stanbury Smokes Another Pipe

Trevelyan was gone, and Bozzle alone knew his address. During the first fortnight of her residence at St Diddulph's Mrs Trevelyan received two letters from Lady Milborough, in both of which she was recommended, indeed tenderly implored, to be submissive to her husband. 'Anything,' said Lady Milborough, 'is better than separation.' In answer to the second letter Mrs Trevelyan told the old lady that she had no means by which she could show any submission to her husband, even if she were so minded. Her husband had gone away, she did not know whither, and she had no means by which she could communicate with him. And then came a packet to her from her father and mother, despatched from the islands after the receipt by Lady Rowley of the melancholy tidings of the journey to Nuncombe Putney. Both Sir Marmaduke and Lady Rowley were full of anger against Trevelyan, and wrote as though the husband could certainly be brought back to a sense of his duty, if they only were present. This packet had been at Nuncombe Putney, and contained a sealed note from Sir Marmaduke addressed to Mr Trevelyan. Lady Rowley explained that it was impossible that they should get to England earlier than in the spring. 'I would come myself at once and leave papa to follow,' said Lady Rowley, 'only for the children. If I were to bring them, I must take a house for them, and the expense would ruin us. Papa has written to Mr Trevelyan in a way that he thinks will bring him to reason.'

But how was this letter, by which the husband was to be brought to reason, to be put into the husband's hands? Mrs Trevelyan applied to Mr Bideawhile and to Lady Milborough, and to Stanbury, for Trevelyan's address; but was told by each of them that nothing was known of his whereabouts. She did not apply to Mr Bozzle, although Mr Bozzle was more than once in her neighbourhood; but as yet she knew nothing of Mr Bozzle. The replies from Mr Bideawhile and from Lady Milborough came by the post; but Hugh Stanbury thought that duty required him to make another journey to St Diddulph's and carry his own answer with him.

And on this occasion Fortune was either very kind to him, – or very unkind. Whichever it was, he found himself alone for a few seconds in the parsonage parlour with Nora Rowley. Mr Outhouse was away at the time. Emily had gone up-stairs for the boy; and Mrs Outhouse, suspecting nothing, had followed her. 'Miss Rowley,' said he, getting up from his seat, 'if you think it will do any good I will follow Trevelyan till I find him.'

'How can you find him? Besides, why should you give up your own business?'

'I would do anything – to serve your sister.' This he said with hesitation in his voice, as though he did not dare to speak all that he desired to have spoken.

'I am sure that Emily is very grateful,' said Nora; 'but she would not wish to give you such trouble as that.'

'I would do anything for your sister,' he repeated, ' – for your sake, Miss Rowley.' This was the first time that he had ever spoken a word to her in such a strain, and it would be hardly too much to say that her heart was sick for some such expression. But now that it had come, though there was a sweetness about it that was delicious to her, she was absolutely silenced by it. And she was at once not only silent, but stern, rigid, and apparently cold. Stanbury could not but feel as he looked at her that he had offended her. 'Perhaps I ought not to say as much,' said he; 'but it is so.'

'Mr Stanbury,' said she, 'that is nonsense. It is of my sister, not of me, that we are speaking.'

Then the door was opened and Emily came in with her child, followed by her aunt. There was no other opportunity, and perhaps it was well for Nora and for Hugh that there should have been no other. Enough had been said to give her comfort; and more might have led to his discomposure. As to that matter on which he was presumed to have come to St Diddulph's, he could do nothing. He did not know Trevelyan's address, but did know that Trevelyan had abandoned the chambers in Lincoln's Inn. And then he found himself compelled to confess that he had quarrelled with Trevelyan, and that they had parted in anger on the day of their joint visit to the East. 'Everybody who knows him must quarrel with him,' said Mrs Outhouse. Hugh when he took his leave was treated by them all as a friend who had been gained. Mrs Outhouse was gracious to him. Mrs Trevelyan whispered a word to him of her own trouble. 'If I can hear anything of him, you may be sure that I will let you know,' he said. Then it was Nora's turn to bid him adieu. There was nothing to be said. No word could be spoken before others that should be of any avail. But as he took her hand in his he remembered the reticence of her fingers on that former day, and thought that he was sure there was a difference.

On this occasion he made his journey back to the end of Chancery Lane on the top of an omnibus; and as he lit his little pipe, disregarding altogether the scrutiny of the public, thoughts passed through his mind similar to those in which he had indulged as he sat smoking on the corner of the churchyard wall at Nuncombe Putney. He declared to himself that he did love this girl; and as it was so, would it not be better, at any rate more manly, that he should tell her so honestly, than go on groping about with half-expressed words when he saw her, thinking of her and yet hardly daring to go near her, bidding himself to forget her although he knew that such forgetting was impossible, hankering after the sound of her voice and the touch of her hand, and something of the tenderness of returned affection, – and yet regarding her as a prize altogether out of his reach! Why should she be out of his reach? She had no money, and he had not a couple of hundred pounds in the world. But he was earning an income which would give them both shelter and clothes and bread and cheese.

What reader is there, male or female, of such stories as is this, who has not often discussed in his or her own mind the different sides of this question of love and marriage? On either side enough may be said by any arguer to convince at any rate himself. It must be wrong for a man, whose income is both insufficient and precarious also, not only to double his own cares and burdens, but to place the weight of that doubled burden on other shoulders besides his own, – on shoulders that are tender and soft, and ill adapted to the carriage of any crushing weight. And then that doubled burden, – that burden of two mouths to be fed, of two backs to be covered, of two minds to be satisfied, is so apt to double itself again and again. The two so speedily become four, and six! And then there is the feeling that that kind of semi-poverty, which has in itself something of the pleasantness of independence, when it is borne by a man alone, entails the miseries of a draggle-tailed and querulous existence when it is imposed on a woman who has in her own home enjoyed the comforts of affluence. As a man thinks of all this, if he chooses to argue with himself on that side, there is enough in the argument to make him feel that not only as a wise man but as an honest man, he had better let the young lady alone. She is well as she is, and he sees around him so many who have tried the chances of marriage and who are not well! Look at Jones with his wan, worn wife and his five children, Jones who is not yet thirty, of whom he happens to know that the wretched man cannot look his doctor in the face, and that the doctor is as necessary to the man's house as is the butcher! What heart can Jones have for his work with such a burden as this upon his shoulders? And so the thinker, who argues on that side, resolves that the young lady shall go her own way for him.

But the arguments on the other side are equally cogent, and so much more alluring! And they are used by the same man with reference to the same passion, and are intended by him to put himself right in his conduct in reference to the same dear girl. Only the former line of thoughts occurred to him on a Saturday, when he was ending his week rather gloomily, and this other way of thinking on the same subject has come upon him on a Monday, as he is beginning his week with renewed hope. Does this young girl of his heart love him? And if so, their affection for each other being thus reciprocal, is she not entitled to an expression of her opinion and her wishes on this difficult subject? And if she be willing to run the risk and to encounter the dangers, – to do so on his behalf, because she is willing to share everything with him, – is it becoming in him, a man, to fear what she does not fear? If she be not willing let her say so. If there be any speaking, he must speak first; – but she is entitled, as much as he is, to her own ideas respecting their great outlook into the affairs of the world. And then is it not manifestly God's ordinance that a man should live together with a woman? How poor a creature does the man become who has shirked his duty in this respect, who has done nothing to keep the world going, who has been willing to ignore all affection so that he might avoid all burdens, and who has put into his own belly every good thing that has come to him, either by the earning of his own hands or from the bounty and industry of others! Of course there is a risk; but what excitement is there in anything in which there is none? So on the Tuesday he speaks his mind to the young lady, and tells her candidly that there will be potatoes for the two of them, – sufficient, as he hopes, of potatoes, but no more. As a matter of course the young lady replies that she for her part will be quite content to take the parings for her own eating. Then they rush deliciously into each others arms and the matter is settled. For, though the convictions arising from the former line of argument may be set aside as often as need be, those reached from the latter are generally conclusive. That such a settlement will always be better for the young gentle- man and the young lady concerned than one founded on a sterner prudence is more than one may dare to say; but we do feel sure that that country will be most prosperous in which such leaps in the dark are made with the greatest freedom.

Our friend Hugh, as he sat smoking on the knife-board of the omnibus, determined that he would risk everything. If it were ordained that prudence should prevail, the prudence should be hers. Why should he take upon himself to have prudence enough for two, seeing that she was so very discreet in all her bearings? Then he remembered the touch of her hand, which he still felt upon his palm as he sat handling his pipe, and he told himself that after that he was bound to say a word more. And moreover he confessed to himself that he was compelled by a feeling that mastered him altogether. He could not get through an hour's work without throwing down his pen and thinking of Nora Rowley. It was his destiny to love her, – and there was, to his mind, a mean, pettifogging secrecy, amounting almost to daily lying, in his thus loving her and not telling her that he loved her. It might well be that she should rebuke him; but he thought that he could bear that. It might well be that he had altogether mistaken that touch of her hand. After all it had been the slightest possible motion of no more than one finger. But he would at any rate know the truth. If she would tell him at once that she did not care for him, he thought that he could get over it; but life was not worth having while he lived in this shifty, dubious, and uncomfortable state. So he made up his mind that he would go to St Diddulph's with his heart in his hand.

In the mean time, Mr Bozzle had been twice to St Diddulph's; – and now he made a third journey there, two days after Stanbury's visit. Trevelyan, who, in truth, hated the sight of the man, and who suffered agonies in his presence, had, nevertheless, taught himself to believe that he could not live without his assistance. That it should be so was a part of the cruelty of his lot. Who else was there that he could trust? His wife had renewed her intimacy with Colonel Osborne the moment that she had left him. Mrs Stanbury, who had been represented to him as the most correct of matrons, had at once been false to him and to her trust, in allowing Colonel Osborne to enter her house. Mr and Mrs Outhouse, with whom his wife had now located herself, not by his orders, were, of course, his enemies. His old friend, Hugh Stanbury, had gone over to the other side, and had quarrelled with him purposely, with malice prepense, because he would not submit himself to the caprices of the wife who had injured him. His own lawyer had refused to act for him; and his fast and oldest ally, the very person who had sounded in his ear the earliest warning note against that odious villain, whose daily work it was to destroy the peace of families, – even Lady Milborough had turned against him! Because he would not follow the stupid prescription which she, with pig-headed obstinacy, persisted in giving, – because he would not carry his wife off to Naples, – she was ill-judging and inconsistent enough to tell him that he was wrong! Who was then left to him but Bozzle? Bozzle was very disagreeable. Bozzle said things, and made suggestions to him which were as bad as pins stuck into his flesh. But Bozzle was true to his employer, and could find out facts. Had it not been for Bozzle, he would have known nothing of the Colonel's journey to Devonshire. Had it not been for Bozzle, he would never have heard of the correspondence; and, therefore, when he left London, he gave Bozzle a roving commission; and when he went to Paris, and from Paris onwards, over the Alps into Italy, he furnished Bozzle with his address. At this time, in the midst of all his misery, it never occurred to him to inquire of himself whether it might be possible that his old friends were right, and that he himself was wrong. From morning to night he sang to himself melancholy silent songs of inward wailing, as to the cruelty of his own lot in life; – and, in the mean time, he employed Bozzle to find out for him how far that cruelty was carried.

Mr Bozzle was, of course, convinced that the lady whom he was employed to watch was – no better than she ought to be. That is the usual Bozzlian language for broken vows, secrecy, intrigue, dirt, and adultery. It was his business to obtain evidence of her guilt. There was no question to be solved as to her innocency. The Bozzlian mind would have regarded any such suggestion as the product of a green softness, the possession of which would have made him quite unfit for his profession. He was aware that ladies who are no better than they should be are often very clever, – so clever, as to make it necessary that the Bozzles who shall at last confound them should be first-rate Bozzles, Bozzles quite at the top of their profession, – and, therefore, he went about his work with great industry and much caution. Colonel Osborne was at the present moment in Scotland. Bozzle was sure of that. He was quite in the north of Scotland. Bozzle had examined his map, and had found that Wick, which was the Colonel's post-town, was very far north indeed. He had half a mind to run down to Wick, as he was possessed by a certain honest zeal, which made him long to do something hard and laborious; but his experience told him that it was very easy for the Colonel to come up to the neighbourhood of St Diddulph's, whereas the lady could not go down to Wick, unless she were to decide upon throwing herself into her lover's arms, – whereby Bozzle's work would be brought to an end. He, therefore, confined his immediate operations to St Diddulph's.

He made acquaintance with one or two important persons in and about Mr Outhouse's parsonage. He became very familiar with the postman. He arranged terms of intimacy, I am sorry to say, with the housemaid; and, on the third journey, he made an alliance with the potboy at the Full Moon. The potboy remembered well the fact of the child being brought to 'our 'ouse,' as he called the Full Moon; and he was enabled to say, that the same 'gent as had brought the boy backards and forrards,' had since that been at the parsonage. But Bozzle was quite quick enough to perceive that all this had nothing to do with the Colonel. He was led, indeed, to fear that his 'governor,' as he was in the habit of calling Trevelyan in his half-spoken soliloquies, – that his governor was not as true to him as he was to his governor. What business had that meddling fellow Stanbury at St Diddulph's? – for Trevelyan had not thought it necessary to tell his satellite that he had quarrelled with his friend. Bozzle was grieved in his mind when he learned that Stanbury's interference was still to be dreaded; and wrote to his governor, rather severely, to that effect; but, when so writing, he was able to give no further information. Facts, in such cases, will not unravel themselves without much patience on the part of the investigators.

34
Priscilla's Wisdom

On the night after the dinner party in the Close, Dorothy was not the only person in the house who laid awake thinking of what had taken place. Miss Stanbury also was full of anxiety, and for hour after hour could not sleep as she remembered the fruitlessness of her efforts on behalf of her nephew and niece.

It had never occurred to her when she had first proposed to herself that Dorothy should become Mrs Gibson that Dorothy herself would have any objection to such a step in life. Her fear had been that Dorothy would have become over-radiant with triumph at the idea of having a husband, and going to that husband with a fortune of her own. That Mr Gibson might hesitate, she had thought very likely. It is thus, in general, that women regard the feelings, desires, and aspirations of other women. You will hardly ever meet an elderly lady who will not speak of her juniors as living in a state of breathless anxiety to catch husbands. And the elder lady will speak of the younger as though any kind of choice in such catching was quite disregarded. The man must be a gentleman, – or, at least, gentleman-like, – and there must be bread. Let these things be given, and what girl won't jump into what man's arms? Female reader, is it not thus that the elders of your sex speak of the younger? When old Mrs Stanbury heard that Nora Rowley had refused Mr Glascock, the thing was to her unintelligible; and it was now quite unintelligible to Miss Stanbury that Dorothy should prefer a single life to matrimony with Mr Gibson.

It must be acknowledged, on Aunt Stanbury's behalf, that Dorothy was one of those yielding, hesitating, submissive young women, trusting others but doubting ever of themselves, as to whom it is natural that their stronger friends should find it expedient to decide for them. Miss Stanbury was almost justified in thinking that unless she were to find a husband for her niece, her niece would never find one for herself. Dorothy would drift into being an old maid, like Priscilla, simply because she would never assert herself, – never put her best foot foremost. Aunt Stanbury had therefore taken upon herself to put out a foot; and having carefully found that Mr

Gibson was 'willing,' had conceived that all difficulties were over. She would be enabled to do her duty by her niece, and establish comfortably in life, at any rate, one of her brother's children. And now Dorothy was taking upon herself to say that she did not like the gentleman! Such conduct was almost equal to writing for a penny newspaper!

On the following morning, after breakfast, when Brooke Burgess was gone out to call upon his uncle, – which he insisted upon doing openly, and not under the rose, in spite of Miss Stanbury's great gravity on the occasion, – there was a very serious conversation, and poor Dorothy had found herself to be almost silenced. She did argue for a time; but her arguments seemed, even to herself, to amount to so little! Why shouldn't she love Mr Gibson? That was a question which she found it impossible to answer. And though she did not actually yield, though she did not say that she would accept the man, still, when she was told that three days were to be allowed to her for consideration, and that then the offer would be made to her in form, she felt that, as regarded the anti-Gibson interest, she had not a leg to stand upon. Why should not such an insignificant creature, as was she, love Mr Gibson, – or any other man, who had bread to give her, and was in some degree like a gentleman? On that night, she wrote the following letter to her sister:

The Close, Tuesday

Dearest Priscilla,

I do so wish that you could be with me, so that I could talk to you again. Aunt Stanbury is the most affectionate and kindest friend in the world; but she has always been so able to have her own way, because she is both clever and good, that I find myself almost like a baby with her. She has been talking to me again about Mr Gibson; and it seems that Mr Gibson really does mean it. It is certainly very strange; but I do think now that it is true. He is to come on Friday. It seems very odd that it should all be settled for him in that way; but then Aunt Stanbury is so clever at settling things!

He sat next to me almost all the evening yesterday; but he didn't say anything about it, except that he hoped I agreed with him about going to church, and all that. I suppose I do; and I am quite sure that if I were to be a clergyman's wife, I should endeavour to do whatever my husband thought right about religion. One ought to try to do so, even if the clergyman is not one's husband. Mr Burgess has come, and he was so very amusing all the evening, that perhaps that was the reason Mr Gibson said so little. Mr Burgess is a very nice man, and I think Aunt Stanbury is more fond of him than of anybody. He is not at all the sort of person that I expected.

But if Mr Gibson does come on Friday, and does really mean it, what am I to say to him? Aunt Stanbury will be very angry if I do not take her advice. I am quite sure that she intends it all for my happiness; and then, of course, she knows so much more about the world than I do. She asks me what it is that I expect. Of course, I do not expect anything. It is a great compliment from Mr Gibson, who is a clergyman, and thought well of by everybody. And nothing could be more respectable. Aunt Stanbury says that with the money she would give us we should be quite comfortable; and she wants us to live in this house. She says that there are thirty girls round Exeter who would give their eyes for such a chance; and, looking at it in that light, of course, it is a very great thing for me. Only think how poor we have been! And then, dear Priscilla, perhaps he would let me be good to you and dear mamma!

But, of course, he will ask me whether I – love him; and what am I to say? Aunt Stanbury says that I am to love him. "Begin to love him at once," she said this morning. I would if I could, partly for her sake, and because I do feel that it would be so respectable. When I think of it, it does seem such a pity that poor I should throw away such a chance. And I must say that Mr Gibson is very good, and most obliging; and everybody says that he has an excellent temper, and that he is a most prudent, well-dispositioned man. I declare, dear Priscilla, when I think of it, I cannot bring myself to believe that such a man should want me to be his wife.

But what ought I to do? I suppose when a girl is in love she is very unhappy if the gentleman does not propose to her. I am sure it would not make me at all unhappy if I were told that Mr Gibson had changed his mind.

Dearest Priscilla, you must write at once, because he is to be here on Friday. Oh, dear; Friday does seem to be so near! And I shall never know what to say to him, either one way or the other.

> Your most affectionate sister,
> Dorothy Stanbury

PS – Give my kindest love to mamma; but you need not tell her unless you think it best.

Priscilla received this letter on the Wednesday morning, and felt herself bound to answer it on that same afternoon. Had she postponed her reply for a day, it would still have been in Dorothy's hands before Mr Gibson could have come to her on the dreaded Friday morning. But still that would hardly give her time enough to consider the matter with any degree of deliberation after she should have been armed with what wisdom Priscilla might be able to send her. The post left Nuncombe Putney at three; and therefore the letter had to be written before their early dinner.

So Priscilla went into the garden and sat herself down under an old cedar that she might discuss the matter with herself in all its bearings. She felt that no woman could be called upon to write a letter that should be of more importance. The whole welfare in life of the person who was dearest to her would probably depend upon it. The weight upon her was so great that she thought for a while she would take counsel with her mother; but she felt sure that her mother would recommend the marriage; and that if she afterwards should find herself bound to oppose it, then her mother would be a miserable woman. There could be no use to her in taking counsel with her mother, because her mother's mind was known to her beforehand. The responsibility was thrown upon her, and she alone must bear it.

She tried hard to persuade herself to write at once and tell her sister to marry the man. She knew her sister's heart so well as to be sure that Dorothy would learn to love the man who was her husband. It was almost impossible that Dorothy should not love those with whom she lived. And then her sister was so well adapted to be a wife and mother. Her temper was so sweet, she was so pure, so unselfish, so devoted, and so healthy withal! She was so happy when she was acting for others; and so excellent in action when she had another one to think for her! She was so trusting and trustworthy that any husband would adore her! Then Priscilla walked slowly into the house, got her prayer-book, and returning to her seat under the tree, read the marriage service. It was one o'clock when she went up-stairs to write her letter, and it had not yet struck eleven when she first seated herself beneath the tree. Her letter, when written, was as follows:

Nuncombe Putney, August 25, 186 —

Dearest Dorothy,

I got your letter this morning, and I think it is better to answer it at once, as the time is very short. I have been thinking about it with all my mind, and I feel almost awe-stricken lest I should advise you wrongly. After all, I believe that your own dear sweet truth and honesty would guide you better than anybody else can guide you. You may be sure of this, that whichever way it is, I shall think that you have done right. Dearest sister, I suppose there can be no doubt that for most women a married life is happier than a single one. It is always thought so, as we may see by the anxiety of others to get married; and when an opinion becomes general, I think that the world is most often right. And then, my own one, I feel sure that you are adapted both for the cares and for the joys of married life. You would do your duty as a married woman happily, and would be a comfort to your husband; – not a thorn in his side, as are so many women.

But, my pet, do not let that reasoning of Aunt Stanbury's about the thirty young girls who would give their eyes for Mr Gibson, have any weight with you. You should not take him because thirty other young girls would be glad to have him. And do not think too much of that respectability of which you speak. I would never advise my Dolly to marry any man unless she could be respectable in her new position; but that alone should go for nothing. Nor should our poverty. We shall not starve. And even if we did, that would be but a poor excuse.

I can find no escape from this, – that you should love him before you say that you will take him. But honest, loyal love need not, I take it, be of that romantic kind which people write about in novels and poetry. You need not think him to be perfect, or the best or grandest of men. Your heart will tell you whether he is dear to you. And remember, Dolly, that I shall remember that love itself must begin at some precise time. Though you had not learned to love him when you wrote on Tuesday, you may have begun to do so when you get this on Thursday.

If you find that you love him, then say that you will be his wife. If your heart revolts from such a declaration as being false; – if you cannot bring yourself to feel that you prefer him to others as the partner of your life, – then tell him, with thanks for his courtesy, that it cannot be as he would have it.

Yours always and ever most affectionately,
Priscilla

35
Mr Gibson's Good Fortune

'I'll bet you half-a-crown, my lad, you're thrown over at last, like the rest of them. There's nothing she likes so much as taking some one up in order that she may throw him over afterwards.' It was thus that Mr Bartholomew Burgess cautioned his nephew Brooke.

'I'll take care that she shan't break my heart, Uncle Barty. I will go my way and she may go hers, and she may give her money to the hospital if she pleases.'

On the morning after his arrival Brooke Burgess had declared aloud in Miss Stanbury's parlour that he was going over to the bank to see his uncle. Now there was in this almost a breach of contract. Miss Stanbury, when she invited the young man to Exeter, had stipulated that there should be no intercourse between her house and the bank. 'Of course, I shall not need to know where you go or where you don't go,' she had written; 'but after all that has passed there must not be any positive intercourse between my house and the bank.' And now he had spoken of going over to C and B, as he called them, with the utmost indifference. Miss Stanbury had looked very grave, but had said nothing. She had determined to be on her guard, so that she should not be driven to quarrel with Brooke if she could avoid it.

Bartholomew Burgess was a tall, thin, ill-tempered old man, as well-known in Exeter as the cathedral, and respected after a fashion. No one liked him. He said ill-natured things of all his neighbours, and had never earned any reputation for doing good-natured acts. But he had lived in Exeter for nearly seventy years, and had achieved that sort of esteem which comes from long tenure. And he had committed no great iniquities in the course of his fifty years of business. The bank had never stopped payment, and he had robbed no one. He had not swallowed up widows and orphans, and had done his work in the firm of Cropper and Burgess after the old-fashioned safe manner, which leads neither to riches nor to ruin. Therefore he was respected. But he was a discontented, sour old man, who believed himself to have been injured by all his own friends, who disliked his own partners because they had bought that which had, at any rate, never belonged to him; – and whose strongest passion it was to hate Miss Stanbury of the Close.

'She's got a parson by the hand now,' said the uncle, as he continued his caution to the nephew.

'There was a clergyman there last night.'

'No doubt, and she'll play him off against you, and you against him; and then she'll throw you both over. I know her.'

'She has got a right to do what she likes with her own, Uncle Barty.'

'And how did she get it? Never mind. I'm not going to set you against her, if you're her favourite for the moment. She has a niece with her there, – hasn't she?'

'One of her brother's daughters.'

'They say she's going to make that clergyman marry her.'

'What; – Mr Gibson?'

'Yes. They tell me he was as good as engaged to another girl, – one of the Frenches of Heavitree. And therefore dear Jemima could do nothing better than interfere. When she has succeeded in breaking the girl's heart – '

'Which girl's heart, Uncle Barty?'

'The girl the man was to have married; when that's done she'll throw Gibson over. You'll see. She'll refuse to give the girl a shilling.

She took the girl's brother by the hand ever so long, and then she threw him over. And she'll throw the girl over too, and send her back to the place she came from. And then she'll throw you over.'

'According to you, she must be the most malicious old woman that ever was allowed to live!'

'I don't think there are many to beat her, as far as malice goes. But you'll find out for yourself. I shouldn't be surprised if she were to tell you before long that you were to marry the niece.'

'I shouldn't think that such very hard lines either,' said Brooke Burgess.

'I've no doubt you may have her if you like,' said Barty, 'in spite of Mr Gibson. Only I should recommend you to take care and get the money first.'

When Brooke went back to the house in the Close, Miss Stanbury was quite fussy in her silence. She would have given much to have been told something about Barty, and, above all, to have learned what Barty had said about herself. But she was far too proud even to mention the old man's name of her own accord. She was quite sure that she had been abused. She guessed, probably with tolerable accuracy, the kind of things that had been said of her, and suggested to herself what answer Brooke would make to such accusations. But she had resolved to cloak it all in silence, and pretended for awhile not to remember the young man's declared intention when he left the house. 'It seems odd to me,' said Brooke, 'that Uncle Barty should always live alone as he does. He must have a dreary time of it.'

'I don't know anything about your Uncle Barty's manner of living.'

'No; — I suppose not. You and he are not friends.'

'By no means, Brooke.'

'He lives there all alone in that poky bank-house, and nobody ever goes near him. I wonder whether he has any friends in the city?'

'I really cannot tell you anything about his friends. And, to tell you the truth, Brooke, I don't want to talk about your uncle. Of course, you can go to see him when you please, but I'd rather you didn't tell me of your visits afterwards.'

'There is nothing in the world I hate so much as a secret,' said he. He had no intention in this of animadverting upon Miss Stanbury's secret enmity, nor had her purposed to ask any question as to her relations with the old man. He had alluded to his dislike of having secrets of his own. But she misunderstood him.

'If you are anxious to know – ' she said, becoming very red in the face.

'I am not at all curious to know. You quite mistake me.'

'He has chosen to believe, – or to say that he believed, – that I wronged him in regard to his brother's will. I nursed his brother when he was dying, – as I considered it to be my duty to do. I cannot tell you all that story. It is too long, and too sad. Romance is very pretty in novels, but the romance of a life is always a melancholy matter. They are most happy who have no story to tell.'

'I quite believe that.'

'But your Uncle Barty chose to think, – indeed, I hardly know what he thought. He said that the will was a will of my making. When it was made I and his brother were apart; we were not even on speaking terms. There had been a quarrel, and all manner of folly. I am not very proud when I look back upon it. It is not that I think myself better than others; but your Uncle Brooke's will was made before we had come together again. When he was ill it was natural that I should go to him, – after all that had passed between us. Eh, Brooke?'

'It was womanly.'

'But it made no difference about the will. Mr Bartholomew Burgess might have known that at once, and must have known it afterwards. But he has never acknowledged that he was wrong; – never even yet.'

'He could not bring himself to do that, I should say.'

'The will was no great triumph to me. I could have done without it. As God is my judge, I would not have lifted up my little finger to get either a part or the whole of poor Brooke's money. If I had known that a word would have done it, I would have bitten my tongue out before it should have been spoken.' She had risen from her seat, and was speaking with a solemnity that almost filled her listener with awe. She was a woman short of stature; but now, as she stood over him, she seemed to be tall and majestic. 'But when the man was dead,' she continued, 'and the will was there, – the property was mine, and I was bound in duty to exercise the privileges and hear the responsibilities which the dead man had conferred upon me. It was Barty, then, who sent a low attorney to me, offering me a compromise. What had I to compromise? Compromise! No. If it was not mine by all the right the law could give, I would sooner have starved than have had a crust of bread out of the money.' She had now clenched both her fists, and was shaking them rapidly as she stood over him, looking down upon him.

'Of course it was your own.'

'Yes. Though they asked me to compromise, and sent messages to me to frighten me; – both Barty and your Uncle Tom; ay, and your father too, Brooke; they did not dare to go to law. To law, indeed! If ever there was a good will in the world, the will of your Uncle Brooke was good. They could talk, and malign me, and tell lies as to dates, and strive to make my name odious in the county; but they knew that the will was good. They did not succeed very well in what they did attempt.'

'I would try to forget it all now, Aunt Stanbury.'

'Forget it! How is that to be done? How can the mind forget the history of its own life? No, – I cannot forget it. I can forgive it.'

'Then why not forgive it?'

'I do. I have. Why else are you here?'

'But forgive old Uncle Barty also!'

'Has he forgiven me? Come now. If I wished to forgive him, how should I begin? Would he be gracious if I went to him? Does he love me, do you think, – or hate me? Uncle Barty is a good hater. It is the best point about him. No, Brooke, we won't try the farce of a reconciliation after a long life of enmity. Nobody would believe us, and we should not believe each other.'

'Then I certainly would not try.'

'I do not mean to do so. The truth is, Brooke, you shall have it all when I'm gone, if you don't turn against me. You won't take to writing for penny newspapers, will you, Brooke?' As she asked the question she put one of her hands softly on his shoulder.

'I certainly shan't offend in that way.'

'And you won't be a Radical?'

'No, not a Radical.'

'I mean a man to follow Beales and Bright,* a republican, a utter-down of the Church, a hater of the Throne. You won't take up that line, will you, Brooke?'

'It isn't my way at present, Aunt Stanbury. But a man shouldn't promise.'

'Ah me! It makes me sad when I think what the country is coming to. I'm told there are scores of members of Parliament who don't pronounce their h's. When I was young, a member of Parliament used to be a gentleman; – and they've taken to ordaining all manner of people. It used to be the case that when you met a clergyman you met a gentleman. By-the-bye, Brooke, what do you think of Mr Gibson?'

'Mr Gibson! To tell the truth, I haven't thought much about him yet.'

'But you must think about him. Perhaps you haven't thought about my niece, Dolly Stanbury?'

'I think she's an uncommonly nice girl.'

'She's not to be nice for you, young man. She's to be married to Mr Gibson.'

'Are they engaged?'

'Well, no; but I intend that they shall be. You won't begrudge that I should give my little savings to one of my own name?'

'You don't know me, Aunt Stanbury, if you think that I should begrudge anything that you might do with your money.'

'Dolly has been here a month or two. I think it's three months since she came, and I do like her. She's soft and womanly, and hasn't taken up those vile, filthy habits which almost all the girls have adopted. Have you seen those Frenches with the things they have on their heads?'

'I was speaking to them yesterday.'

'Nasty sluts! You can see the grease on their foreheads when they try to make their hair go back in the dirty French fashion. Dolly is not like that; – is she?'

'She is not in the least like either of the Miss Frenches.'

'And now I want her to become Mrs Gibson. He is quite taken.'

'Is he?'

'Oh dear, yes. Didn't you see him the other night at dinner and afterwards? Of course he knows that I can give her a little bit of money, which always goes for something, Brooke. And I do think it would be such a nice thing for Dolly.'

'And what does Dolly think about it?'

'There's the difficulty. She likes him well enough; I'm sure of that. And she has no stuck-up ideas about herself. She isn't one of those who think that almost nothing is good enough for them. But –'

'She has an objection.'

'I don't know what it is. I sometimes think she is so bashful and modest she doesn't like to talk of being married, – even to an old woman like me.'

'Dear me! That's not the way of the age; – is it, Aunt Stanbury?'

'It's coming to that, Brooke, that the girls will ask the men soon. Yes, – and that they won't take a refusal either. I do believe that Camilla French did ask Mr Gibson.'

'And what did Mr Gibson say?'

'Ah; I can't tell you that. He knows too well what he's about to take her. He's to come here on Friday at eleven, and you must be out of the way. I shall be out of the way too. But if Dolly says a word to you before that, mind you make her understand that she ought to accept Gibson.'

'She's too good for him, according to my thinking.'

'Don't you be a fool. How can any young woman be too good for a gentleman and a clergyman? Mr Gibson is a gentleman. Do you know, – only you must not mention this, – that I have a kind of idea we could get Nuncombe Putney for him. My father had the living, and my brother; and I should like it to go on in the family.'

No opportunity came in the way of Brooke Burgess to say anything in favour of Mr Gibson to Dorothy Stanbury. There did come to be very quickly a sort of intimacy between her and her aunt's favourite; but she was not one prone to talk about her own affairs. And as to such an affair as this, – a question as to whether she should or should not give herself in marriage to her suitor, – she, who could not speak of it even to her own sister without a blush, who felt confused and almost confounded when receiving her aunt's admonitions and instigations on the subject, would not have endured to hear Brooke Burgess speak on the matter. Dorothy did feel that a person easier to know than Brooke had never come in her way. She had already said as much to him as she had spoken to Mr Gibson in the three months that she had made his acquaintance. They had talked about Exeter, and about Mrs MacHugh, and the cathedral, and Tennyson's poems, and the London theatres, and Uncle Barty, and the family quarrel. They had become quite confidential with each other on some matters. But on this heavy subject of Mr Gibson and his proposal of marriage not a word had been said. When Brooke once mentioned Mr Gibson on the Thursday morning, Dorothy within a minute had taken an opportunity of escaping from the room.

But circumstances did give him an opportunity of speaking to Mr Gibson. On the Wednesday afternoon both he and Mr Gibson were invited to drink tea at Mrs French's house on that evening. Such invitations at Exeter were wont to be given at short dates, and both the gentlemen had said that they would go. Then Arabella French had called in the Close and had asked Miss Stanbury and Dorothy. It was well understood by Arabella that Miss Stanbury herself would not drink tea at Heavitree. And it may be that Dorothy's company was not in truth desired. The ladies both declined. 'Don't you stay at home for me, my dear,' Miss Stanbury said to her niece. But Dorothy had not been out without her aunt since she had been at Exeter, and understood perfectly that it would not be wise to commence the practice at the house of the Frenches. 'Mr Brooke is coming, Miss Stanbury; and Mr Gibson,' Miss French said. And

Miss Stanbury had thought that there was some triumph in her tone. 'Mr Brooke can go where he pleases, my dear,' Miss Stanbury replied. 'And as for Mr Gibson, I am not his keeper.' The tone in which Miss Stanbury spoke would have implied great imprudence, had not the two ladies understood each other so thoroughly, and had not each known that it was so.

There was the accustomed set of people in Mrs French's drawing-room; – the Crumbies, and the Wrights, and the Apjohns. And Mrs MacHugh came also, – knowing that there would be a rubber. 'Their naked shoulders don't hurt me,' Mrs MacHugh said, when her friend almost scolded her for going to the house. 'I'm not a young man. I don't care what they do to themselves.' 'You might say as much if they went naked altogether,' Miss Stanbury had replied in anger. 'If nobody else complained, I shouldn't,' said Mrs MacHugh. Mrs MacHugh got her rubber; and as she had gone for her rubber, on a distinct promise that there should be a rubber, and as there was a rubber, she felt that she had no right to say ill-natured things. 'What does it matter to me,' said Mrs MacHugh, 'how nasty she is ? She's not going to be my wife.' 'Ugh !' exclaimed Miss Stanbury, shaking her head both in anger and disgust.

Camilla French was by no means so bad as she was painted by Miss Stanbury, and Brooke Burgess rather liked her than otherwise. And it seemed to him that Mr Gibson did not at all dislike Arabella, and felt no repugnance at either the lady's noddle or shoulders now that he was removed from Miss Stanbury's influence. It was clear enough also that Arabella had not given up the attempt, although she must have admitted to herself that the claims of Dorothy Stanbury were very strong. On this evening it seemed to have been specially permitted to Arabella, who was the elder sister, to take into her own hands the management of the case. Beholders of the game had hitherto declared that Mr Gibson's safety was secured by the constant coupling of the sisters. Neither would allow the other to hunt alone. But a common sense of the common danger had made some special strategy necessary, and Camilla hardly spoke a word to Mr Gibson during the evening. Let us hope that she found some temporary consolation in the presence of the stranger.

'I hope you are going to stay with us ever so long, Mr Burgess ?' said Camilla.

'A month. That is ever so long; – isn't it ? Why I mean to see all Devonshire within that time. I feel already that I know Exeter thoroughly and everybody in it.'

'I'm sure we are very much flattered.'

'As for you, Miss French, I've heard so much about you all my life, that I felt that I knew you before I came here.'

'Who can have spoken to you about me?'

'You forget how many relatives I have in the city. Do you think my Uncle Barty never writes to me?'

'Not about me.'

'Does he not? And do you suppose I don't hear from Miss Stanbury?'

'But she hates me. I know that.'

'And do you hate her?'

'No, indeed. I've the greatest respect for her. But she is a little odd; isn't she, now, Mr Burgess? We all like her ever so much; and we've known her ever so long, six or seven years, – since we were quite young things. But she has such queer notions about girls.'

'What sort of notions?'

'She's like them all to dress just like herself; and she thinks that they should never talk to young men. If she was here she'd say I was flirting with you, because we're sitting together.'

'But you are not; are you?'

'Of course I am not.'

'I wish you would,' said Brooke.

'I shouldn't know how to begin. I shouldn't, indeed. I don't know what flirting means, and I don't know who does know. When young ladies and gentleman go out, I suppose they are intended to talk to each other.'

'But very often they don't, you know.'

'I call that stupid,' said Camilla. 'And yet, when they do, all the old maids say that the girls are flirting. I'll tell you one thing, Mr Burgess. I don't care what any old maid says about me. I always talk to people that I like, and if they choose to call me a flirt, they may. It's my opinion that still waters run the deepest.'

'No doubt the noisy streams are very shallow,' said Brooke.

'You may call me a shallow stream if you like, Mr Burgess.'

'I meant nothing of the kind.'

'But what do you call Dorothy Stanbury? That's what I call still water. She runs deep enough.'

'The quietest young lady I ever saw in my life.'

'Exactly. So quiet, but so – clever. What do you think of Mr Gibson?'

'Everybody is asking me what I think of Mr Gibson.'

'You know what they say. They say he is to marry Dorothy

Stanbury. Poor man! I don't think his own consent has ever been asked yet; – but, nevertheless, it's settled.'

'Just at present he seems to me to be, – what shall I say? – I oughtn't to say flirting with your sister; ought I?'

'Miss Stanbury would say so if she were here, no doubt. But the fact is, Mr Burgess, we've known him almost since we were infants, and of course we take an interest in his welfare. There has never been anything more than that. Arabella is nothing more to him than I am. Once, indeed – ; but, however – ; that does not signify. It would be nothing to us, if he really liked Dorothy Stanbury. But as far as we can see, – and we do see a good deal of him, – there is no such feeling on his part. Of course we haven't asked. We should not think of such a thing. Mr Gibson may do just as he likes for us. But I am not quite sure that Dorothy Stanbury is just the girl that would make him a good wife. Of course when you've known a person seven or eight years you do get anxious about his happiness. Do you know, we think her, – perhaps a little, – sly.'

In the meantime, Mr Gibson was completely subject to the undivided charms of Arabella. Camilla had been quite correct in a part of her description of their intimacy. She and her sister had known Mr Gibson for seven or eight years; but nevertheless the intimacy could not with truth be said to have commenced during the infancy of the young ladies, even if the word were used in its legal sense. Seven or eight years, however, is a long acquaintance; and there was, perhaps, something of a real grievance in this Stanbury intervention. If it be a recognised fact in society that young ladies are in want of husbands, and that an effort on their part towards matrimony is not altogether impossible, it must be recognised also that failure will be disagreeable, and interference regarded with animosity. Miss Stanbury the elder was undoubtedly interfering between Mr Gibson and the Frenches; and it is neither manly nor womanly to submit to interference with one's dearest prospects. It may, perhaps, be admitted that the Miss Frenches had shown too much open ardour in their pursuit of Mr Gibson. Perhaps there should have been no ardour and no pursuit. It may be that the theory of womanhood is right which forbids to women any such attempts, -- which teaches them that they must ever be the pursued, never the pursuers. As to that there shall be no discourse at present. But it must be granted that whenever the pursuit has been attempted, it is not in human nature to abandon it without an effort. That the French girls should be very angry with Miss Stanbury, that they should put their heads together with the intention of thwarting her, that they should think evil things of poor Dorothy, that they should half despise Mr Gibson, and yet resolve to keep their hold upon him as a chattel and a thing of value that was almost their own, was not perhaps much to their discredit.

'You are a good deal at the house in the Close now,' said Arabella, in her lowest voice, – in a voice so low that it was almost melancholy.

'Well; yes. Miss Stanbury, you know, has always been a staunch friend of mine. And she takes an interest in my little church.' People say that girls are sly; but men can be sly, too, sometimes.

'It seems that she has taken you so much away from us, Mr Gibson.'

'I don't know why you should say that, Miss French.'

'Perhaps I am wrong. One is apt to be sensitive about one's friends. We seem to have known you so well. There is nobody else in Exeter that mamma regards as she does you. But, of course, if you are happy with Miss Stanbury that is every thing.'

'I am speaking of the old lady,' said Mr Gibson, who, in spite of his slyness, was here thrown a little off his guard.

'And I am speaking of the old lady too,' said Arabella. 'Of whom else should I be speaking?'

'No; of course not.'

'Of course,' continued Arabella, 'I hear what people say about the niece. One cannot help what one hears, you know, Mr Gibson; but I don't believe that, I can assure you.' As she said this, she looked into his face, as though waiting for an answer; but Mr Gibson had no answer ready. Then Arabella told herself that if anything was to be done it must be done at once. What use was there in beating round the bush, when the only chance of getting the game was to be had by dashing at once into the thicket. 'I own I should be glad,' she said, turning her eyes away from him, 'if I could hear from your own mouth that it is not true.'

Mr Gibson's position was not one to be envied. Were he willing to tell the very secrets of his soul to Miss French with the utmost candour, he could not answer her question either one way or the other, and he was not willing to tell her any of his secrets. It was certainly the fact, too, that there had been tender passages between him and Arabella. Now, when there have been such passages, and the gentleman is cross-examined by the lady, as Mr Gibson was being cross-examined at the present moment, – the gentleman usually teaches himself to think that a little falsehood is permissible. A gentleman can hardly tell a lady that he has become tired of her, and has changed his mind. He feels the matter, perhaps, more keenly even than she does; and though, at all other times he may be a very Paladin in the cause of truth, in such straits as this he does allow himself some latitude.

'You are only joking, of course,' he said.

'Indeed, I am not joking. I can assure you, Mr Gibson, that the welfare of the friends whom I really love can never be a matter of joke to me. Mrs Crumbie says that you positively are engaged to marry Dorothy Stanbury.'

'What does Mrs Crumbie know about it?'

'I dare say nothing. It is not so; – is it?'

'Certainly not.'

'And there is nothing in it; – is there?'

'I wonder why people make these reports,' said Mr Gibson, prevaricating.

'It is a fabrication from beginning to end, then?' said Arabella, pressing the matter quite home. At this time she was very close to him, and though her words were severe, the glance from her eyes was soft. And the scent from her hair was not objectionable to him as it would have been to Miss Stanbury. And the mode of her head-dress was not displeasing to him. And the folds of her dress, as they fell across his knee, were welcome to his feelings. He knew that he was as one under temptation, but he was not strong enough to bid the tempter avaunt. 'Say that it is so, Mr Gibson!'

'Of course, it is not so,' said Mr Gibson – lying.

'I am so glad. For, of course, Mr Gibson, when we heard it we thought a great deal about it. A man's happiness depends so much on whom he marries; – doesn't it? And a clergyman's more than anybody else's. And we didn't think she was quite the sort of woman that you would like. You see, she has had no advantages, poor thing! She has been shut up in a little country cottage all her life; – just a labourer's hovel, no more; – and though it wasn't her fault, of course, and we all pitied her, and were so glad when Miss Stanbury brought her to the Close; – still, you know, as a wife, – and for such a dear, dear friend – ' She went on, and said many other things with equal enthusiasm, and then wiped her eyes, and then smiled and laughed. After that she declared that she was quite happy, – so happy; and so she left him. The poor man, after the falsehood had been extracted from him, said nothing more; but sat, in patience, listening to the raptures and enthusiasm of his friend. He knew that he had disgraced himself; and he knew also that his disgrace would be known, if Dorothy Stanbury should accept his offer on the morrow. And yet how hardly he had been used! What answer could he have given compatible both with the truth and with his own personal dignity?

About half an hour afterwards, he was walking back to Exeter with Brooke Burgess, and then Brooke did ask him a question or two.

'Nice girls those Frenches, I think,' said Brooke.

'Very nice,' said Mr Gibson.

'How Miss Stanbury does hate them,' says Brooke.

'Not hate them, I hope,' said Mr Gibson.

'She doesn't love them; – does she ?'

'Well, as for love; – yes; in one sense, – I hope she does. Miss Stanbury, you know, is a woman who expresses herself strongly.'

'What would she say, if she were told that you and I were going to marry those two girls ? We are both favourites, you know.'

'Dear me ! What a very odd supposition,' said Mr Gibson.

'For my part, I don't think I shall,' said Brooke.

'I don't suppose I shall either,' said Mr Gibson, with a gravity which was intended to convey some smattering of rebuke.

'A fellow might do worse, you know,' said Brooke. 'For my part, I rather like girls with chignons, and all that sort of get-up. But the worst of it is, one can't marry two at a time.'

'That would be bigamy,' said Mr Gibson.

'Just so,' said Brooke.

36
Miss Stanbury's Wrath

Punctually at eleven o'clock on the Friday morning Mr Gibson knocked at the door of the house in the Close. The reader must not imagine that he had ever wavered in his intention with regard to Dorothy Stanbury, because he had been driven into a corner by the pertinacious ingenuity of Miss French. He never for a moment thought of being false to Miss Stanbury the elder. Falseness of that nature would have been ruinous to him, – would have made him a marked man in the city all his days, and would probably have reached even to the bishop's ears. He was neither bad enough, nor audacious enough, nor foolish enough, for such perjury as that. And, moreover, though the wiles of Arabella had been potent with him, he very much preferred Dorothy Stanbury. Seven years of flirtation with a young lady is more trying to the affection than any duration of matrimony. Arabella had managed to awaken something of the old glow, but Mr Gibson, as soon as he was alone, turned from her mentally in disgust. No ! Whatever little trouble there might be in his way, it was clearly his duty to marry Dorothy Stanbury. She had the sweetest tongue in the world, and blushed with the prettiest blush ! She would have, moreover, two thousand pounds on the day she married, and there was no saying what other and greater pecuniary advantages might follow. His mind was quite made up ; and during the whole morning he had been endeavouring to drive all disagreeable reminiscences of Miss French from his memory, and to arrange the words with which he would make his offer to Dorothy. He was aware that he need not be very particular about his words, as Dorothy, from the bashfulness of her nature, would be no judge of eloquence at such a time. But still, for his own sake, there should be some form of expression, some propriety of diction. Before eleven o'clock he had it all by heart, and had nearly freed himself from the uneasiness of his falsehood to Arabella. He had given much serious thought to the matter, and had quite resolved that he was right in his purpose, and that he could marry Dorothy with a pure conscience, and with a true promise of a husband's love. 'Dear Dolly !' he said to himself, with something of enthusiasm as he walked across the Close. And he looked up to the house as he came to it. There was to be his future home. There was not one of the prebends who had a better house. And there was a dovelike softness about Dorothy's eyes, and a winning obedience in her manner, that were charming. His lines had fallen to him in very pleasant places.* Yes – he would go up to her and take her at once by the hand, and ask her whether she would be his, now and for ever. He would not let go her hand, till he had brought her so close to him that she could hide her blushes on his shoulder. The whole thing had been so well conceived, had become so clear to his mind, that he felt no hesitation or embarrassment as he knocked at the door. Arabella French would, no doubt, hear of it soon. Well; – she must hear of it. After all she could do him no injury.

He was shown up at once into the drawing-room, and there he found – Miss Stanbury the elder. 'Oh, Mr Gibson !' she said at once.

'Is anything the matter with – dear Dorothy ?'

'She is the most obstinate, pig-headed young woman I ever came across since the world began.'

'You don't say so ! But what is it, Miss Stanbury ?'

'What is it ? Why just this. Nothing on earth that I can say to her will induce her to come down and speak to you.'

'Have I offended her ?'

'Offended a fiddlestick ! Offence indeed ! An offer from an honest man, with her friends' approval, and a fortune at her back as though she had been born with a gold spoon in her mouth! And she tells me that she can't, and won't, and wouldn't, and shouldn't, as though I were asking her to walk the streets. I declare I don't know what has come to the young women; – or what it is they want. One would have thought that butter wouldn't melt in her mouth.'

'But what is the reason, Miss Stanbury?'

'Oh, reason! You don't suppose people give reasons in these days. What reason have they when they dress themselves up with bandboxes on their sconces? Just simply the old reason – "I do not like thee, Dr Fell; – why I cannot tell."'*

'May I not see her myself, Miss Stanbury.'

'I can't make her come down-stairs to you. I've been at her the whole morning, Mr Gibson, ever since daylight pretty nearly. She came into my room before I was up and told me she'd made up her mind. I've coaxed, and scolded, and threatened, and cried; – but if she'd been a milestone it couldn't have been of less use. I told her she might go back to Nuncombe, and she just went off to pack up.'

'But she's not to go?'

'How can I say what such a young woman will do? I'm never allowed a way of my own for a moment. There's Brooke Burgess been scolding me at that rate I didn't know whether I stood on my head or my heels. And I don't know now.'

Then there was a pause, while Mr Gibson was endeavouring to decide what would not be his best course of action. 'Don't you think she'll ever come round, Miss Stanbury?'

'I don't think she'll ever come any way that anybody wants her to come, Mr Gibson.'

'I didn't think she was at all like that,' said Mr Gibson, almost in tears.

'No, – nor anybody else. I have been seeing it come all the same. It's just the Stanbury perversity. If I'd wanted to keep her by herself to take care of me and had set my back up at her if she spoke to a man, and made her understand that she wasn't to think of getting married, she'd have been making eyes at every man that came into the house. It's just what one gets for going out of one's way. I did think she'd be so happy, Mr Gibson, living here as your wife. She and I between us could have managed for you so nicely.'

Mr Gibson was silent for a minute or two, during which he walked up and down the room, – contemplating, no doubt, the picture of married life which Miss Stanbury had painted for him, – a picture which, as it seemed, was not to be realised. 'And what had I better do, Miss Stanbury?' he asked at last.

'Do ! I don't know what you're to do. I'm groom enough to bring a mare to water, but I can't make her drink.'

'Will waiting be any good ?'

'How can I say ? I'll tell you one thing not to do. Don't go and philander with those girls at Heavitree. It's my belief that Dorothy has been thinking of them. People talk to her, of course.'

'I wish people would hold their tongues. People are so indiscreet. People don't know how much harm they may do.'

'You've given them some excuse, you know, Mr Gibson.'

This was very ill-natured, and was felt by Mr Gibson to be so rude, that he almost turned upon his patroness in anger. He had known Dolly for not more than three months, and had devoted himself to her, to the great anger of his older friends. He had come this morning true to his appointment, expecting that others would keep their promises to him, as he was ready to keep those which he had made; – and now he was told that it was his fault ! 'I do think that's rather hard, Miss Stanbury,' he said.

'So you have,' said she; – 'nasty, slatternly girls, without an idea inside their noddles. But it's no use your scolding me.'

'I didn't mean to scold, Miss Stanbury.'

'I've done all that I could.'

'And you think she won't see me for a minute ?'

'She says she won't. I can't bid Martha carry her down.'

'Then, perhaps, I had better leave you for the present,' said Mr Gibson, after another pause. So he went, a melancholy, blighted man. Leaving the Close, he passed through into Southernhay, and walked across by the new streets towards the Heavitree road. He had no design in taking this route, but he went on till he came in sight of the house in which Mrs French lived. As he walked slowly by it, he looked up at the windows, and something of a feeling of romance came across his heart. Were his young affections buried there, or were they not ? And, if so, with which of those fair girls were they buried ? For the last two years, up to last night, Camilla had certainly been in the ascendant. But Arabella was a sweet young woman; and there had been a time, – when those tender passages were going on, – in which he had thought that no young woman ever was so sweet. A period of romance, an era of enthusiasm, a short-lived, delicious holiday of hot-tongued insanity had been permitted to him in his youth; – but all that was now over. And yet here he was, with three strings to his bow, – so he told himself, – and he had not as yet settled for himself the great business of matrimony. He was inclined to think, as he walked on, that he would walk his life alone, an active, useful, but a melancholy man. After such experiences as his, how should he ever again speak of his heart to a woman? During this walk, his mind recurred frequently to Dorothy Stanbury; and, doubtless, he thought that he had often spoken of his heart to her. He was back at his lodgings before three, at which hour he ate an early dinner, and then took the afternoon cathedral service at four. The evening he spent at home, thinking of the romance of his early days. What would Miss Stanbury have said, had she seen him in his easy chair behind the 'Exeter Argus,' – with a pipe in his mouth?

In the meantime, there was an uncomfortable scene in progress between Dorothy and her aunt. Brooke Burgess, as desired, had left the house before eleven, having taken upon himself, when consulted, to say in the mildest terms, that he thought that, in general, young women should not be asked to marry if they did not like to; – which opinion had been so galling to Miss Stanbury that she had declared that he had so scolded her, that she did not know whether she was standing on her head or her heels. As soon as Mr Gibson left her, she sat herself down, and fairly cried. She had ardently desired this thing, and had allowed herself to think of her desire as of one that would certainly be accomplished. Dorothy would have been so happy as the wife of a clergyman! Miss Stanbury's standard for men and women was not high. She did not expect others to be as self-sacrificing, as charitable, and as good as herself. It was not that she gave to herself credit for such virtues; but she thought of herself as one who, from the peculiar circumstances of life, was bound to do much for others. There was no end to her doing good for others, – if only the others would allow themselves to be governed by her. She did not think that Mr Gibson was a great divine; but she perceived that he was a clergyman, living decently, – of that secret pipe Miss Stanbury knew nothing, – doing his duty punctually, and, as she thought, very much in want of a wife. Then there was her niece, Dolly, – soft, pretty, feminine, without a shilling, and much in want of some one to comfort and take care of her. What could be better than such a marriage! And the overthrow to the girls with the big chignons would be so complete! She had set her mind upon it, and now Dorothy said that it couldn't, and it wouldn't, and it shouldn't be accomplished! She was to be thrown over by this chit of a girl, as she had been thrown over by the girl's brother! And, when she complained, the girl simply offered to go away!

At about twelve Dorothy came creeping down into the room in which her aunt was sitting, and pretended to occupy herself on some piece of work. For a considerable time, – for three minutes perhaps, – Miss Stanbury did not speak. She had resolved that she would not speak to her niece again, – at least, not for that day. She would let the ungrateful girl know how miserable she had been made. But at the close of the three minutes her patience was exhausted. 'What are you doing there?' she said.

'I am quilting your cap, Aunt Stanbury.'

'Put it down. You shan't do anything for me. I won't have you touch my things any more. I don't like pretended service.'

'It is not pretended, Aunt Stanbury.'

'I say it is pretended. Why did you pretend to me that you would have him when you had made up your mind against it all the time?'

'But I hadn't – made up my mind.'

'If you had so much doubt about it, you might have done what I wanted you.'

'I couldn't, Aunt Stanbury.'

'You mean you wouldn't. I wonder what it is you do expect.'

'I don't expect anything, Aunt Stanbury.'

'No; and I don't expect anything. What an old fool I am ever to look for any comfort. Why should I think anybody would care for me?'

'Indeed, I do care for you.'

'In what sort of way do you show it? You're just like your brother Hugh. I've disgraced myself to that man, – promising what I could not perform. I declare it makes me sick when I think of it. Why did you not tell me at once?' Dorothy said nothing further, but sat with the cap on her lap. She did not dare to resume her needle, and she did not like to put the cap aside, as by doing so it would seem as though she had accepted her aunt's prohibition against her work. For half an hour she sat thus, during which time Miss Stanbury dropped asleep. She woke with a start, and began to scold again. 'What's the good of sitting there all the day, with your hands before you, doing nothing?'

But Dorothy had been very busy. She had been making up her mind, and had determined to communicate her resolution to her aunt. 'Dear aunt,' she said, 'I've been thinking of something.'

'It's too late now,' said Miss Stanbury.

'I see I've made you very unhappy.'

'Of course you have.'

'And you think that I'm ungrateful. I'm not ungrateful, and I don't think that Hugh is.'

'Never mind Hugh.'

'Only because it seems so hard that you should take so much trouble about us, and that then there should be so much vexation.'

'I find it very hard.'

'So I think that I'd better go back to Nuncombe.'

'That's what you call gratitude.'

'I don't like to stay here and make you unhappy. I can't think that I ought to have done what you asked me, because I did not feel at all in that way about Mr Gibson. But as I have only disappointed you, it will be better that I should go home. I have been very happy here, – very.'

'Bother !' exclaimed Miss Stanbury.

'I have, – and I do love you, though you won't believe it. But I am sure I oughtn't to remain to make you unhappy. I shall never forget all that you have done for me; and though you call me ungrateful, I am not. But I know that I ought not to stay, as I cannot do what you wish. So, if you please, I will go back to Nuncombe.'

'You'll not do anything of the kind,' said Miss Stanbury.

'But it will be better.'

'Yes, of course ; no doubt. I suppose you're tired of us all.'

'It is not that I'm tired, Aunt Stanbury. It isn't that at all.' Dorothy had now become red up to the roots of her hair, and her eyes were full of tears. 'But I cannot stay where people think that I am ungrateful. If you please, Aunt Stanbury, I will go.' Then, of course, there was a compromise. Dorothy did at last consent to remain in the Close, but only on condition that she should be forgiven for her sin in reference to Mr Gibson, and be permitted to go on with her aunt's cap.

37

Mont Cenis

The night had been fine and warm, and it was now noon on a fine September day when the train from Paris reached Saint Michel, on the route to Italy by Mont Cenis, – as all the world knows Saint Michel is, or was a year or two back, the end of railway travelling in that direction. At the time Mr Fell's grand project* of carrying a line of rails over the top of the mountain was only in preparation, and the journey from Saint Michel to Susa was still made by the diligences, – those dear old continental coaches which are now nearly as extinct as our own, but which did not deserve death so fully as did our abominable vehicles. The coupé of a diligence, or, better still, the banquette, was a luxurious mode of travelling as compared with anything that our coaches offered. There used indeed to be a certain halo of glory round the occupant of the box of a mail-coach. The man who had secured that seat was supposed to know something about the world, and to be such a one that the passengers sitting behind him would be proud to be allowed to talk to him. But the prestige of the position was greater than the comfort. A night on the box of a mail-coach was but a bad time, and a night inside a mail-coach was a night in purgatory. Whereas a seat up above, on the banquette of a diligence passing over the Alps, with room for the feet, and support for the back, with plenty of rugs and plenty of tobacco, used to be on the Mont Cenis, and still is on some other mountain passes, a comfortable mode of seeing a mountain route. For those desirous of occupying the coupé, or the three front seats of the body of the vehicle, it must be admitted that difficulties frequently arose; and that such difficulties were very common at Saint Michel. There would be two or three of those enormous vehicles preparing to start for the mountain, whereas it would appear that twelve or fifteen passengers had come down from Paris armed with tickets assuring them that this preferable mode of travelling should be theirs. And then assertions would be made, somewhat recklessly, by the officials, to the effect that all the diligence was coupé. It would generally be the case that some middle-aged Englishman who could not speak French would go to the wall, together with his wife. Middle-aged Englishmen with their wives, who can't speak French, can nevertheless be very angry, and threaten loudly, when they suppose themselves to be ill-treated. A middle-aged Englishman, though he can't speak a word of French, won't believe a French official who tells him that the diligence is all coupé, when he finds himself with his unfortunate partner in a round-about place behind with two priests, a dirty man who looks like a brigand, a sick maid-servant, and three agricultural labourers. The attempt, however, was frequently made, and thus there used to be occasionally a little noise round the bureau at Saint Michel.

On the morning of which we are speaking, two Englishmen had just made good their claim, each independently of the other, each without having heard or seen the other, when two American ladies, coming up very tardily, endeavoured to prove their rights. The ladies were without other companions, and were not fluent with their French, but were clearly entitled to their seats. They were told that the conveyance was all coupé, but perversely would not believe the statement. The official shrugged his shoulders and signified that his ultimatum had been pronounced. What can an official do in such circumstances, when more coupé passengers are sent to him than the coupés at his command will hold? 'But we have paid for the coupé,' said the elder American lady, with considerable indignation, though her French was imperfect; – for American ladies understand their rights. 'Bah; yes; you have paid and you shall go. What would you have?' 'We would have what we have paid for,' said the American lady. Then the official rose from his stool and shrugged his shoulders again, and made a motion with both his hands, intended to shew that the thing was finished. 'It is a robbery,' said the elder American lady to the younger. 'I should not mind, only you are so unwell.' 'It will not kill me, I dare say,' said the younger. Then one of the English gentlemen declared that his place was very much at the service of the invalid, – and the other Englishman declared that his also was at the service of the invalid's companion. Then, and not till then, the two men recognised each other. One was Mr Glascock, on his way to Naples, and the other was Mr Trevelyan, on his way, – he knew not whither.

Upon this, of course, they spoke to each other. In London they had been well acquainted, each having been an intimate guest at the house of old Lady Milborough. And each knew something of the other's recent history. Mr Glascock was aware, as was all the world, that Trevelyan had quarrelled with his wife; and Trevelyan was aware that Mr Glascock had been spoken of as a suitor to his own sister-in-law. Of that visit which Mr Glascock had made to Nuncombe Putney, and of the manner in which Nora had behaved to her lover, Trevelyan knew nothing. Their greetings spoken, their first topic of conversation was, of course, the injury proposed to be done to the American ladies, and which would now fall upon them. They went into the waiting-room together, and during such toilet as they could make there, grumbled furiously. They would take post horses over the mountain, not from any love of solitary grandeur, but in order that they might make the company pay for its iniquity. But it was soon apparent to them that they themselves had no ground of complaint, and as everybody was very civil, and as a seat in the banquette over the heads of the American ladies was provided for them, and as the man from the bureau came and apologised, they consented to be pacified, and ended, of course, by tipping half-a-dozen of the servants about the yard. Mr Glascock had a man of his own with him, who was very nearly being put on to the same seat with his master as an extra civility; but this inconvenience was at last avoided. Having settled these little difficulties, they went into breakfast in the buffet.

There could be no better breakfast than used to be given in the buffet at the railway terminus at Saint Michel. The company might occasionally be led into errors about that question of coupé seats, but in reference to their provisions, they set an example which might be of great use to us here in England. It is probably the case that breakfasts for travellers are not so frequently needed here as they are on the Continent; but, still, there is often to be found a crowd of people ready to eat if only the wherewithal were there. We are often told in our newspapers that England is disgraced by this and by that; by the unreadiness of our army, by the unfitness of our navy, by the irrationality of our laws, by the immobility of our prejudices, and what not; but the real disgrace of England is the railway sandwich, − that whited sepulchre, fair enough outside, but so meagre, poor, and spiritless within, such a thing of shreds and parings, such a dab of food, telling us that the poor bone whence it was scraped had been made utterly bare before it was sent into the kitchen for the soup pot. In France one does get food at the railway stations, and at Saint Michel the breakfast was unexceptional.

Our two friends seated themselves near to the American ladies, and were, of course, thanked for their politeness. American women are taught by the habits of their country to think that men should give way to them more absolutely than is in accordance with the practices of life in Europe. A seat in a public conveyance in the States, when merely occupied by a man, used to be regarded by any woman as being at her service as completely as though it were vacant. One woman indicating a place to another would point with equal freedom to a man or a space. It is said that this is a little altered now, and that European views on this subject are spreading themselves. Our two ladies, however, who were pretty, clever-looking, and attractive even after the night's journey, were manifestly more impressed with the villainy of the French officials than they were with the kindness of their English neighbours.

'And nothing can be done to punish them?' said the younger of them to Mr Glascock.

'Nothing, I should think,' said he. 'Nothing will, at any rate.'

'And you will not get back your money?' said the elder, − who, though the elder, was probably not much above twenty.

'Well; − no. Time is money, they say. It would take thrice the value of the time in money, and then one would probably fail. They have done very well for us, and I suppose there are difficulties.'

'It couldn't have taken place in our country,' said the younger lady. 'All the same, we are very much obliged to you. It would not have been nice for us to have to go up into the banquette.'

'They would have put you into the interior.'

'And that would have been worse. I hate being put anywhere, – as if I were a sheep. It seems so odd to us, that you here should be all so tame.'

'Do you mean the English, or the French, or the world in general on this side of the Atlantic?'

'We mean Europeans,' said the younger lady, who was better after her breakfast. 'But then we think that the French have something of compensation, in their manners, and their ways of life, their climate, the beauty of their cities, and their general management of things.'

'They are very great in many ways, no doubt,' said Mr Glascock.

'They do understand living better than you do,' said the elder.

'Everything is so much brighter with them,' said the younger.

'They contrive to give a grace to every-day existence,' said the elder.

'There is such a welcome among them for strangers,' said the younger.

'Particularly in reference to places taken in the coupé,' said Trevelyan, who had hardly spoken before.

'Ah, that is an affair of honesty,' said the elder. 'If we want honest, I believe we must go back to the stars and stripes.'

Mr Glascock looked up from his plate almost aghast. He said nothing, however, but called for the waiter, and paid for his breakfast. Nevertheless, there was a considerable amount of travelling friendship engendered between the ladies and our two friends before the diligence had left the railway yard. They were two Miss Spaldings, going on to Florence, at which place they had an uncle, who was minister from the States to the kingdom of Italy;* and they were not at all unwilling to receive such little civilities as gentlemen can give to ladies when travelling. The whole party intended to sleep at Turin that night, and they were altogether on good terms with each other when they started on the journey from Saint Michel.

'Clever women those,' said Mr Glascock, as soon as they had arranged their legs and arms in the banquette.

'Yes, indeed.'

'American women always are clever, – and are almost always pretty.'

'I do not like them,' said Trevelyan, – who in these days was in a mood to like nothing. 'They are exigeant; – and then they are so hard. They want the weakness that a woman ought to have.'

'That comes from what they would call your insular prejudice. We are accustomed to less self-assertion on the part of women than is customary with them. We prefer women to rule us by seeming to yield. In the States, as I take it, the women never yield, and the men have to fight their own battles with other tactics.'

'I don't know what their tactics are.'

'They keep their distance. The men live much by themselves, as though they knew they would not have a chance in the presence of their wives and daughters. Nevertheless they don't manage these things badly. You very rarely hear of an American being separated from his wife.'

The words were no sooner out of his mouth, than Mr Glascock knew, and remembered, and felt what he had said. There are occasions in which a man sins so deeply against fitness and the circumstances of the hour, that it becomes impossible for him to slur over his sin as though it had not been committed. There are certain little peccadilloes in society which one can manage to throw behind one, – perhaps with some difficulty, and awkwardness; but still they are put aside, and conversation goes on, though with a hitch. But there are graver offences, the gravity of which strikes the offender so seriously that it becomes impossible for him to seem even to ignore his own iniquity. Ashes must be eaten publicly, and sackcloth worn before the eyes of men. It was so now with poor Mr Glascock. He thought about it for a moment, – whether or no it was possible that he should continue his remarks about the American ladies, without betraying his own consciousness of the thing that he had done; and he found that it was quite impossible. He knew that he was red up to his hairs, and hot, and that his blood tingled. His blushes, indeed, would not be seen in the seclusion of the banquette; but he could not overcome the heat and the tingling. There was silence for about three minutes, and then he felt that it would be best for him to confess his own fault. 'Trevelyan,' he said, 'I am very sorry for the allusion that I made. I ought to have been less awkward, and I beg your pardon.'

'It does not matter,' said Trevelyan. 'Of course I know that everybody is talking of it behind my back. I am not to expect that people will be silent because I am unhappy.'

'Nevertheless I beg your pardon,' said the other.

There was but little further conversation between them till they reached Lanslebourg, at the foot of the mountains, at which place they occupied themselves with getting coffee for the two American ladies. The Miss Spaldings took their coffee almost with as much grace as though it had been handed to them by Frenchmen. And indeed they were very gracious, – as is the nature of American ladies in spite of that hardness of which Trevelyan had complained.

They assume an intimacy readily, with no appearance of impropriety, and are at their ease easily. When, therefore, they were handed out of their carriage by Mr Glascock, the bystanders at Lanslebourg might have thought that the whole party had been travelling together from New York. 'What should we have done if you hadn't taken pity on us?' said the elder lady. 'I don't think we could have climbed up into that high place; and look at the crowd that have come out of the interior. A man has some advantages after all.'

'I am quite in the dark as to what they are,' said Mr Glascock.

'He can give up his place to a lady, and can climb up into a banquette.'

'And he can be a member of Congress,' said the younger. 'I'd sooner be senator from Massachusets than be the Queen of England.'

'So would I,' said Mr Glascock. 'I'm glad we can agree about one thing.'

The two gentlemen agreed to walk up the mountain together, and with some trouble induced the conductor to permit them to do so. Why conductors of diligences should object to such relief to their horses the ordinary Englishman can hardly understand. But in truth they feel so deeply the responsibility which attaches itself to their shepherding of their sheep, that they are always fearing lest some poor lamb should go astray on the mountain side. And though the road be broad and very plainly marked, the conductor never feels secure that his passenger will find his way safely to the summit. He likes to know that each of his flock is in his right place, and disapproves altogether of an erratic spirit. But Mr Glascock at last prevailed, and the two men started together up the mountain. When the permission has been once obtained the walker may be sure that his guide and shepherd will not desert him.

'Of course I know,' said Trevelyan, when the third twist up the mountain had been overcome, 'that people talk about me and my wife. It is a part of the punishment for the mistake that one makes.'

'It is a sad affair altogether.'

'The saddest in the world. Lady Milborough has no doubt spoken to you about it.'

'Well; — yes; she has.'

'How could she help it? I am not such a fool as to suppose that people are to hold their tongues about me more than they do about others. Intimate as she is with you, of course she has spoken to you.'

'I was in hopes that something might have been done by this time.'

'Nothing has been done. Sometimes I think I shall put an end to myself, it makes me so wretched.'

'Then why don't you agree to forget and forgive and have done with it?'

'That is so easily said; — so easily said.' After this they walked on in silence for a considerable distance. Mr Glascock was not anxious to talk about Trevelyan's wife, but he did wish to ask a question or two about Mrs Trevelyan's sister, if only this could be done without telling too much of his own secret. 'There's nothing I think so grand, as walking up a mountain,' he said after a while.

'It's all very well,' said Trevelyan, in a tone which seemed to imply that to him in his present miserable condition all recreations, exercises, and occupations were mere leather and prunella.*

'I don't mean, you know, in the Alpine Club way,' said Glascock. 'I'm too old and too stiff for that. But when the path is good, and the air not too cold, and when it is neither snowing, nor thawing, nor raining, and when the sun isn't hot, and you've got plenty of time, and know that you can stop any moment you like and be pushed up by a carriage, I do think walking up a mountain is very fine, — if you've got proper shoes, and a good stick, and it isn't too soon after dinner. There's nothing like the air of Alps.' And Mr Glascock renewed his pace, and stretched himself against the hill at the rate of three miles an hour.

'I used to be very fond of Switzerland,' said Trevelyan, 'but I don't care about it now. My eye has lost all its taste.'

'It isn't the eye,' said Glascock.

'Well; no. The truth is that when one is absolutely unhappy one cannot revel in the imagination. I don't believe in the miseries of poets.'

'I think myself,' said Glascock, 'that a poet should have a good digestion. By-the-bye, Mrs Trevelyan and her sister went down to Nuncombe Putney, in Devonshire.'

'They did go there.'

'Have they moved since? A very pretty place is Nuncombe Putney.'

'You have been there, then?'

Mr Glascock blushed again. He was certainly an awkward man, saying things that he ought not to say, and telling secrets which ought not to have been told. 'Well; — yes. I have been there, — as it happens.'

'Just lately do you mean?'

Mr Glascock paused, hoping to find his way out of the scrape, but soon perceived that there was no way out. He could not lie, even in an affair of love, and was altogether destitute of those honest subterfuges, — subterfuges honest in such position, — of which a dozen would have been at once at the command of any woman, and with one of which, sufficient for the moment, most men would have been able to arm themselves. 'Indeed, yes,' he said, almost stammering as he spoke. 'It was lately; — since your wife went there.' Trevelyan, though he had been told of the possibility of Mr Glascock's courtship, felt himself almost aggrieved by this man's intrusion on his wife's retreat. Had he not sent her there that she might be private; and what right had any one to invade such privacy? 'I suppose I had better tell the truth at once,' said Mr Glascock. 'I went to see Miss Rowley.'

'Oh, indeed.'

'My secret will be safe with you, I know.'

'I did not know that there was a secret,' said Trevelyan. 'I should have thought that they would have told me.'

'I don't see that. However, it doesn't matter much. I got nothing by my journey. Are the ladies still at Nuncombe Putney?'

'No, they have moved from there to London.'

'Not back to Curzon Street?'

'Oh dear, no. There is no house in Curzon Street for them now.' This was said in a tone so sad that it almost made Mr Glascock weep. 'They are staying with an aunt of theirs, — out to the east of the city.'

'At St Diddulph's?'

'Yes; — with Mr Outhouse, the clergyman there. You can't conceive what it is not to be able to see your own child; and yet, how can I take the boy from her?'

'Of course not. He's only a baby.'

'And yet all this is brought to me solely by her obstinacy. God knows, however, I don't want to say a word against her. People choose to say that I am to blame, and they may say so for me. Nothing that any one may say can add anything to the weight that I have to bear.' Then they walked to the top of the mountain in silence, and in due time were picked up by their proper shepherd and carried down to Susa at a pace that would give an English coachman a concussion of the brain.

Why passengers for Turin, who reach Susa dusty, tired, and sleepy, should be detained at that place for an hour and a half instead of being forwarded to their beds in the great city, is never made very apparent. All travelling officials on the continent of

Europe are very slow in their manipulation of luggage; but as they are equally correct we will find the excuse for their tardiness in the latter quality. The hour and a half, however, is a necessity, and it is very grievous. On this occasion the two Miss Spaldings ate their supper, and the two gentlemen waited on them. The ladies had learned to regard at any rate Mr Glascock as their own property, and received his services, graciously indeed, but quite as a matter of course. When he was sent from their peculiar corner of the big, dirty refreshment room to the supper-table to fetch an apple, and then desired to change it because the one which he had brought was spotted, he rather liked it. And when he sat down with his knees near to theirs, actually trying to eat a large Italian apple himself simply because they had eaten one, and discussed with them the passage over the Mont Cenis, he began to think that Susa was, after all, a place in which an hour and a half might be whiled away without much cause for complaint.

'We only stay one night at Turin,' said Caroline Spalding, the elder.

'And we shall have to start at ten, – to get through to Florence to-morrow,' said Olivia, the younger. 'Isn't it cruel, wasting all this time when we might be in bed?'

'It is not for me to complain of the cruelty,' said Mr Glascock.

'We should have fared infinitely worse if we hadn't met you,' said Caroline Spalding.

'But our republican simplicity won't allow us to assert that even your society is better than going to bed, after a journey of thirty hours,' said Olivia.

In the meantime Trevelyan was roaming about the station moodily by himself, and the place is one not apt to restore cheerfulness to a moody man by any resources of its own. When the time for departure came Mr Glascock sought him and found him; but Trevelyan had chosen a corner for himself in a carriage, and declared that he would rather avoid the ladies for the present. 'Don't think me uncivil to leave you,' he said, 'but the truth is, I don't like American ladies.'

'I do rather,' said Mr Glascock.

'You can say that I've got a headache,' said Trevelyan. So Mr Glascock returned to his friends, and did say that Mr Trevelyan had a headache. It was the first time that a name had been mentioned between them.

'Mr Trevelyan! What a pretty name. It sounds like a novel,' said Olivia.

'A very clever man,' said Mr Glascock, 'and much liked by his own circle. But he has had trouble, and is unhappy.'

'He looks unhappy,' said Caroline.

'The most miserable looking man I ever saw in my life,' said Olivia. Then it was agreed between them as they went up to Trompetta's hotel, that they would go on together by the ten o'clock train to Florence.

38

Verdict of the Jury — 'Mad, My Lord'

Trevelyan was left alone at Turin when Mr Glascock went on to Florence with his fair American friends. It was imperatively necessary that he should remain at Turin, though he had no business there of any kind whatever, and did not know a single person in the city. And of all towns in Italy Turin has perhaps less of attraction to offer to the solitary visitor than any other. It is new and parallelogrammatic as an American town, is very cold in cold weather, very hot in hot weather, and now that it has been robbed of its life as a capital,* is as dull and uninteresting as though it were German or English. There is the Armoury, and the river Po, and a good hotel. But what are these things to a man who is forced to live alone in a place for four days, or perhaps a week? Trevelyan was bound to remain at Turin till he should hear from Bozzle. No one but Bozzle knew his address; and he could do nothing till Bozzle should have communicated to him tidings of what was being done at St Diddulph's.

There is perhaps no great social question so imperfectly understood among us at the present day as that which refers to the line which divides sanity from insanity. That this man is sane and that other unfortunately mad we do know well enough; and we know also that one man may be subject to various hallucinations, — may fancy himself to be a teapot, or what not, — and yet be in such a condition of mind as to call for no intervention either on behalf of his friends, or of the law; while another may be in possession of intellectual faculties capable of lucid exertion for the highest purposes, and yet be so mad that bodily restraint upon him is indispensable. We know that the sane man is responsible for what he does, and that the insane man is irresponsible; but we do not know, — we only guess wildly, at the state of mind of those, who now and again act like madmen, though no court or council of experts has declared them to be mad. The bias of the public mind is to press heavily on such men till the law attempts to touch them, as though they were thoroughly responsible; and then, when the law interferes, to screen them as though they were altogether irresponsible. The same juryman who would find a man mad who has murdered a young woman, would in private life express a desire that the same young man should be hung, crucified, or skinned alive, if he had moodily and without reason broken his faith to the young woman in lieu of killing her. Now Trevelyan was, in truth, mad on the subject of his wife's alleged infidelity. He had abandoned everything that he valued in the world, and had made himself wretched in every affair of life, because he could not submit to acknowledge to himself the possibility of error on his own part. For that, in truth, was the condition of his mind. He had never hitherto believed that she had been false to her vow, and had sinned against him irredeemably; but he had thought that in her regard for another man she had slighted him; and, so thinking, he had subjected her to a severity of rebuke which no high-spirited woman could have borne. His wife had not tried to bear it, – in her indignation had not striven to cure the evil. Then had come his resolution that she should submit, or part from him; and, having so resolved, nothing could shake him. Though every friend he possessed was now against him, – including even Lady Milborough, – he was certain that he was right. Had not his wife sworn to obey him, and was not her whole conduct one tissue of disobedience? Would not the man who submitted to this find himself driven to submit to things worse? Let her own her fault, let her submit, and then she should come back to him.

He had not considered, when his resolutions to this effect were first forming themselves, that a separation between a man and his wife once effected cannot be annulled, and as it were cured, so as to leave no cicatrice behind. Gradually, as he spent day after day in thinking on this one subject, he came to feel that even were his wife to submit, to own her fault humbly, and to come back to him, this very coming back would in itself be a new wound. Could he go out again with his wife on his arm to the houses of those who knew that he had repudiated her because of her friendship with another man? Could he open again that house in Curzon Street, and let things go on quietly as they had gone before? He told himself that it was impossible; – that he and she were ineffably disgraced; – that, if reunited, they must live buried out of sight in some remote distance. And he told himself, also, that he could never be with her

again night or day without thinking of the separation. His happiness
had been shipwrecked.

Then he had put himself into the hands of Mr Bozzle, and Mr
Bozzle had taught him that women very often do go astray. Mr
Bozzle's idea of female virtue was not high, and he had opportunities of implanting his idea on his client's mind. Trevelyan hated
the man. He was filled with disgust by Bozzle's words, and was
made miserable by Bozzle's presence. Yet he came gradually to
believe in Bozzle. Bozzle alone believed in him. There were none
but Bozzle who did not bid him to submit himself to his disobedient
wife. And then, as he came to believe in Bozzle, he grew to be more
and more assured that no one but Bozzle could tell him facts. His
chivalry, and love, and sense of woman's honour, with something
of manly pride on his own part, – so he told himself, – had taught
him to believe it to be impossible that his wife should have sinned.
Bozzle, who knew the world, thought otherwise. Bozzle, who had
no interest in the matter, one way or the other, would find out
facts. What if his chivalry, and love, and manly pride had deceived
him? There were women who sinned. Then he prayed that his wife
might not be such a woman; and got up from his prayers almost
convinced that she was a sinner.

His mind was at work upon it always. Could it be that she was
so base as this – so vile a thing, so abject, such dirt, pollution, filth?
But there were such cases. Nay, were they not almost numberless?
He found himself reading in the papers records of such things from
day to day, and thought that in doing so he was simply acquiring
experience necessary for himself. If it were so, he had indeed done
well to separate himself from a thing so infamous. And if it were
not so, how could it be that that man had gone to her in
Devonshire? He had received from his wife's hands a short note
addressed to the man, in which the man was desired by her not to
go to her, or to write to her again, because of her husband's
commands. He had shown this to Bozzle, and Bozzle had smiled.
'It's just the sort of thing they does,' Bozzle had said. 'Then they
writes another by post.' He had consulted Bozzle as to the sending
on of that letter, and Bozzle had been strongly of opinion that it
should be forwarded, a copy having been duly taken and attested
by himself. It might be very pretty evidence by-and-by. If the letter
were not forwarded, Bozzle thought that the omission to do so
might be given in evidence against his employer. Bozzle was very
careful, and full of 'evidence.' The letter therefore was sent on to
Colonel Osborne. 'If there's billy-dous going between 'em we shall

nobble 'em,' said Bozzle. Trevelyan tore his hair in despair, but believed that there would be billy-dous.

He came to believe everything; and, though he prayed fervently that his wife might not be led astray, that she might be saved at any rate from utter vice, yet he almost came to hope that it might be otherwise; — not, indeed, with the hope of the sane man, who desires that which he tells himself to be for his advantage; but with the hope of the insane man, who loves to feed his grievance, even though the grief should be his death. They who do not understand that a man may be brought to hope that which of all things is the most grievous to him, have not observed with sufficient closeness the perversity of the human mind. Trevelyan would have given all that he had to save his wife; would, even now, have cut his tongue out before he would have expressed to anyone, — save to Bozzle, — a suspicion that she could in truth have been guilty; was continually telling himself that further life would be impossible to him, if he, and she, and that child of theirs, should be thus disgraced; — and yet he expected it, believed it, and, after a fashion, he almost hoped it.

He was to wait at Turin till tidings should come from Bozzle, and after that he would go on to Venice; but he would not move from Turin till he should have received his first communication from England. When he had been three days at Turin they came to him, and, among other letters in Bozzle's packet, there was a letter addressed in his wife's handwriting. The letter was simply directed to Bozzle's house. In what possible way could his wife have found out ought of his dealings with Bozzle, — where Bozzle lived, or could have learned that letters intended for him should be sent to the man's own residence? Before, however, we inspect the contents of Mr Bozzle's dispatch, we will go back and see how Mrs Trevelyan had discovered the manner of forwarding a letter to her husband.

The matter of the address was, indeed, very simple. All letters for Trevelyan were to be redirected from the house in Curzon Street, and from the chambers in Lincoln's Inn, to the Acrobats' Club; to the porter of the Acrobats' Club had been confided the secret, not of Bozzle's name, but of Bozzle's private address, No. 55, Stony Walk, Union Street, Borough. Thus all letters reching the Acrobats', were duly sent to Mr Bozzle's house. It may be remembered that Hugh Stanbury, on the occasion of his last visit to the parsonage of St Diddulph's, was informed that Mrs Trevelyan had a letter from her father for her husband, and that she knew not whither to send it. It may well be that, had the matter assumed no other interest in Stanbury's eyes than that given to it by Mrs Trevelyan's very moderate anxiety to have the letter forwarded, he would have thought nothing about it; but having resolved, as he sat upon the knifeboard of the omnibus, – the reader will, at any rate, remember those resolutions made on the top of the omnibus while Hugh was smoking his pipe, – having resolved that a deed should be done at St Diddulph's, he resolved also that it should be done at once. He would not allow the heat of his purpose to be cooled by delay. He would go to St Diddulph's at once, with his heart in his hand. But it might, he thought, be as well that he should have an excuse for his visit. So he called upon the porter at the Acrobats', and was successful in learning Mr Trevelyan's address. 'Stony Walk, Union Street, Borough,' he said to himself, wondering; then it occurred to him that Bozzle, and Bozzle only among Trevelyan's friends, could live at Stony Walk in the Borough. Thus armed, he set out for St Diddulph's; – and, as one of the effects of his visit to the East, Sir Marmaduke's note was forwarded to Louis Trevelyan at Turin.

39
Miss Nora Rowley is Maltreated

Hugh Stanbury, when he reached the parsonage, found no difficulty in making his way into the joint presence of Mrs Outhouse, Mrs Trevelyan, and Nora. He was recognised by the St Diddulph's party as one who had come over to their side, as a friend of Trevelyan who had found himself constrained to condemn his friend in spite of his friendship, and was consequently very welcome. And there was no difficulty about giving the address. The ladies wondered how it came to pass that Mr Trevelyan's letters should be sent to such a locality, and Hugh expressed his surprise also. He thought it discreet to withhold his suspicions about Mr Bozzle, and simply expressed his conviction that letters sent in accordance with the directions given by the club-porter would reach their destination. Then the boy was brought down, and they were all very confidential and very unhappy together. Mrs Trevelyan could see no end to the cruelty of her position, and declared that her father's anger against her husband was so great that she anticipated his coming with almost more of fear than of hope. Mrs Outhouse expressed an opinion that Mr Trevelyan must surely be mad; and Nora suggested that the possibility of such perversity on the part of a man made it almost unwise in any woman to trust herself to the power of a husband. 'But there are not many like him, thank God,' said Mrs

Outhouse, bridling in her wrath. Thus they were very friendly together, and Hugh was allowed to feel that he stood upon comfortable terms in the parsonage; – but he did not as yet see how he was to carry out his project for the present day.

At last Mrs Trevelyan went away with the child. Hugh felt that he ought to go, but stayed courageously. He thought he could perceive that Nora suspected the cause of his assiduity; but it was quite evident that Mrs Outhouse did not do so. Mrs Outhouse, having reconciled herself to the young man, was by no means averse to his presence. She went on talking about the wickedness of Trevelyan, and her brother's anger, and the fate of the little boy, till at last the little boy's mother came back into the room. Then Mrs Outhouse went. They must excuse her for a few minutes, she said. If only she would have gone a few minutes sooner, how well her absence might have been excused. Nora understood it all now; and though she became almost breathless, she was not surprised, when Hugh got up from his chair and asked her sister to go away. 'Mrs Trevelyan,' he said, 'I want to speak a few words to your sister. I hope you will give me the opportunity.'

'Nora !' exclaimed Mrs Trevelyan.

'She knows nothing about it,' said Hugh.

'Am I to go ?' said Mrs Trevelyan to her sister. But Nora said never a word. She sat perfectly fixed, not turning her eyes from the object on which she was gazing.

'Pray, – pray do,' said Hugh.

'I cannot think that it will be for any good,' said Mrs Trevelyan; 'but I know that she may be trusted. And I suppose it ought to be so, if you wish it.'

'I do wish it, of all things,' said Hugh, still standing up, and almost turning the elder sister out of the room by the force of his look and voice. Then, with another pause of a moment, Mrs Trevelyan rose from her chair and left the room, closing the door after her.

Hugh, when he found that the coast was clear for him, immediately began his task with a conviction that not a moment was to be lost. He had told himself a dozen times that the matter was hopeless, that Nora had shown him by every means in her power that she was indifferent to him, that she with all her friends would know that such a marriage was out of the question; and he had in truth come to believe that the mission which he had in hand was one in which success was not possible. But he thought that it was his duty to go on with it. 'If a man love a woman, even though it be the king and the beggar-woman reversed, – though it be a beggar and a queen, he should tell her of it. If it be so, she has a right to know it and to take her choice. And he has a right to tell her, and to say what he can for himself.' Such was Hugh's doctrine in the matter; and, acting upon it, he found himself alone with his mistress.

'Nora,' he said, speaking perhaps with more energy than the words required, 'I have come here to tell you that I love you, and to ask you to be my wife.'

Nora, for the last ten minutes, had been thinking that this would come, – that it would come at once; and yet she was not at all prepared with an answer. It was now weeks since she had confessed to herself frankly that nothing else but this, – this one thing which was now happening, this one thing which had now happened, – that nothing else could make her happy, or could touch her happiness. She had refused a man whom she otherwise would have taken, because her heart had been given to Hugh Stanbury. She had been bold enough to tell that other suitor that it was so, though she had not mentioned the rival's name. She had longed for some expression of love from this man when they had been at Nuncombe together, and had been fiercely angry with him because no such expression had come from him. Day after day, since she had been with her aunt, she had told herself that she was a broken-hearted woman, because she had given away all that she had to give and had received nothing in return. Had he said a word that might have given her hope, how happy could she have been in hoping. Now he had come to her with a plain-spoken offer, telling her that he loved her, and asking her to be his wife, – and she was altogether unable to answer. How could she consent to be his wife, knowing as she did that there was no certainty of an income on which they could live ? How could she tell her father and mother that she had engaged herself to marry a man who might or might not make £400 a year, and who already had a mother and sister depending on him ?

In truth, had he come more gently to her, his chance of a happy answer, – of an answer which might be found to have in it something of happiness, – would have been greater. He might have said a word which she could not but have answered softly; – and then from that constrained softness other gentleness would have followed, and so he would have won her in spite of her discretion. She would have surrendered gradually, accepting on the score of her great love all the penalties of a long and precarious engagement. But when she was asked to come and be his wife, now and at once, she felt that in spite of her love it was impossible that she could accede to a request so sudden, so violent, so monstrous. He stood over her as though expecting an instant answer; and then, when she had sat dumb before him for a minute, he repeated his demand. 'Tell me, Nora, can you love me? If you know how thoroughly I have loved you, you would at least feel something for me.'

To tell him that she did not love him was impossible to her. But how was she to refuse him without telling him either a lie, or the truth? Some answer she must give him; and as to that matter of marrying him, the answer must be a negative. Her education had been of that nature which teaches girls to believe that it is a crime to marry a man without an assured income. Assured morality in a husband is a great thing. Assured good temper is very excellent. Assured talent, religion, amiability, truth, honesty, are all desirable. But an assured income is indispensable. Whereas, in truth, the income may come hereafter; but the other things, unless they be there already, will hardly be forthcoming. 'Mr Stanbury,' she said, 'your suddenness has quite astounded me.'

'Ah, yes; but how should I not be sudden? I have come here on purpose to say this to you. If I do not say it now – '

'You heard what Emily said.'

'No; – what did she say?'

'She said that it would not be for good that you should speak to me thus.'

'Why not for good? But she is unhappy, and looks gloomily at things.'

'Yes, indeed.'

'But all the world need not be sad for ever because she has been unfortunate.'

'Not all the world, Mr Stanbury; – but you must not be surprised if it affects me.'

'But would that prevent your loving me, – if you did love me? But, Nora, I do not expect you to love me, – not yet. I do not say that I expect it, – ever. But if you would – Nora, I can do no more than tell you the simple truth. Just listen to me for a minute. You know how I came to be intimate with you all in Curzon Street. The first day I saw you I loved you; and there has come no change yet. It is months now since I first knew that I loved you. Well; I told myself more than once, – when I was down at Nuncombe for instance, – that I had no right to speak to you. What right can a poor devil like me have, who lives from hand to mouth, to ask such a girl as you to be his wife? And so I said nothing, – though it was on my lips every moment that I was there.' Nora remembered at the moment how she had looked to his lips, and had not seen the words there. 'But I think there is something unmanly in this. If you cannot give me a grain of hope; – if you tell me that there never can be hope, it is my misfortune. It will be very grievous, but I will bear it. But that will be better than puling and moping about without daring to tell my tale. I am not ashamed of it. I have fallen in love with you, Nora, and I think it best to come for an answer.'

He held out his arms as though he thought that she might perhaps come to him. Indeed he had no idea of any such coming on her part; but she, as she looked at him, almost thought that it was her duty to go. Had she a right to withhold herself from him, she who loved him so dearly? Had he stepped forward and taken her in his arms, it might be that all power of refusal would soon have been beyond her power.

'Mr Stanbury,' she said, 'you have confessed yourself that it is impossible.'

'But do you love me; – do you think that it is possible that you should ever love me?'

'You know, Mr Stanbury, that you should not say anything further. You know that it cannot be.'

'But do you love me?'

'You are ungenerous not to take an answer without driving me to be uncourteous.'

'I do not care for courtesy. Tell me the truth. Can you ever love me? With one word of hope I will wait, and work, and feel myself to be a hero. I will not go till you tell me that you cannot love me.'

'Then I must tell you so.'

'What is it you will tell me, Nora? Speak it. Say it. If I knew that a girl disliked me, nothing should make me press myself upon her. Am I odious to you, Nora?'

'No; not odious, – but very, very unfair.'

'I will have the truth if I be ever sir,' he said. And by this time probably some inkling of the truth had reached his intelligence. There was already a tear in Nora's eye, but he did not pity her. She owed it to him to tell him the truth, and he would have it from her if it was to be reached. 'Nora,' he said, 'listen to me again. All my heart and soul are in this. It is everything to me. If you can love me you are bound to say so. By Jove, I will believe you do, unless you swear to me that it is not so!' He was now holding her by the hand and looking closely into her face.

'Mr Stanbury,' she said, 'let me go; pray, pray let me go.'

'Not till you say that you love me. Oh, Nora, I believe that you love me. You do; yes; you do love me. Dearest, dearest Nora, would you not say a word to make me the happiest man in the world?' And now he had his arm round her waist.

'Let me go,' she said, struggling through her tears and covering her face with her hands. 'You are very, very wicked. I will never speak to you again. Nay, but you shall let me go!' And then she was out of his arms and had escaped from the room before he had managed to touch her face with his lips.

As he was thinking how he also might escape now, – might escape and comfort himself with his triumph, – Mrs Outhouse returned to the chamber. She was very demure, and her manner towards him was considerably changed since she had left the chamber. 'Mr Stanbury,' she said, 'this kind of thing mustn't go any further indeed; – at least not in my house.'

'What kind of thing, Mrs Outhouse?'

'Well; – what my elder niece has told me. I have not seen Miss Rowley since she left you. I am quite sure she has behaved with discretion.'

'Indeed she has, Mrs Outhouse.'

'The fact is my nieces are in grief and trouble, and this is no time or place for love-making. I am sorry to be uncivil, but I must ask you not to come here any more.'

'I will stay away from this house, certainly, if you bid me.'

'I am very sorry; but I must bid you. Sir Marmaduke will be home in the spring, and if you have anything to say to him of course you can see him.'

Then Hugh Stanbury took his leave of Mrs Outhouse; but as he went home, again on the knifeboard of an omnibus, he smoked the pipe of triumph rather than the pipe of contemplation.

40

C. G.

The Miss Spaldings were met at the station at Florence by their uncle, the American Minister, by their cousin, the American Secretary of Legation, and by three or four other dear friends and relations, who were there to welcome the newcomers to sunny Italy. Mr Glascock, therefore, who ten minutes since had been, and had felt himself to be, quite indispensable to their comfort, suddenly became as though he were nothing and nobody. Who is there that has not felt these sudden disruptions to the intimacies and friendships of a long journey? He bowed to them, and they to him, and then they were whirled away in their grandeur. He put himself into a small, open hackney-carriage, and had himself driven to the York Hotel, feeling himself to be deserted and desolate. The two Miss

Spaldings were the daughters of a very respectable lawyer at Boston, whereas Mr Glascock was heir to a peerage, to an enormous fortune, and to one of the finest places in England. But he thought nothing of this at the time. As he went, he was meditating which young woman was the most attractive, Nora Rowley or Caroline Spalding. He had no doubt but that Nora was the prettier, the pleasanter in manner, the better dressed, the more engaging in all that concerned the outer woman; but he thought that he had never met any lady who talked better than Caroline Spalding. And what was Nora Rowley's beauty to him? Had she not told him that she was the property of some one else; or, for the matter of that, what was Miss Spalding to him? They had parted, and he was going on to Naples in two days. He had said some half-defined word as to calling at the American Embassy, but it had not been taken up by either of the ladies. He had not pressed it, and so they had parted without an understanding as to a future meeting.

The double journey, from Turin to Bologna and from Bologna to Florence, is very long, and forms ample time for a considerable intimacy. There had, too, been a long day's journeying together before that; and with no women is a speedy intimacy so possible, or indeed so profitable, as with Americans. They fear nothing, – neither you nor themselves; and talk with as much freedom as though they were men. It may, perhaps, be assumed to be true as a rule, that women's society is always more agreeable to men than that of other men, – except for the lack of ease. It undoubtedly is so when the women be young and pretty. There is a feeling, however, among pretty women in Europe that such freedom is dangerous, and it is withheld. There is such danger, and more or less of such withholding is expedient; but the American woman does not recognise the danger; and, if she withhold the grace of her countenance and the pearls of her speech, it is because she is not desirous of the society which is proffered to her. These two American sisters had not withholden their pearls from Mr Glascock. He was much their senior in age; he was gentle in his manners, and they probably recognised him to be a safe companion. They had no idea who he was, and had not heard his name when they parted from him. But it was not probable that they should have been with him so long, and that they should leave him without further thought of him, without curiosity, or a desire to know more of him. They had seen 'C. G.,' in large letters, on his dressing-bag, and that was all they had learned as to his identity. He had known their names well, and had once called Olivia by hers, in the hurry of speaking to her sister. He had apologised, and there had been a little laugh, and a discussion about the use of Christian names, – such as is very conducive to intimacy between gentlemen and ladies. When you can talk to a young lady about her own Christian name, you are almost entitled for the nonce to use it.

Mr Glascock went to his hotel, and was very moody and desolate. His name was very soon known there, and he received the honours due to his rank and station. 'I should like to travel in America,' he said to himself, 'if I could be sure that no one would find out who I was.' He had received letters at Turin, stating that his father was better, and, therefore, he intended to remain two days at Florence. The weather was still very hot, and Florence in the middle of September is much preferable to Naples.

That night, when the two Miss Spaldings were alone together, they discussed their fellow-traveller thoroughly. Something, of course, had been said about him to their uncle the minister, to their aunt the minister's wife, and to their cousin the secretary of legation. But travellers will always observe that the dear new friends they have made on their journey are not interesting to the dear old friends whom they meet afterwards. There may be some touch of jealousy in this; and then, though you, the traveller, are fully aware that there has been something special in the case which has made this new friendship more peculiar than others that have sprung up in similar circumstances, fathers and brothers and wives and sisters do not see it in that light. They suspect, perhaps, that the new friend was a bagman, or an opera dancer, and think that the affair need not be made of importance. The American Minister had cast his eye on Mr Glascock during that momentary parting, and had not thought much of Mr Glascock. 'He was, certainly, a gentleman,' Caroline had said. 'There are a great many English gentlemen,' the minister had replied.

'I thought you would have asked him to call,' Olivia said to her sister. 'He did offer.'

'Why didn't you tell him he might come?'

'Because we are not in Boston, Livy. It might be the most horrible thing in the world to do here in Florence; and it may make a difference, because Uncle Jonas is minister.'

'Why should that make a difference? Do you mean that one isn't to see one's own friends? That must be nonsense.'

'But he isn't a friend, Livy.'

'It seems to me as if I'd known him for ever. That soft, monotonous voice, which never became excited and never disagreeable, is as familiar to me as though I had lived with it all my life.'

'I thought him very pleasant.'

'Indeed, you did, Carry. And he thought you pleasant too. Doesn't it seem odd? You were mending his glove for him this very afternoon, just as if he were your brother.'

'Why shouldn't I mend his glove?'

'Why not, indeed? He was entitled to have everything mended after getting us such a good dinner at Bologna. By-the-bye, you never paid him.'

'Yes, I did, – when you were not by.'

'I wonder who he is! C. G.! That fine man in the brown coat was his servant, you know. I thought at first that C. G. must have been cracked, and that the tall man was his keeper.'

'I never knew any one less like a madman.'

'No; – but the man was so queer. He did nothing, you know. We hardly saw him, if you remember, at Turin. All he did was to tie the shawls at Bologna. What can any man want with another man about with him like that, unless he is cracked either in body or mind?'

'You'd better ask C. G. yourself.'

'I shall never see C. G. again, I suppose. I should like to see him again. I guess you would too, Carry. Eh?'

'Of course, I should; – why not?'

'I never knew a man so imperturbable, and who had yet so much to say for himself. I wonder what he is? Perhaps he's on business, and that man was a kind of a clerk.'

'He had livery buttons on,' said Carry.

'And does that make a difference?'

'I don't think they put clerks into livery, even in England.'

'Nor yet mad doctors,' said Olivia. 'Well, I like him very much; and the only thing against him is that he should have a man, six feet high, going about with him doing nothing.'

'You'll make me angry, Livy, if you talk in that way. It's uncharitable.'

'In what way?'

'About a mad doctor.'

'It's my belief,' said Olivia, 'that he's an English swell, a lord, or a duke; – and it's my belief, too, that he's in love with you.'

'It's my belief, Livy, that you're a regular ass;' – and so the conversation was ended on that occasion.

On the next day, about noon, the American Minister, as a part of the duty which he owed to his country, read in a publication of that day, issued for the purpose, the names of the new arrivals at Florence. First and foremost was that of the Honourable Charles Glascock, with his suite, at the York Hotel, en route to join his father, Lord Peterborough, at Naples. Having read the news first to himself, the minister read it out loud in the presence of his nieces.

'That's our friend C. G.,' said Livy.

'I should think not,' said the minister, who had his own ideas about an English lord.

'I'm sure it is, because of the tall man with the buttons,' said Olivia.

'It's very unlikely,' said the secretary of the legation. 'Lord Peterborough is a man of immense wealth, very old, indeed. They say he is dying in Naples. This man is his eldest son.'

'Is that any reason why he shouldn't have been civil to us?' asked Olivia.

'I don't think he is the sort of man likely to sit up in the banquette; and he would have posted over the Alps. Moreover, he had his suite with him.'

'His suite was Buttons,' said Olivia. 'Only fancy, Carry, we've been waited on for two days by a lord as is to be, and didn't know it! And you have mended the tips of his lordship's glove!' But Carry said nothing at all.

Late on that same evening, they met Mr Glascock close to the Duomo, under the shade of the Campanile. He had come out as they had done, to see by moonlight that loveliest of all works made by man's hands. They were with the minister, but Mr Glascock came up and shook hands with them.

'I would introduce you to my uncle, Mr Spalding,' said Olivia, – 'only, – as it happens, – we have never yet heard your name.'

'My name is Glascock,' said he, smiling. Then the introduction was made; and the American Minister took off his hat, and was very affable.

41

Showing What Took Place at St Diddulph's

Nora Rowley, when she escaped from the violence of her lover, at once rushed up to her own room, and managed to fasten herself in before she had been seen by any one. Her elder sister had at once gone to her aunt when, at Hugh's request, she had left the room, thinking it right that Mrs Outhouse should know what was being done in her own house. Mrs Outhouse had considered the matter patiently for awhile, giving the lovers the benefit of her hesitation, and had then spoken her mind to Stanbury, as we have already heard. He had, upon the whole, been so well pleased with what had occurred, that he was not in the least angry with the parson's wife when he left the parsonage. As soon as he was gone Mrs Outhouse was at once joined by her elder niece, but Nora remained for a while alone in her room.

Had she committed herself; and if so, did she regret it? He had behaved very badly to her, certainly, taking her by the hand and putting his arm round her waist. And then had he not even attempted to kiss her? He had done all this, although she had been resolute in refusing to speak to him one word of kindness, – though she had told him with all the energy and certainty of which she was mistress, that she would never be his wife. If a girl were to be subjected to such treatment as this when she herself had been so firm, so discreet, so decided, then indeed it would be unfit that a girl should trust herself with a man. She had never thought that he had been such a one as that, to ill-use her, to lay a hand on her in violence, to refuse to take an answer. She threw herself on the bed and sobbed, and then hid her face, – and was conscious that in spite of this acting before herself she was the happiest girl alive. He had behaved very badly; – of course, he had behaved most wickedly, and she would tell him so some day. But was he not the dearest fellow living? Did ever man speak with more absolute conviction of love in every tone of his voice? Was it not the finest, noblest heart that ever throbbed beneath a waistcoat? Had not his very wickedness come from the overpowering truth of his affection for her? She would never quite forgive him because it had been so very wrong; but she would be true to him for ever and ever. Of course they could not marry. What! – would she go to him and be a clog round his neck, and a weight upon him for ever, bringing him down to the gutter by the burden of her own useless and unworthy self? No. She would never so injure him. She would not even hamper him by an engagement. But yet she would be true to him. She had an idea that in spite of all her protestations, – which, as she looked back upon them, appeared to her to have been louder than they had been, – that through the teeth of her denials, something of the truth had escaped from her. Well, – let it be so. It was the truth, and why should he now know it? Then she pictured to herself a long romance, in which the heroine lived happily on the simple knowledge that she had been beloved. And the reader may be sure that in this romance Mr Glascock with his splendid prospects filled one of the characters.

She had been so wretched at Nuncombe Putney when she had felt herself constrained to admit to herself that this man for whom she had sacrificed herself did not care for her, that she could not now but enjoy her triumph. After she had sobbed upon the bed, she got up and walked about the room smiling; and she would now press her hands to her forehead, and then shake her tresses, and then clasp her own left hand with her right, as though he were still holding it. Wicked man! Why had he been so wicked and so violent? And why, why, why had she not once felt his lips upon her brow?

And she was pleased with herself. Her sister had rebuked her because she had refused to make her fortune by marrying Mr Glascock; and, to own the truth, she had rebuked herself on the same score when she found that Hugh Stanbury had not had a word of love to say to her. It was not that she regretted the grandeur which she had lost, but that she should, even within her own thoughts, with the consciousness of her own bosom, have declared herself unable to receive another man's devotion because of her love for this man who neglected her. Now she was proud of herself. Whether it might be accounted as good or ill-fortune that she had ever seen Hugh Stanbury, it must at any rate be right that she should be true to him now that she had seen him, and had loved him. To know that she loved and that she was not loved again had nearly killed her. But such was not her lot. She too had been successful with her quarry, and had struck her game, and brought down her dear. He had been very violent with her, but his violence had at least made the matter clear. He did love her. She would be satisfied with that, and would endeavour so to live that that alone should make life happy for her. How should she get his photograph, – and a lock of his hair? – and when again might she have the pleasure of placing her own hand within his great, rough, violent grasp? Then she kissed the hand which he had held, and opened the door of her room, at which her sister was now knocking.

'Nora, dear, will you not come down?'

'Not yet, Emily. Very soon I will.'

'And what has happened, dearest?'

'There is nothing to tell, Emily.'

'There must be something to tell What did he say to you?'

'Of course you know what he said.'

'And what answer did you make?'

'I told him that it could not be.'

'And did he take that, – as final, Nora?'

'Of course not. What man ever takes a No as final?'

'When you said No to Mr Glascock he took it.'

'That was different, Emily.'

'But how different? I don't see the difference, except that if you could have brought yourself to like Mr Glascock, it would have been the greatest thing in the world for you, and for all of them.'

'Would you have me take a man, Emily, that I didn't care one straw for, merely because he was a lord? You can't mean that.'

'I'm not talking about Mr Glascock now, Nora.'

'Yes, you are. And what's the use? He is gone, and there's an end of it.'

'And is Mr Stanbury gone?'

'Of course.'

'In the same way?' asked Mrs Trevelyan.

'How can I tell about his ways? No; it is not in the same way. There! He went in a very different way.'

'How was it different, Nora?'

'Oh, so different. I can't tell you how. Mr Glascock will never come back again.'

'And Mr Stanbury will?' said the elder sister. Nora made no reply, but after a while nodded her head. 'And you want him to come back?' She paused again, and again nodded her head. 'Then you have accepted him?'

'I have not accepted him. I have refused him. I have told him that it was impossible.'

'And yet you wish him back again!' Nora again nodded her head. 'That is a state of things I cannot at all understand,' said Mrs Trevelyan, 'and would not believe unless you told me so yourself.'

'And you think me very wrong, of course. I will endeavour to do nothing wrong, but it is so. I have not said a word of encouragement to Mr Stanbury; but I love him with all my heart. Ought I to tell you a lie when you question me? Or is it natural that I should never wish to see again a person whom I love better than all the world? It seems to me that a girl can hardly be right if she have any choice of her own. Here are two men, one rich and the other poor. I shall fall to the ground between them. I know that. I have fallen to the ground already. I like the one I can't marry. I don't care a straw for the one who could give me a grand house. That is falling to the ground. But I don't see that it is hard to understand, or that I have disgraced myself.'

'I said nothing of disgrace, Nora.'

'But you looked it.'

'I did not intend to look it, dearest.'

'And remember this, Emily, I have told you everything because you asked me. I do not mean to tell anybody else, at all. Mamma would not understand me. I have not told him, and I shall not.'

'You mean Mr Stanbury?'

'Yes; I mean Mr Stanbury. As to Mr Glascock, of course I shall tell mamma that. I have no secret there. That is his secret, and I suppose mamma should know it. But I will have nothing told about the other. Had I accepted him, or even hinted to him that I cared for him, I would tell mamma at once.'

After that there came something of a lecture, or something, rather, of admonition, from Mrs Outhouse. That lady did not attempt to upbraid, or to find any fault; but observed that as she understood that Mr Stanbury had no means whatsoever, and as Nora herself had none, there had better be no further intercourse between them, till, at any rate, Sir Marmaduke and Lady Rowley should be in London. 'So I told him that he must not come here any more, my dear,' said Mrs Outhouse.

'You are quite right, aunt. He ought not to come here.'

'I am so glad that you agree with me.'

'I agree with you altogether. I think I was bound to see him when he asked to see me; but the thing is altogether out of the question. I don't think he'll come any more, aunt.' Then Mrs Outhouse was quite satisfied that no harm had been done.

A month had now passed since anything had been heard at St Diddulph's from Mr Trevelyan, and it seemed that many months might go on in the same dull way. When Mrs Trevelyan first found herself in her uncle's house, a sum of two hundred pounds had been sent to her; and since that she had received a letter from her husband's lawyer saying that a similar amount would be sent to her every three months, as long as she was separated from her husband. A portion of this she had given over to Mr Outhouse; but this pecuniary assistance by no means comforted that unfortunate gentleman in his trouble. 'I don't want to get into debt,' he said, 'by keeping a lot of people whom I haven't the means to feed. And I don't want to board and lodge my nieces and their family at so much a head. It's very hard upon me either way.' And so it was. All the comfort of his home was destroyed, and he was driven to sacrifice his independence by paying his tradesmen with a portion of Mrs Trevelyan's money. The more he thought of it all, and the more he discussed the matter with his wife, the more indignant they became with the truant husband. 'I can't believe,' he said, 'but what Mr Bideawhile could make him come back, if he chose to do his duty.'

'But they say that Mr Trevelyan is in Italy, my dear.'

'And if I went to Italy, might I leave you to starve, and take my income with me?'

'He doesn't leave her quite to starve, my dear.'

'But isn't a man bound to stay with his wife? I never heard of such a thing, – never. And I'm sure that there must be something wrong. A man can't go away and leave his wife to live with her uncle and aunt. It isn't right.'

'But what can we do?'

Mr Outhouse was forced to acknowledge that nothing could be done. He was a man to whom the quiescence of his own childless house was the one pleasure of his existence. And of that he was robbed because this wicked madman chose to neglect all his duties, and leave his wife without a house to shelter her. 'Supposing that she couldn't have come here, what then?' said Mr Outhouse. 'I did tell him, as plain as words could speak, that we couldn't receive them.' 'But here they are,' said Mrs Outhouse, 'and here they must remain till my brother comes to England.' 'It's the most monstrous thing that I ever heard of in all my life,' said Mr Outhouse. 'He ought to be locked up; – that's what he ought.'

It was hard, and it became harder, when a gentleman, whom Mr Outhouse certainly did not wish to see, called upon him about the latter end of September. Mr Outhouse was sitting alone, in the gloomy parlour of his parsonage, – for his own study had been given up to other things, since this great inroad had been made upon his family; – he was sitting alone on one Saturday morning, preparing for the duties of the next day, with various manuscript sermons lying on the table around him, when he was told that a gentleman had called to see him. Had Mr Outhouse been an incumbent at the West-end of London, or had his maid been a West-end servant, in all probability the gentleman's name would have been demanded; but Mr Outhouse was a man who was not very ready in foreseeing and preventing misfortune, and the girl who opened the door was not trained to discreet usages in such matters. As she announced the fact that there was a gentleman, she pointed to the door, to show that the gentleman was there; and before Mr Outhouse had been able to think whether it would be prudent for him to make some preliminary inquiry, Colonel Osborne was in the room. Now, as it happened, these two men had never hitherto met each other, though one was the brother-in-law of Sir Marmaduke Rowley, and the other had been his very old friend. 'My name, Mr Outhouse, is Colonel Osborne,' said the visitor, coming forward, with his hand out. The clergyman, of course, took his hand, and asked him to be seated. 'We have known each other's names very long,' continued the Colonel, 'though I do not think we have ever yet had an opportunity of becoming acquainted.'

'No,' said Mr Outhouse; 'we have never been acquainted, I believe.' He might have added, that he had no desire whatever to make such acquaintance; and his manner, over which he himself had no control, did almost say as much. Indeed, this coming to his house of the suspected lover of his niece appeared to him to be a heavy addition to his troubles; for, although he was disposed to take his niece's part against her husband to any possible length, – even to the locking up of the husband as a madman, if it were possible, – nevertheless, he had almost as great a horror of the Colonel, as though the husband's allegations as to the lover had been true as gospel. Because Trevelyan had been wrong altogether, Colonel Osborne was not the less wrong. Because Trevelyan's suspicions were to Mr Outhouse wicked and groundless, he did not the less regard the presumed lover to be an iniquitous roaring lion, going about seeking whom he might devour. Elderly unmarried men of fashion generally, and especially colonels, and majors, and members of parliament, and such like, were to him as black sheep or roaring lions. They were 'fruges consumere nati;'* men who stood on club doorsteps talking naughtily and doing nothing, wearing sleek clothing, for which they very often did not pay, and never going to church. It seemed to him, – in his ignorance, – that such men had none of the burdens of this world upon their shoulders, and that, therefore, they stood in great peril of the burdens of the next. It was, doubtless, his special duty to deal with men in such peril; – but those wicked ones with whom he was concerned were those whom he could reach. Now, the Colonel Osbornes of the earth were not to be got at by any clergyman, or, as far as Mr Outhouse could see, by any means of grace. That story of the rich man and the camel seemed to him to be specially applicable to such people. How was such a one as Colonel Osborne to be shown the way through the eye of a needle? To Mr Outhouse, his own brother-in-law, Sir Marmaduke, was almost of the same class, – for he frequented clubs when in London, and played whist, and talked of the things of the world, – such as the Derby, and the levées, and West-end dinner parties, – as though they were all in all to him. He, to be sure, was weighted with so large a family that there might be hope for him. The eye of the needle could not be closed against him as a rich man; but he savoured of the West-end, and was worldly, and consorted with such men as this Colonel Osborne. When Colonel Osborne introduced himself to Mr Outhouse, it was almost as though Apollyon had made his way into the parsonage of St Diddulph's.

'Mr Outhouse,' said the Colonel, 'I have thought it best to come to you the very moment that I got back to town from Scotland.' Mr Outhouse bowed, and was bethinking himself slowly what manner of speech he would adopt. 'I leave town again to-morrow for Dorsetshire. I am going down to my friends, the Brambers, for partridge shooting.' Mr Outhouse knitted his thick brows, in further inward condemnation. Partridge shooting! yes; – this was September, and partridge shooting would be the probable care and occupation of such a man at such a time. A man without a duty in the world! Perhaps, added to this there was a feeling that, whereas Colonel Osborne could shoot Scotch grouse in August, and Dorsetshire partridges in September, and go about throughout the whole year like a roaring lion, he, Mr Outhouse, was forced to remain at St Diddulph's-in-the-East, from January to December, with the exception of one small parson's week spent at Margate, for the benefit of his wife's health. If there was such a thought, or, rather, such a feeling, who will say that it was not natural? 'But I could not go through London without seeing you,' continued the Colonel. 'This is a most frightful infatuation of Trevelyan!'

'Very frightful, indeed,' said Mr Outhouse.

'And, on my honour as a gentleman, not the slightest cause in the world.'

'You are old enough to be the lady's father,' said Mr Outhouse, managing in that to get one blow at the gallant Colonel.

'Just so. God bless my soul!' Mr Outhouse shrunk visibly at this profane allusion to the Colonel's soul. 'Why, I've known her father ever so many years. As you say, I might almost be her father myself.' As far as age went, such certainly might have been the case, for the Colonel was older than Sir Marmaduke. 'Look here, Mr Outhouse, here is a letter I got from Emily – '

'From Mrs Trevelyan?'

'Yes, from Mrs Trevelyan; and as well as I can understand, it must have been sent to me by Trevelyan himself. Did you ever hear of such a thing? And now I'm told he has gone away, nobody knows where, and has left her here.'

'He has gone away, – nobody knows where.'

'Of course, I don't ask to see her.'

'It would be imprudent, Colonel Osborne; and could not be permitted in this house.'

'I don't ask it. I have known Emily Trevelyan since she was an infant, and have always loved her. I'm her godfather, for aught I know, – though one forgets things of that sort.' Mr Outhouse again knit his eyebrows and shuddered visibly. 'She and I have been fast friends, – and why not? But, of course, I can't interfere.'

'If you ask me, Colonel Osborne, I should say that you can do nothing in the matter; – except to remain away from her. When Sir Marmaduke is in England, you can see him, if you please.'

'See him; – of course, I shall see him. And, by George, Louis Trevelyan will have to see him, too! I shouldn't like to have to stand up before Rowley if I had treated a daughter of his in such a fashion. You know Rowley, of course?'

'Oh, yes; I know him.'

'He's not the sort of man to bear this sort of thing. He'll about tear Trevelyan in pieces if he gets hold of him. God bless my soul – ' the eye brows went to work again, – 'I never heard of such a thing in all my life! Does he pay anything for them, Mr Outhouse?'

This was dreadful to the poor clergyman. 'That is a subject which we surely need not discuss,' said he. Then he remembered that such speech on his part was like to a subterfuge, and he found it necessary to put himself right. 'I am repaid for the maintenance here of my nieces, and the little boy, and their attendants. I do not know why the question should be asked, but such is the fact.'

'Then they are here by agreement between you and him?'

'No, sir; they are not. There is no such agreement. But I do not like these interrogatives from a stranger as to matters which should be private.'

'You cannot wonder at my interest, Mr Outhouse.'

'You had better restrain it, sir, till Sir Marmaduke arrives. I shall then wash my hands of the affair.'

'And she is pretty well; – Emily, I mean?'

'Mrs Trevelyan's health is good.'

'Pray tell her though I could not – might not ask to see her, I came to inquire after her the first moment that I was in London. Pray tell her how much I feel for her; – but she will know that. When Sir Marmaduke is here, of course, we shall meet. When she is once more under her father's wing, she need not be restrained by any absurd commands from a husband who has deserted her. At present, of course, I do not ask to see her.'

'Of course, you do not, Colonel Osborne.'

'And give my love to Nora; – dear little Nora! There can be no reason why she and I should not shake hands.'

'I should prefer that it should not be so in this house,' said the clergyman, who was now standing, – in expectation that his unwelcome guest would go.

'Very well; – so be it. But you will understand I could not be in London without coming and asking after them.' Then the Colonel at last took his leave, and Mr Outhouse was left to his solitude and his sermons.

Mrs Outhouse was very angry when she heard of the visit. 'Men of that sort,' she said, 'think it a fine thing, and talk about it. I believe the poor girl is as innocent as I am, but he isn't innocent. He likes it.'

'"It is easier,"' said Mr Outhouse solemnly, '"for a camel to go through the eye of a needle, than for a rich man to enter into the kingdom of God."'*

'I don't know that he is a rich man,' said Mrs Outhouse; 'but he wouldn't have come here if he had been honest.'

Mrs Trevelyan was told of the visit, and simply said that of course it was out of the question that she should have seen Colonel Osborne. Nevertheless she seemed to think it quite natural that he should have called, and defended him with some energy when her aunt declared that he had been much to blame. 'He is not bound to obey Mr Trevelyan because I am,' said Emily.

'He is bound to abstain from evil doing,' said Mrs Outhouse; 'and he oughtn't to have come. There; let that be enough, my dear. Your uncle doesn't wish to have it talked about.' Nevertheless it was talked about between the two sisters. Nora was of opinion that Colonel Osborne had been wrong, whereas Emily defended him. 'It seems to me to have been the most natural thing in life,' said she.

Had Colonel Osborne made the visit as Sir Marmaduke's friend, feeling himself to be an old man, it might have been natural. When a man has come to regard himself as being, on the score of age, about as fit to be a young lady's lover as though he were an old woman instead of an old man, – which some men will do when they are younger even than was Colonel Osborne, – he is justified in throwing behind him as utterly absurd the suspicions of other people. But Colonel Osborne cannot be defended altogether on that plea.

42

Miss Stanbury and Mr Gibson Become Two

There came to be a very gloomy fortnight at Miss Stanbury's house in the Close. For two or three days after Mr Gibson's dismissal at the hands of Miss Stanbury herself, Brooke Burgess was still in the house, and his presence saved Dorothy from the full weight of her aunt's displeasure. There was the necessity of looking after Brooke, and scolding him, and of praising him to Martha, and of dispraising him, and of seeing that he had enough to eat, and of watching whether he smoked in the house, and of quarrelling with him about everything under the sun, which together so employed Miss Stanbury that she satisfied herself with glances at Dorothy which were felt to be full of charges of ingratitude. Dorothy was thankful that it should be so, and bore the glances with abject submission. And then there was a great comfort to her in Brooke's friendship. On the second day after Mr Gibson had gone she found herself talking to Brooke quite openly upon the subject. 'The fact was, Mr Burgess, that I didn't really care for him. I know he's very good and all that, and of course Aunt Stanbury meant it all for the best. And I would have done it if I could, but I couldn't.' Brooke patted her on the back, – not in the flesh but in the spirit, – and told her that she was quite right. And he expressed an opinion too that it was not expedient to yield too much to Aunt Stanbury. 'I would yield to her in anything that was possible to me,' said Dorothy. 'I won't,' said he; 'and I don't think I should do any good if I did. I like her, and I like her money. But I don't like either well enough to sell myself for a price.'

A great part too of the quarrelling which went on from day to day between Brooke and Miss Stanbury was due to the difference of their opinions respecting Dorothy and her suitor. 'I believe you put her up to it,' said Aunt Stanbury.

'I neither put her up nor down, but I think that she was quite right.'

'You've robbed her of a husband, and she'll never have another chance. After what you've done you ought to take her yourself.'

'I shall be ready to-morrow,' said Brooke.

'How can you tell such a lie?' said Aunt Stanbury.

But after two or three days Brooke was gone to make a journey through the distant parts of the county, and see the beauties of Devonshire. He was to be away for a fortnight, and then come back for a day or two before he returned to London. During that fortnight things did not go well with poor Dorothy at Exeter.

'I suppose you know your own business best,' her aunt said to her one morning. Dorothy uttered no word of reply. She felt it to be equally impossible to suggest either that she did or that she did not know her own business best. 'There may be reasons which I don't understand,' exclaimed Aunt Stanbury; 'but I should like to know what it is you expect.'

'Why should I expect anything, Aunt Stanbury?'

'That's nonsense. Everybody expects something. You expect to have your dinner by-and-by, – don't you?'

'I suppose I shall,' said Dorothy, to whom it occurred at the moment that such expectation was justified by the fact that on every day of her life hitherto some sort of a dinner had come in her way.

'Yes, – and you think it comes from heaven, I suppose.'

'It comes by God's goodness, and your bounty, Aunt Stanbury.'

'And how will it come when I'm dead? Or how will it come if things should go in such a way that I can't stay here any longer? You don't ever think of that.'

'I should go back to mamma, and Priscilla.'

'Psha! As if two months were not enough to eat all the meal there is in that tub. If there was a word to say against the man, I wouldn't ask you to have him; if he drank or smoked, or wasn't a gentleman, or was too poor, or anything you like. But there's nothing. It's all very well to tell me you don't love him, but why don't you love him? I don't like a girl to go and throw herself at a man's head, as those Frenches have done; but when everything has been prepared for you and made proper, it seems to me to be like turning away from good victuals.' Dorothy could only offer to go home if she had offended her aunt, and then Miss Stanbury scolded her for making the offer. As this kind of thing went on at the house in the Close for a fortnight, during which there was no going out, and no society at home, Dorothy began to be rather tired of it.

At the end of the fortnight, on the morning of the day on which Brooke Burgess was expected back, Dorothy, slowly moving into the sitting room with her usual melancholy air, found Mr Gibson talking to her aunt. 'There she is herself,' said Miss Stanbury, jumping up briskly; 'and now you can speak to her. Of course I have no authority, – none in the least. But she knows what my wishes are.' And, having so spoken, Miss Stanbury left the room.

It will be remembered that hitherto no word of affection had been whispered by Mr Gibson into Dorothy's ears. When he came before to press his suit she had been made aware of his coming, and had fled, leaving her answer with her aunt. Mr Gibson had then expressed himself as somewhat injured in that no opportunity of pouring forth his own eloquence had been permitted to him. On that occasion Miss Stanbury, being in a snubbing humour, had snubbed him. She had in truth scolded him almost as much as she had scolded Dorothy, telling him that he went about the business in hand as though butter wouldn't melt in his mouth. 'You're stiff as a chair-back,' she had said to him, with a few other compliments, and these amenities had for awhile made him regard the establishment at Heavitree as being, at any rate, pleasanter than that in the Close. But since that cool reflection had come. The proposal was not that he should marry Miss Stanbury, senior, who certainly could be severe on occasions, but Miss Stanbury, junior, whose temper was as sweet as primroses in March. That which he would have to take from Miss Stanbury, senior, was a certain sum of money, as to which her promise was as good as any bond in the world. Things had come to such a pass with him in Exeter, – from the hints of his friend the Prebend, from a word or two which had come to him from the Dean, from certain family arrangements proposed to him by his mother and sisters, – things had come to such a pass that he was of a mind that he had better marry some one. He had, as it were, three strings to his bow. There were the two French strings, and there was Dorothy. He had not breadth of genius enough to suggest to himself that yet another woman might be found. There was a difficulty on the French score even about Miss Stanbury; but it was clear to him that, failing her, he was due to one of the two Miss Frenches. Now it was not only that the Miss Frenches were empty-handed, but he was beginning to think himself that they were not as nice as they might have been in reference to the arrangement of their head gear. Therefore, having given much thought to the matter, and remembering that he had never yet had play for his own eloquence with Dorothy, he had come to Miss Stanbury asking that he might have another chance. It had been borne in upon him that he had perhaps hitherto regarded Dorothy as too certainly his own, since she had been offered to him by her aunt, – as being a prize that required no eloquence in the winning; and he thought that if he could have an opportunity of amending that fault, it might even yet be well with his suit. So he prepared himself, and asked permission, and now found himself alone with the young lady.

'When last I was in this house, Miss Stanbury,' he began, 'I was not fortunate enough to be allowed an opportunity of pleading my cause to yourself.' Then he paused, and Dorothy was left to consider how best she might answer him. All that her aunt had said to her had not been thrown away upon her. The calls upon that slender meal-tub at home she knew were quite sufficient. And Mr Gibson was, she believed, a good man. And how better could she dispose of herself in life? And what was she that she should scorn the love of an honest gentleman? She would take him, she thought, – if she could. But then there came upon her, unconsciously, without work of thought, by instinct rather than by intelligence, a feeling of the closeness of a wife to her husband. Looking at in in general she could not deny that it would be very proper that she should become Mrs Gibson. But when there came upon her a remembrance that she would be called upon for demonstration of her love, – that he would embrace her, and hold her to his heart, and kiss her, – she revolted and shuddered. She believed that she did not want to marry any man, and that such a state of things would not be good for her. 'Dear young lady,' continued Mr Gibson, 'you will let me now make up for the loss which I then experienced?'

'I thought it was better not to give you trouble,' said Dorothy.

'Trouble, Miss Stanbury! How could it be trouble? The labour we delight in physics pain.* But to go back to the subject-matter. I hope you do not doubt that my affection for you is true, and honest, and genuine.'

'I don't want to doubt anything, Mr Gibson; but – '

'You needn't, dearest Miss Stanbury; indeed you needn't. If you could read my heart you would see written there true love very plainly; – very plainly. And do you not think it a duty that people should marry?' It may be surmised that he had here forgotten some connecting link which should have joined without abruptness the declaration of his own love, and his social view as to the general expediency of matrimony. But Dorothy did not discover the hiatus.

'Certainly, – when they like each other, and if their friends think it proper.'

'Our friends think it proper, Miss Stanbury, – may I say Dorothy? – all of them. I can assure you that on my side you will be welcomed by a mother and sisters only too anxious to receive you with open arms. And as regards your own relations, I need hardly allude to your revered aunt. As to your own mother and sister, – and your brother, who, I believe, gives his mind chiefly to other things, – I am assured by Miss Stanbury that no opposition need be feared from them. Is that true, dearest Dorothy?'

'It is true.'

'Does not all that plead in my behalf? Tell me, Dorothy.'

'Of course it does.'

'And you will be mine?' As far as eloquence could be of service,

Mr Gibson was sufficiently eloquent. To Dorothy his words appeared good, and true, and affecting. All their friends did wish it. There were many reasons why it should be done. If talking could have done it, his talking was good enough. Though his words were in truth cold, and affected, and learned by rote, they did not offend her; but his face offended her; and the feeling was strong within her that if she yielded, it would soon be close to her own. She couldn't do it. She didn't love him, and she wouldn't do it. Priscilla would not grudge her her share out of that meagre meal-tub. Had not Priscilla told her not to marry the man if she did not love him? She found that she was further than ever from loving him. She would not do it. 'Say that you will be mine,' pleaded Mr Gibson, coming to her with both his hands outstretched.

'Mr Gibson, I can't,' she said. She was sobbing now, and was half choked by tears.

'And why not, Dorothy?'

'I don't know, but I can't. I don't feel that I want to be married at all.'

'But it is honourable.'

'It's no use, Mr Gibson; I can't, and you oughtn't to ask me any more.'

'Must this be your very last answer?'

'What's the good of going over it all again and again. I can't do it.'

'Never, Miss Stanbury?'

'No; – never.'

'That is cruel, very cruel. I fear that you doubt my love.'

'It isn't cruel, Mr Gibson. I have a right to have my own feelings, and I can't. If you please, I'll go away now.' Then she went, and he was left standing alone in the room. His first feeling was one of anger. Then there came to be mixed with that a good deal of wonder, – and then a certain amount of doubt. He had during the last fortnight discussed the matter at great length with a friend, a gentleman who knew the world, and who took upon himself to say that he specially understood female nature. It was by advice from this friend that he had been instigated to plead his own cause. 'Of course she means to accept you,' the friend had said. 'Why the mischief shouldn't she? But she has some flimsy, old-fashioned country idea that it isn't maidenly to give in at first. You tell her roundly that she must marry you.' Mr Gibson was just reaching that roundness which his friend had recommended when the lady left him and he was alone.

Mr Gibson was no doubt very much in love with Dorothy

Stanbury. So much, we may take for granted. He, at least, believed that he was in love with her. He would have thought it wicked to propose to her had he not been in love with her. But with his love was mingled a certain amount of contempt which had induced him to look upon her as an easy conquest. He had been perhaps a little ashamed of himself for being in love with Dorothy, and had almost believed the Frenches when they had spoken of her as a poor creature, a dependant, one born to be snubbed, – as a young woman almost without an identity of her own. When, therefore, she so pertinaciously refused him, he could not but be angry. And it was natural that he should be surprised. Though he was to have received a fortune with Dorothy, the money was not hers. It was to be hers, – or rather theirs, – only if she would accept him. Mr Gibson thoroughly understood this point. He knew that Dorothy had nothing of her own. The proposal made to her was as rich as though he had sought her down at Nuncombe Putney, with his preferment, plus the £2000, in his own pocket. And his other advantages were not hidden from his own eyes. He was a clergyman, well thought of, not bad-looking certainly, considerably under forty, – a man, indeed, who ought to have been, in the eyes of Dorothy, such an Orlando as she would have most desired. He could not therefore but wonder. And then came the doubt. Could it be possible that all those refusals were simply the early pulses of hesitating compliance produced by maidenly reserve? Mr Gibson's friend had expressed a strong opinion that almost any young woman would accept any young man if he put his 'com 'ether' upon her strong enough. For Mr Gibson's friend was an Irishman. As to Dorothy the friend had not a doubt in the world. Mr Gibson, as he stood alone in the room after Dorothy's departure, could not share his friend's certainty; but he thought it just possible that the pulsations of maidenly reserve were yet at work. As he was revolving these points in his mind, Miss Stanbury entered the room.

'It's all over now,' she said.

'As how, Miss Stanbury?'

'As how! She's given you an answer; hasn't she?'

'Yes, Miss Stanbury, she has given me an answer. But it has occurred to me that young ladies are sometimes, – perhaps a little – '

'She means it, Mr Gibson; you may take my word for that. She is quite in earnest. She can take the bit between her teeth as well as another, though she does look so mild and gentle. She's a Stanbury all over.'

'And must this be the last of it, Miss Stanbury?'

'Upon my word, I don't know what else you can do, – unless you send the Dean and Chapter to talk her over. She's a pig-headed, foolish young woman; – but I can't help that. The truth is, you didn't make enough of her at first, Mr Gibson. You thought the plum would tumble into your mouth.'

This did seem cruel to the poor man. From the first day in which the project had been opened to him by Miss Stanbury, he had yielded a ready acquiescence, – in spite of those ties which he had at Heavitree, – and had done his very best to fall into her views. 'I don't think that is at all fair, Miss Stanbury,' he said, with some tone of wrath in his voice.

'It's true, – quite true. You always treated her as though she were something beneath you.' Mr Gibson stood speechless, with his mouth open. 'So you did. I saw it all. And now she's had spirit enough to resent it. I don't wonder at all; I don't, indeed. It's no good your standing there any longer. The thing is done.'

Such intolerable ill-usage Mr Gibson had never suffered in his life. Had he been untrue, or very nearly untrue, to those dear girls at Heavitree for this? 'I never treated her as anything beneath me,' he said at last.

'Yes, you did. Do you think that I don't understand? Haven't I eyes in my head, and ears? I'm not deaf yet, nor blind. But there's an end of it. If any young woman ever meant anything, she means it. The truth is, she don't like you.'

Was ever a lover despatched in so uncourteous a way! Then, too, he had been summoned thither as a lover, had been specially encouraged to come there as a lover, had been assured of success in a peculiar way, had had the plum actually offered to him! He had done all that this old woman had bidden him, – something, indeed, to the prejudice of his own heart; he had been told that the wife was ready for him; and now, because this foolish young woman didn't know her own mind, – this was Mr Gibson's view of the matter, – he was reviled and abused, and told that he had behaved badly to the lady. 'Miss Stanbury,' he said, 'I think that you are forgetting yourself.'

'Highty, tighty!' said Miss Stanbury. 'Forgetting myself! I shan't forget you in a hurry, Mr Gibson.'

'Nor I you, Miss Stanbury. Good morning, Miss Stanbury.' Mr Gibson, as he went from the hall-door into the street, shook the dust off his feet,* and resolved that for the future he and Miss Stanbury should be two. There would arise great trouble in Exeter; but, nevertheless, he and Miss Stanbury must be two. He could justify himself in no other purpose after such conduct as he had received.

43

Laburnum Cottage

There had been various letters passing, during the last six weeks, between Priscilla Stanbury and her brother, respecting the Clock House at Nuncombe Putney. The ladies at Nuncombe had, certainly, gone into the Clock House on the clear understanding that the expenses of the establishment were to be incurred on behalf of Mrs Trevelyan. Priscilla had assented to the movement most doubtingly. She had disliked the idea of taking the charge of a young married woman who was separated from her husband, and she had felt that a going down after such an uprising, – a fall from the Clock House back to a cottage, – would be very disagreeable. She had, however, allowed her brother's arguments to prevail, and there they were. The annoyance which she had anticipated from the position of their late guest had fallen upon them: it had been felt grievously, from the moment in which Colonel Osborne called at the house; and now that going back to the cottage must be endured. Priscilla understood that there had been a settlement between Trevelyan and Stanbury as to the cost of the establishment so far; – but that must now be at an end. In their present circumstances, she would not continue to live there, and had already made inquiries as to some humble roof for their shelter. For herself she would not have cared had it been necessary for her to hide herself in a hut, – for herself, as regarded any feeling as to her own standing in the village. For herself, she was ashamed of nothing. But her mother would suffer, and she knew what Aunt Stanbury would say to Dorothy. To Dorothy at the present moment, if Dorothy should think of accepting her suitor, the change might be very deleterious; but still it should be made. She could not endure to live there on the very hard-earned proceeds of her brother's pen, – proceeds which were not only hard-earned, but precarious. She gave warning to the two servants who had been hired, and consulted with Mrs Crocket as to a cottage, and was careful to let it be known throughout Nuncombe Putney that the Clock House was to be abandoned. The Clock House had been taken furnished for six months, of which half were not yet over; but there were other expenses of living there much greater than the rent, and go she would. Her mother sighed and assented; and Mrs

Crocket, having strongly but fruitlessly advised that the Clock House should be inhabited at any rate for the six months, promised her assistance. 'It has been a bad business, Mrs Crocket,' said Priscilla; 'and all we can do now is to get out of it as well as we can. Every mouthful I eat chokes me while I stay there.' 'It ain't good, certainly, miss, not to know as you're all straight the first thing as you wakes in the morning,' said Mrs Crocket, – who was always able to feel when she woke that everything was straight with her.

Then there came the correspondence between Priscilla and Hugh. Priscilla was at first decided, indeed, but mild in the expression of her decision. To this, and to one or two other missives couched in terms of increasing decision, Hugh answered with manly, self-asserting, overbearing arguments. The house was theirs till Christmas; between this and then he would think about it. He could very well afford to keep the house on till next Midsummer, and then they might see what had best be done. There was plenty of money, and Priscilla need not put herself into a flutter. In answer to that word flutter, Priscilla wrote as follows:

Clock House, September 16, 186 –

Dear Hugh,

I know very well how good you are, and how generous, but you must allow me to have feelings as well as yourself. I will not consent to have myself regarded as a grand lady out of your earnings. How should I feel when some day I heard that you had run yourself into debt? Neither mamma nor I could endure it. Dorothy is provided for now, at any rate for a time, and what we have is enough for us. You know I am not too proud to take anything you can spare to us, when we are ourselves placed in a proper position; but I could not live in this great house, while you are paying for everything, – and I will not. Mamma quite agrees with me, and we shall go out of it on Michaelmas-day. Mrs Crocket says she thinks she can get you a tenant for the three months, out of Exeter, – if not for the whole rent, at least for part of it. I think we have already got a small place for eight shillings a week, a little out of the village, on the road to Cockchaffington. You will remember it. Old Soames used to live there. Our old furniture will be just enough. There is a mite of a garden, and Mrs Crocket says she thinks we can get it for seven shillings, or perhaps for six and sixpence, if we stay there. We shall go in on the 29th. Mrs Crocket will see about having somebody to take care of the house.

Your most affectionate sister,
Priscilla

On the receipt of this letter, Hugh proceeded to Nuncombe. At this time he was making about ten guineas a week, and thought that he saw his way to further work. No doubt the ten guineas were precarious; – that is, the 'Daily Record' might discontinue his services to-morrow, if the 'Daily Record' thought fit to do so. The greater part of his earnings came from the 'D. R.,' and the editor had only to say that things did not suit any longer, and there would be an end of it. He was not as a lawyer or a doctor with many clients who could not all be supposed to withdraw their custom at once; but leading articles were things wanted with at least as much regularity as physic or law; and Hugh Stanbury, believing in himself, did not think it probable that an editor, who knew what he was about, would withdraw his patronage. He was proud of his weekly ten guineas, feeling sure that a weekly ten guineas would not as yet have been his had he stuck to the Bar as a profession. He had calculated, when Mrs Trevelyan left the Clock House, that two hundred a year would enable his mother to continue to reside there, the rent of the place furnished, or half-furnished, being only eighty; and he thought that he could pay the two hundred easily. He thought so still, when he received Priscilla's last letter; but he knew something of the stubbornness of his dear sister, and he, therefore, went down to Nuncombe Putney, in order that he might use the violence of his logic on his mother.

He had heard of Mr Gibson from both Priscilla and from Dorothy, and was certainly desirous that 'dear old Dolly,' as he called her, should be settled comfortably. But when dear old Dolly wrote to him declaring that it could not be so, that Mr Gibson was a very nice gentleman, of whom she could not say that she was particularly fond, – 'though I really do think that he is an excellent man, and if it was any other girl in the world, I should recommend her to take him,' – and that she thought that she would rather not get married, he wrote to her the kindest brotherly letter in the world, telling her that she was 'a brick,' and suggesting to her that there might come some day some one who would suit her taste better than Mr Gibson. 'I'm not very fond of parsons myself,' said Hugh, 'but you must not tell that to Aunt Stanbury.' Then he suggested that as he was going down to Nuncombe, Dorothy should get leave of absence and come over and meet him at the Clock House. Dorothy demanded the leave of absence somewhat imperiously, and was at home at the Clock House when Hugh arrived.

'It was a pity,' said Mrs Stanbury, plaintively. She had been very plaintive on the subject. What a thing it would have been for her, could she have seen Dorothy so well established!

'There's no help for spilt milk, mother,' said Hugh. Mrs Stanbury shook her head.

'Dorothy was quite right,' said Priscilla.

'Of course she was right,' said Hugh. 'Who doubts her being right? Bless my soul! What's any girl to do if she don't like a man except to tell him so? I honour you, Dolly, – not that I ever should have doubted you. You're too much of a chip off the old block to say you liked a man when you didn't.'

'He is a very excellent young man,' said Mrs Stanbury.

'An excellent fiddlestick, mother. Loving and liking don't go by excellence. Besides, I don't know about his being any better than anybody else, just because he's a clergyman.'

'A clergyman is more likely to be steady than other men,' said the mother.

'Steady, yes; and as selfish as you please.'

'Your father was a clergyman, Hugh.'

'I don't mean to say that they are not as good as others; but I won't have it that they are better. They are always dealing with the Bible, till they think themselves apostles. But when money comes up, or comfort, or, for the matter of that either, a pretty woman with a little money, then they are as human as the rest of us.'

If the truth had been told on that occasion, Hugh Stanbury would have had to own that he had written lately two or three rather stinging articles in the 'Daily Record,' as 'to the assumed merits and actual demerits of the clergy of the Church of England.' It is astonishing how fluent a man is on a subject when he has lately delivered himself respecting it in this fashion.

Nothing on that evening was said about the Clock House, or about Priscilla's intentions. Priscilla was up early on the next morning, intending to discuss it in the garden with Hugh before breakfast; but Hugh was aware of her purpose and avoided her. It was his intention to speak first to his mother; and though his mother was, as he knew, very much in awe of her daughter, he thought that he might carry his point, at any rate for the next three months, by forcing an assent from the elder lady. So he managed to waylay Mrs Stanbury before she descended to the parlour.

'We can't afford it, my dear; – indeed we can't,' said Mrs Stanbury.

'That's not the question, mother. The rent must be paid up to Christmas, and you can live here as cheap as you can anywhere.'

'But Priscilla – '

'Oh, Priscilla! Of course we know what Priscilla says. Priscilla has been writing to me about it in the most sensible manner in the world; but what does it all come to? If you are ashamed of taking assistance from me, I don't know who is to do anything for anybody. You are comfortable here?'

'Very comfortable; only Priscilla feels – '

'Priscilla is a tyrant mother; and a very stern one. Just make up your mind to stay here till Christmas. If I tell you that I can afford it, surely that ought to be enough.' Then Dorothy entered the room, and Hugh appealed to her. Dorothy had come to Nuncombe only on the day before, and had not been consulted on the subject. She had been told that the Clock House was to be abandoned, and had been taken down to inspect the cottage in which old Soames had lived; – but her opinions had not been asked. Priscilla had quite made up her mind, and why should she ask an opinion of any one? But now Dorothy's opinion was demanded. 'It's what I call the rhodomontade of independence,' said Hugh.

'I suppose it is very expensive,' suggested Dorothy.

'The house must be paid for,' said Hugh; – 'and if I say that I've got the money, is not that enough? A miserable, dirty little place, where you'll catch your death of lumbago, mother.'

'Of course it's not a comfortable house,' said Mrs Stanbury, – who, of herself, was not at all indifferent to the comforts of her present residence.

'And it is very dirty,' said Dorothy.

'The nastiest place I ever saw in my life. Come, mother; if I say that I can afford it, ought not that to be enough for you? If you think you can't trust me, there's an end of everything, you know.' And Hugh, as he thus expressed himself, assumed an air of injured virtue.

Mrs Stanbury had very nearly yielded, when Priscilla came in among them. It was impossible not to continue the conversation, though Hugh would much have preferred to have forced an assent from his mother before he opened his mouth on the subject to his sister. 'My mother agrees with me,' said he abruptly, 'and so does Dolly, that it will be absurd to move away from this house at present.'

'Mamma!' exclaimed Priscilla.

'I don't think I said that, Hugh,' murmured Dorothy, softly.

'I am sure I don't want anything for myself,' said Mrs Stanbury.

'It's I that want it,' said Hugh. 'And I think that I've a right to have my wishes respected, so far as that goes.'

'My dear Hugh,' said Priscilla, 'the cottage is already taken, and we shall certainly go into it. I spoke to Mrs Crocket yesterday about a cart for moving the things. I'm sure mamma agrees with me. What possible business can people have to live in such a house as this with about twenty-four shillings a week for every thing? I won't do it. And as the thing is settled, it is only making trouble to disturb it.'

'I suppose, Priscilla,' said Hugh, 'you'll do as your mother chooses?'

'Mamma chooses to go. She has told me so already.'

'You have talked her into it.'

'We had better go, Hugh,' said Mrs Stanbury. 'I'm sure we had better go.'

'Of course we shall go,' said Priscilla. 'Hugh is very kind and very generous, but he is only giving trouble for nothing about this. Had we not better go down to breakfast?'

And so Priscilla carried the day. They went down to breakfast, and during the meal Hugh would speak to nobody. When the gloomy meal was over he took his pipe and walked out to the cottage. It was an untidy-looking, rickety place, small and desolate, with a pretension about it of the lowest order, a pretension that was evidently ashamed of itself. There was a porch. And the one sitting-room had what the late Mr Soames had always called his bow window. But the porch looked as though it were tumbling down, and the bow window looked as though it were tumbling out. The parlour and the bedroom over it had been papered; – but the paper was torn and soiled, and in sundry places was hanging loose. There was a miserable little room called a kitchen to the right as you entered the door, in which the grate was worn out, and behind this was a shed with a copper. In the garden there remained the stumps and stalks of Mr Soames's cabbages, and there were weeds in plenty, and a damp hole among some elder bushes called an arbour. It was named Laburnum Cottage, from a shrub that grew at the end of the house. Hugh Stanbury shuddered as he stood smoking among the cabbage-stalks. How could a man ask such a girl as Nora Rowley to be his wife, whose mother lived in a place like this? While he was still standing in the garden, and thinking of Priscilla's obstinacy and his own ten guineas a week, and the sort of life which he lived in London, – where he dined usually at his club, and denied himself nothing in the way of pipes, beer, and beefsteaks, he heard a step behind him, and turning round, saw his elder sister.

'Hugh,' she said, 'you must not be angry with me.'

'But I am angry with you.'

'I know you are; but you are unjust. I am doing what I am sure is right.'

'I never saw such a beastly hole as this in all my life.'

'I don't think it beastly at all. You'll find that I'll make it nice. Whatever we want here you shall give us. You are not to think that I am too proud to take anything at your hands. It is not that.'

'It's very like it.'

'I have never refused anything that is reasonable, but it is quite unreasonable that we should go on living in such a place as that, as though we had three or four hundred a year of our own. If mamma got used to the comfort of it, it would be hard then upon her move. You shall give her what you can afford, and what is reasonable; but it is madness to think of living there. I couldn't do it.'

'You're to have your way at any rate, it seems.'

'But you must not quarrel with me, Hugh. Give me a kiss. I don't have you often with me; and yet you are the only man in the world that I ever speak to, or even know. I sometimes half think that the bread is so hard and the water so bitter, that life will become impossible. I try to get over it; but if you were to go away from me in anger, I should be so beaten for a week or two that I could do nothing.'

'Why won't you let me do anything?'

'I will; – whatever you please. But kiss me.' Then he kissed her, as he stood among Mr Soames's cabbage-stalks. 'Dear Hugh; you are such a god to me!'

'You don't treat me like a divinity.'

'But I think of you as one when you are absent. The gods were never obeyed when they showed themselves. Let us go and have a walk. Come; – shall we get as far as Ridleigh Mill?' Then they started together, and all unpleasantness was over between them when they returned to the Clock House.

44

Brooke Burgess takes leave of Exeter

The time had arrived at which Brooke Burgess was to leave Exeter. He had made his tour through the county, and returned to spend his two last nights at Miss Stanbury's house. When he came back Dorothy was still at Nuncombe, but she arrived in the Close the day before his departure. Her mother and sister had wished her to stay at Nuncombe. 'There is a bed for you now, and a place to be comfortable in,' Priscilla had said, laughing, 'and you may as well see the last of us.' But Dorothy declared that she had named a day to her aunt, and that she would not break her engagement. 'I suppose you can stay if you like,' Priscilla had urged. But Dorothy was of opinion that she ought not to stay. She said not a word about Brooke Burgess; but it may be that it would have been matter of regret to her not to shake hands with him once more. Brooke declared to her that had she not come back he would have gone over to Nuncombe to see her; but Dorothy did not consider herself entitled to believe that.

On the morning of the last day Brooke went over to his uncle's office. 'I've come to say Good-bye, Uncle Barty,' he said.

'Good-bye, my boy. Take care of yourself.'

'I mean to try.'

'You haven't quarrelled with the old woman, – have you?' said Uncle Barty.

'Not yet; – that is to say, not to the knife.'

'And you still believe that you are to have her money?'

'I believe nothing one way or the other. You may be sure of this, – I shall never count it mine till I've got it; and I shall never make myself so sure of it as to break my heart because I don't get it. I suppose I've got as good a right to it as anybody else, and I don't see why I shouldn't take it if it come in my way.'

'I don't think it ever will,' said the old man, after a pause.

'I shall be none the worse,' said Brooke.

'Yes, you will. You'll be a broken-hearted man. And she means to break your heart. She does it on purpose. She has no more idea of leaving you her money than I have. Why should she?'

'Simply because she takes the fancy.'

'Fancy! Believe me, there is very little fancy about it. There isn't one of the name she wouldn't ruin if she could. She'd break all our hearts if she could get at them. Look at me and my position. I'm little more than a clerk in the concern. By God; – I'm not so well off as a senior clerk in many a bank. If there came a bad time, I must lose as the others would lose; – but a clerk never loses. And my share in the business is almost a nothing. It's just nothing, – compared to what it would have been, only for her.'

Brooke had known that his uncle was a disappointed, or at least a discontented man; but he had never known much of the old man's circumstances, and certainly had not expected to hear him speak in the strain that he had now used. He had heard often that his Uncle Barty disliked Miss Stanbury, and had not been surprised at former sharp, biting little words spoken in reference to that lady's character. But he had not expected such a tirade of abuse as the banker had now poured out. 'Of course I know nothing about the bank,' said he; 'but I did not suppose that she had had anything to do with it.'

'Where do you think the money came from that she has got? Did you ever hear that she had anything of her own? She never had a penny, – never a penny. It came out of this house. It is the capital on which this business was founded, and on which it ought to be carried on to this day. My brother had thrown her off; by heavens, yes; – had thrown her off. He had found out what she was, and had got rid of her.'

'But he left her his money.'

'Yes; – she got near him when he was dying, and he did leave her his money; – his money, and my money, and your father's money.'

'He could have given her nothing, Uncle Barty, that wasn't his own.'

'Of course that's true; – it's true in one way. You might say the same of a man who was cozened into leaving every shilling away from his own children. I wasn't in Exeter when the will was made. We none of us were here. But she was here; and when we came to see him die, there we found her. She had had her revenge upon him, and she means to have it on all of us. I don't believe she'll ever leave you a shilling, Brooke. You'll find her out yet, and you'll talk of her to your nephews as I do to you.'

Brooke made some ordinary answer to this, and bade his uncle adieu. He had allowed himself to entertain a half chivalrous idea that he could produce a reconciliation between Miss Stanbury and his uncle Barty; and since he had been at Exeter he had said a word, first to the one and then to the other, hinting at the subject; – but his hints had certainly not been successful. As he walked from the bank into the High Street he could not fail to ask himself whether there were any grounds for the terrible accusations which he had just heard from his uncle's lips. Something of the same kind, though in form much less violent, had been repeated to him very often by others of the family. Though he had as a boy known Miss Stanbury well, he had been taught to regard her as an ogress. All the Burgesses had regarded Miss Stanbury as an ogress since that unfortunate will had come to light. But she was an ogress from whom something might be gained, – and the ogress had still persisted in saying that a Burgess should be her heir. It had therefore come to pass that Brooke had been brought up half to revere her and half to abhor her. 'She is a dreadful woman,' said his branch of the family, 'who will not scruple at anything evil. But as it seems that you may probably reap the advantage of the evil that she does, it will become you to put up with her iniquity.' As he had become old enough to understand the nature of her position, he had determined to judge for himself; but his judgment hitherto simply amounted to this, – that Miss Stanbury was a very singular old woman, with a kind heart and good instincts, but so capricious withal that no sensible man would risk his happiness on expectations formed on her promises. Guided by this opinion, he had resolved to be attentive to her and, after a certain fashion, submissive; but certainly not to become her slave. She had thrown over her nephew. She was constantly complaining of him to her niece. Now and again she would say a very bitter word to him about himself. When he had left Exeter on his little excursion, no one was so much in favour with her as Mr Gibson. On his return he found that Mr Gibson had been altogether discarded, and was spoken of in terms of almost insolent abuse. 'If I were ever so humble to her,' he had said to himself, 'it would do no good; and there is nothing I hate so much as humility.' He had thus determined to take the goods the gods provided,* should it ever come to pass that such godlike provision was laid before him out of Miss Stanbury's coffers; – but not to alter his mode of life or put himself out of his way in obedience to her behests, as a man might be expected to do who was destined to receive so rich a legacy. Upon this idea he had acted, still believing the old woman to be good, but believing at the same time that she was very capricious. Now he had heard what his Uncle Bartholomew Burgess had had to say upon the matter, and he could not refrain from asking himself whether his uncle's accusations were true.

In a narrow passage between the High Street and the Close he met Mr Gibson. There had come to be that sort of intimacy between the two men which grows from closeness of position rather than from any social desire on either side, and it was natural that Burgess should say a word of farewell. On the previous evening Miss Stanbury had relieved her mind by turning Mr Gibson into ridicule in her description to Brooke of the manner in which the clergyman had carried on his love affair; and she had at the same time declared that Mr Gibson had been most violently impertinent to herself. He knew, therefore, that Miss Stanbury and Mr Gibson had become two, and would on this occasion have passed on without a word relative to the old lady had Mr Gibson allowed him to do so. But Mr Gibson spoke his mind freely.

'Off to-morrow, are you?' he said. 'Good-bye. I hope we may meet again; but not in the same house, Mr Burgess.'

'There or anywhere I shall be very happy,' said Brooke.

'Not there, certainly. While you were absent Miss Stanbury

treated me in such a way that I shall certainly never put my foot in her house again.'

'Dear me! I thought that you and she were such great friends.'

'I knew her very well, of course; — and respected her. She is a good churchwoman, and is charitable in the city; but she has got such a tongue in her head that there is no bearing it when she does what she calls giving you a bit of her mind.'

'She has been indulgent to me, and has not given me much of it.'

'Your time will come, I've no doubt,' continued Mr Gibson. 'Every body has always told me that it would be so. Even her oldest friends knew it. You ask Mrs MacHugh, or Mrs French, at Heavitree.'

'Mrs French!' said Brooke, laughing. 'That would hardly be fair evidence.'

'Why not? I don't know a better judge of character in all Exeter than Mrs French. And she and Miss Stanbury have been intimate all their lives. Ask your uncle at the bank.'

'My uncle and Miss Stanbury never were friends,' said Brooke.

'Ask Hugh Stanbury what he thinks of her. But I don't suppose I want to say a word against her. I wouldn't for the world do such a thing. Only, as we've met there and all that, I thought it best to let you know that she had treated me in such a way, and has been altogether so violent, that I never will go there again.' So saying, Mr Gibson passed on, and was of opinion that he had spoken with great generosity of the old woman who had treated him so badly.

In the afternoon Brooke Burgess went over to the further end of the Close, and called on Mrs MacHugh; and from thence he walked across to Heavitree, and called on the Frenches. It may be doubted whether he would have been so well behaved to these ladies had they not been appealed to by Mr Gibson as witnesses to the character of Miss Stanbury. He got very little from Mrs MacHugh. That lady was kind and cordial, and expressed many wishes that she might see him again in Exeter. When he said a few words about Mr Gibson, Mrs MacHugh only laughed, and declared that the gentleman would soon find a plaister for that sore. 'There are more fishes than one in the sea,' she said.

'But I'm afraid they've quarrelled, Mrs MacHugh.'

'So they tell me. What should we have to talk about here if somebody didn't quarrel sometimes? She and I ought to get up a quarrel for the good of the public, — only they know that I never can quarrel with anybody. I never see anybody interesting enough to quarrel with.' But Mrs MacHugh said nothing about Miss

Stanbury, except that she sent over a message with reference to a rubber of whist for the next night but one.

He found the two French girls sitting with their mother, and they all expressed their great gratitude to him for coming to say good-bye before he went. 'It is so very nice of you, Mr Burgess,' said Camilla, 'and particularly just at present.'

'Yes, indeed,' said Arabella, 'because you know things have been so unpleasant.'

'My dears, never mind about that,' said Mrs French. 'Miss Stanbury has meant everything for the best, and it is all over now.'

'I don't know what you mean by its being all over, mamma,' said Camilla. 'As far as I can understand, it has never been begun.'

'My dear, the least said the soonest mended,' said Mrs French.

'That's of course, mamma,' said Camilla ; 'but yet one can't hold one's tongue altogether. All the city is talking about it, and I dare say Mr Burgess has heard as much as anybody else.'

'I've heard nothing at all,' said Brooke.

'Oh yes, you have,' continued Camilla. Arabella conceived herself at this moment to be situated in so delicate a position, that it was best that her sister should talk about it, and that she herself should hold her tongue, – with the exception, perhaps, of a hint here and there which might be of assistance ; for Arabella completely under-stood that the prize was now to be hers, if the prize could be rescued out of the Stanbury clutches. She was aware, – no one better aware, – how her sister had interfered with her early hopes, and was sure, in her own mind, that all her disappointment had come from fratricidal rivalry on the part of Camilla. It had never, however, been open to her to quarrel with Camilla. There they were, linked together, and together they must fight their battles. As two pigs may be seen at the same trough, each striving to take the delicacies of the banquet from the other, and yet enjoying always the warmth of the same dunghill in amicable contiguity, so had these young ladies lived in sisterly friendship, while each was striving to take a husband from the other. They had understood the position, and, though for years back they had talked about Mr Gibson, they had never quarrelled ; but now, in these latter days of the Stanbury interference, there had come tacitly to be something of an understanding between them that, if any fighting were still possible on the subject, one must be put forward and the other must yield. There had been no spoken agreement, but Arabella quite understood that she was to be put forward. It was for her to take up the running, and to win, if possible, against the Stanbury filly. That was her view, and she was inclined to give Camilla credit for acting in accordance with it with honesty and zeal. She felt, therefore, that her words on the present occasion ought to be few. She sat back in her corner of the sofa, and was intent on her work, and shewed by the pensiveness of her brow that there were thoughts within her bosom of which she was not disposed to speak. 'You must have heard a great deal,' said Camilla, laughing. 'You must know how poor Mr Gibson has been abused, because he wouldn't – '

'Camilla, don't be foolish,' said Mrs French.

'Because he wouldn't what?' asked Brooke. 'What ought he to have done that he didn't do?'

'I don't know anything about ought,' said Camilla. 'That's a matter of taste altogether.'

'I'm the worst hand in the world at a riddle,' said Brooke.

'How sly you are,' continued Camilla, laughing; 'as if dear Aunt Stanbury hadn't confided all her hopes to you.'

'Camilla, dear, – don't,' said Arabella.

'But when a gentleman is hunted, and can't be caught, I don't think he ought to be abused to his face.'

'But who hunted him, and who abused him?' asked Brooke.

'Mind, I don't mean to say a word against Miss Stanbury, Mr Burgess. We've known her and loved her all our lives; – haven't we, mamma?'

'And respected her,' said Arabella.

'Quite so,' continued Camilla. 'But you know, Mr Burgess, that she likes her own way.'

'I don't know anybody that does not,' said Brooke.

'And when she's disappointed, she shows it. There's no doubt she is disappointed now, Mr Burgess.'

'What's the good of going on, Camilla?' said Mrs French. Arabella sat silent in her corner, with a conscious glow of satisfaction, as she reflected that the joint disappointment of the elder and the younger Miss Stanbury had been caused by a tender remembrance of her own charms. Had not dear Mr Gibson told her, in the glowing language of truth, that there was nothing further from his thoughts than the idea of taking Dorothy Stanbury for his wife?

'Well, you know,' continued Camilla, 'I think that when a person makes an attempt, and comes by the worst of it, that person should put up with the defeat, and not say all manner of ill-natured things. Everybody knows that a certain gentleman is very intimate in this house.'

'Don't, dear,' said Arabella, in a whisper.

'Yes, I shall,' said Camilla. 'I don't know why people should hold their tongues, when other people talk so loudly. I don't care a bit what anybody says about the gentleman and us. We have known him for ever so many years, and mamma is very fond of him.'

'Indeed I am, Camilla,' said Mrs French.

'And for the matter of that, so am I, — very,' said Camilla, laughing bravely. 'I don't care who knows it.'

'Don't be so silly, child,' said Arabella. Camilla was certainly doing her best, and Arabella was grateful.

'We don't care what people may say,' continued Camilla again. 'Of course we heard, as everybody else heard too, that a certain gentleman was to be married to a certain lady. It was nothing to us whether he was married or not.'

'Nothing at all,' said Arabella.

'We never spoke ill of the young lady. We did not interfere. If the gentleman liked the young lady, he was quite at liberty to marry her, as far as we were concerned. We had been in the habit of seeing him here, almost as a brother, and perhaps we might feel that a connection with that particular young lady would take him from us; but we never hinted so much even as that, — to him or to anyone else. Why should we? It was nothing to us. Now it turns out that the gentleman never meant anything of the kind, whereupon he is pretty nearly kicked out of the house, and all manner of ill-natured things are said about us everywhere.' By this time Camilla had become quite excited, and was speaking with much animation.

'How can you be so foolish, Camilla?' said Arabella.

'Perhaps I am foolish,' said Camilla, 'to care what anybody says.'

'What can it all be to Mr Burgess?' said Mrs French.

'Only this, that as we all like Mr Burgess, and as he is almost one of the family in the Close, I think he ought to know why we are not quite so cordial as we used to be. Now that the matter is over I have no doubt things will get right again. And as for the young lady, I'm sure we feel for her. We think it was the aunt who was indiscreet.'

'And then she has such a tongue,' said Arabella.

Our friend Brooke, of course, knew the whole truth; — knew the nature of Mr Gibson's failure, and knew also how Dorothy had acted in the affair. He was inclined, moreover, to believe that the ladies who were now talking to him were as well instructed on the subject as was he himself. He had heard, too, of the ambition of the two young ladies now before him, and believed that that ambition was not yet dead. But he did not think it incumbent on him to fight a battle even on behalf of Dorothy. He might have declared that Dorothy, at least, had not been disappointed, but he thought it better to be silent about Dorothy. 'Yes,' he said, 'Miss Stanbury has a tongue; but I think it speaks as much good as it does evil, and perhaps that is a great deal to say for any lady's tongue.'

'We never speak evil of anybody,' said Camilla; 'never. It is a rule with us.' Then Brooke took his leave, and the three ladies were cordial and almost affectionate in their farewell greetings.

Brooke was to start on the following morning before anybody would be up except Martha, and Miss Stanbury was very melancholy during the evening. 'We shall miss him very much; shall we not?' she said, appealing to Dorothy. 'I am sure you will miss him very much,' said Dorothy. 'We are so stupid here alone,' said Miss Stanbury. When they had drank their tea, she sat nearly silent for half an hour, and then summoned him up into her own room. 'So you are going, Brooke?' she said.

'Yes; I must go now. They would dismiss me if I stayed an hour longer.'

'It was good of you to come to the old woman; and you must let me hear of you from time to time.'

'Of course I'll write.'

'And, Brooke, – '

'What is it, Aunt Stanbury?'

'Do you want any money, Brooke?'

'No; – none, thank you. I've plenty for a bachelor.'

'When you think of marrying, Brooke, mind you tell me.'

'I'll be sure to tell you; – but I can't promise yet when that will be.' She said nothing more to him, though she paused once more as though she were going to speak. She kissed him and bade him good-bye, saying that she would not go down-stairs again that evening. He was to tell Dorothy to go to bed. And so they parted.

But Dorothy did not go to bed for an hour after that. When Brooke came down into the parlour with his message she intended to go at once, and put up her work, and lit her candle, and put out her hand to him, and said good-bye to him. But, for all that, she remained there for an hour with him. At first she said very little, but by degrees her tongue was loosened, and she found herself talking with a freedom which she could hardly herself understand. She told him how thoroughly she believed her aunt to be a good woman – how sure she was that her aunt was at any rate honest. 'As for me,' said Dorothy, 'I know that I have displeased her about Mr Gibson; – and I would go away, only that I think she would be so desolate.' Then Brooke begged her never to allow the idea of leaving Miss Stanbury to enter her head. Because Miss Stanbury was capricious, he said, not on that account should her caprices either be indulged or permitted. That was his doctrine respecting Miss Stanbury, and he declared that, as regarded himself, he would never be either disrespectful to her or submissive. 'It is a great mistake,' he said, 'to think that anybody is either an angel or a devil.' When Dorothy expressed an opinion that with some people angelic tendencies were predominant, and with others diabolic tendencies, he assented; but declared that it was not always easy to tell the one tendency from the other. At last, when Dorothy had made about five attempts to go, Mr Gibson's name was mentioned. 'I am very glad that you are not going to be Mrs Gibson,' said he.

'I don't know why you should be glad.'

'Because I should not have liked your husband, − not as your husband.'

'He is an excellent man, I'm sure,' said Dorothy.

'Nevertheless I am very glad. But I did not think you would accept him, and I congratulate you on your escape. You would have been nothing to me as Mrs Gibson.'

'Shouldn't I?' said Dorothy, not knowing what else to say.

'But now I think we shall always be friends.'

'I'm sure I hope so, Mr Burgess. But indeed I must go now. It is ever so late, and you will hardly get any sleep. Good night.' Then he took her hand, and pressed it very warmly, and referring to a promise before made to her, he assured her that he would certainly make acquaintance with her brother as soon as he was back in London. Dorothy, as she went up to bed, was more than ever satisfied with herself, in that she had not yielded in reference to Mr Gibson.

45

Trevelyan at Venice

Trevelyan passed on moodily and alone from Turin to Venice, always expecting letters from Bozzle, and receiving from time to time the dispatches which that functionary forwarded to him, as must be acknowledged, with great punctuality. For Mr Bozzle did his work, not only with a conscience, but with a will. He was now, as he had declared more than once, altogether devoted to Mr Trevelyan's interest; and as he was an active, enterprising man, always on the alert to be doing something, and as he loved the work of writing dispatches, Trevelyan received a great many letters from Bozzle. It is not exaggeration to say that every letter made him for the time a very wretched man. This ex-policeman wrote of the wife of his bosom, – of her who had been the wife of his bosom, and who was the mother of his child, who was at this very time the only woman whom he loved, – with an entire absence of delicacy. Bozzle would have thought reticence on his part to be dishonest. We remember Othello's demand of Iago.* That was the demand which Bozzle understood that Trevelyan had made of him, and he was minded to obey that order. But Trevelyan, though he had in truth given the order, was like Othello also in this, – that he would have preferred before all the prizes of the world to have had proof brought home to him exactly opposite to that which he demanded. But there was nothing so terrible to him as the grinding suspicion that he was to be kept in the dark. Bozzle could find out facts. Therefore he gave, in effect, the same order that Othello gave; – and Bozzle went to work determined to obey it. There came many dispatches to Venice, and at last there came one, which created a correspondence which shall be given here at length. The first is a letter from Mr Bozzle to his employer:

> 55, Stony Walk, Union Street, Borough,
> September 29, 186 – , 4.30 p.m.

Hond. Sir,

Since I wrote yesterday morning, something has occurred which, it may be, and I think it will, will help to bring this melancholly affair to a satisfactory termination and conclusion. I had better explain, Mr Trevelyan, how I have been at work from the beginning about whatching the Colonel. I couldn't do nothing with the porter at the Albany, which he is always mostly muzzled with beer, and he wouldn't have taken my money, not on the square. So, when it was tellegrammed to me as the Colonel was on the move in the North, I put on two boys as knows the Colonel, at eighteenpence a day, at each end, one Piccadilly end, and the other Saville Row end, and yesterday morning, as quick as ever could be, after the Limited Express Edinborough Male Up was in, there comes the Saville Row End Boy here to say as the Colonel was lodged safe in his downey. Then I was off immediate myself to St Diddulph's, because I knows what it is to trust to Inferiors when matters gets dellicate. Now, there hadn't been no letters from the Colonel, nor none to him as I could make out, though that mightn't be so sure. She might have had 'em addrressed to A. Z., or the like of that, at any of the Post-offices as was distant, as nobody could give the notice to 'em all. Barring the money, which I know ain't an object when the end is so dessirable, it don't do to be too ubiketous, because things will go astray. But I've kept my eye uncommon open, and I don't think there have been no letters since that last which was sent, Mr Trevelyan, let any of 'em, parsons or what not, say what they will. And I don't see as parsons are better than other folk when they has to do with a lady as likes her fancy-man.'

Trevelyan, when he had read as far as this, threw down the letter and tore his hair in despair. 'My wife,' he exclaimed, 'Oh, my wife!' But it was essential that he should read Bozzle's letter, and he persevered.

Well; I took to the ground myself as soon as ever I heard that the Colonel was among us, and I hung out at the Full Moon. They has been quite on the squair with me at the Full Moon, which I mention, because, of course, it has to be remembered, and it do come up as a hitem. And I'm proud, Mr Trevelyan, as I did take to the ground myself; for what should happen but I see the Colonel as large as life ringing at the parson's bell at 1.47 p.m. He was let in at 1.49, and he was let out at 2.17. He went away in a cab which it was kept, and I followed him till he was put down at the Arcade, and I left him having his 'ed washed and greazed at Trufitt's rooms, half-way up. It was a wonder to me when I see this, Mr Trevelyan, as he didn't have his 'ed done first, as they most of 'em does when they're going to see their ladies; but I couldn't make nothing of that, though I did try to put too and too together, as I always does.

What he did at the parson's, Mr Trevelyan, I won't say I saw, and I won't say I know. It's my opinion the young woman there isn't on the squair, though she's been remembered too, and is a hitem of course. And, Mr Trevelyan, it do go against the grain with me when they're remembered and ain't on the squair. I doesn't expect too much of Human Nature, which is poor, as the saying goes; but when they're remembered and ain't on the square after that, it's too bad for Human Nature. It's more than poor. It's what I calls beggarly.

He ain't been there since, Mr Trevelyan, and he goes out of town to-morrow by the 1.15 p.m. express to Bridport. So he lets on; but of course I shall see to that. That he's been at St Diddulph's, in the house from 1.47 to 2.17, you may take as a fact. There won't be no shaking of that, because I have it in my mem. book, and no Counsel can get the better of it. Of course he went there to see her, and it's my belief he did. The young woman as was remembered says he didn't, but she isn't on the squair. They never is when a lady wants to see her gentleman, though they comes round afterwards, and tell up everything when comes before his ordinary lordship.

If you ask me, Mr Trevelyan, I don't think it's ripe yet for the court, but we'll have it ripe before long. I'll keep a look-out, because it's just possible she may leave town. If she do, I'll be down upon them together, and no mistake.

Yours most respectful,
S. Bozzle

Every word in the letter had been a dagger to Trevelyan, and yet he felt himself to be under an obligation to the man who had written it. No one else would or could make facts known to him. If she were innocent, let him know that she were innocent, and he would proclaim her innocence, and believe in her innocence, – and sacrifice himself to her innocence, if such sacrifice were necessary. But if she were guilty, let him also know that. He knew how bad it was, all that bribing of postmen and maidservants, who took his money, and her money also, very likely. It was dirt, all of it. But who had put him into the dirt? His wife had, at least, deceived him, – had deceived him and disobeyed him, and it was necessary that he should know the facts. Life without a Bozzle would now have been to him a perfect blank.

The Colonel had been to the parsonage at St Diddulph's, and had been admitted! As to that he had no doubt. Nor did he really doubt that his wife had seen the visitor. He had sent his wife first into a remote village on Dartmoor, and there she had been visited by her – lover! How was he to use any other word? Iago; – oh, Iago! The pity of it, Iago!* Then, when she had learned that this was discovered, she had left the retreat in which he had placed her, – without permission from him, – and had taken herself to the house of a relative of hers. Here she was visited again by her – lover! Oh, Iago; the pity of it, Iago! And then there had been between them an almost constant correspondence. So much he had ascertained as fact; but he did not for a moment believe that Bozzle had learned all the facts. There might be correspondence, or even visits, of which Bozzle could learn nothing. How could Bozzle know where Mrs Trevelyan was during all those hours which Colonel Osborne passed in London? That which he knew, he knew absolutely, and on that he could act; but there was, of course, much of which he knew nothing. Gradually the truth would unveil itself, and then he would act. He would tear that Colonel into fragments, and throw his wife form him with all the ignominy which the law made possible to him.

But in the meantime he wrote a letter to Mr Outhouse. Colonel Osborne, after all that had been said, had been admitted at the parsonage, and Trevelyan was determined to let the clergyman know what he thought about it. The oftener he turned the matter in his mind, as he walked slowly up and down the piazza of St Mark, the more absurd it appeared to him to doubt that his wife had seen the man. Of course she had seen him. He walked there nearly the whole night, thinking of it, and as he dragged himself off at last to his inn, had almost come to have but one desire, – namely, that he should find her out, that the evidence should be conclusive, that it should be proved, and so brought to an end. Then he would destroy her, and destroy that man, – and afterwards destroy himself, so bitter to him would be his ignominy. He almost revelled in the idea of the tragedy he would make. It was three o'clock before he was in his bedroom, and then he wrote his letter to Mr Outhouse before he took himself to his bed. It was as follows:

Venice, Oct. 4, 186 –

Sir,

Information of a certain kind, on which I can place a firm reliance, has reached me, to the effect that Colonel Osborne has been allowed to visit at your house during the sojourn of my wife under your roof. I will thank you to inform me whether this be true; as, although I am confident of my facts, it is necessary, in reference to my ulterior conduct, that I should have from you either an admission or a denial of my assertion. It is of course open to you to leave my letter unanswered. Should you think proper to do so, I shall know also how to deal with that fact.

As to your conduct in admitting Colonel Osborne into your house while my wife is there, – after all that has passed, and all that you know that has passed, – I am quite unable to speak with anything like moderation of feeling. Had the man succeeded in forcing himself into your residence, you should have been the first to give me notice of it. As it is, I have been driven to ascertain the fact from other sources. I think that you have betrayed the trust that a husband has placed in you, and that you will find from the public voice that you will be regarded as having disgraced yourself as a clergyman.

In reference to my wife herself, I would wish her to know, that after what has now taken place, I shall not feel myself justified in leaving our child longer in her hands, even tender as are his years. I shall take steps for having him removed. What further I shall do to vindicate myself, and extricate myself as far as may be possible from the slough of despond in which I have been submerged, she and you will learn in due time.

Your obedient servant,
L. Trevelyan

A letter addressed 'poste restante, Venice,' will reach me here.

If Trevelyan was mad when he wrote this letter, Mr Outhouse was very nearly as mad when he read it. He had most strongly desired to have nothing to do with his wife's niece when she was separated from her husband. He was a man honest, charitable, and sufficiently affectionate; but he was timid, and disposed to think ill of those whose modes of life were strange to him. Actuated by these

feelings, he would have declined to offer the hospitality of his roof
to Mrs Trevelyan, had any choice been left to him. But there had
been no choice. She had come thither unasked, with her boy and
baggage, and he could not send her away. His wife had told him
that it was his duty to protect these women till their father came,
and he recognised the truth of what his wife said. There they were,
and there they must remain throughout the winter. It was hard
upon him, – especially as the difficulties and embarrassments as to
money were so disagreeable to him; – but there was no help for it.
His duty must be done though it were ever so painful. Then that
horrid Colonel had come. And now had come this letter, in which
he was not only accused of being an accomplice between his married
niece and her lover, but was also assured that he should be held up
to public ignominy and disgrace. Though he had often declared that
Trevelyan was mad, he would not remember that now. Such a letter
as he had received should have been treated by him as the
production of a madman. But he was not sane enough himself to
see the matter in that light. He gnashed his teeth, and clenched his
fist, and was almost beside himself as he read the letter a second
time.

There had been a method in Trevelyan's madness;* for, though
he had declared to himself that without doubt Bozzle had been right
in saying that as the Colonel had been at the parsonage, therefore,
as a certainty, Mrs Trevelyan had met the Colonel there, yet he had
not so stated in his letter. He had merely asserted that Colonel
Osborne had been at the house, and had grounded his accusation
upon that alleged fact. The alleged fact had been in truth a fact. So
far Bozzle had been right. The Colonel had been at the parsonage ;
and the reader knows how far Mr Outhouse had been to blame for
his share in the matter ! He rushed off to his wife with the letter,
declaring at first that Mrs Trevelyan, Nora, and the child, and the
servant, should be sent out of the house at once. But at last Mrs
Outhouse succeeded in showing him that he would not be justified
in ill-using them because Trevelyan had ill-used him. 'But I will
write to him,' said Mr Outhouse. 'He shall know what I think
about it.' And he did write his letter that day, in spite of his wife's
entreaties that he would allow the sun to set upon his wrath. And
his letter was as follows :

St Diddulph's, October 8, 186 –

Sir,
I have received your letter of the 4th, which is more iniquitous, unjust,
and ungrateful, than anything I ever before saw written. I have been

surprised from the first at your gross cruelty to your unoffending wife;
but even that seems to me more intelligible than your conduct in writing
such words as those which you have dared to send to me.

For your wife's sake, knowing that she is in a great degree still in
your power, I will condescend to tell you what has happened. When
Mrs Trevelyan found herself constrained to leave Nuncombe Putney by
your aspersions on her character, she came here, to the protection of
her nearest relatives within reach, till her father and mother should be
in England. Sorely against my will I received them into my home,
because they had been deprived of other shelter by the cruelty or
madness of him who should have been their guardian. Here they are,
and here they shall remain till Sir Marmaduke Rowley arrives. The
other day, on the 29th of September, Colonel Osborne, who is their
father's old friend, called, not on them, but on me. I may truly say that
I did not wish to see Colonel Osborne. They did not see him, nor did
he ask to see them. If his coming was a fault, – and I think it was a
fault, – they were not implicated in it. He came, remained a few
minutes, and went without seeing any one but myself. That is the
history of Colonel Osborne's visit to my house.

I have not thought fit to show your letter to your wife, or to make
her acquainted with this further proof of your want of reason. As to
the threads which you hold out of removing her child from her, you
can of course do nothing except by law. I do not think that even you
will be sufficiently audacious to take any steps of that description.
Whatever protection the law may give her and her child from your
tyranny and misconduct cannot be obtained till her father shall be here.

I have only further to request that you will not address any further
communication to me. Should you do so, it will be refused.

Yours, in deep indignation,
Oliphant Outhouse

Trevelyan had also written two other letters to England, one to
Mr Bideawhile, and the other to Bozzle. In the former he acquainted
the lawyer that he had discovered that his wife still maintained her
intercourse with Colonel Osborne, and that he must therefore
remove his child from her custody. He then inquired what steps
would be necessary to enable him to obtain possession of his little
boy. In the letter to Bozzle he sent a cheque, and his thanks for the
ex-policeman's watchful care. He desired Bozzle to continue his
precautions, and explained his intentions about his son. Being
somewhat afraid that Mr Bideawhile might not be zealous on his
behalf, and not himself understanding accurately the extent of his
power with regard to his own child, or the means whereby he might
exercise it, he was anxious to obtain assistance from Bozzle also on

this point. He had no doubt that Bozzle knew all about it. He had great confidence in Bozzle. But still he did not like to consult the ex-policeman. He knew that it became him to have some regard for his own dignity. He therefore put the matter very astutely to Bozzle, – asking no questions, but alluding to his difficulty in a way that would enable Bozzle to offer advice.

And where was he to get a woman to take charge of his child? If Lady Milborough would do it, how great would be the comfort! But he was almost sure that Lady Milborough would not do it. All his friends had turned against him, and Lady Milborough among the number. There was nobody left to him, but Bozzle. Could he entrust Bozzle to find some woman for him who would take adequate charge of the little fellow, till he himself could see to the child's education? He did not put this question to Bozzle in plain terms; but he was very astute, and wrote in such a fashion that Bozzle could make a proposal, if any proposal were within his power.

The answer from Mr Outhouse came first. To this Mr Trevelyan paid very little attention. It was just what he expected. Of course, Mr Outhouse's assurance about Colonel Osborne went for nothing. A man who would permit intercourse in his house between a married lady and her lover, would not scruple to deny that he had permitted it. Then came Mr Bideawhile's answer, which was very short. Mr Bideawhile said that nothing could be done about the child till Mr Trevelyan should return to England; – and that he could give no opinion as to what should be done then till he knew more of the circumstances. It was quite clear to Trevelyan that he must employ some other lawyer. Mr Bideawhile had probably been corrupted by Colonel Osborne. Could Bozzle recommend a lawyer?

From Bozzle himself there came no other immediate reply than, 'his duty, and that he would make further inquiries.'

46

The American Minister

In the second week in October, Mr Glascock returned to Florence, intending to remain there till the weather should have become bearable at Naples. His father was said to be better, but was in such a condition as hardly to receive much comfort from his son's presence. His mind was gone, and he knew no one but his nurse; and, though Mr Glascock was unwilling to put himself altogether out of the reach of returning at a day's notice, he did not find himself obliged to remain in Naples during the heat of the autumn. So Mr Glascock returned to the hotel in Florence, accompanied by the tall man who wore the buttons. The hotel-keeper did not allow such a light to remain long hidden under a bushel, and it was soon spread far and wide that the Honourable Charles Glascock and his suite were again in the beautiful city.

And the fact was soon known to the American Minister and his family. Mr Spalding was a man who at home had been very hostile to English interests. Many American gentlemen are known for such hostility. They make anti-English speeches about the country, as though they thought that war with England would produce certain triumph to the States, certain increase to American trade, and certain downfall to a tyranny which no Anglo-Saxon nation ought to endure. But such is hardly their real opinion. There, in the States, as also here in England, you shall from day to day hear men propounding, in very loud language, advanced theories of political action, the assertion of which is supposed to be necessary to the end which they have in view. Men whom we know to have been as mild as sucking doves in the political aspiratino of their whole lives, suddenly jump up, and with infuriated gestures declare themselves the enemies of everything existing. When they have obtained their little purpose, – or have failed to do so, – they revert naturally into their sucking-dove elements. It is so with Americans as frequently as with ourselves, – and there is no political subject on which it is considered more expedient to express pseudo-enthusiasm than on that of the sins of England. It is understood that we do not resent it. It is presumed that we regard it as the Irishman regarded his wife's cuffs. In the States a large party, which consists chiefly of those who have lately left English rule, and who are keen to prove to themselves how wise they have been in doing so, is pleased by this strong language against England; and, therefore, the strong language is spoken. But the speakers, who are, probably, men knowing something of the world, mean it not at all; they have no more idea of war with England than they have of war with all Europe; and their respect for England and for English opinion is unbounded. In their political tones of speech and modes of action they strive to be as English as possible. Mr Spalding's aspirations were of this nature. He had uttered speeches against England which would make the hair stand on end on the head of an uninitiated English reader. He had told his countrymen that Englishmen hugged their chains, and would do so until American hammers had knocked those chains from off their wounded wrists and bleeding ankles. He had declared that, if certain American claims were not satisfied,* there was nothing left for Americans to do but to cross the ferry with such a sheriff's officer as would be able to make distraint on the great English household. He had declared that the sheriff's officer would have very little trouble. He had spoken of Canada as an outlying American territory, not yet quite sufficiently redeemed from savage life to be received into the Union as a State. There is a multiplicity of subjects of this kind ready to the hand of the American orator. Mr Spalding had been quite successful, and was now Minister at Florence; but, perhaps, one of the greatest pleasures coming to him from his prosperity was the enjoyment of the society of well-bred Englishmen, in the capital to which he had been sent. When, therefore, his wife and nieces pointed out to him the fact that it was manifestly his duty to call upon Mr Glascock after what had passed between them on that night under the Campanile, he did not rebel for an instant against the order given to him. His mind never reverted for a moment to that opinion which had gained for him such a round of applause, when expressed on the platform of the Temperance Hall at Nubbly Creek, State of Illinois, to the effect that the English aristocrat, thorough-born and thorough-bred, who inherited acres and title from his father, could never be fitting company for a thoughtful Christian American citizen. He at once had his hat brushed, and took up his best gloves and umbrella, and went off to Mr Glascock's hotel. He was strictly enjoined by the ladies to fix a day on which Mr Glascock would come and dine at the American embassy.

'"C. G." has come back to see you,' said Olivia to her elder sister. They had always called him 'C. G.' since the initials had been seen on the travelling bag.

'Probably,' said Carry. 'There is so very little else to bring people to Florence, that there can hardly be any other reason for his coming. They do say it's terribly hot at Naples just now; but that can have had nothing to do with it.'

'We shall see,' said Livy. 'I'm sure he's in love with you. He looked to me just like a proper sort of lover for you, when I saw his long legs creeping up over our heads into the banquette.'

'You ought to have been very much obliged to his long legs; – so sick as you were at the time.'

'I like him amazingly,' said Livy, 'legs and all. I only hope Uncle Jonas won't bore him, so as to prevent his coming.'

'His father is very ill,' said Carry, 'and I don't suppose we shall see him at all.'

But the American Minister was successful. He found Mr Glascock sitting in his dressing-gown, smoking a cigar, and reading a newspaper. The English aristocrat seemed very glad to see his visitor, and assumed no airs at all. The American altogether forgot his speech at Nubbly Creek, and found the aristocrat's society to be very pleasant. He lit a cigar, and they talked about Naples, Rome, and Florence. Mr Spalding, when the marbles of old Rome were mentioned, was a little too keen in insisting on the merits of Story, Miss Hosmer, and Hiram Powers, and hardly carried his listener with him in the parallel which he drew between Greenough and Phidias;* and he was somewhat repressed by the apathetic curtness of Mr Glascock's reply, when he suggested that the victory gained by the gunboats at Vicksburg, on the Mississippi, was vividly brought to mind by an account which he had just been reading of the battle of Actium;* but he succeeded in inducing Mr Glascock to accept an invitation to dinner for the next day but one, and the two gentlemen parted on the most amicable terms.

Everybody meets everybody in Florence every day. Carry and Livy Spalding had met Mr Glascock twice before the dinner at their uncle's house, so that they met at dinner as intimate friends. Mrs Spalding had very large rooms, up three flights of stairs, on the Lungarno. The height of her abode was attributed by Mrs Spalding to her dread of mosquitoes. She had not yet learned that people in Florence require no excuse for being asked to walk up three flights of stairs. The rooms, when they were reached, were very lofty, floored with what seemed to be marble, and were of a nature almost to warrant Mrs Spalding in feeling that nature had made her more akin to an Italian countess than to a matron of Nubbly Creek, State of Illinois, where Mr Spalding had found her and made her his own. There was one other Englishman present, Mr Harris Hyde Granville Gore, from the Foreign Office, now serving temporarily at the English Legation in Florence; and an American, Mr Jackson Unthank, a man of wealth and taste, who was resolved on having such a collection of pictures at his house in Baltimore that no English private collection should in any way come near to it; and a Tuscan, from the Italian Foreign Office, to whom nobody could speak except Mr Harris Hyde Granville Gore, – who did not indeed seem to enjoy the efforts of conversation which were expected of him. The Italian, who had a handle to his name, – he was Count Buonarosci, – took Mrs Spalding into dinner. Mrs Spalding had been at great trouble to ascertain whether this was proper, or whether she should not entrust herself to Mr Glascock. There were different points to be considered in the matter. She did not quite know whether she was in Italy or in America. She had glimmerings on the subject of her privilege to carry her own nationality into her own drawing-room. And then she was called upon to deal between an Italian Count with an elder brother, and an English Honourable, who had no such encumbrance. Which of the two was possessed of the higher rank ? 'I've found it all out, Aunt Mary,' said Livy. 'You must take the Count.' For Livy wanted to give her sister every chance. 'How have you found it out ?' said the aunt. 'You may be sure it is so,' said Livy. And the lady in her doubt yielded the point. Mrs Spalding, as she walked along the passage on the Count's arm, determined that she would learn Italian. She would have given all Nubbly Creek to have been able to speak a word to Count Buonarosci. To do her justice, it must be admitted that she had studied a few words. But her courage failed her, and she could not speak them. She was very careful, however, that Mr H. H. G. Gore was placed in the chair next to the Count.

'We are very glad to see you here,' said Mr Spalding, addressing himself especially to Mr Glascock, as he stood up at his own seat at the round table. 'In leaving my own country, sir, there is nothing that I value more than the privilege of becoming acquainted with those whose historic names and existing positions are of such inestimable value to the world at large.' In saying this, Mr Spalding was not in the least insincere, nor did his conscience at all prick him in reference to that speech at Nubbly Creek. On both occasions he half thought as he spoke, – or thought that he thought so. Unless it be on subjects especially endeared to us the thoughts of but few of us go much beyond this.

Mr Glascock, who sat between Mrs Spalding and her niece, was soon asked by the elder lady whether he had been in the States. No ; he had not been in the States. 'Then, you must come, Mr Glascock,' said Mrs Spalding, 'though I will not say, dwelling as we now are in the metropolis of the world of art, that we in our own homes have as much of the outer beauty of form to charm the stranger as is to be found in other lands. Yet I think that the busy lives of men, and the varied institutions of a free country, must always have an interest peculiarly their own.' Mr Glascock declared that he quite agreed with her, and expressed a hope that he might some day find himself in New York.

'You wouldn't like it at all,' said Carry; 'because you are an aristocrat. I don't mean that it would be your fault.'

'Why should that prevent my liking it, – even if I were an aristocrat ?'

'One half of the people would run after you, and the other half would run away from you,' said Carry.

'Then I'd take to the people who ran after me, and would not regard the others.'

'That's all very well, – but you wouldn't like it. And then you would become unfair to what you saw. When some of our speechi-fying people talked to you about our institutions through their noses, you would think that the institutions themselves must be bad. And we have nothing to show except our institutions.'

'What are American institutions?' asked Mr Glascock.

'Everything is an institution. Having iced water to drink in every room of the house is an institution. Having hospitals in every town is an institution. Travelling altogether in one class of railway cars is an institution. Saying sir, is an institution. Teaching all the children mathematics is an institution. Plenty of food is an institution. Getting drunk is an institution in a great many towns. Lecturing is an institution. There are plenty of them, and some are very good; – but you wouldn't like it.'

'At any rate, I'll go and see,' said Mr Glascock.

'If you do, I hope we may be at home,' said Miss Spalding.

Mr Spalding, in the mean time, with the assistance of his countryman, the man of taste, was endeavouring to explain a certain point in American politics to the count. As, in doing this, they called upon Mr Gore to translate every speech they made into Italian, and as Mr Gore had never offered his services as an interpreter, and as the Italian did not quite catch the subtle meanings of the Americans in Mr Gore's Tuscan version, and did not in the least wish to understand the things that were explained to him, Mr Gore and the Italian began to think that the two Americans were bores. 'The truth is, Mr Spalding,' said Mr Gore, 'I've got such a cold in my head, that I don't think I can explain it any more.' Then Livy Spalding laughed aloud, and the two Ameri-can gentlemen began to eat their dinner. 'It sounds ridiculous, don't it?' said Mr Gore, in a whisper.

'I ought not to have laughed, I know,' said Livy.

'The very best thing you could have done. I shan't be troubled any more now. The fact is, I know just nine words of Italian. Now there is a difficulty in having to explain the whole theory of American politics to an Italian, who doesn't want to know anything about it, with so very small a repertory of words at one's command.'

'How well you did it!'

'Too well. I felt that. So well that, unless I had stopped it, I shouldn't have been able to say a word to you all through dinner. Your laughter clenched it, and Buonarosci and I will be grateful to you for ever.'

After the ladies went there was rather a bad half hour for Mr Glascock. He was button-holed by the minister, and found it oppressive before he was enabled to escape into the drawing-room. 'Mr Glascock,' said the minister, 'an English gentleman, sir, like you, who has the privilege of an hereditary seat in your parliament,' – Mr Glascock was not quite sure whether he were being accused of having an hereditary seat in the House of Commons, but he would not stop to correct any possible error on that point, – 'and who has been born to all the gifts of fortune, rank, and social eminence, should never think that his education is complete till he has visited our great cities in the west.' Mr Glascock hinted that he by no means conceived his education to be complete; but the minister went on without attending to this. 'Till you have seen, sir, what men can do who are placed upon the earth with all God's gifts of free intelligence, free air, and a free soil, but without any of those other good things which we are accustomed to call the gifts of fortune, you can never become aware of the infinite ingenuity of man.' There had been much said before, but just at this moment Mr Gore and the American left the room, and the Italian followed them briskly. Mr Glascock at once made a decided attempt to bolt; but the minister was on the alert, and was too quick for him. And he was by no means ashamed of what he was doing. He had got his guest by the coat, and openly declared his intention of holding him. 'Let me keep you for a few minutes, sir,' said he, 'while I dilate on this point in one direction. In the drawing-room female spells are too potent for us male orators. In going among us, Mr Glascock, you must not look for luxury or refinement, for you will find them not. Nor must you hope to encounter the highest order of erudition. The lofty summits of acquired knowledge tower in your country with an altitude we have not reached yet.'

'It's very good of you to say so,' said Mr Glascock.

'No, sir. In our new country and in our new cities we still lack the luxurious perfection of fastidious civilisation. But, sir, regard our level. That is what I say to every unprejudiced Britisher that comes among us; – look at our level. And when you have looked at our level, I think that you will confess that we live on the highest table-land that the world has yet afforded to mankind. You follow my meaning, Mr Glascock?' Mr Glascock was not sure that he did, but the minister went on to make that meaning clear. 'It is the multitude that with us is educated. Go into their houses, sir, and see how they thumb their books. Look at the domestic correspondence of our helps and servants, and see how they write and spell. We haven't got the mountains, sir, but our table-lands are the highest on which the bright sun of our Almighty God has as yet shone with its illuminating splendour in this improving world of ours! It is because we are a young people, sir – with nothing as yet near to us of the decrepitude of age. The weakness of age, sir, is the penalty paid by the folly of youth. We are not so wise, sir, but what we too shall suffer from its effects as years roll over our heads.' There was a great deal more, but at last Mr Glascock did escape into the drawing-room.

'My uncle has been saying a few words to you perhaps,' said Carry Spalding.

'Yes; he has,' said Mr Glascock.

'He usually does,' said Carry Spalding.

47

About Fishing, and Navigation, and Head-dresses

The feud between Miss Stanbury and Mr Gibson raged violently in Exeter, and produced many complications which were very difficult indeed of management. Each belligerent party felt that a special injury had been inflicted upon it. Mr Gibson was quite sure that he had been grossly misused by Miss Stanbury the elder, and strongly suspected that Miss Stanbury the younger had had a hand in this misconduct. It had been positively asserted to him, – at least so he thought, but in this was probably in error, – that the lady would accept him if he proposed to her. All Exeter had been made aware of the intended compact. He, indeed, had denied its existence to Miss French, comforting himself, as best he might, with the reflection that all is fair in love and war; but when he counted over his injuries he did not think of this denial. All Exeter, so to say, had known of it. And yet, when he had come with his proposal, he had been refused without a moment's consideration, first by the aunt, and then by the niece; – and, after that, had been violently abused, and at last turned out of the house! Surely, no gentleman had ever before been subjected to ill-usage so violent! But Miss Stanbury the elder was quite as assured that the injury had been done to her. As to the matter of the compact itself, she knew very well that she had been as true as steel. She had done everything in her power to bring about the marriage. She had been generous in her offers of money. She had used all her powers of persuasion on Dorothy, and she had given every opportunity to Mr Gibson. It was not her fault if he had not been able to avail himself of the good things which she had put in his way. He had first been, as she thought, ignorant and arrogant, fancying that the good things ought to be made his own without any trouble on his part; – and then awkward, not knowing how to take the trouble when trouble was necessary. And as to that matter of abusive language and turning out of the house, Miss Stanbury was quite convinced that she was sinned again, and not herself the sinner. She declared to Martha, more than once, that Mr Gibson had used such language to her that, coming out of a clergyman's mouth, it had quite dismayed her. Martha, who knew her mistress, probably felt that Mr Gibson had at least received as good as he gave; but she had made no attempt to set her mistress right on that point.

But the cause of Miss Stanbury's sharpest anger was not to be found in Mr Gibson's conduct either before Dorothy's refusal of his offer, or on the occasion of his being turned out of the house. A base rumour was spread about the city that Dorothy Stanbury had been offered to Mr Gibson, that Mr Gibson had civilly declined the offer, – and that hence had arisen the wrath of the Juno of the Close. Now this was not to be endured by Miss Stanbury. She had felt even in the moment of her original anger against Mr Gibson that she was bound in honour not to tell the story against him. She had brought him into the little difficulty, and she at least would hold her tongue. She was quite sure that Dorothy would never boast of her triumph. And Martha had been strictly cautioned, – as indeed, also, had Brooke Burgess. The man had behaved like an idiot, Miss Stanbury said; but he had been brought into a little dilemma, and nothing should be said about it from the house in the Close. But when the other rumour reached Miss Stanbury's ears, when Mrs Crumbie condoled with her on her niece's misfortune, when Mrs MacHugh asked whether Mr Gibson had not behaved rather badly to the young lady, then our Juno's celestial mind was filled with a divine anger. But even then she did not declare the truth. She asked a question of Mrs Crumbie, and was enabled, as she thought, to trace the falsehood to the Frenches. She did not think that Mr Gibson could on a sudden have become so base a liar.* 'Mr Gibson fast and loose with my niece!' she said to Mrs MacHugh. 'You have not got the story quite right, my dear friend. Pray, believe me; – there has been nothing of that sort.' 'I dare say not,' said Mrs MacHugh, 'and I'm sure I don't care. Mr Gibson has been going to marry one of the French girls for the last ten years, and I think he ought to make up his mind and do it at last.'

'I can assure you he is quite welcome as far as Dorothy is concerned,' said Miss Stanbury.

Without a doubt the opinion did prevail throughout Exeter that Mr Gibson, who had been regarded time out of mind as the property of the Miss Frenches, had been angled for by the ladies in the Close, that he had nearly been caught, but that he had slipped the hook out of his mouth, and was now about to subside quietly into the net which had been originally prepared for him. Arabella French had not spoken loudly on the subject, but Camilla had declared in more than one house that she had most direct authority for stating that the gentleman had never dreamed of offering to the young lady. 'Why he should not do so if he pleases, I don't know,' said Camilla. 'Only the fact is that he has not pleased. The rumour of course has reached him, and, as we happen to be very old friends, we have authority for denying it altogether.' All this came round to Miss Stanbury's, and she was divine in her wrath.

'If they drive me to it,' she said to Dorothy, 'I'll have the whole truth told by the bellman through the city, or I'll publish it in the County Gazette.'

'Pray don't say a word about it, Aunt Stanbury.'

'It is those odious girls. He's there now every day.'

'Why shouldn't he go there, Aunt Stanbury?'

'If he's fool enough, let him go. I don't care where he goes. But I do care about these lies. They wouldn't dare to say it only they think my mouth is closed. They've no honour themselves, but they screen themselves behind mine.'

'I'm sure they won't find themselves mistaken in what they trust to,' said Dorothy, with a spirit that he aunt had not expected from her. Miss Stanbury at this time had told nobody that the offer to her niece had been made and repeated and finally rejected; – but she found it very difficult to hold her tongue.

In the meantime Mr Gibson spent a good deal of his time at Heavitree. It should not perhaps be asserted broadly that he had made up his mind that marriage would be good for him; but he had made up his mind, at least, to this, that it was no longer to be postponed without a balance of disadvantage. The Charybdis in the Close drove him helpless into the whirlpool of the Heavitree Scylla. He had no longer an escape from the perils of the latter shore. He had been so mauled by the opposite waves, that he had neither spirit nor skill left to him to keep in the middle track. He was almost daily at Heavitree, and did not attempt to conceal from himself the approach of his doom.

But still there were two of them. He knew that he must become a prey, but was there any choice left to him as to which siren should have him? He had been quite aware in his more gallant days, before he had been knocked about on that Charybdis rock, that he might sip, and taste, and choose between the sweets. He had come to think lately that the younger young lady was the sweeter. Eight years ago indeed the passages between him and the elder had been tender; but Camilla had then been simply a romping girl; hardly more than a year or two beyond her teens. Now, with her matured charms, Camilla was certainly the more engaging, as far as outward form went. Arabella's cheeks were thin and long, and her front teeth had come to show themselves. Her eyes were no doubt still bright, and what she had of hair was soft and dark. But it was very thin in front, and what there was of supplemental mass behind, – the bandbox by which Miss Stanbury was so much aggrieved, – was worn with an indifference to the lines of beauty, which Mr Gibson himself found to be very depressing. A man with a fair burden on his back is not a grievous sight; but when we see a small human being attached to a bale of goods which he can hardly manage to move, we feel that the poor fellow has been cruelly overweighted. Mr Gibson certainly had that sensation about Arabella's chignon. And as he regarded it in a nearer and a dearer light, – as a chignon that might possibly become his own, as a burden which in one sense he might himself be called upon to bear, as a domestic utensil of which he himself might be called upon to inspect, and, perhaps, to aid the shifting on and the shifting off, he did begin to think that that side of the Scylla gulf ought to be avoided if possible. And probably this propensity on his part, this feeling that he would like to reconsider the matter dispassionately before he gave himself up for good to his old love, may have been increased by Camilla's apparent withdrawal of her claims. He felt mildly grateful to the Heavitree household in general for accepting him in this time of his affliction, but he could not admit to himself that they had a right to decide upon him in private conclave, and allot him either to the one or to the other nuptials without consultation with himself. To be swallowed up by Scylla he now recognised as his doom; but he thought he ought to be asked on which side of the gulf he would prefer to go down. The way in which Camilla spoke of him as a thing that wasn't hers, but another's; and the way in which Arabella looked at him, as though he were hers and could never be another's, wounded his manly pride. He had always understood that he might have his choice, and he could not understand that the little mishap which had befallen him in the Close was to rob him of that privilege.

He used to drink tea at Heavitree in those days. On one evening on going in he found himself alone with Arabella. 'Oh, Mr Gibson,' she said, 'we weren't sure whether you'd come. And mamma and Camilla have gone out to Mrs Camadge's.' Mr Gibson muttered some word to the effect that he hoped he had kept nobody at home; and, as he did so, he remembered that he had distinctly said that he would come on this evening. 'I don't know that I should have gone,' said Arabella, 'because I am not quite, – not quite myself at present. No, not ill; not at all. Don't you know what it is, Mr Gibson, to be, – to be, – to be, – not quite yourself? Mr Gibson said that he had very often felt like that. 'And one can't get over it; – can one?' continued Arabella. 'There comes a presentiment that something is going to happen, and a kind of belief that something has happened, though you don't know what; and the heart refuses to be light, and the spirit becomes abashed, and the mind, though it creates new thoughts, will not settle itself to its accustomed work. I suppose it's what the novels have called Melancholy.'

'I suppose it is,' said Mr Gibson. 'But there's generally some cause for it. Debt for instance – '

'It's nothing of that kind with me. It's no debt, at least, that can be written down in the figures of ordinary arithmetic. Sit down, Mr Gibson, and we will have some tea.' Then, as she stretched forward to ring the bell, he thought that he never in his life had seen anything so unshapely as that huge wen at the back of her head. 'Monstrum horrendum, informe, ingens!'* He could not help quoting the words to himself. She was dressed with some attempt at being smart, but her ribbons were soiled, and her lace was tawdry, and the fabric of her dress was old and dowdy. He was quite sure that he would feel no pride in calling her Mrs Gibson, no pleasure in having her all to himself at his own hearth. 'I hope we shall escape the bitterness of Miss Stanbury's tongue if we drink tea téte-a-téte,' she said, with her sweetest smile.

'I don't suppose she'll know anything about it.'

'She knows about everything, Mr Gibson. It's astonishing what she knows. She has eyes and ears everywhere. I shouldn't care, if she didn't see and hear so very incorrectly. I'm told now that she declares – ; but it doesn't signify.'

'Declares what?' asked Mr Gibson.

'Never mind. But wasn't it odd how all Exeter believed that you were going to be married in that house, and to live there all the rest of your life, and be one of Miss Stanbury's slaves. I never believed it, Mr Gibson.' This she said with a sad smile, that ought to have brought him on his knees, in spite of the chignon.

'One can't help these things,' said Mr Gibson.

'I never could have believed it; – not even if you had not given me an assurance so solemn, and so sweet, that there was nothing in it.' The poor man had given the assurance, and could not deny the solemnity and the sweetness. 'That was a happy moment for us, Mr Gibson; because, though we never believed it, when it was dinned into our ears so frequently, when it was made such a triumph in the Close, it was impossible not to fear that there might be something in it.' He felt that he ought to make some reply, but he did not know what to say. He was thoroughly ashamed of the lie he had told, but he could not untell it. 'Camilla reproached me afterwards for asking you,' whispered Arabella, in her softest, tenderest voice. 'She said that it was unmaidenly. I hope you did not think it unmaidenly, Mr Gibson?'

'Oh dear no; – not at all,' said he.

Arabella French was painfully alive to the fact that she must do something. She had her fish on the hook; but of what use is a fish on your hook, if you cannot land him? When could she have a better opportunity than this of landing the scaly darling out of the fresh and free waters of his bachelor stream, and sousing him into the pool of domestic life, to be ready there for her own household purposes? 'I had known you so long, Mr Gibson,' she said, 'and had valued your friendship so – so deeply.' As he looked at her, he could see nothing but the shapeless excrescence to which his eyes had been so painfully called by Miss Stanbury's satire. It is true that he had formerly been very tender with her, but she had not then carried about with her that distorted monster. He did not believe himself to be at all bound by anything which had passed between them in circumstances so very different. But yet he ought to say something. He ought to have said something; but he said nothing. She was patient, however, very patient; and she went on playing him with her hook. 'I am so glad that I did not go out to-night with mamma. It has been such a pleasure to me to have this conversation with you. Camilla, perhaps, would say that I am – unmaidenly.'

'I don't think so.'

'That is all that I care for, Mr Gibson. If you acquit me, I do not mind who accuses. I should not like to suppose that you thought me unmaidenly. Anything would be better than that; but I can throw all such considerations to the wind when true – true – friendship is concerned. Don't you think that one ought, Mr Gibson?'

If it had not been for the thing at the back of her head, he would have done it now. Nothing but that gave him courage to abstain. It grew bigger and bigger, more shapeless, monstrous, absurd, and abominable, as he looked at it. Nothing should force upon him the necessity of assisting to carry such an abortion through the world. 'One ought to sacrifice everything to friendship,' said Mr Gibson, 'except self-respect.'

He meant nothing personal. Something special, in the way of an opinion, was expected of him; and, therefore, he had striven to say something special. But she was in tears in a moment. 'Oh, Mr Gibson,' she exclaimed; 'oh, Mr Gibson!'

'What is the matter, Miss French?'

'Have I lost your respect? Is it that that you mean?'

'Certainly not, Miss French.'

'Do not call me Miss French, or I shall be sure that you condemn me. Miss French sounds so very old. You used to call me – Bella.' That was quite true; but it was long ago, thought Mr Gibson, – before the monster had been attached. 'Will you not call me Bella now?'

He thought that he had rather not; and yet, how was he to avoid it? On a sudden he became very crafty. Had it not been for the sharpness of his mother wit, he would certainly have been landed at that moment. 'As you truly observed just now,' he said, 'the tongues of people are so malignant. There are little birds that hear everything.'

'I don't care what the little birds hear,' said Miss French, through her tears. 'I am a very unhappy girl; – I know that; and I don't care what anybody says. It is nothing to me what anybody says. I know what I feel.' At this moment there was some dash of truth about her. The fish was so very heavy on hand that, do what she would, she could not land him. Her hopes before this had been very low, – hopes that had once been high; but they had been depressed gradually; and, in the slow, dull routine of her daily life, she had learned to bear disappointment by degrees, without sign of outward suffering, without consciousness of acute pain. The task of her life had been weary, and the wished-for goal was ever becoming more and more distant; but there had been still a chance, and she had fallen away into a lethargy of lessening expectation, from which joy, indeed, had been banished, but in which there had been nothing of agony. Then had come upon the whole house at Heavitree the great Stanbury peril, and, arising out of that, had sprung new hopes to Arabella, which made her again capable of all the miseries of a foiled ambition. She could again be patient, if patience might be of any service; but in such a condition an eternity of patience is simply suicidal. She was willing to work hard, but how could she work harder than she had worked. Poor young woman, – perishing beneath an incubus which a false idea of fashion had imposed on her!

'I hope I have said nothing that makes you unhappy,' pleaded Mr Gibson. 'I'm sure I haven't meant it.'

'But you have,' she said. 'You make me very unhappy. You condemn me. I see you do. And if I have done wrong it has been all because – Oh dear, oh dear, oh dear!'

'But who says you have done wrong?'

'You won't call me, Bella, – because you say the little birds will hear it. If I don't care for the little birds, why should you?'

There is no question more difficult than this for a gentleman to answer. Circumstances do not often admit of its being asked by a lady with that courageous simplicity which had come upon Miss French in this moment of her agonising struggle; but nevertheless it is one which, in a more complicated form, is often put, and to which some reply, more or less complicated, is expected. 'If I, a woman, can dare, for your sake, to encounter the public tongue, will you, a man, be afraid?' The true answer, if it could be given, would probably be this; 'I am afraid, though a man, because I have much to lose and little to get. You are not afraid, though a woman, because you have much to get and little to lose.' But such an answer would be uncivil, and is not often given. Therefore men shuffle and lie, and tell themselves that in love, – love here being taken to mean all antinuptial contests between man and woman, – everything is fair. Mr Gibson had the above answer in his mind, though he did not frame it into words. He was neither sufficiently brave nor sufficiently cruel to speak to her in such language. There was nothing for him, therefore, but that he must shuffle and lie.

'I only meant,' said he, 'that I would not for worlds do anything to make you uneasy.'

She did not see how she could again revert to the subject of her own Christian name. She had made her little tender, loving request, and it had been refused. Of course she knew that it had been refused as a matter of caution. She was not angry with him because of his caution, as she had expected him to be cautious. The barriers over which she had to climb were no more than she had expected to find in her way; – but they were so very high and so very difficult! Of course she was aware that he would escape if he could. She was not angry with him on that account. Anger could not have helped her. Indeed, she did not price herself highly enough to make her feel that she would be justified in being angry. It was natural enough that he shouldn't want her. She knew herself to be a poor,

thin, vapid, tawdry creature, with nothing to recommend her to any
man except a sort of second-rate, provincial-town fashion which, –
infatuated as she was, – she attributed in a great degree to the thing
she carried on her head. She knew nothing. She could do nothing.
She possessed nothing. She was not angry with him because he so
evidently wished to avoid her. But she thought that if she could
only be successful she would be good and loving and obedient, –
and that it was fair for her at any rate to try. Each created animal
must live and get its food by the gifts which the Creator has given
to it, let those gifts be as poor as they may, – let them be even as
distasteful as they may to other members of the great created family.
The rat, the toad, the slug, the flea, must each live according to its
appointed mode of existence. Animals which are parasites by nature
can only live by attaching themselves to life that is strong. To
Arabella Mr Gibson would be strong enough, and it seemed to her
that if she could fix herself permanently upon his strength, that
would be her proper mode of living. She was not angry with him
because he resisted the attempt, but she had nothing of conscience
to tell her that she should spare him as long as there remained to
her a chance of success. And should not her plea of excuse, her
justification be admitted? There are tormentors as to which no man
argues that they are iniquitous, though they be very troublesome.
He either rids himself of them, or suffers as quiescently as he may.

'We used to be such – great – friends,' she said, still crying, 'and
I am afraid you don't like me a bit now.'

'Indeed I do; – I have always like you. But – '

'But what? Do tell me what the but means. I will do anything
that you bid me.'

Then it occurred to him that if, after such a promise, he were to
confide to her his feeling that the chignon which she wore was ugly
and unbecoming, she would probably be induced to change her
mode of head-dress. It was a foolish idea, because, had he followed
it out, he would have seen that compliance on her part in such a
matter could only be given with the distinct understanding that a
certain reward should be the consequence. When an unmarried
gentleman calls upon an unmarried lady to change the fashion of
her personal adornments, the unmarried lady has a right to expect
that the unmarried gentleman means to make her his wife. But Mr
Gibson had no such meaning; and was led into error by the
necessity for sudden action. When she offered to do anything that
he might bid her do, he could not take up his hat and go away. She
looked up into his face, expecting that he would give her some
order; – and he fell into the temptation that was spread for him.

'If I might say a word, – ' he began.

'You may say anything,' she exclaimed.

'If I were you I don't think – '

'You don't think what, Mr Gibson ?'

He found it to be a matter very difficult to approach. 'Do you know, I don't think the fashion that has come up about wearing your hair quite suits you, – not so well as the way you used to do it.' She became on a sudden very red in the face, and he thought that she was angry. Vexed she was, but still accompanying her vexation, there was a remembrance that she was achieving victory even by her own humiliation. She loved her chignon; but she was ready to abandon even that for him. Nevertheless she could not speak for a moment or two, and he was forced to continue his criticism. 'I have no doubt those things are very becoming and all that, and I dare say they are comfortable.'

'Oh, very,' she said.

'But there was a simplicity that I liked about the other.'

Could it be then that for the last five years he had stood aloof from her because she had arrayed herself in fashionable attire ? She was still very red in the face, still suffering from wounded vanity, still conscious of that soreness which affects us all when we are made to understand that we are considered to have failed there, where we have most thought that we excelled. But her woman's art enabled her quickly to conceal the pain. 'I have made a promise,' she said, 'and you will find that I will keep it.'

'What promise ?' asked Mr Gibson.

'I said that I would do as you bade me, and so I will. I would have done it sooner if I had known that you wished it. I would never have worn it at all if I had thought that you disliked it.'

'I think that a little of them is very nice,' said Mr Gibson. Mr Gibson was certainly an awkward man. But there are men so awkward that it seems to be their especial province to say always the very worst thing at the very worst moment.

She became redder than ever as she was thus told of the hugeness of her favourite ornament. She was almost angry now. But she restrained herself, thinking perhaps of how she might teach him taste in days to come as he was teaching her now. 'I will change it to-morrow,' she said with a smile. 'You come and see to-morrow.'

Upon this he got up and took his hat and made his escape, assuring her that he would come and see her on the morrow. She let him go now without any attempt at further tenderness. Certainly she had gained much during the interview. He had as good as told her in what had been her offence, and of course, when she had remedied that offence, he could hardly refuse to return to her. She got up as soon as she was alone, and looked at her head in the glass, and told herself that the pity would be great. It was not that the chignon was in itself a thing of beauty, but that it imparted so unmistakable an air of fashion! It divested her of that dowdiness which she feared above all things, and enabled her to hold her own among other young women, without feeling that she was absolutely destitute of attraction. There had been a certain homage paid to it, which she had recognised and enjoyed. But it was her ambition to hold her own, not among young women, but among clergymen's wives, and she would certainly obey his orders. She could not make the attempt now because of the complications; but she certainly would make it before she laid her head on the pillow, – and would explain to Camilla that it was a little joke between herself and Mr Gibson.

48

Mr Gibson is Punished

Miss Stanbury was divine in her wrath, and became more and more so daily as new testimony reached her of dishonesty on the part of the Frenches and of treachery on the part of Mr Gibson. And these people, so empty, so vain, so weak, were getting the better of her, were conquering her, were robbing her of her prestige and her ancient glory, simply because she herself was too generous to speak out and tell the truth! There was a martyrdom to her in this which was almost unendurable.

Now there came to her one day at luncheon time, – on the day succeeding that on which Miss French had promised to sacrifice her chignon, – a certain Mrs Clifford from Budleigh Salterton, to whom she was much attached. Perhaps the distance of Budleigh Salterton from Exeter added somewhat to this affection, so that Mrs Clifford was almost closer to our friend's heart even than Mrs MacHugh, who lived just at the other end of the cathedral. And in truth Mrs Clifford was a woman more serious in her mode of thought than Mrs MacHugh, and one who had more in common with Miss Stanbury than that other lady. Mrs Clifford had been a Miss Noel of Doddiscombe Leigh, and she and Miss Stanbury had been engaged to be married at the same time, – each to a man of fortune. One match had been completed in the ordinary course of matches. What had been the course of the other we already know. But the friendship had been maintained on very close terms. Mrs MacHugh was a Gallio* at heart, anxious chiefly to remove from herself, – and from her friends also, – all the troubles of life, and make things smooth and easy. She was one who disregarded great questions; who cared little or nothing what people said of her; who considered nothing worth the trouble of a fight; – Epicuri de grege porca.* But there was nothing swinish about Mrs Clifford of Budleigh Salterton. She took life thoroughly in earnest. She was a Tory who sorrowed heartily for her country, believing that it was being brought to ruin by the counsels of evil men. She prayed daily to be delivered from dissenters, radicals, and wolves in sheep's clothing, – by which latter bad name she meant especially a certain leading politician of the day who had, with the cunning of the devil, tempted and perverted the virtue of her own political friends.* And she was one who thought that the slightest breath of scandal on a young woman's name should be stopped at once. An antique, pure-minded, anxious, self-sacrificing matron was Mrs Clifford, and very dear to the heart of Miss Stanbury.

After lunch was over on the day in question Mrs Clifford got Miss Stanbury into some closet retirement, and there spoke her mind as to the things which were being said. It had been asserted in her presence by Camilla French that she, Camilla, was authorised by Mr Gibson to declare that he had never thought of proposing to Dorothy Stanbury, and that Miss Stanbury had been 'labouring under some strange misapprehension in the matter.' 'Now, my dear, I don't care very much for the young lady in question,' said Mrs Clifford, alluding to Camilla French.

'Very little, indeed, I should think,' said Miss Stanbury, with a shake of her head.

'Quite true, my dear, – but that does not make the words out of her mouth the less efficacious for evil. She clearly insinuated that you had endeavoured to make up a match between this gentleman and your niece, and that you had failed.' So much was at least true. Miss Stanbury felt this, and felt also that she could not explain the truth, even to her dear old friend. In the midst of her divine wrath she had acknowledged to herself that she had brought Mr Gibson into his difficulty, and that it would not become her to tell any one of his failure. And in this matter she did not herself accuse Mr Gibson. She believed that the lie originated with Camilla French, and it was against Camilla that her wrath raged the fiercest.

'She is a poor, mean, disappointed thing,' said Miss Stanbury.

'Very probably; – but I think I should ask her to hold her tongue about Miss Dorothy,' said Mrs Clifford.

The consultation in the closet was carried on for about half-an-hour, and then Miss Stanbury put on her bonnet and shawl and descended into Mrs Clifford's carriage. The carriage took the Heavitree road, and deposited Miss Stanbury at the door of Mrs French's house. The walk home from Heavitree would be nothing, and Mrs Clifford proceeded on her way, having given this little help in counsel and conveyance to her friend. Mrs French was at home, and Miss Stanbury was shown up into the room in which the three ladies were sitting.

The reader will doubtless remember the promise which Arabella had made to Mr Gibson. That promise she had already fulfilled, – to the amazement of her mother and sister; and when Miss Stanbury entered the room the elder daughter of the family was seen without her accustomed head gear. If the truth is to be owned, Miss Stanbury gave the poor young woman no credit for her new simplicity, but put down the deficiency to the charge of domestic slatternliness. She was unjust enough to declare afterwards that she had found Arabella French only half dressed at between three and four o'clock in the afternoon! From which this lesson may surely be learned, – that though the way down Avernus* may be, and customarily is, made with great celerity, the return journey, if made at all, mut be made slowly. A young woman may commence in chignons by attaching any amount of an edifice to her head; but the reduction should be made by degrees. Arabella's edifice had, in Miss Stanbury's eyes, been the ugliest thing in art that she had known; but, now, its absence offended her, and she most untruly declared that she had come upon the young woman in the middle of the day just out of her bedroom and almost in her dressing-gown.

And the whole French family suffered a diminution of power from the strange phantasy which had come upon Arabella. They all felt, in sight of the enemy, that they had to a certain degree lowered their flag. One of the ships, at least, had shown signs of striking, and this element of weakness made itself felt through the whole fleet. Arabella, herself, when she saw Miss Stanbury, was painfully conscious of her head, and wished that she had postponed the operation till the evening. She smiled with a faint watery smile, and was aware that something ailed her.

The greetings at first were civil, but very formal, as are those between nations which are nominally at peace, but which are waiting for a sign at which each may spring at the other's throat. In this instance the Juno from the Close had come quite prepared to declare her casus belli* as complete, and to fling down her gauntlet,

unless the enemy should at once yield to her everything demanded
with an abject submission. 'Mrs French,' she said, 'I have called to-
day for a particular purpose, and I must address myself chiefly to
Miss Camilla.'

'Oh, certainly,' said Mrs French.

'I shall be delighted to hear anything from you, Miss Stanbury,
said Camilla, – not without an air of bravado. Arabella said
nothing, but she put her hand up almost convulsively to the back of
her head.

'I have been told to-day by a friend of mine, Miss Camilla,' began
Miss Stanbury, 'that you declared yourself, in her presence, authorised by Mr Gibson to make a statement about my niece Dorothy.'

'May I ask who was your friend ?' demanded Mrs French.

'It was Mrs Clifford, of course,' said Camilla. 'There is nobody
else would try to make difficulties.'

'There need be no difficulty at all, Miss Camilla,' said Miss
Stanbury, 'if you will promise me that you will not repeat the
statement. It can't be true.'

'But it is true,' said Camilla.

'What is true ?' asked Miss Stanbury, surprised by the audacity
of the girl.

'It is true that Mr Gibson authorised us to state what I did state
when Mrs Clifford heard me.'

'And what was that ?'

'Only this, – that people had been saying all about Exeter that he
was going to be married to a young lady, and that as the report was
incorrect, and as he had never had the remotest idea in his mind of
making the young lady his wife, – ' Camilla, as she said this, spoke
with a great deal of emphasis, putting forward her chin and shaking
her head, – 'and as he thought it was uncomfortable both for the
young lady and for himself, and as there was nothing in it the least
in the world, – nothing at all, no glimmer of a foundation for the
report, it would be better to have it denied everywhere. That is
what I said ; and we had authority from the gentleman himself.
Arabella can say the same, and so can mamma ; – only mamma did
not hear him.' Nor had Camilla heard him, but that incident she
did not mention.

The circumstances were, in Miss Stanbury's judgment, becoming
very remarkable. She did not for a moment believe Camilla. She did
not believe that Mr Gibson had given to either of the Frenches any
justification for the statement just made. But Camilla had been so
much more audacious than Miss Stanbury had expected, that that
lady was for a moment struck dumb. 'I'm sure, Miss Stanbury,' said

Mrs French, 'we don't want to give any offence to your niece, – very far from it.'

'My niece doesn't care about it two straws,' said Miss Stanbury. 'It is I that care. And I care very much. The things that have been said have been altogether false.'

'How false, Miss Stanbury?' asked Camilla.

'Altogether false, – as false as they can be.'

'Mr Gibson must know his own mind,' said Camilla.

'My dear, there's a little disappointment,' said Miss French, 'and it don't signify.'

'There's no disappointment at all,' said Miss Stanbury, 'and it does signify very much. Now that I've begun, I'll go to the bottom of it. If you say that Mr Gibson told you to make these statements, I'll go to Mr Gibson. I'll have it out somehow.'

'You may have what you like out for us, Miss Stanbury,' said Camilla.

'I don't believe Mr Gibson said anything of the kind.'

'That's civil,' said Camilla.

'But why shouldn't he?' asked Arabella.

'There were the reports, you know,' said Mrs French.

'And why shouldn't he deny them when there wasn't a word of truth in them?' continued Camilla. 'For my part, I think the gentleman is bound for the lady's sake to declare that there's nothing in it when there is nothing in it.' This was more than Miss Stanbury could bear. Hitherto the enemy had seemed to have the best of it. Camilla was firing broadside after broadside, as though she was assured of victory. Even Mrs French was becoming courageous; and Arabella was forgetting the place where her chignon ought to have been. 'I really do not know what else there is for me to say,' remarked Camilla, with a toss of her head, and an air of impudence that almost drove poor Miss Stanbury frantic.

It was on her tongue to declare the whole truth, but she refrained. She had schooled herself on this subject vigorously. She would not betray Mr Gibson. Had she known all the truth, – or had she believed Camilla French's version of the story, – there would have been no betrayal. But looking at the matter with such knowledge as she had at present, she did not even yet feel herself justified in declaring that Mr Gibson had offered his hand to her niece, and had been refused. She was, however, sorely tempted. 'Very well, ladies,' she said. 'I shall now see Mr Gibson, and ask him whether he did give you authority to make such statements as you have been spreading abroad everywhere.' Then the door of the room was opened, and in a moment Mr Gibson was among them. He was true to his promise, and had come to see Arabella with her altered head-dress; – but he had come at this hour thinking that escape in the morning would be easier and quicker than it might have been in the evening. His mind had been full of Arabella and her head-dress even up to the moment of his knocking at the door; but all that was driven out of his brain at once when he saw Miss Stanbury.

'Here is Mr Gibson himself,' said Mrs French.

'How do you do, Mr Gibson?' said Miss Stanbury, with a very stately courtesy. They had never met since the day on which he had been, as he stated, turned out of Miss Stanbury's house. He now bowed to her; but there was no friendly greeting, and the Frenches were able to congratulate themselves on the apparent loyalty to themselves of the gentleman who stood among them. 'I have come here, Mr Gibson,' continued Miss Stanbury, 'to put a small matter right in which you are concerned.'

'It seems to me to be the most insignificant thing in the world,' said Camilla.

'Very likely,' said Miss Stanbury. 'But it is not insignificant to me. Miss Camilla French has asserted publicly that you have authorised her to make a statement about my niece Dorothy.'

Mr Gibson looked into Camilla's face doubtingly, inquisitively, almost piteously. 'You had better let her go on,' said Camilla. 'She will make a great many mistakes, no doubt, but you had better let her go on to the end.'

'I have made no mistake as yet, Miss Camilla. She so asserted, Mr Gibson, in the hearing of a friend of mine, and she repeated the assertion here in this room to me just before you came in. She says that you have authorised her to declare that – that – that, – I had better speak it out plainly at once.'

'Much better,' said Camilla.

'That you never entertained an idea of offering your hand to my niece.' Miss Stanbury paused, and Mr Gibson's jaw fell visibly. But he was not expected to speak as yet; and Miss Stanbury continued her accusation. 'Beyond that, I don't want to mention my niece's name, if it can be avoided.'

'But it can't be avoided,' said Camilla.

'If you please, I will continue. Mr Gibson will understand me. I will not, if I can help it, mention my niece's name again, Mr Gibson. But I still have that confidence in you that I do not think that you would have made such a statement in reference to yourself and any young lady, – unless it were some young lady who had absolutely thrown herself at your head.' And in saying this she paused, and looked very hard at Camilla.

'That's just what Dorothy Stanbury has been doing,' said Camilla.

'She has been doing nothing of the kind, and you know she hasn't,' said Miss Stanbury, raising her arm as though she were going to strike her opponent. 'But I am quite sure, Mr Gibson, that you never could have authorised these young ladies to make such an assertion publicly on your behalf. Whatever there may have been of misunderstanding between you and me, I can't believe that of you.' Then she paused for a reply. 'If you will be good enough to set us right on that point, I shall be obliged to you.'

Mr Gibson's position was one of great discomfort. He had given no authority to any one to make such a statement. He had said nothing about Dorothy Stanbury to Camilla; but he had told Arabella, when hard pressed by that lady, that he did not mean to propose to Dorothy. He could not satisfy Miss Stanbury because he feared Arabella. He could not satisfy the Frenches because he feared Miss Stanbury. 'I really do not think,' said he, 'that we ought to talk about a young lady in this way.'

'That's my opinion, too,' said Camilla; 'but Miss Stanbury will.'

'Exactly so. Miss Stanbury will,' said that lady. 'Mr Gibson, I insist upon it, that you tell me whether you did give any such authority to Miss Camilla French, or to Miss French.'

'I wouldn't answer her, if I were you,' said Camilla.

'I really don't think this can do any good,' said Mrs French.

'And it is so very harassing to our nerves,' said Arabella.

'Nerves! Pooh!' exclaimed Miss Stanbury. 'Now, Mr Gibson, I am waiting for an answer.'

'My dear Miss Stanbury, I really think it better, – the situation is so peculiar, and, upon my word, I hardly know how not to give offence, which I wouldn't do for the world.'

'Do you mean to tell me that you won't answer my question?' demanded Miss Stanbury.

'I really think that I had better hold my tongue,' pleaded Mr Gibson.

'You are quite right, Mr Gibson,' said Camilla.

'Indeed, it is wisest,' said Mrs French.

'I don't see what else he can do,' said Arabella.

Then was Miss Stanbury driven altogether beyond her powers of endurance. 'If that be so,' said she, 'I must speak out, though I should have preferred to hold my tongue. Mr Gibson did offer to my niece the week before last, – twice, and was refused by her. My niece, Dorothy, took it into her head that she did not like him; and, upon my word, I think she was right. We should have said nothing about this, – not a word; but when these false assertions are made on Mr Gibson's alleged authority, and Mr Gibson won't deny it, I must tell the truth.' Then there was silence among them for a few seconds, and Mr Gibson struggled hard, but vainly, to clothe his face in a pleasant smile. 'Mr Gibson, is that true?' said Miss Stanbury. But Mr Gibson made no reply. 'It is as true as heaven,' said Miss Stanbury, striking her hand upon the table. 'And now you have better, all of you, hold your tongues about my niece, and she will hold her tongue about you. And as for Mr Gibson, – anybody who wants him after this is welcome to him for us. Good-morning, Mrs French; good-morning, young ladies.' And so she stalked out of the room, and out of the house, and walked back to her house in the Close.

'Mamma,' said Arabella as soon as the enemy was gone, 'I have got such a headache that I think I will go up-stairs.'

'And I will go with you, dear,' said Camilla.

Mr Gibson, before he left the house, confided his secret to the maternal ears of Mrs French. He certainly had been allured into making an offer to Dorothy Stanbury, but was ready to atone for this crime by marrying her daughter, – Camilla, – as soon as might be convenient. He was certainly driven to make this declaration by intense cowardice. He knew not how else; – not to excuse himself, for in that there could be no excuse; – but how else should he dare to suggest that he might as well leave the house? 'Shall I tell the dear girl?' asked Mrs French. But Mr Gibson requested a fortnight, in which to consider how the proposition had best be made.'

49

Mr Brooke Burgess after Supper

Brooke Burgess was a clerk in the office of the Ecclesiastical Commissioners in London, and as such had to do with things very solemn, grave, and almost melancholy. He had to deal with the rents of episcopal properties, to correspond with clerical claimants, and to be at home with the circumstances of underpaid vicars and perpetual curates with much less than £300 a-year; but yet he was as jolly and pleasant at his desk as though he were busied about the collection of the malt tax, or wrote his letters to admirals and captains instead of to deans and prebendaries. Brooke Burgess had risen to be a senior clerk, and was held in some respect in his office; but it was not perhaps for the amount of work he did, nor yet on account of the gravity of his demeanour, nor for the brilliancy of his intellect. But if not clever, he was sensible; though he was not a dragon of official virtue, he had a conscience; – and he possessed those small but most valuable gifts by which a man becomes popular among men. And thus is had come to pass in all those battles as to competitive merit which had taken place in his as in other public offices, that no one had ever dreamed of putting a junior over the head of Brooke Burgess. He was tractable, easy, pleasant, and therefore deservedly successful. All his brother clerks called him Brooke, – except the young lads who, for the first year or two of their service, still denominated him Mr Burgess.

'Brooke,' said one of his juniors, coming into his room and standing before the fireplace with a cigar in his mouth, 'have you heard who is to be the new Commissioner?'

'Colenso, to be sure,' said Brooke.

'What a lark that would be. And I don't see why he shouldn't. But it isn't Colenso.* The name has just come down.'

'And who is it?'

'Old Proudie, from Barchester.'*

'Why, we had him here years ago, and he resigned.'

'But he's to come on again now for a spell. It always seems to me that the bishops ain't a bit of use here. They only get blown up, and snubbed, and shoved into corners by the others.'

'You young reprobate, – to talk of shoving an archbishop into a corner.'

'Well, – don't they? It's only for the name of it they have them. There's the Bishop of Broomsgrove; – he's always sauntering about the place, looking as though he'd be so much obliged if somebody would give him something to do. He's always smiling, and so gracious, – just as if he didn't feel above half sure that he had any right to be where he is, and he thought that perhaps somebody was going to kick him.'

'And so old Proudie is coming up again,' said Brooke. 'It certainly is very much the same to us whom they send. He'll get shoved into a corner, as you call it, – only that he'll go into the corner without any shoving.' Then there came in a messenger with a card, and Brooke learned that Hugh Stanbury was waiting for him in the strangers' room. In performing the promise made to Dorothy, he had called upon her brother as soon as he was back in London, but had not found him. This now was the return visit.

'I thought I was sure to find you here,' said Hugh.

'Pretty nearly sure from eleven till five,' said Brooke. 'A hard stepmother like the Civil Service does not allow one much chance of relief. I do get across to the club sometimes for a glass of sherry and a biscuit, – but here I am now, at any rate; and I'm very glad you have come.' Then there was some talk between them about affairs at Exeter; but as they were interrupted before half an hour was over their heads by a summons brought for Burgess from one of the secretaries, it was agreed that they should dine together at Burgess's club on the following day. 'We can manage a pretty good beef-steak,' said Brooke, 'and have a fair glass of sherry. I don't think you can get much more than that anywhere nowadays, – unless you want a dinner for eight at three guineas a head. The magnificence of men has become so intolerable now that one is driven to be humble in one's self-defence.' Stanbury assured his acquaintance that he was anything but magnificent in his own ideas, that cold beef and beer was his usual fare, and at last allowed the clerk to wait upon the secretary.

'I wouldn't have any other fellow to meet you,' said Brooke as they sat at their dinners, 'because in this way we can talk over the dear old woman at Exeter. Yes, our fellow does make good soup, and it's about all that he does do well. As for getting a potato properly boiled, that's quite out of the question. Yes, it is a good glass of sherry. I told you we'd a fairish tap of sherry on. Well, I was there, backwards and forwards, for nearly six weeks.'

'And how did you get on with the old woman?'

'Like a house on fire,' said Brooke.

'She didn't quarrel with you?'

'No, – upon the whole she did not. I always felt that it was touch and go. She might or she might not. Every now and then she looked at me, and said a sharp word, as though it was about to come. But I had determined when I went there altogether to disregard that kind of thing.'

'It's rather important to you, – is it not?'

'You mean about her money?'

'Of course, I mean about her money,' said Stanbury.

'It is important; – and so it was to you.'

'Not in the same degree, or nearly so. And as for me, it was not on the cards that we shouldn't quarrel. I am so utterly a Bohemian in all my ideas of life, and she is so absolutely the reverse, that not to have quarrelled would have been hypocritical on my part or on hers. She had got it into her head that she had a right to rule my life; and, of course, she quarrelled with me when I made her understand that she should do nothing of the kind. Now, she won't want to rule you.'

'I hope not.'

'She has taken you up,' continued Stanbury, 'on altogether a different understanding. You are to her the representative of a family to whom she thinks she owes the restitution of the property which she enjoys. I was simply a member of her own family, to which she owes nothing. She thought it well to help one of us out of what she regarded as her private purse, and she chose me. But the matter is quite different with you.'

'She might have given everything to you, as well as to me,' said Brooke.

'That's not her idea. She conceives herself bound to leave all she has back to a Burgess, except anything she may save, – as she says, off her own back, or out of her own belly. She has told me so a score of times.'

'And what did you say?'

'I always told her that, let her do as she would, I should never ask any question about her will.'

'But she hates us all like poison, – except me,' said Brooke. 'I never knew people so absurdly hostile as are your aunt and my uncle Barty. Each thinks the other the most wicked person in the world.'

'I suppose your uncle was hard upon her once.'

'Very likely. He is a hard man, – and has, very warmly, all the feelings of an injured man. I suppose my uncle Brooke's will was a cruel blow to him. He professes to believe that Miss Stanbury will never leave me a shilling.'

'He is wrong, then,' said Stanbury.

'Oh yes; – he's wrong, because he thinks that that's her present intention. I don't know that he's wrong as to the probable result.'

'Who will have it, then?'

'There are ever so many horses in the race,' said Brooke. 'I'm one.'

'You're the favourite,' said Stanbury.

'For the moment I am. Then there's yourself.'

'I've been scratched, and am altogether out of the betting.'

'And your sister,' continued Brooke.

'She's only entered to run for the second money; and, if she'll trot over the course quietly, and not go the wrong side of the posts, she'll win that.'

'She may do more than that. Then there's Martha.'

'My aunt will never leave her money to a servant. What she may give Martha would come from her own savings.'

'The next is a dark horse, but one that wins a good many races of this kind. He's apt to come in with a fatal rush at the end.'

'Who is it ?'

'The hospitals. When an old lady finds in her latter days that she hates everybody, and fancies that the people around her are all thinking of her money, she's uncommon likely to indulge herself in a little bit of revenge, and solace herself with large-handed charity.'

'But she's so good a woman at heart,' said Hugh.

'And what can a good woman do better than promote hospitals ?'

'She'll never do that. She's too strong. It's a maudlin sort of thing, after all, for a person to leave everything to a hospital.'

'But people are maudlin when they're dying,' said Brooke, – 'or even when they think they're dying. How else did the Church get the estates, of which we are now distributing so bountifuly some of the last remnants down at our office ? Come into the next room, and we'll have a smoke.'

They had their smoke, and then they went at half-price to the play ; and, after the play was over, they ate three or four dozen of oysters between them. Brooke Burgess was a little too old for oysters at midnight in September ; but he went through his work like a man. Hugh Stanbury's powers were so great, that he could have got up and done the same thing again, after he had been an hour in bed, without any serious inconvenience.

But, in truth, Brooke Burgess had still another word or two to say before he went to his rest. They supped somewhere near the Haymarket, and then he offered to walk home with Stanbury, to his chambers in Lincoln's Inn. 'Do you know that Mr Gibson at Exeter ?' he asked, as they passed through Leicester Square.

'Yes ; I knew him. He was a sort of tame-cat parson at my aunt's house, in my days.'

'Exactly ; – but I fancy that has come to an end now. Have you heard anything about him lately ?'

'Well ; – yes I have,' said Stanbury, feeling that dislike to speak of his sister which is common to most brothers when in company with other men.

'I suppose you've heard of it, and, as I was in the middle of it all, of course I couldn't but know all about it too. Your aunt wanted him to marry your sister.'

'So I was told.'

'But your sister didn't see it,' said Brooke.

'So I understand,' said Stanbury. 'I believe my aunt was exceedingly liberal, and meant to do the best she could for poor Dorothy ; but, if she didn't like him, I suppose she was right not to have him,' said Hugh.

'Of course she was right,' said Brooke, with a good deal of enthusiasm.

'I believe Gibson to be a very decent sort of fellow,' said Stanbury.

'A mean, paltry dog,' said Brooke. There had been a little whisky-toddy after the oysters, and Mr Burgess was perhaps moved to a warmer expression of feeling than he might have displayed had he discussed this branch of the subject before supper. 'I knew from the first that she would have nothing to say to him. He is such a poor creature !'

'I always thought well of him,' said Stanbury, 'and was inclined to think that Dolly might have done worse.'

'It is hard to say what is the worse a girl might do ; but I think she might do, perhaps, a little better.'

'What do you mean ?' said Hugh.

'I think I shall go down, and ask her to take myself.'

'Do you mean it in earnest ?'

'I do,' said Brooke. 'Of course, I hadn't a chance when I was there. She told me – '

'Who told you; – Dorothy ?'

'No, your aunt; – she told me that Mr Gibson was to marry your sister. You know you aunt's way. She spoke of it as though the thing were settled as soon as she had got into her own head ; and she was as hot upon it as though Mr Gibson had been an archbishop. I had nothing to do then but to wait and see.'

'I had no idea of Dolly being fought for by rivals.'

'Brothers never think much of their sisters,' said Brooke Burgess.

'I can assure you I think a great deal of Dorothy,' said Hugh. 'I believe her to be as sweet a woman as God ever made. She hardly knows that she has a self belonging to herself.'

'I'm sure she doesn't,' said Brooke.

'She is a dear, loving, sweet-tempered creature, who is only too ready to yield in all things.'

'But she wouldn't yield about Gibson,' said Brooke.

'How did she and my aunt manage ?'

'Your sister simply said she couldn't, – and then that she wouldn't. I never thought from the first moment that she'd take that fellow. In the first place he can't say boo to a goose.'

'But Dolly wouldn't want a man to say – boo.'

'I'm not so sure of that, old fellow. At any rate I mean to try myself. Now, – what'll the old woman say ?'

'She'll be pleased as Punch, I should think,' said Stanbury.

'Either that; – or else she'll swear that she'll never speak another word to either of us. However, I shall go on with it.'

'Does Dorothy know anything of this?' asked Stanbury.

'Not a word,' said Brooke. 'I came away a day or so after Gibson was settled; and as I had been talked to all through the affair by both of them, I couldn't turn round and offer myself the moment he was gone. You won't object; – will you?'

'Who; I?' said Stanbury. 'I shall have no objection as long as Dolly pleases herself. Of course you know that we haven't as much as a brass farthing among us?'

'That won't matter if the old lady takes it kindly,' said Brooke. Then they parted, at the corner of Lincoln's Inn Fields, and Hugh as he went up to his own rooms, reflected with something of wonderment on the success of Dorothy's charms. She had always been the poor one of the family, the chick out of the nest which would most require assistance from the stronger birds; but it now appeared that she would become the first among all the Stanburys. Wealth had first flowed down upon the Stanbury family from the will of old Brooke Burgess; and it now seemed probable that poor Dolly would ultimately have the enjoyment of it all.

END OF VOLUME ONE

VOLUME II

50

Camilla Triumphant

It was now New Year's day, and there was some grief and perhaps more excitement in Exeter, – for it was rumoured that Miss Stanbury lay very ill at her house in the Close. But in order that our somewhat uneven story may run as smoothly as it may be made to do, the little history of the French family for the intervening months shall be told in this chapter, in order that it may be understood how matters were with them when the tidings of Miss Stanbury's severe illness first reached their house at Heavitree.

After that terrible scene in which Miss Stanbury had so dreadfully confounded Mr Gibson by declaring the manner in which he had been rebuffed by Dorothy, the unfortunate clergyman had endeavoured to make his peace with the French family by assuring the mother that in very truth it was the dearest wish of his heart to make her daughter Camilla his wife. Mrs French, who had ever been disposed to favour Arabella's ambition, well knowing its priority and ancient right, and who of late had been taught to consider that even Camilla had consented to waive any claim that she might have once possessed, could not refrain from the expression of some surprise. That he should be recovered at all out of the Stanbury clutches was very much to Mrs French, – was so much that, had time been given her for consideration, she would have acknowledged to herself readily that the property had best be secured at once to the family, without incurring that amount of risk which must unquestionably attend any attempt on her part to direct Mr Gibson's purpose hither or thither. But the proposition came so suddenly, that time was not allowed to her to be altogether wise. 'I thought it was poor Bella,' she said, with something of a piteous whine in her voice. At the moment Mr Gibson was so humble, that he was half inclined to give way even on that head. He felt himself to have been brought so low in the market by that terrible story of Miss Stanbury's, – which he had been unable either to contradict or to explain, – that there was but little power of fighting left in him. He was, however, just able to speak a word for himself, and that sufficed. 'I hope there has been no mistake,' he said; 'but really it is Camilla that has my heart.' Mrs French made no rejoinder to this. It was so much to her to know that Mr Gibson's heart was among them at all after what had occurred in the Close, that she acknowledged to herself after that moment of reflection that Arabella must be sacrificed for the good of the family interests. Poor, dear, loving, misguided, and spiritless mother! She would have given the blood out of her bosom to get husbands for her daughters, though it was not of her own experience that she had learned that of all worldly goods a husband is the best. But it was the possession which they had from their earliest years thought of acquiring, which they had first expected, for which they had then hoped, and afterwards worked and schemed and striven with every energy, – and as to which they had at last almost despaired. And now Arabella's fire had been rekindled with a new spark, which, alas, was to be quenched so suddenly! 'And am I to tell them?' asked Mrs French, with a tremor in her voice. To this, however, Mr Gibson demurred. He said that for certain reasons he should like a fortnight's grace; and that at the end of the fortnight he would be prepared to speak. The interval was granted without further questions, and Mr Gibson was allowed to leave the house.

After that Mrs French was not very comfortable at home. As soon as Mr Gibson had departed, Camilla at once returned to her mother and desired to know what had taken place. Was it true that the perjured man had proposed to that young woman in the Close? Mrs French was not clever at keeping a secret, and she could not keep this by her own aid. She told all that happened to Camilla, and between them they agreed that Arabella should be kept in ignorance till the fatal fortnight should have passed. When Camilla was interrogated as to her own purpose, she said she should like a day to think of it. She took the twenty-four hours, and then made the following confession of her passion to her mother. 'You see, mamma, I always liked Mr Gibson, – always.'

'So did Arabella, my dear, – before you thought of such things.'

'I dare say that may be true, mamma; but that is not my fault. He came here among us on such sweetly intimate terms that the feeling grew up with me before I knew what it meant. As to any idea of cutting out Arabella, my conscience is quite clear. If I thought there had been anything really between them I would have gone anywhere, – to the top of a mountain, – rather than rob my sister of a heart that belonged to her.'

'He has been so slow about it,' said Mrs French.

'I don't know about that,' said Camilla. 'Gentleman have to be slow, I suppose, when they think of their incomes. He only got St Peter's-cum-Pumkin three years ago, and didn't know for the first year whether he could hold that and the minor canonry together. Of course a gentleman has to think of these things before he comes forward.'

'My dear, he has been very backward.'

'If I'm to be Mrs Gibson, mamma, I beg that I mayn't hear

anything said against him. Then there came all this about that young woman; and when I saw that Arabella took on so, – which I must say was very absurd, – I'm sure I put myself out of the way entirely. If I'd buried myself under the ground I couldn't have done it more. And it's my belief that what I've said, all for Arabella's sake, has put the old woman into such a rage that it has made a quarrel between him and the niece; otherwise that wouldn't be off. I don't believe a word of her refusing him, and never shall. It is in the course of things, mamma?' Mrs French shook her head. 'Of course not. Then when you question him, – very properly, – he says that he's devoted to – poor me. If I was to refuse him, he wouldn't put up with Bella.'

'I suppose not,' said Mrs French.

'He hates Bella. I've known it all along, though I wouldn't say so. If I were to sacrifice myself ever so it wouldn't be of any good, – and I shan't to it.' In this way the matter was arranged.

At the end of the fortnight, however, Mr Gibson did not come, – nor at the end of three weeks. Inquiries had of course been made, and it was ascertained that he had gone into Cornwall for a parson's holiday of thirteen days. That might be all very well. A man might want the recruiting vigour of some change of air after such scenes as those Mr Gibson had gone through with the Stanburys, and before his proposed encounter with new perils. And he was a man so tied by the leg that his escape could not be for any long time. He was back on the appointed Sunday, and on the Wednesday Mrs French, under Camilla's instruction, wrote to him a pretty little note. He replied that he would be with her on the Saturday. It would then be nearly four weeks after the great day with Miss Stanbury, but no one would be inclined to quarrel with so short a delay as that. Arabella in the meantime had become fidgety and unhappy. She seemed to understand that something was expected, being quite unable to guess what that something might be. She was true throughout these days to the simplicity of head-gear which Mr Gibson had recommended to her, and seemed in her questions to her mother and to Camilla to be more fearful of Dorothy Stanbury than of any other enemy. 'Mamma, I think you ought to tell her,' said Camilla more than once. But she had not been told when Mr Gibson came on the Saturday. It may truly be said that the poor mother's pleasure in the prosects of one daughter was altogether destroyed by the anticipation of the other daughter's misery. Had Mr Gibson made Dorothy Stanbury his wife they could have all comforted themselves together by the heat of their joint animosity.

He came on the Saturday, and it was so managed that he was

closeted with Camilla before Arabella knew that he was in the house. There was a quarter of an hour during which his work was easy, and perhaps pleasant. When he began to explain his intention Camilla, with the utmost frankness, informed him that her mother had told her all about it. Then she turned her face on one side and put her hand in his; he got his arm round her waist, gave her a kiss, and the thing was done. Camilla was fully resolved that after such a betrothal it should not be undone. She had behaved with sisterly forbearance, and would not now lose the reward of virtue. Not a word was said of Arabella at this interview till he was pressed to come and drink tea with them all that night. He hesitated a moment; and then Camilla declared, with something perhaps of imperious roughness in her manner, that he had better face it all at once. 'Mamma will tell her, and she will understand,' said Camilla. He hesitated again, but at last promised that he would come.

Whilst he was yet in the house Mrs French had told the whole story to her poor elder daughter. 'What is he doing with Camilla?' Arabella had asked with feverish excitement.

'Bella, darling; – don't you know?' said the mother.

'I know nothing. Everybody keeps me in the dark, and I am badly used. What is it that he is doing?' Then Mrs French tried to take the poor young woman in her arms, but Arabella would not submit to be embraced. 'Don't!' she exclaimed. 'Leave me alone. Nobody likes me, or cares a bit about me! Why is Cammy with him there, all alone?'

'I suppose he is asking her – to be – his wife.' Then Arabella threw herself in despair upon the bed, and wept without any further attempt at control over her feelings. It was a death-blow to her last hope, and all the world, as she looked upon the world then, was over for her. 'If I could have arranged it the other way, you know that I would,' said the mother.

'Mamma,' said Arabella jumping up, 'he shan't do it. He hasn't a right. And as for her, – Oh, that she should treat me in this way! Didn't he tell me the other night, when he drank tea here with me alone – '

'What did he tell you, Bella?'

'Never mind. Nothing shall ever make me speak to him again; – not if he married her three times over; nor to her. She is a nasty, sly, good-for-nothing thing!'

'But, Bella – '

'Don't talk to me, mamma. There never was such a thing done before since people – were – people at all. She has been doing it all the time. I know she has.'

Nevertheless Arabella did sit down to tea with the two lovers that night. There was a terrible scene between her and Camilla ; but Camilla held her own ; and Arabella, being the weaker of the two, was vanquished by the expenditure of her own small energies. Camilla argued that as her sister's chance was gone, and as the prize had come in her own way, there was no good reason why it should be lost to the family altogether, because Arabella could not win it. When Arabella called her a treacherous vixen and a heartless, profligate hussy, she spoke out freely, and said that she wasn't going to be abused. A gentleman to whom she was attached has asked her for her hand, and she had given it. If Arabella chose to make herself a fool she might, – but what would be the effect ? Simply that all the world would know that she, Arabella, was disappointed. Poor Bella at last gave way, put on her discarded chignon, and came down to tea. Mr Gibson was already in the room when she entered it. 'Arabella,' he said, getting up to meet her, 'I hope you will congratulate me.' He had planned his little speech and his manner of making it, and had wisely decided that in this way might be best get over the difficulty.

'Oh yes ; – of course,' she said, with a little giggle, and then a sob, and then a flood of tears.

'Dear Bella feels these things so strongly,' said Mrs French.

'We have never been parted yet,' said Camilla. Then Arabella tapped the head of the sofa three or four times sharply with her knuckles. It was the only protest against the reading of the scene which Camilla had given of which she was capable at that moment. After that Mrs French gave out the tea, Arabella curled herself upon the sofa as though she were asleep, and the two lovers settled down to proper lover-like conversation.

The reader may be sure that Camilla was not slow in making the fact of her engagement notorious through the city. It was not probably true that the tidings of her success had anything to do with Miss Stanbury's illness ; but it was reported by many that such was the case. It was in November that the arrangement was made, and it certainly was true that Miss Stanbury was rather ill about the same time. 'You know, you naughty Lothario, that you did give her some ground to hope that she might dispose of her unfortunate niece,' said Camilla playfully to her own one, when this illness was discussed between them. 'But you are caught now, and your wings are clipped, and you are never to be a naughty Lothario again.' The clerical Don Juan bore it all, awkwardly indeed, but with good humour, and declared that all his troubles of that sort were over, now and for ever. Nevertheless he did not name the day, and

Camilla began to feel that there might be occasion for a little more of that imperious roughness which she had at her command.

November was nearly over and nothing had been fixed about the day. Arabella never condescended to speak to her sister on the subject; but on more than one occasion made some inquiry of her mother. And she came to perceive, or to think that she perceived, that her mother was still anxious on the subject. 'I shouldn't wonder if he wasn't off some day now,' she said at last to her mother.

'Don't say anything so dreadful, Bella.'

'It would serve Cammy quite right, and it's just what he's likely to do.'

'It would kill me,' said the mother.

'I don't know about killing,' said Arabella; 'it's nothing to what I've had to go through. I shouldn't pretend to be sorry if he were to go to Hong-Kong to-morrow.'

But Mr Gibson had no idea of going to Hong-Kong. He was simply carrying out his little scheme for securing the advantages of a 'long-day'. He was fully resolved to be married, and was contented to think that his engagement was the best thing for him. To one or two male friends he spoke of Camilla as the perfection of female virtue, and entertained no smallest idea of ultimate escape. But a 'long day' is often a convenience. A bill at three months sits easier on a man than one at sixty days; and a bill at six months is almost as little of a burden as no bill at all.

But Camilla was resolved that some day should be fixed. 'Thomas,' she said to her lover one morning, as they were walking home together after service at the cathedral, 'isn't this rather a fool's Paradise of ours?'

'How a fool's Paradise?' asked the happy Thomas.

'What I mean is, dearest, that we ought to fix something. Mamma is getting uneasy about her own plans.'

'In what way, dearest?'

'About a thousand things. She can't arrange anything till our plans are made. Of course there are little troubles about money when people ain't rich.' Then it occurred to her that this might seem to be a plea for postponing rather than for hurrying the marriage, and she mended her argument. 'The truth is, Thomas, she wants to know when the day is to be fixed, and I've promised to ask. She said she'd ask you herself, but I wouldn't let her do that.'

'We must think about it, of course,' said Thomas.

'But, my dear, there has been plenty of time for thinking. What do you say to January?' This was on the last day of November.

'January!' exclaimed Thomas, in a tone that betrayed no triumph. 'I couldn't get my services arranged for in January.'

'I thought a clergyman could always manage that for his marriage,' said Camilla.

'Not in January. Besides, I was thinking you would like to be away in warmer weather.'

They were still in November, and he was thinking of postponing it till the summer! Camilla immediately perceived how necessary it was that she should be plain with him. 'We shall not have warm weather, as you call it, for a very long time, Thomas; – and I don't think that it would be wise to wait for the weather at all. Indeed, I've begun to get my things for doing it in the winter. Mamma said that she was sure January would be the very latest. And it isn't as though we had to get furniture or anything of that kind. Of course a lady shouldn't be pressing.' She smiled sweetly and leaned on his arm as she said this. 'But I hate all girlish nonsense and that kind of thing. It is such a bore to be kept waiting. I'm sure there's nothing to prevent it coming off in February.'

The 31st of March was fixed before they reached Heavitree, and Camilla went into her mother's house a happy woman. But Mr Gibson, as he went home, thought that he had been hardly used. Here was a girl who hadn't a shilling of money, – not a shilling till her mother died, – and who already talked about his house, and his furniture, and his income as if it were all her own! Circumstanced as she was, what right had she to press for an early day? He was quite sure that Arabella would have been more discreet and less exacting. He was very angry with his dcar Cammy as he went across the Close to his house.

51

Showing what happened during Miss Stanbury's Illness

It was on Christmas-day that Sir Peter Mancrudy, the highest authority on such matters in the west of England, was sent for to see Miss Stanbury; and Sir Peter had acknowledged that things were very serious. He took Dorothy on one side, and told her that Mr Martin, the ordinary practitioner, had treated the case, no doubt, quite wisely throughout; that there was not a word to be said against Mr Martin, whose experience was great, and whose discretion was undeniable; but, nevertheless, – at least it seemed to Dorothy that this was the only meaning to be attributed to Sir Peter's words, – Mr Martin had in his case taken one line of treatment, when he ought to have taken another. The plan of action was undoubtedly changed, and Mr Martin became very fidgety, and ordered nothing without Sir Peter's sanction. Miss Stanbury was suffering from bronchitis, and a complication of diseases about her throat and chest. Barty Burgess declared to more than one acquaintance in the little parlour behind the bank, that she would go on drinking four or five glasses of new port wine every day, in direct opposition to Martin's request. Camilla French heard the report, and repeated it to her lover, and perhaps another person or two, with an expression of her assured conviction that it must be false, – at any rate, as regarded the fifth glass. Mrs MacHugh, who saw Martha daily, was much frightened. The peril of such a friend disturbed equally the repose and the pleasures of her life. Mrs Clifford was often at Miss Stanbury's bed-side, – and would have sat there reading for hours together, had she not been made to understand by Martha that Miss Stanbury preferred that Miss Dorothy should read to her. The sick woman received the Sacrament weekly, – not from Mr Gibson, but from the hands of another minor canon; and, though she never would admit her own danger, or allow others to talk to her of it, it was known to them all that she admitted it to herself because she had, with much personal annoyance, caused a codicil to be added to her will. 'As you didn't marry that man,' she said to Dorothy, 'I must change it again.' It was in vain that Dorothy begged her not to trouble herself with such thoughts. 'That's trash,' said Miss Stanbury, angrily. 'A person who has it is bound to trouble himself about it. You don't suppose I'm afraid of dying; – do you?' she added. Dorothy answered her with some commonplace, – declaring how strongly they all expected to see her as well as ever. 'I'm not a bit afraid to die,' said the old woman, wheezing, struggling with such voice as she possessed; 'I'm not afraid of it, and I don't think I shall die this time; but I'm not going to have mistakes when I'm gone.' This was on the eve of the new year, and on the same night she asked Dorothy to write to Brooke Burgess, and request him to come to Exeter. This was Dorothy's letter:

Exeter, 31 December, 18C – .

My Dear Mr Burgess,

Perhaps I ought to have written before, to say that Aunt Stanbury is not as well as we could wish her; but, as I know that you cannot very well leave your office, I have thought it best not to say anything to frighten you. But to-night Aunt herself has desired me to tell you that she thinks you ought to know that she is ill, and that she wishes you to come to Exeter for a day or two, if it is possible. Sir Peter Mancrudy has been here every day since Christmas-day, and I believe he thinks she may get over it. It is chiefly in the throat; – what they call bronchitis, – and she has got to be very weak with it, and at the same time very liable to inflammation. So I know that you will come if you can.

Yours very truly,
Dorothy Stanbury.

Perhaps I ought to tell you that she had her lawyer here with her the day before yesterday; but she does not seem to think that she herself is in danger. I read to her a good deal, and I think she is generally asleep; when I stop she wakes, and I don't believe she gets any other rest at all.

When it was known in Exeter that Brooke Burgess had been sent for, then the opinion became general that Miss Stanbury's days were numbered. Questions were asked of Sir Peter at every corner of the street; but Sir Peter was a discreet man, who could answer such questions without giving any information. If it so pleased God, his patient would die; but it was quite possible that she might live. That was the tenor of Sir Peter's replies, – and they were read in any light, according to the idiosyncrasies of the reader. Mrs MacHugh was quite sure that the danger was over, and had a little game of cribbage on the sly with old Miss Wright; – for, during the severity of Miss Stanbury's illness, whist was put on one side in the vicinity of the Close. Barty Burgess was still obdurate, and shook his head. He was of opinion that they might soon gratify their curiosity, and see the last crowning iniquity of this wickedest of old women. Mrs Clifford declared that it was all in the hands of God; but that she saw no reason why Miss Stanbury should not get about again. Mr Gibson thought that it was all up with his late friend; and Camilla wished that at their last interview there had been more of charity on the part of one whom she had regarded in past days with respect and esteem. Mrs French, despondent about everything, was quite despondent in this case. Martha almost despaired, and already was burdened with the cares of a whole wardrobe of solemn funereal clothing. She was seen peering in for half-an-hour at the windows and doorway of a large warehouse for the sale of mourning. Giles Hickbody would not speak above his breath, and took his beer standing; but Dorothy was hopeful, and really believed that her aunt would recover. Perhaps Sir Peter had spoken to her in terms less oracular than those which he used towards the public.

Brooke Burgess came, and had an interview with Sir Peter, and to him Sir Peter was under some obligation to speak plainly, as being the person whom Miss Stanbury recognised as her heir. So Sir Peter declared that his patient might perhaps live, and perhaps might die. 'The truth is, Mr Burgess,' said Sir Peter, 'a doctor doesn't know so very much more about these things than other people.' It was understood that Brooke was to remain three days in Exeter, and then return to London. He would, of course, come again if – if anything should happen. Sir Peter had been quite clear in his opinion, that no immediate result was to be anticipated, – either in the one direction or the other. His patient was doomed to a long illness; she might get over it, or she might succumb to it.

Dorothy and Brooke were thus thrown much together during these three days. Dorothy, indeed, spent most of her hours beside her aunt's bed, instigating sleep by the reading of a certain series of sermons in which Miss Stanbury had great faith; but nevertheless, there were some minutes in which she and Brooke were necessarily together. They eat their meals in each other's company, and there was a period in the evening, before Dorothy began her night-watch in her aunt's room, at which she took her tea while Martha was nurse in the room above. At this time of the day she would remain an hour or more with Brooke; and a great deal may be said between a man and a woman in an hour when the will to say it is there. Brooke Burgess had by no means changed his mind since he had declared it to Hugh Stanbury under the midnight lamps of Long Acre, when warmed by the influence of oysters and whisky toddy. The whisky toddy had in that instance brought out truth and not falsehood, – as is ever the nature of whisky toddy and similar dangerous provocatives. There is no saying truer than that which declares that there is truth in wine. Wine is a dangerous thing, and should not be made the exponent of truth, let the truth be good as it may; but it has the merit of forcing a man to show his true colours. A man who is a gentleman in his cups may be trusted to be a gentleman at all times. I trust that the severe censor will not turn upon me, and tell me that no gentleman in these days is ever to be seen in his cups. There are cups of different degrees of depth; and cups do exist, even among gentlemen, and seem disposed to hold their own let the censor be ever so severe. The gentleman in his cups is a gentleman always; and the man who tells his friend in his cups that he is in love, does so because the fact has been very present to himself in his cooler and calmer moments. Brooke Burgess, who had seen Hugh Stanbury on two or three occasions since that of the oysters and toddy, had not spoken again of his regard for Hugh's sister; but not the less was he determined to carry out his plan and make Dorothy his wife if she would accept him. But could he ask her while the old lady was, as it might be, dying in the house? He had put this question to himself as he travelled down to Exeter, and had told himself that he must be guided for an answer by circumstances as they might occur. Hugh had met him at the station as he started for Exeter, and there had been a consultation between them as to the propriety of bringing about, or of attempting to bring about, an interview between Hugh and his aunt. 'Do whatever you like,' Hugh had said. 'I would go down to her at a moment's warning, if she should express a desire to see me.'

On the first night of Brooke's arrival this question had been discussed between him and Dorothy. Dorothy had declared herself unable to give advice. If any message were given to her she would deliver it to her aunt; but she thought that anything said to her aunt on the subject had better come from Brooke himself. 'You evidently are the person most important to her,' Dorothy said, 'and she would listen to you when she would not let any one else say a word.' Brooke promised that he would think of it; and then Dorothy tripped up to relieve Martha, dreaming nothing at all of that other doubt to which the important personage down-stairs was now subject. Dorothy was, in truth, very fond of the new friend she had made; but it had never occurred to her that he might be a possible suitor to her. Her old conception of herself, – that she was beneath the notice of any man, – had only been partly disturbed by the absolute fact of Mr Gibson's courtship. She had now heard of his engagement to Camilla French, and saw in that complete proof that the foolish man had been induced to offer his hand to her by the promise of her aunt's money. If there had been a moment of exaltation, – a period in which she had allowed herself to think that she was, as other women, capable of making herself dear to a man, – it had been but a moment. And now she rejoiced greatly that she had not acceded to the wishes of one to whom it was so manifest that she had not made herself in the least dear.

On the second day of his visit, Brooke was summoned to Miss Stanbury's room at noon. She was forbidden to talk, and during a great portion of the day could hardly speak without an effort; but there would be half hours now and again in which she would become stronger than usual, at which time nothing that Martha and Dorothy could say would induce her to hold her tongue. When Brooke came to her on this occasion he found her sitting up in bed with a great shawl round her; and he at once perceived she was much more like her own self than on the former day. She told him that she had been an old fool for sending for him, that she had nothing special to say to him, that she had made no alteration in her will in regard to him, — except that I have done something for Dolly that will have to come out of your pocket, Brooke.' Brooke declared that too much could not be done for a person so good, and dear, and excellent as Dorothy Stanbury, let it come out of whose pocket it might. 'She is nothing to you, you know,' said Miss Stanbury.

'She is a great deal to me,' said Brooke.

'What is she?' asked Miss Stanbury.

'Oh; — a friend; a great friend.'

'Well; yes. I hope it may be so. But she won't have anything that I haven't saved,' said Miss Stanbury. 'There are two houses at St Thomas's; but I bought them myself, Brooke; — out of the income.' Brooke could only declare that as the whole property was hers, to do what she liked with it as completely as though she had inherited it from her own father, no one could have any right to ask questions as to when or how this or that portion of the property had accrued. 'But I don't think I'm going to die yet, Brooke,' she said. 'If it is God's will, I am ready. Not that I'm fit, Brooke. God forbid that I should ever think that. But I doubt whether I shall ever be fitter. I can go without repining if He thinks best to take me.' Then he stood up by her bed-side, with his hand upon hers, and after some hesitation asked her whether she would wish to see her nephew Hugh. 'No,' said she, sharply. Brooke went on to say how pleased Hugh would have been to come to her. 'I don't think much of death-bed reconciliations,' said the old woman grimly. 'I loved him dearly, but he didn't love me, and I don't know what good we should do each other.' Brooke declared that Hugh did love her; but he could not press the matter, and it was dropped.

On that evening at eight Dorothy came down to her tea. She had dined at the same table with Brooke that afternoon, but a servant had been in the room at the time and nothing had been said between them. As soon as Brooke has got his tea he began to tell the story of his failure about Hugh. He was sorry, he said, that he had spoken on the subject as it had moved Miss Stanbury to an acrimony which he had not expected.

'She always declares that he never loved her,' said Dorothy. 'She has told me so twenty times.'

'There are people who fancy that nobody cares for them,' said Brooke.

'Indeed there are, Mr Burgess; and it is so natural.'

'Why natural?'

'Just as it is natural that there should be dogs and cats that are petted and loved and made much of, and others that have to crawl through life as they can, cuffed and kicked and starved.'

'That depends on the accident of possession,' said Brooke.

'So does the other. How many people there are that don't seem to belong to anybody, – and if they do, they're no good to anybody. They're not cuffed exactly, or starved; but – '

'You mean that they don't get their share of affection?'

'They get perhaps as much as they deserve,' said Dorothy.

'Because they're cross-grained, or ill-tempered, or disagreeable?'

'Not exactly that.'

'What then?' asked Brooke.

'Because they're just nobodies. They are not anything particular to anybody, and so they go on living till they die. You know what I mean, Mr Burgess. A man who is a nobody can perhaps make himself somebody, – or, at any rate, he can try; but a woman has no means of trying. She is a nobody, and a nobody she must remain. She has her clothes and her food, but she isn't wanted anywhere. People put up with her, and that is about the best of her luck. If she were to die somebody perhaps would be sorry for her, but nobody would be worse off. She doesn't earn anything or do any good. She is just there and that's all.'

Brooke had never heard her speak after this fashion before, had never known her to utter so many consecutive words, or to put forward any opinion of her own with so much vigour. And Dorothy herself, when she had concluded her speech, was frightened by her own energy and grew red in the face, and showed very plainly that she was half ashamed of herself. Brooke thought that he had never seen her look so pretty before, and was pleased by her enthusiasm. He understood perfectly that she was thinking of her own position, though she had entertained no idea that he would so read her meaning; and he felt that it was incumbent on him to undeceive her, and make her know that she was not one of these women who are 'just there and that's all.' 'One does see such a woman as that now and again,' he said.

'There are hundreds of them,' said Dorothy. 'And of course it can't be helped.'

'Such as Arabella French,' said he, laughing.

'Well, – yes; if she is one. It is very easy to see the difference. Some people are of use and are always doing things. There are others, generally women, who have nothing to do, but who can't be got rid of. It is a melancholy sort of feeling.'

'You at least are not one of them.

'I didn't mean to complain about myself,' she said. 'I have got a great deal to make me happy.'

'I don't suppose you regard yourself as an Arabella French,' said he.

'How angry Miss French would be if she heard you. She considers herself to be one of the reigning beauties of Exeter.'

'She has had a very long reign, and dominion of that sort to be successful ought to be short.'

'That is spiteful, Mr Burgess.'

'I don't feel spiteful against her, poor woman. I own I do not love Camilla. Not that I begrudge Camilla her present prosperity.'

'Nor I either, Mr Burgess.'

'She and Mr Gibson will do very well together, I dare say.'

'I hope they will,' said Dorothy, 'and I do not see any reason against it. They have known each other a long time.'

'A very long time,' said Brooke. Then he paused for a minute, thinking how he might best tell her that which he had now resolved should be told on this occasion. Dorothy finished her tea and got up as though she were about to go to her duty up-stairs. She had been as yet hardly an hour in the room, and the period of her relief was not fairly over. But there had come something of a personal flavour in their conversation which prompted her, unconsciously, to leave him. She had, without any special indication of herself, included herself among that company of old maids who are born and live and die without that vital interest in the affairs of life which nothing but family duties, the care of children, or at least of a husband, will give to a woman. If she had not meant this she had felt it. He had understood her meaning, or at least her feeling, and had taken upon himself to assure her that she was not one of the company whose privations she had endeavoured to describe. Her instinct rather than her reason put her at once upon her guard, and she prepared to leave the room. 'You are not going yet,' he said.

'I think I might as well. Martha has so much to do, and she comes to me again at five in the morning.'

'Don't go quite yet,' he said, pulling out his watch. 'I know all about the hours, and it wants twenty minutes to the proper time.'

'There is no proper time, Mr Burgess.'

'Then you can remain a few minutes longer. The fact is, I've got something I want to say to you.'

He was now standing between her and the door, so that she

could not get away from him; but at this moment she was absolutely ignorant of his purpose, expecting nothing of love from him more than she would from Sir Peter Mancrudy. Her face had become flushed when she made her long speech, but there was no blush on it as she answered him now. 'Of course, I can wait,' she said, 'if you have anything to say to me.'

'Well; – I have. I should have said it before, only that that other man was here.' He was blushing now, – up to the roots of his hair, and felt that he was in a difficulty. There are men, to whom such moments of their lives are pleasurable, but Brooke Burgess was not one of them. He would have been glad to have had it done and over, – so that then he might take pleasure in it.

'What man?' asked Dorothy, in perfect innocence.

'Mr Gibson, to be sure. I don't know that there is anybody else.'

'Oh, Mr Gibson. He never comes here now, and I don't suppose he will again. Aunt Stanbury is so very angry with him.'

'I don't care whether he comes or not. What I mean is this. When I was here before, I was told that you were going – to marry him.'

'But I wasn't.'

'How was I to know that, when you didn't tell me? I certainly did know it after I came back from Dartmoor.' He paused a moment, as though she might have a word to say. She had no word to say, and did not in the least know what was coming. She was so far from anticipating the truth, that she was composed and easy in her mind. 'But all that is of no use at all,' he continued. 'When I was here before Miss Stanbury wanted you to marry Mr Gibson; and, of course, I had nothing to say about it. Now I want you – to marry me.'

'Mr Burgess!'

'Dorothy, my darling, I love you better than all the world. I do, indeed.' As soon as he had commenced his protestations he became profuse enough with them, and made a strong attempt to support them by the action of his hands. But she retreated from him step by step, till she had regained her chair by the tea-table, and there she seated herself, – safely, as she thought; but he was close to her, over her shoulder, still continuing his protestations, offering up his vows, and imploring her to reply to him. She, as yet, had not answered him by a word, save by that one half-terrified exclamation of his name. 'Tell me, at any rate, that you believe me, when I assure you that I love you,' he said. The room was going round with Dorothy, and the world was going round, and there had come upon her so strong a feeling of the disruption of things in general, that she was at the moment anything but happy. Had it been possible for her to find that the last ten minutes had been a dream, she would at this moment have wished that it might become one. A trouble had come upon her, out of which she did not see her way. To dive among the waters in warm weather is very pleasant; there is nothing pleasanter. But when the young swimmer first feels the thorough immersion of his plunge, there comes upon him a strong desire to be quickly out again. He will remember afterwards how joyous it was; but now, at this moment, the dry land is everything to him. So it was with Dorothy. She had thought of Brooke Burgess as one of those bright ones of the world, with whom everything is happy and pleasant, whom everybody loves, who may have whatever they please, whose lines have been laid in pleasant places. She thought of him as a man who might some day make some woman very happy as his wife. To be the wife of such a man was, in Dorothy's estimation, one of those blessed chances which come to some women, but which she never regarded as being within her own reach. Though she had thought much about him, she had never thought of him as a possible possession for herself; and now that he was offering himself to her, she was not at once made happy by his love. Her ideas of herself and of her life were all dislocated for the moment, and she required to be alone, that she might set herself in order, and try herself all over, and find whether her bones were broken. 'Say that you believe me,' he repeated.

'I don't know what to say,' she whispered.

'I'll tell you what to say. Say at once that you will be my wife.'

'I can't say that, Mr Burgess.'

'Why not? Do you mean that you cannot love me?'

'I think, if you please, I'll go up to Aunt Stanbury. It is time for me; indeed it is; and she will be wondering, and Martha will be put out. Indeed I must go.'

'And will you not answer me?'

'I don't know what to say. You must give me a little time to consider. I don't quite think you're serious.'

'Heaven and earth!' began Brooke.

'And I'm sure it would never do. At any rate, I must go now. I must, indeed.'

And so she escaped, and went up to her aunt's room, which she reached at ten minutes after her usual time, and before Martha had began to be put out. She was very civil to Martha, as though Martha had been injured; and she put her hand on her aunt's arm, with a soft, caressing, apologetic touch, feeling conscious that she had given cause for offence. 'What has he been saying to you?' said her aunt, as soon as Martha had closed the door. This was a question which Dorothy, certainly, could not answer. Miss Stanbury meant nothing by it, – nothing beyond a sick woman's desire that something of the conversation of those who were not sick should be retailed to her; but to Dorothy the question meant so much! How should her aunt have known that he had said anything? She sat herself down and waited, giving no answer to the question. 'I hope he gets his meals comfortably,' said Miss Stanbury.

'I am sure he does,' said Dorothy, infinitely relieved. Then, knowing how important it was that her aunt should sleep, she took up the volume of Jeremy Taylor, and, with so great a burden on her mind, she went on painfully and distinctly with the second sermon on the Marriage Ring.* She strove valiantly to keep her mind to the godliness of the discourse, so that it might be of some possible service to herself; and to keep her voice to the tone that might be of service to her aunt. Presently she heard the grateful sound which indicated her aunt's repose, but she knew of experience that were she to stop, the sound and the sleep would come to an end also. For a whole hour she persevered, reading the sermon of the Marriage Ring with such attention to the godly principles of the teaching as she could give, – with that terrible burden upon her mind.

'Thank you; – thank you; that will do, my dear. Shut it up,' said the sick woman. 'It's time now for the draught.' Then Dorothy moved quietly about the room, and did her nurse's work with soft hand, and soft touch, and soft tread. After that her aunt kissed her, and bade her sit down and sleep.

'I'll go on reading, aunt, if you'll let me,' said Dorothy. But Miss Stanbury, who was not a cruel woman, would have no more of the reading, and Dorothy's mind was left at liberty to think of the proposition that had been made to her. To one resolution she came very quickly. The period of her aunt's illness could not be a proper time for marriage vows, or the amenities of love-making. She did not feel that he, being a man, had offended; but she was quite sure that were she, a woman, the niece of so kind an aunt, the nurse at the bed-side of such an invalid, – were she at such a time to consent to talk of love, she would never deserve to have a lover. And from this resolve she got great comfort. It would give her an excuse for making no more assured answer at present, and would enable her to reflect at leisure as to the reply she would give him, should he ever by any chance, renew his offer. If he did not, – and probably he would not, – then it would have been very well that he should not have been made the victim of a momentary generosity. She had complained of the dulness of her life, and that complaint from her had produced his noble, kind, generous, dear, enthusiastic benevolence towards her. As she thought of it all, – and by degrees she took great pleasure in thinking of it, – her mind bestowed upon him all manner of eulogies. She could not persuade herself that he really loved her, and yet she was full at heart of gratitude to him for the expression of his love. And as for herself, could she love him ? We who are looking on of course know that she loved him; – that from this moment there was nothing belonging to him, down to his shoe-tie, that would not be dear to her heart and an emblem so tender as to force a tear from her. He had already become her god, though she did not know it. She made comparisons between him and Mr Gibson, and tried to convince herself that the judgment, which was always pronounced very clearly in Brooke's favour, came from anything but her heart. And thus through the long watches of the night she became very happy, feeling but not knowing that the whole aspect of the world was changed to her by those few words which her lover had spoken to her. She thought now that it would be consolation enough to her in future to know that such a man as Brooke Burgess had once asked her to be the partner of his life, and that it would be almost ungenerous in her to push her advantage further and attempt to take him at his word. Besides, there would be obstacles. Her aunt would dislike such a marriage for him, and he would be bound to obey her aunt in such a matter. She would not allow herself to think that she could ever become Brooke's wife, but nothing could rob her of the treasure of the offer which he had made her. Then Martha came to her at five o'clock, and she went to her bed to dream for an hour or two of Brooke Burgess and her future life.

On the next morning she met him at breakfast. She went down stairs later than usual, not till ten, having hung about her aunt's room, thinking that thus she would escape him for the present. She would wait till he was gone out, and then she would go down. She did wait ; but she could not hear the front door, and then her aunt murmured something about Brooke's breakfast. She was told to go down, and she went. But when on the stairs she slunk back to her own room, and stood there for awhile, aimless, motionless, not knowing what to do. Then one of the girls came to her, and told her that Mr Burgess was waiting breakfast for her. She knew not what excuse to make, and at last descended slowly to the parlour. She was very happy, but had it been possible for her to have run away she would have gone.

'Dear Dorothy,' he said at once. 'I may call you so, – may I not ?'
'Oh yes.'
'And you will love me; – and be my own, own wife ?'

'No, Mr Burgess.'

'No?'

'I mean; – that is to say –'

'Do you love me, Dorothy?'

'Only think how ill Aunt Stanbury is, Mr Burgess; – perhaps dying! How can I have any thought now except about her? It wouldn't be right; – would it?'

'You may say that you love me.'

'Mr Burgess, pray, pray don't speak of it now. If you do I must go away.'

'But do you love me?'

'Pray, pray don't, Mr Burgess!'

There was nothing more to be got from her during the whole day than that. He told her in the evening that as soon as Miss Stanbury was well, he would come again; – that in any case he would come again. She sat quite still as he said this, with a solemn face, – but smiling at heart, laughing at heart, so happy! When she got up to leave him, and was forced to give him her hand, he seized her in his arms and kissed her. 'That is very, very wrong,' she said, sobbing, and then ran to her room, – the happiest girl in all Exeter. He was to start early on the following morning, and she knew that she would not be forced to see him again. Thinking of him was so much pleasanter than seeing him!

52

Mr Outhouse Complains that it's Hard

Life had gone on during the winter at St Diddulph's Parsonage in a dull, weary, painful manner. There had come a letter in November from Trevelyan to his wife, saying that as he could trust neither her nor her uncle with the custody of his child, he should send a person armed with due legal authority, addressed to Mr Outhouse, for the recovery of the boy, and desiring that little Louis might be at once surrendered to the messenger. Then of course there had arisen great trouble in the house. Both Mrs Trevelyan and Nora Rowley had learned by this time that, as regarded the master of the house, they were not welcome guests at St Diddulph's. When the threat was shown to Mr Outhouse, he did not say a word to indicate that the child should be given up. He muttered something, indeed, about impotent nonsense, which seemed to imply that the threat could be of no avail; but there was none of that reassurance to be obtained from him which a positive promise on his part to hold the bairn against all comers would have given. Mrs Outhouse told her niece more than once that the child would be given to no messenger whatever; but even she did not give the assurance with that energy which the mother would have liked. 'They shall drag him away from me by force if they do take him!' said the mother, gnashing her teeth. Oh, if her father would but come! For some weeks she did not let the boy out of her sight; but when no messenger had presented himself by Christmas time, they all began to believe that the threat had in truth meant nothing, – that it had been part of the ravings of a madman.

But the threat had meant something. Early on one morning in January Mr Outhouse was told that a person in the hall wanted to see him, and Mrs Trevelyan, who was sitting at breakfast, the child being at the moment up-stairs, started from her seat. The maid described the man as being 'All as one as a gentleman,' though she would not go so far as to say that he was a gentleman in fact. Mr Outhouse slowly rose from his breakfast, went out to the man in the passage, and bade him follow into the little closet that was now used as a study. It is needless perhaps to say that the man was Bozzle.

'I dare say, Mr Houthouse, you don't know me,' said Bozzle. Mr Outhouse, disdaining all complimentary language, said that he certainly did not. 'My name, Mr Houthouse, is Samuel Bozzle, and I live at No. 55, Stony Walk, Union Street, Borough. I was in the Force once, but I work on my own 'ook now.'

'What do you want with me, Mr Bozzle?'

'It isn't so much with you, sir, as it is with a lady as is under your protection; and it isn't so much with the lady as it is with her infant.'

'Then you may go away, Mr Bozzle,' said Mr Outhouse, impatiently. 'You may as well go away at once.'

'Will you please read them few lines, sir,' said Mr Bozzle. 'They is in Mr Trewilyan's handwriting, which will no doubt be familiar characters, – leastways to Mrs T., if you don't know the gent's fist.' Mr Outhouse, after looking at the paper for a minute, and considering deeply what in this emergency he had better do, did take the paper and read it. The words ran as follows: 'I hereby give full authority to Mr Samuel Bozzle, of 55, Stony Walk, Union Street, Borough, to claim and to enforce possession of the body of my child, Louis Trevelyan; and I require that any person whatsoever who may now have the custody of the said child, whether it be my wife or any of her friends, shall at once deliver him up to Mr

Bozzle on the production of this authority. – LOUIS TREVELYAN.'
It may be explained that before this document had been written
there had been much correspondence on the subject between Bozzle
and his employer. To give the ex-policeman his due, he had not at
first wished to meddle in the matter of the child. He had a wife at
home who expressed an opinion with much vigour that the boy
should be left with its mother, and that he, Bozzle, should he
succeed in getting hold of the child, would not know what to do
with it. Bozzle was aware, moreover, that it was his business to find
out facts, and not to perform actions. But his employer had become
very urgent with him. Mr Bideawhile had positively refused to move
in the matter; and Trevelyan, mad as he was, had felt a disinclina-
tion to throw his affairs into the hands of a certain Mr Skint, of
Stamford Street, whom Bozzle had recommended to him as a
lawyer. Trevelyan had hinted, moreover, that if Bozzle would make
the application in person, that application, if not obeyed, would act
with usefulness as a preliminary step for further personal measures
to be taken by himself. He intended to return to England for the
purpose, but he desired that the order for the child's rendition
should be made at once. Therefore Bozzle had come. He was an
earnest man, and had now worked himself up to a certain degree of
energy in the matter. He was a man loving power, and specially
anxious to enforce obedience from those with whom he came in
contact by the production of the law's mysterious authority. In his
heart he was ever tapping people on the shoulder, and telling them
that they were wanted. Thus, when he displayed his document to
Mr Outhouse, he had taught himself at least to desire that that
document should be obeyed.

Mr Outhouse read the paper and turned up his nose at it. 'You
had better go away,' said he, as he thrust it back into Bozzle's hand.

'Of course I shall go away when I have the child.'

'Psha!' said Mr Outhouse.

'What does that mean, Mr Houthouse? I presume you'll not
dispute the paternal parent's legal authority.'

'Go away, sir,' said Mr Outhouse.

'Go away!'

'Yes; – out of this house. It's my belief that you're a knave.'

'A knave, Mr Houthouse?'

'Yes; – a knave. No one who was not a knave would lend a hand
towards separating a little child from its mother. I think you are a
knave, but I don't think you are fool enough to suppose that the
child will be given up to you.'

'It's my belief that knave is hactionable,' said Bozzle, – whose respect, however, for the clergyman was rising fast. 'Would you mind ringing the bell, Mr Houthouse, and calling me a knave again before the young woman?'

'Go away,' said Mr Outhouse.

'If you have no objection, sir, I should be glad to see the lady before I goes.'

'You won't see any lady here; and if you don't get out of my house when I tell you, I'll send for a real policeman.' Then was Bozzle conquered; and, as he went, he admitted to himself that he had sinned against all the rules of his life in attempting to go beyond the legitimate line of his profession. As long as he confined himself to the getting up of facts nobody could threaten him with a 'real policeman.' But one fact he had learned to-day. The clergyman of St Diddulph's, who had been represented to him as a weak, foolish man, was anything but that. Bozzle was much impressed in favour of Mr Outhouse, and would have been glad to have done that gentleman a kindness had an opportunity come in his way.

'What does he want, Uncle Oliphant?' said Mrs Trevelyan at the foot of the stairs, guarding the way up to the nursery. At this moment the front door had just been closed behind the back of Mr Bozzle.

'You had better ask no questions,' said Mr Outhouse.

'But is it about Louis?'

'Yes, he came about him.'

'Well? Of course you must tell me, Uncle Oliphant. Think of my condition.'

'He had some stupid paper in his hand from your husband, but it meant nothing.'

'He was the messenger, then?'

'Yes, he was the messenger. But I don't suppose he expected to get anything. Never mind. Go up and look after the child.' Then Mrs Trevelyan returned to her boy, and Mr Outhouse went back to his papers.

It was very hard upon him, Mr Outhouse thought, – very hard. He was threatened with an action now, and most probably would become subject to one. Though he had been spirited enough in presence of the enemy, he was very much out of spirits at this moment. Though he had admitted to himself that his duty required him to protect his wife's niece, he had never taken the poor woman to his heart with a loving, generous feeling of true guardianship. Though he would not give up the child to Bozzle, he thoroughly wished that the child was out of his house. Though he called Bozzle a knave and Trevelyan a madman, still he considered that Colonel

Osborne was the chief sinner, and that Emily Trevelyan had behaved badly. He constantly repeated to himself the old adage, that there was no smoke without fire; and lamented the misfortune that had brought him into close relation with things and people that were so little to his taste. He sat for awhile, with a pen in his hand, at the miserable little substitute for a library table which had been provided for him, and strove to collect his thoughts and go on with his work. But the effort was in vain. Bozzle would be there, presenting his document, and begging that the maid might be rung for, in order that she might hear him called a knave. And then he knew that on this very day his niece intended to hand him money, which he could not refuse. Of what use would it be to refuse it now, after it had been once taken? As he could not write a word, he rose and went away to his wife.

'If this goes on much longer,' said he, 'I shall be in Bedlam.'

'My dear, don't speak of it in that way!'

'That's all very well. I suppose I ought to say that I like it. There has been a policeman here who is going to bring an action against me.'

'A policeman!'

'Some one that her husband has sent for the child.'

'The boy must not be given up, Oliphant.'

'It's all very well to say that, but I suppose we must obey the law. The Parsonage of St Diddulph's isn't a castle in the Apennines.* When it comes to this, that a policeman is sent here to fetch any man's child, and threatens me with an action because I tell him to leave my house, it is very hard upon me, seeing how very little I've had to do with it. It's all over the parish now that my niece is kept here away from her husband, and that a lover comes to see her. This about the policeman will be known now, of course. I only say it is hard; that's all.' The wife did all that she could to comfort him, reminding him that Sir Marmaduke would be home soon, and that then the burden would be taken from his shoulders. But she was forced to admit that it was very hard.

53

Hugh Stanbury is shown to be no Conjuror

Many weeks had now passed since Hugh Stanbury had paid his visit to St Diddulph's, and Nora Rowley was beginning to believe that her rejection of her lover had been so firm and decided that she would never see him or hear from him more; — and she had long since confessed to herself that if she did not see him or hear from him soon, life would not be worth a straw to her. To all of us a single treasure counts for much more when the outward circumstances of our life are dull, unvaried, and melancholy, than it does when our days are full of pleasure, or excitement, or even of business. With Nora Rowley at St Diddulph's life at present was very melancholy. There was little or no society to enliven her. Her sister was sick at heart, and becoming ill in health under the burden of her troubles. Mr Outhouse was moody and wretched; and Mrs Outhouse, though she did her best to make her house comfortable to her unwelcome inmates, could not make it appear that their presence there was a pleasure to her. Nora understood better than did her sister how distasteful the present arrangement was to their uncle, and was consequently very uncomfortable on that score. And in the midst of that unhappiness, she of course told herself that she was a young woman miserable and unfortunate altogether. It is always so with us. The heart when it is burdened, though it may have ample strength to bear the burden, loses its buoyancy and doubts its own power. It is like the springs of a carriage which are pressed flat by the superincumbent weight. But, because the springs are good, the weight is carried safely, and they are the better afterwards for their required purposes because of the trial to which they have been subjected.

Nora had sent her lover away, and now at the end of three months from the day of his dismissal she had taught herself to believe that he would never come again. Amidst the sadness of her life at St Diddulph's some confidence in a lover expected to come again would have done much to cheer her. The more she thought of Hugh Stanbury, the more fully she became convinced that he was the man who as a lover, as a husband, and as a companion, would just suit all her tastes. She endowed him liberally with a hundred good gifts in the disposal of which Nature had been much more sparing. She made for herself a mental portrait of him more gracious in its flattery than ever was canvas coming from the hand of a Court limner. She gave him all gifts of manliness, honesty, truth, and energy, and felt regarding him that he was a Paladin, — such as Paladins are in this age, that he was indomitable, sure of success, and fitted in all respects to take the high position which he would certainly win for himself. But she did not presume him to be endowed with such a constancy as would make him come to seek her hand again. Had Nora at this time of her life been living at the West-end of London, and going out to parties three or four times a week, she would have been quite easy about his coming. The springs would not have been weighted so heavily, and her heart would have been elastic.

No doubt she had forgotten many of the circumstances of his visit and of his departure. Immediately on his going she had told her sister that he would certainly come again, but had said at the same time that his coming could be of no use. He was so poor a man; and she, – though poorer than he, – had been so little accustomed to poverty of life, that she had then acknowledged to herself that she was not fit to be his wife. Gradually, as the slow weeks went by her, there had come a change in her ideas. She now thought that he never would come again; but that if he did she would confess to him that her own views about life were changed. 'I would tell him frankly that I could eat a crust with him in any garret in London.' But this was said to herself; – never to her sister. Emily and Mrs Outhouse had determined together that it would be wise to abstain from all mention of Hugh Stanbury's name. Nora had felt that her sister had so abstained, and this reticence had assisted in producing the despair which had come upon her. Hugh, when he had left her, had certainly given her encouragement to expect that he would return. She had been sure then that he would return. She had been sure of it, though she had told him that it would be useless. But now, when those sad weeks had slowly crept over her head, when during the long hours of the long days she had thought of him continually, – telling herself that it was impossible that she should ever become the wife of any man if she did not become his, – she assured herself that she had seen and heard the last of him. She must surely have forgotten his hot words and that daring embrace.

Then there came a letter to her. The question of the management of letters for young ladies is handled very differently in different houses. In some establishments the post is as free to young ladies as it is to the reverend seniors of the household. In others it is considered to be quite a matter of course that some experienced discretion should sit in judgment on the correspondence of the daughters of the family. When Nora Rowley was living with her sister in Curzon Street, she would have been very indignant indeed had it been suggested to her that there was any authority over her letters vested in her sister. But now, circumstanced as she was at St Diddulph's, she did understand that no letter would reach her without her aunt knowing that it had come. All this was distasteful to her, – as were indeed all the details of her life at St Diddulph's; – but she could not help herself. Had her aunt told her that she should never be allowed to receive a letter at all, she must have submitted till her mother had come to her relief. The letter which reached her now was put into her hands by her sister, but it had been given to Mrs Trevelyan by Mrs Outhouse. 'Nora,' said Mrs Trevelyan, 'here is a letter for you. I think it is from Mr Stanbury.'

'Give it me,' said Nora greedily.

'Of course I will give it you. But I hope you do not intend to correspond with him.'

'If he has written to me I shall answer him of course,' said Nora, holding her treasure.

'Aunt Mary thinks that you should not do so till papa and mamma have arrived.'

'If Aunt is afraid of me let her tell me so, and I will contrive to go somewhere else.' Poor Nora knew that this threat was futile. There was no house to which she could take herself.

'She is not afraid of you at all, Nora. She only says that she thinks you should not write to Mr Stanbury.' Then Nora escaped to the cold but solitary seclusion of her bedroom and there she read her letter.

The reader may remember that Hugh Stanbury when he last left St Diddulph's had not been oppressed by any of the gloomy reveries of a despairing lover. He had spoken his mind freely to Nora, and had felt himself justified in believing that he had not spoken in vain. He had had her in his arms, and she had found it impossible to say that she did not love him. But then she had been quite firm in her purpose to give him no encouragement that she could avoid. She had said no word that would justify him in considering that there was any engagement between them; and, moreover, he had been warned not to come to the house by its mistress. From day to day he thought of it all, now telling himself that there was nothing to be done but to trust in her fidelity till he should be in a position to offer her a fitting home, and then reflecting that he could not expect such a girl as Nora Rowley to wait for him, unless he could succeed in making her understand that he at any rate intended to wait for her. On one day he would think that good faith and proper consideration for Nora herself required him to keep silent; on the next he would tell himself that such maudlin chivalry as he was proposing to himself was sure to go to the wall and be neither rewarded nor recognised. So at last he sat down and wrote the following letter:

Lincoln's Inn Fields, January, 186 – .

Dearest Nora,

Ever since I last saw you at St Diddulph's, I have been trying to teach myself what I ought to do in reference to you. Sometimes I think that because I am poor I ought to hold my tongue. At others I feel sure that I ought to speak out loud, because I love you so dearly. You may presume that just at this moment the latter opinion is in the ascendant.

As I do write I mean to be very bold; – so bold that if I am wrong you will be thoroughly disgusted with me and will never willingly see me again. But I think it best to be true, and to say what I think. I do believe that you love me. According to all precedent I ought not to say so; – but I do believe it. Ever since I was at St Diddulph's that belief has made me happy, – though there have been moments of doubt. If I thought that you did not love me, I would trouble you no further. A man may win his way to love when social circumstances are such as to throw him and the girl together; but such is not the case with us; and unless you love me now, you never will love me. I do – I do! said Nora, pressing the letter to her bosom. If you do, I think that you owe it me to say so, and to let me have all the joy and all the feeling of responsibility which such an assurance will give me. I will tell him so, said Nora; I don't care what may come afterwards, but I will tell him the truth. I know, continued Hugh, that an engagement with me now would be hazardous, because what I earn is both scanty and precarious; but it seems to me that nothing could ever be done without some risk. There are risks of different kinds, – She wondered whether he was thinking when he wrote this of the rock on which her sister's barque had been split to pieces; – and we may hardly hope to avoid them all. For myself, I own that life would be tame to me, if there were no dangers to be overcome.

If you do love me, and will say so, I will not ask you to be my wife till I can give you a proper home; but the knowledge that I am the master of the treasure which I desire will give me a double energy, and will make me feel that when I have gained so much I cannot fail of adding to it all other smaller things that may be necessary.

Pray, – pray send me an answer. I cannot reach you except by writing, as I was told by your aunt not to come to the house again.

> Dearest Nora, pray believe
> That I shall always be truly yours only,
> Hugh Stanbury.

Write to him! Of course she would write to him. Of course she would confess to him the truth. 'He tells me that I owe it to him to say so, and I acknowledge the debt,' she said aloud to herself. 'And as for a proper home, he shall be the judge of that.' She resolved that she would not be a fine lady, not fastidious, not coy, not afraid to take her full share of the risk of which he spoke in such manly terms. 'It is quite true. As he has been able to make me love him, I have no right to stand aloof, – even if I wished it.' As she was walking up and down the room so resolving her sister came to her.

'Well, dear !' said Emily. 'May I ask what it is he says ?'

Nora paused a moment, holding the letter tight in her hand, and then she held it out to her sister. 'There it is. You may read it.' Mrs Trevelyan took the letter and read it slowly, during which Nora stood looking out of the window. She would not watch her sister's face, as she did not wish to have to reply to any outward signs of disapproval. 'Give it me back,' she said, when she heard by the refolding of the paper that the perusal was finished.

'Of course I shall give it you back, dear.'

'Yes; – thanks. I did not mean to doubt you.'

'And what will you do, Nora ?'

'Answer it of course.'

'I would think a little before I answered it,' said Mrs Trevelyan.

'I have thought, – a great deal, already.'

'And how will you answer it ?'

Nora paused again before she replied. 'As nearly as I know how to do in such words as he would put into my mouth. I shall strive to write just what I think he would wish me to write.'

'Then you will engage yourself to him, Nora ?'

'Certainly I shall. I am engaged to him already. I have been ever since he came here.'

'You told me that there was nothing of the kind.'

'I told you that I loved him better than anybody in the world, and that ought to have made you know what it must come to. When I am thinking of him every day, and every hour, how can I not be glad to have an engagement settled with him ? I couldn't marry anybody else, and I don't want to remain as I am.' The tears came into the married sister's eyes, and rolled down her cheeks, as this was said to her. Would it not have been better for her had she remained as she was ? 'Dear Emily,' said Nora, 'you have got Louey still.'

'Yes; – and they mean to take him from me. But I do not wish to speak of myself. Will you postpone your answer till mamma is here ?'

'I cannot do that, Emily. What ; receive such a letter as that, and send no reply to it !'

'I would write a line for you, and explain – '

'No, indeed, Emily. I choose to answer my own letters. I have shewn you that, because I trust you ; but I have fully made up my mind as to what I shall write. It will have been written and sent before dinner.'

'I think you will be wrong, Nora.'

'Why wrong ! When I came over here to stay with you, would mamma ever have thought of directing me not to accept any offer till her consent had been obtained all the way from the Mandarins? She would never have dreamed of such a thing.'

'Will you ask Aunt Mary?'

'Certainly not. What is Aunt Mary to me? We are here in her house for a time, under the press of circumstances; but I owe her no obedience. She told Mr Stanbury not to come here; and he has not come; and I shall not ask him to come. I would not willingly bring any one into Uncle Oliphant's house, that he and she do not wish to see. But I will not admit that either of them have any authority over me.'

'Then who has, dearest?'

'Nobody; – except papa and mamma; and they have chosen to leave me to myself.'

Mrs Trevelyan found it impossible to shake her sister's firmness, and could herself do nothing, except tell Mrs Outhouse what was the state of affairs. When she said that she should do this, there almost came to be a flow of high words between the two sisters; but at last Nora assented. 'As for knowing, I don't care if all the world knows it. I shall do nothing in a corner. I don't suppose Aunt Mary will endeavour to prevent my posting my letter.'

Emily at last went to seek Mrs Outhouse, and Nora at once sat down to her desk. Neither of the sisters felt at all sure that Mrs Outhouse would not attempt to stop the emission of the letter from her house; but, as it happened, she was out, and did not return till Nora had come back from her journey to the neighbouring post-office. She would trust her letter, when written, to no hands but her own; and as she herself dropped it into the safe custody of the Postmaster-General, it also shall be revealed to the public:

Parsonage, St Diddulph's, January 186 – .

Dear Hugh,

For I suppose I may as well write to you in that way now. I have been made so happy by your affectionate letter. Is not that a candid confession for a young lady? But you tell me that I owe you the truth, and so I tell you the truth. Nobody will ever be anything to me, except you; and you are everything. I do love you; and should it ever be possible, I will become your wife.

I have said so much, because I feel that I ought to obey the order you have given me; but pray do not try to see me or write to me till mamma has arrived. She and papa will be here in the spring, – quite early in the spring, we hope; and then you may come to us. What they may say, of course, I cannot tell; but I shall be true to you.

Your own, with truest affection,
Nora.

Of course, you knew that I loved you, and I don't think that you are a conjuror at all.

As soon as ever the letter was written, she put on her bonnet, and went forth with it herself to the post-office. Mrs Trevelyan stopped her on the stairs, and endeavoured to detain her, but Nora would not be detained. 'I must judge for myself about this,' she said. 'If mamma were here, it would be different, but, as she is not here, I must judge for myself.'

What Mrs Outhouse might have done had she been at home at the time, it would be useless to surmise. She was told what had happened when it occurred, and questioned Nora on the subject. 'I thought I understood from you,' she said, with something of severity in her countenance, 'that there was to be nothing between you and Mr Stanbury – at any rate, till my brother came home ?'

'I never pledged myself to anything of the kind, Aunt Mary,' Nora said. 'I think he promised that he would not come here, and I don't suppose that he means to come. If he should do so, I shall not see him.'

With this Mrs Outhouse was obliged to be content. The letter was gone, and could not be stopped. Nor, indeed, had any authority been delegated to her by which she would have been justified in stopping it. She could only join her husband in wishing that they both might be relieved, as soon as possible, from the terrible burden which had been thrown upon them. 'I call it very hard,' said Mr Outhouse; – 'very hard, indeed. If we were to desire them to leave the house, everybody would cry out upon us for our cruelty ; and yet, while they remains here, they will submit themselves to no authority. As far as I can see, they may, both of them, do just what they please, and we can't stop it.'

54
Mr Gibson's Threat

Miss Stanbury for a long time persisted in being neither better nor worse. Sir Peter would not declare her state to be precarious, nor would he say that she was out of danger ; and Mr Martin had been so utterly prostrated by the nearly-fatal effects of his own mistake that he was quite unable to rally himself and talk on the subject with any spirit or confidence. When interrogated he would simply reply that Sir Peter said this and Sir Peter said that, and thus add to, rather than diminish, the doubt, and excitement, and varied opinion which prevailed through the city. On one morning it was absolutely asserted within the limits of the Close that Miss Stanbury was dying, – and it was believed for half a day at the bank that she was then lying in articulo mortis. There had got about, too, a report that a portion of the property had only been left to Miss Stanbury for her life, that the Burgesses would be able to reclaim the houses in the city, and that a will had been made altogether in favour of Dorothy, cutting out even Brooke from any share in the inheritance; – and thus Exeter had a good deal to say respecting the affairs and state of health of our old friend. Miss Stanbury's illness, however, was true enough. She was much too ill to hear anything of what was going on; – too ill to allow Martha to talk to her at all about the outside public. When the invalid herself would ask questions about the affairs of the world, Martha would be very discreet and turn away from the subject. Miss Stanbury, for instance, ill as she was, exhibited a most mundane interest, not exactly in Camilla French's marriage, but in the delay which that marriage seemed destined to encounter. 'I dare say he'll slip out of it yet,' said the sick lady to her confidential servant. Then Martha had thought it right to change the subject, feeling it to be wrong that an old lady on her death-bed should be taking joy in the disappointment of her young neighbour. Martha changed the subject, first to jelly, and then to the psalms of the day. Miss Stanbury was too weak to resist; but the last verse of the last psalm of the evening had hardly been finished before she remarked that she would never believe it till she saw it. 'It's all in the hands of Him as is on high, mum,' said Martha, turning her eyes up to the ceiling, and closing the book at the same time, with a look strongly indicative of displeasure.

Miss Stanbury understood it all as well as though she were in perfect health. She knew her own failings, was conscious of her worldly tendencies, and perceived that her old servant was thinking of it. And then sundry odd thoughts, half-digested thoughts, ideas too difficult for her present strength, crossed her brain. Had it been wicked of her when she was well to hope that a scheming woman should not succeed in betraying a man by her schemes into an ill-assorted marriage; and if not wicked then, was it wicked now because she was ill? And from that thought her mind travelled on to the ordinary practices of death-bed piety. Could an assumed devotion be of use to her now, – such a devotion as Martha was enjoining upon her from hour to hour, in pure and affectionate solicitude for her soul? She had spoken one evening of a game of cards, saying that a game of cribbage would have consoled her.

Then Martha, with a shudder, had suggested a hymn, and had had recourse at once to a sleeping draught. Miss Stanbury had submitted, but had understood it all. If cards were wicked, she had indeed been a terrible sinner. What hope could there be now, on her death-bed, for one so sinful? And she could not repent of her cards, and would not try to repent of them, not seeing the evil of them; and if they were innocent, why should she not have the consolation now, – when she so much wanted it? Yet she knew that the whole household, even Dorothy, would be in arms against her, were she to suggest such a thing. She took the hymn and the sleeping draught, telling herself that it would be best for her to banish such ideas from her mind. Pastors and masters had laid down for her a mode of living, which she had followed, but indifferently perhaps, but still with an intention of obedience. They had also laid down a mode of dying, and it would be well that she should follow that as closely as possible. She would say nothing more about cards. She would think nothing more of Camilla French. But, as she so resolved, with intellect half asleep, with her mind wandering between fact and dream, she was unconsciously comfortable with an assurance that if Mr Gibson did marry Camilla French, Camilla French would lead him the very devil of a life.

During three days Dorothy went about the house as quiet as a mouse, sitting nightly at her aunt's bedside, and tending the sick woman with the closest care. She, too, had been now and again somewhat startled by the seeming worldliness of her aunt in her illness. Her aunt talked to her about rents, and gave her messages for Brooke Burgess on subjects which seemed to Dorothy to be profane when spoken of on what might perhaps be a death-bed. And this struck her the more strongly, because she had a matter of her own on which she would have much wished to ascertain her aunt's opinion, if she had not thought that it would have been exceedingly wrong of her to trouble her aunt's mind at such a time by any such matter. Hitherto she had said not a word of Brooke's proposal to any living being. At present it was a secret with herself, but a secret so big that it almost caused her bosom to burst with the load that it bore. She could not, she thought, write to Priscilla till she had told her aunt. If she were to write a word on the subject to any one, she could not fail to make manifest the extreme longing of her own heart. She could not have written Brooke's name on paper, in reference to his words to herself, without covering it with epithets of love. But all that must be known to no one if her love was to be of no avail to her. And she had an idea that her aunt would not wish Brooke to marry her, – would think that Brooke should do better; and she was quite clear that in such a matter as this her aunt's wishes must be law. Had not her aunt the power of disinheriting Brooke altogether? And what then if her aunt should die, – should die now, – leaving Brooke at liberty to do as he pleased? There was something so distasteful to her in this view of the matter that she would not look at it. She would not allow herself to think of any success which might possibly accrue to herself by reason of her aunt's death. Intense as was the longing in her heart for permission from those in authority over her to give herself to Brooke Burgess, perfect as was the earthly Paradise which appeared to be open to her when she thought of the good thing which had befallen her in that matter, she conceived that she would be guilty of the grossest ingratitude were she in any degree to curtail even her own estimate of her aunt's prohibitory powers because of her aunt's illness. The remembrance of the words which Brooke had spoken to her was with her quite perfect. She was entirely conscious of the joy which would be hers, if she might accept those words as properly sanctioned; but she was a creature in her aunt's hands, – according to her own ideas of her own duties; and while her aunt was ill she could not even learn what might be the behests which she would be called on to obey.

She was sitting one evening alone, thinking of all this, having left Martha with her aunt, and was trying to reconcile the circumstances of her life as it now existed with the circumstances as they had been with her in the old days at Nuncombe Putney, wondering at herself in that she should have a lover, and trying to convince herself that for her this little episode of romance could mean nothing serious, when Martha crept down into the room to her. Of late days, – the alteration might perhaps be dated from the rejection of Mr Gibson, – Martha, who had always been very kind, had become more respectful in her manner to Dorothy than had heretofore been usual with her. Dorothy was quite aware of it, and was not unconscious of a certain rise in the world which was thereby indicated. 'If you please, miss,' said Martha, 'who do you think is here?'

'But there is nobody with my aunt?' said Dorothy.

'She is sleeping like a babby, and I came down just for a moment. Mr Gibson is here, miss, – in the house! He asked for your aunt, and when, of course, he could not see her, he asked for you.' Dorothy for a few minutes was utterly disconcerted, but at last she consented to see Mr Gibson. 'I think it is best,' said Martha, 'because it is bad to be fighting, and missus so ill. "Blessed are the peace-makers,"* miss, "for they shall be called the children of God."' Convinced by this argument, or by the working of her own mind, Dorothy directed that Mr Gibson might be shown into the room. When he came, she found herself unable to address him. She remembered the last time in which she had seen him, and was lost in wonder that he should be there. But she shook hands with him, and went through some form of greeting in which no word was uttered.

'I hope you will not think that I have done wrong,' said he, 'in calling to ask after my old friend's state of health?'

'Oh dear, no,' said Dorothy, quite bewildered.

'I have known her for so very long, Miss Dorothy, that now in the hour of her distress, and perhaps mortal malady, I cannot stop to remember the few harsh words that she spoke to me lately.'

'She never means to be harsh, Mr Gibson.'

'Ah; well; no, – perhaps not. At any rate I have learned to forgive and forget. I am afraid your aunt is very ill, Miss Dorothy.'

'She is ill, certainly, Mr Gibson.'

'Dear, dear! We are all as the grass of the field, Miss Dorothy, – here to-day and gone to-morrow, as sparks fly upwards. Just fit to be cut down and cast into the oven.* Mr Jennings has been with her, I believe?' Mr Jennings was the other minor canon.

'He comes three times a week, Mr Gibson.'

'He is an excellent young man, – a very good young man. It has been a great comfort to me to have Jennings with me. But he's very young, Miss Dorothy; isn't he?' Dorothy muttered something, purporting to declare that she was not acquainted with the exact circumstances of Mr Jennings' age. 'I should be so glad to come if my old friend would allow me,' said Mr Gibson, almost with a sigh. Dorothy was clearly of opinion that any change at the present would be bad for her aunt, but she did not know how to express her opinion; so she stood silent and looked at him. 'There needn't be a word spoken, you know, about the ladies at Heavitree,' said Mr Gibson.

'Oh dear, no,' said Dorothy. And yet she knew well that there would be such words spoken if Mr Gibson were to make his way into her aunt's room. Her aunt was constantly alluding to the ladies at Heavitree, in spite of all the efforts of her old servant to restrain her.

'There was some little misunderstanding,' said Mr Gibson; 'but all that should be over now. We both intended for the best, Miss Dorothy; and I'm sure nobody here can say that I wasn't sincere.' But Dorothy, though she could not bring herself to answer Mr Gibson plainly, could not be induced to assent to his proposition. She muttered something about her aunt's weakness, and the great attention which Mr Jennings showed. Her aunt had become very fond of Mr Jennings, and she did at last express her opinion with some clearness, that her aunt should not be disturbed by any changes at present. 'After that I should not think of pressing it, Miss Dorothy,' said Mr Gibson; 'but, still, I do hope that I may have the privilege of seeing her yet once again in the flesh. And touching my approaching marriage, Miss Dorothy – ' He paused, and Dorothy felt that she was blushing up to the roots of her hair. 'Touching my marriage,' continued Mr Gibson, 'which however will not be solemnized till the end of March;' – it was manifest that he regarded this as a point that would in that household be regarded as an argument in his favour, – 'I do hope that you will look upon it in the most favourable light, – and your excellent aunt also, if she be spared to us.'

'I am sure we hope that you will be happy, Mr Gibson.'

'What was I do to, Miss Dorothy? I know that I have been very much blamed; – but so unfairly! I have never meant to be untrue to a mouse, Miss Dorothy.' Dorothy did not at all understand whether she were the mouse, or Camilla French, or Arabella. 'And it is so hard to find that one is ill-spoken of because things have gone a little amiss.' It was quite impossible that Dorothy should make any answer to this, and at last Mr Gibson left her, assuring her with his last word that nothing would give him so much pleasure as to be called upon once more to see his old friend in her last moments.

Though Miss Stanbury had been described as sleeping 'like a babby,' she had heard the footsteps of a strange man in the house, and had made Martha tell her whose footsteps they were. As soon as Dorothy went to her, she darted upon the subject with all her old keenness. 'What did he want here, Dolly?'

'He said he would like to see you, aunt, – when you are a little better, you know. He spoke a good deal of his old friendship and respect.'

'He should have thought of that before. How am I to see people now?'

'But when you are better, aunt – ?'

'How do I know that I shall ever be better? He isn't off with those people at Heavitree, – is he?'

'I hope not, aunt.'

'Psha! A poor, weak, insufficient creature; – that's what he is. Mr Jennings is worth twenty of him.' Dorothy, though she put the question again in its most alluring form of Christian charity and forgiveness, could not induce her aunt to say that she would see Mr

Gibson. 'How can I see him, when you know that Sir Peter has forbidden me to see anybody, except Mrs Clifford and Mr Jennings?'

Two days afterwards there was an uncomfortable little scene at Heavitree. It must, no doubt, have been the case, that the same train of circumstances which had produced Mr Gibson's visit to the Close, produced also the scene in question. It was suggested by some who were attending closely to the matter that Mr Gibson had already come to repent his engagement with Camilla French; and, indeed, there were those who pretended to believe that he was induced, by the prospect of Miss Stanbury's demise, to transfer his allegiance yet again, and to bestow his hand upon Dorothy at last. There were many in the city who could never be persuaded that Dorothy had refused him, – these being, for the most part, ladies in whose estimation the value of a husband was counted so great, and a beneficed clergyman so valuable among suitors, that it was to their thinking impossible that Dorothy Stanbury should in her sound senses have rejected such an offer. 'I don't believe a bit of it,' said Mrs Crumbie to Mrs Apjohn; 'is it likely?' The ears of all the French family were keenly alive to rumours, and to rumours of rumours. Reports of these opinions respecting Mr Gibson reached Heavitree, and had their effect. As long as Mr Gibson was behaving well as a suitor, they were inoperative there. What did it matter to them how the prize might have been struggled for, – might still be struggled for elsewhere, while they enjoyed the consciousness of possession? But when the consciousness of possession became marred by a cankerous doubt, such rumours were very important. Camilla heard of the visit in the Close, and swore that she would have justice done her. She gave her mother to understand that, if any trick were played upon her, the diocese should be made to ring of it, in a fashion that would astonish them all, from the bishop downwards. Whereupon Mrs French, putting much faith in her daughter's threats, sent for Mr Gibson.

'The truth is, Mr Gibson,' said Mrs French, when the civilities of their first greeting had been completed, 'my poor child is pining.'

'Pining, Mrs French!'

'Yes; – pining, Mr Gibson. I am afraid that you little understand how sensitive is that young heart. Of course, she is your own now. To her thinking, it would be treason to you for her to indulge in conversation with any other gentleman; but, then, she expects that you should spend your evenings with her, – of course!'

'But, Mrs French, – think of my engagements as a clergyman.'

'We know all about that, Mr Gibson. We know what a clergy-man's calls are. It isn't like a doctor's, Mr Gibson.'

'It's very often worse, Mrs French.'

'Why should you go calling in the Close, Mr Gibson ?' Here was the gist of the accusation.

'Wouldn't you have me make my peace with a poor dying sister ?' pleaded Mr Gibson.

'After what has occurred,' said Mrs French, shaking her head at him, 'and while things are just as they are now, it would be more like an honest man of you to stay away. And, of course, Camilla feels it. She feels it very much; – and she won't put up with it neither.'

'I think this is the cruellest, cruellest thing I ever heard,' said Mr Gibson.

'It is you that are cruel, sir.'

Then the wretched man turned at bay. 'I tell you what it is, Mrs French; – if I am treated in this way, I won't stand it. I won't, indeed. I'll go away. I'm not going to be suspected, nor yet blown up. I think I've behaved handsomely, at any rate to Camilla.'

'Quite so, Mr Gibson, if you would come and see her on evenings,' said Mrs French, who was falling back into her usual state of timidity.

'But, if I'm to be treated in this way, I will go away. I've thoughts of it as it is. I've been already invited to go to Natal, and if I hear anything more of these accusations, I shall certainly make up my mind to go.' Then he left the house, before Camilla could be down upon him from her perch on the landing-place.

55

The Republican Browning

Mr Glascock had returned to Naples after his sufferings in the dining-room of the American Minister, and by the middle of February was back again in Florence. His father was still alive, and it was said that the old lord would now probably live through the winter. And it was understood that Mr Glascock would remain in Italy. He had declared that he would pass his time between Naples, Rome, and Florence ; but it seemed to his friends that Florence was, of the three, the most to his taste. He liked his room, he said, at the York Hotel, and he liked being in the capital. That was his own statement. His friends said that he liked being with Carry Spalding, the niece of the American Minister; but none of them, then in Italy, were sufficiently intimate with him to express that opinion to himself.

It had been expressed more than once to Carry Spalding. The world in general says such things to ladies more openly than it does to men, and the probability of a girl's success in matrimony is canvassed in her hearing by those who are nearest to her with a freedom which can seldom be used in regard to a man. A man's most intimate friend hardly speaks to him of the prospect of his marriage till he himself has told that the engagement exists. The lips of no living person had suggested to Mr Glascock that the American girl was to become his wife; but a great deal had been said to Carry Spalding about the conquest she had made. Her uncle, her aunt, her sister, and her great friend Miss Petrie, the poetess, – the Republican Browning as she was called, – had all spoken to her about it frequently. Olivia had declared her conviction that the thing was to be. Miss Petrie had, with considerable eloquence, explained to her friend that that English title, which was but the clatter of a sounding brass, should be regarded as a drawback rather than as an advantage. Mrs Spalding, who was no poetess, would undoubtedly have welcomed Mr Glascock as her niece's husband with all an aunt's energy. When told by Miss Petrie that old Lord Peterborough was a tinkling cymbal* she snapped angrily at her gifted countrywoman. But she was too honest a woman, and too conscious also of her niece's strength, to say a word to urge her on. Mr Spalding as an American minister, with full powers at the court of a European sovereign, felt that he had full as much to give as to receive; but he was well inclined to do both. He would have been much pleased to talk about his nephew Lord Peterborough, and he loved his niece dearly. But by the middle of February he was beginning to think that the matter had been long enough in training. If the Honourable Glascock meant anything, why did he not speak out his mind plainly? The American Minister in such matters was accustomed to fewer ambages then were common in the circles among which Mr Glascock had lived.

In the meantime Caroline Spalding was suffering. She had allowed herself to think that Mr Glascock intended to propose to her, and had acknowledged to herself that were he to do so she would certainly accept him. All that she had seen of him, since the day on which he had been courteous to her about the seat in the diligence, had been pleasant to her. She had felt the charm of his manner, his education, and his gentleness; and had told herself that with all her love for her own country, she would willingly become an Englishwoman for the sake of being that man's wife. But nevertheless the warnings of her great friend, the poetess, had not been thrown away upon her. She would put away from herself as far as she could any desire to become Lady Peterborough. There should be no bias in the man's favour on that score. The tinkling cymbal and the sounding brass should be nothing to her. But, yet, — yet what a chance was there here for her? 'They are dishonest, and rotten at the core,' said Miss Petrie, trying to make her friend understand that a free American should under no circumstances place trust in an English aristocrat. 'Their country, Carry, is a game played out, while we are still breasting the hill with our young lungs full of air.' Carry Spalding was proud of her intimacy with the Republican Browning; but nevertheless she liked Mr Glascock; and when Mr Glascock had been ten days in Florence, on his third visit to the city, and had been four or five times at the embassy without expressing his intentions in the proper form, Carry Spalding began to think that she had better save herself from a heartbreak while salvation might be within her reach. She perceived that her uncle was gloomy and almost angry when he spoke of Mr Glascock, and that her aunt was fretful with disappointment. The Republican Browning had uttered almost a note of triumph; and had it not been that Olivia persisted, Carry Spalding would have consented to go away with Miss Petrie to Rome. 'The old stones are rotten too,' said the poetess; 'but their dust tells no lies.' That well known piece of hers — 'Ancient Marbles, while ye crumble,' was written at this time, and contained an occult reference to Mr Glascock and her friend.

But Livy Spalding clung to the alliance. She probably knew her sister's heart better than did the others; and perhaps also had a clearer insight into Mr Glascock's character. She was at any rate clearly of opinion that there should be no running away. 'Either you do like him, or you don't. If you do, what are you to get by going to Rome?' said Livy.

'I shall get quit of doubt and trouble.'

'I call that cowardice. I would never run away from a man, Carry. Aunt Sophie forgets that they don't manage these things in England just as we do.'

'I don't know why there should be a difference.'

'Nor do I; — only that there is. You haven't read so many of their novels as I have.'

'Who would ever think of learning to live out of an English novel?' said Carry.

'I am not saying that. You may teach him to live how you like afterwards. But if you have anything to do with people it must be well to know what their manners are. I think the richer sort of people in England slide into these things more gradually than we do. You stand your ground, Carry, and hold your own, and take the goods the gods provide you.'* Though Caroline Spalding opposed her sister's arguments, and was particularly hard upon that allusion to 'the richer sort of people,' – which, as she knew, Miss Petrie would have regarded as evidence of reverence for sounding brasses and tinkling cymbals, – nevertheless she loved Livy dearly for what she said, and kissed the sweet counsellor, and resolved that she would for the present decline the invitation of the poetess. Then was Miss Petrie somewhat indignant with her friend, and threw out her scorn in those lines which have been mentioned.

But the American Minister hardly knew how to behave himself when he met Mr Glascock, or even when he was called upon to speak of him. Florence no doubt is a large city, and is now the capital of a great kingdom; but still people meet in Florence much more frequently than they do in Paris or in London. It may almost be said that they whose habit it is to go into society, and whose circumstances bring them into the same circles, will see each other every day. Now the American Minister delighted to see and to be seen in all places frequented by persons of a certain rank and position in Florence. Having considered the matter much, he had convinced himself that he could thus best do his duty as minister from the great Republic of Free States to the newest and, – as he called, – 'the free-est of the European kingdoms.' The minister from France was a marquis; he from England was an earl; from Spain had come a count, – and so on. In the domestic privacy of his embassy Mr Spalding would be severe enough upon the sounding brasses and the tinkling cymbals, and was quite content himself to be the Honourable Jonas G. Spalding, – Honourable because selected by his country for a post of honour; but he liked to be heard among the cymbals and seen among the brasses, and to feel that his position was as high as theirs. Mr Glascock also was frequently in the same circles, and thus it came to pass that the two gentlemen saw each other almost daily. That Mr Spalding knew well how to bear himself in his high place no one could doubt; but he did not quite know how to carry himself before Mr Glascock. At home at Boston he would have been more completely master of the situation.

He thought too that he began to perceive that Mr Glascock avoided him, though he would hear on his return home that that gentleman had been at the embassy, or had been walking in the

Casino with his nieces. That their young ladies should walk in public places with unmarried gentlemen is nothing to American fathers and guardians. American young ladies are accustomed to choose their own companions. But the minister was tormented by his doubts as to the ways of Englishmen, and as to the phase in which English habits might most probably exhibit themselves in Italy. He knew that people were talking about Mr Glascock and his niece. Why then did Mr Glascock avoid him? It was perhaps natural that Mr Spalding should have omitted to observe that Mr Glascock was not delighted by those lectures on the American constitution which formed so large a part of his ordinary conversation with Englishmen.

It happened one afternoon that they were thrown together so closely for nearly an hour that neither could avoid the other. They were both at the old palace in which the Italian parliament is held, and were kept waiting during some long delay in the ceremonies of the place. They were seated next to each other, and during such delay there was nothing for them but to talk. On the other side of each of them was a stranger, and not to talk in such circumstances would be to quarrel. Mr Glascock began by asking after the ladies.

'They are quite well, sir, thank you,' said the minister. 'I hope that Lord Peterborough was pretty well when last you heard from Naples, Mr Glascock.' Mr Glascock explained that his father's condition was not much altered, and then there was silence for a moment.

'Your nieces will remain with you through the spring I suppose?' said Mr Glascock.

'Such is their intention, sir.'

'They seem to like Florence, I think.'

'Yes; — yes; I think they do like Florence. They see this capital, sir, perhaps under more favourable circumstances than are accorded to most of my countrywomen. Our republican simplicity, Mr Glascock, has this drawback, that away from home it subjects us somewhat to the cold shade of unobserved obscurity. That it possesses merits which much more than compensate for this trifling evil I should be the last man in Europe to deny.' It is to be observed that American citizens are always prone to talk of Europe. It affords the best counterpoise they know to that other term, America, — and America and the United States are of course the same. To speak of France or of England as weighing equally against their own country seems to an American to be an absurdity, — and almost an insult to himself. With Europe he can compare himself, but even this is done generally in the style of the Republican Browning when she addressed the Ancient Marbles.

'Undoubtedly,' said Mr Glascock, 'the family of a minister abroad has great advantages in seeing the country to which he is accredited.'

'That is my meaning, sir. But, as I was remarking, we carry with us as a people no external symbols of our standing at home. The wives and daughters, sir, of the most honoured of our citizens have no nomenclature different than that which belongs to the least noted among us. It is perhaps a consequence of this that Europeans who are accustomed in their social intercourse to the assistance of titles, will not always trouble themselves to inquire who and what are the American citizens who may sit opposite to them at table. I have known, Mr Glascock, the wife and daughter of a gentleman who has been thrice sent as senator from his native State to Washington, to remain as disregarded in the intercourse of a European city, as though they had formed part of the family of some grocer from your Russell Square !'

'Let the Miss Spaldings go where they will,' said Mr Glascock, 'they will not fare in that way.'

'The Miss Spaldings, sir, are very much obliged to you,' said the minister with a bow.

'I regard it as one of the luckiest chances of my life that I was thrown in with them at Saint Michel as I was,' said Mr Glascock with something like warmth.

'I am sure, sir, they will never forget the courtesy displayed by you on that occasion,' said the minister bowing again.

'That was a matter of course. I and my friend would have done the same for the grocer's wife and daughter of whom you spoke. Little services such as that do not come from appreciation of merit, but are simply the payment of the debt due by all men to all women.'

'Such is certainly the rule of living in our country, sir,' said Mr Spalding.

'The chances are,' continued the Englishman, 'that no further observation follows the payment of such a debt. It has been a thing of course.'

'We delight to think it so, Mr Glascock, in our own cities.'

'But in this instance it has given rise to one of the pleasantest, and as I hope most enduring friendships that I have ever formed,' said Mr Glascock with enthusiasm. What could the American Minister do but bow again three times ? And what other meaning could he attach to such words than that which so many of his friends had been attributing to Mr Glascock for some weeks past ?

It had occurred to Mr Spalding, even since he had been sitting in his present close proximity to Mr Glascock, that it might possibly be his duty as an uncle having to deal with an Englishman, to ask that gentleman what were his intentions. He would do his duty let it be what it might; but the asking of such a question would be very disagreeable to him. For the present he satisfied himself with inviting his neighbour to come and drink tea with Mrs Spalding on the next evening but one. 'The girls will be delighted, I am sure,' said he, thinking himself to be justified in this friendly familiarity by Mr Glascock's enthusiasm. For Mr Spalding was clearly of opinion that, let the value of republican simplicity be what it might, an alliance with the crumbling marbles of Europe would in his niece's circumstances be not inexpedient. Mr Glascock accepted the invitation with alacrity, and the minister when he was closeted with his wife that evening declared his opinion that after all the Britisher meant fighting. The aunt told the girls that Mr Glascock was coming, and in order that it might not seem that a net was being specially spread for him, others were invited to join the party. Miss Petrie consented to be there, and the Italian, Count Buonarosci, to whose presence, though she could not speak to him, Mrs Spalding was becoming accustomed. It was painful to her to feel that she could not communicate with those around her, and for that reason she would have avoided Italians. But she had an idea that she could not thoroughly realise the advantages of foreign travel unless she lived with foreigners; and, therefore, she was glad to become intimate at any rate with the outside of Count Buonarosci.

'I think your uncle is wrong, dear,' said Miss Petrie early in the day to her friend.

'But why? He has done nothing more than what is just civil.'

'If Mr Glascock kept a store in Broadway he would not have thought it necessary to show the same civility.'

'Yes; — if we all liked the Mr Glascock who kept the store.'

'Caroline,' said the poetess with severe eloquence, 'can you put your hand upon your heart and say that this inherited title, this tinkling cymbal as I call it, has no attraction for you or yours? Is it the unadorned simple man that you welcome to your bosom, or a thing of stars and garters, a patch of parchment, the minion of a throne, the lordling of twenty descents, in which each has been weaker than that before it, the hero of a scutcheon, whose glory is in his quarterings, and whose worldly wealth comes from the sweat of serfs whom the euphonism* of an effete country has learned to decorate with the name of tenants?'

But Caroline Spalding had a spirit of her own, and had already made up her mind that she would not be talked down by Miss Petrie. 'Uncle Jonas,' said she, 'asks him because we like him; and would do so too if he kept the store in Broadway. But if he did keep the store perhaps we should not like him.'

'I trow not,' said Miss Petrie.

Livy was much more comfortable in her tactics, and without consulting anybody sent for a hairdresser. 'It's all very well for Wallachia,' said Livy, – Miss Petrie's name was Wallachia, – 'but I know a nice sort of man when I see him, and the ways of the world are not to be altered because Wally writes poetry.'

When Mr Glascock was announced Mrs Spalding's handsome rooms were almost filled, as rooms in Florence are filled, – obstruction in every avenue, a crowd in every corner, and a block at every doorway, not being among the customs of the place. Mr Spalding immediately caught him, – intercepting him between the passages and the ladies, – and engaged him at once in conversation.

'Your John S. Mill* is a great man,' said the minister.

'They tell me so,' said Mr Glascock. 'I don't read what he writes myself.'

This acknowledgement seemed to the minister to be almost disgraceful, and yet he himself had never read a word of Mr Mill's writings. 'He is a far-seeing man,' continued the minister. 'He is one of the few Europeans who can look forward, and see how the rivers of civilization are running on. He has understood that women must at last be put upon an equality with men.'

'Can he manage that men shall have half the babies?' said Mr Glascock, thinking to escape by an attempt at playfulness.

But the minister was down upon him at once, – had him by the lappet of his coat, though he knew how important it was for his dear niece that he should allow Mr Glascock to amuse himself this evening after another fashion. 'I have an answer ready, sir, for that difficulty,' he said. 'Step aside with me for a moment. The question is important, and I should be glad if you would communicate my ideas to your great philosopher. Nature, sir, has laid down certain laws, which are immutable; and, against them, – '

But Mr Glascock had not come to Florence for this. There were circumstances in his present position which made him feel that he would be justified in escaping, even at the cost of some seeming incivility. 'I must go in to the ladies at once,' he said, 'or I shall never get a word with them.' There came across the minister's brow a momentary frown of displeasure, as though he felt that he were being robbed of that which was justly his own. For an instant his grasp fixed itself more tightly to the coat. It was quite within the scope of his courage to hold a struggling listener by physical strength; – but he remembered that there was a purpose, and he relaxed his hold.

'I will take another opportunity,' said the minister. 'As you have raised that somewhat trite objection of the bearing of children, which we in our country, sir, have altogether got over, I must put you in possession of my views on that subject; but I will find another occasion.' Then Mr Glascock began to reflect whether an American lady, married in England, would probably want to see much of her uncle in her adopted country.

Mrs Spalding was all smiles when her guest reached her. 'We did not mean to have such a crowd of people,' she said, whispering; 'but you know how one thing leads to another, and people here really like short invitations.' Then the minister's wife bowed very low to an Italian lady, and for the moment wished herself in Beacon Street. It was a great trouble to her that she could not pluck up courage to speak a word in Italian. 'I know more about it than some that are glib enough,' she would say to her niece Livy, 'but these Tuscans are so particular with their Bocca Toscana.'

It was almost spiteful on the part of Miss Petrie, – the manner in which, on this evening, she remained close to her friend Caroline Spalding. It is hardly possible to believe that it came altogether from high principle, – from a determination to save her friend from an impending danger. One's friend has no right to decide for one what is, and what is not dangerous. Mr Glascock after awhile found himself seated on a fixed couch, that ran along the wall, between Carry Spalding and Miss Petrie; but Miss Petrie was almost as bad to him as had been the minister himself. 'I am afraid,' she said, looking up into his face with some severity, and rushing upon her subject with audacity, 'that the works of your Browning have not been received in your country with that veneration to which they are entitled.'

'Do you mean Mr or Mrs Browning?' asked Mr Glascock, – perhaps with some mistaken idea that the lady was out of her depth, and did not know the difference.

'Either; – both; for they are one, the same, and indivisible.* The spirit and gorm of each is so reflected in the outcome of the other, that one sees only the result of so perfect a combination, and one is tempted to acknowledge that here and there a marriage may have been arranged in Heaven. I don't think that in your country you have perceive ! this, Mr Glascock.'

'I am not quite sure that we have,' said Mr Glascock.

'Yours is not altogether an inglorious mission,' continued Miss Petrie.

'I've got no mission,' said Mr Glascock, – 'either from the Foreign Office, or from my own inner convictions.'

Miss Petrie laughed with a scornful laugh. 'I spoke, sir, of the mission of that small speck on the earth's broad surface, of which you think so much, and which we call Great Britain.'

'I do think a good deal of it,' said Mr Glascock.

'It has been more thought of than any other speck of the same size,' said Carry Spalding.

'True,' said Miss Petrie, sharply, – 'because of its iron and coal. But the mission I spoke of was this.' And she put forth her hand with an artistic motion as she spoke. 'It utters prophecies, though it cannot read them. It sends forth truth, though it cannot understand it. Though its own ears are deaf as adder's, it is the nursery of poets, who sing not for their own countrymen, but for the higher sensibilities and newer intelligences of lands, in which philanthropy has made education as common as the air that is breathed.'

'Wally,' said Olivia, coming up to the poetress, in anger that was almost apparent, 'I want to take you, and introduce you to the Marchesa Pulti.'

But Miss Petrie no doubt knew that the eldest son of an English lord was at least as good as an Italian marchesa. 'Let her come here,' said the poetess, with her grandest smile.

56
Withered Grass

When Caroline Spalding perceived how direct an attempt had been made by her sister to take the poetess away in order that she might thus be left alone with Mr Glascock, her spirit revolted against the manœuvre, and she took herself away amidst the crowd. If Mr Glascock should wish to find her again he could do so. And there came across her mind something of a half-formed idea that, perhaps after all her friend Wallachia was right. Were this man ready to take her and she ready to be taken, would such an arrangement be a happy one for both of them? His high-born, wealthy friends might very probably despise her, and it was quite possible that she also might despise them. To be Lady Peterborough, and have the spending of a large fortune, would not suffice for her happiness. She was sure of that. It would be a leap in the dark, and all such leaps must needs be dangerous, and therefore should be avoided. But she did like the man. Her friend was untrue to her and cruel in those allusions to tinkling cymbals. It might be well for her to get over her liking, and to think no more of one who was to her a foreigner and a stranger, – of whose ways of living in his own home she knew so little, whose people might be antipathetic to her, enemies instead of friends, among whom her life would be one long misery; but it was not on that ground that Miss Petrie had recommended her to start for Rome as soon as Mr Glascock had reached Florence. 'There is no reason,' she said to herself, 'why I should not marry a man if I like him, even though he be a lord. And of him I should not be the least afraid. It's the women that I fear.' And then she called to mind all that she had ever heard of English countesses and duchesses. She thought that she knew that they were generally cold and proud, and very little given to receive outsiders graciously within their ranks. Mr Glascock had an aunt who was a Duchess, and a sister who would be a Countess. Caroline Spalding felt how her back would rise against these new relations, if it should come to pass that they should look unkindly upon her when she was taken in her own home; – how she would fight with them, giving them scorn for scorn; how unutterably miserable she would be; how she would long to be back among her own equals, in spite even of her love for her husband. 'How grand a thing it is,' she said, 'to be equal with those whom you love !' And yet she was to some extent allured by the social position of the man. She could perceive that he had a charm of manner which her countrymen lacked. He had read, perhaps, less than her uncle; – knew, perhaps, less than most of those men with whom she had been wont to associate in her own city life at home; – was not braver, or more virtuous, or more self-denying than they; but there was a softness and an ease in his manner which was palatable to her, and an absence of that too visible effort of the intellect which is so apt to mark and mar the conversation of Americans. She almost wished that she had been English, in order that the man's home and friends might have suited her. She was thinking of all this as she stood pretending to talk to an American lady, who was very eloquent on the delights of Florence.

In the meantime Olivia and Mr Glascock had moved away together, and Miss Petrie was left alone. This was no injury to Miss Petrie, as her mind at once set itself to work on a sonnet touching the frivolity of modern social gatherings; and when she complained afterwards to Caroline that it was the curse of their mode of life that no moment could be allowed for thought, – in which she referred specially to a few words that Mr Gore had addressed to her at this moment of her meditations, – she was not wilfully a hypocrite. She was painfully turning her second set of rhymes, and really believed that she had been subjected to a hardship. In the meantime Olivia and Mr Glascock were discussing her at a distance.

'You were being put through your facings, Mr Glascock,' Olivia had said.

'Well; yes; and your dear friend, Miss Petrie, is rather a stern examiner.'

'She is Carry's ally, – not mine,' said Olivia. Then she remembered that by saying this she might be doing her sister an injury. Mr Glascock might object to such a bosom friend for his wife. 'That is to say, of course we are all intimate with her, but just at this moment Carry is most in favour.'

'She is very clever, I am quite sure,' said he.

'Oh yes; – she's a genius. You must not doubt that on the peril of making every American in Italy your enemy.'

'She is a poet, – is she not?'

'Mr Glascock!'

'Have I said anything wrong?' he asked.

'Do you mean to look me in the face and tell me that you are not acquainted with her works, – that you don't know pages of them by heart, – that you don't sleep with them under your pillow, don't travel about with them in your dressing-bag? I'm afraid we have mistaken you, Mr Glascock.'

'Is it so great a sin?'

'If you'll own up honestly, I'll tell you something, – in a whisper. You have not read a word of her poems?'

'Not a word.'

'Neither have I. Isn't it horrible? But, perhaps, if I heard Tennyson talking every day, I shouldn't read Tennyson. Familiarity does breed contempt; – doesn't it? And then poor dear Wallachia is such a bore. I sometimes wonder, when English people are listening to her, whether they think that American girls generally talk like that.'

'Not all, perhaps, with that perfected eloquence.'

'I dare say you do,' continued Olivia, craftily. 'That is just the way in which people form their opinions about foreigners. Some specially self-asserting American speaks his mind louder than other people, and then you say that all Americans are self-asserting.'

'But you are a little that way given, Miss Spalding.'

'Because we are always called upon to answer accusations against us, expressed or unexpressed. We don't think ourselves a bit better than you; or, if the truth were known, half as good. We are always struggling to be as polished and easy as the French, or as sensible and dignified as the English; but when our defects are thrown in our teeth – '

'Who throws them in your teeth, Miss Spalding?'

'You look it, – all of you, – if you do not speak it out. You do assume a superiority, Mr Glascock; and that we cannot endure.'

'I do not feel that I assume anything,' said Mr Glascock, meekly.

'If three gentlemen be together, an Englishman, a Frenchman, and an American, is not the American obliged to be on his mettle to prove that he is somebody among the three? I admit that he is always claiming to be the first; but he does so only that he may not be too evidently the last. If you knew us, Mr Glascock, you would find us to be very mild, and humble, and nice, and good, and clever, and kind, and charitable, and beautiful, – in short, the finest people that have as yet been created on the broad face of God's smiling earth.' These last words she pronounced with a nasal twang, and in a tone of voice which almost seemed to him to be a direct mimicry of the American Minister. The upshot of the conversation, however, was that the disgust against Americans which, to a certain degree, had been excited in Mr Glascock's mind by the united efforts of Mr Spalding and the poetess, had been almost entirely dispelled. From all of which the reader ought to understand that Miss Olivia Spalding was a very clever young woman.

But nevertheless Mr Glascock had not quite made up his mind to ask the elder sister to be his wife. He was one of those men to whom love-making does not come very easy, although he was never so much at his ease as when he was in company with ladies. He was sorely in want of a wife, but he was aware that at different periods during the last fifteen years he had been angled for as a fish. Mothers in England had tried to catch him, and of such mothers he had come to have the strongest possible detestation. He had seen the hooks, – or perhaps had fancied that he saw them when they were not there. Lady Janes and Lady Sarahs had been hard upon him, till he learned to buckle himself into triple armour when he went amongst them, and yet he wanted a wife; – no man more sorely wanted one. The reader will perhaps remember how he went down to Nuncombe Putney in quest of a wife, but all in vain. The lady in that case had been so explicit with him that he could not hope for a more favourable answer; and, indeed, he would not have cared to marry a girl who had told him that she preferred another man to himself, even if it had been possible for him to do so. Now he had met a lady very different from those with whom he had hitherto associated, – but not the less manifestly a lady. Caroline Spalding was bright, pleasant, attractive, very easy to talk to, and yet quite able to hold her own. But the American Minister was – a bore; and Miss Petrie was – unbearable. He had often told himself that in this matter of marrying a wife he would please himself altogether, that he would allow himself to be tied down by no consideration of family pride, – that he would consult nothing but his own heart and feelings. As for rank, he could give that to his wife. As for money, he had plenty of that also. He wanted a woman that was not blasée with the world, that was not a fool, and who would respect him. The more he thought of it, the more sure he was that he had seen none who pleased him so well as Caroline Spalding; and yet he was a little afraid of taking a step that would be irrevocable. Perhaps the American Minister might express a wish to end his days at Monkhams, and might think it desirable to have Miss Petrie always with him as a private secretary in poetry!

'Between you and us, Mr Glascock, the spark of sympathy does not pass with a strong flash,' said a voice in his ear. As he turned round rapidly to face his foe, he was quite sure, for the moment, that under no possible circumstances would he ever take an American woman to his bosom as his wife.

'No,' said he; 'no, no. I rather think that I agree with you.'

'The antipathy is one,' continued Miss Petrie, 'which has been common on the face of the earth since the clown first trod upon the courtier's heels. It is the instinct of fallen man to hate equality, to desire ascendancy, to crush, to oppress, to tyrannise, to enslave. Then, when the slave is at last free, and in his freedom demands – equality, man is not great enough to take his enfranchised brother to his bosom.'

'You mean negroes,' said Mr Glascock, looking round and planning for himself a mode of escape.

'Not negroes only, – not the enslaved blacks, who are now enslaved no more, – but the rising nations of white men wherever they are to be seen. You English have no sympathy with a people who claim to be at least your equals. The clown has trod upon the courtier's heels till the clown is clown no longer, and the courtier has hardly a court in which he may dangle his sword-knot.'

'If so the clown might as well spare the courtier,' not meaning the rebuke which his words implied.

'Ah – h, – but the clown will not spare the courtier, Mr Glascock. I understand the gibe, and I tell you that the courtier shall be spared no longer; – because he is useless. He shall be cut down together with the withered grasses and thrown into the oven, and there shall be an end of him.' Then she turned round to appeal to an American gentleman who had joined them, and Mr Glascock made his escape. 'I hold it to be the holiest duty which I owe to my country never to spare one of them when I meet him.'

'They are all very well in their way,' said the American gentleman.

'Down with them, down with them!' exclaimed the poetess, with a beautiful enthusiasm. In the meantime Mr Glascock had made up his mind that he could not dare to ask Caroline Spalding to be his wife. There were certain forms of the American female so dreadful that no wise man would wilfully come in contact with them. Miss Petrie's ferocity was distressing to him, but her eloquence and enthusiasm were worse even than her ferocity. The personal incivility of which she had been guilty in calling him a withered grass was distasteful to him, as being opposed to his ideas of the customs of society; but what would be his fate if his wife's chosen friend should be for ever dinning her denunciation of withered grasses into his ear?

He was still thinking of all this when he was accosted by Mrs Spalding. 'Are you going to dear Lady Banbury's to-morrow?' she asked. Lady Banbury was the wife of the English Minister.

'I suppose I shall be there in the course of the evening.'

'How very nice she is; is she not? I do like Lady Banbury; – so soft, and gentle, and kind.'

'One of the pleasantest old ladies I know,' said Mr Glascock.

'It does not strike you so much as it does me,' said Mrs Spalding, with one of her sweetest smiles. 'The truth is, we all value what we have not got. There are no Lady Banburys in our country, and therefore we think the more of them when we meet them here. She is talking of going to Rome for the Carnival, and has asked Caroline to go with her. I am so pleased to find that my dear girl is such a favourite.'

Mr Glascock immediately told himself that he saw the hook. If he were to be fished for by this American aunt as he had been fished for by English mothers, all his pleasure in the society of Caroline Spalding would be at once over. It would be too much, indeed, if in this American household he were to find the old vices of an aristocracy superadded to young republican sins! Nevertheless Lady Banbury was, as he knew well, a person whose opinion about young people was supposed to be very good. She noticed those only who were worthy of notice; and to have been taken by the hand by Lady Banbury was acknowledged to be a passport into good society. If Caroline Spalding was in truth going to Rome with Lady Banbury, that fact was in itself a great confirmation of Mr Glascock's good opinion of her. Mrs Spalding had perhaps understood this; but had not understood that having just hinted that it was so, she should have abstained from saying a word more about her dear girl. Clever and well-practised must, indeed, be the hand of the fisherwoman in matrimonial waters who is able to throw her fly without showing any glimpse of the hook to the fish for whom she angles. Poor Mrs Spalding, though with kindly instincts towards her niece she did on this occasion make some slight attempt at angling, was innocent of any concerted plan. It seemed to her to be so natural to say a good word in praise of her niece to the man whom she believed to be in love with her niece.

Caroline and Mr Glascock did not meet each other again till late in the evening, and just as he was about to take his leave. As they came together each of them involuntarily looked round to see whether Miss Petrie was near. Had she been there nothing would have been said beyond the shortest farewell greeting. But Miss Petrie was afar off, electrifying some Italian by the vehemence of her sentiments, and the audacious volubility of a language in which all arbitrary restrictions were ignored. 'Are you going?' she asked.

'Well; – I believe I am. Since I saw you last I've encountered Miss Petrie again, and I'm rather depressed.'

'Ah; – you don't know her. If you did you wouldn't laugh at her.'

'Laugh at her! Indeed I do not to that; but when I'm told that I'm to be thrown into the oven and burned because I'm such a worn-out old institution – '

'You don't mean to say that you mind that!'

'Not much, when it comes up in the ordinary course of conversation; but it palls upon one when it is asserted for the fourth or fifth time in an evening.'

'Alas, alas!' exclaimed Miss Spalding, with mock energy.

'And why, alas?'

'Because it is so impossible to make the oil and vinegar of the old world and of the new mix together and suit each other.'

'You think it is impossible, Miss Spalding?'

'I fear so. We are so terribly tender, and you are always pinching us on our most tender spot. And we never meet you without treading on your gouty toes.'

'I don't think my toes are gouty,' said he.

'I apologise for your own, individually, Mr Glascock; but I must assert that nationally you are subject to the gout.'

'That is, when I'm told over and over again that I'm to be cut down and thrown into the oven – '

'Never mind the oven now, Mr Glascock. If my friend has been over-zealous I will beg pardon for her. But it does seem to me, indeed it does, with all the reverence and partiality I have for everything European,' – the word European was an offence to him, and he showed that was so by his countenance, – 'that the idiosyncrasies of you and of us are so radically different, that we cannot be made to amalgamate and sympathise with each other thoroughly.'

He paused for some seconds before he answered her, but it was so evident by his manner that he was going to speak, that she could neither leave him nor interrupt him. 'I had thought that it might have been otherwise,' he said at last, and the tone of his voice was so changed as to make her know that he was in earnest.

But she did not change her voice by a single note. 'I'm afraid it cannot be so,' she said, speaking after her old fashion – half in earnest, half in banter. 'We may make up our minds to be very civil to each other when we meet. The threats of the oven may no doubt be dropped on our side, and you may abstain from expressing in words your sense of our inferiority.'

'I never expressed anything of the kind,' he said, quite in anger.

'I am taking you simply as the sample Englishman, not as Mr Glascock, who helped me and my sister over the mountains. Such of us as have to meet in society may agree to be very courteous; but courtesy and cordiality are not only not the same, but they are incompatible.'

'Why so?'

'Courtesy is an effort, and cordiality is free. I must be allowed to contradict the friend that I love; but I assent, – too often falsely, – to what is said to me by a passing acquaintance. In spite of what the Scripture says, I think it is one of the greatest privileges of a brother that he may call his brother a fool.'*

'Shall you desire to call your husband a fool?'

'My husband!'

'He will, I suppose, be at least as dear to you as a brother?'

'I never had a brother.'

'Your sister, then! It is the same, I suppose?'

'If I were to have a husband, I hope he would be the dearest to me of all. Unless he were so, he certainly would not be my husband. But between a man and his wife there does not spring up that playful, violent intimacy admitting of all liberties, which comes from early nursery assocations; and, then, there is the difference of sex.'

'I should not like my wife to call me a fool,' he said.

'I hope she may never have occasion to do so, Mr Glascock.

Marry an English wife in your own class, – as, of course, you will, – and then you will be safe.'

'But I have set my heart fast on marrying an American wife,' he said.

'Then I can't tell what may befall you. It's like enough, if you do that, that you may be called by some name you will think hard to bear. But you'll think better of it. Like should pair with like, Mr Glascock. If you were to marry one of our young women, you would lose in dignity as much as she would lose in comfort.' Then they parted, and she went off to say farewell to other guests. The manner in which she had answered what he had said to her had certainly been of a nature to stop any further speech of the same kind. Had she been gentle with him, then he would certainly have told her that she was the American woman whom he desired to take with him to his home in England.

57

Dorothy's Fate

Towards the end of February Sir Peter Mancrudy declared Miss Stanbury to be out of danger, and Mr Martin began to be sprightly on the subject, taking himself no inconsiderable share of the praise accruing to the medical faculty in Exeter generally for the saving of a life so valuable to the city. 'Yes, Mr Burgess,' Sir Peter said to old Barty of the bank, 'our friend will get over it this time, and without any serious damage to her constitution, if she will only take care of herself.' Barty made some inaudible grunt, intended to indicate his own indifference on the subject, and expressed his opinion to the chief clerk that old Jemima Wideawake, – as he was pleased to call her, – was one of those tough customers who would never die. 'It would be nothing to us, Mr Barty, one way or the other,' said the clerk; to which Barty Burgess assented with another grunt.

Camilla French declared that she was delighted to hear the news. At this time there had been some sort of a reconciliation between her and her lover. Mrs French had extracted from him a promise that he would not go to Natal; and Camilla had commenced the preparations for her wedding. His visits to Heavitree were as few and far between as he could make them with any regard to decency; but the 31st of March was coming on quickly, and as he was to be made a possession of then for ever, it was considered to be safe and well to allow him some liberty in his present condition. 'My dear, if they are driven, there is no knowing what they won't do,' Mrs French said to her daughter. Camilla had submitted with compressed lips and a slight nod of her head. She had worked very hard, but her day of reward was coming. It was impossible not to perceive, – both for her and her mother, – that the scantiness of Mr Gibson's attention to his future bride was cause of some weak triumph to Arabella. She said that it was very odd that he did not come, – and once added with a little sigh that he used to come in former days, alluding to those happy days in which another love was paramount. Camilla could not endure this with an equal mind. 'Bella, dear,' she said, 'we know what all that means. He has made his choice, and if I am satisified with what he does now, surely you need not grumble.' Miss Stanbury's illness had undoubtedly been a great source of contentment to the family at Heavitree, as they had all been able to argue that her impending demise was the natural consequences of her great sin in the matter of Dorothy's proposed marriage. When, however, they heard from Mr Martin that she would certainly recover, that Sir Peter's edict to that effect had gone forth, they were willing to acknowledge that Providence, having so far punished the sinner, was right in staying its hand and abstaining from the final blow. 'I'm sure we are delighted,' said Mrs French, 'for though she had said cruel things of us, – and so untrue too, – yet of course it is our duty to forgive her. And we do forgive her.'

Dorothy had written three or four notes to Brooke since his departure, which contained simple bulletins of her aunt's health. She always began her letters with 'My dear Mr Burgess,' and ended them with 'yours truly.' She never made any allusion to Brooke's declaration of love, or gave the slightest sign in her letters to show that she even remembered it. At last she wrote to say that her aunt was convalescent; and, in making this announcement, she allowed herself some enthusiasm of expression. She was so happy, and was so sure that Mr Burgess would be equally so! And her aunt had asked after her 'dear Brooke,' expressing her great satisfaction with him, in that he had come down to see her when she had been almost too ill to see anyone. In answer to this there came to her a real love-letter from Brooke Burgess. It was the first occasion on which he had written to her. The little bulletins had demanded no replies, and had received none. Perhaps there had been a shade of disappointment on Dorothy's side, in that she had written thrice, and had been made rich with no word in return. But, although her heart had palpitated on hearing the postman's knock, and had palpitated in vain, she had told herself that it was all as it should be. She wrote to him, because she possessed information which it was necessary that she should communicate. He did not write to her, because there was nothing for him to tell. Then had come the love-letter, and in the love-letter there was an imperative demand for a reply.

What was she to do? To have recourse to Priscilla for advice was her first idea; but she herself believed that she owed a debt of gratitude to her aunt, which Priscilla would not take into account, – the existence of which Priscilla would by no means admit. She knew Priscilla's mind in this matter, and was sure that Priscilla's advice, whatever it might be, would be given without any regard to her aunt's view. And then Dorothy was altogether ignorant of her aunt's views. Her aunt had been very anxious that she should marry Mr Gibson, but had clearly never admitted into her mind the idea that she might possibly marry Brooke Burgess; and it seemed to her that she herself would be dishonest, both to her aunt and to her lover, if she were to bind this man to herself without her aunt's knowledge. He was to be her aunt's heir, and she was maintained by her aunt's liberality! Thinking of all this, she at last resolved that she would take the bull by the horns, and tell her aunt. She felt that the task would be one almost beyond her strength. Thrice she went into her aunt's room, intending to make a clean breast. Thrice her courage failed her, and she left the room with her tale untold, excusing herself on various pretexts. Her aunt had seemed to be not quite so well, or had declared herself to be tired, or had been a little cross; – or else Martha had come in at the nick of time. But there was Brooke Burgess's letter unanswered, – a letter that was read night and morning, and which was never for an instant out of her mind. He had demanded a reply, and he had a right at least to that. The letter had been with her for four entire days before she had ventured to speak to her aunt on the subject.

On the first of March Miss Stanbury came out of her bed-room for the first time. Dorothy, on the previous day, had decided on postponing her communication for this occasion; but, when she found herself sitting in the little sitting-room up-stairs close at her aunt's elbow, and perceived the signs of weakness which the new move had made conspicuous, and heard the invalid declare that the little journey had been almost too much for her, her heart misgave her. She ought to have told her tale while her aunt was still in bed. But presently there came a question, which put her into such a flutter that she was for the time devoid of all resolution. 'Has Brooke written?' said Miss Stanbury.

'Yes, – aunt; he has written.'

'And what did he say?' Dorothy was struck quite dumb. 'Is there anything wrong?' And now, as Miss Stanbury asked the question, she seemed herself to have forgotten that she had two minutes before declared herself to be almost too feeble to speak. 'I'm sure there is something wrong. What is it ? I will know.'

'There is nothing wrong, Aunt Stanbury.'

'Where is the letter ? Let me see it.'

'I mean there is nothing wrong about him.'

'What is it, then ?'

'He is quite well, Aunt Stanbury.'

'Show me the letter. I will see the letter. I know that there is something the matter. Do you mean to say you won't show me Brooke's letter ?'

There was a moment's pause before Dorothy answered. 'I will show you his letter; – though I am sure he didn't mean that I should show it to anyone.'

'He hasn't written evil of me ?'

'No; no; no. He would sooner cut his hand off than say a word bad of you. He nevers says or writes anything bad of anybody. But – . Oh, aunt; I'll tell you everything. I should have told you before, only that you were ill.'

Then Miss Stanbury was frightened. 'What is it ?' she said hoarsely, clasping the arms of the great chair, each with a thin, shrivelled hand.

'Aunt Stanbury, Brooke, – Brooke, – wants me to be his – wife !'

'What !'

'You cannot be more surprised than I have been. Aunt Stanbury; and there has been no fault of mine.'

'I don't believe it,' said the old woman.

'Now you may read the letter,' said Dorothy, standing up. She was quite prepared to be obedient, but she felt that her aunt's manner of receiving the information was almost an insult.

'He must be a fool,' said Miss Stanbury.

This was hard to bear, and the colour went and came rapidly across Dorothy's cheeks as she gave herself a few moments to prepare an answer. She already perceived that her aunt would be altogether adverse to the marriage, and that therefore the marrige could never take place. She had never for a moment allowed herself to think otherwise, but, nevertheless, the blow was heavy on her. We all know how constantly hope and expectation will rise high within our own bosoms in opposition to our own judgment, – how we become sanguine in regard to events which we almost know can never come to pass. So it had been with Dorothy. Her heart had been almost in a flutter of happiness since she had had Brooke's letter in her possession, and yet she never ceased to declare to herself her own conviction that that letter could lead to no good result. In regard to her own wishes on the subject she had never asked herself a single question. As it had been quite beyond her power to bring herself to endure the idea of marrying Mr Gibson, so it had been quite impossible to her not to long to be Brooke's wife from the moment in which a suggestion to that effect had fallen from his lips. This was a state of things so certain, so much a matter of course, that, though she had not spoken a word to him in which she owned her love, she had never for a moment doubted that he knew the truth, – and that everybody else concerned would know it too. But she did not suppose that her wishes would go for anything with her aunt. Brooke Burgess was to become a rich man as her aunt's heir, and her aunt would of course have her own ideas about Brooke's advancement in life. She was quite prepared to submit without quarrelling when her aunt should tell her that the idea must not be entertained. But the order might be given, the prohibition might be pronounced, without an insult to her own feelings as a woman. 'He must be a fool,' Miss Stanbury had said, and Dorothy took time to collect her thoughts before she would reply. In the meantime her aunt finished the reading of the letter.

'He may be foolish in this,' Dorothy said; 'but I don't think you should call him a fool.'

'I shall call him what I please. I suppose this was going on at the time when you refused Mr Gibson.'

'Nothing was going on. Nothing has gone on at all,' said Dorothy, with as much indignation as she was able to assume.

'How can you tell me that? That is an untruth.'

'It is not – an untruth,' said Dorothy, almost sobbing, but driven at the same time to much anger.

'Do you mean to say that this is the first you ever heard of it?' And she held out the letter, shaking it in her thin hand.

'I have never said so, Aunt Stanbury.'

'Yes, you did.'

'I said that nothing – was – going on, when Mr Gibson – was – If you choose to suspect me, Aunt Stanbury, I'll go away. I won't stay here if you suspect me. When Brooke spoke to me, I told him you wouldn't like it.'

'Of course I don't like it.' But she gave no reason why she did not like it.

'And there was nothing more till this letter came. I couldn't help his writing to me. It wasn't my fault.'

'Psha!'

'If you are angry, I am very sorry. But you haven't a right to be angry.'

'Go on, Dorothy; go on. I'm so weak that I can hardly stir myself; it's the first moment that I've been out of my bed for weeks; – and of course you can say what you please. I know what it will be. I shall have to take to my bed again, and then, – in a very little time, – you can both – make fools of yourselves, – just as you like.'

This was an argument against which Dorothy of course found it to be quite impossible to make continued combat. She could only shuffle her letter back into her pocket, and be, if possible, more assiduous than ever in her attentions to the invalid. She knew that she had been treated most unjustly, and there would be a question to be answered as soon as her aunt should be well as to the possibility of her remaining in the Close subject to such injustice; but let her aunt say what she might, or do what she might, Dorothy could not leave her for the present. Miss Stanbury sat for a considerable time quite motionless, with her eyes closed, and did not stir or make signs of life till Dorothy touched her arm, asking her whether she would not take some broth which had been prepared for her. 'Where's Martha? Why does not Martha come?' said Miss Stanbury. This was a hard blow, and from that moment Dorothy believed that it would be expedient that she should return to Nuncombe Putney. The broth, however, was taken, while Dorothy sat by in silence. Only one word further was said that evening by Miss Stanbury about Brooke and his love affair. 'There must be nothing more about this, Dorothy; remember that; nothing at all. I won't have it.' Dorothy made no reply. Brooke's letter was in her pocket, and it should be answered that night. On the following day she would let her aunt know what she had said to Brooke. Her aunt should not see the letter, but should be made acquainted with its purport in reference to Brooke's proposal of marriage.

'I won't have it!' That had been her aunt's command. What right had her aunt to give any command upon the matter? Then crossed Dorothy's mind, as she thought of this, a glimmering of an idea that no one can be entitled to issue commands who cannot enforce obedience. If Brooke and she chose to become man and wife by mutual consent, how could her aunt prohibit the marriage? Then there followed another idea, that commands are enforced by the threatening and, if necessary, by the enforcement of penalties. Her aunt had within her hand no penalty of which Dorothy was afraid on her own behalf; but she had the power of inflicting a terrible punishment on Brooke Burgess. Now Dorothy conceived that she herself would be the meanest creature alive if she were actuated by fears as to money in her acceptance or rejection of a man whom she loved as she did Brooke Burgess. Brooke had an income of his own which seemed to her to be ample for all purposes. But that which would have been sordid in her, did not seem to her to have any stain of sordidness for him. He was a man, and was bound to be rich if he could. And, moreover, what had she to offer in herself, – such a poor thing as was she, – to make compensation to him for the loss of fortune? Her aunt could inflict this penalty, and therefore the power was hers, and the power must be obeyed. She would write to Brooke in a manner that should convey to him her firm decision. But not the less on that account would she let her aunt know that she thought herself to have been ill-used. It was an insult to her, a most ill-natured insult, – that telling her that Brooke had been a fool for loving her. And then that accusation against her of having been false, of having given one reason for refusing Mr Gibson, while there was another reason in her heart, – of having been cunning and then untrue, was not to be endured. What would her aunt think of her if she were to bear such allegations without indignant protest? She would writer her letter, and speak her mind to her aunt as soon as her aunt should be well enough to hear it.

As she had resolved, she wrote her letter that night before she went to bed. She wrote it with floods of tears, and a bitterness of heart which almost conquered her. She too had heard of love, and had been taught to feel that the success or failure of a woman's life depended upon that, – whether she did, or whether she did not, by such gifts as God might have given to her, attract to herself some man strong enough, and good enough, and loving enough to make straight for her her paths, to bear for her her burdens, to be the father of her children, the staff on which she might lean, and the wall against which she might grow, feeling the sunshine, and sheltered from the wind. She had ever estimated her own value so lowly as to have told herself often that such success could never come in her way. From her earliest years she had regarded herself as outside the pale within which such joys are to be found. She had so strictly taught herself to look forward to a blank existence, that she had learned to do so without active misery. But not the less did she know where happiness lay; and when the good thing came almost within her reach, when it seemed that God had given her gifts which might have sufficed, when a man had sought her hand whose nature was such that she could have leaned on him with a true worship, could have grown against him as against a wall with perfect confidence, could have lain with her head upon his bosom,

and have felt that of all spots that in the world was the most fitting
for her, – when this was all but grasped, and must yet be
abandoned, there came upon her spirit an agony so bitter that she
had not before known how great might be the depth of human
disappointment. But the letter was at last written, and when finished
was as follows :

The Close, Exeter, March 1, 186 –

Dear Brooke
There had been many doubts about this ; but at last they were
conquered, and the name was written.

I have shown your letter to my aunt, as I am sure you will think was
best. I should have answered it before, only that I thought that she was
not quite well enought to talk about it. She says, as I was sure she
would, that what you propose is quite out of the question. I am aware
that I am bound to obey her ; and as I think that you also ought to do
so, I shall think no more of what you have said to me and have written.
It is quite impossible now, even if it might have been possible under
other circumstances. I shall always remember your great kindness to
me. Perhaps I ought to say that I am very grateful for the compliment
you have paid me. I shall think of you always ; – till I die.
                                   Believe me to be,
                                   Your very sincere friend,
                                   Dorothy Stanbury.

The next day Miss Stanbury again came out of her room, and on
the third day she was manifestly becoming stronger. Dorothy had
as yet not spoken of her letter, but was prepared to do so as soon
as she thought that a fitting opportunity had come. She had a word
or two to say for herself ; but she must not again subject herself to
being told that she was taking her will of her aunt because her aunt
was too ill to defend herself. But on the third day Miss Stanbury
herself asked the question. 'Have you written anything to Brooke ?'
she asked.
    'I have answered his letter, Aunt Stanbury.'
    'And what have you said to him ?'
    'I have told him that you disapproved of it, and that nothing
more must be said about it.'
    'Yes ; – of course you made me out to be an ogre.'
    'I don't know what you mean by that, aunt. I am sure that I told
him the truth.'
    'May I see the letter ?'
    'It has gone.'
    'But you have kept a copy,' said Miss Stanbury.

'Yes; I have got a copy,' replied Dorothy; 'but I would rather not show it. I told him just what I tell you.'

'Dorothy, it is not at all becoming that you should have a correspondence with any young man of such a nature that you should be ashamed to show it to your aunt.'

'I am not ashamed of anything,' said Dorothy sturdily.

'I don't know what young women in these days have come to,' continued Miss Stanbury. 'There is no respect, no subjection, no obedience, and too often – no modesty.'

'Does that mean me, Aunt Stanbury?' asked Dorothy.

'To tell you the truth, Dorothy, I don't think you ought to have been receiving love-letters from Brooke Burgess when I was lying ill in bed. I didn't expect it of you. I tell you fairly that I didn't expect it of you.'

Then Dorothy spoke out her mind. 'As you think that, Aunt Stanbury, I had better go away. And if you please I will, – when you are well enough to spare me.'

'Pray don't think of me at all,' said her aunt.

'And as for love-letters, – Mr Burgess has written to me once. I don't think that there can be anything immodest in opening a letter when it comes by the post. And as soon as I had it I determined to show it to you. As for what happened before, when Mr Burgess spoke to me, which was long, long after all that about Mr Gibson was over, I told him that it couldn't be so; and I thought there would be no more about it. You were so ill that I could not tell you. Now you know it all.'

'I have not seen your letter to him.'

'I shall never show it to anybody. But you have said things, Aunt Stanbury, that are very cruel.'

'Of course! Everything I say is wrong.'

'You have told me that I was telling untruths, and you have called me – immodest. That is a terrible word.'

'You shouldn't deserve it then.'

'I never have deserved it, and I won't bear it. No; I won't. If Hugh heard me called that word, I believe he'd tear the house down.'

'Hugh, indeed! He's to be brought in between us; – is he?'

'He's my brother, and of course I'm obliged to think of him. And if you please, I'll go home as soon as you are well enough to spare me.'

Quickly after this there were very many letters coming and going between the house in the Close and the ladies at Nuncombe Putney, and Hugh Stanbury, and Brooke Burgess. The correspondent of

Brooke Burgess was of course Miss Stanbury herself. The letters to Hugh and to Nuncombe Putney were written by Dorothy. Of the former we need be told nothing at the present moment; but the upshot of all poor Dolly's letters was, that on the tenth of March she was to return home to Nuncombe Putney, share once more her sister's bed and mother's poverty, and abandon the comforts of the Close. Before this became a definite arrangement Miss Stanbury had given way in a certain small degree. She had acknowledged that Dorothy had intended no harm. But this was not enough for Dorothy, who was conscious of no harm either done or intended. She did not specify her terms, or require specifically that her aunt should make apology for that word, immodest, or at least withdraw it; but she resolved that she would go unless it was most absolutely declared to have been applied to her without the slightest reason. She felt, moreover, that her aunt's house ought to be open to Brooke Burgess, and that it could not be open to them both. And so she went; — having resided under her aunt's roof between nine and ten months.

'Good-bye, Aunt Stanbury,' said Dorothy, kissing her aunt, with a tear in her eye and a sob in her throat.

'Good-bye, my dear, good-bye.' And Miss Stanbury, as she pressed her niece's hand, left in it a bank-note.

'I'm much obliged, aunt; I am indeed; but I'd rather not.' And the bank-note was left on the parlour table.

58

Dorothy at Home

Dorothy was received at home with so much affection and such expressions of esteem as to afford her much consolation in her misery. Both her mother and her sister approved of her conduct. Mrs Stanbury's approval was indeed accompanied by many expressions of regret as to the good things lost. She was fully alive to the fact that life in the Close at Exeter was better for her daughter than life in their little cottage at Nuncombe Putney. The outward appearance which Dorothy bore on her return home was proof of this. Her clothes, the set of her hair, her very gestures and motions had framed themselves on town ideas. The faded, wildered, washed-out look, the uncertain, purposeless bearing which had come from her secluded life and subjection to her sister had vanished from her. She had lived among people, and had learned something of their gait and carriage. Money we know will do almost everything, and no doubt money had had much to do with this. It is very pretty to talk of the alluring simplicity of a clean calico gown; but poverty will show itself to be meagre, dowdy, and draggled in a woman's dress, let the woman be ever so simple, ever so neat, ever so independent, and ever so high-hearted. Mrs Stanbury was quite alive to all that her younger daughter was losing. Had she not received two offers of marriage while she was at Exeter? There was no possibility that offers of marriage should be made in the cottage at Nuncombe Putney. A man within the walls of the cottage would have been considered as much out of place as a wild bull. It had been matter of deep regret to Mrs Stanbury that her daughter should not have found herself able to marry Mr Gibson. She knew that there was no matter for reproach in this, but it was a misfortune, – a great misfortune. And in the mother's breast there had been a sad, unrepressed feeling of regret that young people should so often lose their chances in the world through over-fancifulness, and ignorance as to their own good. Now when she heard the story of Brooke Burgess, she could not but think that had Dorothy remained at Exeter, enduring patiently such hard words as her aunt might speak, the love affair might have been brought at some future time to a happy conclusion. She did not say all this; but there came on her a silent melancholy, made expressive by contrast little shakings of the head and a continued reproachful sadness of demeanour, which was quite as intelligible to Priscilla as would have been any spoken words. But Priscilla's approval of her sister's conduct was clear, outspoken, and satisfactory. She had been quite sure that her sister had been right about Mr Gibson; and was equally sure that she was now right about Brooke Burgess. Priscilla had in her mind an idea that if B. B., as they called him, was half as good as her sister represented him to be, – for indeed Dorothy endowed him with every virtue consistent with humanity, – he would not be deterred from his pursuit either by Dolly's letter or by Aunt Stanbury's commands. But of this she thought it wise to say nothing. She paid Dolly the warm and hitherto unaccustomed compliment of equality, assuming to regard her sister's judgment and persistent independence to be equally strong with her own; and, as she knew well, she could not have gone further than this. 'I never shall agree with you about Aunt Stanbury,' she said. 'To me she seems to be so imperious, so exacting, and also so unjust, as to be unbearable.'

'But she is affectionate,' said Dolly.

'So is the dog that bites you, and, for aught I know, the horse that kicks you. But it is ill living with biting dogs and kicking horses. But all that matters little as you are still your own mistress. How strange these nine months have been, with you in Exeter, while we have been at the Clock House. And here we are, together again in the old way, just as though nothing had happened.' But Dorothy knew well that a great deal had happened, and that her life could never be as it had been heretofore. The very tone in which her sister spoke to her was proof of this. She had an infinitely greater possession in herself than had belonged to her before her residence at Exeter; but that possession was so heavily mortgaged and so burthened as to make her believe that the change was to be regretted.

At the end of the first week there came a letter from Aunt Stanbury to Dorothy. It began by saying that Dolly had left behind her certain small properties which had now been made up in a parcel and sent by the railway, carriage paid. 'But they weren't mine at all,' said Dolly, alluding to certain books in which she had taken delight. 'She means to give them to you,' said Priscilla, 'and I think you must take them.' 'And the shawl is no more mine than it is yours, though I wore it two or three times in the winter.' Priscilla was of opinion that the shawl must be taken also. Then the letter spoke of the writer's health, and at last fell into such a strain of confidential gossip that Mrs Stanbury, when she read it, could not understand that there had been a quarrel. 'Martha says that she saw Camilla French in the street to-day, such a guy in her new finery as never was seen before except on May-day.' Then in the postscript Dorothy was enjoined to answer this letter quickly. 'None of your short scraps, my dear,' said Aunt Stanbury.

'She must mean you to go back to her,' said Mrs Stanbury.

'No doubt she does,' said Priscilla; 'but Dolly need not go because my aunt means it. We are not her creatures.'

But Dorothy answered her aunt's letter in the spirit in which it had been written. She asked after her aunt's health, thanked her aunt for the gift of the books, – in each of which her name had been clearly written, protested about the shawl, sent her love to Martha and her kind regards to Jane, and expressed a hope that C. F. enjoyed her new clothes. She described the cottage, and was funny about the cabbage stumps in the garden, and at last succeeded in concocting a long epistle. 'I suppose there will be a regular correspondence,' said Priscilla.

Two days afterwards, however, the correspondence took altogether another form. The cottage in which they now lived was supposed to be beyond the beat of the wooden-legged postman, and therefore it was necessary that they should call at the post-office for their letters. On the morning in question Priscilla obtained a thick letter from Exeter for her mother, and knew that it had come from her aunt. Her aunt could hardly have found it necessary to correspond with Dorothy's mother so soon after that letter to Dorothy had been written and there not arisen some very peculiar cause. Priscilla, after much meditation, thought it better that the letter should be opened in Dorothy's absence, and in Dorothy's absence the following letter was read both by Priscilla and her mother.

The Close, March 19, 186 –

Dear Sister Stanbury,
After much consideration, I think it best to send under cover to you the enclosed letter from Mr Brooke Burgess, intended for your daughter Dorothy. You will see that I have opened it and read it, – as I was clearly entitled to do, the letter having been addressed to my niece while she was supposed to be under my care. I do not like to destroy the letter, though, perhaps, that would be best; but I would advise you to do so, if it be possible, without showing it to Dorothy. I have told Mr Brooke Burgess what I have done.

I have also told him that I cannot sanction a marriage between him and your daughter. There are many reasons of old date, – not to speak of present reasons also, – which would make such a marriage highly inexpedient. Mr Brooke Burgess is, of course, his own master, but your daughter understands completely how the matter stands.

Yours truly,
Jemima Stanbury

'What a wicked old woman!' said Priscilla. Then there arose a question whether they should read Brooke's letter, or whether they should give it unread to Dorothy. Priscilla denounced her aunt in the strongest language she could use for having broken the seal. '"Clearly entitled," – because Dorothy had been living with her!' exclaimed Priscilla. 'She can have no proper conception of honour or of honesty. She had no more right to open Dorothy's letter than she had to take her money.' Mrs Stanbury was very anxious to read Brooke's letter, alleging that they would then be able to judge whether it should be handed over to Dorothy. But Priscilla's sense of right would not admit of this. Dorothy must receive the letter from her lover with no further stain from unauthorised eyes than that to which it had been already subjected. She was called in, therefore, from the kitchen, and the whole packet was given to her. 'Your aunt has read the enclosure, Dolly; but we have not opened it.'

Dorothy took the packet without a word and sat herself down. She first read her aunt's letter very slowly. 'I understand perfectly,' she said, folding it up, almost listlessly, while Brooke's letter lay still unopened on her lap. Then she took it up, and held it awhile in both hands, while her mother and Priscilla watched her. 'Priscilla,' she said, 'do you read it first.'

Priscilla was immediately at her side, kissing her. 'No, my darling; no,' she said; 'it is for you to read it.' Then Dorothy took the precious contents from the envelope, and opened the folds of the paper. When she had read a dozen words, her eyes were so suffused with tears, that she could hardly make herself mistress of the contents of the letter; but she knew that it contained renewed assurances of her lover's love, and assurance on his part that he would take no refusal from her based on any other ground than that of her own indifference to him. He had written to Miss Stanbury to the same effect; but he had not thought it necessary to explain this to Dorothy; nor did Miss Stanbury in her letter tell them that she had received any communication from him. 'Shall I read it now?' said Priscilla, as soon as Dorothy again allowed the letter to fall into her lap.

Both Priscilla and Mrs Stanbury read it, and for awhile they sat with the two letters among them without much speech about them. Mrs Stanbury was endeavouring to make herself believe that her sister-in-law's opposition might be overcome, and that thus Dorothy might be married. Priscilla was inquiring of herself whether it would be well that Dorothy should defy her aunt, – so much, at any rate, would be well, – and marry the man, even to his deprivation of the old woman's fortune. Priscilla had her doubts about this, being very strong in her ideas of self-denial. That her sister should put up with the bitterest disappointment rather than injure the man she loved was right; – but then it would also be so extremely right to defy Aunt Stanbury to her teeth! But Dorothy, in whose character was mixed with her mother's softness much of the old Stanbury strength, had no doubt in her mind. It was very sweet to be so loved. What gratitude did she not owe to a man who was so true to her! What was she that she should stand in his way? To lay herself down that she might be crushed in his path was no more than she owed to him. Mrs Stanbury was the first to speak.

'I suppose he is a very good young man,' she said.

'I am sure he is; – a noble, true-hearted man,' said Priscilla.

'And why shouldn't he marry whom he pleases, as long as she is respectable?' said Mrs Stanbury.

'In some people's eyes poverty is more disreputable than vice,' said Priscilla.

'Your aunt has been so fond of Dorothy,' pleaded Mrs Stanbury.

'Just as she is of her servants,' said Priscilla.

But Dorothy said nothing. Her heart was too full to enable her to defend her aunt; nor at the present moment was she strong enough to make her mother understand that no hope was to be entertained. In the course of the day she walked out with her sister on the road towards Ridleigh, and there, standing among the rocks and ferns, looking down upon the river, with the buzz of the little mill within her ears, she explained the feelings of her heart and her many thoughts with a flow of words stronger, as Priscilla thought, than she had ever used before.

'It is not what he would suffer now, Pris, or what he would feel, but what he would feel ten, twenty years hence, when he would know that his children would have been all provided for, had he not lost his fortune by marrying me.'

'He must be the only judge whether he prefers you to the old woman's money,' said Priscilla.

'No, dear; not the only judge. And it isn't that, Pris, – not which he likes best now, but which it is best for him that he should have. What could I do for him?'

'You can love him.'

'Yes; – I can do that.' And Dorothy paused a moment, to think how exceedingly well she could do that one thing. 'But what is that? As you said the other day, a dog can do that. I am not clever. I can't play, or talk French, or do things that men like their wives to do. And I have lived here all my life; and what am I, that for me he should lose a great fortune?'

'That is his look out.'

'No, dearest; – it is mine, and I will look out. I shall be able, at any rate, to remember always that I have loved him, and have not injured him. He may be angry with me now,' – and there was a feeling of pride at her heart, as she thought that he would be angry with her, because she did not go to him, – 'but he will know at last that I have been as good to him as I knew how to be.'

Then Priscilla wound her arms round Dorothy, and kissed her. 'My sister,' she said; 'my own sister!' They walked on further, discussing the matter in all its bearings, talking of the act of self-denial which Dorothy was called on to perform, as though it were some abstract thing, the performance of which was, or perhaps was not, imperatively demanded by the laws which should govern humanity; but with no idea on the mind of either of them that there was any longer a doubt as to this special matter in hand. They were away from home over three hours; and, when they returned, Dorothy at once wrote her two letters. They were very simple, and very short. She told Brooke, whom she now addressed as 'Dear Mr Burgess,' that it could not be as he would have it; and she told her aunt, – with some terse independence of expression, which Miss Stanbury quite understood, – that she had considered the matter, and had thought it right to refuse Mr Burgess's offer.

'Don't you think she is very much changed?' said Mrs Stanbury to her eldest daughter.

'Not changed in the least, mother; but the sun has opened the bud, and now we see the fruit.'

59
Mr Bozzle at Home

It had now come to pass that Trevelyan had not a friend in the world to whom he could apply in the matter of his wife and family. In the last communication which he had received from Lady Milborough she had scolded him, in terms that were for her severe, because he had not returned to his wife and taken her off with him to Naples. Mr Bideawhile had found himself obliged to decline to move in the matter at all. With Hugh Stanbury Trevelyan had had a direct quarrel. Mr and Mrs Outhouse he regarded as bitter enemies, who had taken the part of his wife without any regard to the decencies of life. And now it had come to pass that his sole remaining ally, Mr Samuel Bozzle, the ex-policeman, was becoming weary of his service. Trevelyan remained in the north of Italy up to the middle of March, spending a fortune in sending telegrams to Bozzle, instigating Bozzle by all the means in his power to obtain possession of the child, desiring him at one time to pounce down upon the parsonage of St Diddulph's with a battalion of policemen armed to the teeth with the law's authority, and at another time suggesting to him to find his way by stratagem into Mr Outhouse's castle and carry off the child in his arms. At last he sent word to say that he himself would be in England before the end of March, and would see that the majesty of the law should be vindicated in his favour.

Bozzle had in truth made but one personal application for the child at St Diddulph's. In making this he had expected no success, though, from the energetic nature of his disposition, he had made the attempt with some zeal. But he had never applied again at the parsonage, disregarding the letters, the telegrams, and even the promises which had come to him from his employer with such frequency. The truth was that Mrs Bozzle was opposed to the proposed separation of the mother and the child, and that Bozzle was a man who listened to the words of his wife. Mrs Bozzle was quite prepared to admit that Madame T., – as Mrs Trevelyan had come to be called at No 55, Stony Walk, – was no better than she should be. Mrs Bozzle was disposed to think that ladies of quality, among whom Madame T. was entitled in her estimation to take rank, were seldom better than they ought to be, and she was quite willing that her husband should earn his bread by watching the lady or the lady's lover. She had participated in Bozzle's triumph when he had discovered that the Colonel had gone to Devonshire, and again when he had learned that the Lothario had been at St Diddulph's. And had the case been brought before the judge ordinary by means of her husband's exertions, she would have taken pleasure in reading every word of the evidence, even though her husband should have been ever so roughly handled by the lawyers. But now, when a demand was made upon Bozzle to violate the sanctity of the clergyman's house, and withdraw the child by force or stratagem, she began to perceive that the palmy days of the Trevelyan affair were over for them, and that it would be wise on her husband's part gradually to back out of the gentleman's employment. 'Just put it on the fireback, Bozzle,' she said one morning, as her husband stood before her reading for the second time a somewhat lengthy epistle which had reached him from Italy, while he held the baby over his shoulder with his left arm. He had just washed himself at the sink, and though his face was clean, his hair was rough, and his shirt sleeves were tucked up.

'That's all very well, Maryanne; but when a party has took a gent's money, a party is bound to go through with the job.'

'Gammon, Bozzle.'

'It's all very well to say gammon; but his money has been took, – and there's more to come.'

'And ain't you worked for the money, – down to Hexeter one time, across the water pretty well day and night watching that ere clergyman's 'ouse like a cat? What more'd he have? As to the child, I won't hear of it, B. The child shan't come here. We'd all be showed up in the papers as that black, that they'd hoot us along the streets. It ain't the regular line of business, Bozzle; and there ain't no good to be got, never, by going off the regular line.' Whereupon Bozzle scratched his head and again read the letter. A distinct promise of a

hundred pounds was made to him, if he would have the child ready
to hand over to Trevelyan on Trevelyan's arrival in England.

'It ain't to be done, you know,' said Bozzle.

'Of course it ain't,' said Mrs Bozzle.

'It ain't to be done anyways; – not in my way of business. Why
didn't he go to Skint, as I told him, when his own lawyer was too
dainty for the job? The paternal parent has a right to his hinfants,
no doubt.' That was Bozzle's law.

'I don't believe it, B.'

'But he have, I tell you.'

'He can't suckle 'em; – can he? I don't believe a bit of his rights.'

'When a married woman has followers, and the husband don't
go the wrong side of the post too, or it ain't proved again him that
he do, they'll never let her have nothing to do with the children. It's
been before the court a hundred times. He'll get the child fast
enough if he'll go before the court.'

'Anyways it ain't your business, Bozzle, and don't you meddle
nor make. The money's good money as long as it's honest earned;
but when you come to rampaging and breaking into a gent's house,
then I say money may be had a deal too hard.' In this special letter,
which had now come to hand, Bozzle was not instructed to
'rampage.' He was simply desired to make a further official requisi-
tion for the boy at the parsonage, and to explain to Mr Outhouse,
Mrs Outhouse, and Mrs Trevelyan, or to as many of them as he
could contrive to see, that Mr Trevelyan was immediately about to
return to London, and that he would put the law into execution if
his son were not given up to him at once. 'I'll tell you what it is, B.,'
exclaimed Mrs Bozzle, 'it's my belief as he ain't quite right up here;'
and Mrs Bozzle touched her forehead.

'It's love for her as has done it then,' said Bozzle, shaking his
head.

'I'm not a taking of her part, B. A woman as has a husband as
finds her with her wittels regular, and with what's decent and
comfortable beside, ought to be contented. I've never said no other
than that. I ain't no patience with your saucy madames as can't
remember as they're eating an honest man's bread. Drat 'em all;
what is it they wants? They don't know what they wants. It's just
hidleness, – cause there ain't a ha'porth for 'em to do. It's that as
makes 'em – , I won't say what. But as for this here child, B. – ' At
that moment there came a knock at the door. Mrs Bozzle going into
the passage, opened it herself, and saw a strange gentleman. Bozzle,
who had stood at the inner door, saw that the gentleman was Mr
Trevelyan.

The letter, which was still in the ex-policeman's hand, had reached Stony Walk on the previous day; but the master of the house had been absent, finding out facts, following up his profession, and earning an honest penny. Trevelyan had followed his letter quicker than he had intended when it was written, and was now with his prime minister, before his prime minister had been able to take any action on the last instruction received. 'Does one Mr Samuel Bozzle live here?' asked Trevelyan. Then Bozzle came forward and introduced his wife. There was no one else present except the baby, and Bozzle intimated that let matters be as delicate as they might, they could be discussed with perfect security in his wife's presence. But Trevelyan was of a different opinion, and he was disgusted and revolted, – most unreasonably, – by the appearance of his minister's domestic arrangements. Bozzle had always waited upon him with a decent coat, and a well-brushed hat, and clean shoes. It is very much easier for such men as Mr Bozzle to carry decency of appearance about with them than to keep it at home. Trevelyan had never believed his ally to be more than an ordinary ex-policeman, but he had not considered how unattractive might be the interior of a private detective's private residence. Mrs Bozzle had set a chair for him, but he had declined to sit down. The room was dirty, and very close, – as though no breath of air was ever allowed to find entrance there. 'Perhaps you could put on your coat, and walk out with me for a few minutes,' said Trevelyan. Mrs Bozzle, who well understood that business was business, and that wives were not business, felt no anger at this, and handed her husband his best coat. The well-brushed hat was fetched from a cupboard, and it was astonishing to see how easily and how quickly the outer respectability of Bozzle was restored.

'Well?' said Trevelyan, as soon as they were together in the middle of Stony Walk.

'There hasn't been nothing to be done, sir,' said Bozzle.

'Why not?' Trevelyan could perceive at once that the authority which he had once respected had gone from the man. Bozzle away from his own home, out on business, with his coat buttoned over his breast, and his best hat in his hand, was aware that he commanded respect, – and he could carry himself accordingly. He knew himself to be somebody, and could be easy, self-confident, confidential, severe, authoritative, or even arrogant, as the circumstances of the moment might demand. But he had been found with his coat off, and a baby in his arms, and he could not recover himself. 'I do not suppose that anybody will question my right to have the care of my own child,' said Trevelyan.

'If you would have gone to Mr Skint, sir – ,' suggested Bozzle. 'There aint no smarter gent in all the profession, sir, than Mr Skint.'

Mr Trevelyan made no reply to this, but walked on in silence, with his minister at his elbow. He was very wretched, understanding well the degradation to which he was subjecting himself in discussing his wife's conduct with this man; – but with whom else would he discuss it ? The man seemed to be meaner now than he had been before he had been seen in his own home. And Trevelyan was conscious too that he himself was not in outward appearance as he used to be; – that he was ill-dressed, and haggard, and worn, and visibly a wretched being. How can any man care to dress himself with attention who is always alone, and always miserable when alone ? During the months which had passed over him since he had sent his wife away from him, his very nature had been altered, and he himself was aware of the change. As he went about, his eyes were ever cast downwards, and he walked with a quick shuffling gait, and he suspected others, feeling that he himself was suspected. And all work had ceased with him. Since she had left him he had not read a single book that was worth the reading. And he knew it all. He was conscious that he was becoming disgraced and degraded. He would sooner have shot himself than have walked into his club, or even have allowed himself to be seen by daylight in Pall Mall, or Piccadilly. He had taken in his misery to drinking little drops of brandy in the morning, although he knew well that there was no shorter road to the devil than that opened by such a habit. He looked up for a moment at Bozzle, and then asked him a question. 'Where is he now ?'

'You mean the Colonel, sir. He's up in town, sir, a minding of his parliamentary duties. He have been up all this month, sir.'

'They haven't met ?'

Bozzle paused a moment before he replied, and then smiled as he spoke. 'It is so hard to say, sir. Ladies is so cute and cunning. I've watched as sharp as watching can go, pretty near. I've put a youngster on at each hend, and both of 'em 'd hear a mouse stirring in his sleep. I ain't got no evidence, Mr Trevelyan. But if you ask me my opinion, why in course they've been together somewhere. It stands to reason, Mr Trevelyan; don't it ?' And Bozzle as he said this smiled almost aloud.

'D – n and b – t it all for ever !' said Trevelyan, gnashing his teeth, and moving away into Union Street as fast as he could walk. And he did go away, leaving Bozzle standing in the middle of Stony Walk.

'He's disturbed in his mind, – quite 'orrid,' Bozzle said when he got back to his wife. 'He cursed and swore as made even me feel bad.'

'B.,' said his wife, 'do you listen to me. Get in what's a howing, and don't you have nothing more to do with it.'

60

Another Struggle

Sir Marmaduke and Lady Rowley were to reach England about the end of March or the beginning of April, and both Mrs Trevelyan and Nora Rowley were almost sick for their arrival. Both their uncle and aunt had done very much for them, had been true to them in their need, and had submitted to endless discomforts in order that their nieces might have respectable shelter in their great need; but nevertheless their conduct had not been of a kind to produce either love or friendship. Each of the sisters felt that she had been much better off at Nuncombe Putney, and that either the weakness of Mrs Stanbury, or the hardness of Priscilla, was preferable to the repulsive forbearance of their clerical host. He did not scold them. He never threw it in Mrs Trevelyan's teeth that she had been separated from her husband by her own fault; he did not tell them of his own discomfort. But he showed it in every gesture, and spoke of it in every tone of his voice; – so that Mrs Trevelyan could not refrain from apologising for the misfortune of her presence.

'My dear,' he said, 'things can't be pleasant and unpleasant at the same time. You were quite right to come here. I am glad for all our sakes that Sir Marmaduke will be with us so soon.'

She had almost given up in her mind the hope that she had long cherished, that she might some day be able to live again with her husband. Every step which he now took in reference to her seemed to be prompted by so bitter an hostility, that she could not but believe that she was hateful to him. How was it possible that a husband and his wife should again come together, when there had been between them such an emissary as a detective policeman? Mrs Trevelyan had gradually come to learn that Bozzle had been at Nuncombe Putney, watching her, and to be aware that she was still under the surveillance of his eye. For some months past now she had neither seen Colonel Osborne, nor heard from him. He had certainly by his folly done much to produce the ruin which had fallen upon her; but it never occurred to her to blame him. Indeed she did not know that he was liable to blame. Mr Outhouse always spoke of him with indignant scorn, and Nora had learned to think that much of their misery was due to his imprudence. But Mrs Trevelyan would not see this, and, not seeing it, was more widely separated from her husband than she would have been had she acknowledged that any excuse for his misconduct had been afforded by the vanity and folly of the other man.

Lady Rowley had written to have a furnished house taken for them from the first of April, and a house had been secured in Manchester Street. The situation in question is not one which is of itself very charming, nor is it supposed to be in a high degree fashionable; but Nora looked forward to her escape from St Diddulph's to Manchester Street as though Paradise were to be re-opened to her as soon as she should be there with her father and mother. She was quite clear now as to her course about Hugh Stanbury. She did not doubt but that she could so argue the matter as to get the consent of her father and mother. She felt herself to be altogether altered in her views of life, since experience had come upon her, first at Nuncombe Putney, and after that, much more heavily and seriously, at St Diddulph's. She looked back as though to a childish dream to the ideas which had prevailed with her when she had told herself, as she used to do so frequently, that she was unfit to be a poor man's wife. Why should she be more unfit for such a position than another? Of course there were many thoughts in her mind, much of memory if nothing of regret, in regard to Mr Glascock and the splendour that had been offered to her. She had had her chance of being a rich man's wife, and had rejected it, – had rejected it twice, with her eyes open. Readers will say that if she loved Hugh Stanbury with all her heart, there could be nothing of regret in her reflections. But we are perhaps accustomed in judging for ourselves and of others to draw the lines too sharply, and to say that on this side lie vice, folly, heartlessness, and greed, – and on the other honour, love, truth, and wisdom, – the good and the bad each in its own domain. But the good and the bad mix themselves so thoroughly in our thoughts, even in our aspirations, that we must look for excellence rather in overcoming evil than in freeing ourselves from its influence. There had been many moments of regret with Nora; – but none of remorse. At the very moment in which she had sent Mr Glascock away from her, and had felt that he had now been sent away for always, she had been full of regret. Since that there had been many hours in which she had thought of her own self-lesson, of that teaching by which she had striven to convince herself that she could never fitly become a poor man's wife. But the upshot of it all was a healthy pride in what she had done, and a strong resolution that she would make shirts and hem towels for her husband if he required it. It had been given her to choose, and she had chosen. She had found herself unable to tell a man that she loved him when she did not love him, – and equally unable to conceal the love which she did feel. 'If he wheeled a barrow of turnips about the street, I'd marry him to-morrow,' she said to her sister one afternoon as they were sitting together in the room which ought to have been her uncle's study.

'If he wheeled a big barrow, you'd have to wheel a little one,' said her sister.

'Then I'd do it. I shouldn't mind. There has been this advantage in St Diddulph's, that nothing can be triste, nothing dull, nothing ugly after it.'

'It may be so with you, Nora; – that is in imagination.'

'What I mean is that living here has taught me much that I never could have learned in Curzon Street. I used to think myself such a fine young woman, – but, upon my word, I think myself a finer one now.'

'I don't quite know what you mean.'

'I don't quite know myself; but I nearly know. I do know this, that I've made up my own mind about what I mean to do.'

'You'll change it, dear, when Mamma is here, and things are comfortable again. It's my believe that Mr Glascock would come to you again to-morrow if you would let him.' Mrs Trevelyan was, naturally, in complete ignorance of the experience of transatlantic excellence which Mr Glascock had encountered in Italy.

'But I certainly should not let him. How would it be possible after what I wrote to Hugh?'

'All that might pass away,' said Mrs Trevelyan, – slowly, after a long pause.

'All what might pass away? Have I not given him a distinct promise? Have I not told him that I loved him, and sworn that I would be true to him? Can that be made to pass away, – even if one wished it?'

'Of course it can. Nothing need be fixed for you till you have stood at the altar with a man and been made his wife. You may choose still. I can never choose again.'

'I never will, at any rate,' said Nora.

Then there was another pause. 'It seems strange to me, Nora,' said the elder sister, 'that after what you have seen you should be so keen to be married to any one.'

'What is a girl to do?'

'Better drown herself than do as I have done. Only think what there is before me. What I have gone through is nothing to it. Of course I must go back to the Islands. Where else am I to live? Who else will take me?'

'Come to us,' said Nora.

'Us, Nora! Who are the us? But in no way would that be possible. Papa will be here, perhaps, for six months.' Nora thought it quite possible that she might have a home of her own before six months were passed, – even though she might be wheeling the smaller barrow, – but she would not say so. 'And by that time everything must be decided.'

'I suppose it must.'

'Of course papa and mamma must go back,' said Mrs Trevelyan. 'Papa might take a pension. He's entitled to a pension now.'

'He'll never do that as long as he can have employment. They'll go back, and I must go with them. Who else would take me in?'

'I know who would take you in, Emily.'

'My darling, that is romance. As for myself, I should not care where I went. If it were even to remain here, I could bear it.'

'I could not,' said Nora, decisively.

'It is so different with you, dear. I don't suppose it is possible I should take my boy with me to the Islands; and how – am I – to go – anywhere – without him?' Then she broke down, and fell into a paroxysm of sobs, and was in very truth a broken-hearted woman.

Nora was silent for some minutes, but at last she spoke. 'Why do you not go back to him, Emily?'

'How am I to go back to him? What am I to do to make him take me back?' At this very moment Trevelyan was in the house, but they did not know it.

'Write to him,' said Nora.

'What am I to say? In very truth I do believe that he is mad. If I write to him, should I defend myself or accuse myself? A dozen times I have striven to write such a letter, – not that I might send it, but that I might find what I could say should I ever wish to send it. And it is impossible. I can only tell him how unjust he has been, how cruel, how mad, how wicked!'

'Could you not say to him simply this? – "Let us be together, wherever it may be; and let bygones be bygones."'

'While he is watching me with a policeman? While he is still thinking that I entertain a – lover? While he believes that I am the base thing that he has dared to think me?'

'He has never believed it.'

'Then how can he be such a villain as to treat me like this? I could not go to him, Nora; – not unless I went to him as one who was known to be mad, over whom in his wretched condition it would be my duty to keep watch. In no other way could I overcome my abhorrence of the outrages to which he has subjected me.'

'But for the child's sake, Emily.'

'Ah, yes! If it were simply to grovel in the dust before him it should be done. If humiliation would suffice, – or any self-abasement that were possible to me! But I should be false if I said that I look forward to any such possibility. How can he wish to have me back again after what he has said and done? I am his wife, and he has disgraced me before all men by his own words. And what have I done, that I should not have done; – what left undone on his behalf that I should have done?* It is hard that the foolish workings of a weak man's mind should be able so completely to ruin the prospects of a woman's life!'

Nora was beginning to answer this by attempting to show that the husband's madness was, perhaps, only temporary, when there came a knock at the door, and Mrs Outhouse was at once in the room. It will be well that the reader should know what had taken place at the parsonage while the two sisters had been together up-stairs, so that the nature of Mrs Outhouse's mission to them may explain itself. Mr Outhouse had been in his closet down-stairs, when the maid-servant brought word to him that Mr Trevelyan was in the parlour, and was desirous of seeing him.

'Mr Trevelyan!' said the unfortunate clergyman, holding up both his hands. The servant understood the tragic importance of the occasion quite as well as did her master, and simply shook her head. 'Has your mistress seen him?' said the master. The girl again shook her head. 'Ask your mistress to come to me,' said the clergyman. Then the girl disappeared; and in a few minutes Mrs Outhouse, equally imbued with the tragic elements of the day, was with her husband.

Mr Outhouse began by declaring that no consideration should induce him to see Trevelyan, and commissioned his wife to go to the man and tell him that he must leave the house. When the unfortunate woman expressed an opinion that Trevelyan had some legal rights upon which he might probably insist, Mr Outhouse asserted roundly that he could have no legal right to remain in that parsonage against the will of the rector. 'If he wants to claim his wife and child, he must do it by law, – not by force; and thank God, Sir Marmaduke will be here before he can do that.' 'But I can't make him go,' said Mrs Outhouse. 'Tell him that you'll send for a policeman,' said the clergyman.

It had come to pass that there had been messages backwards and forwards between the visitor and the master of the house, all carried by that unfortunate lady. Treveylan did not demand that his wife and child should be given up to him; – did not even, on this occasion, demand that his boy should be surrendered to him, – now, at once. He did say, very repeatedly, that of course he must have his boy, but seemed to imply that, under certain circumstances, he would be willing to take his wife to live with him again. This appeared to Mrs Outhouse to be so manifestly the one thing that was desirable, – to be the only solution of the difficulty that could be admitted as a solution at all, – that she went to work on that hint, and ventured to entertain a hope that a reconciliation might be effected. She implored her husband to lend a hand to the work; – by which she intended to imply that he should not only see Trevelyan, but consent to meet the sinner on friendly terms. But Mr Outhouse was on the occasion even more than customarily obstinate. His wife might do what she liked. He would neither meddle nor make. He would not willingly see Mr Trevelyan in his own house; – unless, indeed, Mr Trevelyan should attempt to force his way up into the nursery. Then he said that which left no doubt on his wife's mind that, should any violence be attempted, her husband would manfully join the mêlée.

But it soon became evident that no such attempt was to be made on that day. Trevelyan was lachrymose, heartbroken, and a sight pitiable to behold. When Mrs Outhouse loudly asserted that his wife had not sinned against him in the least, – 'not in a tittle, Mr Trevelyan,' she repeated over and over again, – he began to assert himself, declaring that she had seen the man in Devonshire, and corresponded with him since she had been at St Diddulph's; and when the lady had declared that the latter assertion was untrue, he had shaken his head, and had told her that perhaps she did not know all. But the misery of the man had its effect upon her, and at last she proposed to be the bearer of a message to his wife. He had demanded to see his child, offering to promise that he would not attempt to take the boy by force on this occasion, – saying, also, that his claim by law was so good, that no force could be necessary. It was proposed by Mrs Outhouse that he should first see the mother, – and to this he at last assented. How blessed a thing would it be if these two persons could be induced to forget the troubles of the last twelve months, and once more to love and trust each other! 'But, sir,' said Mrs Outhouse, putting her hand upon his arm; – 'you must not upbraid her, for she will not bear it.' 'She knows nothing of what is due to a husband,' said Trevelyan, gloomily. The task was not hopeful; but, nevertheless, the poor woman resolved to do her best.

And now Mrs Outhouse was in her niece's room, asking her to go down and see her husband. Little Louis had at the time been with the nurse, and the very moment that the mother heard that the child's father was in the house, she jumped up and rushed away to get possession of her treasure. 'Has he come for baby?' Nora asked in dismay. Then Mrs Outhouse, anxious to obtain a convert to her present views, boldly declared that Mr Trevelyan had no such intention. Mrs Trevelyan came back at once with the boy, and then listened to all her aunt's arguments. 'But I will not take baby with me,' she said. At last it was decided that she should go down alone, and that the child should afterwards be taken to his father in the drawing-room; Mrs Outhouse pledging herself that the whole household should combine in her defence if Mr Trevelyan should attempt to take the child out of that room. 'But what am I to say to him?' she asked.

'Say as little as possible,' said Mrs Outhouse, – 'except to make him understand that he has been in error in imputing fault to you.'

'He will never understand that,' said Mrs Trevelyan.

A considerable time elapsed after that before she could bring herself to descend the stairs. Now that her husband was so near her, and that her aunt had assured her that she might reinstate herself in her position, if she could only abstain from saying hard words to him, she wished that he was away from her again, in Italy. She knew that she could not refrain from hard words. How was it possible that she should vindicate her own honour, without asserting with all her strength that she had been ill-used; and, to speak truth on the matter, her love for the man, which had once been true and eager, had been quelled by the treatment she had received. She had clung to her love in some shape, in spite of the accusations made against her, till she had heard that the policeman had been set upon her heels. Could it be possible that any woman should love a man, or at least that any wife should love a husband, after such usage as that? At last she crept gently down the stairs, and stood at the parlour-door. She listened, and could hear his steps, as he paced backwards and forwards through the room. She looked back, and could see the face of the servant peering round from the kitchen-stairs. She could not endure to be watched in her misery, and, thus driven, she opened the parlour-door. 'Louis,' she said, walking into the room, 'Aunt Mary has desired me to come to you.'

'Emily!' he exclaimed, and ran to her and embraced her. She did not seek to stop him, but she did not return the kiss which he gave her. Then he held her by her hands, had looked into her face, and she could see how strangely he was altered. She thought that she would hardly have known him, had she not been sure that it was he. She herself was also changed. Who can bear sorrow without such change, till age has fixed the lines of the face, or till care has made them hard and unmalleable? But the effect on her was as nothing to that which grief, remorse, and desolation had made on him. He had had no child with him, no sister, no friend. Bozzle had been his only refuge, – a refuge not adapted to make life easier to such a man as Trevelyan; and he, – in spite of the accusations made by himself against his wife, within his own breast hourly since he had left her, – had found it to be very difficult to satisfy his own conscience. He told himself from hour to hour that he knew that he was right; – but in very truth he was ever doubting his own conduct.

'You have been ill, Louis,' she said, looking at him.

'Ill at ease, Emily; – very ill at ease! A sore heart will make the face thin, as well as fever or ague. Since we parted I have not had much to comfort me.'

'Nor have I, – nor any of us,' said she. 'How was comfort to come from such a parting?'

Then they both stood silent together. He was still holding her by the hand, but she was careful not to return his pressure. She would not take her hand away from him; but she would show him no sign of softness till he should have absolutely acquitted her of the accusation he had made against her. 'We are man and wife,' he said after awhile. 'In spite of all that has come and gone I am yours, and you are mine.'

'You should have remembered that always, Louis.'

'I have never forgotten it, – never. In no thought have I been untrue to you. My heart has never changed since first I gave it you.' There came a bitter frown upon her face, of which she was so conscious herself, that she turned her face away from him. She still remembered her lesson, that she was not to anger him, and, therefore, she refrained from answering him at all. But the answer was there, hot within her bosom. Had he loved her, – and yet suspected that she was false to him and to her vows, simply because she had been on terms of intimacy with an old friend? Had he loved her, and yet turned her from his house? Had he loved her, – and set a policeman to watch her? Had he loved her, and yet spoken evil of her to all their friends? Had he loved her, and yet striven to rob her of her child? 'Will you come to me?' he said.

'I suppose it will be better so,' she answered slowly.

'Then you will promise me – ' He paused, and attempted to turn her towards him, so that he might look her in the face.

'Promise what?' she said, quickly glancing round at him, and drawing her hand away from him as she did so.

'That all intercourse with Colonel Osborne shall be at an end.'

'I will make no promise. You come to me to add one insult to another. Had you been a man, you would not have named him to me after what you have done to me.'

'That is absurd. I have a right to demand from you such a pledge. I am willing to believe that you have not – '

'Have not what?'

'That you have not utterly disgraced me.'

'God in heaven, that I should hear this!' she exclaimed. 'Louis Trevelyan, I have not disgraced you at all, – in thought, in word, in deed, in look, or in gesture. It is you that have disgraced yourself, and ruined me, and degraded even your own child.'

'Is this the way in which you welcome me?'

'Certainly it is, – in this way and in no other if you speak to me of what is past, without acknowledging your error.' Her brow became blacker and blacker as she continued to speak to him. 'It would be best that nothing should be said, – not a word. That it all should be regarded as an ugly dream. But, when you come to me and at once go back to it all, and ask me for a promise – '

'Am I to understand then that all idea of submission to your husband is to be at an end?'

'I will submit to no imputation on my honour, – even from you. One would have thought that it would have been for you to preserve it untarnished.'

'And you will give me no assurance as to your future life?'

'None; – certainly none. If you want promises from me, there can be no hope for the future. What am I to promise? That I will not have – a lover? What respect can I enjoy as your wife if such a promise be needed? If you should choose to fancy that it had been broken you would set your policeman to watch me again! Louis, we can never live together again ever with comfort, unless you acknowledge in your own heart that you have used me shamefully.'

'Were you right to see him in Devonshire?'

'Of course I was right. Why should I not see him, – or any one?'

'And you will see him again?'

'When papa comes, of course I shall see him.'

'Then it is hopeless,' said he, turning away from her.

'If that man is to be a source of disquiet to you, it is hopeless,' she answered. 'If you cannot so school yourself that he shall be the same to you as other men, it is quite hopeless. You must still be mad, – as you have been mad hitherto.'

He walked about the room restlessly for a time, while she stood with assumed composure near the window. 'Send me my child,' he said at last.

'He shall come to you, Louis, – for a little; but he is not to be taken out from hence. Is that a promise?'

'You are to exact promises from me, where my own rights are concerned, while you refuse to give me any, though I am entitled to demand them! I order you to send the boy to me. Is he not my own?'

'Is he not mine too? And is he not all that you have left to me?'

He paused again, and then gave the promise. 'Let him be brought to me. He shall not be removed now. I intend to have him. I tell you so fairly. He shall be taken from you unless you come back to me with such assurances as to your future conduct as I have a right to demand. There is much that the law cannot give me. It cannot procure wife-like submission, love, gratitude, or even decent matronly conduct. But that which it can give me, I will have.'

She walked off to the door, and then as she was quitting the room she spoke to him once again. 'Alas, Louis,' she said, 'neither can the law, nor medicine, nor religion, restore to you that fine intellect which foolish suspicions have destroyed.' Then she left him and returned to the room in which her aunt, and Nora, and the child were all clustered together, waiting to learn the effects of the interview. The two women asked their questions with their eyes, rather than with spoken words. 'It is all over,' said Mrs Trevelyan. 'There is nothing left for me but to go back to papa. I only hear the same accusations, repeated again and again, and make myself subject to the old insults.' Then Mrs Outhouse knew that she could interfere no further, and that in truth nothing could be done till the return of Sir Marmaduke should relieve her and her husband from all further active concern in the matter.

But Trevelyan was still down-stairs waiting for the child. At last it was arranged that Nora should take the boy into the drawing-room, and that Mrs Outhouse should fetch the father up from the parlour to the room above it. Angry as was Mrs Trevelyan with her husband, not the less was she anxious to make the boy good-looking and seemly in his father's eyes. She washed the child's face, put on him a clean frill and a pretty ribbon; and, as she did so, she bade him kiss his papa, and speak nicely to him, and love him. 'Poor papa is unhappy,' she said, 'and Louey must be very good to him.' The boy, child though he was, understood much more of what was passing around him than his mother knew. How was he to love papa when mamma did not do so? In some shape that idea had framed itself in his mind; and, as he was taken down, he knew it was impossible that he should speak nicely to his papa. Nora did as she was bidden, and went down to the first-floor. Mrs Outhouse, promising that even if she were put out of the room by Mr Trevelyan she would not stir from the landing outside the door, descended to the parlour and quickly returned with the unfortunate father. Mr Outhouse, in the meantime, was still sitting in his closet, tormented with curiosity, but yet determined not to be seen till the intruder should have left his house.

'I hope you are well, Nora,' he said, as he entered the room with Mrs Outhouse.

'Quite well, thank you, Louis.'

'I am sorry that our troubles should have deprived you of the home you had been taught to expect.' To this Nora made no reply, but escaped, and went up to her sister. 'My poor little boy,' said Trevelyan, taking the child and placing it on his knee. 'I suppose you have forgotten your unfortunate father.' The child, of course, said nothing, but just allowed himself to be kissed.

'He is looking very well,' said Mrs Outhouse.

'Is he? I dare say he is well. Louey, my boy, are you happy?' The question was asked in a voice that was dismal beyond compare, and it also remained unanswered. He had been desired to speak nicely to his papa; but how was it possible that a child should speak nicely under such a load of melancholy? 'He will not speak to me,' said Trevelyan. 'I suppose it is what I might have expected.' Then the child was put off his knee on to the floor, and began to whimper. 'A few months since he would sit there for hours, with his head upon my breast,' said Trevelyan.

'A few months is a long time in the life of such an infant,' said Mrs Outhouse.

'He may go away,' said Trevelyan. Then the child was led out of the room, and sent up to his mother.

'Emily has done all she can to make the child love your memory,' said Mrs Outhouse.

'To love my memory! What; – as though I were dead. I will teach him to love me as I am, Mrs Outhouse. I do not think that it is too late. Will you tell your husband from me, with my compliments, that I shall cause him to be served with a legal demand for the restitution of my child?'

'But Sir Marmaduke will be here in a few days.'

'I know nothing of that. Sir Marmaduke is nothing to me now.

My child is my own, – and so is my wife. Sir Marmaduke has no authority over either one or the other. I find my child here, and it is here that I must look for him. I am sorry that you should be troubled, but the fault does not rest with me. Mr Outhouse has refused to give me up my own child, and I am driven to take such steps for his recovery as the law has put within my reach.'

'Why did you turn your wife out of doors, Mr Trevelyan?' asked Mrs Outhouse boldly.

'I did not turn her out of doors. I provided a fitting shelter for her. I gave her everything that she could want. You know what happened. That man went down and was received there. I defy you, Mrs Outhouse, to say that it was my fault.'

Mrs Outhouse did attempt to show him that it was his fault; but while she was doing so he left the house. 'I don't think she could go back to him,' said Mrs Outhouse to her husband. 'He is quite insane upon this matter.'

'I shall be insane, I know,' said Mr Outhouse, 'if Sir Marmaduke does not come home very quickly.' Nevertheless he quite ignored any legal power that might be brought to bear against him as to the restitution of the child to its father.

61

Parker's Hotel, Mowbray Street

Within a week of the occurrence which is related in the last chapter, there came a telegram from Southampton to the parsonage at St Diddulph's, saying that Sir Marmaduke and Lady Rowley had reached England. On the evening of that day they were to lodge at a small family hotel in Baker Street, and both Mrs Trevelyan and Nora were to be with them. The leave-taking at the parsonage was painful, as on both sides there existed a feeling that affection and sympathy were wanting. The uncle and aunt had done their duty, and both Mrs Trevelyan and Nora felt that they ought to have been demonstrative and cordial in their gratitude; – but they found it impossible to become so. And the rector could not pretend but that he was glad to be rid of his guests. There were, too, some last words about money to be spoken, which were grievous thorns in the poor man's flesh. Two bank notes, however, were put upon his table, and he knew that unless he took them he could not pay for the provisions which his unwelcome visitors had consumed. Surely there never was a man so cruelly ill-used as had been Mr Outhouse in all this matter. 'Another such winter as that would put me in my grave,' he said, when his wife tried to comfort him after they were gone. 'I know that they have both been very good to us,' said Mrs Trevelyan, as she and her sister, together with the child and the nurse, hurried away towards Baker Street in a cab, 'but I have never for a moment felt that they were glad to have us.' 'But how could they have been glad to have us,' she added afterwards, 'when we brought such trouble with us?' But they to whom they were going now would receive her with joy; − would make her welcome with all her load of sorrows, would give to her a sympathy which it was impossible that she should receive from others. Though she might not be happy now, − for in truth how could she be ever really happy again, − there would be a joy to her in placing her child in her mother's arms, and in receiving her father's warm caresses. That her father would be very vehement in his anger against her husband she knew well, − for Sir Marmaduke was a vehement man. But there would be some support for her in the very violence of his wrath, and at this moment it was such support that she most needed. As they journeyed together in the cab, the married sister seemed to be in the higher spirits of the two. She was sure, at any rate, that those to whom she was going would place themselves on her side. Nora had her own story to tell about Hugh Stanbury, and was by no means so sure that her tale would be received with cordial agreement. 'Let me tell them myself,' she whispered to her sister. 'Not to-night, because they will have so much to say to you; but I shall tell mamma to-morrow.'

The train by which the Rowleys were to reach London was due at the station at 7.30 p.m., and the two sisters timed their despatch from St Diddulph's so as to enable them to reach the hotel at eight. 'We shall be there now before mamma,' said Nora, 'becuase they will have so much luggage, and so many things, and the trains are always late.' When they started from the door of the parsonage, Mr Outhouse gave the direction to the cabman, 'Gregg's Hotel, Baker Street.' Then at once he began to console himself in that they were gone.

It was a long drive from St Diddulph's in the east, to Marylebone in the west, of London. None of the party in the cab knew anything of the region through which they passed. The cabman took the line by the back of the bank, and Finsbury Square and the City Road, thinking it best, probably, to avoid the crush at Holborn Hill, though at the expense of something of a circuit. But of this Mrs Trevelyan and Nora knew nothing. Had their way taken them along Piccadilly, or through Mayfair, or across Grosvenor Square, they would have known where they were; but at present they were not thinking of those once much-loved localities. The cab passed the Angel, and up and down the hill at Pentonville, and by the King's Cross stations, and through Euston Square, – and then it turned up Gower Street. Surely the man should have gone on along the New Road,* now that he had come so far out of his way. But of this the two ladies knew nothing, – nor did the nurse. It was a dark, windy night, but the lamps in the streets had given them light, so that they had not noticed the night. Nor did they notice it now as the streets became narrower and darker. They were hardly thinking that their journey was yet at an end, and the mother was in the act of covering her boy's face as he lay asleep on the nurse's lap, when the car was stopped. Nora looking out through the window, saw the word 'Hotel' over a doorway, and was satisfied. 'Shall I take the child, ma'am?' said a man in black, and the child was handed out. Nora was the first to follow, and she then perceived that the door of the hotel was not open. Mrs Trevelyan followed; and then they looked round them, – and the child was gone. They heard the rattle of another cab as it was carried away at a gallop round a distant corner; – and then some inkling of what had happened came upon them. The father had succeeded in getting possession of his child.

It was a narrow, dark street, very quiet, having about it a certain air of poor respectability, – an obscure, noiseless street, without even a sign of life. Some unfortunate one had endeavoured here to keep an hotel; – but there was no hotel kept there now. There had been much craft in selecting the place in which the child had been taken from them. As they looked around them, perceiving the terrible misfortune which had befallen them, there was not a human being near them save the cabman, who was occupied in unchaining, or pretending to unchain the heavy mass of luggage on the roof. The windows of the house before which they were stopping, were closed, and Nora perceived at once that the hotel was not inhabited. The cabman must have perceived it also. As for the man who had taken the child, the nurse could only say that he was dressed in black, like a waiter, that he had a napkin under his arm, and no hat on his head. He had taken the boy tenderly in his arms, – and then she had seen nothing further. The first thing that Nora had seen, as she stood on the pavement, was the other cab moving off rapidly.

Mrs Trevelyan had staggered against the railings, and was soon screaming in her wretchedness. Before long there was a small crowd around them, comprising three or four women, a few boys, an old man or two, – and a policeman. To the policeman Nora had soon told the whole story, and the cabman was of course attacked. But the cabman played his part very well. He declared that he had done just what he had been told to do. Nora was indeed sure that she had heard her uncle desire him to drive to Gregg's Hotel in Baker Street. The cabman in answer to this, declared that he had not clearly heard the old gentleman's directions; but that a man whom he had conceived to be a servant, had very plainly told him to drive to Parker's Hotel, Mowbray Street, Gower Street. 'I comed ever so far out of my way,' said the cabman, 'to avoid the rumpus with the homnibuses at the hill, – cause the ladies' things is so heavy we'd never got up if the 'orse had once jibbed.' All which, though it had nothing to do with the matter, seemed to impress the policeman with the idea that the cabman, if not a true man, was going to be too clever for them on this occasion. And the crafty cabman went on to declare that his horse was so tired with the load that he could not go on to Baker Street. They must get another cab. Take his number! Of course they could take his number. There was his number. His fare was four and six, – that is if the ladies wouldn't pay him anything extra for the terrible load; and he meant to have it. It would be sixpence more if they kept him there many minutes longer. The number was taken, and another cab was got, and the luggage was transferred, and the money was paid, while the unhappy mother was still screaming in hysterics against the railings. What had been done was soon clear enough to all those around her. Nora had told the policeman, and had told one of the women, thinking to obtain their sympathy and assistance. 'It's the kid's dada as has taken it,' said one man, 'and there ain't nothing to be done.' There was nothing to be done; – nothing at any rate then and there.

Nora had been very eager that the cabman should be arrested; but the policeman assured her that such an arrest was out of the question, and would have been useless had it been possible. The man would be forthcoming if his presence should be again desired, but he had probably, – so said the policeman, – really been desired to drive to Mowbray Street. 'They knows where to find me if they want's me, – only I must be paid my time,' said the cabman confidently. And the policeman was of opinion that as the boy had been kidnapped on behalf of the father, no legal steps could be taken either for the recovery of the child or for the punishment of the perpetrators of the act. He got up, however, on the box of the cab, and accompanied the party to the hotel in Baker Street. They reached it almost exactly at the same time with Sir Marmaduke and Lady Rowley, and the reader must imagine the confusion, the anguish, and the disappointment of that meeting. Mrs Trevelyan was hardly in possession of her senses when she reached her mother, and could not be induced to be tranquil even when she was assured by her father that her son would suffer no immediate evil by being transferred to his father's hands. She in her frenzy declared that she would never see her little one again, and seemed to think that the father might not improbably destroy the child. 'He is mad, papa, and does not know what he does. Do you mean to say that a madman may do as he pleases ? – that he may rob my child from me in the streets ? – that he may take him out of my very arms in that way ?' And she was almost angry with her father because no attempt was made that night to recover the boy.

Sir Marmaduke, who was not himself a good lawyer, had been closeted with the policeman for a quarter of an hour, and had learned the policeman's views. Of course, the father of the child was the person who had done the deed. Whether the cabman had been in the plot or not, was not matter of much consequence. There could be no doubt that some one had told the man to go to Parker's Hotel, as the cab was starting ; and it would probably be impossible to punish him in the teeth of such instructions. Sir Marmaduke, however, could doubtless have the cabman summoned. And as for the absolute abduction of the child, the policeman was of opinion that a father could not be punished for obtaining possession of his son by such a stratagem, unless the custody of the child had been made over to the mother by some court of law. The policeman, indeed, seemed to think that nothing could be done, and Sir Marmaduke was inclined to agree with him. When this was explained to Mrs Trevelyan by her mother, she again became hysterical in her agony, and could hardly be restrained from going forth herself to look for her lost treasure.

It need hardly be further explained that Trevelyan had planned the stratagem in concert with Mr Bozzle. Bozzle, though strongly cautioned by his wife to keep himself out of danger in the matter, was sorely tempted by his employer's offer of a hundred pounds. He positively refused to be a party to any attempt at violence at St Diddulph's ; but when he learned, as he did learn, that Mrs Trevelyan, with her sister and baby, were to be transferred from St Diddulph's in a cab to Baker Street, and that the journey was luckily to be made during the shades of evening, his active mind went to work, and he arranged the plan. There were many difficulties, and even some pecuniary difficulty. He bargained that he should have his hundred pounds clear of all deduction for expenses, – and then the attendant expenses were not insignificant. It was necessary that there should be four men in the service, all good and true; and men require to be well paid for such goodness and truth. There was the man, himself an ex-policeman, who gave the instructions to the first cabman, as he was starting. The cabman would not undertake the job at all unless he were so instructed on the spot, asserting that in this way he would be able to prove that the orders he obeyed came from the lady's husband. And there was the crafty pseudo-waiter, with the napkin and no hat, who had carried the boy to the cab in which his father was sitting. And there were the two cabmen. Bozzle planned it all, and with some difficulty arranged the preliminaries. How successful was the scheme, we have seen; and Bozzle, for a month, was able to assume a superiority over his wife, which that honest woman found to be very disagreeable. 'There ain't no fraudulent abduction in it at all,' Bozzle exclaimed, 'because a wife ain't got no rights again her husband, – not in such a matter as that.' Mrs Bozzle implied that if her husband were to take her child away from her without her leave, she'd let him know something about it. But as the husband had in his possession the note for a hundred pounds, realized, Mrs Bozzle had not much to say in support of her view of the case.

On the morning after the occurrence, while Sir Marmaduke was waiting with his solicitor upon a magistrate to find whether anything could be done, the following letter was brought to Mrs Trevelyan at Gregg's Hotel:

Our child is safe with me, and will remain so. If you care to obtain legal advice you will find that I as his father have a right to keep him under my protection. I shall do so; but will allow you to see him as soon as I shall have received a full guarantee that you have no idea of withdrawing him from my charge.

A home for yourself with me is still open to you, – on condition that you will give me the promise that I have demanded from you; and as long as I shall not hear that you again see or communicate with the person to whose acquaintance I object. While you remain away from me I will cause you to be paid £50 a month, as I do not wish that you should be a burden on others. But this payment will depend also on your not seeing or holding any communication with the person to whom I have alluded.

> Your affectionate and offended husband,
> Louis Trevelyan

A letter addressed to The Acrobats Club will reach me.

Sir Rowley came home dispirited and unhappy, and could not give much comfort to his daughter. The magistrate had told him that though the cabman might probably be punished for taking the ladies otherwise than as directed, – if the direction to Baker Street could be proved, – nothing could be done to punish the father. The magistrate explained that under a certain Act of Parliament the mother might apply to the Court of Chancery for the custody of any children under seven years of age, and that the court would probably grant such custody, – unless it were shown that the wife had left her husband without sufficient cause. The magistrate could not undertake to say whether or no sufficient cause had here been given; – or whether the husband was in fault or the wife. It was, however, clear that nothing could be done without application to the Court of Chancery. It appeared, – so said the magistrate, – that the husband had offered a home to his wife, and that in offering it he had attempted to impose no conditions which could be shown to be cruel before a judge. The magistrate thought that Mr Trevelyan had done nothing illegal in taking the child from the cab. Sir Marmaduke, on hearing this, was of opinion that nothing could be gained by legal interference. His private desire was to get hold of Trevelyan and pull him limb from limb. Lady Rowley thought that her daughter had better go back to her husband, let the future consequences be what they might. And the poor desolate mother herself had almost brought herself to offer to do so, having in her brain some idea that she would after a while be able to escape with her boy. As for love for her husband, certainly there was none now left in her bosom. Nor could she teach herself to think it possible that she should ever live with him again on friendly terms. But she would submit to anything with the object of getting back her boy. Three or four letters were written to Mr Trevelyan in as many days from his wife, from Lady Rowley, and from Nora; in which various overtures were made. Trevelyan wrote once again to his wife. She knew, he said, already the terms on which she might come back. These terms were still open to her. As for the boy, he certainly should not leave his father. A meeting might be planned on condition that he, Trevelyan, were provided with a written assurance from his wife that she would not endeavour to remove the boy, and that he himself should be present at the meeting.

Thus the first week was passed after Sir Marmaduke's return, – and a most wretched time it was for all the party at Gregg's Hotel.

62

Lady Rowley Makes an Attempt

Nothing could be more uncomfortable than the state of Sir Marmaduke Rowley's family for the first ten days after the arrival in London of the Governor of the Mandarin Islands. Lady Rowley had brought with her two of her girls, – the third and fourth, – and, as we know, had been joined by the two eldest, so that there was a large family of ladies gathered together. A house had been taken in Manchester Street, to which they had intended to transfer themselves after a single night passed at Gregg's Hotel. But the trouble and sorrow inflicted upon them by the abduction of Mrs Trevelyan's child, and the consequent labours thrust upon Sir Marmaduke's shoulders had been so heavy, that they had slept six nights at the hotel, before they were able to move themselves into the house prepared for them. By that time all idea had been abandoned of recovering the child by any legal means to be taken as a consequence of the illegality of the abduction. The boy was with his father, and the lawyers seemed to think that the father's rights were paramount, – as he had offered a home to his wife without any conditions which a court of law would adjudge to be cruel. If she could show that he had driven her to live apart from him by his own bad conduct, then probably the custody of her boy might be awarded to her, until the child should be seven years old. But when the circumstances of the case were explained to Sir Marmaduke's lawyer by Lady Rowley, that gentleman shook his head. Mrs Trevelyan had, he said, no case with which she could go into court. Then by degrees there were words whispered as to the husband's madness. The lawyer said that that was a matter for the doctors. If a certain amount of medical evidence could be obtained to show that the husband was in truth mad, the wife could, no doubt, obtain the custody of the child. When this was reported to Mrs Trevelyan, she declared that conduct such as her husband's must suffice to prove any man to be mad; but at this Sir Marmaduke shook his head, and Lady Rowley sat, sadly silent, with her daughter's hand within her own. They would not dare to tell her that she could regain her child by that plea.

During those ten days they did not learn whither the boy had been carried, nor did they know even where the father might be found. Sir Marmaduke followed up the address as given in the letter, and learned from the porter at 'The Acrobats' that the gentleman's letters were sent to No 55, Stony Walk, Union Street, Borough. To this uncomfortable locality Sir Marmaduke travelled more than once. Thrice he went thither, intent on finding his son-in-law's residence. On the two first occasions he saw no one but Mrs Bozzle; and the discretion of that lady in declining to give any information was most admirable. 'Trewillian!' Yes, she had heard the name certainly. It might be that her husband had business engagements with a gent of that name. She would not say even that for certain, as it was not her custom ever to make any inquiries as to her husband's business engagements. Her husband's business engagements were, she said, much too important for the 'likes of she' to know anything about them. When was Bozzle likely to be at home? Bozzle was never likely to be at home. According to her showing, Bozzle was of all husbands the most erratic. He might perhaps come in for an hour or two in the middle of the day on a Wednesday, or perhaps would take a cup of tea at home on Friday evening. But anything so fitful and uncertain as were Bozzle's appearances in the bosom of his family was not to be conceived in the mind of woman. Sir Marmaduke then called in the middle of the day on Wednesday, but Bozzle was reported to be away in the provinces. His wife had no idea in which of the provinces he was at that moment engaged. The persevering governor from the islands called again on the Friday evening, and then, by chance, Bozzle was found at home. But Sir Marmaduke succeeded in gaining very little information even from Bozzle. The man acknowledged that he was employed by Mr Trevelyan. Any letter or parcel left with him for Mr Trevelyan should be duly sent to that gentleman. If Sir Marmaduke wanted Mr Trevelyan's address, he could write to Mr Trevelyan and ask for it. If Mr Trevelyan declined to give it, was it likely that he, Bozzle, should betray it? Sir Marmaduke explained who he was at some length. Bozzle with a smile assured the governor that he knew very well who he was. He let drop a few words to show that he was intimately acquainted with the whole course of Sir Marmaduke's family affairs. He knew all about the Mandarins, and Colonel Osborne, and Gregg's Hotel, – not that he said anything about Parker's Hotel, – and the Colonial Office. He spoke of Miss Nora, and even knew the names of the other two young ladies, Miss Sophia and Miss Lucy. It was a weakness with Bozzle, – that of displaying his information. He would have much liked to be able to startle Sir Marmaduke by describing the Government House in the island, or by telling him something of his old carriage-horses. But of such information as Sir Marmaduke desired, Sir Marmaduke got none.

And there were other troubles which fell very heavily upon the poor governor, who had come home as it were for a holiday, and who was a man hating work naturally, and who, from the circumstances of his life, had never been called on to do much work. A man may govern the Mandarins and yet live in comparative idleness. To do such governing work well a man should have a good presence, a flow of words which should mean nothing, an excellent temper, and a love of hospitality. With these attributes Sir Rowley was endowed; for, though his disposition was by nature hot, for governing purposes it had been brought by practice under good control. He had now been summoned home through the machinations of his dangerous old friend Colonel Osborne, in order that he might give the results of his experience in governing before a committee of the House of Commons. In coming to England on this business he had thought much more of his holiday, of his wife and children, of his daughters at home, of his allowance per day while he was to be away from his government, and of his salary to be paid to him entire during his absence, instead of being halved as it would be if he were away on leave, – he had thought much more in coming home on these easy and pleasant matters, than he did on the work that was to be required from him when he arrived. And then it came to pass that he felt himself almost injured, when the Colonial Office demanded his presence from day to day, and when clerks bothered him with questions as to which they expected ready replies, but in replying to which Sir Marmaduke was by no means ready. The working men at the Colonial Office had not quite thought that Sir Marmaduke was the most fitting man for the job in hand. There was a certain Mr Thomas Smith at another set of islands in quite another part of the world, who was supposed by these working men at home to be a very paragon of a governor. If he had been had home, – so said the working men, – no Committee of the House would have been able to make anything of him. They might have asked him questions week after week, and he would have answered them all fluently and would have committed nobody. He knew all the ins and outs of governing, – did Mr Thomas Smith, – and was a match for the sharpest Committee that ever sat at Westminster. Poor Sir Marmaduke was a man of a very different sort; all of which was known by the working men; but the Parliamentary interest had been too strong, and here was Sir Marmaduke at home. But the working men were not disposed to make matters so pleasant for Sir Marmaduke, as Sir Marmaduke had expected. The Committee would not examine Sir Marmaduke till after Easter, in the middle of April; but it was expected of him that he should read blue-books without number, and he was so catechised by the working men that he almost began to wish himself back at the Mandarins. In this way the new establishment in Manchester Street was not at first in a happy or even in a contented condition.

At last, after about ten days, Lady Rowley did succeed in obtaining an interview with Trevelyan. A meeting was arranged through Bozzle, and took place in a very dark and gloomy room at an inn in the City. Why Bozzle should have selected the Bremen Coffee House, in Poulter's Alley, for this meeting no fit reason can surely be given, unless it was that he conceived himself bound to select the most dreary locality within his knowledge on so melancholy an occasion. Poulter's Alley is a narrow dark passage somewhere behind the Mansion House; and the Bremen Coffee House, – why so called no one can now tell, – is one of those strange houses of public resort in the City at which the guests seem never to eat, never to drink, never to sleep, but to come in and out after a mysterious and almost ghostly fashion, seeing their friends, – or perhaps their enemies, in nooks and corners, and carrying on their conferences in low melancholy whispers. There is an aged waiter at the Bremen Coffee House; and there is certainly one private sitting-room up-stairs. It was a dingy, ill-furnished room, with an old large mahogany table, an old horse-hair sofa, six horse-hair chairs, two old round mirrors, and an old mahogany press in a corner. It was a chamber so sad in its appearance that no wholesome useful work could have been done within it; nor could men have eaten there with any appetite, or have drained the flowing bowl with any touch of joviality. It was generally used for such purposes as that to which it was not appropriated, and no doubt had been taken by Bozzle on more than one previous occasion. Here Lady Rowley arrived precisely at the hour fixed, and was told that the gentleman was waiting up-stairs for her.

There had, of course, been many family consultations as to the manner in which this meeting should be arranged. Should Sir Marmaduke accompany his wife; – or, perhaps, should Sir Marmaduke go alone? Lady Rowley had been very much in favour of meeting Mr Trevelyan without any one to assist her in the conference. As for Sir Marmaduke, no meeting could be concluded between him and his son-in-law without a personal, and probably a violent quarrel. Of that Lady Rowley had been quite sure. Sir Marmaduke, since he had been home, had, in the midst of his various troubles, been driven into so vehement a state of indignation against his son-in-law as to be unable to speak of the wretched man without strongest terms of opprobrium. Nothing was too bad to be said by him of one who had ill-treated his dearest daughter. It must be admitted that Sir Marmaduke had heard only one side of the question. He had questioned his daughter, and had constantly seen his old friend Osborne. The colonel's journey down to Devonshire had been made to appear the most natural proceeding in the world. The correspondence of which Trevelyan thought so much had been shown to consist of such notes as might pass between any old gentleman and any young woman. The promise which Trevelyan had endeavoured to exact, and which Mrs Trevelyan had declined to give, appeared to the angry father to be a monstrous insult. He knew that the colonel was an older man than himself, and his Emily was still to him only a young girl. It was incredible to him that anybody should have regarded his old comrade as his daughter's lover. He did not believe that anybody had, in truth, so regarded the man. The tale had been a monstrous invention on the part of the husband, got up because he had become tired of his young wife. According to Sir Marmaduke's way of thinking, Trevelyan should either be thrashed within an inch of his life, or else locked up in a mad-house. Colonel Osborne shook his head, and expressed a conviction that the poor man was mad.

But Lady Rowley was more hopeful. Though she was as confident about her daughter as was the father, she was less confident about the old friend. She, probably, was alive to that fact that a man of fifty might put on the airs and assume the character of a young lover; and acting on that suspicion, entertaining also some hope that bad as matters now were they might be mended, she had taken care that Colonel Osborne and Mrs Trevelyan should not be brought together. Sir Marmaduke had fumed, but Lady Rowley had been firm. 'If you think so, mamma,' Mrs Trevelyan had said, with something of scorn in her tone, – 'of course let it be so.' Lady Rowley had said that it would be better so; and the two had not seen each other since the memorable visit to Nuncombe Putney. And now Lady Rowley was about to meet her son-in-law with some slight hope that she might arrange affairs. She was quite aware that present indignation, though certainly a gratification, might be indulged in at much too great a cost. It would be better for all reasons that Emily should go back to her husband and her home, and that Trevelyan should be forgiven for his iniquities.

Bozzle was at the tavern during the interview, but he was not seen by Lady Rowley. He remained seated down-stairs, in one of the dingy corners, ready to give assistance to his patron should assistance be needed. When Lady Rowley was shown into the gloomy sitting-room by the old waiter, she found Trevelyan alone, standing in the middle of the room, and waiting for her. 'This is a sad occasion,' he said, as he advanced to give her his hand.

'A very sad occasion, Louis.'

'I do not know what you may have heard of what has occurred, Lady Rowley. It is natural, however, to suppose that you must have heard me spoken of with censure.'

'I think my child has been ill used, Louis,' she replied.

'Of course you do. I could not expect that it should be otherwise. When it was arranged that I should meet you here, I was quite aware that you would have taken the side against me before you had heard my story. It is I that have been ill used, – cruelly misused; but I do not expect that you should believe me. I do not wish you to do. I would not for worlds separate the mother from her daughter.'

'But why have you separated your own wife from her child?'

'Because it was my duty. What! Is a father not to have the charge of his own son. I have done nothing, Lady Rowley, to justify a separation which is contrary to the laws of nature.'

'Where is the boy, Louis?'

'Ah; – that is just what I am not prepared to tell any one who has taken my wife's side till I know that my wife has consented to pay to me that obedience which I, as her husband, have a right to demand. If Emily will do as I request of her, – as I command her,' – as Trevelyan said this, he spoke in a tone which was intended to give the highest possible idea of his own authority and dignity, – 'then she may see her child without delay.'

'What is it you request of my daughter?'

'Obedience; – simply that. Submission to my will, which is surely a wife's duty. Let her beg my pardon for what has occurred, – '

'She cannot do that, Louis.'

'And solemnly promise me,' continued Trevelyan, not deigning to notice Lady Rowley's interruption, 'that she will hold no further intercourse with that snake in the grass who wormed his way into my house, – let her be humble, and penitent, and affectionate, and then she shall be restored to her husband and to her child.' He said this walking up and down the room, and waving his hand, as though he were making a speech that was intended to be eloquent, – as though he had conceived that he was to overcome his mother-in-law by the weight of his words and the magnificence of his demeanour. And yet his demeanour was ridiculous, and his words would have had no weight had they not tended to show Lady Rowley how little prospect there was that she should be able to heal this breach. He himself, too, was so altered in appearance since she had last seen him, bright with the hopes of his young married happiness, that she would hardly have recognised him had she met him in the street. He was thin, and pale, and haggard, and mean. And as he stalked up and down the room, it seemed to her that the very character of the man was changed. She had not previously known him to be pompous, unreasonable, and absurd. She did not answer him at once, as she perceived that he had not finished his address; – and, after a moment's pause, he continued. 'Lady Rowley, there is nothing I would not have done for your daughter, – for my wife. All that I had was hers. I did not dictate to her any mode of life; I required from her no sacrifices; I subjected her to no caprices; but I was determined to be master in my own house.'

'I do not think, Louis, that she has ever denied your right to be master.'

'To be master in my own house, and to be paramount in my influence over her. So much I had a right to demand.'

'Who has denied your right?'

'She has submitted herself to the counsels and to the influences of a man who has endeavoured to undermine me in her affection. In saying that I make my accusation as light against her as is possible. I might make it much heavier, and yet not sin against the truth.'

'This is an illusion, Louis.'

'Ah; – well. No doubt it becomes you to defend your child. Was it an illusion when he went to Devonshire? Was it an illusion when he corresponded with her, – contrary to my express orders, – both before and after that unhallowed journey? Lady Rowley, there must be no more such illusions. If my wife means to come back to me, and to have her child in her own hands, she must be penitent as regards the past, and obedient as regards the future.'

There was a wicked bitterness in that word penitent which almost maddened Lady Rowley. She had come to this meeting believing that Trevelyan would be rejoiced to take back his wife, if details could be arranged for his doing so which should not subject him to the necessity of crying, peccavi;* but she found him speaking of his wife as though he would be doing her the greatest possible favour in allowing her to come back to him dressed in sackcloth, and with ashes on her head. She could understand from what she had heard that his tone and manner were much changed since he obtained possession of the child, and that he now conceived that he had his wife within his power. That he should become a tyrant because he had the power to tyrannise was not in accordance with her former conception of the man's character; – but then he was so changed, that she felt that she knew nothing of the man who now stood before her. 'I cannot acknowledge that my daughter has done anything that requires penitence,' said Lady Rowley.

'I dare say not; – but my view is different.'

'She cannot admit herself to be wrong when she knows herself to be right. You would not have her confess to a fault, the very idea of which has always been abhorrent to her ?'

'She must be crushed in spirit, Lady Rowley, before she can again become a pure and happy woman.'

'This is more than I can bear,' said Lady Rowley, now, at last, worked up to a fever of indignation. 'My daughter, sir, is as pure a woman as you have ever known, or are likely to know. You, who should have protected her against the world, will some day take blame to yourself as you remember that you have so cruelly maligned her.' Then she walked away to the door, and would not listen to the words which he was hurling after her. She went down the stairs, and out of the house, and at the end of Poulter's Alley found the cab which was waiting for her.

Trevelyan, as soon as he was alone, rang the bell, and sent for Bozzle. And while the waiter was coming to him, and until his myrmidon had appeared, he continued to stalk up and down the room, waving his hand in the air as though he were continuing his speech. 'Bozzle,' said he, as soon as the man had closed the door, 'I have changed my mind.'

'As how, Mr Trewillian ?'

'I shall make no further attempt. I have done all that man can do, and have done it in vain. Her father and mother uphold her in her conduct, and she is lost to me, – for ever.'

'But the boy, Mr T. ?'

'I have my child. Yes, – I have my child. Poor infant. Bozzle, I look to you to see that none of them learn our retreat.'

'As for that, Mr Trewillian, – why facts is to be come at by one party pretty well as much as by another. Now, suppose the things was changed, wicey warsey, – and as I was hacting for the Colonel's party.'

'D – the Colonel !' exclaimed Trevelyan.

'Just so, Mr Trewillian ; but if I was hacting for the other party, and they said to me, "Bozzle, – where's the boy ?" why, in three days I'd be down on the facts. Facts is open, Mr Trewillian, if you knows where to look for them.'

'I shall take him abroad, – at once.'

'Think twice of it, Mr T. The boy is so young, you see, and a mother's 'art is softer and lovinger than anything. I'd think twice of it, Mr T., before I kept 'em apart.' This was a line of thought which

Mr Bozzle's conscience had not forced him to entertain to the prejudice of his professional arrangements; but now, as he conversed with his employer, and became by degrees aware of the failure of Trevelyan's mind, some shade of remorse came upon him, and made him say a word on behalf of the 'other party.'

'Am I not always thinking of it? What else have they left me to think of? That will do for to-day. You had better come down to me to-morrow afternoon.' Bozzle promised obedience to these instructions, and as soon as his patron had started he paid the bill, and took himself home.

Lady Rowley, as she travelled back to her house in Manchester Street, almost made up her mind that the separation between her daughter and her son-in-law had better be continued. It was a very sad conclusion to which to come, but she could not believe that any high-spirited woman could long continue to submit herself to the caprices of a man so unreasonable and dictatorial as he to whom she had just been listening. Were it not for the boy, there would, she felt, be no doubt upon the matter. And now, as matters stood, she thought that it should be their great object to regain possession of the child. Then she endeavoured to calculate what would be the result to her daughter, if in very truth it should be found that the wretched man was mad. To hope for such a result seemed to her to be very wicked; — and yet she hardly knew how not to hope for it.

'Well, mamma,' said Emily Trevelyan, with a faint attempt at a smile, 'you saw him?'

'Yes, dearest, I saw him. I can only say that he is a most unreasonable man.'

'And he would tell you nothing of Louey?'

'No dear, — not a word.'

63

Sir Marmaduke at Home

Nora Rowley had told her lover that there was to be no further communication between them till her father and mother should be in England; but in telling him so, had so frankly confessed her own affection for him and had so sturdily promised to be true to him, that no lover could have been reasonably aggrieved by such an interdiction. Nora was quite conscious of this, and was aware that Hugh Stanbury had received such encouragement as ought at any rate to bring him to the new Rowley establishment, as soon as he should learn where it had fixed itself. But when at the end of ten days he had not shown himself, she began to feel doubts. Could it be that he had changed his mind, that he was unwilling to encounter refusal from her father, or that he had found, on looking into his own affairs more closely, that it would be absurd for him to propose to take a wife to himself while his means were so poor and so precarious? Sir Marmaduke during this time had been so unhappy, so fretful, so indignant, and so much worried, that Nora herself had become almost afraid of him; and, without much reasoning on the matter, had taught herself to believe that Hugh might be actuated by similar fears. She had intended to tell her mother of what had occurred between her and Stanbury the first moment that she and Lady Rowley were together; but then there had fallen upon them that terrible incident of the loss of the child, and the whole family had become at once so wrapped up in the agony of the bereaved mother, and so full of rage against the unreasonable father, that there seemed to Nora to be no possible opportunity for the telling of her own love-story. Emily herself appeared to have forgotten it in the midst of her own misery, and had not mentioned Hugh Stanbury's name since they had been in Manchester Street. We have all felt how on occasions our own hopes and fears, nay, almost our own individuality, become absorbed in and obliterated by the more pressing cares and louder voices of those around us. Nora hardly dared to allude to herself while her sister's grief was still so prominent, and while her father was daily complaining of his own personal annoyances at the Colonial Office. It seemed to her that at such a moment she could not introduce a new matter for dispute, and perhaps a new subject of dismay.

Nevertheless, as the days passed by, and as she saw nothing of Hugh Stanbury, her heart became sore and her spirit vexed. It seemed to her that if she were now deserted by him, all the world would be over for her. The Glascock episode in her life had passed by, — that episode which might have been her history, which might have been a history so prosperous, so magnificent, and probably so happy. As she thought of herself and of circumstances as they had happened to her, of the resolutions which she had made as to her own career when she first came to London, and of the way in which she had thrown all those resolutions away in spite of the wonderful success which had come in her path, she could not refrain from thinking that she had brought herself to shipwreck by her own indecision. It must not be imagined that she regretted what she had done. She knew very well that to have acted otherwise than she did when Mr Glascock came to her at Nuncombe Putney would have proved her to be heartless, selfish, and unwomanly. Long before that time she had determined that it was her duty to marry a rich man, – and, if possible, a man in high position. Such a one had come to her, – one endowed with all the good things of the world beyond her most sanguine expectation, – and she had rejected him! She knew that she had been right because she had allowed herself to love the other man. She did not repent what she had done, the circumstances being as they were, but she almost regretted that she had been so soft in heart, so susceptible of the weakness of love, so little able to do as she pleased with herself. Of what use to her was it that she loved this man with all her strength of affection when he never came to her, although the time at which he had been told that he might come was now ten days past?

She was sitting one afternoon in the drawing-room listlessly reading, or pretending to read, a novel, when, on a sudden, Hugh Stanbury was announced. The circumstances of the moment were most unfortunate for such a visit. Sir Marmaduke, who had been down at Whitehall in the morning, and from thence had made a journey to St Diddulph's-in-the-East and back, was exceedingly cross and out of temper. They had told him at his office that they feared he would not suffice to carry through the purpose for which he had been brought home. And his brother-in-law, the parson, had expressed to him an opinion that he was in great part responsible for the misfortune of his daughter, by the encouragement which he had given to such a man as Colonel Osborne. Sir Marmaduke had in consequence quarrelled both with the chief clerk and with Mr Outhouse, and had come home surly and discontented. Lady Rowley and her eldest daughter were away, closeted at the moment with Lady Milborough, with whom they were endeavouring to arrange some plan by which the boy might at any rate be given back. Poor Emily Trevelyan was humble enough now to Lady Milborough, – was prepared to be humble to any one, and in any circumstances, so that she should not be required to acknowledge that she had entertained Colonel Osborne as her lover. The two younger girls, Sophy and Lucy, were in the room when Stanbury was announced, as were also Sir Marmaduke, who at that very moment was uttering angry growls at the obstinacy and want of reason with which he had been treated by Mr Outhouse. Now Sir Marmaduke had not so much as heard the name of Hugh Stanbury as yet; and Nora, though her listlessness was all at an end, at once felt how impossible it would be to explain any of the circumstances of her case in such an interview as this. While, however, Hugh's dear steps were heard upon the stairs, her feminine mind at once went to work to ascertain in what best mode, with what most attractive reason for his presence, she might introduce the young man to her father. Had not the girls been then present, she thought that it might have been expedient to leave Hugh to tell his own story to Sir Marmaduke. But she had no opportunity of sending her sisters away; and, unless chance should remove them, this could not be done.

'He is son of the lady we were with at Nuncombe Putney,' she whispered to her father as she got up to move across the room to welcome her lover. Now Sir Marmaduke had expressed great disapproval of that retreat to Dartmoor, and had only understood respecting it that it had been arranged between Trevelyan and the family in whose custody his two daughters had been sent away into banishment. He was not therefore specially disposed to welcome Hugh Stanbury in consequence of this mode of introduction.

Hugh, who had asked for Lady Rowley and Mrs Trevelyan and had learned that they were out before he had mentioned Miss Rowley's name, was almost prepared to take his sweetheart into his arms. In that half-minute he had taught himself to expect that he would meet her alone, and had altogether forgotten Sir Marmaduke. Young men when they call at four o'clock in the day never expect to find papas at home. And of Sophia and Lucy he had either heard nothing or had forgotten what he had heard. He repressed himself however in time, and did not commit either Nora or himself by any very vehement demonstration of affection. But he did hold her hand longer than he should have done, and Sir Marmaduke saw that he did so.

'This is papa,' said Nora. 'Papa, this is our friend, Mr Hugh Stanbury.' The introduction was made in a manner almost absurdly formal, but poor Nora's difficulties lay heavy upon her. Sir Marmaduke muttered something; – but it was little more than a grunt. 'Mamma and Emily are out,' continued Nora. 'I dare say they will be in soon.' Sir Marmaduke looked round sharply at the man. Why was he to be encouraged to stay till Lady Rowley should return? Lady Rowley did not want to see him. It seemed to Sir Marmaduke, in the midst of his troubles, that this was no time to be making new acquaintances. 'These are my sisters, Mr Stanbury,' continued Nora. 'This is Sophia, and this is Lucy.' Sophia and Lucy would have been thoroughly willing to receive their sister's lover with genial kindness if they had been properly instructed, and if the time had been opportune; but, as it was, they had nothing to say. They, also, could only mutter some little sound intended to be more courteous than their father's grunt. Poor Nora!

'I hope you are comfortable here,' said Hugh.

'The house is all very well,' said Nora, 'but we don't like the neighbourhood.'

Hugh also felt that conversation was difficult. He had soon come to perceive, – before he had been in the room half a minute, – that the atmosphere was not favourable to his mission. There was to be no embracing or permission for embracing on the present occasion. Had he been left alone with Sir Marmaduke he would probably have told his business plainly, let Sir Marmaduke's manner to him have been what it might; but it was impossible for him to do this with three young ladies in the room with him. Seeing that Nora was embarrassed by her difficulties, and that Nora's father was cross and silent, he endeavoured to talk to the other girls, and asked them concerning their journey and the ship in which they had come. But it was very up-hill work. Lucy and Sophy could talk as glibly as any young ladies home from any colony, – and no higher degree of fluency can be expressed; – but now they were cowed. Their elder sister was shamefully and most undeservedly disgraced, and this man had had something, – they knew not what, – to do with it. 'Is Priscilla quite well?' Nora asked at last.

'Quite well. I heard from her yesterday. You know they have left the Clock House.'

'I had not heard it.'

'Of yes; – and they are living in a small cottage just outside the village. And what else do you think has happened?'

'Nothing bad, I hope, Mr Stanbury.'

'My sister Dorothy has left her aunt, and is living with them again at Nuncombe.'

'Has there been a quarrel, Mr Stanbury?'

'Well, yes; – after a fashion there has, I suppose. But it is a long story and would not interest Sir Marmaduke. The wonder is that Dorothy should have been able to stay so long with my aunt. I will tell it you all some day.' Sir Marmaduke could not understand why a long story about this man's aunt and sister should be told to his daughter. He forgot, – as men always do in such circumstances forget, – that, while he was living in the Mandarins, his daughter, living in England, would of course pick up new interest and become intimate with new histories. But he did not forget that pressure of the hand which he had seen, and he determined that his daughter Nora could not have any worse lover than the friend of his elder daughter's husband.

Stanbury had just determined that he must go, that there was no possibility for him either to say or do anything to promote his cause at the present moment, when the circumstances were all changed by the return home of Lady Rowley and Mrs Trevelyan. Lady Rowley knew, and had for some days known, much more of Stanbury than had come to the ears of Sir Marmaduke. She understood in the first place that the Stanburys had been very good to her daughters, and she was aware that Hugh Stanbury had thoroughly taken her daughter's part against his old friend Trevelyan. She would therefore have been prepared to receive him kindly had he not on this very morning been the subject of special conversation between her and Emily. But, as it had happened, Mrs Trevelyan had this very day told Lady Rowley the whole story of Nora's love. The elder sister had not intended to be treacherous to the younger; but in the thorough confidence which mutual grief and close conference had created between the mother and daughter, everything had at last come out, and Lady Rowley had learned the story, not only of Hugh Stanbury's courtship, but of those rich offers which had been made by the heir to the barony of Peterborough.

It must be acknowledged that Lady Rowley was greatly grieved and thoroughly dismayed. It was not only that Mr Glascock was the eldest son of a peer, but that he was represented by the poor suffering wife of the ill-tempered man to be a man blessed with a disposition sweet as an angel's. 'And she would have liked him,' Emily had said, 'if it had not been for this unfortunate young man.' Lady Rowley was not worse than are other mothers, not more ambitious, or more heartless, or more worldly. She was a good mother, loving her children, and thoroughly anxious for their welfare. But she would have liked to be the mother-in-law of Lord Peterborough, and she would have liked, dearly, to see her second daughter removed from the danger of those rocks against which her eldest child had been shipwrecked. And when she asked after Hugh Stanbury, and his means of maintaining a wife, the statement which Mrs Trevelyan made was not comforting. 'He writes for a penny newspaper, – and, I believe, writes very well,' Mrs Trevelyan had said.

'For a penny newspaper! Is that respectable?'

'His aunt, Miss Stanbury, seemed to think not. But I suppose men of education do write for such things now. He says himself that it is very precarious as an employment.'

'It must be precarious, Emily. And has he got nothing?'

'Not a penny of his own,' said Mrs Trevelyan.

Then Lady Rowley had thought again of Mr Glascock, and of the family title, and of Monkhams. And she thought of her present troubles, and of the Mandarins, and the state of Sir Marmaduke's balance at the bankers; – and of the other girls, and of all there was before her to do. Here had been a very Apollo among suitors kneeling at her child's feet, and the foolish girl had sent him away for the sake of a young man who wrote for a penny newspaper! Was it worth the while of any woman to bring up daughters with such results? Lady Rowley, therefore, when she was first introduced to Hugh Stanbury, was not prepared to receive him with open arms.

On this occasion the task of introducing him fell to Mrs Trevelyan, and was done with much graciousness. Emily knew that Hugh Stanbury was her friend, and would sympathise with her respecting her child. 'You have heard what has happened to me?' she said. Stanbury, however, had heard nothing of that kidnapping of the child. Though to the Rowleys it seemed that such a deed of iniquity, done in the middle of London, must have been known to all the world, he had not as yet been told of it; – and now the story was given to him. Mrs Trevelyan herself told it, with many tears and an agony of fresh grief; but still she told it as to one whom she regarded as a sure friend, and from whom she knew that she would receive sympathy. Sir Marmaduke sat by the while, still gloomy and out of humour. Why was their family sorrow to be laid bare to this stranger?

'It is the cruellest thing I ever heard,' said Hugh.

'A dastardly deed,' said Lady Rowley.

'But we all feel that for the time he can hardly know what he does,' said Nora.

'And where is the child?' Stanbury asked.

'We have not the slightest idea,' said Lady Rowley. 'I have seen him, and he refuses to tell us. He did say that my daughter should see her boy; but he now accompanies his offer with such conditions that it is impossible to listen to him.'

'And where is he?'

'We do not know where he lives. We can reach him only through a certain man – '

'Ah, I know the man,' said Stanbury; 'one who was a policeman once. His name is Bozzle.'

'That is the man,' said Sir Marmaduke. 'I have seen him.'

'And of course he will tell us nothing but what he is told to tell us,' continued Lady Rowley. 'Can there be anything so horrible as this, – that a wife should be bound to communicate with her own husband respecting her own child through such a man as that?'

'One might possibly find out where he keeps the child,' said Hugh.

'If you could manage that, Mr Stanbury!' said Lady Rowley.

'I hardly see that it would do much good,' said Hugh. 'Indeed I do not know why he should keep the place a secret. I suppose he has a right to the boy until the mother shall have made good her claim before the court.' He promised, however, that he would do his best to ascertain where the child was kept, and where Trevelyan resided, and then, – having been nearly an hour at the house, – he was forced to get up and take his leave. He had said not a word to any one of the business that had brought him there. He had not even whispered an assurance of his affections to Nora. Till the two elder ladies had come in, and the subject of the taking of the boy had been mooted, he had sat there as a perfect stranger. He thought that it was manifest enough that Nora had told her secret to no one. It seemed to him that Mrs Trevelyan must have forgotten it; – that Nora herself must have forgotten it, if such forgetting could be possible! He got up, however, and took his leave, and was comforted in some slight degree by seeing that there was a tear in Nora's eye.

'Who is he?' demanded Sir Marmaduke, as soon as the door was closed.

'He is a young man who was an intimate friend of Louis's,' answered Mrs Trevelyan; 'but he is so no longer, because he sees how infatuated Louis has been.'

'And why does he come here?'

'We know him very well,' continued Mrs Trevelyan. 'It was he that arranged our journey down to Devonshire. He was very kind about it, and so were his mother and sister. We have every reason to be grateful to Mr Stanbury.' This was all very well, but Nora nevertheless felt that the interview had been anything but successful.

'Has he any profession?' asked Sir Marmaduke.

'He writes for the press,' said Mrs Trevelyan.

'What do you mean; – books?'

'No; – for a newspaper.'

'For a penny newspaper,' said Nora boldly; – 'for the Daily Record.'

'Then I hope he won't come here any more,' said Sir Marmaduke. Nora paused a moment, striving to find words for some speech which might be true to her love and yet not unseemly, – but finding no such words ready, she got up from her seat and walked out of the room. 'What is the meaning of it all?' asked Sir Marmaduke. There was a silence for a while, and then he repeated his question in another form. 'Is there any reason for his coming here, – about Nora?'

'I think he is attached to Nora,' said Mrs Trevelyan.

'My dear,' said Lady Rowley, 'perhaps we had better not speak about it just now.'

'I suppose he has not a penny in the world,' said Sir Marmaduke.

'He has what he earns,' said Mrs Trevelyan.

'If Nora understands her duty she will never let me hear his name again,' said Sir Marmaduke. Then there was nothing more said and as soon as they could escape, both Lady Rowley and Mrs Trevelyan left the room.

'I should have told you everything,' said Nora to her mother that night. 'I had no intention to keep anything a secret from you. But we have all been so unhappy about Louey, that we have had no heart to talk of anything else.'

'I understand all that, my darling.'

'And I had meant that you should tell papa, for I supposed that he would come. And I meant that he should go to papa himself. He intended that himself, – only, to-day, – as things turned out – '

'Just so, dearest; – but it does not seem that he has got any income. It would be very rash, – wouldn't it?'

'People must be rash sometimes. Everybody can't have an income without earning it. I suppose people in professions do marry without having fortunes.'

'When they have settled professions, Nora.'

'And why is not his a settled profession? I believe he receives quite as much at seven and twenty as Uncle Oliphant does at sixty.'

'But your Uncle Oliphant's income is permanent.'

'Lawyers don't have permanent incomes, or doctors, – or merchants.'

'But those professions are regular and sure. They don't marry, without fortunes, till they have made their incomes sure.'

'Mr Stanbury's income is sure. I don't know why it shouldn't be sure. He goes on writing and writing every day, and it seems to me that of all professions in the world it is the finest. I'd much sooner write for a newspaper than be one of those old musty, fusty lawyers, who'll say anything that they're paid to say.'

'My dearest Nora, all that is nonsense. You know as well as I do that you should not marry a man when there is a doubt whether he can keep a house over your head; – that is his position.'

'It is good enough for me, mamma.'

'And what is his income from writing?'

'It is quite enough for me, mamma. The truth is I have promised, and I cannot go back from it. Dear, dear, mamma, you won't quarrel with us, and oppose us, and make papa hard against us. You can do what you like with papa. I know that. Look at poor Emily. Plenty of money has not made her happy.'

'If Mr Glascock had only asked you a week sooner,' said Lady Rowley, with a handkerchief to her eyes.

'But you see he didn't, mamma.'

'When I think of it I cannot but weep;' – and the poor mother burst out into a full flood of tears – 'such a man, so good, so gentle, and so truly devoted to you.'

'Mamma, what's the good of that now?'

'Going down all the way to Devonshire after you!'

'So did Hugh, mamma.'

'A position that any girl in England would have envied you. I cannot but feel it. And Emily says she is sure he would come back, if he got the very slightest encouragement.'

'That is quite impossible, mamma.'

'Why should it be impossible? Emily declares that she never saw a man so much in love in her life; – and she says also that she believes he is abroad now simply because he is broken-hearted about it.'

'Mr Glascock, mamma, was very nice and good and all that; but indeed he is not the man to suffer from a broken heart. And Emily is quite mistaken. I told him the whole truth.'

'What truth?'

'That there was somebody else that I did love. Then he said that of course that put an end to it all, and he wished me good-bye ever so calmly.'

'How could you be so infatuated? Why should you have cut the ground away from your feet in that way?'

'Because I chose that there should be an end to it. Now there has been an end to it; and it is much better, mamma, that we should not think about Mr Glascock any more. He will never come again to me, – and if he did, I could only say the same thing.'

'You mustn't be surprised, Nora, if I'm unhappy; that is all. Of course I must feel it. Such a connection as it would have been for your sisters! Such a home for poor Emily in her trouble! And as for this other man – '

'Mamma, don't speak ill of him.'

'If I say anything of him, I must say the truth,' said Lady Rowley.

'Don't say anything against him, mamma, because he is to be my husband. Dear, dear mamma, you can't change me by anything you say. Perhaps I have been foolish; but it is settled now. Don't make me wretched by speaking against the man whom I mean to love all my life better than all the world.'

'Think of Louis Trevelyan.'

'I will think of no one but Hugh Stanbury. I tried not to love him, mamma. I tried to think that it was better to make believe that I loved Mr Glascock. But he got the better of me, and conquered me, and I will never rebel against him. You may help me, mamma; — but you can't change me.'

64

Sir Marmaduke at his Club

Sir Marmaduke had come away from his brother-in-law the parson in much anger, for Mr Outhouse, with that mixture of obstinacy and honesty which formed his character, had spoken hard words of Colonel Osborne, and words which by implication had been hard also against Emily Trevelyan. He had been very staunch to his niece when attacked by his niece's husband; but when his sympathies and assistance were invoked by Sir Marmaduke it seemed as though he had transferred his allegiance to the other side. He pointed out to the unhappy father that Colonel Osborne had behaved with great cruelty in going to Devonshire, that the Stanburys had been untrue to their trust in allowing him to enter the house, and that Emily had been 'indiscreet' in receiving him. When a young woman is called indiscreet by her friends it may be assumed that her character is very seriously assailed. Sir Marmaduke had understood this, and on hearing the word had become wroth with his brother-in-law. There had been hot words between them, and Mr Outhouse would not yield an inch or retract a syllable. He conceived it to be his duty to advise the father to caution his daughter with severity, to quarrel absolutely with Colonel Osborne, and to let Trevelyan know that this had been done. As to the child, Mr Outhouse expressed a strong opinion that the father was legally entitled to the custody of his boy, and that nothing could be done to recover the child, except what might be done with the father's consent. In fact, Mr Outhouse made himself exceedingly disagreeable, and sent away Sir Marmaduke with a very heavy heart. Could it rally be possible that his old friend Fred Osborne, who seven or eight-and-twenty years ago had been potent among young ladies, had really been making love to his old friend's married daughter? Sir Marmaduke looked into himself, and conceived it to be quite out of the question that he should make love to any one. A good dinner, good wine, a good cigar, an easy chair, and a rubber of whist, – all these things, with no work to do, and men of his own standing around him were the pleasures of life which Sir Marmaduke desired. Now Fred Osborne was an older man than he, and though Fred Osborne did keep up a foolish system of padded clothes and dyed whiskers, still, – at fifty-two or fifty-three, – surely a man might be reckoned safe. And then, too, that ancient friendship! Sir Marmaduke, who had lived all his life in the comparative seclusion of a colony, thought perhaps more of that ancient friendship than did the Colonel, who had lived amidst the blaze of London life, and who had had many opportunities of changing his friends. Some inkling of all this made its way into Sir Marmaduke's bosom, as he thought of it with bitterness; and he determined that he would have it out with his friend.

Hitherto he had enjoyed very few of those pleasant hours which he had anticipated on his journey homewards. He had had no heart to go his club, and he had fancied that Colonel Osborne had been a little backward in looking him up, and providing him with amusement. He had suggested this to his wife, and she had told him that the Colonel had been right not to come to Manchester Street. 'I have told Emily,' said Lady Rowley, 'that she must not meet him, and she is quite of the same opinion.' Nevertheless, there had been remissness. Sir Marmaduke felt that it was so, in spite of his wife's excuses. In this way he was becoming sore with everybody, and very unhappy. It did not at all improve his temper when he was told that his second daughter had refused an offer from Lord Peterborough's eldest son. 'Then she may go into the workhouse for me,' the angry father had said, declaring at the same time that he would never give his consent to her marriage with the man who 'did dirty work' for the Daily Record, – as he, with his paternal wisdom, chose to express it. But this cruel phrase was not spoken in Nora's hearing, nor was it repeated to her. Lady Rowley knew her husband, and was aware that he would on occasions change his opinion.

It was not till two or three days after his visit to St Diddulph's that he met Colonel Osborne.* The Easter recess was then over, and Colonel Osborne had just returned to London. They met on the door-steps of 'The Acrobats,' and the Colonel immediately began with an apology. 'I have been so sorry to be away just when you are here; – upon my word I have. But I was obliged to go down to the duchess's. I had promised early in the winter; and those people are so angry if you put them off. By George, it's almost as bad as putting of royalty.'

'D — n the duchess,' said Sir Marmaduke.

'With all my heart,' said the Colonel; — 'only I thought it as well that I should tell you the truth.'

'What I mean is, that the duchess and her people make no difference to me. I hope you had a pleasant time; that's all.'

'Well; — yes, we had. One must get away somewhere at Easter. There is no one left at the club, and there's no House, and no one asks one to dinner in town. In fact, if one didn't go away one wouldn't know what to do. There were ever so many people there that I liked to meet. Lady Glencora was there, and uncommon pleasant she made it. That woman has more to say for herself than any half-dozen men that I know. And Lord Cantrip, your chief, was there.* He said a word or two to me about you.'

'What sort of a word?'

'He says he wishes you would read up some blue books, or papers, or reports, or something of that kind, which he says that some of his fellows have sent you. It seems that there are some new rules, or orders, or fashions, which he wants you to have at your finger's ends. Nothing could be more civil than he was, — but he just wished me to mention this, knowing that you and I are likely to see each other.'

'I wish I had never come over,' said Sir Marmaduke.

'Why so?'

'They didn't bother me with their new rules and fashions over there. When the papers came somebody read them, and that was enough. I could do what they wanted me to do there.'

'And so you will here, — after a bit.'

'I'm not so sure of that. Those young fellows seem to forget that an old dog can't learn new tricks. They've got a young brisk fellow there who seems to think that a man should be an encyclopedia of knowledge because he has lived in a colony over twenty years.'

'That's the new under-secretary.'

'Never mind who it is. Osborne, just come up to the library, will you? I want to speak to you.' Then Sir Marmaduke, with considerable solemnity, led the way up to the most deserted room in the club, and Colonel Osborne followed him, well knowing that something was to be said about Emily Trevelyan.

Sir Marmaduke seated himself on a sofa, and his friend sat close beside him. The room was quite deserted. It was four o'clock in the afternoon, and the club was full of men. There were men in the morning-room, and men in the drawing-room, and men in the card-room, and men in the billiard-room; but no better choice of a chamber for a conference intended to be silent and secret could have been made in all London than that which had induced Sir Marmaduke to take his friend into the library of 'The Acrobats.' And yet a great deal of money had been spent in providing this library for 'The Acrobats.' Sir Marmaduke sat for awhile silent, and had he sat silent for an hour, Colonel Osborne would not have interrupted him. Then, at last, he began, with a voice that was intended to be serious, but which struck upon the ear of his companion as being affected and unlike the owner of it. 'This is a very sad thing about my poor girl,' said Sir Marmaduke.

'Indeed it is. There is only one thing to be said about it, Rowley.'

'And what's that?'

'The man must be mad.'

'He is not so mad as to give us any relief by his madness, – poor as such comfort would be. He has got Emily's child away from her, and I think it will about kill her. And what is to become of her? As to taking her back to the islands without her child, it is out of the question. I never knew anything so cruel in my life.'

'And so absurd, you know.'

'Ah, – that's just the question. If anybody had asked me, I should have said that you were the man of all men whom I could have best trusted.'

'Do you doubt it now?'

'I don't know what to think.'

'Do you mean to say that you suspect me, – and your daughter too?'

'No; – by heavens! Poor dear. If I suspected her, there would be an end of all things with me. I could never get over that. No; – I don't suspect her!' Sir Marmaduke had now dropped his affected tone, and was speaking with natural energy.

'But you do me?'

'No; – if I did, I don't suppose I should be sitting with you here; but they tell me – .'

'They tell you what?'

'They tell me that, – that you did not behave wisely about it. Why could you not let her alone when you found out how matters were going?'

'Who has been telling you this, Rowley?'

Sir Marmaduke considered for awhile, and then, remembering that Colonel Osborne could hardly quarrel with a clergyman, told him the truth. 'Outhouse says that you have done her an irretrievable injury by going down to Devonshire to her, and by writing to her.'

'Outhouse is an ass.'

'That is easily said; – but why did you go?'

'And why should I not go? What the deuce! Because a man like that chooses to take vagaries into his head I am not to see my own godchild!' Sir Marmaduke tried to remember whether the Colonel was in fact the godfather of his eldest daughter, but he found that his mind was quite a blank about his children's godfathers and godmothers. 'And as for the letters; – I wish you could see them. The only letters which had in them a word of importance were those about your coming home. I was anxious to get that arranged, not only for your sake, but because she was so eager about it.'

'God bless her, poor child,' said Sir Marmaduke, rubbing the tears away from his eyes with his red silk pocket-handkerchief.

'I will acknowledge that those letters, – there may have been one or two, – were the beginning of the trouble. It was these that made this man show himself to be a lunatic. I do admit that. I was bound not to talk about your coming, and I told her to keep the secret. He went spying about, and found her letters, I suppose, – and then he took fire, because there was to be a secret from him. Dirty, mean dog! And now I'm to be told by such a fellow as Outhouse that it's my fault, that I have caused all the trouble, because, when I happened to be in Devonshire, I went to see your daughter!' We must do the Colonel the justice of supposing that he had by this time quite taught himself to believe that the church porch at Cock-chaffington had been the motive cause of his journey into Devonshire. 'Upon my word it is too hard,' continued he indignantly. 'As for Outhouse, – only for the gown upon his back, I'd pull his nose. And I wish that you would tell him that I say so.'

'There is trouble enough without that,' said Sir Marmaduke.

'But it is hard. By G – , it is hard. There is this comfort; – if it hadn't been me, it would have been some one else. Such a man as that couldn't have gone two or three years, without being jealous of some one. And as for poor Emily, she is better off perhaps with an accusation so absurd as this, than she might have been had her name been joined with a younger man, or with one whom you would have less reason for trusting.'

There was so much that seemed to be sensible in this, and it was spoken with so well assumed a tone of injured innocence, that Sir Marmaduke felt that he had nothing more to say. He muttered something further about the cruelty of the case, and then slunk away out of the club, and made his way home to the dull gloomy house in Manchester Street. There was no comfort for him there; — but neither was there any comfort for him at the club. And why did that vexatious Secretary of State send him messages about blue books? As he went, he expressed sundry wishes that he was back at the Mandarins, and told himself that it would be well that he should remain there till he died.

65

Mysterious Agencies

When the thirty-first of March arrived, Exeter had not as yet been made gay with the marriage festivities of Mr Gibson and Camilla French. And this delay had not been the fault of Camilla. Camilla had been ready, and when, about the middle of the month, it was hinted to her that some postponement was necessary, she spoke her mind out plainly, and declared that she was not going to stand that kind of thing. The communication had not been made to her by Mr Gibson in person. For some days previously he had not been seen at Heavitree, and Camilla had from day to day become more black, gloomy, and harsh in her manners both to her mother and her sisters. Little notes had come and little notes had gone, but no one in the house, except Camilla herself, knew what those notes contained. She would not condescend to complain to Arabella; nor did she say much in condemnation of her lover to Mrs French, till the blow came. With unremitting attention she pursued the great business of her wedding garments, and exacted from the unfortunate Arabella an amount of work equal to her own, — of thankless work, as is the custom of embryo brides with their unmarried sisters. And she drew with great audacity on the somewhat slender means of the family for the amount of feminine gear necessary to enable her to go into Mr Gibson's house with something of the éclat of a well-provided bride. When Mrs French hesitated, and then expostulated, Camilla replied that she did not except to be married above once, and that in no cheaper or more productive way than this could her mother allow her to consume her share of the family resources. 'What matter, mamma, if you do have to borrow a little money? Mr Burgess will let you have it when he knows why. And as I shan't be eating and drinking at home any more, nor yet getting my things here, I have a right to expect it.' And she ended by expressing an opinion, in Arabella's hearing, that any daughter of a house who proves herself to be capable of getting a husband for herself, is entitled to expect that those left at home shall pinch themselves for a time, in order that she may go forth to the world in a respectable way, and be a credit to the family.

Then came the blow. Mr Gibson had not been at the house for some days, but the notes had been going and coming. At last Mr Gibson came himself; but, as it happened, when he came Camilla was out shopping. In these days she often did go out shopping between eleven and one, carrying her sister with her. It must have been but a poor pleasure for Arabella, this witnessing the purchases made, seing the pleasant draperies and handling the real linens and admiring the fine cambrics spread out before them on the shop counters by obsequious attendants. And the questions asked of her by her sister, whether this was good enough for so august an occasion, or that sufficiently handsome, must have been harassing. She could not have failed to remember that it ought all to have been done for her, – that had she not been treated with monstrous injustice, with most unsisterly cruelty; all these good things would have been spread on her behoof. But she went on and endured it, and worked diligently with her needle, and folded and unfolded as she was desired, and became as it were quite a younger sister in the house, – creeping out by herself now and again into the purlieus of the city, to find such consolation as she might receive from her solitary thoughts.

But Arabella and Camilla were both away when Mr Gibson called to tell Mrs French of his altered plans. And as he asked, not for his lady-love, but for Mrs French herself, it is probable that he watched his opportunity and that he knew to what cares his Camilla was then devoting herself. 'Perhaps it is quite as well that I should find you alone,' he said, after sundry preludes, to his future mother-in-law, 'because you can make Camilla understand this better than I can. I must put off the day for about three weeks.'

'Three weeks, Mr Gibson?'

'Or a month. Perhaps we had better say the 29th of April.' Mr Gibson had by this time thrown off every fear that he might have entertained of the mother, and could speak to her of such an unwarrantable change of plans with tolerable equanimity.

'But I don't know that that will suit Camilla at all.'

'She can name any other day she pleases, of course; – that is, in May.'

'But why is this to be?'

'There are things about money, Mrs French, which I cannot arrange sooner. And I find that unfortunately I must go up to London.' Though many other questions were asked, nothing further was got out of Mr Gibson on that occasion; and he left the house with a perfect understanding on his own part, – and on that of Mrs French, – that the marriage was postponed till some day still to be fixed, but which could not and should not be before the 29th of April. Mrs French asked him why he did not come up and see Camilla. He replied, – false man that he was, – that he had hoped to have seen her this morning, and that he would come again before the week was over.

Then it was that Camilla spoke her mind out plainly. 'I shall go to his house at once,' she said, 'and find out all about it. I don't understand it. I don't understand it at all; and I won't put up with it. He shall know who he has to deal with, if he plays tricks upon me. Mamma, I wonder you let him out of the house, till you had made him come back to his old day.'

'What could I do, my dear?'

'What could you do? Shake him out of it, – as I would have done. But he didn't dare to tell me, – because he is a coward.'

Camilla in all this showed her spirit; but she allowed her anger to hurry her away into an indiscretion. Arabella was present, and Camilla should have repressed her rage.

'I don't think he's at all a coward,' said Arabella.

'That's my business. I suppose I'm entitled to know what he is better than you.'

'All the same I don't think Mr Gibson is at all a coward,' said Arabella, again pleading the cause of the man who had misused her.

'Now, Arabella, I won't take any interference from you; mind that. I say it was cowardly, and he should have come to me. It's my concern, and I shall go to him. I'm not going to be stopped by any shilly-shally nonsense, when my future respectability, perhaps, is at stake. All Exeter knows that the marriage is to take place on the 31st of this month.'

On the next day Camilla absolutely did go to Mr Gibson's house at an early hour, at nine, when, as she thought, he would surely be at breakfast. But he had flown. He had left Exeter that morning by an early train, and his servant thought that he had gone to London. On the next morning Camilla got a note from him, written in London. It affected to be very cheery and affectionate, beginning 'Dearest Cammy,' and alluding to the postponement of his wedding as though it were a thing so fixed as to require no further question. Camilla answered this letter, still in much wrath, complaining, protesting, expostulating; – throwing in his teeth the fact that the day had been fixed by him, and not by her. And she added a postscript in the following momentous words; – 'If you have any respect for the name of your future wife, you will fall back upon your first arrangement.' To this she got simply a line of an answer, declaring that this falling back was impossible, and then nothing was heard of him for ten days. He had gone from Tuesday to Saturday week; – and the first that Camilla saw of him was his presence in the reading desk when he chaunted the cathedral service as priest-vicar on the Sunday.

At this time Arabella was very ill, and was confined to her bed. Mr Martin declared that her system had become low from over anxiety, – that she was nervous, weak, and liable to hysterics, – that her feelings were in fact too many for her, – and that her efforts to overcome them, and to face the realities of the world, had exhausted her. This was, of course, not said openly, at the town-cross of Exeter; but such was the opinion which Mr Martin gave in confidence to the mother. 'Fiddle-de-dee!' said Camilla, when she was told of feelings, susceptibilities, and hysterics. At the present moment she had a claim to the undivided interest of the family, and she believed that her sister's illness was feigned in order to defraud her of her rights. 'My dear, she is ill,' said Mrs French. 'Then let her have a dose of salts,' said the stern Camilla. This was on the Sunday afternoon. Camilla had endeavoured to see Mr Gibson as he came out of the cathedral, but had failed. Mr Gibson had been detained within the building, – no doubt by duties connected with the choral services. On that evening he got a note from Camilla, and quite early on the Monday morning he came up to Heavitree.

'You will find her in the drawing-room,' said Mrs French, as she opened the hall-door for him. There was a smile on her face as she spoke, but it was a forced smile. Mr Gibson did not smile at all.

'Is it all right with her?' he asked.

'Well; – you had better go to her. You see, Mr Gibson, young ladies, when they are going to be married, think that they ought to have their own way a little, just for the last time, you know.' He took no notice of the joke, but went with slow steps up to the drawing-room. It would be inquiring too curiously to ask whether Camilla, when she embraced him, discerned that he had fortified his courage that morning with a glass of curacoa.

'What does all this mean, Thomas?' was the first question that Camilla asked when the embrace was over.

'All what mean, dear?'

'This untoward delay? Thomas, you have almost broken my heart. You have been away, and I have not heard from you.'

'I wrote twice, Camilla.'

'And what sort of letters? If there is anything the matter, Thomas, you had better tell me at once.' She paused, but Thomas held his tongue. 'I don't suppose you want to kill me.'

'God forbid,' said Thomas.

'But you will. What must everybody think of me in the city when they find that it is put off. Poor mamma has been dreadful; – quite dreadful! And here is Arabella now laid up on a bed of sickness.' This, too, was indiscreet. Camilla should have said nothing about her sister's sickness.

'I have been so sorry to hear about dear Bella,' said Mr Gibson.

'I don't suppose she's very bad,' said Camilla, 'but of course we all feel it. Of course we're upset. As for me, I bear up; because I've that spirit that I won't give way if it's ever so; but, upon my word, if tries me hard. What is the meaning of it, Thomas?'

But Thomas had nothing to say beyond what he had said before to Mrs French. He was very particular, he said, about money; and certain money matters made it incumbent on him not to marry before the 29th of April. When Camilla suggested to him that as she was to be his wife, she ought to know all about his money matters, he told her that she should, – some day. When they were married, he would tell her all. Camilla talked a great deal, and said some things that were very severe. Mr Gibson did not enjoy his morning, but he endured the upbraidings of his fair one with more firmness than might perhaps have been expected from him. He left all the talking to Camilla; but when he got up to leave her, the 29th of April had been fixed, with some sort of assent from her, as the day on which she was really to become Mrs Gibson.

When he left the room, he again met Mrs French on the landing-place. She hesitated a moment, waiting to see whether the door would be shut; but the door could not be shut, as Camilla was standing in the entrance. 'Mr Gibson,' said Mrs French, in a voice that was scarcely a whisper, 'would you mind stepping in and seeing poor Bella for a moment?'

'Why; – she is in bed,' said Camilla.

'Yes; – she is in bed; but she thinks it would be a comfort to her. She has seen nobody these four days except Mr Martin, and she thinks it would comfort her to have a word or two with Mr Gibson.' Now Mr Gibson was not only going to be Bella's brother-in-law, but he was also a clergyman. Camilla in her heart believed that the half-clerical aspect which her mother had given to the request was false and hypocritical. There were special reasons why Bella should not have wished to see Mr Gibson in her bedroom, at any rate till Mr Gibson had become her brother-in-law. The expression of such a wish at the present moment was almost indecent.

'You'll be there with them?' said Camilla. Mr Gibson blushed up to his ears as he heard the suggestion. 'Of course you'll be there with them, mamma.'

'No, my dear, I think not. I fancy she wishes him to read to her, – or something of that sort.' Then Mr Gibson, without speaking a word, but still blushing up to his ears, was taken to Arabella's room; and Camilla, flouncing into the drawing-room, banged the door behind her. She had hitherto fought her battle with considerable skill and with great courage; – but her very success had made her imprudent. She had become so imperious in the great position which she had reached, that she could not control her temper or wait till her power was confirmed. The banging of that door was heard through the whole house, and every one knew why it was banged. She threw herself on to a sofa, and then, instantly rising again, paced the room with quick step. Could it be possible that there was treachery? Was it on the cards that that weak, poor creature, Bella, was intriguing once again to defraud her of her husband? There were different things that she now remembered. Arabella, in that moment of bliss in which she had conceived herself to be engaged to Mr Gibson, had discarded her chignon. Then she had resumed it, – in all its monstrous proportions. Since that it had been lessened by degrees, and brought down, through various interesting but abnormal shapes, to a size which would hardly have drawn forth any anathema from Miss Stanbury. And now, on this very morning, Arabella had put on a clean nightcap, with muslin frills. It is perhaps not unnatural that a sick lady, preparing to receive a clergyman in her bedroom, should put on a clean nightcap, – but to suspicious eyes small causes suffice to create alarm. And if there were any such hideous wickedness in the wind, had Arabella any colleague in her villainy? Could it be that the mother was plotting against her daughter's happiness and respectability? Camilla was well aware that her mamma would at first have preferred to give Arabella to Mr Gibson, had the choice in the matter been left to her. But now, when the thing had been settled before all the world, would not such treatment on a mother's part be equal to infanticide? And then as to Mr Gibson himself! Camilla was not prone to think little of her own charms, but she had been unable not to perceive that her lover had become negligent in his personal attentions to her. An accepted lover, who deserves to have been accepted, should devote every hour at his command to his mistress. But Mr Gibson had of late been so chary of his presence at

Heavitree, that Camilla could not but have known that he took no delight in coming thither. She had acknowledged this to herself; but she had consoled herself with the reflection that marriage would make this all right. Mr Gibson was not the man to stray from his wife, and she could trust herself to obtain a sufficient hold upon her husband hereafter, partly by the strength of her tongue, partly by the ascendancy of her spirit, and partly, also, by the comforts which she would provide for him. She had not doubted but that it would be all well when they should be married; – but how if, even now, there should be no marriage for her? Camilla French had never heard of Creusa and of Jason, but as she paced her mother's drawing-room that morning she was a Medea in spirit.* If any plot of that kind should be in the wind, she would do such things that all Devonshire should hear of her wrongs and of her revenge!

In the meantime Mr Gibson was sitting by Arabella's bedside, while Mrs French was trying to make herself busy in her own chamber, next door. There had been a reading of some chapter of the Bible, – or of some portion of a chapter. And Mr Gibson, as he read, and Arabella, as she listened, had endeavoured to take to their hearts and to make use of the word which they heard. The poor young woman, when she begged her mother to send to her the man who was so dear to her, did so with some half-formed conviction that it would be good for her to hear a clergyman read to her. But now the chapter had been read, and the book was back in Mr Gibson's pocket, and he was sitting with his hand on the bed. 'She is so very arrogant,' said Bella, – and so domineering.' To this Mr Gibson made no reply. 'I'm sure I have endeavoured to bear it well, though you must have known what I have suffered, Thomas. Nobody can understand it so well as you do.'

'I wish I had never been born,' said Mr Gibson tragically.

'Don't say that, Thomas, – because it's wicked.'

'But I do. See all the harm I have done; – and yet I did not mean it.'

'You must try and do the best you can now. I am not saying what that should be. I am not dictating to you. You are a man, and, of course, you must judge for yourself. But I will say this. You shouldn't do anything just because it is the easiest. I don't suppose I should live after it. I don't indeed. But that should not signify to you.'

'I don't suppose that any man was ever before in such a terrible position since the world began.'

'It is difficult; – I am sure of that, Thomas.'

'And I have meant to be so true. I fancy sometimes that some mysterious agency interferes with the affairs of a man and drives him on, – and on, – and on, – almost, – till he doesn't know where it drives him.' As he said this in a voice that was quite sepulchral in its tone, he felt some consolation in the conviction that this mysterious agency could not affect a man without embuing him with a certain amount of grandeur, – very uncomfortble, indeed, in its nature, but still having considerable value as a counterpoise. Pride must bear pain; – but pain is recompensed by pride.

'She is so strong, Thomas, that she can put up with anything,' said Arabella, in a whisper.

'Strong; – yes,' said he, with a shudder; – 'she is strong enough.'

'And as for love – '

'Don't talk about it,' said he, getting up from his chair. 'Don't talk about it. You will drive me frantic.'

'You know what my feelings are, Thomas; you have always known them. There has been no change since I was the young thing you first knew me.' As she spoke, she just touched his hand with hers; but he did not seem to notice this, sitting with his elbow on the arm of his chair and his forehead on his hand. In reply to what she said to him, he merely shook his head, – not intending to imply thereby any doubt of the truth of her assertion. 'You have now to make up your mind, and to be bold, Thomas,' continued Arabella. 'She says that you are a coward; but I know that you are no coward. I told her so, and she said that I was interfering. Oh, – that she should be able to tell me that I interfere when I defend you !'

'I must go,' said Mr Gibson, jumping up from his chair. 'I must go. Bella, I cannot stand this any longer. It is too much for me. I will pray that I may decide aright. God bless you !' Then he kissed her brow as she lay in bed, and hurried out of the room.

He had hoped to go from the house without further converse with any of its inmates; for his mind was disturbed, and he longed to be at rest. But he was not allowed to escape so easily. Camilla met him at the dining-room door, and accosted him with a smile. There had been time for much meditation during the last half hour, and Camilla had meditated. 'How do you find her, Thomas ?' she asked.

'She seems weak, but I believe she is better. I have been reading to her.'

'Come in, Thomas; – will you not ? It is bad for us to stand talking on the stairs. Dear Thomas, don't let us be so cold to each other.' He had no alternative but to put his arm around her waist, and kiss her, thinking, as he did so, of the mysterious agency which afflicted him. 'Tell me that you love me, Thomas,' she said.

'Of course I love you.' The question is not a pleasant one when put by a lady to a gentleman whose affections towards her are not strong, and it requires a very good actor to produce an efficient answer.

'I hope you do, Thomas. It would be sad, indeed, if you did not. You are not weary of your Camilla, – are you?'

For a moment there came upon him an idea that he would confess that he was weary of her, but he found at once that such an effort was beyond his powers. 'How can you ask such a question?' he said.

'Because you do not – come to me.' Camilla, as she spoke, laid her head upon his shoulder and wept. 'And now you have been five minutes with me and nearly an hour with Bella.'

'She wanted me to read to her,' said Mr Gibson; – and he hated himself thoroughly as he said it.

'And now you want to get away as fast as you can,' continued Camilla.

'Because of the morning service,' said Mr Gibson. This was quite true, and yet he hated himself again for saying it. As Camilla knew the truth of the last plea, she was obliged to let him go; but she made him swear before he went that he loved her dearly. 'I think it's all right,' she said to herself as he went down the stairs. 'I don't think he'd dare make it wrong. If he does; – o-oh!'

Mr Gibson, as he walked into Exeter, endeavoured to justify his own conduct to himself. There was no moment, he declared to himself, in which he had not endeavoured to do right. Seeing the manner in which he had been placed among these two young women, both of whom had fallen in love with him, how could he have saved himself from vacillation? And by what untoward chance had it come to pass that he had now learned to dislike so vigorously, almost to hate, the one whom he had been for a moment sufficiently infatuated to think that he loved?

But with all his arguments he did not succeed in justifying to himself his own conduct, and he hated himself.

66

Of a Quarter of Lamb

Miss Stanbury, looking out of her parlour window, saw Mr Gibson hurrying towards the cathedral, down the passage which leads from Southernhay into the Close. 'He's just come from Heavitree, I'll be bound,' said Miss Stanbury to Martha, who was behind her.

'Like enough, ma'am.'

'Though they do say that the poor fool of a man has become quite sick of his bargain already.'

'He'll have to be sicker yet, ma'am,' said Martha.

'They were to have been married last week, and nobody ever knew why it was put off. It's my belief he'll never marry her. And she'll be served right; – quite right.'

'He must marry her now, ma'am. She's been buying things all over Exeter, as though there was no end of their money.'

'They haven't more than enough to keep body and soul together,' said Miss Stanbury. 'I don't see why I mightn't have gone to service this morning, Martha. It's quite warm now out in the Close.'

'You'd better wait, ma'am, till the east winds is over. She was at Puddock's only the day before yesterday, buying bed-linen, – the finest they had, and that wasn't good enough.'

'Psha !' said Miss Stanbury.

'As though Mr Gibson hadn't things of that kind good enough for her,' said Martha.

Then there was silence in the room for awhile. Miss Stanbury was standing at one window, and Martha at the other, watching the people as they passed backwards and forwards, in and out of the Close. Dorothy had now been away at Nuncombe Putney for some weeks, and her aunt felt her loneliness with a heavy sense of weakness. Never had she entertained a companion in the house who had suited her as well as her niece, Dorothy. Dorothy would always listen to her, would always talk to her, would always bear with her. Since Dorothy had gone, various letters had been interchanged beteen them. Though there had been anger about Brooke Burgess, there had been no absolute rupture; but Miss Stanbury had felt that she could not write and beg her niece to come back to her. She had not sent Dorothy away. Dorothy had chosen to go, because her aunt had had an opinion of her own as to what was fitting for her heir; and as Miss Stanbury would not give up her opinion, she could not ask her niece to return to her. Such had been her resolution, sternly expressed to herself a dozen times during these solitary weeks; but time and solitude had acted upon her, and she longed for the girl's presence in the house. 'Martha,' she said at last, 'I think I shall get you to go over to Nuncombe Putney.'

'Again, ma'am ?'

'Why not again ? It's not so far, I suppose, that the journey will hurt you.'

'I don't think it'd hurt me, ma'am; – only what good will I do ?'

'If you'll go rightly to work, you may do good. Miss Dorothy was a fool to go the way she did; — a great fool.'

'She stayed longer than I thought she would, ma'am.'

'I'm not asking you what you thought. I'll tell you what. Do you send Giles to Winslow's, and tell them to send in early to-morrow a nice fore-quarter of lamb. Or it wouldn't hurt you if you went and chose it yourself.'

'It wouldn't hurt me at all, ma'am.'

'You get it nice; — not too small, because meat is meat at the price things are now; and how they ever see butcher's meat at all is more than I can understand.'

'People as has to be careful, ma'am, makes a little go a long way.'

'You get it a good size, and take it over in a basket. It won't hurt you, done up clean in a napkin.'

'It won't hurt me at all, ma'am.'

'And you give it to Miss Dorothy with my love. Don't you let 'em think I sent it to my sister-in-law.'

'And is that to be all, ma'am?'

'How do you mean all?'

'Because, ma'am, the railway and the carrier would take it quite ready, and there would be a matter of ten or twelve shillings saved in the journey.'

'Whose affair is that?'

'Not mine, ma'am, of course.'

'I believe you're afraid of the trouble, Martha. Or else you don't like going because they're poor.'

'It ain't fair, ma'am, of you to say so; — that it ain't. All I ask is, — is that to be all? When I've give'em the lamb, am I just to come away straight, or am I to say anything? It will look so odd if I'm just to put down the basket and come away without e'er a word.'

'Martha!'

'Yes, ma'am.'

'You're a fool.'

'That's true, too, ma'am.'

'It would be like you to go about in that dummy way, — wouldn't it; — and you that was so fond of Miss Dorothy.'

'I was fond of her, ma'am.'

'Of course you'll be talking to her; — and why not? And if she should say anything about returning — .'

'Yes, ma'am.'

'You can say that you know her old aunt wouldn't, — wouldn't refuse to have her back again. You can put it your own way, you know. You needn't make me find words for you.'

'But she won't, ma'am.'

'Won't what?'

'Won't say anything about returning.'

'Yes, she will, Martha, if you talk to her rightly.' The servant didn't reply for a while, but stood looking out of the window. 'You might as well go about the lamb at once, Martha.'

'So I will, ma'am, when I've got it out, all clear.'

'Why, – just this, ma'am. May I tell Miss Dolly straight out that you want her to come back, and that I've been sent to say so?'

'No, Martha.'

'Then how am I to do it, ma'am?'

'Do it out of your own head, just as it comes up at the moment?'

'Out of my own head, ma'am?'

'Yes; – just as you feel, you know.'

'Just as I feel, ma'am?'

'You understand what I mean, Martha.'

'I'll do my best, ma'am, and I can't say no more. And if you scolds me afterwards, ma'am, – why, of course, I must put up with it.'

'But I won't scold you, Martha.'

'Then I'll go out to Winslow's about the lamb at once, ma'am.'

'Very nice, and not too small, Martha.'

Martha went out and ordered the lamb, and packed it as desired quite clean in a napkin, and fitted it into the basket, and arranged with Giles Hickbody to carry it down for her early in the morning to the station, so that she might take the first train to Lessboro'. It was understood that she was to hire a fly at Lessboro' to take her to Nuncombe Putney. Now that she understood the importance of her mission and was aware that the present she took with her was only the customary accompaniment of an ambassadress entrusted with a great mission, Martha said nothing even about the expense. The train started for Lessboro' at seven, and as she was descending from her room at six, Miss Stanbury in her flannel dressing-gown stepped out of the door of her own room. 'Just put this in the basket,' said she, handing a note to her servant. 'I thought last night I'd write a word. Just put it in the basket and say nothing about it.' The note which she sent was as follows:

The Close, 8th April, 186 –

My Dear Dorothy, –

As Martha talks of going over to pay you a visit, I've thought that I'd just get her to take you a quarter of lamb, which is coming in now very nice. I do envy her going to see you, my dear, for I had gotten somehow to love to see your pretty face. I'm getting almost strong again; but Sir Peter, who was here this afternoon, just calling as a friend, was uncivil enough to say that I'm too much of an old woman to go out in the east wind. I told him it didn't much matter; – for the sooner old women made way for young ones, the better.

I am very desolate and solitary here. But I rather think that women who don't get married are intended to be desolate; and perhaps it is better for them, if they bestow their time and thoughts properly, – as I hope you do, my dear. A woman with a family of children has almost too many of the cares of this world, to give her mind as she ought to the other. What shall we say then of those who have no such cares, and yet do not walk uprightly? Dear Dorothy, be not such a one. For myself, I acknowledge bitterly the extent of my shortcomings. Much has been given to me; but if much be expected, how shall I answer the demand?

I hope I need not tell you that whenever it may suit you to pay a visit to Exeter, your room will be ready for you, and there will be a warm welcome. Mrs MacHugh always asks after you; and so has Mrs Clifford. I won't tell you what Mrs Clifford said about your colour, because it would make you vain. The Heavitree affair has all been put off; – of course you have heard that. Dear, dear, dear! You know what I think, so I need not repeat it.

Give my respects to your mamma and Priscilla, – and for yourself, accept the affectionate love of

> Your loving old aunt,
> Jemima Stanbury

PS – If Martha should say anything to you, you may feel sure that she knows my mind.

Poor old soul. She felt an almost uncontrollable longing to have her niece back again, and yet she told herself that she was bound not to send a regular invitation, or to suggest an unconditional return. Dorothy had herself decided to take her departure, and if she chose to remain away, – so it must be. She, Miss Stanbury, could not demean herself by renewing her invitation. She read her letter before she added to it the postscript, and felt that it was too solemn in its tone to suggest to Dorothy that which she wished to suggest. She had been thinking much of her own past life when she wrote those words about the state of an unmarried woman, and was vacillating between two minds, – whether it were better for a young woman to look forward to the cares and affections, and perhaps hard usage, of a marriage life; or to devote herself to the easier and safer course of an old maid's career. But an old maid is nothing if she be not kind and good. She acknowledged that, and, acknowledging it, added the postscript to her letter. What though there was a certain blow to her pride in the writing of it! She did tell herself that in thus referring her niece to Martha for an expression of her own mind, – after that conversation which she and Martha had had in the parlour, – she was in truth eating her own words. But the postscript was written, and though she took the letter up with her to her own room in order that she might alter the words if she repented of them in the night, the letter was sent as it was written, – postscript and all.

She spent the next day with very sober thoughts. When Mrs MacHugh called upon her and told her that there were rumours afloat in Exeter that the marriage between Camilla French and Mr Gibson would certainly be broken off, in spite of all purchases that had been made, she merely remarked that they were two poor, feckless things, who didn't know their own minds. 'Camilla knows hers plain enough,' said Mrs MacHugh sharply; but even this did not give Miss Stanbury any spirit. She waited, and waited patiently, till Martha should return, thinking of the sweet pink colour which used to come and go in Dorothy's cheeks, – which she had been wont to observe so frequently, not knowing that she had observed it and loved it.

67

River's Cottage

Three days after Hugh Stanbury's visit to Manchester Street, he wrote a note to Lady Rowley, telling her of the address at which might be found both Trevelyan and his son. As Bozzle had acknowledged, facts are things which may be found out. Hugh had gone to work somewhat after the Bozzlian fashion, and had found out this fact. 'He lives at a place called River's Cottage, at Willesden,' wrote Stanbury. 'If you turn off the Harrow Road to the right, about a mile beyond the cemetery, you will find the cottage on the left hand side of the lane, about a quarter of a mile from the Harrow road. I believe you can go to Willesden by railway, but you had better take a cab from London.' There was much consultation respecting this letter between Lady Rowley and Mrs Trevelyan, and it was decided that it should not be shown to Sir Marmaduke. To see her child was at the present moment the most urgent necessity of the poor mother, and both the ladies felt that Sir Marmaduke in his wrath might probably impede rather than assist her in this desire. If told where he might find Trevelyan, he would probably insist on starting in quest of his son-in-law himself, and the distance between the mother and her child might become greater in consequence, instead of less. There were many consultations; and the upshot of these was, that Lady Rowley and her daughter determined to start for Willesden without saying anything to Sir Marmaduke of the purpose they had in hand. When Emily expressed her conviction that if Trevelyan should be away from home they would probably be able to make their way into the house, – so as to see the child, Lady Rowley with some hesitation acknowledged that such might be the case. But the child's mother said nothing to her own mother of a scheme which she had half formed of so clinging to her boy that no human power should separate them.

They started in a cab, as advised by Stanbury, and were driven to a point on the road from which a lane led down to Willesden, passing by River's Cottage. They asked as they came along, and met no difficulty in finding their way. At the point on the road indicated, there was a country inn for hay-waggoners, and here Lady Rowley proposed that they should leave their cab, urging that it might be best to call at the cottage in the quietest manner possible; but Mrs Trevelyan, with her scheme in her head for the recapture of their child, begged that the cab might go on; – and thus they were driven up to the door.

River's Cottage was not a prepossessing abode. It was a new building, of light-coloured bricks, with a door in the middle and one window on each side. Over the door was a stone tablet, bearing the name, – River's Cottage. There was a little garden between the road and the house, across which there was a straight path to the door. In front of one window was a small shrub, generally called a puzzle-monkey, and in front of the other was a variegated laurel. There were two small morsels of green turf, and a distant view round the corner of the house of a row of cabbage stumps. If Trevelyan were living there, he had certainly come down in the world since the days in which he had occupied the house in Curzon Street. The two ladies got out of the cab, and slowly walked across the little garden. Mrs Trevelyan was dressed in black, and she wore a thick veil. She had altogether been unable to make up her mind as to what should be her conduct to her husband should she see him. That must be governed by circumstances as they might occur. Her visit was made not to him, but to her boy.

The door was opened before they knocked, and Trevelyan himself was standing in the narrow passage. Lady Rowley was the first to speak. 'Louis,' she said, 'I have brought your wife to see you.'

'Who told you that I was here?' he asked, still standing in the passage.

'Of course a mother would find out where was her child,' said Lady Rowley.

'You should not have come here without notice,' he said. 'I was careful to let you know the conditions on which you should come.'

'You do not mean that I shall not see my child,' said the mother. 'Oh, Louis, you will let me see him.'

Trevelyan hesitated a moment, still keeping his position firmly in the doorway. By this time an old woman, decently dressed and of comfortable appearance, had taken her place behind him, and behind her was a slip of a girl about fifteen years of age. This was the owner of River's Cottage and her daughter, and all the inhabitants of the cottage were now there, standing in the passage. 'I ought not to let you see him,' said Trevelyan; 'you have intruded upon me in coming here! I had not wished to see you here, – till you had complied with the order I had given you.' What a meeting between a husband and a wife who had not seen each other now for many months,* – between a husband and a wife who were still young enough not to have outlived the first impulses of their early love! He still stood there guarding the way, and had not even put out his hand to greet her. He was guarding the way lest she should, without his permission, obtain access to her own child! She had not removed her veil, and now she hardly dared to step over the threshold of her husband's house. At this moment, she perceived that the woman behind was pointing to the room on the left, as the cottage was entered, and Emily at once understood that her boy was there. Then at that moment she heard her son's voice, as, in his solitude, the child began to cry. 'I must go in,' she said; 'I will go in;' and rushing on she tried to push aside her husband. Her mother aided her, nor did Trevelyan attempt to stop her with violence, and in a moment she was kneeling at the foot of a small sofa, with her child in her arms. 'I had not intended to hinder you,' said Trevelyan, 'but I require from you a promise that you will not attempt to remove him.'

'Why should she not take him home with her?' said Lady Rowley.

'Because I will not have it so,' replied Trevelyan. 'Because I choose that it should be understood that I am to be the master of my own affairs.'

Mrs Trevelyan had now thrown aside her bonnet and her veil, and was covering her child with caresses. The poor little fellow,

whose mind had been utterly dismayed by the events which had
occurred to him since his capture, though he returned her kisses,
did so in fear and trembling. And he was still sobbing, rubbing his
eyes with his knuckles, and by no means yielding himself with his
whole heart to his mother's tenderness, – as she would have had
him do. 'Louey,' she said, whispering to him, 'you know mamma;
you haven't forgotten mamma?' He half murmured some little
infantine word through his sobs, and then put his cheek up to be
pressed against his mother's face. 'Louey will never, never forget his
own mamma; – will he, Louey?' The poor boy had no assurances
to give, and could only raise his cheek again to be kissed. In the
meantime Lady Rowley and Trevelyan were standing by, not
speaking to each other, regarding the scene in silence.

She, – Lady Rowley, – could see that he was frightfully altered in
appearance, even since the day on which she had so lately met him
in the City. His cheeks were thin and haggard, and his eyes were
deep and very bright, – and he moved them quickly from side to
side, as though ever suspecting something. He seemed to be smaller
in stature, – withered, as it were, as though he had melted away.
And, though he stood looking upon his wife and child, he was not
for a moment still. He would change the posture of his hands and
arms, moving them quickly with little surreptitious jerks; and
would shuffle his feet upon the floor, almost without altering his
position. His clothes hung about him, and his linen was soiled and
worn. Lady Rowley noticed this especially, as he had been a man
peculiarly given to neatness of apparel. He was the first to speak.
'You have come down here in a cab?' said he.

'Yes, – in a cab, from London,' said Lady Rowley.

'Of course you will go back in it? You cannot stay here. There is
no accommodation. It is a wretched place, but it suits the boy. As
for me, all places are now alike.'

'Louis,' said his wife, springing up from her knees, coming to
him, and taking his right hand between both her own, 'you will let
me take him with me. I know you will let me take him with me.'

'I cannot do that, Emily; it would be wrong.'

'Wrong to restore a child to his mother? Oh, Louis, think of it.
Why must my life be without him, – or you?'

'Don't talk of me. It is too late for that.'

'Not if you will be reasonable, Louis, and listen to me. Oh,
heavens, how ill you are!' As she said this she drew nearer to him,
so that her face was almost close to his. 'Louis, come back; come
back, and let it all be forgotten. It shall be a dream, a horrid dream,
and nobody shall speak of it.' He left his hand within hers and

stood looking into her face. He was well aware that his life since he had left her had been one long hour of misery. There had been to him no alleviation, no comfort, no consolation. He had not a friend left to him. Even his satellite, the policeman, was becoming weary of him and manifestly suspicious. The woman with whom he was now lodging, and whose resources were infinitely benefited by his payments to her, had already thrown out hints that she was afraid of him. And as he looked at his wife, he knew that he loved her. Everything for him now was hot and dry and poor and bitter. How sweet would it be again to sit with her soft hand in his, to feel her cool brow against his own, to have the comfort of her care, and to hear the music of loving words! The companionship of his wife had once been to him everything in the world; but now, for many months past, he had known no companion. She bade him come to her, and look upon all his trouble as a dream not to be mentioned. Could it be possible that it should be so, and that they might yet be happy together, — perhaps in some distant country, where the story of all their misery might not be known? He felt all this truly and with a keen accuracy. If he were mad, he was not all mad. 'I will tell you of nothing that is past,' said she, hanging to him, and coming still nearer to him, and embracing his arm.

Could she have condescended to ask him not to tell her of the past; — had it occurred to her so to word her request, — she might perhaps have prevailed. But who can say how long the tenderness of his heart would have saved him from further outbreak; — and whether such prevailing on her part would have been of permanent service? As it was, her words wounded him in that spot of his inner self which was most sensitive, — on that spot from whence had come all his fury. A black cloud came upon his brow, and he made an effort to withdraw himself from her grasp. It was necessary to him that she should in some fashion own that he had been right, and now she was promising him that she would not tell him of his fault! He could not thus swallow down all the convictions by which he had fortified himself to bear the misfortunes which he had endured. Had he not quarrelled with every friend he possessed on this score; and should he now stultify himself in all those quarrels by admitting that he had been cruel, unjust, and needlessly jealous? And did not truth demand of him that he should cling to his old assurances? Had she not been disobedient, ill-conditioned, and rebellious? Had she not received the man, both him personally and his letters, after he had explained to her that his honour demanded that it should not be so? How could he come into such terms as those now proposed to him, simply because he longed to enjoy the rich sweetness of her soft hand, to feel the fragrance of her breath, and to quench the heat of his forehead in the cool atmosphere of her beauty? 'Why have you driven me to this by your intercourse with that man?' he said. 'Why, why, why did you do it?'

She was still clinging to him. 'Louis,' she said, 'I am your wife.'

'Yes; you are my wife.'

'And will you still believe such evil of me without any cause?'

'There has been cause, – horrible cause. You must repent, – repent, – repent.'

'Heaven help me,' said the woman, falling back from him, and returning to the boy who was now seated in Lady Rowley's lap. 'Mamma, do you speak to him. What can I say? Would he think better of me were I to own myself to have been guilty, when there has been no guilt, – no slightest fault? Does he wish me to purchase my child by saying that I am not fit to be his mother?'

'Louis,' said Lady Rowley, 'if any man was ever wrong, mad, madly mistaken, you are so now.'

'Have you come out here to accuse me again, as you did before in London?' he asked. 'Is that the way in which you and she intend to let the past be, as she says, like a dream? She tells me that I am ill. It is true. I am ill, – and she is killing me, killing me, by her obstinacy.'

'What would you have me do?' said the wife, again rising from her child.

'Acknowledge your transgressions, and say that you will amend your conduct for the future.'

'Mamma, mamma, – what shall I say to him?'

'Who can speak to a man that is beside himself?' replied Lady Rowley.

'I am not so beside myself as yet, Lady Rowley, but that I know how to guard my own honour and to protect my own child. I have told you, Emily, the terms on which you can come back to me. You had better now return to your mother's house; and if you wish again to have a house of your own, and your husband, and your boy, you know by what means you may acquire them. For another week I shall remain here; – after that I shall remove far from hence.'

'And where will you go, Louis?'

'As yet I know not. To Italy I think, – or perhaps to America. It matters little where for me.'

'And will Louey be taken with you?'

'Certainly he will go with me. To strive to bring him up so that he may be a happier man than his father is all that there is now left for me in life.' Mrs Trevelyan had now got the boy in her arms, and her mother was seated by her on the sofa. Trevelyan was standing away from them, but so near the door that no sudden motion on their part would enable them to escape with the boy without his interposition. It now again occurred to the mother to carry off her prize in opposition to her husband; – but she had no scheme to that effect laid with her mother, and she could not reconcile herself to the idea of a contest with him in which personal violence would be necessary. The woman of the house had, indeed, seemed to sympathise with her, but she could not dare in such a matter to trust to assistance from a stranger. 'I do not wish to be uncourteous,' said Trevelyan, 'but if you have no assurance to give me, you had better – leave me.'

Then there came to be a bargaining about time, and the poor woman begged almost on her knees that she might be allowed to take her child up-stairs and be with him alone for a few minutes. It seemed to her that she had not seen her boy till she had had him to herself, in absolute privacy, till she had kissed his limbs, and had her hand upon his smooth back, and seen that he was white and clean and bright as he had ever been. And the bargain was made. She was asked to pledge her word that she would not take him out of the house, – and she pledged her word, feeling that there was no strength in her for that action which she had meditated. He, knowing that he might still guard the passage at the bottom of the stairs, allowed her to go with the boy to his bedroom, while he remained below with Lady Rowley. A quarter of an hour was allowed to her, and she humbly promised that she would return when that time was expired.

Trevelyan held the door open for her as she went, and kept it open during her absence. There was hardly a word said between him and Lady Rowley, but he paced from the passage into the room and from the room into the passage with his hands behind his back. 'It is cruel,' he said once. 'It is very cruel.'

'It is you that are cruel,' said Lady Rowley.

'Of course; – of course. That is natural from you. I expect that from you.' To this she made no answer, and he did not open his lips again.

After a while Mrs Trevelyan called to her mother, and Lady Rowley was allowed to go up-stairs. The quarter of an hour was of course greatly stretched, and all the time Trevelyan continued to pace in and out of the room. He was patient, for he did not summon them; but went on pacing backwards and forwards, looking now and again to see that the cab was at its place, – that no deceit was being attempted, no second act of kidnapping being perpetrated. At last the two ladies came down the stairs, and the boy was with them, – and the woman of the house.

'Louis,' said the wife, going quickly up to her husband, 'I will do anything, if you will give me my child.'

'What will you do?'

'Anything; – say what you want. He is all the world to me, and I cannot live if he be taken from me.'

'Acknowledge that you have been wrong.'

'But how; – in what words; – how am I to speak it?'

'Say that you have sinned; – and that you will sin no more.'

'Sinned, Louis; – as the woman did, – in the Scripture?* Would you have me say that?'

'He cannot think that it is so,' said Lady Rowley.

But Trevelyan had not understood her. 'Lady Rowley, I should have fancied that my thoughts at any rate were my own. But this is useless now. The child cannot go with you to-day, nor can you remain here. Go home and think of what I have said. If then you will do as I would have you, you shall return.'

With many embraces, with promises of motherly love, and with prayers for love in return, the poor woman did at last leave the house, and return to the cab. As she went there was a doubt on her own mind whether she should ask to kiss her husband; but he made no sign, and she at last passed out without any mark of tenderness. He stood by the cab as they entered it, and closed the door upon them, and then went slowly back to his room. 'My poor bairn,' he said to the boy; 'my poor bairn.'

'Why for mamma go?' sobbed the child.

'Mamma goes – ; oh, heaven and earth, why should she go? She goes because her spirit is obstinate, and she will not bend. She is stiff-necked, and will not submit herself. But Louey must love mamma always; – and mamma some day will come back to him, and be good to him.'

'Mamma is good, – always,' said the child. Trevelyan had intended on this very afternoon to have gone up to town, – to transact business with Bozzle; for he still believed, though the aspect of the man was bitter to him as wormwood, that Bozzle was necessary to him in all his business. And he still made appointments with the man, sometimes at Stony Walk, in the Borough, and sometimes at the tavern in Poulter's Court, even though Bozzle not unfrequently neglected to attend the summons of his employer. And he would go to his banker's and draw out money, and then walk about the crowded lanes of the City, and afterwards return to his desolate lodgings at Willesden, thinking that he had been transacting business, – and that this business was exacted from him by the unfortunate position of his affairs. But now he gave up his journey. His retreat had been discovered; and there came upon him at once a fear that if he left the house his child would be taken. His landlady told him on this very day that the boy ought to be sent to his mother, and had made him understand that it would not suit her to find a home any longer for one who was so singular in his proceedings. He believed that his child would be given up at once, if he were not there to guard it. He stayed at home, therefore, turning in his mind many schemes. He had told his wife that he should go either to Italy or to America at once; but in doing so he had had no formed plan in his head. He had simply imagined at the moment that such a threat would bring her to submission. But now it became a question whether he could do better than go to America. He suggested to himself that he should go to Canada, and fix himself with his boy on some remote farm, – far away from any city; and would then invite his wife to join him if she would. She was too obstinate, as he told himself, ever to yield, unless she should be absolutely softened and brought down to the ground by the loss of her child. What would do this so effectually as the interposition of the broad ocean between him and her? He sat thinking of this for the rest of the day, and Louey was left to the charge of the mistress of River's Cottage.

'Do you think he believes it, mamma?' Mrs Trevelyan said to her mother when they had already made nearly half their journey home in the cab. There had been nothing spoken hitherto between them, except some half-formed words of affection intended for consolation to the young mother in her great affliction.

'He does not know what he believes, dearest.'

'You heard what he said. I was to own that I had – sinned.'

'Sinned; – yes; because you will not obey him like a slave. That is sin – to him.'

'But I asked him, mamma. Did you not hear me? I could not say the word plainer, – but I asked him whether he meant that sin. He must have known, and he would not answer me. And he spoke of my – transgression. Mamma, if he believed that, he would not let me come back at all.'

'He did not believe it, Emily.'

'Could he possibly then so accuse me, – the mother of his child! If his heart be utterly hard and false towards me, if it is possible that he should be cruel to me with such cruelty as that, – still he must love his boy. Why did he not answer me, and say that he did not think it?'

'Simply because his reason has left him.'

'But if he be mad, mamma, ought we to leave him like that? And, then, did you see his eyes, and his face, and his hands? Did you observe how thin he is, – and his back, how bent? And his clothes, – how they were torn and soiled. It cannot be right that he should be left like that.'

'We will tell papa when we get home,' said Lady Rowley, who was herself beginning to be somewhat frightened by what she had seen. It is all very well to declare that a friend is mad when one simply desires to justify one's self in opposition to that friend; – but the matter becomes much more serious when evidence of the friend's insanity becomes true and circumstantial. 'I certainly think that a physician should see him,' continued Lady Rowley. On their return home Sir Marmaduke was told of what had occurred, and there was a long family discussion in which it was decided that Lady Milborough should be consulted, as being the oldest friend of Louis Trevelyan himself with whom they were acquainted. Trevelyan had relatives of his own name living in Cornwall; but Mrs Trevelyan herself had never even met one of that branch of the family.

Sir Marmaduke, however, resolved that he himself would go out and see his son-in-law. He too had called Trevelyan mad, but he did not believe that the madness was of such a nature as to interfere with his own duties in punishing the man who had ill used his daughter. He would at any rate see Trevelyan himself; – but of this he said nothing either to his wife or to his child.

68

Major Magruder's Committee

Sir Marmaduke could not go out to Willesden on the morning after Lady Rowley's return from River's Cottage, because on that day he was summoned to attend at twelve o'clock before a Committee of the House of Commons, to give his evidence and the fruit of his experience as to the government of British colonies generally; and as he went down to the House in a cab from Manchester Street he thoroughly wished that his friend Colonel Osborne had not been so efficacious in bringing him home. The task before him was one which he thoroughly disliked, and of which he was afraid. He dreaded the inquisitors before whom he was to appear, and felt that though he was called there to speak as a master of his art of governing, he would in truth be examined as a servant, – and probably as a servant who did not know his business. Had his sojourn at home been in other respects happy, he might have been able to balance the advantage against the inquiry; – but there was no such balancing for him now. And, moreover, the expense of his own house in Manchester Street was so large that his journey, in a pecuniary point of view, would be of but little service to him. So he went down to the House in an unhappy mood; and when he shook hands in one of the passages with his friend Osborne who was on the Committee, there was very little cordiality in his manner. 'This is the most ungrateful thing I ever knew,' said the Colonel to himself; 'I have almost disgraced myself by having this fellow brought home; and now he quarrels with me because that idiot, his son-in-law, has quarrelled with his wife.' And Colonel Osborne really did feel that he was a martyr to the ingratitude of his friend.

The Committee had been convoked by the House in compliance with the eager desires of a certain ancient pundit of the constitution, who had been for many years a member, and who had been known as a stern critic of our colonial modes of government. To him it certainly seemed that everything that was, was bad, – as regarded our national dependencies. But this is so usually the state of mind of all parliamentary critics, it is so much a matter of course that the members who take up the army or the navy, guns, India, our relations with Spain, or workhouse management, should find everything to be bad, rotten, and dishonest, that the wrath of the member for Killicrankie against colonial peculation and idleness, was not thought much of in the open House. He had been at the work for years, and the Colonial Office were so used to it that they rather liked him. He had made himself free of the office, and the clerks were always glad to see him. It was understood that he said bitter things in the House, – that was Major Magruder's line of business; but he could be quite pleasant when he was asking questions of a private secretary, or telling the news of the day to a senior clerk. As he was now between seventy and eighty, and had been at the work for at least twenty years, most of those concerned had allowed themselves to think that he would ride his hobby harmlessly to the day of his parliamentary death. But the drop from a house corner will hollow a stone by its constancy, and Major Magruder at last persuaded the House to grant him a Committee of Inquiry. Then there came to be serious faces at the Colonial Office, and all the little pleasantries of a friendly opposition were at an end. It was felt that the battle must now become a real fight, and Secretary and Under-Secretary girded up their loins.

Major Magruder was chairman of his own committee, and being a man of a laborious turn of mind, much given to blue-books, very patient, thoroughly conversant with the House, and imbued with a strong belief in the efficacy of parliamentary questionings to carry a point, if not to elicit a fact, had a happy time of it during this session. He was a man who always attended the House from 4 p.m. to the time of its breaking up, and who never missed a division. The slight additional task of sitting four hours in a committee-room three days a week, was only a delight the more, – especially as during those four hours he could occupy the post of chairman. Those who knew Major Magruder well did not doubt but that the Committee would sit for many weeks, and that the whole theory of colonial government, or rather of imperial control supervising such government, would be tested to the very utmost. Men who had heard the old Major maunder on for years past on his pet subject, hardly knew how much vitality would be found in him when his maundering had succeeded in giving him a committee.

A Governor from one of the greater colonies had already been under question for nearly a week, and was generally thought to have come out of the fire unscathed by the flames of the Major's criticism. This Governor had been a picked man, and he had made it appear that the control of Downing Street was never more harsh and seldom less refreshing and beautifying than a spring shower in April. No other lands under the sun were so blest, in the way of government, as were the colonies with which he had been acquainted; and, as a natural consequence, their devotion and loyalty to the mother country were quite a passion with them. Now the Major had been long of a mind that one or two colonies had better simply be given up to other nations, which were more fully able to look after them than was England, and that three or four more should be allowed to go clear, – costing England nothing, but owing England nothing. But the well-chosen Governor who had now been before the Committee, had rather staggered the Major, – and things altogether were supposed to be looking up for the Colonial Office.

And now had come the day of Sir Marmaduke's martyrdom. He was first requested, with most urbane politeness, to explain the exact nature of the government which he exercised in the Mandarins. Now it certainly was the case that the manner in which the legislative and executive authorities were intermingled in the affairs of these islands, did create a complication which it was difficult for any man to understand, and very difficult indeed for any man to explain to others. There was a Court of Chancery, so called, which

Sir Marmaduke described as a little parliament. When he was asked whether the court exercised legislative or executive functions, he said at first that it exercised both, and then that it exercised neither. He knew that it consisted of nine men, of whom five were appointed by the colony and four by the Crown. Yet he declared that the Crown had the control of the court; – which, in fact, was true enough no doubt, as the five open members were not perhaps, all of them, immaculate patriots; but on this matter poor Sir Marmaduke was very obscure. When asked who exercised the patronage of the Crown in nominating the four members, he declared that the four members exercised it themselves. Did he appoint them? No; – he never appointed anybody himself. He consulted the Court of Chancery for everything. At last it came out that the chief justice of the islands, and three other officers, always sat in the court; – but whether it was required by the constitution of the islands that this should be so, Sir Marmaduke did not know. It had worked well; – that was to say, everybody had complained of it, but he, Sir Marmaduke, would not recommend any change. What he thought best was that the Colonial Secretary should send out his orders, and that the people in the colonies should mind their business and grow coffee. When asked what would be the effect upon the islands, under his scheme of government, if an incoming Colonial Secretary should change the policy of his predecessor, he said that he didn't think it would much matter if the people did not know anything about it.

In this way the Major had a field day, and poor Sir Marmaduke was much discomfited. There was present on the Committee a young Parliamentary Under-Secretary, who with much attention had studied the subject of the Court of Chancery in the Mandarins, and who had acknowledged to his superiors in the office that it certainly was of all legislative assemblies the most awkward and complicated. He did what he could, by questions judiciously put, to pull Sir Marmaduke through his difficulties; but the unfortunate Governor had more than once lost his temper in answering the chairman; and in his heavy confusion was past the power of any Under-Secretary, let him be ever so clever, to pull him through. Colonel Osborne sat by the while and asked no questions. He had been put on the Committee as a respectable dummy; but there was not a member sitting there who did not know that Sir Marmaduke had been brought home as his friend; – and some of them, no doubt, had whispered that this bringing home of Sir Marmaduke was part of the payment made by the Colonel for the smiles of the Governor's daughter. But no one alluded openly to the inefficiency of the evidence given. No one asked why a Governor so incompetent had been sent to them. No one suggested that a job had been done. There are certain things of which opposition members of Parliament complain loudly; – and there are certain other things as to which they are silent. The line between these things is well known; and should an ill-conditioned, a pig-headed, an underbred, or an ignorant member not understand this line and transgress it, by asking questions which should not be asked, he is soon put down from the Treasury bench, to the great delight of the whole House.

Sir Marmaduke, after having been questioned for an entire afternoon, left the House with extreme disgust. He was so con-vinced of his own failure, that he felt that his career as a Colonial Governor must be over. Surely they would never let him go back to his islands after such an exposition as he had made of his own ignorance. He hurried off into a cab, and was ashamed to be seen of men. But the members of the Committee thought little or nothing about it. The Major, and those who sided with him, had been anxious to entrap their witness into contradictions and absurdities, for the furtherance of their own object; and for the furtherance of theirs, the Under-Secretary from the Office and the supporters of Government had endeavoured to defend their man. But, when the affair was over, if no special admiration had been elicited for Sir Marmaduke, neither was there expressed any special reprobation. The Major carried on his Committee over six weeks, and succeeded in having his blue-book printed; but, as a matter of course, nothing further came of it; and the Court of Chancery in the Mandarin Islands still continues to hold its own, and to do its work, in spite of the absurdities displayed in its construction. Major Magruder has had his day of success, and now feels that Othello's occupation is gone.* He goes no more to the Colonial Office, lives among his friends on the memories of his Committee, – not always to their gratification, – and is beginning to think that as his work is done he may as well resign Killicrankie to some younger politician. Poor Sir Marmaduke remembered his defeat with soreness long after it had been forgotten by all others who had been present, and was astonished when he found that the journals of the day, though they did in some curt fashion report the proceedings of the Committee, never uttered a word of censure against him, as they had not uttered a word of praise for that pearl of a Governor who had been examined before him.

On the following morning he went to the Colonial Office by appointment, and then he saw the young Irish Under-Secretary whom he had so much dreaded. Nothing could be more civil than was the young Irish Under-Secretary, who told him that he had better of course stay in town till the Committee was over, though it was not probable that he would be wanted again. When the Committee had done its work he would be allowed to remain six weeks on service to prepare for his journey back. If he wanted more time after that he could ask for leave of absence. So Sir Marmaduke left the Colonial Office with a great weight off his mind, and blessed that young Irish Secretary as he went.

69
Sir Marmaduke at Willesden

On the next day Sir Marmaduke purposed going to Willesden. He was in great doubt whether or no he would first consult that very eminent man Dr Trite Turbury, as to the possibility, and, – if possible, – as to the expediency, of placing Mr Trevelyan under some control. But Sir Maramduke, though he would repeatedly declare that his son-in-law was mad, did not really believe in this madness. He did not, that is, believe that Trevelyan was so mad as to be fairly exempt from the penalties of responsibility; and he was therefore desirous of speaking his own mind out fully to the man, and, as it were, of having his own personal revenge, before he might be deterred by the interposition of medical advice. He resolved therefore that he would not see Sir Trite Turbury, at any rate till he had come back from Willesden. He also went down in a cab, but he left the cab at the public-house at the corner of the road, and walked to the cottage.

When he asked whether Mr Trevelyan was at home, the woman of the house hesitated and then said that her lodger was out. 'I particularly wish to see him,' said Sir Marmaduke, feeling that the woman was lying to him. 'But he ain't to be seen, sir,' said the woman. 'I know he is at home,' said Sir Marmaduke. But the argument was soon cut short by the appearance of Trevelyan behind the woman's shoulder.

'I am here, Sir Marmaduke Rowley,' said Trevelyan. 'If you wish to see me you may come in. I will not say that you are welcome, but you can come in.' Then the woman retired, and Sir Marmaduke followed Trevelyan into the room in which Lady Rowley and Emily had been received; – but the child was not now in the chamber.

'What are these charges that I hear against my daughter?' said Sir Marmaduke, rushing at once into the midst of his indignation.

'I do not know what charges you have heard.'

'You have put her away.'

'In strict accuracy that is not correct, Sir Marmaduke.'

'But she is put away. She is in my house now because you have no house of your own for her. Is not that so? And when I came home she was staying with her uncle, because you had put her away. And what was the meaning of her being sent down into Devonshire. What has she done? I am her father, and I expect to have an answer?'

'You shall have an answer, certainly.'

'And a true one. I will have no hocus-pocus, no humbug, no Jesuitry.'

'Have you come here to insult me, Sir Marmaduke? Because, if so, there shall be an end to this interview at once.'

'There shall not be an end: – by G – , no, not till I have heard what is the meaning of all this. Do you know what people are saying of you; – that you are mad, and that you must be locked up, and your child taken away from you, and your property?'

'Who are the people that say so? Yourself; – and, perhaps, Lady Rowley? Does my wife say so? Does she think that I am mad. She did not think so on Thursday, when she prayed that she might be allowed to come back and live with me.'

'And you would not let her come?'

'Pardon me,' said Trevelyan. 'I would wish that she should come, – but it must be on certain conditions.'

'What I want to know is why she was turned out of your house?'

'She was not turned out.'

'What has she done that she should be punished?' urged Sir Marmaduke, who was unable to arrange his questions with the happiness which had distinguished Major Magruder. 'I insist upon knowing what it is that you lay to her charge. I am her father, and I have a right to know. She has been barbarously, shamefully ill-used, and by G – I will know.'

'You have come here to bully me, Sir Marmaduke Rowley.'

'I have come here, sir, to do the duty of a parent to his child; to protect my poor girl against the cruelty of a husband who in an unfortunate hour was allowed to take her from her home. I will know the reason why my daughter has been treated as though, – as though, – as though – '

'Listen to me for a minute,' said Trevelyan.

'I am listening.'

'I will tell you nothing; I will answer you not a word.'

'You will not answer me?'

'Not when you come to me in this fashion. My wife is my wife, and my claim to her is nearer and closer than is yours, who are her father. She is the mother of my child, and the only being in the world, – except that child, – whom I love. Do you think that with such motives on my part for tenderness towards her, for loving care, for the most anxious solicitude, that I can be made more anxious, more tender, more loving by coarse epithets from you ? I am the most miserable being under the sun because our happiness has been interrupted, and is it likely that such misery should be cured by violent words and gestures ? If your heart is wrung for her, so is mine. If she be much to you, she is more to me. She came here the other day, almost as a stranger, and I thought that my heart would have burst beneath its weight of woe. What can you do that can add an ounce to the burden that I bear ? You may as well leave me, – or at least be quiet.'

Sir Marmaduke had stood and listened to him, and he, too, was so struck by the altered appearance of the man that the violence of his indignation was lessened by the pity which he could not suppress. When Trevelyan spoke of his wretchedness, it was impossible not to believe him. He was as wretched a being to look at as it might have been possible to find. His contracted cheeks, and lips always open, and eyes glowing in their sunken caverns, told a tale which even Sir Marmaduke, who was not of nature quick in deciphering such stories, could not fail to read. And then the twitching motion of the man's hands, and the restless shuffling of his feet, produced a nervous feeling that if some remedy were not applied quickly, some alleviation given to the misery of the suffering wretch, human power would be strained too far, and the man would break to pieces, – or else the mind of the man. Sir Marmaduke, during his journey in the cab, had resolved that, old as he was, he would take this sinner by the throat, this brute who had striven to stain his daughter's name, – and would make him there and then acknowledge his own brutality. But it was now very manifest to Sir Marmaduke that there could be no taking by the throat in this case. He could not have brought himself to touch the poor, weak, passionate creature before him. Indeed, even the fury of his words was stayed, and after that last appeal he stormed no more. 'But what is to be the end of it ?' he said.

'Who can tell ? Who can say ? She can tell. She can put an end to it all. She has but to say a word, and I will devote my life to her. But that word must be spoken.' As he said this, he dashed his hand upon the table, and looked up with an air that would have been comic with its assumed magnificence had it not been for the true tragedy of the occasion.

'You had better, at any rate, let her have her child for the present.'

'No; – my boy shall go with me. She may go, too, if she pleases, but my boy shall certainly go with me. If I had put her from me, as you said just now, it might have been otherwise. But she shall be as welcome to me as flowers in May, – as flowers in May! She shall be as welcome to me as the music of heaven.'

Sir Marmaduke felt that he had nothing more to urge. He had altogether abandoned that idea of having his revenge at the cost of the man's throat, and was quite convinced that reason could have no power with him. He was already thinking that he would go away, straight to his lawyer, so that some step might be taken at once to stop, if possible, the taking away of the boy to America, when the lock of the door was gently turned, and the landlady entered the room.

'You will excuse me, sir,' said the woman, 'but if you be anything to this gentleman – '

'Mrs Fuller, leave the room,' said Trevelyan. 'I and the gentleman are engaged.'

'I see you be engaged, and I do beg pardon. I ain't one as would intrude wilful, and, as for listening, or the likes of that, I scorn it. But if this gentleman be anything to you, Mr Trevelyan – '

'I am his wife's father,' said Sir Marmaduke.

'Like enough. I was thinking perhaps so. His lady was down here on Thursday, – as sweet a lady as any gentleman need wish to stretch by his side.'

'Mrs Fuller,' said Trevelyan, marching up towards her, 'I will not have this, and I desire that you will retire from my room.'

But Mrs Fuller escaped round the table, and would not be banished. She got round the table, and came closely opposite to Sir Marmaduke. 'I don't want to say nothing out of my place, sir,' said she, 'but something ought to be done. He ain't fit to be left to hisself, – not alone, – not as he is at present. He ain't, indeed, and I wouldn't be doing my duty if I didn't say so. He has them sweats at night as'd be enough to kill any man; and he eats nothing, and he don't do nothing; and as for that poor little boy as in now in my own bed upstairs, if it wasn't that I and my Bessy is fond of children, I don't know what would become of that boy.'

Trevelyan, finding it impossible to get rid of her, had stood quietly, while he listened to her. 'She has been good to my child,' he said. 'I acknowledge it. As for myself, I have not been well. It is true. But I am told that travel will set me on my feet again. Change of air will do it.' Not long since he had been urging the wretchedness of his own bodily health as a reason why his wife should yield to him; but now, when his sickness was brought as a charge against him, – was adduced as a reason why his friends should interfere, and look after him, and concern themselves in his affairs, he saw at once that it was necessary that he should make little of his ailments.

'Would it not be best, Trevelyan, that you should come with me to a doctor,' said Sir Marmaduke.

'No; – no. I have my own doctor. That is, I know the course which I should follow. This place, though it is good for the boy, has disagreed with me, and my life has not been altogether pleasant; – I may say, by no means pleasant. Troubles have told upon me, but change of air will mend it all.'

'I wish you would come with me, at once, to London. You shall come back, you know. I will not detain you.'

'Thank you, – no. I will not trouble you. That will do, Mrs Fuller. You have intended to do your duty, no doubt, and now you can go.' Whereupon Mrs Fuller did go. 'I am obliged for your care, Sir Marmaduke, but I can really do very well without troubling you.'

'You cannot suppose, Trevelyan, that we can allow things to go on like this.'

'And what do you mean to do?'

'Well; – I shall take advice. I shall go to a lawyer, – and to a doctor, and perhaps to the Lord Chancellor, and all that kind of thing. We can't let things go on like this.'

'You can do as you please,' said Trevelyan, 'but as you have threatened me, I must ask you to leave me.'

Sir Marmaduke could do no more, and could say no more, and he took his leave, shaking hands with the man, and speaking to him with a courtesy which astonished himself. It was impossible to maintain the strength of his indignation against a poor creature who was so manifestly unable to guide himself. But when he was in London he drove at once to the house of Dr Trite Turbury, and remained there till the doctor returned from his round of visits. According to the great authority, there was much still to be done before even the child could be rescued out of the father's hands. 'I can't act without the lawyers,' said Dr Turbury. But he explained to Sir Marmaduke what steps should be taken in such a matter.

Trevelyan, in the mean time, clearly understanding that hostile measures would now be taken against him, set his mind to work to think how best he might escape at once to America with his boy.

70

Showing What Nora Rowley Thought
About Carriages

Sir Marmaduke, on his return home from Dr Turbury's house, found that he had other domestic troubles on hand over and above those arising from his elder daughter's position. Mr Hugh Stanbury had been in Manchester Street during his absence, and had asked for him, and, finding that he was away from home, had told his story to Lady Rowley. When he had been shown up-stairs all the four daughters had been with their mother; but he had said a word or two signifying his desire to speak to Lady Rowley, and the three girls had left the room. In this way it came to pass that he had to plead his cause before Nora's mother and her elder sister. He had pleaded it well, and Lady Rowley's heart had been well disposed towards him; but when she asked of his house and his home, his answer had been hardly more satisfactory than that of Alan-a-Dale.* There was little that he could call his own beyond 'The blue vault of heaven.' Had he saved any money? No, – not a shilling; – that was to say, – as he himself expressed it, – nothing that could be called money. He had a few pounds by him, just to go on with. What was his income? Well, – last year he had made four hundred pounds, and this year he hoped to make something more. He thought he could see his way plainly to five hundred a year. Was it permanent; and if not, on what did it depend? He believed it to be as permanent as most other professional incomes, but was obliged to confess that, as regarded the source from whence it was drawn at the present moment, it might be brought to an abrupt end any day by a disagreement between himself and the editor of the D. R. Did he think that this was a fixed income? He did think that if he and the editor of the D. R. were to fall out, he could come across other editors who would gladly employ him. Would he himself feel safe in giving his own sister to a man with such an income? In answer to this question, he started some rather bold doctrines on the subject of matrimony in general, asserting that safety was not desirable, that energy, patience, and mutual confidence would be increased by the excitement of risk, and that in his opinion it behoved young men and young women to come together and get themselves married, even though there might be some not remote danger of distress before them. He admitted that starvation would be disagreeable, – especially for children, in the eyes of their parents, – but alleged that children as a rule were not starved, and quoted the Scripture to prove that honest laborious men were not to be seen begging their bread in the streets.* He was very eloquent, but his eloquence itself was against him. Both Lady Rowley and Mrs Trevelyan were afraid of such advanced opinions; and, although everything was of course to be left, nominally, to the decision of Sir Marmaduke, they both declared that they could not recommend Sir Marmaduke to consent. Lady Rowley said a word as to the expediency of taking Nora back with her to the Mandarins, pointing out what appeared to her then to be the necessity of taking Mrs Trevelyan with them also; and in saying this she hinted that if Nora were disposed to stand by her engagement, and Mr Stanbury equally so disposed, there might be some possibility of a marriage at a future period. Only, in such case, there must be no correspondence. In answer to this Hugh declared that he regarded such a scheme as being altogether bad. The Mandarins were so very far distant that he might as well be engaged to an angel in heaven. Nora, if she were to go away now, would perhaps never come back again; and if she did come back, would be an old woman, with hollow cheeks. In replying to this proposition, he let fall an opinion that Nora was old enough to judge for herself. He said nothing about her actual age, and did not venture to plead that the young lady had a legal right to do as she liked with herself; but he made it manifest that such an idea was in his mind. In answer to this, Lady Rowley asserted that Nora was a good girl, and would do as her father told her; but she did not venture to assert that Nora would give up her engagement. Lady Rowley at last undertook to speak to Sir Rowley, and to speak also to her daughter. Hugh was asked for his address, and gave that of the office of the D. R. He was always to be found there between three and five; and after that, four times a week, in the reporters' gallery of the House of Commons. Then he was at some pains to explain to Lady Rowley that though he attended the reporters' gallery, he did not report himself. It was his duty to write leading political articles, and, to enable him to do so, he attended the debates.

Before he went Mrs Trevelyan thanked him most cordially for the trouble he had taken in procuring for her the address at Willesden, and gave him some account of the journey which she and her mother had made to River's Cottage. He argued with both of them that the unfortunate man must now be regarded as being altogether out of his mind, and something was said as to the great wisdom and experience of Dr Trite Turbury. Then Hugh Stanbury took his leave; and even Lady Rowley bade him adieu with kind cordiality. 'I don't wonder, mamma, that Nora should like him,' said Mrs Trevelyan.

'That is all very well, my dear, and no doubt he is pleasant, and manly, and all that; – but really it would be almost like marrying a beggar.'

'For myself,' said Mrs Trevelyan, 'if I could begin life again, I do not think that any temptation would induce me to place myself in a man's power.'

Sir Marmaduke was told of all this on his return home, and he asked many questions as to the nature of Stanbury's work. When it was explained to him, – Lady Rowley repeating as nearly as she could all that Hugh had himself said about it, he expressed his opinion that writing for a penny newspaper was hardly more safe as a source of income than betting on horse races. 'I don't see that it is wrong,' said Mrs Trevelyan.

'I say nothing about wrong. I simply assert that it is uncertain. The very existence of such a periodical must in itself be most insecure.' Sir Marmaduke, amidst the cares of his government at the Mandarins, had, perhaps, had no better opportunity of watching what was going on the world of letters than had fallen to the lot of Miss Stanbury at Exeter.

'I think your papa is right,' said Lady Rowley.

'Of course I am right. It is out of the question; and so Nora must be told.' He had as yet heard nothing about Mr Glascock.* Had that misfortune been communicated to him his cup would indeed have been filled with sorrow to overflowing.

In the evening Nora was closeted with her father. 'Nora, my dear, you must understand, once and for all, that this cannot be,' said Sir Marmaduke. The Governor, when he was not disturbed by outward circumstances, could assume a good deal of personal dignity, and could speak, especially to his children, with an air of indisputable authority.

'What can't be, papa?' said Nora.

Sir Marmaduke perceived at once that there was no indication of obedience in his daughter's voice, and he prepared himself for battle. He conceived himself to be very strong, and thought that his objections were so well founded that no one would deny their truth and that his daughter had not a leg to stand on. 'This, that your mamma tells me of about Mr Stanbury. Do you know, my dear, that he has not a shilling in the world?'

'I know that he has no fortune, papa, – if you mean that.'

'And no profession either; – nothing that can be called a profession. I do not wish to argue it, my dear, because there is no room for argument. The whole thing is preposterous. I cannot but think ill of him for having proposed it to you; for he must have known, – must have known, that a young man without an income cannot be accepted as a fitting suitor for a gentleman's daughter. As for yourself, I can only hope that you will get the little idea out of your head very quickly; – but mamma will speak to you about that. What I want you to understand from me is this, – that there must be an end to it.'

Nora listened to this speech in perfect silence, standing before her father, and waiting patiently till the last word of it should be pronounced. Even when he had finished she still paused before she answered him. 'Papa,' she said at last, – and hesitated again before she went on.

'Well, my dear.'

'I can not give it up.'

'But you must give it up.'

'No, papa. I would do anything I could for you and mamma, but that is impossible.'

'Why is it impossible ?'

'Because I love him so dearly.'

'That is nonsense. That is what all girls say when they choose to run against their parents. I tell you that it shall be given up. I will not have him here. I forbid you to see him. It is quite out of the question that you should marry such a man. I do hope, Nora, that you are not going to add to mamma's difficulties and mine by being obstinate and disobedient.' He paused a moment, and then added, 'I do not think that there is anything more to be said.'

'Papa.'

'My dear, I think you had better say nothing further about it. If you cannot bring yourself at the present moment to promise that there shall be an end of it, you had better hold your tongue. You have heard what I say, and you have heard what mamma says. I do not for a moment suppose that you dream of carrying on a communication with this gentleman in opposition to our wishes.'

'But I do.'

'Do what ?'

'Papa, you had better listen to me.' Sir Marmaduke, when he heard this, assumed an air of increased authority, in which he intended that paternal anger should be visible; but he seated himself, and prepared to receive, at any rate, some of the arguments with which Nora intended to bolster up her bad cause. 'I have promised Mr Stanbury that I will be his wife.'

'That is all nonsense.'

'Do listen to me, papa. I have listened to you and you ought to listen to me. I have promised him, and I must keep my promise. I shall keep my promise if he wishes it. There is a time when a girl must be supposed to know what is best for herself, — just as there is for a man.'

'I never heard such stuff in all my life. Do you mean that you'll go out and marry him like a beggar, with nothing but what you stand up in, with no friend to be with you, an outcast, thrown off by your mother, — with your father's — curse?'

'Oh, papa, do not say that. You would not curse me. You could not.'

'If you do it at all, that will be the way.'

'That will not be the way, papa. You could not treat me like that.'

'And how are you proposing to treat me?'

'But, papa, in whatever way I do it, I must do it. I do not say to-day or to-morrow; but it must be the intention and purpose of my life, and I must declare that it is, everywhere. I have made up my mind about it. I am engaged to him, and I shall always say so, — unless he breaks it. I don't care a bit about fortune. I thought I did once, but I have changed all that.'

'Because this scoundrel has talked sedition to you.'

'He is not a scoundrel, papa, and he has not talked sedition. I don't know what sedition is. I thought it meant treason, and I'm sure he is not a traitor. He has made me love him, and I shall be true to him.'

Hereupon Sir Marmaduke began almost to weep. There came first a half-smothered oath and then a sob, and he walked about the room, and struck the table with his fist, and rubbed his bald head impatiently with his hand. 'Nora,' he said, 'I thought you were so different from this! If I had believed this of you, you never should have come to England with Emily.'

'It is too late for that now, papa.'

'Your mamma always told me that you had such excellent ideas about marriage.'

'So I have, — I think,' said she, smiling.

'She always believed that you would make a match that would be a credit to the family.'

'I tried it, papa; — the sort of match that you mean. Indeed I was mercenary enough in what I believed to be my views of life. I meant to marry a rich man, — if I could, and did not think much whether I should love him or not. But when the rich man came — '

'What rich man?'

'I suppose mamma has told you about Mr Glascock.'

'Who is Mr Glascock? I have not heard a word about Mr

Glascock.' Then Nora was forced to tell her story, – was called upon to tell it with all its aggravating details. By degrees Sir Marmaduke learned that this Mr Glascock, who had desired to be his son-in-law, was in very truth the heir to the Peterborough title and estates, – would have been such a son-in-law as almost to compensate, by the brilliance of the connection, for that other unfortunate alliance. He could hardly control his agony when he was made to understand that this embryo peer had in truth been in earnest. 'Do you mean that he went down after you into Devonshire ?'

'Yes, papa.'

'And you refused him then, – a second time ?'

'Yes, papa.'

'Why; – why; – why ? You say yourself that you liked him; – that you thought that you would accept him.'

'When it came to speaking the word, papa, I found that I could not pretend to love him when I did not love him. I did not care for him, – and I liked somebody else so much better ! I just told him the plain truth, – and so he went away.'

The thought of all that he had lost, of all that might so easily have been his, for a time overwhelmed Sir Marmaduke, and drove the very memory of Hugh Stanbury almost out of his head. He could understand that a girl should not marry a man whom she did not like ; but he could not understand how any girl should not love such a suitor as was Mr Glascock. And had she accepted this pearl of men, with her position, with her manners and beauty and appearance, such a connection would have been as good as an assured marriage for every one of Sir Marmaduke's numerous daughters. Nora was just the woman to look like a great lady, a lady of high rank, – such a lady as could almost command men to come and throw themselves at her unmarried sisters' feet. Sir Marmaduke had believed in his daughter Nora, had looked forward to see her do much for the family ; and, when the crash had come upon the Trevelyan household, had thought almost as much of her injured prospects as he had of the misfortune of her sister. But now it seemed that more than all the good things of what he had dreamed had been proposed to this unruly girl, in spite of that great crash, and had been rejected ! And he saw more than this, – as he thought. These good things would have been accepted had it not been for this rascal of a penny-a-liner, this friend of that other rascal Trevelyan, who had come in the way of their family to destroy the happiness of them all ! Sir Marmaduke, in speaking of Stanbury after this, would constantly call him a penny-a-liner, thinking that the contamination of the penny communicated itself to all transactions of the Daily Record.

'You have made your bed for yourself, Nora, and you must lie upon it.'

'Just so, papa.'

'I mean that, as you have refused Mr Glascock's offer, you can never again hope for such an opening in life.'

'Of course I cannot. I am not such a child as to suppose that there are many Mr Glascocks to come and run after me. And if there were ever so many, papa, it would be no good. As you say, I have chosen for myself, and I must put up with it. When I see the carriages going about in the streets, and remember how often I shall have to go home in an omnibus, I do think about it a good deal.'

'I'm afraid you will think when it is too late.'

'It isn't that I don't like carriages, papa. I do like them; and pretty dresses, and brooches, and men and women who have nothing to do, and balls, and the opera; but – I love this man, and that is more to me than all the rest. I cannot help myself, if it were ever so. Papa, you mustn't be angry with me. Pray, pray, pray do not say that horrid word again.'

This was the end of the interview, Sir Marmaduke found that he had nothing further to say. Nora, when she reached her last prayer to her father, referring to that curse with which he had threatened her, was herself in tears, and was leaning on him with her head against his shoulder. Of course he did not say a word which could be understood as sanctioning her engagement with Stanbury. He was as strongly determined as ever that it was his duty to save her from the perils of such a marriage as that. But, nevertheless, he was so far overcome by her as to be softened in his manners towards her. He kissed her as he left her, and told her to go to her mother. Then he went out and thought of it all, and felt as though Paradise had been opened to his child and she had refused to enter the gate.

71

Showing What Hugh Stanbury Thought About the Duty of Man

In the conference which took place between Sir Marmaduke and his wife after the interview between him and Nora, it was his idea that nothing further should be done at all. 'I don't suppose the man will come here if he be told not,' said Sir Marmaduke,' and if he does, Nora of course will not see him.' He then suggested that Nora would of course go back with them to the Mandarins, and that when once there she would not be able to see Stanbury any more. 'There must be no correspondence or anything of that sort, and so the thing will die away.' But Lady Rowley declared that this would not quite suffice. Mr Stanbury had made his offer in due form, and must be held to be entitled to an answer. Sir Marmaduke, therefore, wrote the following letter to the 'penny-a-liner,' mitigating the asperity of his language in compliance with his wife's counsels.

                                    Manchester Street, April 10th 186 –
My Dear Sir, –
Lady Rowley has told me of your proposal to my daughter Nora ; and she has told me also what she learned from you as to your circumstances in life. I need hardly point out to you that no father would be justified in giving his daughter to a gentleman upon so small an income, and upon an income so very insecure.

I am obliged to refuse my consent, and I must therefore ask you to abstain from visiting and from communicating with my daughter.

                                    Yours faithfully,
                                    Marmaduke Rowley
Hugh Stanbury, Esq

This letter was directed to Stanbury at the office of the D. R., and Sir Marmaduke, as he wrote the pernicious address, felt himself injured in that he was compelled to write about his daughter to a man so circumstanced. Stanbury, when he got the letter, read it hastily and then threw it aside. He knew what it would contain before he opened it. He had heard enough from Lady Rowley to be aware that Sir Marmaduke would not welcome him as a son-in-law. Indeed, he had never expected such welcome. He was half-ashamed of his own suit because of the lowliness of his position, – half-regretful that he should have induced such a girl as Nora Rowley to give up for his sake her hopes of magnificence and splendour. But Sir Marmaduke's letter did not add anything to this feeling. He read it again, and smiled as he told himself that the father would certainly be very weak in the hands of his daughter. Then he went to work again at his article with a persistent resolve that so small a trifle as such a note should have no effect upon his daily work. Of course Sir Marmaduke would refuse his consent. Of course it would be for him, Stanbury, to marry the girl he loved in opposition to her father. Her father indeed ! If Nora chose to take him, – and as to that he was very doubtful as to Nora's wisdom, – but if Nora would take him, what was any father's opposition to him. He wanted nothing from Nora's father. He was not looking for money with his wife; – nor for fashion, nor countenance. Such a Bohemian was he that he would be quite satisfied if his girl would walk out to him, and become his wife, with any morning-gown on and with any old hat that might come readiest to hand. He wanted neither cards, nor breakfast, nor carriages, nor fine clothes. If his Nora should choose to come to him as she was, he having had all previous necessary arrangements duly made, – such as calling of banns or procuring of licence if possible, – he thought that a father's opposition would almost add something to the pleasure of the occasion. So he pitched the letter on one side, and went on with his article. And he finished his article; but it may be doubted whether it was completed with the full strength and pith needed for moving the pulses of the national mind, – as they should be moved by leading articles in the D. R. As he was writing he was thinking of Nora, – and thinking of the letter which Nora's father had sent to him. Trivial as was the letter, he could not keep himself from repeating the words of it to himself. ' "Need hardly point out," – oh; needn't he. Then why does he? Refusing his consent! I wonder what the old buffers think is the meaning of their consent, when they are speaking of daughters old enough to manage for themselves? Abstain from visiting or communicating with her! But if she visits and communicates with me; – what then? I can't force my way into the house, but she can force her way out. Does he imagine that she can be locked up in the nursery or put into the corner.' So he argued with himself, and by such arguments he brought himself to the conviction that it would be well for him to answer Sir Marmaduke's letter. This he did at once, – before leaving the office of the D.R.

250, Fleet Street, 20th April

My Dear Sir Marmaduke Rowley, –

I have just received your letter, and am indeed sorry that its contents should be so little favourable to my hopes. I understand that your objection to me is simply in regard to the smallness and insecurity of my income. On the first point I may say that I have fair hopes that it may be at once increased. As to the second, I believe I may assert that it is as sure at least as the income of other professional men, such as barristers, merchants, and doctors. I cannot promise to say that I will not see your daughter. If she desires me to do so, of course I shall be guided by her views. I wish that I might be allowed an opportunity of seeing you, as I think I could reverse or at least mitigate some of the objections which you feel to our marriage.

Yours most faithfully,
Hugh Stanbury

On the next day but one Sir Marmaduke came to him. He was sitting at the office of the D. R., in a very small and dirty room at the back of the house, and Sir Marmaduke found his way thither through a confused crowd of compositors, pressmen, and printers' boys. He thought that he had never before been in a place so foul, so dark, so crowded, and so comfortless. He himself was accustomed to do his work, out in the Islands, with many of the appanages of vice-royalty around him. He had his secretary, and his private secretary, and his inner-room, and his waiting-room; and not unfrequently he had the honour of a dusky sentinel walking before the door through which he was to be approached. He had an idea that all gentlemen at their work had comfortable appurtenances around them, – such as carpets, dispatch-boxes, unlimited stationery, easy chairs for temporary leisure, big table-space, and a small world of books around them to give at least a look of erudition to their pursuits. There was nothing of the kind in the miserably dark room occupied by Stanbury. He was sitting at a wretched little table on which there was nothing but a morsel of blotting paper, a small ink-bottle, and the paper on which he was scribbling. There was no carpet there, and no dispatch-box, and the only book in the room was a little dog's-eared dictionary. 'Sir Marmaduke, I am so much obliged to you for coming,' said Hugh. 'I fear you will find this place a little rough, but we shall be all alone.'

'The place, Mr Stanbury, will not signify, I think.'

'Not in the least, – if you don't mind it. I got your letter, you know, Sir Marmaduke.'

'And I have had your reply. I have come to you because you have expressed a wish for an interview; – but I do not see that it will do any good.'

'You are very kind for coming, indeed, Sir Marmaduke; – very kind. I thought I might explain something to you about my income.'

'Can you tell me that you have any permanent income?'

'It goes on regularly from month to month;' – Sir Marmaduke did not feel the slightest respect for an income that was paid monthly. According to his ideas, a gentleman's income should be paid quarterly, or perhaps half-yearly. According to his view, a monthly salary was only one degree better than weekly wages; – 'and I suppose that is permanence,' said Hugh Stanbury.

'I cannot say that I so regard it.'

'A barrister gets his, you know, very irregularly. There is no saying when he may have it.'

'But a barrister's profession is recognised as a profession among gentlemen, Mr Stanbury.'

'And is not ours recognised? Which of us, barristers or men of literature, have the most effect on the world at large. Who is most thought of in London, Sir Marmaduke, – the Lord Chancellor or the Editor of the "Jupiter?" '*

'The Lord Chancellor a great deal,' said Sir Marmaduke, quite dismayed by the audacity of the question.

'By no means, Sir Marmaduke,' said Stanbury, throwing out his hand before him so as to give the energy of action to his words. 'He has the higher rank. I will admit that.'

'I should think so,' said Sir Marmaduke.

'And the larger income.'

'Very much larger, I should say,' said Sir Marmaduke, with a smile.

'And he wears a wig.'

'Yes; – he wears a wig,' said Sir Marmaduke, hardly knowing in what spirit to accept his assertion.

'And nobody cares one brass button for him or his opinions,' said Stanbury, bringing down his hand heavily on the little table for the sake of emphasis.

'What, sir?'

'If you'll think of it, it is so.'

'Nobody cares for the Lord Chancellor!' It certainly is the fact that gentlemen living in the Mandarin Islands do think more of the Lord Chancellor, and the Lord Mayor, and the Lord-Lieutenant, and the Lord Chamberlain, than they whose spheres of life bring them into closer contact with those august functionaries. 'I presume, Mr Stanbury, that a connection with a penny newpaper makes such opinions as these almost a necessity.'

'Quite a necessity, Sir Marmaduke. No man can hold his own in print, now-a-days, unless he can see the difference between tinsel and gold.'

'And the Lord Chancellor, of course, is tinsel.'

'I do not say so. He may be a great lawyer, – and very useful. But his lordship, and his wig, and his woolsack, are tinsel in comparison with the real power possessed by the editor of a leading newspaper. If the Lord Chancellor were to go to bed for a month, would he be much missed?'

'I don't know, sir. I'm not in the secrets of the Cabinet. I should think he would.'

'About as much as my grandmother; – but if the Editor of the "Jupiter" were to be taken ill, it would work quite a commotion. For myself I should be glad, – on public grounds, – because I don't like his mode of business. But it would have an effect, – because he is a leading man.'

'I don't see what all this leads to, Mr Stanbury.'

'Only to this, – that we who write for the press think that our calling is recognised, and must be recognised as a profession. Talk of permanence, Sir Marmaduke, are not the newpapers permanent? Do not they come out regularly every day, – and more of them, and still more of them, are always coming out? You do not expect a collapse among them.'

'There will be plenty of newspapers, I do not doubt; – more than plenty, perhaps.'

'Somebody must write them, – and the writers will be paid.'

'Anybody could write the most of them, I should say.'

'I wish you would try, Sir Marmaduke. Just try your hand at a leading article to-night, and read it yourself to-morrow morning.'

'I've a great deal too much to do, Mr Stanbury.'

'Just so. You have, no doubt, the affairs of your Government to look to. We are all so apt to ignore the work of our neighbours! It seems to me that I could go over and govern the Mandarins without the slightest trouble in the world. But, no doubt, I am mistaken; – just as you are about writing for the newspapers.'

'I do not know,' said Sir Marmaduke, rising from his chair with dignity, 'that I called here to discuss such matters as these. As it happens, you, Mr Stanbury, are not the Governor of the Mandarins, and I have not the honour to write for the columns of the penny newspaper with which you are associated. It is therefore useless to discuss what either of us might do in the position held by the other.'

'Altogether useless, Sir Marmaduke, – except just for the fun of the thing.'

'I do not see the fun, Mr Stanbury. I came here, at your request, to hear what you might have to urge against the decision which I expressed to you in reference to my daughter. As it seems that you have nothing to urge, I will not take up your time further.'

'But I have a great deal to urge, and have urged a great deal.'

'Have you, indeed?'

'You have complained that my work is not permanent. I have shown that it is so permanent that there is no possibility of its coming to an end. There must be newspapers, and the people trained to write them must be employed. I have been at it now about two years. You know what I earn. Could I have got so far in so short a time as a lawyer, a doctor, a clergyman, a soldier, a sailor, a Government clerk, or in any of those employments which you choose to call professions? I think that is urging a great deal. I think it is urging everything.'

'Very well, Mr Stanbury. I have listened to you, and in a certain degree I admire your, – your, – your zeal and ingenuity, shall I say.'

'I didn't mean to call for admiration, Sir Marmaduke; but suppose you say, – good sense and discrimination.'

'Let that pass. You must permit me to remark that your position is not such as to justify me in trusting my daughter to your care. As my mind on that matter is quite made up, as is that also of Lady Rowley, I must ask you to give me your promise that your suit to my daughter shall be discontinued.'

'What does she say about it, Sir Marmaduke?'

'What she has said to me has been for my ears, and not for yours.'

'What I say is for her ears and for yours, and for her mother's ears, and for the ears of any who may choose to hear it. I will never give up my suit to your daughter till I am forced to do so by a full conviction that she has given me up. It is best to be plain, Sir Marmaduke, of course.'

'I do not understand this, Mr Stanbury.'

'I mean to be quite clear.'

'I have always thought that when a gentleman was told by the head of a family that he could not be made welcome in that family, it was considered to be the duty of that gentleman, – as a gentleman, – to abandon his vain pursuit. I have been brought up with that idea.'

'And I, Sir Marmaduke, have been brought up in the idea that when a man has won the affections of a woman, it is the duty of that man, – as a man, – to stick to her through thick and thin; and I mean to do my duty, according to my idea.'

'Then, sir, I have nothing further to say, but to take my leave. I must only caution you not to enter my doors.' As the passages were dark and intricate, it was necessary that Stanbury should show Sir Marmaduke out, and this he did in silence. When they parted each of them lifted his hat, and not a word more was said.

That same night there was a note put into Nora's hands as she was following her mother out of one of the theatres. In the confusion she did not even see the messenger who had handed it to her. Her sister Lucy saw that she had taken the note, and questioned her about it afterwards, – with discretion, however, and in privacy. This was the note:

Dearest Love,
I have seen your father, who is stern, – after the manner of fathers. What granite equals a parent's flinty bosom! For myself, I do not prefer clandestine arrangements and rope-ladders; and you, dear, have nothing of the Lydia about you.* But I do like my own way, and like it especially when you are at the end of the path. It is quite out of the question that you should go back to those islands. I think I am justified in already assuming enough of the husband to declare that such going back must not be held for a moment in question. My proposition is that you should authorise me to make such arrangements as may be needed, in regard to licence, banns, or whatever else, and that you should then simply walk from the house to the church and marry me. You are of age, and can do as you please. Neither your father nor mother can have any right to stop you. I do not doubt but that your mother would accompany you, if she were fully satisfied of your purpose. Write to me to the D. R.

> Your own, ever and ever, and always,
> H. S.

I shall try and get this given to you as you leave the theatre. If it should fall into other hands, I don't much care. I'm not in the least ashamed of what I am doing; and I hope that you are not.'

72

The Delivery of the Lamb

It is hoped that a certain quarter of lamb will not have been forgotten, – a quarter of lamb that was sent as a peace-offering from Exeter to Nuncombe Putney by the hands of Miss Stanbury's Martha, not with purposes of corruption, not intended to buy back the allegiance of Dorothy, – folded delicately and temptingly in one of the best table napkins, with no idea of bribery, but sent as presents used to be sent of old in the trains of great ambassadors as signs of friendship and marks of true respect. Miss Stanbury was, no doubt, most anxious that her niece should return to her, but was not, herself, low spirited enough to conceive that a quarter of lamb could be efficacious in procuring such return. If it might be that Dorothy's heart could be touched by mention of the weariness of her aunt's solitary life; and if, therefore, she would return, it would be very well; but it could not be well so, unless the offer should come from Dorothy herself. All of which Martha had been made to understand by her mistress, considerable ingenuity having been exercised in the matter on each side.

On her arrival at Lessboro', Martha had hired a fly, and been driven out to Nuncombe Putney; but she felt, she knew not why, a dislike to be taken in her carriage to the door of the cottage; and was put down in the middle of the village, from whence she walked out to Mrs Stanbury's abode, with the basket upon her arm. It was a good half mile, and the lamb was heavy, for Miss Stanbury had suggested that a bottle of sherry should be put in under the napkin, – and Martha was becoming tired of her burden, when, – whom should she see on the road before her but Brooke Burgess! As she said herself afterwards, it immediately occurred to her, 'that all the fat was in the fire.' Here had this young man come down, passing through Exeter without even a visit to Miss Stanbury, and had clandestinely sought out the young woman whom he wasn't to marry; and here was the young woman herself flying in her aunt's face, when one scratch of a pen might ruin them both! Martha entertained a sacred, awful, overcoming feeling about her mistress's will. That she was to have something herself she supposed, and her anxiety was not on that score; but she had heard so much about it, had realised so fully the great power which Miss Stanbury possessed, and had had her own feelings so rudely invaded by alterations in Miss Stanbury's plans, that she had come to entertain an idea that all persons around her should continually bear that will in their memory. Hugh had undoubtedly been her favourite, and, could Martha have dictated the will herself, she would still have made Hugh the heir; but she had realised the resolution of her mistress so far as to confess that the bulk of the property was to go back to a Burgess. But there were very many Burgesses; and here was the one who had been selected flying in the very face of the testatrix! What was to be done? Were she to go back and not tell her mistress that she had seen Brooke Burgess at Nuncombe then, – should the fact be found out, – would the devoted anger of Miss Stanbury fall upon her own head? It would be absolutely necessary that she should tell the story, let the consequences be what they might; – but the consequences, probably, would be very dreadful. 'Mr Brooke, that is not you?' she said, as she came up to him, putting her basket down in the middle of the dusty road.

'Then who can it be?' said Brooke, giving her his hand to shake.

'But what do bring you here, Mr Brooke? Goodness me, what will the missus say?'

'I shall make that all straight. I'm going back to Exeter tomorrow.' Then there were many questions and many answers. He was sojourning at Mrs Crocket's, and had been there for the last two days. 'Dear, dear, dear,' she said over and over again. 'Deary me, deary me!' and then she asked him whether it was 'all along of Miss Dorothy' that he had come. Of course, it was all along of Miss Dorothy. Brooke made no secret about it. He had come down to see Dorothy's mother and sister, and to say a bit of his own mind about future affairs; – and to see the beauties of the country. When he talked about the beauties of the country, Martha looked at him as the people of Lessboro' and Nuncombe Putney should have looked at Colonel Osborne, when he talked of the church porch at Cockchaffington. 'Beauties of the country, Mr Brooke; – you ought to be ashamed of yourself!' said Martha.

'But I ain't, – the least in the world,' said Brooke.

Then Martha took up her basket, and went on to the cottage, which had been close in sight during their conversation in the road. She felt angry with Dorothy. In such matters a woman is always angry with the woman, – who has probably been quite passive, and rarely with the man, who is ever the real transgressor. Having a man down after her at Nuncombe Putney! It had never struck Martha as very horrible that Brooke Burgess should fall in love with Dorothy in the city; – but this meeting, in the remoteness of the country, out of sight even of the village, was almost indecent; and all, too, with Miss Stanbury's will just, as one might say, on the balance! Dorothy ought to have buried herself rather than have allowed Brooke to see her at Nuncombe Putney; and Dorothy's mother and Priscilla must be worse. She trudged on, however, with her lamb, and soon found herself in the presence of the three ladies.

'What, – Martha!' said Dorothy.

'Yes, miss, – here I am. I'd have been here half-an-hour ago amost, if I hadn't been stopped on the road.'

'And who stopped you?' asked Priscilla.

'Why, – Mr Brooke, of course.'

'And what did Mr Brooke say to you?' asked Dorothy.

Martha perceived at once that Dorothy was quite radiant. She told her mistress that she had never seen Miss Dorothy look half so comely before. 'Laws, ma'am, she brightened up and speckled about, till it did your heart good to see her in spite of all.' But this was some time afterwards.

'He didn't say very much,' replied Martha, gravely.

'But I've got very much to tell you,' continued Dorothy. 'I'm engaged to be married to Mr Brooke, and you must congratulate me. It is settled now, and mamma and my sister know all about it.'

Martha, when she was thus asked directly for congratulation, hardly knew at once how to express herself. Being fully aware of Miss Stanbury's objection to the marriage, she could not venture to express her approbation of it. It was very improper, in Martha's mind, that any young woman should have a follower, when the 'missus' didn't approve of it. She understood well enough that, in that matter of followers, privileges are allowed to young ladies which are not accorded to maid servants. A young lady may do things, have young men to walk and talk with them, to dance with them and embrace them, and perhaps even more than this, – when for half so much a young woman would be turned into the streets without a character. Martha knew all this, and knew also that Miss Dorothy, though her mother lived in a very little cottage, was not altogether debarred, in the matter of followers, from the privileges of a lady. But yet Miss Dorothy's position was so very peculiar! Look at that will, – or, rather, at that embryo will, which might be made any day, which now probably would be made, and which might affect them both so terribly! People who have not got money should not fly in the face of those who have. Such at least was Martha's opinion very strongly. How could she congratulate Miss Dorothy under the existing circumstances. 'I do hope you will be happy, miss; – that you knows,' said Martha, in her difficulty. 'And now, ma'am; – miss, I mean,' she added, correcting herself, in obedience to Miss Stanbury's direct orders about the present, – 'missus has just sent me over with a bit of lamb, and a letter as is here in the basket, and to ask how you is, – and the other ladies.'

'We are very much obliged,' said Mrs Stanbury, who had not understood the point of Martha's speech.

'My sister is, I'm sure,' said Priscilla, who had understood it.

Dorothy had taken the letter, and had gone aside with it, and was reading it very carefully. It touched her nearly, and there had come tears into both her eyes, as she dwelt upon it. There was something in her aunt's allusion to the condition of unmarried women which came home to her especially. She knew her aunt's past history, and now she knew, or hoped that she knew, something of her own future destiny. Her aunt was desolate, whereas upon her the world smiled most benignly. Brooke had just informed her that he intended to make her his wife as speedily as possible, – with her aunt's consent if possible, but if not, then without it. He had ridiculed the idea of his being stopped by Miss Stanbury's threats, and had said all this in such fashion that even Priscilla herself had only listened and obeyed. He had spoken not a word of his own income, and none of them had dreamed even of asking him a question. He had been as a god in the little cottage, and all of them had been ready to fall down and worship him. Mrs Stanbury had not known how to treat him with sufficient deference, and, at the same time, with sufficient affection. He had kissed them all round, and Priscilla had felt an elation which was hardly intelligible to herself. Dorothy, who was so much honoured, had come to enjoy a status in her mother's estimation very different from that which she had previously possessed, and had grown to be quite beautiful in her mother's eyes.

There was once a family of three ancient maiden ladies, much respected and loved in the town in which they lived. Their manners of life were well known among their friends, and excited no surprise; but a stranger to the locality once asked of the elder why Miss Matilda, the younger, always went first out of the room? 'Matilda once had an offer of marriage,' said the dear simple old lady, who had never been so graced, and who felt that such an episode in life was quite sufficient to bestow brevet rank. It was believed by Mrs Stanbury that Dorothy's honours would be carried further than those of Miss Matilda, but there was much of the same feeling in the bosom of the mother towards the fortunate daughter, who, in the eyes of a man, had seemed goodly enough to be his wife.

With this swelling happiness round her heart, Dorothy read her aunt's letter, and was infinitely softened. 'I had gotten somehow to love to see your pretty face.' Dorothy had thought little enough of her own beauty, but she liked being told by her aunt that her face had been found to be pretty. 'I am very desolate and solitary here,' her aunt said; and then had come those words about the state of maiden women; – and then those other words, about women's duties, and her aunt's prayer on her behalf. 'Dear Dorothy, be not such an one.' She held the letter to her lips and to her bosom, and could hardly continue its perusal because of her tears. Such prayers from the aged addressed to the young are generally held in light esteem, but this adjuration was valued by the girl to whom it was addressed. She put together the invitation, – or rather the permission accorded to her, to make a visit to Exeter, – and the intimation in the postscript that Martha knew her mistress's mind; and then she returned to the sitting-room, in which Martha was still seated with her mother, and took the old servant apart. 'Martha,' she said, 'is my aunt happy now?'

'Well, – miss.'

'She is strong again; is she not?'

'Sir Peter says she is getting well; and Mr Martin — ; but Mr Martin isn't much account.'

'She eats and drinks again?'

'Pretty well; – not as it used to be, you know, miss. I tell her she ought to go somewheres, – but she don't like moving nowhow. She never did. I tell her if she'd go to Dawlish, – just for a week. But she don't think there's a bed fit to sleep on, nowhere, except just her own.'

'She would go if Sir Peter told her.'

'She says that these movings are newfangled fashions, and that the air didn't use to want changing for folk when she was young. I heard her tell Sir Peter herself, that if she couldn't live at Exeter, she would die there. She won't go nowheres, Miss Dorothy. She ain't careful to live.'

'Tell me something, Martha; will you?'

'What is it, Miss Dorothy?'

'Be a dear good woman now, and tell me true. Would she be better if I were with her?'

'She don't like being alone, miss. I don't know nobody as does.'

'But now, about Mr Brooke, you know.'

'Yes; Mr Brooke! That's it.'

'Of course, Martha, I love him better than anything in all the world. I can't tell you how it was, but I think I loved him the very first moment I saw him.'

'Dear, dear, dear!'

'I couldn't help it, Martha; – but it's no good talking about it, for of course I shan't try to help it now. Only this, – that I would do anything in the world for my aunt, – except that.'

'But she don't like it, Miss Dorothy. That is the truth, you know.'

'It can't be helped now, Martha; and of course she'll be told at once. Shall I go and tell her? I'd go to-day if you think she would like it.'

'And Mr Brooke?'

'He is to go to-morrow.'

'And will you leave him here?'

'Why not? Nobody will hurt him. I don't mind a bit about having him with me now. But I can tell you this. When he went away from us once it made me very unhappy. Would Aunt Stanbury be glad to see me, Martha?'

Martha's reserve was at last broken down, and she expressed herself in strong language. There was nothing on earth her mistress wanted so much as to have her favourite niece back again. Martha acknowledged that there were great difficulties about Brooke Burgess, and she did not see her way clearly through them. Dorothy declared her purpose of telling her aunt boldly, – at once. Martha shook her head, admiring the honesty and courage, but doubting the result. She understood better than did any one else the peculiarity of mind which made her mistress specially anxious that none of the Stanbury family should enjoy any portion of the Burgess money, beyond that which she herself had saved out of the income. There had been moments in which Martha had hoped that this prejudice might be overcome in favour of Hugh; but it had become stronger as the old woman grew to be older and more feeble, – and it was believed now to be settled as Fate. 'She'd sooner give it all to old Barty over the way,' Martha had once said, 'than let it go to her own kith and kin. And if she do hate any human creature, she do hate Barty Burgess.' She assented, however, to Dorothy's proposal; and, though Mrs Stanbury and Priscilla were astounded by the precipitancy of the measure they did not attempt to oppose it.

'And what am I to do?' said Brooke, when he was told.

'You'll come to-morrow, of course,' said Dorothy.

'But it may be that the two of us together will be too many for the dear old lunatic.'

'You shan't call her a lunatic, Brooke. She isn't so much a lunatic as you are, to run counter to her, and disobey her, and all that kind of thing.'

'And how about yourself?'

'How can I help it, Brooke? It is you that say it must be so.'

'Of course it must. Who is to be stayed from doing what is reasonable because an old woman has a bee in her bonnet. I don't believe in people's wills.'

'She can do what she likes about it, Brooke.'

'Of course she can, and of course she will. What I mean is that it never pays to do this or that because somebody may alter his will, or may make a will, or may not make a will. You become a slave for life, and then your dead tyrant leaves you a mourning-ring, and grins at you out of his grave. All the same she'll kick up a row, I fancy, and you'll have to bear the worst of it.'

'I'll tell her the truth, and if she be very angry, I'll just come home again. But I think I'll come home to-morrow any way, so that I'll pass you on the road. That will be best. She won't want us both together. Only then, Brooke, I shan't see you again.'

'Not till June.'

'And is it to be really in June?'

'You say you don't like May.'

'You are such a goose, Brooke. It will be May almost to-morrow. I shall be such a poor wife for you, Brooke. As for getting my things ready, I shall not have hardly, any things at all. Have you thought what it is to take a body so very poor?'

'I own I haven't thought as much about it, Dolly, – as I ought to have done, perhaps.'

'It is too late now, Brooke.'

'I suppose it is.'

'Quite too late. A week ago I could have borne it. I had almost got myself to think that it would be better that I should bear it. But you have come, and banished all the virtue out of my head. I am ashamed of myself, because I am so unworthy; but I would put up with that shame rather than lose you now. Brooke, Brooke, I will so try to be good to you!'

In the afternoon Martha and Dorothy started together for Exeter, Brooke and Priscilla accompanying them as far as Mrs Crocket's, where the Lessboro' fly was awaiting them. Dorothy said little or nothing during the walk, nor, indeed, was she very communicative during the journey into Exeter. She was going to her aunt, instigated simply by the affection of her full heart; but she was going with a tale in her mouth which she knew would be very unwelcome. She could not save herself from feeling that, in having accepted Brooke, and in having not only accepted him but even fixed the day for her marriage, she had been ungrateful to her aunt. Had it not been for her aunt's kindness and hospitality, she would never have seen Brooke Burgess. And as she had been under her aunt's care at Exeter, she doubted whether she had not been guilty of some great fault in falling in love with this man, in opposition as it were to express orders. Should her aunt still declare that she would in no way countenance the marriage, that she would still oppose it and use her influence with Brooke to break it off, then would Dorothy return on the morrow to her mother's cottage at Nuncombe Putney, so that her lover might be free to act with her aunt as he might think fit. And should he yield, she would endeavour, – she would struggle hard, to think that he was still acting for the best. 'I must tell her myself, Martha,' said Dorothy, as they came near to Exeter.

'Certainly, miss; – only you'll do it to-night.'

'Yes; – at once. As soon after I get there as possible.'

73

Dorothy Returns to Exeter

Miss Stanbury perfectly understood that Martha was to come back by the train reaching Exeter at 7 p.m., and that she might be expected in the Close about a quarter-of-an-hour after that time. She had been nervous and anxious all day, – so much so that Mr Martin had told her that she must be very careful. 'That's all very well,' the old woman had said, 'but you haven't got any medicine for my complaint, Mr Martin.' The apothecary had assured her that the worst of her complaint was in the east wind, and had gone away begging her to be very careful. 'It is not God's breezes that are hard to any one,' the old lady had said to herself, – 'but our own hearts.' After her lonely dinner she had fidgeted about the room, and had rung twice for the girl, not knowing what order to give when the servant came to her. She was very anxious about her tea, but would not have it brought to her till after Martha should have arrived. She was half-minded to order that a second cup and saucer should be placed there, but she had not the courage to face the disappointment which would fall upon her, should the cup and saucer stand there for no purpose. And yet, should she come, how nice it would be to show her girl that her old aunt had been ready for her. Thrice she went to the window after the cathedral clock had struck seven, to see whether her ambassador was returning. From her window there was only one very short space of pathway on which she could have seen her, – and, as it happened, there came the ring at the door, and no ambassador had as yet been viewed. Miss Stanbury was immediately off her seat, and out upon the landing. 'Here we are again, Miss Dorothy,' said Martha. Then Miss Stanbury could not restrain herself, – but descended the stairs, moving as she had never moved since she had first been ill. 'My bairn,' she said; 'my dearest bairn! I thought that perhaps it might be so. Jane, another tea-cup and saucer up-stairs.' What a pity that she had not ordered it before! 'And get a hot cake, Jane. You will be ever so hungry, my darling, after your journey.'

'Are you glad to see me, Aunt Stanbury?' said Dorothy.

'Glad, my pretty one!' Then she put up her hands, and smoothed down the girl's cheeks, and kissed her, and patted Martha on the back, and scolded her at the same time for not bringing Miss Dorothy from the station in a cab. 'And what is the meaning of that little bag?' she said. 'You shall go back for the rest yourself, Martha, because it is your own fault.' Martha knew that all this was pleasant enough; – but then her mistress's moods would sometimes be changed so suddenly! How would it be when Miss Stanbury knew that Brooke Burgess had been left behind at Nuncombe Putney?

'You see I didn't stay to eat any of the lamb,' said Dorothy, smiling.

'You shall have a calf instead, my dear,' said Miss Stanbury, 'because you are a returned prodigal.'*

All this was very pleasant, and Miss Stanbury was so happy dispensing her tea, and the hot cake, and the clotted cream, and was so intent upon her little methods of caressing and petting her niece, that Dorothy had no heart to tell her story while the plates and cups were still upon the table. She had not, perhaps, cared much for the hot cake, having such a weight upon her mind, but she had seemed to care, understanding well that she might so best conduce to her aunt's comfort. Miss Stanbury was a woman who could not bear that the good things which she had provided for a guest should not be enjoyed. She could taste with a friend's palate, and drink with a friend's throat. But when debarred these vicarious pleasures by what seemed to her to be the caprice of her guests, she would be offended. It had been one of the original sins of Camilla and Arabella French that they would declare at her tea-table that they had dined late and could not eat tea-cake. Dorothy knew all this, – and did her duty; – but with a heavy heart. There was the story to be told, and she had promised Martha that it should be told to-night. She was quite aware, too, independently of her promise, that it was necessary that it should be told to-night. It was very sad, – very grievous that the dear old lady's happiness should be disturbed so soon; but it must be done. When the tea-things were being taken away her aunt was still purring round her, and saying gentle, loving words. Dorothy bore it as well as she could, – bore it well, smiling and kissing her aunt's hand, and uttering now and then some word of affection. But the thing had to be done; and as soon as the room was quiet for a moment, she jumped up from her chair and began. 'Aunt Stanbury, I must tell you something at once. Who, do you think, is at Nuncombe Putney?'

'Not Brooke Burgess?'

'Yes, he is. He is there now, and is to be here with you to-morrow.'

The whole colour and character of Miss Stanbury's face was changed in a moment. She had been still purring up to the moment in which this communication had been made to her. Her gratification had come to her from the idea that her pet had come back to her from love of her, – as in very truth had been the case; but now it seemed that Dorothy had returned to ask for a great favour for herself. And she reflected at once that Brooke had passed through Exeter without seeing her. If he was determined to marry without reference to her, he might at any rate have had the grace to come to her and say so. She, in the fulness of her heart, had written words of affection to Dorothy; – and both Dorothy and Brooke had at once taken advantage of her expressions for their own purposes. Such was her reading of the story of the day. 'He need not trouble himself to come here now,' she said.

'Dear aunt, do not say that.'

'I do say it. He need not trouble himself to come now. When I said that I should be glad to see you, I did not intend that you should meet Mr Burgess under my roof. I did not wish to have you both together.'

'How could I help coming, when you wrote to me like that?'

'It is very well, – but he need not come. He knows the way from Nuncombe to London without stopping at Exeter.'

'Aunt Stanbury, you must let me tell it you all.'

'There is no more to tell, I should think.'

'But there is more. You knew what he thought about me, and what he wished.'

'He is his own master, my dear; – and you are your own mistress.'

'If you speak to me like that you will kill me, Aunt Stanbury. I did not think of coming; – only when Martha brought your dear letter I could not help it. But he was coming. He meant to come to-morrow, and he will. Of course he must defend himself, if you are angry with him.'

'He need not defend himself at all.'

'I told them, and I told him, that I would only stay one night, – if you did not wish that we should be here together. You must see him, Aunt Stanbury. You would not refuse to see him.'

'If you please, my dear, you must allow me to judge whom I will see.'

After that the discussion ceased between them for awhile, and Miss Stanbury left the room that she might hold a consultation with Martha. Dorothy went up to her chamber, and saw that everything had been prepared for her with most scrupulous care. Nothing could be whiter, neater, cleaner, nicer than was everything that surrounded her. She had perceived while living under her aunt's roof, how, gradually, small delicate feminine comforts had been increased for her. Martha had been told that Miss Dorothy ought to have this, and that Miss Dorothy ought to have that; till at last she, who had hitherto known nothing of the small luxuries that come from an easy income, had felt ashamed of the prettinesses that had been added to her. Now she could see at once that infinite care had been used to make her room bright and smiling, – only in the hope that she would return. As soon as she saw it all, she sat down on her bed and burst out into tears. Was it not hard upon her that she should be forced into such ingratitude! Every comfort prepared for her was a coal of hot fire upon her head. And yet what had she done that she ought not to have done? Was it unreasonable that she should have loved this man, when they two were brought together? And had she even dared to think of him otherwise than as an acquaintance till he had compelled her to confess her love? And after that had she not tried to separate herself from him, so that they two, – her aunt and her lover, – might be divided by no quarrel? Had not Priscilla told her that she was right in all that she was doing? Nevertheless, in spite of all this, she could not refrain from accusing herself of ingratitude towards her aunt. And she began to think it would have been better for her now to have remained at home, and have allowed Brooke to come alone to Exeter than to have obeyed the impulse which had arisen from the receipt of her aunt's letter. When she went down again she found herself alone in the room, and she was beginning to think that it was intended that she should go to bed without again seeing her aunt; but at last Miss Stanbury came to her, with a sad countenance, but without that look of wrath which Dorothy knew so well. 'My dear,' she said, 'it will be better that Mr Burgess should go up to London to-morrow. I will see him, of course, if he chooses to come, and Martha shall meet him at the station and explain it. If you do not mind, I would prefer that you should not meet him here.'

'I meant only to stay one night, aunt.'

'That is nonsense. If I am to part with either of you, I will part with him. You are dearer to me than he is. Dorothy, you do not know how dear to me you are.'

Dorothy immediately fell on her knees at her aunt's feet, and hid her face in her aunt's lap. Miss Stanbury twined round her fingers the soft hair which she loved so well, – because it was a grace given by God and not bought out of a shop, – and caressed the girl's head, and muttered something that was intended for a prayer. 'If he will let me, aunt, I will give him up,' said Dorothy, looking up into her aunt's face. 'If he will say that I may, though I shall love him always, he may go.'

'He is his own master,' said Miss Stanbury. 'Of course he is his own master.'

'Will you let me return to-morrow, – just for a few days, – and then you can talk to him as you please. I did not mean to come to stay. I wished him good-bye because I knew that I should not meet him here.'

'You always talk of going away, Dorothy, as soon as ever you are in the house. You are always threatening me.'

'I will come again, the moment you tell me. If he goes in the morning, I will be here the same evening. And I will write to him, Aunt Stanbury, and tell him, – that he is – quite free, – quite free, – quite free.'

Miss Stanbury made no reply to this, but sat, still playing with her niece's hair. 'I think I will go to bed,' she said at last. 'It is past ten. You need not go to Nuncombe, Dorothy. Martha shall meet him, and he can see me here. But I do not wish him to stay in the house. You can go over and call on Mrs MacHugh. Mrs MacHugh will take it well of you that you should call on her.' Dorothy made no further opposition to this arrangement, but kissed her aunt, and went to her chamber.

How was it all to be for her? For the last two days she had been radiant with new happiness. Everything had seemed to be settled. Her lover, in his high-handed way, had declared that in no important crisis of life would he allow himself to be driven out of his way by the fear of what an old woman might do in her will. When Dorothy assured him that not for worlds would she, though she loved him dearly, injure his material prospects, he had thrown it all aside, after a grand fashion, that had really made the girl think that all Miss Stanbury's money was as nothing to his love for her. She and Priscilla and her mother had been carried away so entirely by Brooke's oratory as to feel for the time that the difficulties were entirely conquered. But now the aspect of things was so different! Whatever Brooke might owe to Miss Stanbury, she, Dorothy, owed her aunt everything. She would immolate herself, – if Brooke would only let her. She did not quite understand her aunt's stubborn opposition; but she knew that there was some great cause for her aunt's feeling on the matter. There had been a promise made, or an oath sworn, that the property of the Burgess family should not go into the hands of any Stanbury. Dorothy told herself that, were she married, she would be a Stanbury no longer; – that her aunt would still comply with the obligation she had fixed for herself; but, nevertheless, she was ready to believe that her aunt might be right. Her aunt had always declared that it should be so; and Dorothy,

knowing this, confessed to herself that she should have kept her
heart under better control. Thinking of these things, she went to the
table where, paper and ink and pens had all been prepared for her
so prettily, and began her letter to Brooke. 'Dearest, dearest
Brooke.' But then she thought that this was not a fair keeping of
her promise, and she began again. 'My dear Brooke.' The letter,
however, did not get itself written that night. It was almost
impossible for her to write it. 'I think it will be better for you,' she
had tried to say, 'to be guided by my aunt.' But how could she say
this when she did not believe it? It was her wish to make him
understand that she would never think ill of him, for a moment, if
he would make up his mind to abandon her; – but she could not
find the words to express herself, – and she went, at last, to bed,
leaving the half-covered paper upon the table.

She went to bed, and cried herself to sleep. It had been so sweet
to have a lover, – a man of her own, to whom she could say what
she pleased, from whom she had a right to ask for counsel and
protection, a man who delighted to be near her, and to make much
of her. In comparison with her old mode of living, her old ideas of
life, her life with such a lover was passed in an elysium. She had
entered from barren lands into so rich a paradise! But there is no
paradise, as she now found, without apples which must be eaten,
and which lead to sorrow. She regretted in this hour that she had
ever seen Brooke Burgess. After all, with her aunt's love and care
for her, with her mother and sister near her, with the respect of
those who knew her, why should the lands have been barren, even
had there been no entrance for her into that elysium? And did it
not all result in this – that the elysium to be desired should not be
here; that the paradise, without the apples, must be waited for till
beyond the grave? It is when things go badly with us here, and for
most of us only then, that we think that we can see through the
dark clouds into the joys of heaven. But at last she slept, and in her
dreams Brooke was sitting with her in Nidden Park with his arm
tight clasped round her waist.

She slept so soundly, that when a step crept silently into her
room, and when a light was held for awhile over her face, neither
the step nor the light awakened her. She was lying with her head
back upon the pillow, and her arm hung by the bedside, and her
lips were open, and her loose hair was spread upon the pillow. The
person who stood there with the light thought that there never had
been a fairer sight. Everything there was so pure, so sweet, so good!
She was one whose only selfish happiness could come to her from
the belief that others loved her. The step had been very soft, and

even the breath of the intruder was not allowed to pass heavily into the air, but the light of the candle shone upon the eyelids of the sleeper and she moved her head restlessly on the pillow. 'Dorothy, are you awake? Can you speak to me?'

Then the disturbed girl gradually opened her eyes and gazed upwards, and raised herself in her bed, and sat wondering. 'Is anything the matter, aunt?' she said.

'Only the vagaries of an old woman, my pet, – of an old woman who cannot sleep in her bed.'

'But what is it, aunt?'

'Kiss me, dearest.' Then, with something of slumber still about her, Dorothy raised herself in her bed, and placed her arm on her aunt's shoulder and embraced her. 'And now for my news,' said Miss Stanbury.

'What news, aunt. It isn't morning yet; is it?'

'No; – it is not morning. You shall sleep again presently. 'I have thought of it, and you shall be Brooke's wife, and I will have it here, and we will all be friends.'

'What!'

'You will like that; – will you not?'

'And you will not quarrel with him? What am I to say? What am I to do?' She was, in truth, awake now, and, not knowing what she did, she jumped out of bed, and stood holding her aunt by the arm.

'It is not a dream,' said Miss Stanbury.

'Are you sure that it is not a dream? And may he come here to-morrow?'

'Of course he will come to-morrow.'

'And may I see him, Aunt Stanbury?'

'Not if you go home, my dear.'

'But I won't go home. And will you tell him? Oh dear, oh dear! Aunt Stanbury, I do not think that I believe it yet.'

'You will catch cold, my dear, if you stay there trying to believe it. You have nothing on. Get into bed and believe it there. You will have time to think of it before the morning.' 'Then Miss Stanbury went back to her own chamber, and Dorothy was left alone to realise her bliss.

She thought of all her life for the last twelve months, – of the first invitation to Exeter, and the doubts of the family as to its acceptance, of her arrival and of her own doubts as to the possibility of her remaining, of Mr Gibson's courtship and her aunt's disappointment, of Brooke's coming, of her love and of his, – and then of her departure back to Nuncombe. After that had come the triumph of

Brooke's visit, and then the terrible sadness of her aunt's displeasure. But now everything was good and glorious. She did not
care for money herself. She thought that she never could care much
for being rich. But had she made Brooke poor by marrying him,
that must always have been to her matter of regret, if not of
remorse. But now it was all to be smooth and sweet. Now a
paradise was to be opened to her, with no apples which she might
not eat; – no apples which might not, but still must, be eaten. She
thought that it would be impossible that she should sleep again that
night; but she did sleep, and dreamed that Brooke was holding her
in Niddon park, tighter than ever.

When the morning came she trembled as she walked down into
the parlour. Might it not still be possible that it was all a dream?
or what if her aunt should again have changed her purpose? But
the first moment of her aunt's presence told her that there was
nothing to fear. 'How did you sleep, Dorothy?' said the old lady.

'Dear aunt, I do not know. Was it all sleep?'

'What shall we say to Brooke when he comes?'

'You shall tell him.'

'No, dearest, you must tell him. And you must say to him that if
he is not good to my girl, and does not love her always, and cling
to her, and keep her from harm, and be in truth her loving husband,
I will hold him to be the most ungrateful of human beings.' And
before Brooke came, she spoke again. 'I wonder whether he thinks
you as pretty as I do, Dolly?'

'He never said that he thought me pretty at all.'

'Did he not? Then he shall say so, or he shall not have you. It
was your looks won me first, Dolly, – like an old fool as I am. It is
so pleasant to have a little nature after such a deal of foul artifice.'
In which latter remarks it was quite understood that Miss Stanbury
was alluding to her enemies at Heavitree.

74

The Lioness Aroused

Brooke Burgess had been to Exeter and had gone, – for he only
remained there one night, – and everything was apparently settled.
It was not exactly told through Exeter that Miss Stanbury's heir
was to be allowed to marry Miss Stanbury's niece; but Martha
knew it, and Giles Hickbody guessed it, and Dorothy was allowed
to tell her mother and sister, and Brooke himself, in his own careless

way, had mentioned the matter to his uncle Barty. As Miss Stanbury had also told the secret in confidence to Mrs MacHugh, it cannot be said that it was altogether well kept. Four days after Brooke's departure the news reached the Frenches at Heavitree. It was whispered to Camilla by one of the shopmen with whom she was still arranging her marriage trousseau, and was repeated by her to her mother and sister with some additions which were not intended to be good-natured. 'He gets her and the money together as a bargain – of course,' said Camilla. 'I only hope the money won't be found too dear.'

'Perhaps he won't get it after all,' said Arabella.

'That would be cruel,' replied Camilla. 'I don't think that even Miss Stanbury is so false as that.'

Things were going very badly at Heavitree. There was war there, almost everlastingly, though such little playful conversations as the above showed that there might be an occasional lull in the battle. Mr Gibson was not doing his duty. That was clear enough. Even Mrs French, when she was appealed to with almost frantic energy by her younger daughter, could not but acknowledge that he was very remiss as a lover. And Camilla, in her fury, was very imprudent. That very frantic energy which induced her to appeal to her mother was, in itself, proof of her imprudence. She knew that she was foolish, but she could not control her passion. Twice had she detected Arabella in receiving notes from Mr Gibson, which she did not see, and of which it had been intended that she should know nothing. And once, when she spent a night away at Ottery St Mary with a friend, – a visit which was specially prefatory to marriage, and made in reference to bridesmaids' dresses, – Arabella had had, – so at least Camilla was made to believe, – a secret meeting with Mr Gibson in some of the lanes which lead down from Heavitree to the Topsham road.

'I happened to meet him, and spoke two words to him,' said Arabella. 'Would you have me cut him?'

'I'll tell you what it is, Bella; – If there is any underhand game going on that I don't understand, all Exeter shall be on fire before you shall carry it out.'

Bella made no answer to this, but shrugged her shoulders. Camilla was almost at a loss to guess what might be the truth. Would not any sister, so accused on such an occasion, rebut the accusation with awful wrath? But Arabella simply shrugged her shoulders, and went her way. It was now the 15th of April, and there wanted but one short fortnight to their marriage. The man had not the courage to jilt her! She felt sure that he had not heart enough to do a deed of such audacity. And her sister, too, was weak and a coward, and would lack the power to stand on her legs and declare herself to be the perpetrator of such villainy. Her mother, as she knew well, would always have preferred that her elder daughter should be the bride; but her mother was not the woman to have the hardihood, now, in the eleventh hour, to favour such an intrigue. Let her wish be what it might, she would not be strong enough to carry through the accomplishment of it. They would all know that that threat of hers of setting Exeter on fire would be carried out after some fashion that would not be inadequate to the occasion. A sister, a mother, a promised lover, all false, – all so damnably, cruelly false! It was impossible. No history, no novel of most sensational interest, no wonderful villainy that had ever been wrought into prose or poetry, would have been equal to this. It was impossible. She told herself so a score of times a day. And yet the circumstances were so terribly suspicious! Mr Gibson's conduct as a lover was simply disgraceful to him as a man and a clergyman. He was full of excuses, which she knew to be false. He would never come near her if he could help it. When he was with her, he was as cold as an archbishop both in word and in action. Nothing would tempt him to any outward manifestation of affection. He would talk of nothing but the poor women of St Peter's-cum-Pumpkin in the city, and the fraudulent idleness of a certain colleague in the cathedral services, who was always shirking his work. He made her no presents. He never walked with her. He was always gloomy, – and he had indeed so behaved himself in public that people were beginning to talk of 'poor Mr Gibson.' And yet he could meet Arabella on the sly in the lanes, and send notes to her by the green-grocer's boy! Poor Mr Gibson indeed! Let her once get him well over the 29th of April, and the people of Exeter might talk about poor Mr Gibson if they pleased. And Bella's conduct was more wonderful almost than that of Mr Gibson. With all her cowardice, she still held up her head, – held it perhaps a little higher than was usual with her. And when that grievous accusation was made against her, – made and repeated, – an accusation the very thought and sound of which would almost have annihilated her had there been a decent feeling in her bosom, she would simply shrug her shoulders and walk away. 'Camilla,' she had once said, 'you will drive that man mad before you have done.' 'What is it to you how I drive him?' Camilla had answered in her fury. Then Arabella had again shrugged her shoulders and walked away. Between Camilla and her mother, too, there had come to be an almost internecine quarrel on a collateral point. Camilla was still carrying on a vast arrangement which she called the preparation of her trousseau, but which both Mrs French and Bella regarded as a spoliation of the domestic nest, for the proud purposes of one of the younger birds. And this had grown so fearfully that in two different places Mrs French had found herself compelled to request that no further articles might be supplied to Miss Camilla. The bride elect had rebelled, alleging that as no fortune was to be provided for her, she had a right to take with her such things as she could carry away in her trunks and boxes. Money could be had at the bank, she said; and, after all, what were fifty pounds more of less on such an occasion as this? And then she went into a calculation to prove that her mother and sister would be made so much richer by her absence, and that she was doing so much for them by her marriage, that nothing could be more mean in them than that they should hesitate to supply her with such things as she desired to make her entrance into Mr Gibson's house respectable. But Mrs French was obdurate, and Mr Gibson was desired to speak to her. Mr Gibson, in fear and trembling, told her that she ought to repress her spirit of extravagance, and Camilla at once foresaw that he would avail himself of this plea against her should he find it possible at any time to avail himself of any plea. She became ferocious, and, turning upon him, told him to mind his own business. Was it not all for him that she was doing it? 'She was not,' she said, 'disposed to submit to any control in such matters from him till he had assumed his legal right to it by standing with her before the altar.' It came, however, to be known all over Exeter that Miss Camilla's expenditure had been checked, and that, in spite of the joys naturally incidental to a wedding, things were not going well with the ladies at Heavitree.

At last the blow came. Camilla was aware that on a certain morning her mother had been to Mr Gibson's house, and had held a long conference with him. She could learn nothing of what took place there, for at that moment she had taken upon herself to place herself on non-speaking terms with her mother in consequence of those disgraceful orders which had been given to the tradesmen. But Bella had not been at Mr Gibson's house at the time, and Camilla, though she presumed that her own conduct had been discussed in a manner very injurious to herself, did not believe that any step was being then arranged which would be positively antagonistic to her own views. The day fixed was now so very near, that there could, she felt, be no escape for the victim. But she was wrong.

Mr Gibson had been found by Mrs French in a very excited state on that occasion. He had wept, and pulled his hair, and torn open his waistcoat, had spoken of himself as a wretch, — pleading, however, at the same time, that he was more sinned against than sinning, had paced about the room with his hands dashing against his brows, and at last had flung himself prostrate on the ground. The meaning of it all was, that he had tried very hard, and had found at last that 'he couldn't do it.' 'I am ready to submit,' said he, 'to any verdict that you may pronounce against me, but I should deceive you and deceive her if I didn't say at once that I can't do it.' He went on to explain that since he had unfortunately entered into his present engagement with Camilla, — of whose position he spoke in quite a touching manner, — and since he had found what was the condition of his own heart and feelings he had consulted a friend, — who, if any merely human being was capable of advising, might be implicitly trusted for advice in such a matter, — and that this friend had told him that he was bound to give up the marriage let the consequences to himself or to others be what they might. 'Although the skies should fall on me, I cannot stand at the hymeneal altar with a lie in my mouth,' said Mr Gibson immediately upon his rising from his prostrate condition on the floor. In such a position as this a mother's fury would surely be very great! But Mrs French was hardly furious. She cried, and begged him to think better of it, and assured him that Camilla, when she should be calmed down by matrimony, would not be so bad as she seemed; — but she was not furious. 'The truth is, Mr Gibson,' she said through her tears, 'that, after all, you like Bella best.' Mr Gibson owned that he did like Bella best, and although no bargain was made between them then and there, — and such making of a bargain then and there would hardly have been practicable, — it was understood that Mrs French would not proceed to extremities if Mr Gibson would still make himself forthcoming as a husband for the advantage of one of the daughters of the family.

So far Mr Gibson had progressed towards a partial liberation from his thraldom with a considerable amount of courage; but he was well aware that the great act of daring still remained to be done. He had suggested to Mrs French that she should settle the matter with Camilla, — but this Mrs French had altogether declined to do. It must, she said, come from himself. If she were to do it, she must sympathise with her child; and such sympathy would be obstructive of the future arrangements which were still to be made. 'She always knew that I liked Bella best,' said Mr Gibson, — still sobbing, still tearing his hair, still pacing the room with his waistcoat torn open. 'I would not advise you to tell her that,' said Mrs French. Then Mrs French went home, and early on the following morning it was thought good by Arabella that she also should pay a visit at Ottery St Mary's. 'Good-bye, Cammy,' said Arabella as she went. 'Bella,' said Camilla, 'I wonder whether you are a serpent. I do not think you can be so base a serpent as that.' 'I declare, Cammy, you do say such odd things that no one can understand what you mean.' And so she went.

On that morning Mr Gibson was walking at an early hour along the road from Exeter to Cowley, contemplating his position and striving to arrange his plans. What was he to do, and how was he to do it? He was prepared to throw up his living, to abandon the cathedral, to leave the diocese, – to make any sacrifice rather than take Camilla to his bosom. Within the last six weeks he had learned to regard her with almost a holy horror. He could not understand by what miracle of self-neglect he had fallen into so perilous an abyss. He had long known Camilla's temper. But in those days in which he had been beaten like a shuttlecock between the Stanburys and the Frenches, he had lost his head and had done, – he knew not what. 'Those whom the God chooses to destroy, he first maddens,'* said Mr Gibson to himself of himself, throwing himself back upon early erudition and pagan philosophy. Then he looked across to the river Exe, and thought that there was hardly water enough there to cover the multiplicity of his sorrows.

But something must be done. He had proceeded so far in forming a resolution, as he reached St David's Church on his return homewards. His sagacious friend had told him that as soon as he had altered his mind, he was bound to let the lady know of it without delay. 'You must remember,' said the sagacious friend, 'that you will owe her much, – very much.' Mr Gibson was perplexed in his mind when he reflected how much he might possibly be made to owe her if she should decide on appealing to a jury of her countrymen for justice. But anything would be better than his home at St Peter's-cum-Pumpkin with Camilla sitting opposite to him as his wife. Were there not distant lands in which a clergyman, unfortunate but still energetic, might find work to do? Was there not all America? – and were there not Australia, New Zealand, Natal, all open to him? Would not a missionary career among the Chinese be better for him than St Peter's-cum-Pumpkin with Camilla French for his wife? By the time he had reached home his mind was made up. He would write a letter to Camilla at once; and he would marry Arabella at once, – on any day that might be fixed, – on condition that Camilla would submit to her defeat without legal redress. If legal redress should be demanded, he would put in evidence the fact that her own mother had been compelled to caution the tradesmen of the city in regard to her extravagance.

He did write his letter, – in an agony of spirit.

I sit down, Camilla, with a sad heart and a reluctant hand,' he said, 'to communicate to you a fatal truth. But truth should be made to prevail, and there is nothing in man so cowardly, so detrimental, and so unmanly as its concealment. I have looked into myself, and have enquired of myself, and have assured myself, that were I to become your husband, I should not make you happy. It would be of no use for me now to dilate on the reasons which have convinced me; – but I am convinced, and I consider it my duty to inform you so at once. I have been closeted with your mother, and have made her understand that it is so.

I have not a word to say in my own justification but this, – that I am sure I am acting honestly in telling you the truth. I would not wish to say a word animadverting on yourself. If there must be blame in this matter, I am willing to take it all on my own shoulders. But things have been done of late, and words have been spoken, and habits have displayed themselves, which would not, I am sure, conduce to our mutual comfort in this world, or to our assistance to each other in our struggles to reach the happiness of the world to come.

I think that you will agree with me, Camilla, that when a man or a woman has fallen into such a mistake as that which I have now made, it is best that it would be acknowledged. I know well that such a change of arrangements as that which I now propose will be regarded most unfavourably. But will not anything be better than the binding of a matrimonial knot which cannot be again unloosed, and which we should both regret ?

I do not know that I need add anything further. What can I add further ? Only this; – that I am inflexible. Having resolved to take this step, – and to bear the evil things that may be said of me, – for your happiness and for my own tranquility, – I shall not now relinquish my resolution. I do not ask you to forgive me. I doubt much whether I shall ever be quite able to forgive myself. The mistake which I have made is one which should not have been committed. I do not ask you to forgive me ; but I do ask you to pray that I may be forgiven.

Yours, with feelings of the truest friendship,
Thomas Gibson

The letter had been very difficult, but he was rather proud of it than otherwise when it was completed. He had felt that he was writing a letter which not improbably might become public property. It was necessary that he would be firm, that he should accuse himself a little in order that he might excuse himself much, and that he should hint at causes which might justify the rupture, though he should so veil them as not to appear to defend his own delinquency by ungenerous counter accusation. When he had completed the letter, he thought that he had done all this rather well, and he sent the despatch off to Heavitree by the clerk of St Peter's Church, with something of that feeling of expressible relief which attends the final conquest over some fatal and all but insuperable misfortune. He thought that he was sure now that he would not have to marry Camilla on the 29th of the month, – and there would probably be a period of some hours before he would be called upon to hear or read Camilla's reply.

Camilla was alone when she received the letter, but she rushed at once to her mother. 'There,' said she; 'there – I knew that it was coming!' Mrs French took the paper into her hands, and gasped, and gazed at her daughter without speaking. 'You knew of it, mother.'

'Yesterday, – when he told me, I knew of it.'

'And Bella knows it.'

'Not a word of it.'

'She does. I am sure she does. But it is all nothing. I will not accept it. He cannot treat me so. I will drag him there; – but he shall come.'

'You can't make him, my dear.'

'I will make him. And you would help me, mamma, if you had any spirit. What, – a fortnight before the time, when the things are all bought! Look at the presents that have been sent! Mamma, he doesn't know me. And he never would have done it, if it had not been for Bella, – never. She had better take care, or there shall be such a tragedy that nobody ever heard the like. If she thinks that she is going to be that man's wife, – she is – mistaken.' Then there was a pause for a moment. 'Mamma,' she said, 'I shall go to him at once. I do not care in the least what anybody may say. I shall – go to him, – at once.' Mrs French felt that at this moment it was best that she should be silent.

75

The Rowleys Go Over the Alps

By the thirteenth of May the Rowley family had established itself in Florence, purposing to remain either there or at the baths of Lucca till the end of June, at which time it was thought that Sir Marmaduke should begin to make preparations for his journey back to the Islands. Their future prospects were not altogether settled. It was not decided whether Lady Rowley should at once return with him, whether Mrs Trevelyan should return with him, – nor was it settled among them what should be the fate of Nora Rowley. Nora Rowley was quite resolved herself that she would not go back to the Islands, and had said as much to her mother. Lady Rowley had not repeated this to Sir Marmaduke, and was herself in doubt as to what might best be done. Girls are understood by their mothers better than they are by their fathers. Lady Rowley was beginning to be aware that Nora's obstinacy was too strong to be overcome by mere words, and that other steps must be taken if she were to be weaned from her pernicious passion for Hugh Stanbury. Mr Glascock was still in Florence. Might she not be cured by further overtures from Mr Glascock? The chance of securing such a son-in-law was so important, so valuable, that no trouble was too great to be incurred, even though the probability of success might not be great.

It must not, however, be supposed that Lady Rowley carried off all the family to Italy, including Sir Marmaduke, simply in chase of Mr Glascock. Anxious as she was on the subject, she was too proud, and also too well-conditioned, to have suggested to herself such a journey with such an object. Trevelyan had escaped from Willesden with the child, and they had heard, – again through Stanbury, – that he had returned to Italy. They had all agreed that it would be well that they should leave London for awhile, and see something of the continent; and when it was told to them that little Louis was probably in Florence, that alone was reason enough for them to go thither. They would go to the city till the heat was too great and the mosquitoes too powerful, and then they would visit the baths of Lucca for a month. This was their plan of action, and the cause for their plan; but Lady Rowley found herself able to weave into it another little plan of her own of which she said nothing to anybody. She was not running after Mr Glascock; but if Mr Glascock should choose to run after them, – or her, who could say that any harm had been done?

Nora had answered that proposition of her lover's to walk out of the house in Manchester Street, and get married at the next church, in a most discreet manner. She had declared that she would be true and firm, but that she did not wish to draw upon herself the displeasure of her father and mother. She did not, she said look upon a clandestine marriage as a happy resource. But, – this she added at the end of a long and very sensible letter, – she intended to abide by her engagement, and she did not intend to go back to the Mandarins. She did not say what alternative she would choose in the event of her being unable to obtain her father's consent before his return. She did not suggest what was to become of her when Sir Marmaduke's leave of absence should be expired. But her statement that she would not go back to the islands was certainly made with more substantial vigour, though, perhaps, with less of reasoning, than any other of the propositions made in her letter. Then, in her postscript, she told him that they were all going to Italy. 'Papa and mamma think that we ought to follow poor Mr Trevelyan. The lawyer says that nothing can be done while he is away with the boy. We are therefore all going to start to Florence. The journey is delightful. I will not say whose presence will be wanting to make it perfect.'

Before they started there came a letter to Nora from Dorothy, which shall be given entire, because it will tell the reader more of Dorothy's happiness than would be learned from any other mode of narrative.

The Close, Thursday

Dearest Nora,

I have just had a letter from Hugh, and that makes me feel that I should like to write to you. Dear Hugh has told me all about it, and I do so hope that things may come right and that we may be sisters. He is so good that I do not wonder that you should love him. He has been the best son and the best brother in the world, and everybody speaks well of him, – except my dear aunt, who is prejudiced because she does not like newspapers. I need not praise him to you, for I dare say you think quite as well of him as I do. I cannot tell you all the beautiful things he says about you, but I dare say he has told them to you himself.

I seem to know you so well because Priscilla has talked about you so often. She says that she knew that you and my brother were fond of each other because you growled at each other when you were together at the Clock House, and never had any civil words to say before people. I don't know whether growling is a sign of love, but Hugh does growl sometimes when he is most affectionate. He growls at me, and I understand him, and I like to be growled at. I wonder whether you like him to growl at you.

And now I must tell you something about myself, – because if you are to be my sister you ought to know it all. I also am going to be married to a man whom I love, – oh, so dearly ! His name is Mr Brooke Burgess, and he is a great friend of my aunt's. At first she did not like our being engaged, because of some family reason; – but she has got over that, and nothing can be kinder and nicer than she is. We are to be married here, some day in June, – the 11th I think it will be. How I do wish you could have been here to be my bridesmaid. It would have been so nice to have had Hugh's sweetheart with me. He is a friend of Hugh's, and no doubt you will hear all about him. The worst of it is that we must live in London, because my husband as will be, – you see I call him mine already, – is in an office there. And so poor Aunt Stanbury will be left all alone. It will be very sad, and she is so wedded to Exeter that I fear we shall not get her up to London.

I would describe Mr Burgess to you, only I do not suppose you would care to hear about him. He is not so tall as Hugh, but he is a great deal better looking. With you two the good looks are to be with the wife; but, with us, with the husband. Perhaps you think Hugh is handsome. We used to declare that he was the ugliest boy in the country. I don't suppose it makes very much difference. Brooke is handsome, but I don't think I should like him the less if he were ever so ugly.

Do you remember hearing about the Miss Frenches when you were in Devonshire? There has come up such a terrible affair about them. A Mr Gibson, a clergyman, was going to marry the younger; but has changed his mind and wants to take the elder. I think he was in love with her first.' Dorothy did not say a word about the little intermediate stage of attachment to herself. 'All this is making a great noise in the city, and some people think he should be punished severely. It seems to me that a gentleman ought not to make such a mistake; but if he does, he ought to own it. I hope they will let him marry the elder one. Aunt Stanbury says it all comes from their wearing chignons. I wish you knew Aunt Stanbury, because she is so good. Perhaps you wear a chignon. I think Priscilla said that you did. It must not be large, if you come to see Aunt Stanbury.

Pray write to me, – and believe that I hope to be your most affectionate sister,

Dorothy Stanbury

PS – I am so happy, and I do so hope that you will be the same.

This was received only a day before the departure of the Rowleys for Italy, and was answered by a short note promising that Nora would write to her correspondent from Florence.

There could be no doubt that Trevelyan had started with his boy, fearing the result of the medical or legal interference with his affairs which was about to be made at Sir Marmaduke's instance. He had written a few words to his wife, neither commencing nor ending his note after any usual fashion, telling her that he thought it expedient to travel, that he had secured the services of a nurse for the little boy, and that during his absence a certain income would, as heretofore, be paid to her. He said nothing as to his probable return, or as to her future life; nor was there anything to indicate whither he was going. Stanbury, however, had learned from the faithless and frightened Bozzle that Trevelyan's letters were to be sent after him to Florence. Mr Bozzle, in giving this information, had acknowledged that his employer was 'becoming no longer quite himself under his troubles,' and had expressed his opinion that he ought to be 'looked after.' Bozzle had made his money; and now, with a grain of humanity mixed with many grains of faithlessness, reconciled it to himself to tell his master's secrets to his master's enemies. What would a counsel be able to say about his conduct in a court of law? That was the question which Bozzle was always asking himself as to his own business. That he should be abused by a barrister to a jury, and exposed as a spy and a fiend, was, he thought, a matter of course. To be so abused was a part of his profession. But it was expedient for him in all cases to secure some loop-hole of apparent duty by which he might in part escape from such censures. He was untrue to his employer now, because he thought that his employer ought to be 'looked after.' He did, no doubt, take a five pound note from Hugh Stanbury; but then it was necessary that he should live. He must be paid for his time. In this way Trevelyan started for Florence, and within a week afterwards the Rowleys were upon his track.

Nothing had been said by Sir Marmaduke to Nora as to her lover since that stormy interview in which both father and daughter had expressed their opinions very strongly, and very little had been said by Lady Rowley. Lady Rowley had spoken more than once of Nora's return to the Mandarins, and had once alluded to it as a certainty. 'But I do not know that I shall go back,' Nora had said, 'My dear,' the mother had replied, 'unless you are married, I suppose your home must be with your parents.' Nora, having made her protest, did not think it necessary to persevere, and so the matter was dropped. It was known, however, that they must all come back to London before they started for their seat of government, and therefore the subject did not at present assume its difficult aspect. There was a tacit understanding among them that everything should be done to make the journey pleasant to the young mother who was in search of her son; and, in addition to this, Lady Rowley had her own little understanding, which was very tacit indeed, that in Mr Glascock might be found an escape from one of their great family difficulties.

'You had better take this, papa, Mrs Trevelyan had said, when she received from the office of Mr Bideawhile a cheque payable to her order for the money sent to her by her husband's direction.

'I do not want the man's money,' said Sir Marmaduke.

'But you are going to this place for my sake, papa; – and it is right that he should bear the expense for his own wife. And, papa, you must remember always that though his mind is distracted on this horrible business, he is not a bad man. No one is more liberal or more just about money.' Sir Marmaduke's feelings on the matter were very much the same as those which had troubled Mr Outhouse, and he, personally, refused to touch the money; but his daughter paid her own share of the expenses of the journey.

They travelled at their ease, stopping at Paris, and at Geneva, and at Milan. Lady Rowley thought that she was taken very fast, because she was allowed to sleep only two nights at each of these places, and Sir Rowley himself thought that he had achieved something of a Hannibalian enterprise in taking five ladies and two maids over the Simplon and down into the plains of Lombardy, with nobody to protect him but a single courier. He had been a little nervous about it, being unaccustomed to European travelling, and had not at first realised the fact that the journey is to be made with less trouble than one from the Marble Arch to Mile End. 'My dears,' he said to his younger daughters, as they were rattling round the steep downward twists and turns of the great road, 'you must sit quite still on these descents, or you do not know where you may go. The least thing would overset us.' But Lucy and Sophy soon knew better, and became so intimate with the mountain, under the friendly guidance of their courier, that before the plains were reached, they were in and out, and here and there, and up and down, as though they had been bred among the valleys of the pass. There would come a ringing laugh from some rock above their head, and Lady Rowley looking up would see their dresses fluttering on a pinnacle which appeared to her to be fit only for a bird; and there would be the courier behind them, with two parasols, and a shawl, and a cloak, and an eye-glass, and a fine pair of grizzled whiskers. They made an Alpine club of their own, refusing to admit their father because he would not climb up a rock, and Nora thought of the letters about it which she would write to her lover, – only that she had determined that she would not write to him at all without telling her mother, – and Mrs Trevelyan would for moments almost forget that she had been robbed of her child.

From Milan they went on to Forence, and though they were by that time quite at home in Italy, and had become critical judges of Italian inns and Italian railways, they did not find that journey to be quite so pleasant. There is a romance to us still in the name of Italy which a near view of many details in the country fails to realise. Shall we say that a journey through Lombardy is about as interesting as one through the flats of Cambridgeshire and the fens of Norfolk? And the station of Bologna is not an interesting spot in which to spend an hour or two, although it may be conceded that provisions may be had there much better than any that can be procured at our own railway stations. From thence they went, still by rail, over the Apennines, and unfortunately slept during the whole time. The courier had assured them that if they would only look out they would see the castles of which they had read in novels; but the day had been very hot, and Sir Marmaduke had been cross, and Lady Rowley had been weary, and so not a castle was seen. 'Pistoia, me lady, this,' said the courier opening the door; – 'to stop half and hour.' 'Oh, why was it not Florence?' Another hour and a half! So they all went to sleep again, and were very tired when they reached the beautiful city.

During the next day they rested at their inn, and sauntered through the Duomo, and broke their necks looking up at the inimitable glories of the campanile. Such a one as Sir Marmaduke had of course not come to Florence without introductions. The Foreign Office is always very civil to its next-door neighbour of the colonies, – civil and cordial, though perhaps a little patronising. A minister is a bigger man than a governor; and the smallest of the diplomatic fry are greater swells than even secretaries in quite important dependencies. The attaché, though he be unpaid, dwells in a capital, and flirts with a countess. The governor's right-hand man is confined to an island, and dances with a planter's daughter. The distinction is quite understood, but is not incompatible with much excellent good feeling on the part of the superior department. Sir Marmaduke had come to Florence fairly provided with passports to Florentine society, and had been mentioned in more than one letter as the dintinguished Governor of the Mandarins, who had been called home from his seat of government on a special mission of great importance. On the second day he went out to call at the embassy and to leave his cards. 'Have you been able to learn whether he is here?' asked Lady Rowley of her husband in a whisper, as soon as they were alone.

'Who; – Trevelyan?'

'I did not suppose you could learn about him, because he would be hiding himself. But is Mr Glascock here?'

'I forgot to ask,' said Sir Marmaduke.

Lady Rowley did not reproach him. It is impossible that any father should altogether share a mother's anxiety in regard to the marriage of their daughters. But what a thing it would be! Lady

Rowley thought that she could have a daughter married to the future Lord Peterborough. She had been told in England that he was faultless, – not very clever, not very active, not likely to be very famous; but, as a husband, simply faultless. He was very rich, very good-natured, easily managed, more likely to be proud of his wife than of himself, addicted to no jealousies, afflicted by no vices, so respectable in every way that he was sure to become great as an English nobleman by the very weight of his virtues. And it had been represented also to Lady Rowley that this paragon among men had been passionately attached to her daughter! Perhaps she magnified a little the romance of the story; but it seemed to her that this greatly endowed lover had rushed away from his country in despair, because her daughter Nora would not smile upon him. Now they were, as she hoped, in the same city with him. But it was indispensable to her success that she should not seem to be running after him. To Nora, not a word had been said of the prospect of meeting Mr Glascock at Florence. Hardly more than a word had been said to her sister Emily, and that under injunction of strictest secrecy. It must be made to appear to all the world that other motives had brought them to Florence, – as, indeed, other motives had brought them. Not for worlds would Lady Rowley have run after a man for her daughter; but still, still, – still, seeing that the man was himself so unutterably in love with her girl, seeing that he was so full justified by his position to be in love with any girl, seeing that such a maximum of happiness would be the result of such a marriage, she did feel that, even for his sake, she must be doing a good thing to bring them together! Something, though not much of all this, she had been obliged to explain to Sir Marmaduke; – and yet he had not taken the trouble to inquire whether Mr Glascock was in Florence!

On the third day after their arrival, the wife of the British minister came to call upon Lady Rowley, and the wife of the British minister was good-natured, easy-mannered, and very much given to conversation. She preferred talking to listening, and in the course of a quarter of an hour had told Lady Rowley a good deal about Florence; but she had not mentioned Mr Glascock's name. It would have been so pleasant if the requisite information could have been obtained without the asking of any direct question on the subject! But Lady Rowley, who from many years' practice of similar, though perhaps less distinguished, courtesies on her part, knew well the first symptom of the coming end of her guest's visit, found that the minister's wife was about to take her departure without an allusion to Mr Glascock. And yet the names had been mentioned of so many

English residents in Florence, who neither in wealth, rank, or virtue, were competent to hold a candle to that Phœnix! She was forced, therefore to pluck up courage, and to ask the question. 'Have you had a Mr Glascock here this spring?' said Lady Rowley.

'What; – Lord Peterborough's son? Oh, dear, yes. Such a singular being!'

Lady Rowley thought that she could perceive that her phœnix had not made himself agreeable at the embassy. It might perhaps be that he had buried himself away from society because of his love. 'And is here now?' asked Lady Rowley.

'I cannot say at all. He is sometimes here and sometimes with his father at Naples. But when here, he lives chiefly with the Americans. They say he is going to marry an American girl, – their minister's niece. There are three of them, I think, and he is to take the eldest.' Lady Rowley asked no more questions, and let her august visitor go, almost without another word.

76

We Shall be so Poor

Mr Glascock at that moment was not only in Florence, but was occupying rooms in the very hotel in which the Rowleys were staying. Lady Rowley, when she heard that he was engaged to marry an American lady, became suddenly very sick at heart, – sick with a sickness that almost went beyond her heart. She felt ill, and was glad to be alone. The rumour might be untrue. Such rumours generally are untrue. But then, as Lady Rowley knew very well, they generally have some foundation in truth. Mr Glascock, if he were not actually engaged to the American girl, had probably been flirting with her; – and, if so, where was that picture which Lady Rowley had been painting for herself of a love-lorn swain to be brought back to the pleasures and occupations of the world only by the girl of whom he was enamoured? But still she would not quite give up the project. Mr Glascock, if he was in Italy, would no doubt see by the newspapers that Sir Marmaduke and his family were in Florence, – and would probably come to them. Then, if Nora would only behave herself, the American girl might still be conquered.

During two or three days after this nothing was seen or heard of Mr Glascock. Had Lady Rowley thought of mentioning the name to the waiter at the hotel, she would have learned that he was living in the next passage; but it did not occur to her to seek information in that fashion. Nor did she ask direct questions in other quarters about Mr Glascock himself. She did, however, make inquiry about Americans living in Florence, – especially about the American Minister, – and, before a week had passed overhead, had been introduced to the Spaldings. Mrs Spalding was very civil, and invited Lady Rowley and all the girls and Sir Marmaduke to come to her on her 'Fridays.' She received her friends every Friday, and would continue to do so till the middle of June. She had nieces who would, she said, be so happy to make the acquaintance of the Miss Rowleys.

By this time the picture galleries, the churches, and the palaces in Florence had nearly all been visited. Poor Lady Rowley had dragged herself wearily from sight to sight, hoping always to meet with Mr Glascock, ignorant of the fact that residents in a town do not pass their mornings habitually in looking after pictures. During this time inquiries were being made, through the police, respecting Trevelyan; and Sir Marmaduke had obtained information that an English gentleman, with a little boy, had gone on to Siena, and had located himself there. There seemed to be but little doubt that this was Trevelyan, – though nothing had been learned with certainty as to the gentleman's name. It had been decided that Sir Marmaduke, with his courier and Mrs Trevelyan, should go on to Siena, and endeavour to come upon the fugitive, and they had taken their departure on a certain morning. On that same day Lady Rowley was walking with Nora and one of the other girls through the hall of the hotel, when they were met in full face – by Mr Glascock! Lady Rowley and Lucy were in front, and they, of course, did not know the man. Nora had seen him at once, and in her confusion hardly knew how to bear herself. Mr Glascock was passing by her without recognising her, – had passed her mother and sister, and had so far gone on, that Nora had determined to make no sign, when he chanced to look up and see who it was that was so close to him. 'Miss Rowley,' he said, 'who thought of meeting you in Florence!' Lady Rowley, of course, turned round, and there was an introduction. Poor Nora, though she knew nothing of her other's schemes, was confused and ill at ease. Mr Glascock was very civil, but at the same time rather cold. Lady Rowley was all smiles and courtesy. She had, she said, heard his name from her daughters, and was very happy to make his acquaintance. Lucy looked on somewhat astonished to find that the lover whom her sister had been blamed for rejecting, and who was spoken of with so many encomiums, was so old a man. Mr Glascock asked after Mrs

Trevelyan; and Lady Rowley, in a low, melancholy whisper, told him that they were now all in Florence, in the hope of meeting Mr Trevelyan. 'You have heard the sad story, I know, Mr Glascock, – and therefore I do not mind telling you.' Mr Glascock acknowledged that he did know the story, and informed her that he had seen Mr Trevelyan in Florence within the last ten days. This was so interesting, that, at Lady Rowley's request, he went with them up to their rooms, and in this way the acquaintance was made. It turned out that Mr Glascock had spoken to Mr Trevelyan, and that Trevelyan had told him that he meant for the present to take up his residence in some small Italian town. 'And how was he looking, Mr Glascock?'

'Very ill, Lady Rowley; – very ill, indeed.'

'Do not tell her so, Mr Glascock. She has gone now with her father to Siena. We think that he is there, with the boy, – or, at least, that he may be heard of there. And you; – you are living here?' Mr Glascock said that he was living between Naples and florence, – going occasionally to Naples, a place that he hated, to see his father, and coming back at intervals to the capital. Nora sat by, and hardly spoke a word. She was nicely dressed, with an exquisite little bonnet, which had been bought as they came through Paris; and Lady Rowley, with maternal pride, felt that if he was ever in love with her child, that love must come back upon him now. American girls, she had been told, were hard, and dry, and sharp, and angular. She had seen some at the Mandarins, with whom she thought it must be impossible that any Englishman should be in love. There never, surely, had been an American girl like her Nora. 'Are you fond of pictures, Mr Glascock?' she asked. Mr Glascock was not very fond of pictures, and thought that he was rather tired of them. What was he fond of? Of sitting at home and doing nothing. That was his reply, at least; and a very unsatisfactory reply it was, as Lady Rowley could hardly propose that they should come and sit and do nothing with him. Could he have been lured into churches or galleries, Nora might have been once more thrown into his company. Then Lady Rowley took courage, and asked him whether he knew the Spaldings. They were going to Mrs Spalding's that very evening, – she and her daughters. Mr Glascock replied that he did know the Spaldings, and that he also should be at their house. Lady Rowley thought that she discovered something like a blush about his cheekbones and brow, as he made his answer. Then he left them, giving his hand to Nora as he went; – but there was nothing in his manner to justify the slightest hope.

'I don't think he is nice at all,' said Lucy.

'Don't be so foolish, Lucy,' said Lady Rowley angrily.

'I think he is very nice,' said Nora. 'He was only talking nonsense when he said that he liked to sit still and do nothing. He is not at all an idle man; – at least I am told so.'

'But he is as old as Methuselah,' said Lucy.

'He is between thirty and forty,' said Lady Rowley. 'Of course we know that from the peerage.' Lady Rowley, however, was wrong. Had she consulted the peerage, she would have seen that Mr Glascock was over forty.

Nora, as soon as she was alone and could think about it all, felt quite sure that Mr Glascock would never make her another offer. This ought not to have caused her any sorrow, as she was very well aware that she would not accept him, should he do so. Yet, perhaps, there was a moment of some feeling akin to disappointment. Of course she would not have accepted him. How could she? Her faith was so plighted to Hugh Stanbury that she would be a by-word among women for ever, were she to be so false. And, as she told herself, she had not the slightest feeling of affection for Mr Glascock. It was quite out of the question, and a matter simply for speculation. Nevertheless it would have been a very grand thing to be Lady Peterborough, and she almost regretted that she had a heart in her bosom.

She had become fully aware during that interview that her mother still entertained hopes, and almost suspected that Lady Rowley had known something of Mr Glascock's residence in Florence. She had seen that her mother had met Mr Glascock almost as though some such meeting had been expected, and had spoken to him almost as though she had expected to have to speak to him. Would it not be better that she should at once make her mother understand that all this could be of no avail? If she were to declare plainly that nothing could bring about such a marriage, would not her mother desist? She almost made up her mind to do so; but as her mother said nothing to her before they started for Mrs Spalding's house, neither did she say anything to her mother. She did not wish to have angry words if they could be avoided, and she felt that there might be anger and unpleasant words were she to insist upon her devotion to Hugh Stanbury while this rich prize was in sight. If her mother should speak to her, then, indeed, she would declare her own settled purpose; but she would do nothing to accelerate the evil hour.

There were but few people in Mrs Spalding's drawing-room when they were announced, and Mr Glascock was not among them. Miss Wallachia Petrie was there, and in the confusion of the introduction was presumed by Lady Rowley to be one of the nieces introduced. She had been distinctly told that Mr Glascock was to marry the eldest, and this lady was certainly older than the other two. In this way Lady Rowley decided that Miss Wallachia Petrie was her daughter's hated rival, and she certainly was much surprised at the gentleman's taste. But there is nothing, – nothing in the way of an absurd matrimonial engagement, – into which a man will not allow himself to be entrapped by pique. Nora would have a great deal to answer for, Lady Rowley thought, if the unfortunate man should be driven by her cruelty to marry such a woman as this one now before her.

It happened that Lady Rowley soon found herself seated by Miss Petrie, and she at once commenced her questionings. She intended to be very discreet, but the subject was too near her heart to allow her to be altogether silent. 'I believe you know Mr Glascock?' she said.

'Yes,' said Wallachia, 'I do know him.' Now the peculiar nasal twang which our cousins over the water have learned to use, and which has grown out of a certain national instinct which coerces them to express themselves with self-assertion; – let the reader go into his closet and talk through his nose for awhile with steady attention to the effect which is own voice will have, and he will find that this theory is correct; – this intonation, which is so peculiar among intelligent Americans, had been adopted con amore, and, as it were, taken to her bosom by Miss Petrie. Her ears had taught themselves to feel that there could be no vitality in speech without it, and that all utterance unsustained by such tone was effeminate, vapid, useless, unpersuasive, unmusical, – and English. It was a complaint frequently made by her against her friends Caroline and Olivia that they debased their voices, and taught themselves the puling British mode of speech. 'I do know the gentleman,' said Wallachia; – and Lady Rowley shuddered. Could it be that such a woman as this was to reign over Monkhams, and become the future Lady Peterborough?

'He told me that he is acquainted with the family,' said Lady Rowley. 'He is staying at our hotel, and my daughter knew him very well when he was living in London.'

'I dare say. I believe that in London the titled aristocrats do hang pretty much together.' It had never occurred to poor Lady Rowley, since the day in which her husband had been made a knight, at the advice of the Colonial Minister, in order that the inhabitants of some island might be gratified by the opportunity of using the title, that she and her children had thereby become aristocrats. Were her daughter Nora to marry Mr Glascock, Nora would become an aristocrat, – or would, rather, be ennobled, – all which Lady Rowley understood perfectly.

'I don't know that London society is very exclusive in that respect,' said Lady Rowley.

'I guess you are pretty particular,' said Miss Petrie, 'and it seems to me you don't have much regard to intellect or erudition, – but fix things up straight according to birth and money.'

'I hope we are not quite so bad as that,' said Lady Rowley. 'I do not know London well myself, as I have passed my life in very distant places.'

'The distant places are, in my estimation, the best. The further the mind is removed from the contamination incidental to the centre of long-established luxury, the more chance it has of developing itself according to the intention of the Creator, when he bestowed his gifts of intellect upon us.' Lady Rowley, when she heard this eloquence, could hardly believe that such a man as Mr Glascock should really be intent upon marrying such a lady as this who was sitting next to her.

In the meantime, Nora and the real rival were together, and they also were talking of Mr Glascock. Caroline Spalding had said that Mr Glascock had spoken to her of Nora Rowley, and Nora acknowledged that there had been some acquaintance between them in London. 'Almost more than that, I should have thought,' said Miss Spalding, 'if one might judge by his manner of speaking of you.'

'He is a little given to be enthusiastic,' said Nora, laughing.

'The least so of all mankind, I should have said. You must know he is very intimate in this house. It began in this way; – Olivia and I were travelling together, and there was – a difficulty, as we say in our country when three or four gentlemen shoot each other. Then there came up Mr Glascock and another gentleman. By-the-bye, the other gentleman was your brother-in-law.'

'Poor Mr Trevelyan!'

'He is very ill; – is he not?'

'We think so. My sister is with us, you know. That is to say, she is at Siena to-day.'

'I have heard about him, and it is so sad. Mr Glascock knows him. As I said, they were travelling together, when Mr Glascock came to our assistance. Since that, we have seen him very frequently. I don't think he is enthusiastic, – except when he talks of you.'

'I ought to be very proud,' said Nora.

'I think you ought, – as Mr Glascock is a man whose good

opinion is certainly worth having. Here he is. Mr Glascock, I hope your ears are tingling. They ought to do so, because we are saying all manner of fine things about you.'

'I could not be well spoken of by two on whose good word I should set a higher value,' said he.

'And whose do you value the most?' said Caroline.

'I must first know whose eulogium will run the highest.'

Then Nora answered him. 'Mr Glascock, other people may praise you louder than I can do, but no one will ever do so with more sincerity.' There was a pretty earnestness about her as she spoke, which Lady Rowley ought to have heard. Mr Glascock bowed, and Miss Spalding smiled, and Nora blushed.

'If you are not overwhelmed now,' said Miss Spalding, 'you must be so used to flattery, that it has no longer any effect upon you. You must be like a drunkard, to whom wine is as water, and who thinks that brandy is not strong enough.'

'I think I had better go away,' said Mr Glascock, 'for fear the brandy should be watered by degrees.' And so he left them.

Nora had become quite aware, without much process of thinking about it, that her former lover and this American young lady were very intimate with each other. The tone of the conversation had shown that it was so; – and, then, how had it come to pass that Mr Glascock had spoken to this American girl about her, – Nora Rowley? It was evident that he had spoken of her with warmth, and had done so in a manner to impress his hearer. For a minute or two they sat together in silence after Mr Glascock had left them, but neither of them stirred. Then Caroline Spalding turned suddenly upon Nora, and took her by the hand. 'I must tell you something,' said she, 'only it must be a secret for awhile.'

'I will not repeat it.'

'Thank you, dear. I am engaged to him, – as his wife. He asked me this very afternoon, and nobody knows it but my aunt. When I had accepted him, he told me all the story about you. He had very often spoken of you before, and I had guessed how it must have been. He wears his heart so open for those whom he loves, that there is nothing concealed. He had seen you just before he came to me. But perhaps I am wrong to tell you that now. He ought to have been thinking of you again at such a time.'

'I did not want him to think of me again.'

'Of course you did not. Of course I am joking. You might have been his wife if you wished it. He has told me all that. And he especially wants us to be friends. Is there anything to prevent it?'

'On my part? Oh, dear, no; – except that you will be such grand folk, and we shall be so poor.'

'We!' said Caroline, laughing. 'I am so glad that there is a "we."'

77
The Future Lady Peterborough

'If you have not sold yourself for British gold, and for British acres, and for British rank, I have nothing to say against it,' said Miss Wallachia Petrie that same evening to her friend Caroline Spalding.

'You know that I have not sold myself, as you call it,' said Caroline. There had been a long friendship between these two ladies, and the younger one knew that it behoved her to bear a good deal from the elder. Miss Petrie was honest, clever, and in earnest. We in England are not usually favourably disposed to women who take a pride in a certain antagonism to men in general, and who are anxious to show the world that they can get on very well without male assistance; but there are many such in America who have noble aspirations, good intellects, much energy, and who are by no means unworthy of friendship. The hope in regard to all such women, – the hope entertained not by themselves, but by those who are solicitous for them, – is that they will be cured at last by a husband and half-a-dozen children. In regard to Wallachia Petrie there was not, perhaps, much ground for such hope. She was so positively wedded to women's rights in general, and to her own rights in particular, that it was improbable that she should ever succumb to any man; – and where would be the man brave enough to make the effort? From circumstances Caroline Spalding had been the beloved of her heart since Caroline Spalding was a very little girl; and she had hoped that Caroline would through life have borne arms along with her in that contest which she was determined to wage against man, and which she always waged with the greatest animosity against men of the British race. She hated rank; she hated riches; she hated monarchy; – and with a true woman's instinct in battle, felt that she had a specially strong point against Englishmen, in that they submitted themselves to dominion from a woman monarch. And now the chosen friend of her youth, – the friend who had copied out all her poetry, who had learned by heart all her sonnets, who had, as she thought, reciprocated all her ideas, was going to be married, – and to be married to an English lord! She had seen that it was coming for some time, and had spoken out very plainly, hoping that she might still save the brand from the burning. Now the evil was done; and Caroline Spalding, when she told her news, knew well that she would have to bear some heavy reproaches.

'How many of us are there who never know whether we sell ourselves or not?' said Wallachia. 'The senator who longs for office, and who votes this way instead of that in order that he may get it, thinks that he is voting honestly. The minister who calls himself a teacher of God's word, thinks that it is God's word that he preaches when he strains his lungs to fill his church. The question is this, Caroline; – would you have loved the same man had he come to you with a woodman's axe in his hand or a clerk's quill behind his ear? I guess not.'

'As to the woodman's axe, Wally, it is very well in theory; but –'

'Things good in theory, Caroline, will be good also when practised. You may be sure of that. We dislike theory simply because our intelligences are higher than our wills. But we will let that pass.'

'Pray let it pass, Wally. Do not preach me sermons to-night. I am so happy, and you ought to wish me joy.'

'If wishing you joy would get you joy, I would wish it you while I lived. I cannot be happy that you should be taken from us whither I shall never see you again.'

'But you are to come to us. I have told him so, and it is settled.'

'No, dear; I shall not do that. What should I be in the glittering halls of an English baron? Could there be any visiting less fitting, any admixture less appropriate? Could I who have held up my voice in the Music Hall of Lacedæmon, amidst the glories of the West, in the great and free State of Illinois, against the corruption of an English aristocracy, – could I, who have been listened to by two thousand of my countrywomen, – and men, – while I spurned the unmanly, inhuman errors of primogeniture, – could I, think you, hold my tongue beneath the roof of a feudal lord!' Caroline Spalding knew that her friend could not hold her tongue, and hesitated to answer. There had been the fatal triumph of a lecture on the joint rights of men and women, and it had rendered poor Wallachia Petrie unfit for ordinary society.

'You might come there without talking politics, Wally,' said Caroline.

'No, Caroline; no. I will go into the house of no man in which the free expression of my opinion is debarred me. I will not sit even at your table with a muzzled tongue. When you are gone, Caroline,

I shall devote myself to what, after all, must be the work of my life, and I shall finish the biographical history of our great hero in verse, – which I hope may at least be not ephemeral. From month to month I shall send you what I do, and you will not refuse me your friendly criticism, – and, perhaps, some slight need of approbation, – because you are dwelling beneath the shade of a throne. Oh, Caroline, let it not be a upas tree !'

The Miss Petries of the world have this advantage, – an advantage which rarely if ever falls to the lot of a man, – that they are never convinced of error. Men, let them be ever so much devoted to their closets, let them keep their work ever so closely veiled from public scrutiny, still find themselves subjected to criticism, and under the necessity of either defending themselves or of succumbing. If, indeed, a man neither speaks, nor writes, – if he be dumb as regards opinion, – he passes simply as one of the crowd, and is in the way neither of convincing nor of being convinced ; but a woman may speak, and almost write, as she likes, without danger of being wounded by sustained conflict. Who would have the courage to begin with such a one as Miss Petrie, and endeavour to prove to her that she is wrong from the beginning. A little word of half-dissent, a smile, a shrug, and an ambiguous compliment which is misunderstood, are all the forms of argument which can be used against her. Wallachia Petrie, in her heart of hearts conceived that she had fairly discussed her great projects from year to year with indomitable eloquence and unanswerable truth, – and that none of her opponents had had a leg to stand upon. And this she believed because the chivalry of men had given to her sex that protection against which her life was one continued protest.

'Here he is,' said Caroline, as Mr Glascock came up to them. 'Try and say a civil word to him, if he speaks about it. Though he is to be a lord, still he is a man and a brother.'

'Caroline,' said the stern monitress, 'you are already learning to laugh at principles which have been dear to you since you left your mother's breast. Alas, how true it is, "You cannot touch pitch and not be defiled."'

The further progress of these friendly and feminine amenities was stopped by the presence of the gentleman who had occasioned them. 'Miss Petire,' said the hero of the hour, 'Caroline was to tell you of my good fortune, and no doubt she has done so.'

'I cannot wait to hear the pretty things he has to say,' said Caroline, 'and I must look after my aunt's guests. There is poor Signor Bernarosci without a soul to say a syllable to him, and I must go and use my ten Italian words.'

'You are about to take with you to your old country, Mr
Glascock,' said Miss Petrie, 'one of the brightest stars in our young
American firmament.' There could be no doubt, from the tone of
Miss Petrie's voice, that she now regarded this star, however bright,
as one of a sort which is subjected to falling.

'I am going to take a very nice young woman,' said Mr Glascock.

'I hate that word woman, sir, uttered with the half-hidden sneer
which always accompanies its expression from the mouth of a
man.'

'Sneer, Miss Petrie!'

'I quite allow that it is involuntary, and not analysed or understood by yourselves. If you speak of a dog, you intend to do so with
affection, but there is always contempt mixed with it. The so-called
chivalry of man to woman is all begotten in the same spirit. I want
no favour, but I claim to be your equal.'

'I thought that American ladies were generally somewhat exacting
as to those privileges which chivalry gives them.'

'It is true, sir, that the only rank we know in our country is in
that precedence which man gives to woman. Whether we maintain
that, or whether we abandon it, we do not intend to purchase it at
the price of an acknowledgment of intellectual inferiority. For
myself, I hate chivalry; – what you call chivalry. I can carry my
own chair, and I claim the right to carry it whithersoever I may
please.'

Mr Glascock remained with her for some time, but made no
opportunity for giving that invitation to Monkhams of which
Caroline had spoken. As he said afterwards, he found it impossible
to expect her to attend to any subject so trivial; and when,
afterwards, Caroline told him, with some slight mirth, – the
capability of which on such a subject was coming to her with her
new ideas of life, – that, though he was partly saved as a man and
a brother, still he was partly the reverse as a feudal lord, he began
to reflect that Wallachia Petrie would be a guest with whom he
would find it very difficult to make things go pleasantly at Monkhams. 'Does she not bully you horribly?' he asked.

'Of course she bullies me,' Caroline answered; 'and I cannot
expect you to understand as yet how it is that I love her and like
her; but I do. If I were in distress to-morrow, she would give
everything she has in the world to put me right.'

'So would I,' said he.

'Ah, you; – that is a matter of course. That is your business now.
And she would give everything she has in the world to set the world
right. Would you do that?'

'It would depend on the amount of my faith. If I could believe in the result, I suppose I should do it.'

'She would do it on the slightest hope that such giving would have any tendency that way. Her philanthropy is all real. Of course she is a bore to you.'

'I am very patient.'

'I hope I shall find you so, – always. And, of course, she is ridculous – in your eyes. I have learned to see it, and to regret it; but I shall never cease to love her.'

'I have not the slightest objection. Her lessons will come from over the water, and mine will come from – where shall I say? – over the table. If I can't talk her down with so much advantage on my side, I ought to be made a woman's-right man myself.'

Poor Lady Rowley had watched Miss Petrie and Mr Glascock during those moments that they had been together, and had half believed the rumour, and had half doubted, thinking in the moments of her belief that Mr Glascock must be mad, and in the moments of unbelief that the rumours had been set afloat by the English Minister's wife with the express intention of turning Mr Glascock into ridicule. It had never occurred to her to doubt that Wallachia was the eldest of that family of nieces. Could it be possible that a man who had known her Nora, who had undoubtedly loved her Nora, – who had travelled all the way from London to Nuncombe Putney to ask Nora to be his wife, – should within twelve months of that time have resolved to marry a woman whom he must have selected simply as being the most opposite to Nora of any female human being that he could find? It was not credible to her; and if it were not true, there might still be a hope. Nora had met him, and had spoken to him, and it had seemed that for a moment or two they had spoken as friends. Lady Rowley, when talking to Mrs Spalding, had watched them closely; and she had seen that Nora's eyes had been bright, and that there had been something between them which was pleasant. Suddenly she found herself close to Wallachia, and thought that she would trust herself to a word.

'Have you been long in Florence?' asked Lady Rowley in her softest voice.

'A pretty considerable time, ma'am; – that is, since the fall began.'

What a voice; – what an accent; – and what words! Was there a man living with sufficient courage to take this woman to England, and show her to the world as Lady Peterborough?

'Are you going to remain in Italy for the summer?' continued Lady Rowley.

'I guess I shall; – or, perhaps, locate myself in the purer atmosphere of the Swiss mountains.'

'Switzerland in summer must certainly be much pleasanter.'

'I was thinking at the moment of the political atmosphere,' said Miss Petrie; 'for although, certainly, much has been done in this country in the way of striking off shackles and treading sceptres under foot, still, Lady Rowley, there remains here that pernicious thing, – a king. The feeling of the dominion of a single man, – and that of a single woman is, for aught I know, worse, – with me so clouds the air, that the breath I breathe fails to fill my lungs.' Wallachia, as she said this, put forth her hand, and raised her chin, and extended her arm. She paused, feeling that justice demanded that Lady Rowley should have a right of reply. But Lady Rowley had not a word to say, and Wallachia Petrie went on. 'I cannot adapt my body to the sweet savours and the soft luxuries of the outer world with any comfort to my inner self, while the circumstances of the society around me are oppressive to my spirit. When our war was raging all around me* I was light-spirited as the lark that mounts through the morning sky.'

'I should have thought it was very dreadful,' said Lady Rowley.

'Full of dread, of awe, and of horror, were those fiery days of indiscriminate slaughter; but they were not days of desolation, because hope was always there by our side. There was a hope in which the soul could trust, and the trusting soul is ever light and buoyant.'

'I dare say it is,' said Lady Rowley.

'But apathy, and serfdom, and kinghood, and dominion, drain the fountain of its living springs, and the soul becomes like the plummet of lead, whose only tendency is to hide itself in subaqueous mud and unsavoury slush.'

Subaqueous mud and unsavour slush! Lady Rowley repeated the words to herself as she made good her escape, and again expressed to herself her conviction that it could not possibly be so. The 'subaqueous mud and unsavour slush,' with all that had gone before it about the soul was altogether unintelligible to her; but she knew that it was American buncom of a high order of eloquence, and she told herself again and again that it could not be so. She continued to keep her eyes upon Mr Glascock, and soon saw him again talking to Nora. It was hardly possible, she thought, that Nora should speak to him with so much animation, or he to her, unless there was some feeling between them which, if properly handled, might lead to a renewal of the old tenderness. She went up to Nora, having collected the other girls, and said that the carriage was then waiting for them. Mr Glascock immediately offered Lady Rowley his arm, and took her down to the hall. Could it be that she was leaning upon a future son-in-law? There was something in the thought which made her lay her weight upon him with a freedom which she would not otherwise have used. Oh!-that her Nora should live to be Lady Peterborough! We are apt to abuse mothers for wanting high husbands for their daughters; – but can there be any point in which the true maternal instinct can show itself with more affectionate enthusiasm? This poor mother wanted nothing for herself from Mr Glascock. She knew very well that it was her fate to go back to the Mandarins, and probably to die there. She knew also that such men as Mr Glascock, when they marry beneath themselves in rank and fortune, will not ordinarily trouble themselves much with their mothers-in-law. There was nothing desired for herself. Were such a match accomplished, she might, perhaps, indulge herself in talking among the planter's wives of her daughter's coronet; but at the present moment there was no idea even of this in her mind. It was of Nora herself, and of Nora's sisters, that she was thinking, – for them that she was plotting, – that the one might be rich and splendid, and the others have some path opened for them to riches and splendour. Husband-hunting mothers may be injudicious; but surely they are maternal and unselfish. Mr Glascock put her into the carriage, and squeezed her hand; – and then he squeezed Nora's hand. She saw it, and was sure of it. 'I am so glad you are going to be happy,' Nora had said to him before this. 'As far as I have seen her, I like her so much.' 'If you do not come and visit her in her own house, I shall think you have no spirit of friendship,' he said. 'I will,' Nora had replied; – 'I will.' This had been said up-stairs, just as Lady Rowley was coming to them, and on this understanding, on this footing, Mr Glascock had pressed her hand.

As she went home, Lady Rowley's mind was full of doubt as to the course which it was best that she should follow with her daughter. She was not unaware how great was the difficulty before her. Hugh Stanbury's name had not been mentioned since they left London, but at that time Nora was obstinately bent on throwing herself away upon the 'penny-a-liner.' She had never been brought to acknowledge that such a marriage would be even inappropriate, and had withstood gallantly the expression of her father's displeasure. But with such a spirit as Nora's, it might be easier to prevail by silence than by many words. Lady Rowley was quite sure of this, – that it would be far better to say nothing further of Hugh Stanbury. Let the cure come, if it might be possible, from absence and from her daugher's good sense. The only question was whether it would be wise to say any word about Mr Glascock. In the carriage she was not only forbearing but flattering in her manner to Nora. She caressed her girl's hand and spoke to her, – as mothers know how to speak when they want to make much of their girls, and to have it understood that those girls are behaving as girls should behave. There was to be nobody to meet them to-night, as it had been arranged that Sir Marmaduke and Mrs Trevelyan should sleep at Siena. Hardly a word had been spoken in the carriage; but up-stairs, in their drawing-room, there came a moment in which Lucy and Sophie had left them, and Nora was alone wit her mother. Lady Rowley almost knew that it would be most prudent to be silent; – but a word spoken in season; – how good it is! And the thing was so near to her that she could not hold her peace. 'I must say, Nora,' she began, 'that I do like your Mr Glascock.'

'He is not my Mr Glascock, mamma,' said Nora, smiling.

'You know what I mean, dear.' Lady Rowley had not intended to utter a word that should appear like pressure on her daugher at this moment. She had felt how imprudent it would be to do so. But now Nora seemed to be leading the way herself to such discourse. 'Of course, he is not your Mr Glascock. You cannot eat your cake and have it, nor can you throw it away and have it.'

'I have thrown my cake away altogether, and certainly I cannot have it.' She was still smiling as she spoke, and seemed to be quite merry at the idea of regarding Mr Glascock as the cake which she had declined to eat.

'I can see one thing quite plainly, dear.'

'What is that, mamma?'

'That in spite of what you have done, you can still have your cake whenever you choose to take it.'

'Why, mamma, he is engaged to be married!'

'Mr Glascock?'

'Yes, Mr Glascock. It's quite settled. Is it not sad?'

'To whom is he engaged?' Lady Rowley's solemnity as she asked this question was piteous to behold.

'To Miss Spalding, – Caroline Spalding.'

'The eldest of those nieces?'

'Yes; – the eldest.'

'I cannot believe it.'

'Mamma, they both told me so. I have sworn an eternal friendship with her already.'

'I did not see you speaking to her.'

'But I did talk to her a great deal.'

'And he is really going to marry that dreadful woman ?'

'Dreadful, mamma !'

'Perfectly awful ! She talked to me in a way that I have read about in books, but which I did not before believe to be possible. Do you mean that he is going to be married to that hideous old maid, – that bell-clapper ?'

'Oh, mamma, what slander ! I think her so pretty.'

'Pretty !'

'Very pretty. And, mamma, ought I not to be happy that he should have been able to make himself so happy ? It was quite, quite, quite impossible that I should have been his wife. I have thought about it ever so much, and I am so glad of it ! I think she is just the girl that is fit for him.'

Lady Rowley took her candle and went to bed, professing to herself that she could not understand it. But what did it signify ? It was, at any rate, certain now that the man had put himself out of Nora's reach, and if he chose to marry a republican virago, with a red nose, it could now make no difference to Nora. Lady Rowley almost felt a touch of satisfaction in reflecting on the future misery of his married life.

78

Casalunga

Sir Marmaduke had been told at the Florence post-office that he would no doubt be able to hear tidings of Trevelyan, and to learn his address, from the officals in the post-office at Siena. At Florence he had been introduced to some gentleman who was certainly of importance, – a superintendent who had clerks under him and who was a big man. This person had been very courteous to him, and he had gone to Siena thinking that he would find it easy to obtain Trevelyan's address, – or to learn that there was no such person there. But at Siena he and his courier together could obtain no information. They rambled about the huge cathedral and the picturesque market-place of that quaint old city for the whole day, and on the next morning after breakfast they returned to Florence. They had learned nothing. The young man at the post-office had simply protested that he knew nothing of the name of Trevelyan. If letters should come addressed to such a name, he would keep them till they were called for ; but, to the best of his knowledge, he had never seen or heard the name. At the guard-house of the gendarmerie they could not, or would not, give him any information, and Sir Marmaduke came back with an impression that everybody at Siena was ignorant, idiotic, and brutal. Mrs Trevelyan was so dispirited as to be ill, and both Sir Marmaduke and Lady Rowley were disposed to think that the world was all against them. 'You have no conception of the sort of woman that man is going to marry,' said Lady Rowley.

'What man?'

'Mr Glascock! A horrid American female, as old almost as I am, who talks through her nose, and preaches sermons about the rights of women. It is incredible! And Nora might have had him just for lifting up her hand.' But Sir Marmaduke could not interest himself much about Mr Glascock. When he had been told that his daughter had refused the heir to a great estate and a peerage, it had been matter of regret; but he had looked upon the affair as done, and cared nothing now though Mr Glascock should marry a transatlantic Xantippe.* He was angry with Nora because by her obstinacy she was adding to the general perplexities of the family, but he could not make comparisons on Mr Glascock's behalf between her and Miss Spalding, – as his wife was doing, either mentally or aloud, from hour to hour. 'I suppose it is too late now,' said Lady Rowley, shaking her head.

'Of course it is too late. The man must marry whom he pleases. I am beginning to wonder that anybody should ever want to get married. I am indeed.'

'But what are the girls to do?'

'I don't know what anybody is to do. Here is a man as mad as a March hare, and yet nobody can touch him. If it was not for the child, I should advise Emily to put him out of her head altogether.'

But though Sir Marmaduke could not bring himself to take any interest in Mr Glascock's affairs, and would not ask a single question respecting the fearful American female whom this unfortunate man was about to translate to the position of an English peeress, yet circumstances so fell out that before three days were over he and Mr Glascock were thrown together in very intimate relations. Sir Marmaduke had learned that Mr Glascock was the only Englishman in Florence to whom Trevelyan had been known, and that he was the only person with whom Trevelyan had been seen to speak while passing through the city. In his despair, therefore, Sir Marmaduke had gone to Mr Glascock, and it was soon arranged that the two gentlemen should renew the search at Siena together, without having with them either Mrs Trevelyan or the courier. Mr Glascock knew the ways of the people better than did Sir Marmaduke, and could speak the language. He obtained a passport to the good offices of the police at Siena, and went prepared to demand rather than to ask for assistance. They started very early, before breakfast, and on arriving at Siena at about noon, first employed themselves in recruiting exhausted nature. By the time that they had both declared that the hotel at Siena was the very worst in all Italy, and that a breakfast without eatable butter was not to be considered a breakfast at all, they had become so intimate that Mr Glascock spoke of his own intended marriage. He must have done this with the conviction on his mind that Nora Rowley would have told Sir Marmaduke; but he did not feel it to be incumbent on himself to say anything on that subject. He had nothing to excuse. He had behaved fairly and honourably. It was not to be expected that he should remain unmarried for ever for the sake of a girl who had twice refused him. 'Of course there are very many in England,' he said, 'who will think me foolish to marry a girl from another country.'

'It is done every day,' said Sir Marmaduke.

'No doubt it is. I admit, however, that I ought to be more careful than some other persons. There is a title and an estate to be perpetuated, and I cannot, perhaps, be justified in taking quite so much liberty as some other men may do; but I think I have chosen a woman born to have a high position, and who will make her own way in any society in which she may be placed.'

'I have no doubt she will,' said Sir Marmaduke, who had still sounding in his ears the alarming description which his wife had given him of this infatuated man's proposed bride. But he would have been bound to say as much had Mr Glascock intended to marry as lowly as did King Cophetua.

'She is highly educated, gentle-mannered, as sweetly soft as any English girl I ever met, and very pretty. You have met her, I think.'

'I do not remember that I have observed her.'

'She is too young for me, perhaps,' said Mr Glascock; 'but that is a fault on the right side.' Sir Marmaduke, as he wiped his beard after his breakfast, remembered what his wife had told him about the lady's age. But it was nothing to him. 'She is four-and-twenty, I think,' said Mr Glascock. If Mr Glascock chose to believe that his intended wife was four-and-twenty instead of something over forty, that was nothing to Sir Marmaduke.

'The very best age in the world,' said he.

They had sent for an officer of the police, and before they had been three hours in Siena they had been told that Trevelyan lived about seven miles from the town, in a small and very remote country house, which he had hired for twelve months from one of the city hospitals. He had hired it furnished, and had purchased a horse and small carriage from a man in the town. To this man they went, and it soon became evident to them that he of whom they were in search was living at this house, which was called Casalunga, and was not, as the police officer told them, on the way to any place. They must leave Siena by the road for Rome, take a turn to the left about a mile beyond the city gate, and continue on along the country lane till they saw a certain round hill to the right. On the top of that round hill was Casalunga. As the country about Siena all lies in roundhills, this was no adequate description; – but it was suggested that the country people would know all about it. They got a small open carriage in the market-place, and were driven out. Their driver knew nothing of Casalunga, and simply went whither he was told. But by the aid of the country people they got along over the unmade lanes, and in little more than an hour were told, at the bottom of the hill, that they must now walk up to Casalunga. Though the hill was round-topped, and no more than a hill, still the ascent at last was very steep, and was paved with stones set edgeway in a manner that could hardly have been intended to accommodate wheels. When Mr Glascock asserted that the signor who lived there had a carriage of his own, the driver suggested that he must keep it at the bottom of the hill. It was clearly not his intention to attempt to drive up the ascent, and Sir Marmaduke and Mr Glascock were therefore obliged to walk. It was now in the latter half of May, and there was a blazing Italian sky over their heads. Mr Glascock was acclimated to Italian skies, and did not much mind the work; but Sir Marmaduke, who never did much in walking, declared that Italy was infinitely hotter than the Mandarins, and could hardly make his way as far as the house door.

It seemed to both of them to be a most singular abode for such a man as Trevelyan. At the top of the hill there was a huge entrance through a wooden gateway, which seemed to have been constructed with the intention of defying any intruders not provided with warlike ammunition. The gates were, indeed, open at the period of their visit, but it must be supposed that they were intended to be closed at any rate at night. Immediately on the right, as they entered through the gates, there was a large barn, in which two men were coopering wine vats. From thence a path led slanting to the house, of which the door was shut, and all the front windows blocked with shutters. The house was very long, and only of one story for a portion of its length. Over that end at which the door was placed

there were upper rooms, and there must have been space enough
for a large family with many domestics. There was nothing round
or near the residence which could be called a garden, so that its
look of desolation was extreme. There were various large barns and
outhouses, as though it had been intended by the builder that corn
and hay and cattle should be kept there; but it seemed now that
there was nothing there except the empty vats at which the two
men were coopering. Had the Englishmen gone farther into the
granary, they would have seen that there were wine-presses stored
away in the dark corners.

They stopped and looked at the men, and the men halted for a
moment from their work and looked at them; but the men spoke
never a word. Mr Glascock then asked after Mr Trevelyan, and one
of the coopers pointed to the house. Then they crossed over to the
door, and Mr Glascock finding there neither knocker nor bell, first
tapped with his knuckles, and then struck with his stick. But no one
came. There was not a sound in the house, and no shutter was
removed. 'I don't believe that there is a soul here,' said Sir
Marmaduke.

'We'll not give it up till we've seen it all at any rate,' said Mr
Glascock. And so they went round to the other front.

On this side of the house the tilled ground, either ploughed or
dug with the spade, came up to the very windows. there was hardly
even a particle of grass to be seen. A short way down the hill there
were rows of olive trees, standing in prim order and at regular
distances, from which hung the vines that made the coopering of
the vats necessary. Olives and vines have pretty names, and call up
associations of landscape beauty. But here they were in no way
beautiful. The ground beneath them was turned up, and brown,
and arid, so that there was not a blade of grass to be seen. On some
furrows the maize or Indian corn was sprouting, and there were
patches of growth of other kinds, – each patch closely marked by
its own straight lines; and there were narrow paths, so constructed
as to take as little room as possible. But all that had been done had
been done for economy, and nothing for beauty. The occupiers of
Casalunga had thought more of the produce of their land than of
picturesque or attractive appearance.

The sun was blazing fiercely hot, hotter on this side, Sir Marmaduke thought, even than on the other; and there was not a wavelet
of a cloud in the sky. A balcony ran the whole length of the house,
and under this Sir Marmaduke took shelter at once, leaning with
his back against the wall. 'There is not a soul here at all,' said he.

'The men in the barn told us that there was,' said Mr Glascock;

and, at any rate, we will try the windows.' So saying, he walked along the front of the house, Sir Marmaduke following him slowly, till they came to a door, the upper half of which was glazed, and through which they looked into one of the rooms. Two or three of the other windows in this frontage of the house came down to the ground, and were made for egress and ingress; but they had all been closed with shutters, as though the house was deserted. But they now looked into a room which contained some signs of habitation. There was a small table with a marble top, on which lay two or three books, and there were two arm-chairs in the room, with gilded arms and legs, and a morsel of carpet, and a clock on a shelf over a stove, and – a rocking-horse. 'The boy is here, you may be sure,' said Mr Glascock. 'The rocking-horse makes that certain. But how are we to get at any one!'

'I never saw such a place for an Englishman to come and live in before,' said Sir Marmaduke. 'What on earth can he do here all day!' As he spoke the door of the room was opened, and there was Trevelyan standing before them, looking at them through the window. He wore an old red English dressing-gown, which came down to his feet, and a small braided Italian cap on his head. His beard had been allowed to grow, and he had neither collar nor cravat. His trousers were unbraced, and he shuffled in with a pair of slippers, which would hardly cling to his feet. He was paler and still thinner than when he had been visited at Willesden, and his eyes seemed to be larger, and shone almost with a brighter brilliancy.

Mr Glascock tried to open the door, but found that it was closed. 'Sir Marmaduke and I have come to visit you,' said Mr Glascock, aloud. 'Is there any means by which we can get into the house?' Trevelyan stood still and stared at them. 'We knocked at the front door, but nobody came,' continued Mr Glascock. 'I suppose this is the way you usually go in and out.'

'He does not mean to let us in,' whispered Sir Marmaduke.

'Can you open this door,' said Mr Glascock, 'or shall we go round again?' Trevelyan had stood still contemplating them, but at last came forward and put back the bolt. 'That is all right,' said Mr Glascock, entering. 'I am sure you will be glad to see Sir Marmaduke.'

'I should be glad to see him, – or you, if I could entertain you,' said Trevelyan. His voice was harsh and hard, and his words were uttered with a certain amount of intended grandeur. 'Any of the family would be welcome were it not – '

'Were it not what?' asked Mr Glascock.

'It can be nothing to you, sir, what troubles I have here. This is my own abode, in which I had flattered myself that I could be free from intruders. I do not want visitors. I am sorry that you should have had trouble in coming here, but I do not want visitors. I am very sorry that I have nothing that I can offer you, Mr Glascock.'

'Emily is in Florence,' said Sir Marmaduke.

'Who brought her? Did I tell her to come? Let her go back to her home. I have come here to be free from her, and I mean to be free. If she wants my money, let her take it.'

'She wants her child,' said Mr Glascock.

'He is my child,' said Trevelyan, 'and my right to him is better than hers. Let her try it in a court of law, and she shall see. Why did she deceive me with that man? Why has she driven me to this? Look here, Mr Glascock; – my whole life is spent in this seclusion, and it is her fault.'

'Your wife is innocent of all fault, Trevelyan,' said Mr Glascock.

'Any woman can say as much as that; – and all women do say it. Yet, – what are they worth?'

'Do you mean, sir, to take away your wife's character?' said Sir Marmaduke, coming up in wrath. 'Remember that she is my daughter, and that there are things which flesh and blood cannot stand.'

'She is my wife, sir, and that is ten times more. Do you think that you would do more for her than I would do, – drink more of Esill?* You had better go away, Sir Marmaduke. You can do no good by coming here and talking of your daughter. I would have given the world to save her; – but she would not be saved.'

'You are a slanderer!' said Sir Marmaduke, in his wrath.

Mr Glascock turned round to the father, and tried to quiet him. It was so manifest to him that the balance of the poor man's mind was gone, that it seemed to him to be ridiculous to upbraid the sufferer. He was such a piteous sight to behold, that it was almost impossible to feel indignation against him. 'You cannot wonder,' said Mr Glascock, advancing close to the master of the house, 'that the mother should want to see her only child. You do not wish that your wife should be the most wretched woman in the world.'

'Am not I the most wretched of men? Can anything be more wretched than this? Is her life worse than mine? And whose fault was it? Had I any friend to whom she objected? Was I untrue to her in a single thought?'

'If you say that she was untrue, it is a falsehood,' said Sir Marmaduke.

'You allow yourself a liberty of expression, sir, because you are my wife's father,' said Tevelyan, 'which you would not dare to take in other circumstances.'

'I say that it is a false calumny, – a lie! and I would say so to any man on earth who should dare to slander my child's name.'

'Your child, sir! She is my wife; – my wife; – my wife!' Trevelyan, as he spoke, advanced close up to his father-in-law; and at last hissed out his words, with his lips close to Sir Marmaduke's face. 'Your right in her is gone, sir. She is mine, – mine, – mine! And you see the way in which she has treated me, Mr Glascock. Everything I had was hers; but the words of a grey-haired sinner were sweeter to her than all my love. I wonder whether you think that it is a pleasant thing for such a one as I to come out here and live in such a place as this? I have not a friend, – a companion, – hardly a book. There is nothing that I can eat or drink! I do not stir out of the house, – and I am ill; – very ill! Look at me. See what she has brought me to! Mr Glascock, on my honour as a man, I never wronged her in a thought or a word.'

Mr Glascock had come to think that his best chance of doing any good was to get Trevelyan into conversation with himself, free from the interruption of Sir Marmaduke. The father of the injured woman could not bring himself to endure the hard words that were spoken of his daughter. During this last speech he had broken out once or twice; but Trevelyan, not heeding him, had clung to Mr Glascock's arm. 'Sir Marmaduke,' said he, 'would you not like to see the boy?'

'He shall not see the boy,' said Trevelyan. 'You may see him. He shall not. What is he that he should have control over me?'

'This is the most fearful thing I ever heard of,' said Sir Marmaduke. 'What are we to do with him?'

Mr Glascock whispered a few words to Sir Marmaduke, and then declared that he was ready to be taken to the child. 'And he will remain here?' asked Trevelyan. A pledge was then given by Sir Marmaduke that he would not force his way farther into the house, and the two other men left the chamber together. Sir Marmaduke, as he paced up and down the room alone, perspiring at every pore, thoroughly uncomfortable and ill at ease, thought of all the hard positions of which he had ever read, and that his was harder than them all. Here was a man married to his daughter, in possession of his daughter's child, manifestly mad, – and yet he could do nothing to him! He was about to return to the seat of his government, and he must leave his own child in this madman's power! Of course, his daughter could not go with him, leaving her child in this madman's hands. He had been told that even were he to attempt to prove the man to be mad in Italy, the process would be slow; and, before it could be well commenced, Trevelyan would be off with the child elsewhere. There never was an embarrassment, thought Sir Marmaduke, out of which it was so impossible to find a clear way.

In the meantime, Mr Glascock and Trevelyan were visiting the child. It was evident that the father, let him be ever so mad, had discerned the expediency of allowing someone to see that his son was alive and in health. Mr Glascock did not know much of children, and could only say afterwards that the boy was silent and very melancholy, but clean, and apparently well. It appeared that he was taken out daily by his father in the cool hours of the morning, and that his father hardly left him from the time that he was taken up till he was put to bed. But Mr Glascock's desire was to see Trevelyan alone, and this he did after they had left the boy. 'And now, Trevelyan,' he said, 'what do you mean to do?'

'To do?'

'In what way do you propose to live? I want you to be reasonable with me.'

'They do not treat me reasonably.'

'Are you going to measure your own conduct by that of other people? In the first place, you should go back to England. What good can you do here?' Trevelyan shook his head, but remained silent. 'You cannot like this life.'

'No, indeed. But whither can I go now that I shall like to live?'

'Why not home?'

'I have no home.'

'Why not go back to England? Ask your wife to join you, and return with her. She would go at a word.' The poor wretch again shook his head. 'I hope you think that I speak as your friend,' said Mr Glascock.

'I believe you do.'

'I will say nothing of any imprudence; but you cannot believe that she has been untrue to you?' Trevelyan would say nothing to this, but stood silent waiting for Mr Glascock to continue. 'Let her come back to you – here; and then, as soon as you can arrange it, go to your own home.'

'Shall I tell you something?' said Trevelyan.

'What is it?'

He came up close to Mr Glascock, and put his hand upon his visitor's shoulder. 'I will tell you what she would do at once. I dare say that she would come to me. I dare say that she would go with

me. I am sure she would. And directly she got me there, she would
– say that I was – mad! She, – my wife, would do it! He, – that
furious, ignorant old man below, tried to do it before. His wife said
that I was mad.' He paused a moment, as though waiting for a
reply; but Mr Glascock had none to make. It had not been his
object, in the advice which he had given, to entrap the poor fellow
by a snare, and to induce him so to act that he should deliver
himself up to keepers; but he was well aware that wherever
Trevelyan might be, it would be desirable that he should be placed
for awhile in the charge of some physician. He could not bring
himself at the spur of the moment to repudiate the idea by which
Trevelyan was actuated. 'Perhaps you think that she would be
right?' said Trevelyan.

'I am quite sure that she would do nothing that is not for the
best,' said Mr Glascock.

'I can see it all. I will not go back to England, Mr Glascock. I
intend to travel. I shall probably leave this and go to – to – to
Greece, perhaps. It is a healthy place, this, and I like it for that
reason; but I shall not stay here. If my wife likes to travel with me,
she can come. But, – to England I will not go.'

'You will let the child go to his mother?'

'Certainly not. If she wants to see the child, he is here. If she will
come, – without her father, – she shall see him. She shall not take
him from hence. Nor shall she return to live with me, without full
acknowledgment of her fault, and promises of an amended life. I
kow what I am saying, Mr Glascock, and have thought of these
things perhaps more than you have done. I am obliged to you for
coming to me; but now, if you please, I would prefer to be alone.'

Mr Glascock, seeing that nothing further could be done, joined
Sir Marmaduke, and the two walked down to their carriage at the
bottom of the hill. Mr Glascock, as he went, declared his conviction
that the unfortunate man was altogether mad, and that it would be
necessary to obtain some interference on the part of the authorities
for the protection of the child. How this could be done, or whether
it could be done in time to intercept a further flight on the part of
Trevelyan, Mr Glascock could not say. It was his idea that Mrs
Trevelyan should herself go out to Casalunga, and try the force of
her own persuasion.

'I believe that he would murder her,' said Sir Marmaduke.

'He would not do that. There is a glimmer of sense in all his
madness, which will keep him from any actual violence.'

79

I Can Sleep on the Boards

Three days after this there came another carriage to the bottom of
the hill on which Casalunga stood, and a lady got out of it all alone.
It was Emily Trevelyan, and she had come thither from Siena in
quest of her husband and her child. On the previous day Sir
Marmaduke's courier had been at the house with a note from the
wife to the husband, and had returned with an answer, in which
Mrs Trevelyan was told that, if she would come quite alone, she
should see her child. Sir Marmaduke had been averse to any further
intercourse with the man, other than what might be made in
accordance with medical advice, and, if possible, with government
authority. Lady Rowley had assented to her daughter's wish, but
had suggested that she should at least be allowed to go also, – at
any rate, as far as the bottom of the hill. But Emily had been very
firm, and Mr Glascock had supported her. He was confident that
the man would do no harm to her, and he was indisposed to believe
that any interference on the part of the Italian Government could
be procured in such a case with sufficient celerity to be of use. He
still thought it might be possible that the wife might prevail over
the husband, or the mother over the father. Sir Marmaduke was at
last obliged to yield, and Mrs Trevelyan went to Siena with no
other companion but the courier. From Siena she made the journey
quite alone; and having learned the circumstances of the house
from Mr Glascock, she got out of the carriage, and walked up the
hill. There were still the two men coopering at the vats, but she did
not stay to speak to them. She went through the big gates, and
along the slanting path to the door, not doubting of her way; – for
Mr Glascock had described it all to her, making a small plan of the
premises, and even explaining to her the position of the room in
which her boy and her husband slept. She found the door open, and
an Italian maid-servant at once welcomed her to the house, and
assured her that the signor would be with her immediately. She was
sure that the girl knew that she was the boy's mother, and was
almost tempted to ask questions at once as to the state of the
household; but her knowledge of Italian was slight, and she felt
that she was so utterly a stranger in the land that she could dare to
trust no one. Though the heat was great, her face was covered with
a thick veil. Her dress was black, from head to foot, and she was as
a woman who mourned for her husband. She was led into the room
which her father had been allowed to enter through the window;
and here she sat, in her husband's house, feeling that in no position

in the world could she be more utterly separated from the interests of all around her. In a few minutes the door was opened, and her husband was with her, bringing the boy in his hand. He had dressed himself with some care; but it may be doubted whether the garments which he wore did not make him appear thinner even and more haggard than he had looked to be in his old dressing-gown. He had not shaved himself, but his long hair was brushed back from his forehead, after a fashion quaint and very foreign to his former ideas of dress. His wife had not expected that her child would come to her at once, – had thought that some entreaties would be necessary, some obedience perhaps exacted from her, before she would be allowed to see him; and now her heart was softened, and she was grateful to her husband. But she could not speak to him till she had had the boy in her arms. She tore off her bonnet, and then clinging to the child, covered him with kisses. 'Louey, my darling! Louey; you remember mamma?' The child pressed himself close to his mother's bosom, but spoke never a word. He was cowed and overcome, not only by the incidents of the moment, but by the terrible melancholy of his whole life. He had been taught to understand, without actual spoken lessons, that he was to live with his father, and that the former woman-given happinesses of his life were at an end. In this second visit from his mother he did not forget her. He recognised the luxury of her love; but it did not occur to him even to hope that she might have come to rescue him from the evil of his days. Trevelyan was standing by, the while, looking on; but he did not speak till she addressed him.,

'I am so thankful to you for bringing him to me,' she said.

'I told you that you should see him,' he said. 'Perhaps it might have been better that I should have sent him by a servant; but there are circumstances which make me fear to let him out of my sight.'

'Do you think that I did not wish to see you also? Louis, why do you do me so much wrong? Why do you treat me with such cruelty?' Then she threw her arms round his neck, and before he could repulse her, – before he could reflect whether it would be well that he should repulse her or not, – she had covered his brow and cheeks and lips with kisses. 'Louis,' she said; 'Louis, speak to me!'

'It is hard to speak sometimes,' he said.

'You love me, Louis?'

'Yes; – I love you. But I am afraid of you!'

'What is it that you fear? I would give my life for you, if you would only come back to me and let me feel that you believed me to be true.' He shook his head, and began to think, – while she still clung to him. He was quite sure that her father and mother had intended to bring a mad doctor down upon him, and he knew that his wife was in her mother's hands. Should he yield to her now, – should he make her any promise, – might not the result be that he would be shut up in dark rooms, robbed of his liberty, robbed of what he loved better than his liberty, – his power as a man. She would thus get the better of him and take the child, and the world would say that in this contest between him and her he had been the sinning one, and she the one against whom the sin had been done. It was the chief object of his mind, the one thing for which he was eager, that this should never come to pass. Let it once be conceded to him from all sides that he had been right, and then she might do with him almost as she willed. He knew well that he was ill. When he thought of his child, he would tell himself that he was dying. He was at some moments of his miserable existence fearfully anxious to come to terms with his wife, in order that at his death his boy might not be without a protector. Were he to die, then it would be better that his child should be with its mother. In his happy days, immediately after his marriage, he had made a will, in which he had left his entire property to his wife for her life, providing for its subsequent descent to his child, – or children. It had never even occurred to his poor shattered brain that it would be well for him to alter his will. Had he really believed that his wife had betrayed him, doubtelss he would have done so. He would have hated her, have distrusted her altogether, and have believed her to be an evil thing. He had no such belief. But in his desire to achieve empire, and in the sorrows which had come upon him in his unsuccessful struggle, his mind had wavered so frequently, that his spoken words were no true indicators of his thoughts; and in all his arguments he failed to express either his convictions or his desires. When he would say something stronger than he intended, and it would be put to him by his wife, by her father or mother, or by some friend of hers, whether he did believe that she had been untrue to him, he would recoil from the answer which his heart would dictate, lest he should seem to make an acknowledgment that might weaken the ground upon which he stood. Then he would satisfy his own conscience by assuring himself that he had never accused her of such sin. She was still clinging to him now as his mind was working after this fashion. 'Louis,' she said, 'let it all be as though there had been nothing.'

'How can that be, my dear?'

'Not to others; – but to us it can be so. There shall be no word spoken of the past.' Again he shook his head. 'Will it not be best that there should be no word spoken?'

'"Forgiveness may be spoken with the tongue,"'* he said, beginning to quote from a poem which had formerly been frequent in his hands.

'Cannot there be real forgiveness between you and me, – between husband and wife who, in truth, love each other? Do you think that I would tell you of it again?' He felt that in all that she said there was an assumption that she had been right, and that he had been wrong. She was promising to forgive. She was undertaking to forget. She was willing to take him back to the warmth of her love, and the comfort of her kindness, – but was not asking to be taken back. This was what he could not and would not endure. He had determined that if she behaved well to him, he would not be harsh to her, and he was struggling to keep up to his resolve. He would accuse her of nothing, – if he could help it. But he could not say a word that would even imply that she need forget, – that she should forgive. It was for him to forgive; – and he was willing to do it, if she would accept forgiveness. 'I will never speak a word, Louis,' she said, laying her head upon his shoulder.

'Your heart is still hardened,' he replied slowly.

'Hard to you?'

'And your mind is dark. You do not see what you have done. In our religion, Emily, forgiveness is sure, not after penitence, but with repentance.'

'What does that mean?'

'It means this, that though I would welcome you back to my arms with joy, I cannot do so, till you have – confessed your fault.'

'What fault, Louis? If I have made you unhappy, I do, indeed grieve that it has been so.'

'It is of no use,' said he. 'I cannot talk about it. Do you suppose that it does not tear me to the very soul to think of it?'

'What is it that you think, Louis?' As she had been travelling thither, she had determined that she would say anything that he wished her to say, – make any admission that might satisfy him. That she could be happy again as other women are happy, she did not expect; but if it could be conceded between them that bygones should be bygones, she might live with him and do her duty, and at least, have her child with her. Her father had told her that her husband was mad; but she was willing to put up with his madness on such terms as these. What could her husband do to her in his madness that he could not do also to the child? 'Tell me what you want me to say, and I will say it,' she said.

'You have sinned against me,' he said, raising her head gently from his shoulder.

'Never!' she exclaimed. 'As God is my judge, I never have!' As she said this, she retreated and took the sobbing boy again into her arms.

He was at once placed upon his guard, telling himself that he saw the necessity of holding by his child. How could he tell? Might there not be policemen down from Florence, ready round the house, to seize the boy and carry him away. Though all his remaining life should be a torment to him, though infinite plagues should be poured upon his head, though he should die like a dog, alone, unfriended, and in despair, while he was fighting this battle of his, he would not give way. 'That is sufficient,' he said. 'Louey must return now to his own chamber.'

'I may go with him?'

'No, Emily. You cannot go with him now. I will thank you to release him, that I may take him.' She still held the little fellow closely pressed in her arms. 'Do not reward me me for my courtesy by further disobedience,' he said.

'You will let me come again?' To this he made no reply. 'Tell me that I may come again.'

'I do not think that I shall remain here long.'

'And I may not stay now?'

'That would be impossible. There is no accommodation for you.'

'I could sleep on the boards beside his cot,' said Mrs Trevelyan,

'That is my place,' he replied. 'You may know that he is not disregarded. With my own hands I tend him every morning. I take him out myself. I feed him myself. He says his prayers to me. He learns from me, and can say his letters nicely. You need not fear for him. No mother was ever more tender with her child than I am with him.' Then he gently withdrew the boy from her arms, and she let her child go, lest he should learn to know that there was a quarrel between his father and his mother. 'If you will excuse me,' he said, 'I will not come down to you again to-day. My servant will see you to your carriage.'

So he left her; and she, with an Italian girl at her heels, got into her vehicle, and was taken back to Siena. There she passed the night alone at the inn, and on the next morning returned to Florence by the railway.

80

Will They Despise Him?

Gradually the news of the intended marriage between Mr Glascock and Miss Spalding spread itself over Florence, and people talked about it with that energy which subjects of such moment certainly deserve. That Caroline Spalding had achieved a very great triumph, was, of course, the verdict of all men and of all women; and I fear that there was a corresponding feeling that poor Mr Glascock had been triumphed over, and, as it were, subjugated. In some respects he had been remiss in his duties as a bachelor visitor to Florence, — as a visitor to Florence who had manifestly been much in want of a wife.* He had not given other girls a fair chance, but had thrown himself down at the feet of this American female in the weakest possible manner. And then it got about the town that he had been refused over and over again by Nora Rowley. It is too probable that Lady Rowley in her despair and dismay had been indiscreet, and had told secrets which should never have been mentioned by her. And the wife of the English minister, who had some grudges of her own, lifted her eyebrows and shook her head and declared that all the Glascocks at home would be outraged to the last degree. 'My dear Lady Rowley,' she said, 'I don't know whether it won't become a question with them whether they should issue a commission de lunatico.' Lady Rowley did not know what a commission de lunatico meant, but was quite willing to regard poor Mr Glascock as a lunatic. 'And there is poor Lord Peterborough at Naples just at death's door,' continued the British Minister's wife. In this she was perhaps nearly correct; but as Lord Peterborough had now been in the same condition for many months, as his mind had altogether gone, and as the doctor declared that he might live in his present condition for a year, or for years, it could not fairly be said that Mr Glascock was acting without due filial feeling in engaging himself to marry a young lady. 'And she such a creature!' said Lady Rowley, with emphasis. This the British Minister's wife noticed simply by shaking her head. Caroline Spalding was undoubtedly a pretty girl; but, as the British Minister's wife said afterwards, it was not surprising that poor Lady Rowley should be nearly out of her mind.

This had occurred a full week after the evening spent at Mr Spalding's house; and even yet Lady Rowley had never been put right as to that mistake of hers about Wallachia Petrie. That other trouble of hers, and her eldest daughter's journey to Siena, had prevented them from going out; and though the matter had often been discussed between Lady Rowley and Nora, there had not as yet come between them any proper explanation. Nora would declare that the future bride was very pretty and very delightful; and Lady Rowley would throw up her hands in despair and protest that her daughter was insane. 'Why should he not marry whom he likes, mamma?' Nora once said, almost with indignation.

'Because he will disgrace his family.'

'I cannot understand what you mean, mamma. They are, at any rate, as good as we are. Mr Spalding stands quite as high as papa does.'

'She is an American,' said Lady Rowley.

'And her family might say that he is an Englishman,' said Nora.

'My dear, if you do not understand the incongruity between an English peer and a Yankee – female, I cannot help you. I suppose it is because you have been brought up within the limited society of a small colony. If so, it is not your fault. But I had hoped you had been in Europe long enough to have learned what was what. Do you think, my dear, that she will look well when she is presented to her Majesty as Lord Peterborough's wife?'

'Splendid,' said Nora. 'She has just the brow for a coronet.'

'Heavens and earth!' said Lady Rowley, throwing up her hands. 'And you believe that he will be proud of her in England?'

'I am sure he will.'

'My belief is that he will leave her behind him, or that they will settle somewhere in the wilds of America, – out in Mexico, or Massachussetts, or the Rocky Mountains. I do not think that he will have the courage to show her in London.'

The marriage was to take place in the Protestant church at Florence early in June, and then the bride and bridegroom were to go over the Alps, and to remain there subject to tidings as to the health of the old man at Naples. Mr Glascock had thrown up his seat in Parliament, some month or two ago, knowing that he could not get back to his duties during the present session, and feeling that he would shortly be called upon to sit in the other House. he was thus free to use his time and to fix his days as he pleased; and it was certainly clear to those who knew him, that he was not ashamed of his American bride. He spent much of his time at the Spaldings' house, and was always to be seen with them in the Cascine* and at the Opera. Mrs Spalding, the aunt, was, of course, in great glory. A triumphant, happy, or even simply a splendid marriage, for the rising girl of a family is a great glory to the maternal mind. Mrs Spalding could not but be aware that the very air around her seemed to breathe congratulations into her ears. Her friends spoke to her, even on indifferent subjects, as though everything was going well with her, – better with her than with anybody else; and there came upon her in these days a dangerous feeling, that in spite of all the preachings of the preachers, the next world might perhaps be not so very much better than this. She was, in fact, the reverse of the medal of which poor Lady Rowley filled the obverse. And the American Minister was certainly an inch taller than before, and made longer speeches, being much more regardless of interruption. Olivia was delighted at her sister's success, and heard with rapture the description of Monkhams, which came to her second-hand through her sister. It was already settled that she was to spend her next Christmas at Monkhams, and perhaps there might be an idea in her mind that there were other eldest sons of old lords who would like American brides. Everything around Caroline Spalding was pleasant, – except the words of Wallachia Petrie.

Everything around her was pleasant till there came to her a touch of a suspicion that the marriage which Mr Glascock was going to make would be detrimental to her intended husband in his own country. There were many in Florence who were saying this besides the wife of the English Minister and Lady Rowley. Of course Caroline Spalding herself was the last to hear it, and to her the idea was brought by Wallachia Petrie. 'I wish I could think you would make yourself happy, – or him,' Wallachia had said, croaking.

'Why should I fail to make him happy?'

'Because you are not of the same blood, or race, or manners as himself. They say that he is very wealthy in his own country, and that those who live around him will look coldly on you.'

'So that he does not look coldly, I do not care how others may look,' said Caroline proudly.

'But when he finds that he has injured himself by such a marriage in the estimation of all his friends, – how will it be then?'

This set Caroline Spalding thinking of what she was doing. She began to realise the feeling that perhaps she might not be a fit bride for an English lord's son, and in her agony she came to Nora Rowley for counsel. After all, how little was it that she knew of the home and the country to which she was to be carried! She might not, perhaps, get adequate advice from Nora, but she would probably learn something on which she could act. There was no one else among the English at Florence to whom she could speak with freedom. When she mentioned her fears to her aunt, her aunt of course laughed at her. Mrs Spalding told her that Mr Glascock might be presumed to know his own business best, and that she, as an American lady of high standing, – the niece of a minister! – was a fitting match for any Englishman, let him be ever so much a lord. But Caroline was not comforted by this, and in her suspense she went to Nora Rowley. She wrote a line to Nora, and when she called at the hotel, was taken up to her friend's bedroom. She found great difficulty in telling her story, but she did tell it. 'Miss Rowley,' she said, 'if this is a silly thing that he is going to do, I am bound to save him from his own folly. You know your own country better than I do. Will they think that he has disgraced himself?'

'Certainly not that,' said Nora.

'Shall I be a load round his neck? Miss Rowley, for my own sake I would not endure such a position as that, not even though I love him. But for his sake! Think of that. If I find that people think ill of him, – because of me – !'

'No one will think ill of him.'

'Is it esteemed needful that such a one as he should marry a woman of his own rank. I can bear to end it all now; but I shall not be able to bear his humiliation, and my own despair, if I find that I have injured him. Tell me plainly, – is it a marriage that he should not make?' Nora paused for a while before she answered, and as she sat silent the other girl watched her face carefully. Nora on being thus consulted, was very careful that her tongue should utter nothing that was not her true opinion as best she knew how express it. Her sympathy would have prompted her to give such an answer as would at once have made Caroline happy in her mind. She would have been delighted to have been able to declare that these doubts were utterly groundless, and this hesitation needless. But she conceived that she owed it as a duty from one woman to another to speak the truth as she conceived it on so momentous and occasion, and she was not sure but that Mr Glascock would be considered by his friends in England to be doing badly in marrying an American girl. What she did not remember was this – that her very hesitation was in fact an answer, and such an answer as she was most unwilling to give. 'I see that it would be so,' said Caroline Spalding.

'No; – not that.'

'What then? Will they despise him, – and me?'

'No one who knows you can despise you. No one who sees you can fail to admire you.' Nora, as she said this, thought of her mother, but told herself at once that in this matter her mother's judgement had been altogether destroyed by her disappointment. 'What I think will take place will be this. His family, when first they hear of it, will be sorry.'

'Then,' said Caroline, 'I will put an end to it.'

'You can't do that, dear. You are engaged, and you haven't a right. I am engaged to a man, and all my friends object to it. But I shan't put an end to it. I don't think I have a right. I shall not do it any way, however.'

'But if it were for his good?'

'It couldn't be for his good. He and I have got to go along together somehow.'

'You wouldn't hurt him,' said Caroline.

'I won't if I can help it, but he has got to take me along with him any how; and Mr Glascock has got to take you. If I were you I shouldn't ask any more questions.'

'It isn't the same. You said that you were to be poor, but he is very rich. And I am beginning to understand that these titles of yours are something like kings' crowns. The man who has to wear them can't do just as he pleases with them. Noblesse oblige. I can see the meaning of that, even when the obligation itself is trumpery in its nature. If it is a man's duty to marry a Talbot because he's a Howard, I suppose he ought to do his duty.' After a pause she went on again. 'I do believe that I have made a mistake. It seemed to be absurd at the first to think of it, but I do believe it now. Even what you say to me makes me think it.'

'At any rate you can't go back,' said Nora enthusiastically.

'I will try.'

'Go to himself and ask him. You must leave him to decide it at last. I don't see how a girl when she is engaged, is to throw a man over unless he consents. Of course you can throw yourself into the Arno.'

'And get the water into my shoes, – for it wouldn't do much more at present.'

'And you can – jilt him,' said Nora.

'It would not be jilting him.'

'He must decide that. If he so regards it, it will be so. I advise you to think no more about it; but if you speak to anybody it should be to him.' This was at last the result of Nora's wisdom, and then the two girls descended together to the room in which Lady Rowley was sitting with her other daughters. Lady Rowley was very careful in asking after Miss Spalding's sister, and Miss Spalding assured her that Olivia was quite well. Then Lady Rowley made some inquiry about Olivia and Mr Glascock, and Miss Spalding assured her that Olivia was quite well. Then Lady Rowley made some inquiry about Olivia and Mr Glascock, and Miss Spalding assured her that no two persons were ever such allies, and that she believed that they

were together at this moment investigating some old church. Lady
Rowley simpered, and declared that nothing could be more proper,
and expressed a hope that Olivia would like England. Caroline
Spalding, having still in her mind the trouble that had brought her
to Nora, had not much to say about this. 'If she goes gain to
England I am sure she will like it,' replied Miss Spalding.

'But of course she is going,' said Lady Rowley.

'Of course she will some day, and of course she'll like it,' said
Miss Spalding. 'We both of us have been there already.'

'But I mean Monkhams,' said Lady Rowley, still simpering.

'I declare I believe mamma thinks that your sister is to be married
to Mr Glascock!' said Lucy.

'And so she is; – isn't she?' said Lady Rowley.

'Oh, mamma!' said Nora, jumping up. 'It is Caroline; – this one,
this one, this one,' – and Nora took her friend by the arm as she
spoke, – 'it is this one that is to be Mrs Glascock.'

'It is a most natural mistake to make,' said Caroline.

Lady Rowley became very red in the face, and was unhappy. 'I
declare,' she said, 'that they told me it was your elder sister.'

'But I have no elder sister,' said Caroline, laughing.

'Of course she is oldest,' said Nora, – 'and looks to be so, ever so
much. Don't you Miss Spalding?'

'I have always supposed so.'

'I don't understand it at all,' said Lady Rowley, who had no
image before her mind's eye but that of Wallachia Petrie, and who
was beginning to feel that she had disgraced her own judgment by
the criticisms she had expressed everywhere as to Mr Glascock's
bride. 'I don't understand it at all. Do you mean that both your
sisters are younger than you, Miss Spalding?'

'I have only got one, Lady Rowley.'

'Mamma, you are thinking of Miss Petrie,' said Nora, clapping
both her hands together.

'I mean the lady that wears the black bugles.'

'Of course you do; – Miss Petrie. Mamma has all along thought
that Mr Glascock was going to carry away with him the Republican
Browning!'

'Oh, mamma, how can you have made such a blunder!' said
Sophie Rowley. 'Mamma does make such delicious blunders.'

'Sophie, my dear, that is not a proper way of speaking.'

'But, dear mamma, don't you?'

'If somebody has told me wrong, that has not been my fault,'
said Lady Rowley.

The poor woman was so evidently disconcerted that Caroline

Spalding was quite unhappy. 'My dear Lady Rowley, there has been
no fault. And why shouldn't it have been so. Wallachia is so clever,
that it is the most natural thing in the world to have thought.'

'I cannot say that I agree with you there,' said Lady Rowley,
somewhat recovering herself.

'You must know the whole truth now,' said Nora, turning to her
friend, 'and you must not be angry with us if we laugh a little at
your poetess. Mamma has been frantic with Mr Glascock because
he has been going to marry, – whom shall I say, – her edition of
you. She has sworn that he must be insane. When we have sworn
how beautiful you were, and how nice, and how jolly, and all the
rest of it, – she has sworn that you were at least a hundred, and
that you had a red nose. You must admit that Miss Petrie has a red
nose.'

'Is that a sin?'

'Not at all in the woman who has it; but in the man who is going
to marry it, – yes. Can't you see how we have all been at cross-
purposes, and what mamma has been thinking and saying of poor
Mr Glascock? You mustn't repeat it, of course; but we have had
such a battle here about it. We thought that mamma had lost her
eyes and her ears and her knowledge of things in general. And now
it has all come out! You won't be angry?'

'Why should I be angry?'

'Miss Spalding,' said Lady Rowley, 'I am really unhappy at what
has occurred, and I hope that there may be nothing more said about
it. I am quite sure that somebody told me wrong, or I should not
have fallen into such an error. I beg your pardon, – and Mr
Glascock's!'

'Beg Mr Glascock's pardon, certainly,' said Lucy.

Miss Spalding looked very pretty, smiled very gracefully, and
coming up to Lady Rowley to say good-bye, kissed her on her
cheeks. This overcame the spirit of the disappointed mother, and
Lady Rowley never said another word against Caroline Spalding or
her marriage. 'Now, mamma, what do you think of her?' said
Nora, as soon as Caroline was gone.

'Was it odd, my dear, that I should be astonished at his wanting
to marry that other woman?'

'But, mamma, when we told you that she was young and pretty
and bright!'

'I thought that you were all demented. I did indeed. I still think it
a pity that he should take an American. I think that Miss Spalding
is very nice, but there are English girls quite as nice-looking as her.'

After that there was not another word said by Lady Rowley against Caroline Spalding.

Nora, when she thought of it all that night, felt that she had hardly spoken to Miss Spalding as she should have spoken as to the treatment in England which would be accorded to Mr Glascock's wife. She became aware of the effect which her own hesitation must have had, and thought that it was her duty to endeavour to remove it. Perhaps, too, the conversion of her mother had some effect in making her feel that she had been wrong in supposing that there would be any difficulty in Caroline's position in England. She had heard so much adverse criticism from her mother that she had doubted in spite of her own convictions; – but now it had come to light that Lady Rowley's criticisms had all come from a most absurd blunder. 'Only fancy;' – she said to herself; – 'Miss Petrie coming out as Lady Peterborough! Poor mamma!' And then she thought of the reception which would be given to Caroline, and of the place the future Lady Peterborough would fill in the world, and of the glories of Monkhams! Resolving that she would do her best to counteract any evil which she might have done, she seated herself at her desk, and wrote the following letter to Miss Spalding:

My dear Caroline,

I am sure you will let me call you so, as had you not felt towards me like a friend, you would not have come to me to-day and told me of your doubts. I think that I did not answer you as I ought to have done when you spoke to me. I did not like to say anything off-hand, and in that way I misled you. I feel quite sure that you will encounter nothing in England as Mr Glascock's wife to make you uncomfortable, and that he will have nothing to repent. Of course Englishmen generally marry Englishwomen; and, perhaps, there may be some people who will think that such a prize should not be lost to their countrywomen. But that will be all. Mr Glascock commands such universal respect that his wife will certainly be respected, and I do not suppose that anything will ever come in your way that can possibly make you feel that he is looked down upon. I hope you will understand what I mean.

As for your changing now, that is quite impossible. If I were you, I would not say a word about it to any living being; but just go on, – straight forward, – in your own way, and take the good the gods provide you, – as the poet says to the king in the ode.* And I think the gods have provided for you very well, – and for him.

I do hope that I may see you sometimes. I cannot explain to you how very much out of your line 'we' shall be; – for of couse there is a 'we.' People are more separated with us than they are, I suppose, with you. And my 'we' is a very poor man, who works hard at writing in a dingy newspaper office, and we shall live in a garret and have brown sugar in our tea, and eat hashed mutton. And I shall have nothing a year to buy my clothes with. Still I mean to do it; and I don't mean to be long before I do do it. When a girl has made up her mind to be married, she had better go on with it as once, and take it all afterwards as it may come. Nevertheless, perhaps, we may see each other somewhere, and I may be able to introduce you to the dearest, honestest, very best, and most affectionate man in the world. And he is very, very clever.

Yours very affectionately,
Nora Rowley.

Thursday morning.

81

Mr Glascock is Master

Caroline Spalding, when she received Nora's letter, was not disposed to give much weight to it. She declared to herself that the girl's unpremeditated expression of opinion was worth more than her studied words. But she was not the less grateful or the less loving towards her new friend. She thought how nice it would be to have Nora at that splendid abode in England of which she had heard so much, – but she thought also that in that splendid abode she herself ought never to have part or share. If it were the case that this were an unfitting match, it was clearly her duty to decide that there should be no marriage. Nora had been quite right in bidding her speak to Mr Glascock himself, and to Mr Glascock she would go. But it was very difficult for her to determine on the manner in which she would discuss the subject with him. She thought that she could be firm if her mind were once made up. She believed that perhaps she was by nature more firm than he. In all their intercourse together he had ever yielded to her; and though she had been always pleased and grateful, there had grown upon her an idea that he was perhaps too easy, – that he was a man as to whom it was necessary that they who loved him should see that he was not led away by weakness into folly. But she would want to learn something from him before her decision was finally reached, and in this she foresaw a great difficulty. In her trouble she went to her usual counsellor, – the Republican Browning. In such an emergency she could hardly have done worse. 'Wally,' she said, 'we talk about England, and Italy, and France, as though we knew all about them;

but how hard it is to realise the difference between one's own country and others.'

'We can at least learn a great deal that is satisfactory,' said Wallachia. 'About one out of every five Italians can read a book, about two out of every five Englishmen can read a book. Out of every five New Englanders four and four-fifths can read a book. I guess that is knowing a good deal.'

'I don't mean in statistics.'

'I cannot conceive how you are to learn anything about any country except by statistics. I have just discovered that the number of illegitimate children – '

'Oh, Wally, I can't talk about that, – not now at least. What I cannot realise is this, – what sort of a life it is that they will lead at Monkhams.'

'Plenty to eat and drink, I guess ; and you'll always have to go round in fine clothes.'

'And that will be all ?'

'No; – not all. There will be carriages and horses, and all manner of people there who won't care much about you. If he is firm, – very firm; – if he have that firmness which one does not often meet, even in an American man, he will be able, after a while, to give you a position as an English woman of rank.' It is to be feared that Wallachia Petrie had been made aware of Caroline's idea as to Mr Glascock's want of purpose.

'And that will be all ?'

'If you have a baby, they'll let you go and see it two or three times a day. I don't suppose you will be allowed to nurse it, because they never do in England. You have read what the Saturday Review says. In every other respect the Saturday Review has been the falsest of all false periodicals, but I guess it has been pretty true in what it has said about English women.'*

'I wish I knew more about it really.'

'When a man has to leap through a window in the dark, Caroline, of course he doubts whether the feather bed said to be below will be soft enough for him.'

'I shouldn't fear the leap for myself, if it wouldn't hurt him. Do you think it possible that society can be so formed that a man should lose caste because he doesn't marry just one of his own set ?'

'It has been so all over the world, my dear. If like to like is to be true anywhere, it should be true in marriage.'

'Yes; – but with a difference. He and I are like to like. We come of the same race, we speak the same language, we worship the same God, we have the same ideas of culture and of pleasures. The difference is one that is not patent to the eye or to the ear. It is a difference of accidental incident, not of nature or of acquirement.'

'I guess you would find, Caroline, that a jury of English matrons sworn to try you fairly, would not find you to be entitled to come among them as one of themselves.'

'And how will that affect him?'

'Less powerfully than many others, because he is not impassioned. He is, perhaps – lethargic.'

'No, Wally, he is not lethargic.'

'If you ask me I must speak. It would harass some men almost to death; it will not do so with him. He would probably find his happiness best in leaving his old country and coming among your people.'

The idea of Mr Glascock, – the future Lord Peterborough, – leaving England, abandoning Monkhams, deserting his duty in the House of Lords, and going away to live in an American town, in order that he might escape the miseries which his wife had brought upon him in his own country, was more than Caroline could bear. She knew that, at any rate, it would not come to that. The lord of Monkhams would live at Monkhams, though the heavens should fall – in regard to domestic comforts. It was clear to Caroline that Wallachia Petrie had in truth never brought home to her own imagination the position of an English peer. 'I don't think you understand the people at all,' she said angrily.

'You think that you can understand them better because you are engaged to this man!' said Miss Petrie, with well-pronounced irony. 'You have found generally that when the sun shines in your eyes your sight is improved by it! You think that the love-talk of a few weeks gives clearer instruction than the laborious reading of many volumes and thoughtful converse with thinking persons! I hope that you, may find it so, Caroline.' So saying Wallachia Petrie walked off in great dudgeon.

Miss Petrie, not having learned from her many volumes and her much converse with thoughtful persons to read human nature aright, was convinced by this conversation that her friend Caroline was blind to all results, and was determined to go on with this dangerous marriage, having the rays of that sun of Monkhams so full upon her eyes that she could not see at all. She was specially indignant at finding that her own words had no effect. But, unfortunately, her words had had much effect; and Caroline, though she had contested her points, had done so only with the intention of producing her Mentor's admonitions. Of course it was out of the question that Mr Glascock should go and live in

Providence, Rhode Island, from which thriving town Caroline Spalding had come; but, because that was impossible, it was not the less probable that he might be degraded and made miserable in his own home. That suggested jury of British matrons was a frightful conclave to contemplate, and Caroline was disposed to believe that the verdict given in reference to herself would be adverse to her. So she sat and meditated, and spoke not a word further to any one on the subject till she was alone with the man that she loved.

Mr Spalding at this time inhabited the ground floor of a large palace in the city, from which there was access to a garden which at this period of the year was green, bright, and shady, and which as being in the centre of a city was large and luxurious. From one end of the house there projected a covered terrace, or loggia, in which there were chairs and tables, sculptured ornaments, busts, and old monumental relics let into the wall in profusion. It was half chamber and half garden, – such an adjunct to a house as in our climate would give only an idea of cold, rheumatism, and a false romance, but under an Italian sky is a luxury daily to be enjoyed during most months of the year. Here Mr Glascock and Caroline had passed many hours, – and here they were now seated, late in the evening, while all others of the family were away. As far as regarded the rooms occupied by the American Minister, they had the house and garden to themselves, and there never could come a time more appropriate for the saying of a thing difficult to be said. Mr Glascock had heard from his father's physician, and had said that it was nearly certain now that he need not go down to Naples again before his marriage. Caroline was trembling, not knowing how to speak, not knowing how to begin; – but resolved that the thing should be done. 'He will never know you, Carry,' said Mr Glascock. 'It is, perhaps, hardly a sorrow to me, but it is a regret.'

'It would have been a sorrow perhaps to him had he been able to know me,' said she, taking the opportunity of rushing at her subject.

'Why so? Of all human beings he was the softest-hearted.'

'Not softer-hearted than you, Charles. But soft hearts have to be hardened.'

'What do you mean? Am I becoming obdurate?'

'I am, Charles,' she said. 'I have got something to say to you. What will your uncles and aunts and say of me when they see me at Monkhams?'

'They will swear to me that you are charming; and then, – when my back is turned, – they'll pick you to pieces a little among themselves. I believe that is the way of the world, and I don't suppose that we are to do better than others.'

'And if you had married an English girl, a Lady Augusta Somebody, – would they pick her to pieces?'

'I guess they would, – as you say.'

'Just the same?'

'I don't think anybody escapes, as far as I can see. But that won't prevent their becoming your bosom friends in a few weeks time.'

'No one will say that you have been wrong to marry an American girl?'

'Now, Carry, what is the meaning of all this?'

'Do you know any man in your position who ever did marry an American girl; – any man of your rank in England?' Mr Glascock began to think of the case, and could not at the moment remember any instance. 'Charles, I do not think you ought to be the first.'

'And yet somebody must be first, if the thing is every to be done; – and I am too old to wait on the chance of being the second.'

She felt that at the rate she was now progressing she would only run from one little suggestion to another, and that he, either wilfully or in sheer simplicity, would take such suggestions simply as jokes; and she was aware that she lacked the skill to bring the conversation round gradually to the point which she was bound to reach. She must make another dash, let it be ever so sudden. Her mode of doing so would be crude, ugly, – almost vulgar she feared; but she would attain her object and say what she had to say. When once she had warmed herself with the heat which argument would produce, then, she was pretty sure, she would find herself at least as strong as he. 'I don't know that the thing ought to be done at all,' she said. During the last moment or two he had put his arm round her waist; and she, not chosing to bid him desist from embracing her, but unwilling in her present mood to be embraced, got up and stood before him. 'I have thought, and thought, and thought, and feel that it should not be done. In marriage, like should go to like.' She despised herself for using Wallachia's words, but they fitted in so usefully, that she could not refrain from them. 'I was wrong not to know it before, but it is better to know it now, than not to have known it till too late. Everything that I hear and see tells me that it would be so. If you were simply an Englishman, I would go anywhere with you; but I am not fit to be the wife of an English lord. The time would come when I should be a disgrace to you, and then I should die.'

'I think I should go near dying myself,' said he, 'if you were a disgrace to me.' He had not risen from his chair, and sat calmly looking up into her face.

'We have made a mistake, and let us unmake it,' she continued. 'I will always be your friend. I will correspond with you. I will come and see your wife.'

'That will be very kind!'

'Charles, if you laugh at me, I shall be angry with you. It is right that you should look to your future life, as it is right that I should do so also. Do you think that I am joking? Do you suppose that I do not mean it?'

'You have taken an extra dose this morning of Wallachia Petrie, and of course you mean it.'

'If you think that I am speaking her mind and not my own, you do not know me.'

'And what is it you propose?' he said, still keeping his seat and looking calmly up into her face.

'Simply that our engagement should be over.'

'And why?'

'Because it is not a fitting one for you to have made. I did not understand it before, but now I do. It will not be good for you to marry an American girl. It will not add to your happiness, and may destroy it. I have learned, at last, to know how much higher is your position than mine.'

'And I am to be supposed to know nothing about it?'

'Your fault is only this, – that you have been too generous. I can be generous also.'

'Now, look here, Caroline, you must not be angry with me if on such a subject I speak plainly. You must not even be angry if I laugh a little.'

'Pray do not laugh at me! – not now.'

'I must a little, Carry. Why am I to be supposed to be so ignorant of what concerns my own happiness and my own duties? If you will not sit down, I will get up, and we will take a turn together.' He rose from his seat, but they did not leave the covered terrace. They moved on to the extremity, and then he stood hemming her in against a marble table in the corner. 'In making this rather wild proposition, have you considered me at all?'

'I have endeavoured to consider you, and you only.'

'And how have you done it? By the aid of some misty, far-fetched ideas respecting English society, for which you have no basis except your own dreams, – and by the fantasies of a rabid enthusiast.'

'She is not rabid.' said Caroline earnestly; 'other people think just the same.'

'My dear, there is only one person whose thinking on this subject is of any avail, and I am that person. Of course, I can't drag you into church to be married, but practically you can not help yourself from being taken there now. As there need be no question about our marriage, – which is a thing as good as done – '

'It is not done at all,' said Caroline.

'I feel quite satisfied you will not jilt me, and as I shall insist on having the ceremony performed, I choose to regard it as a certainty. Passing that by, then, I will go on to the results. My uncles, and aunts, and cousins, and the people you talk of, were very reasonable folk when I last saw them, and quite sufficiently alive to the fact that they had to regard me as the head of their family. I do not doubt that we shall find them equally reasonable when we get home; but should they be changed, should there be any sign shown that my choice of a wife had occasioned displeasure, – such displeasure would not affect you.'

'But it would affect you.'

'Not at all. In my own house I am master, – and I mean to continue to be so. You will be mistress there, and the only fear touching such a position is that it may be recognised by others too strongly. You have nothing to fear, Carry.'

'It is of you I am thinking.'

'Nor have I. What if some old women, or even some young women, should turn up their noses at the wife I have chosen, because she has not been chosen from among their own country-women, is that to be a cause of suffering to us? Can not we rise above that, – lasting as it would do for a few weeks, a month or two perhaps, – say a year, – till my Caroline shall have made herself known? I think that we are strong enough to live down a trouble so light.' He had come close to her as he was speaking, and had again put his arm round her waist. She tried to escape from his embrace, – not with persistency, not with the strength which always suffices for a woman when the embrace is in truth a thing to be avoided, but clutching at his fingers with hers, pressing them rather than loosening their grasp. 'No, Carry,' he continued; 'we have got to go through with it now, and we will try and make the best of it. You may trust me that we shall not find it difficult, – not, at least, on the ground of your present fears. I can bear a heavier burden than you will bring upon me.'

'I know that I ought to prove to you that I am right,' she said, still struggling with his hand.

'And I know that you can prove nothing of the kind. Dearest, it is fixed between us now, and do not let us be so silly as to raise imaginary difficulties. Of course you would have to marry me, even if there were cause for such fears. If there were any great cause, still the game would be worth the candle. There could be no going back, let the fear be what it might. But there need be no fear if you will only love me.' She felt that he was altogether too strong for her, – that she had mistaken his character in supposing that she could be more firm than he. He was so strong that he treated her almost as a child; – and yet she loved him infinitely the better for so treating her. Of course, she knew now that her objection, whether true or unsubstantial, could not avail. As he stood with his arm round her, she was powerless to contradict him in anything. She had so far acknowledged this that she no longer struggled with him, but allowed her hand to remain quietly within his. If there was no going back from this bargain that had been made, – why, then, there was no need for combating. And when he stooped over her and kissed her lips, she had not a word to say. 'Be good to me,' he said, 'and tell me that I am right.'

'You must be master, I suppose, whether you are right or wrong. A man always thinks himself entitled to his own way.'

'Why, yes. When he has won the battle, he claims his captive. Now, the truth is this, I have won the battle, and your friend, Miss Petrie, has lost it. I hope she will understand that she has been beaten at last out of the field.' As he said this, he heard a step behind them, and turning round saw Wallachia there almost before he could drop his arm.

'I am sorry that I have intruded on you,' she said very grimly.

'Not in the least,' said Mr Glascock. 'Caroline and I have had a little dispute, but we have settled it without coming to blows.'

'I do not suppose that an English gentleman ever absolutely strikes a lady,' said Wallachia Petrie.

'Not except on strong provocation,' said Mr Glascock. 'In reference to wives, a stick is allowed as big as your thumb.'*

'I have heard that it is so by the laws of England,' said Wallachia.

'How can you be so ridiculous, Wally !' said Caroline. 'There is nothing that you would not believe.'

'I hope that it may never be true in your case,' said Wallachia.

A couple of days after this Miss Spalding found that it was absolutely necessary that she should explain the circumstances of her position to Nora. She had left Nora with the purpose of performing a very high-minded action, of sacrificing herself for the sake of her lover, of giving up all her golden prospects, and of becoming once again the bosom friend of Wallachia Petrie, with this simple consolation for her future life, – that she had refused to marry an English nobleman because the English nobleman's condition was unsuited to her. It would have been an episode in female life in which pride might be taken; – but all that was now changed. She had made her little attempt, – had made it, as she felt, in a very languid manner, and had found herself treated as a child for doing so. Of course she was happy in her ill success; of course she would have been broken-hearted had she succeeded. But, nevertheless, she was somewhat lowered in her own esteem, and it was necessary that she should acknowledge the truth to the friend whom she had consulted. A day or two had passed before she found herself alone with Nora, but when she did so she confessed her failure at once.

'You told him all, then?' said Nora.

'Oh yes, I told him all. That is, I could not really tell him. When the moment came I had no words.'

'And what did he say?'

'He had words enough. I never knew him to be eloquent before.'

'He can speak out if he likes,' said Nora.

'So I have found, – with a vengeance. Nobody was ever so put down as I was. Don't you know that there are times when it does not seem to be worth your while to put out your strength against an adversary? So it was with him. He just told me that he was my master, and that I was to do as he bade me.'

'And what did you say?'

'I promised to be a good girl,' said Caroline, 'and not to pretend to have any opinion of my own even again. And so we kissed, and were friends.'

'I dare say there was a kiss, my dear.'

'Of course there was; – and he held me in his arms, and comforted me, and told me how to behave; – just as you would do a little girl. It's all over now, of course; and if there be a mistake, it is his fault. I feel that all responsibility is gone from myself, and that for all the rest of my life I have to do just what he tells me.'

'And what says the divine Wallachia?'

'Poor Wally! She says nothing, but she thinks that I am a castaway and a recreant. I am a recreant, I know; – but yet I think that I was right. I know I could not help myself.'

'Of course you were right, my dear,' said the sage Nora. 'If you had the notion in your head, it was wise to get rid of it; but I knew how it would be when you spoke to him.'

'You were not so weak when he came to you.'

'That was altogether another thing. It was not arranged in heaven that I was to become his captive.'

After that Wallachia Petrie never again tried her influence on her former friend, but admitted to herself that the evil was done, and that it could not be remedied. According to her theory of life, Caroline Spalding had been wrong, and weak, – had shown herself to be comfort-loving and luxuriously-minded, had looked to get her happiness from soft effeminate pleasures rather than from rational work and the useful, independent exercise of her own intelligence. In the privacy of her little chamber Wallachia Petrie shed, – not absolute tears, – but many tearful thoughts over her friend. It was to her a thing very terrible that the chosen one of her heart should prefer the career of an English lord's wife to that of an American citizenness, with all manner of capability for female voting, female speech-making, female poetising, and, perhaps, female political action before her. It was a thousand pities ! 'You may take a horse to water,' – said Wallachia to herself, thinking of the ever-freshly springing fountain of her own mind, at which Caroline Spalding would always have been made welcome freely to quench her thirst, – 'but you cannot make him drink if he be not athirst.' In the future she would have no friend. Never again would she subject herself to the disgrace of such a failure. But the sacrifice was to be made, and she knew that it was bootless to waste her words further on Caroline Spalding. She left Florence before the wedding, and returned alone to the land of liberty. She wrote a letter to Caroline explaining her conduct, and Caroline Spalding showed the letter to her husband, – as one that was both loving and eloquent.

'Very loving and very eloquent,' he said. 'But, nevertheless, one does think of sour grapes.'

'There I am sure you wrong her,' said Caroline.

82

Mrs French's Carving Knife

During these days there were terrible doings at Exeter. Camilla had sworn that if Mr Gibson did not come to, there should be a tragedy, and it appeared that she was inclined to keep her word. Immediately after the receipt of her letter from Mr Gibson she had had an interview with that gentleman in his lodgings, and had asked him his intentions. He had taken measures to fortify himself against such an attack ; but, whatever those measures were, Camilla had broken through them. She had stood before him as he sat in his arm-chair, and he had been dumb in her presence. It had perhaps been well for him that the eloquence of her indignation had been so great that she had hardly been able to pause a moment for a reply. 'Will you take your letter back again?' she had said. 'I should be wrong to do that,' he had lisped out in reply, 'because it is true. As a Christian minister I could not stand with you at the altar with a lie in my mouth.' In no other way did he attempt to excuse himself, – but that, twice repeated, filled up all the pause which she made for him.

There never had been such a case before, – so impudent, so cruel, so gross, so uncalled for, so unmanly, so unnecessary, so unjustifiable, so damnable, – so damned! All this she said to him with loud voice, and clenched fist, and starting eyes, – regardless utterly of any listeners on the stairs, or of outside passers in the street. In very truth she was moved to a sublimity of indignation. Her low nature became nearly poetic under the wrong inflicted upon her. She was almost tempted to tear him with her hands, and inflcit upon him at the moment some terrible vengeance which should be told of for ever in the annals of Exeter. A man so mean as he, so weak, so cowardly, one so little of a hero; – that he should dare to do it, and dare to sit there before her, and to say that he would do it! 'Your gown shall be torn off your back, sir, and the very boys of Exeter shall drag you through the gutters!' To this threat he said nothing, but sat mute, hiding his face in his hands. 'And now tell me this, sir; – is there anything between you and Bella?' But there was no voice in reply. 'Answer my question, sir. I have a right to ask it.' Still he said not a word. 'Listen to me. Sooner than that you and she should be man and wife, I would stab her! Yes, I would; – you poor, paltry, lying, cowardly creature!' She remained with him for more than half an hour, and then banged out of the room flashing back a look of scorn at him as she went. Martha, before that day was over, had learned the whole story from Mr Gibson's cook, and had told her mistress.

'I did not think he had so much spirit in him,' was Miss Stanbury's answer. Throughout Exeter the great wonder arising from the crisis was the amount of spirit which had been displayed by Mr Gibson.

When he was left alone he shook himself, and began to think that if there were danger that such interviews might occur frequently he had better leave Exeter for good. As he put his hand over his forehead, he declared to himself that a very little more of that kind of thing would kill him. When a couple of hours had passed over his head he shook himself again, and sat down and wrote a letter to his intended mother-in-law.

I do not mean to complain, he said, God knows I have no right; but I cannot stand a repetition of what has occurred just now. If your younger daughter comes to see me again I must refuse to see her, and shall leave the town. I am ready to make what reparation may be possible for the mistake into which I have fallen.

T. G.

Mrs French was no doubt much afraid of her younger daughter, but she was less afraid of her than were other people. Familiarity, they say, breeds contempt; and who can be so familiar with a child as its parent? She did not in her heart believe that Camilla would murder anybody, and she fully realised the conviction that, even after all that was come and gone, it would be better that one of her daughters should have a husband than that neither should be so blessed. If only Camilla could be got out of Exeter for a few months, – how good a thing it would be for them all! She had a brother in Gloucester, – if only he could be got to take Camilla for a few months! And then, too, she knew that if the true rights of her two daughters were strictly and impartially examined, Arabella's claim was much stronger than any that Camilla could put forward to the hand of Mr Gibson.

'You must not go there again, Camilla,' the mother said.

'I shall go wherever I please,' replied the fury.

'Now, Camilla, we may as well understand each other. I will not have it done. If I am provoked, I will send to your uncle at Gloucester.' Now the uncle at Gloucester was a timber merchant, a man with protuberant eyes and a great square chin, – known to be a very stern man indeed, and not at all afraid of young women.

'What do I care for my uncle? My uncle would take my part.'

'No, he would not. The truth is, Camilla, you interfered with Bella first.'

'Mamma, how dare you say so!'

'You did, my dear. And these are the consequences.'

'And you mean to say that she is to be Mrs Gibson?'

'I say nothing about that. But I do not see why they shouldn't be married if their hearts are inclined to each other.'

'I will die first!'

'Your dying has nothing to do with it, Camilla.'

'And I will kill her!'

'If you speak to me again in that way I will write to your uncle at Gloucester. I have done the best I could for you both, and I will not bear such treatment.'

'And how am I treated?'

'You should not have interfered with your sister.'

'You are all in a conspiracy together,' shouted Camilla, 'you are! There never was anybody so badly treated, – never, – never, – never! What will everybody say of me?'

'They will pity you, if you will be quiet.'

'I don't want to be pitied; – I won't be pitied. I wish I could die, – and I will die! Anybody else would, at any rate, have had their mother and sister with them!' Then she burst into a flood of real, true, womanly tears.

After this there was a lull at Heavitree for a few days. Camilla did not speak to her sister, but she condescended to hold some intercourse with her mother, and to take her meals at the family table. She did not go out of the house, but she employed herself in her own room, doing no one knew what, with all that new clothing and household gear which was to have been transferred in her train to Mr Gibson's house. Mrs French was somewhat uneasy about the new clothing and household gear, feeling that, in the event of Bella's marriage, at least a considerable portion of it must be transferred to the new bride. But it was impossible at the present moment to open such a subject to Camilla; – it would have been as a proposition to a lioness respecting the taking away of her whelps. Nevertheless, the day must soon come in which something must be said about the clothing and household gear. All the property that had been sent into the house at Camilla's orders could not be allowed to remain as Camilla's perquisites, now that Camilla was not to be married. 'Do you know what she is doing, my dear?' said Mrs French to her elder daughter.

'Perhaps she is picking out the marks,' said Bella.

'I don't think she would do that as yet,' said Mrs French.

'She might just as well leave it alone,' said Bella, feeling that one of the two letters would do for her. But neither of them dared to speak to her of her occupation in these first days of her despair.

Mr Gibson in the meantime remained at home, or only left his house to go to the Cathedral or to visit the narrow confines of his little parish. When he was out he felt that everybody looked at him, and it seemed to him that people whispered about him when they saw him at his usual desk in the choir. His friends passed him merely bowing to him, and he was aware that he had done that which would be regarded by every one around him as unpardonable. And yet, – what ought he to have done? He acknowledged to himself that he had been very foolish, mad, – quite demented at the moment, – when he allowed himself to think it possible that he should marry Camilla French. But having found out how mad he had been at that moment, having satisfied himself that to live with her as his wife would be impossible, was he not right to break the engagement? Could anything be so wicked as marrying a woman whom he – hated? Thus he tried to excuse himself; but yet he knew that all the world would condemn him. Life in Exeter would be impossible, if no way to social pardon could be opened for him. He was willing to do anything within bounds in mitigation of his offence. He would give up fifty pounds a year to Camilla for his life, – or he would marry Bella. Yes; he would marry Bella at once, – if Camilla would only consent, and give up that idea of stabbing some one. Bella French was not very nice in his eyes; but she was quiet, he thought, and it might be possible to live with her. Nevertheless, he told himself over and over again that the manner in which unmarried men with incomes were set upon by ladies in want of husbands was very disgraceful to the country at large. That mission to Natal which had once been offered to him would have had charms for him now, of which he had not recognised the force when he rejected it.

'Do you think that he ever was really engaged to her?' Dorothy said to her aunt. Dorothy was now living in a seventh heaven of happiness, writing love-letters to Brooke Burgess every other day, and devoting to this occupation a number of hours of which she ought to have been ashamed; making her purchases for her wedding, – with nothing, however, of the magnificence of a Camilla, – but discussing everything with her aunt, who urged her on to extravagances which seemed beyond the scope of her own economical ideas; settling, or trying to settle, little difficulties which perplexed her somewhat, and wondering at her own career. She could not of course be married without the presence of her mother and sister, and her aunt, – with something of a grim courtesy, – had intimated that they should be made welcome to the house in the Close for the special occasion. But nothing had been said about Hugh. The wedding was to be in the Cathedral, and Dorothy had a little scheme in her head for meeting her brother among the aisles. He would no doubt come down with Brooke, and nothing perhaps need be said about it to Aunt Stanbury. But still it was a trouble. Her aunt had been so good that Dorothy felt that no step should be taken which would vex the old woman. It was evident enough that when permission had been given for the visit of Mrs Stanbury and Priscilla, Hugh's name had been purposely kept back. There had been no accidental omission. Dorothy, therefore, did not dare to mention it, – and yet it was essential for her happiness that he should be there. At the present moment Miss Stanbury's intense interest in the Stanbury wedding was somewhat mitigated by the excitement occasioned by Mr Gibson's refusal to be married. Dorothy was so shocked that she could not bring herself to believe the statement that had reached them through Martha.

'Of course he was engaged to her. We all knew that,' said Miss Stanbury.

'I think there must have been some mistake,' said Dorothy. 'I don't see how he could do it.'

'There is no knowing what people can do, my dear, when they're hard driven. I suppose we shall have a lawsuit now, and he'll have to pay ever so much money. Well, well, well! see what a deal of trouble you might have saved!'

'But, he'd have done the same to me, aunt; – only, you know, I never could have taken him. Isn't it better as it is, aunt? Tell me.'

'I suppose young women always think it best when they can get their own ways. An old woman like me has only got to do what she is bid.'

'But this was best, aunt; – was it not?'

'My dear, you've had your way, and let that be enough. Poor Camilla French is not allowed to have hers at all. Dear, dear, dear! I didn't think the man would ever have been such a fool to begin with; – or that he would ever have had the heart to get out of it afterwards.' It astonished Dorothy to find that her aunt was not loud in reprobation of Mr Gibson's very dreadful conduct.

In the meantime Mrs French had written to her brother at Gloucester. The maid-servant, in making Miss Camilla's bed, and in 'putting the room to rights,' as she called it, – which description probably was intended to cover the circumstances of an accurate search, – had discovered, hidden among some linen, – a carving knife! such a knife as is used for the cutting up of fowls; and, after two days' interval, had imparted the discovery to Mrs French. Instant visit was made to the pantry, and it was found that a very aged but unbroken and sharply-pointed weapon was missing. Mrs French at once accused Camilla, and Camilla, after some hesitation, admitted that it might be there. Molly, she said, was a nasty, sly, wicked thing, to go looking in her drawers, and she would never leave anything unlocked again. The knife, she declared, had been taken up-stairs, because she had wanted something very sharp to cut, – the bones of her stays. The knife was given up, but Mrs French thought it best to write to her brother, Mr Crump. She was in great doubt about sundry matters. Had the carving knife really pointed to a domestic tragedy; – and if so, what steps ought a poor widow to take with such a daughter? And what ought to be done about Mr Gibson? It ran through Mrs French's mind that unless something were done at once, Mr Gibson would escape scot-free. It was her wish that he should yet become her son-in-law. Poor Bella was entitled to her chance. But if Bella was to be disappointed, – from fear of carving knives, or for other reasons, – then there came the question whether Mr Gibson should not be made to pay in purse for the mischief he had done. With all these thoughts and doubts running through her head, Mrs French wrote to her brother at Gloucester.

There came back an answer from Mr Crump, in which that gentleman expressed a very strong idea that Mr Gibson should be prosecuted for damages with the utmost virulence, and with the least possible delay. No compromise should be accepted. Mr Crump would himself come to Exeter and see the lawyer as soon as he should be told that there was a lawyer to be seen. As to the carving knife, Mr Crump was of opinion that it did not mean anything. Mr Crump was a gentleman who did not believe in strong romance, but who had great trust in all pecuniary claims. The Frenches had always been genteel. The late Captain French had been an officer in the army, and at ordinary times and seasons the Frenches were rather ashamed of the Crump connection. But now the timber merchant might prove himself to be a useful friend.

Mrs French showed her brother's letter to Bella, – and poor Bella was again sore-hearted, seeing that nothing was said in it of her claims. 'It will be dreadful to have it all in the papers!' said Bella.

'But what can we do?'

'Anything would be better than that,' said Bella. 'And you don't want to punish Mr Gibson, mamma.'

'But, my dear, you see what your uncle says. What can I do, except go to him for advice?'

'Why don't you go to Mr Gibson yourself, mamma?'

But nothing was said to Camilla about Mr Crump; – nothing as yet. Camilla did not love Mr Crump, but there was no other house except that of Mr Crump's at Gloucester to which she might be sent, if it could be arranged that Mr Gibson and Bella should be made one. Mrs French took her eldest daughter's advice, and went to Mr Gibson; – taking Mr Crump's letter in her pocket. For herself she wanted nothing, – but was it not the duty of her whole life to fight for her daughters? Poor woman! If somebody would only have taught her how that duty might best be done, she would have endeavoured to obey the teaching. 'You know I do not want to threaten you,' she said to Mr Gibson; 'but you see what my brother says. Of course I wrote to my brother. What could a poor woman do in such circumstances except write to her brother?'

'If you choose to set the bloodhounds of the law at me, of course you can,' said Mr Gibson.

'I do not want to go to law at all; — God knows I do not!' said Mrs French. Then there was a pause. 'Poor dear Bella!' ejaculated Mrs French.

'Dear Bella!' echoed Mr Gibson.

'What do you mean to do about Bella?' asked Mrs French.

'I sometimes think that I had better take poison and have done with it!' said Mr Gibson, feeling himself to be very hard pressed.

83

Bella Victrix

Mr Crump arrived at Exeter. Camilla was not told of his coming till the morning of the day on which he arrived; and then the tidings were communicated, because it was necessary that a change should be made in the bed-rooms. She and her sister had separate rooms when there was no visitor with them, but now Mr Crump must be accommodated. There was a long consultation between Bella and Mrs French, but at last it was decided that Bella should sleep with her mother. There would still be too much of the lioness about Camilla to allow of her being regarded as a safe companion through the watches of the night. 'Why is Uncle Jonas coming now?' she asked.

'I thought it better to ask him,' said Mrs French.

After a long pause, Camilla asked another question. 'Does Uncle Jonas mean to see Mr Gibson?'

'I suppose he will,' said Mrs French.

'Then he will see a low, mean fellow; — the lowest, meanest fellow that ever was heard of! But that won't make much difference to Uncle Jonas. I wouldn't have him now, if he was to ask me ever so; — that I wouldn't!'

Mr Crump came, and kissed his sister and two nieces. The embrace with Camilla was not very affectionate. 'So your Joe has been and jilted you?' said Uncle Jonas; — 'it's like one of them clergymen. They say so many prayers, they think they may do almost anything afterwards. Another man would have had his head punched.'

'The less talk there is about it the better,' said Camilla.

On the following day Mr Crump called by appointment on Mr Gibson, and remained closeted with that gentleman for the greater portion of the morning. Camilla knew well that he was going, and went about the house like a perturbed spirit* during his absence. There was a look about her that made them all doubt whether she was not, in truth, losing her mind. Her mother more than once went to the pantry to see that the knives were right; and, as regarded that sharp-pointed weapon, was careful to lock it up carefully out of her daugher's way. Mr Crump had declared himself willing to take Camilla back to Gloucester, and had laughed at the obstacles which his niece might, perhaps, throw in the way of such an arrangement. 'She mustn't have much luggage; – that is all,' said Mr Crump. For Mr Crump had been made aware of the circumstances of the trousseau. About three o'clock Mr Crump came back from Mr Gibson's, and expressed a desire to be left alone with Camilla. Mrs French was prepared for everything; and Mr Crump soon found himself with his younger niece.

'Camilla, my dear,' said he, 'this has been a bad business.'

'I don't know what business you mean, Uncle Jonas.'

'Yes, you do, my dear; – you know. And I hope it won't come too late to prove to you that young women shouldn't be too keen in setting their caps at the gentlemen. It's better for them to be hunted, than to hunt.'

'Uncle Jonas, I will not be insulted.'

'Stick to that, my dear, and you won't get into a scrape again. Now, look here. This man can never be made to marry you, anyhow.'

'I wouldn't touch him with a pair of tongs, if he were kneeling at my feet!'

'That's right; stick to that. Of course, you wouldn't now, after all that has come and gone. No girl with any spirit would.'

'He's a coward and a thief, and he'll be – damned for what he has done, some of these days!'

'T-ch, t-ch, t-ch! That isn't a proper way for a young lady to talk. That's cursing and swearing.'

'It isn't cursing and swearing; – it's what the Bible says.'

'Then we'll leave him to the Bible. In the meantime, Mr Gibson wants to marry some one else, and that can't hurt you.'

'He may marry whom he likes, – but he shan't marry Bella – that's all!'

'It is Bella that he means to marry.'

'Then he won't. I'll forbid the banns. I'll write to the bishop. I'll go to the church and prevent its being done. I'll make such a noise in the town that it can't be done. It's no use your looking at me like that, Uncle Jonas. I've got my own feelings, and he shall never marry Bella. It's what they have been intending all through, and it shan't be done!'

'It will be done.'

'Uncle Jonas, I'll stab her to the heart, and him too, before I'll see it done! Though I were to be killed the next day, I would. Could you bear it?'

'I'm not a young woman. Now, I'll tell you what I want you to do.'

'I'll not do anything.'

'Just pack up your things, and start with me to Gloucester to-morrow.'

'I – won't!'

'Then you'll be carried, my dear. I'll write to your aunt to say that you're coming; and we'll be as jolly as possible when we get you home.'

'I won't go to Gloucester, Uncle Jonas. I won't go away from Exeter. I won't let it be done. She shall never, never, never be that man's wife!'

Nevertheless, on the day but one after this, Camilla French did go to Gloucester. Before she went, however, things had to be done in that house which almost made Mrs French repent that she had sent for so stern an assistant. Camilla was at last told, in so many words, that the things which she had prepared for her own wedding must be given up for the wedding of her sister; and it seemed that this item in the list of her sorrows troubled her almost more than any other. She swore that whither she went there should go the dresses, and the handkerchiefs, and the hats, the bonnets, and the boots. 'Let her have them,' Bella had pleaded. But Mr Crump was inexorable. He had looked into his sister's affairs, and found that she was already in debt. To his practical mind, it was an absurdity that the unmarried sister should keep things that were wholly unnecessary, and that the sister that was to be married should be without things that were needed. There was a big trunk, of which Camilla had the key, but which, unfortunately for her, had been deposited in her mother's room. Upon this she sat, and swore that nothing should move her but a promise that her plunder should remain untouched. But there came this advantage from the terrible question of the wedding raiments, – that in her energy to keep possession of them, she gradually abandoned her opposition to her sister's marriage. She had been driven from one point to another till she was compelled at last to stand solely upon her possessions.

'Perhaps we had better let her keep them,' said Mrs French. 'Trash and nonsense!' said Mr Crump. 'If she wants a new frock, let her have it; as for the sheets and tablecloths, you'd better keep them yourself. But Bella must have the rest.'

It was found on the eve of the day on which she was told that she was to depart that she had in truth armed herself with a dagger or clasp knife. She actually displayed it when her uncle told her to come away from the chest on which she was sitting. She declared that she would defend herself there to the last gasp of her life; but of course the knife fell from her hand the first moment that she was touched. 'I did think once that she was going to make a poke at me,' Mr Crump said afterwards; 'but she had screamed herself so weak that she couldn't do it.'

When the morning came, she was taken to the fly and driven to the station without any further serious outbreak. She had even condescended to select certain articles, leaving the rest of the hymeneal wealth behind her. Bella, early on that morning of departure, with great humility, implored her sister to forgive her; but no entreaties could induce Camilla to address one gracious word to the proposed bride. 'You've been cheating me all along!' she said; and that was the last word she spoke to poor Bella.

She went, and the field was once more open to the amorous Vicar of St Peter's-cum-Pumpkin. It is astonishing how the greatest dificulties will sink away, and become as it were nothing, when they are encountered face to face. It is certain that Mr Gibson's position had been one most trying to the nerves. He had speculated on various modes of escape; – a curacy in the north of England would be welcome, or the duties of a missionary in New Zealand, – or death. To tell the truth, he had, during the last week or two, contemplated even a return to the dominion of Camilla. That there should ever again be things pleasant for him in Exeter seemed to be quite impossible. And yet, on the evening of the day but one after the departure of Camilla, he was seated almost comfortably with his own Arabella! There is nothing that a man may not do, nothing that he may not achieve, if he have only pluck enough to go through with it.

'You do love me?' Bella said to him. It was natural that she should ask him; but it would have been better perhaps if she had held her tongue. Had she spoken to him about his house, or his income, or the servants, or the duties of his parish church, it would have been easier for him to make a comfortable reply.

'Yes; – I love you,' he replied; 'of course I love you. We have always been friends, and I hope things will go straight now. I have had a great deal to go through, Bella, and so have you; – but God will temper the wind to the shorn lambs.' How was the wind to be tempered for the poor lamb who had gone forth shorn down to the very skin !

Soon after this Mrs French returned to the room, and then there was no more romance. Mrs French had by no means forgiven Mr Gibson all the trouble he had brought into the family, and mixed a certain amount of acrimony with her entertainment of him. She dictated to him, treated him with but scant respect, and did not hesitate to let him understand that he was to be watched very closely till he was actually and absolutely married. The poor man had in truth no further idea of escape. He was aware that he had done that which made it necessary that he should bear a great deal, and that he had no right to resent suspicion. When a day was fixed in June on which he should be married at the church of Heavitree, and it was proposed that he should be married by banns, he had nothing to urge to the contrary. And when it was also suggested to him by one of the prebendaries of the Cathedral that it might be well for him to change his clerical duties for a period with the vicar of a remote parish in the north of Cornwall, – so as to be out of the way of remark from those whom he had scandalised by his conduct, – he had no objection to make to that arrangement. When Mrs MacHugh met him in the Close, and told him that he was a gay Lothario, he shook his head with a melancholy self-abasement, and passed on without even a feeling of anger. 'When they smite me on the right cheek, I turn unto them my left,'* he said to himself, when one of the cathedral vergers remarked to him that after all he was going to be married at last. Even Bella became dominant over him, and assumed with him occasionally the air of one who had been injured.

Bella wrote a touching letter to her sister, – a letter that ought to have touched Camilla, begging for forgiveness, and for one word of sisterly love. Camilla answered the letter, but did not send a word of sisterly love. 'According to my way of thinking, you have been a nasty sly thing, and I don't believe you'll ever be happy. As for him, I'll never speak to him again.' That was nearly the whole of her letter. 'You must leave it to time,' said Mrs French wisely; 'she'll come round some day.' And then Mrs French thought how bad it would be for her if the daughter who was to be her future companion did not 'come round' some day.

And so it was settled that they should be married in Heavitree Church, – Mr Gibson and his first love, – and things went on pretty much as though nothing had been done amiss. The gentleman from

Cornwall came down to take Mr Gibson's place at St Peter's-cum-Pumpkin, while his duties in the Cathedral were temporarily divided among the other priest-vicars, – with some amount of grumbling on their part. Bella commenced her modest preparations without any of the eclat which had attended Camilla's operations, but she felt more certainty of ultimate success than had ever fallen to Camilla's lot. In spite of all that had come and gone, Bella never feared again that Mr Gibson would be untrue to her. In regard to him, it must be doubted whether Nemesis ever fell upon him with a hand sufficiently heavy to punish him for the great sins which he had manifestly committed. He had encountered a bad week or two, and there had been days in which, as has been said, he thought of Natal, of ecclesiastical censures, and even of annihilation; but no real punishment seemed to fall upon him. It may be doubted whether, when the whole arrangement was settled for him, and when he heard that Camilla had yielded to the decrees of Fate, he did not rather flatter himself on being a successful man of intrigue, – whether he did not take some glory to himself for his good fortune with women, and pride himself amidst his self-reproaches for the devotion which had been displayed for him by the fair sex in general. It is quite possible that he taught himself to believe that at one time Dorothy Stanbury was devotedly in love with him, and that when he reckoned up his sins she was one of those in regard to whom he accounted himself to have been a sinner. The spirit of intrigue with women, as to which men will flatter themselves, is customarily so vile, so mean, so vapid a reflection of a feeling, so aimless, resultless, and utterly unworthy! Passion exists and has its sway. Vice has its votaries, – and there is, too, that worn-out longing for vice, 'prurient, yet passionless, cold-studied lewdness,'* which drags on a feeble continuance with the aid of money. But the commonest folly of man in regard to women is a weak taste for intrigue, with little or nothing on which to feed it; – a worse than feminine aptitude for male coquetry, which never assends beyond a desire that somebody shall hint that there is something peculiar; and which is shocked and retreats backwards into its boots when anything like a consequence forces itself on the apprehension. Such men have their glory in their own estimation. We remember how Falstaff flouted the pride of his companion whose victory in the fields of love had been but little glorious. But there are victories going now-a-days so infinitely less glorious, that Falstaff's page was a Lothario, a very Don Juan, in comparison with the heroes whose praises are too often sung by their own lips. There is this recompense, – that their defeats are always sung by lips louder than their own. Mr Gibson, when he found that he was to escape apparently unscathed, – that people standing respectably before the world absolutely dared to whisper words to him of congratulation on this third attempt at marriage within little more than a year, took pride to himself, and bethought himself that he was a gay deceiver. He believed that he had selected his wife, – and that he had done so in circumstances of peculiar difficulty! Poor Mr Gibson, – we hardly know whether most to pity him, or the unfortunate, poor woman who ultimately became Mrs Gibson.

'And so Bella French is to be the fortunate woman after all,' said Miss Stanbury to her niece.

'It does seem to me to be so odd,' said Dorothy. 'I wonder how he looked when he proposed it.'

'Like a fool, – as he always does.'

Dorothy refrained from remarking that Miss Stanbury had not always thought that Mr Gibson looked like a fool, but the idea occurred to her mind. 'I hope they will be happy at last,' she said.

'Pshaw! Such people can't be happy, and can't be unhappy. I don't suppose it much matters which he marries, or whether he marries them both, or neither. They are to be married by banns, they say, – at Heavitree.'

'I don't see anything bad in that.'

'Only Camilla might step out and forbid them,' said Aunt Stanbury. 'I almost wish she would.'

'She has gone away, aunt, – to an uncle who lives at Gloucester.'

'It was well to get her out of the way, no doubt. They'll be married before you now, Dolly.'

'That won't break my heart, aunt.'

'I don't suppose there'll be much of a wedding. They haven't anybody belonging to them, except that uncle at Gloucester.' Then there was a pause. 'I think it is a nice thing for friends to collect together at a wedding,' continued Aunt Stanbury.

'I think it is,' said Dorothy, in the mildest, softest voice.

'I suppose we must make room for that black sheep of a brother of yours, Dolly, – or else you won't be contented.'

'Dear, dear, dearest aunt!' said Dorothy, falling down on her knees at her aunt's feet.

84

Self-Sacrifice

Trevelyan, when his wife had left him, sat for hours in silence pondering over his own position and hers. He had taken his child to an upper room, in which was his own bed and the boy's cot, and before he seated himself, he spread out various toys which he had been at pains to purchase for the unhappy little fellow, – a regiment of Garibaldian soldiers, all with red shirts, and a drum to give the regiment martial spirit, and a soft fluffy Italian ball, and a battledore and a shuttlecock, – instruments enough for juvenile joy, if only there had been a companion with whom the child could use them. But the toys remained where the father had placed them, almost unheeded, and the child sat looking out of the window, melancholy, silent, and repressed. Even the drum did not tempt him to be noisy. Doubtless he did not know why he was wretched, but he was fully conscious of his wretchedness. In the meantime the father sat motionless, in an old worn-out but once handsome leathern arm-chair, with his eyes fixed against the opposite wall, thinking of the wreck of his life.

Thought deep, correct, continued, and energetic is quite compatible with madness. At this time Trevelyan's mind was so far unhinged, his ordinary faculties were so greatly impaired, that they who declared him to be mad were justified in their declaration. His condition was such that the happiness and welfare of no human being, – not even his own, – could safely be entrusted to his keeping. He considered himself to have been so injured by the world, to have been the victim of so cruel a conspiracy among those who ought to have been his friends, that there remained nothing for him but to flee away from them and remain in solitude. But yet, through it all, there was something approaching to a conviction that he had brought his misery upon himself by being unlike to other men; and he declared to himself over and over again that it was better that he should suffer than that others should be punished. When he was alone his reflections respecting his wife were much juster than were his words when he spoke either with her, or to others, of her conduct. He would declare to himself not only that he did not believe her to have been false to him, but that he had never accused her of such crime. He had demanded from her obedience, and she had been disobedient. It had been incumbent upon him, – so ran his own ideas, as expressed to himself in these long unspoken soliloquies, – to exact obedience, or at least compliance, let the consequences be what they might. She had refused to obey or even to comply, and the consequences were very grievous. But, though he pitied himself with a pity that was feminine, yet he acknowledged to himself that her conduct had been the result of his own moody temperament. Every friend had parted from him. All those to whose counsels he had listened, had counselled him that he was wrong. The whole world was against him. Had he remained in England, the doctors and lawyers among them would doubtless have declared him to be mad. He knew all this, and yet he could not yield. He could not say that he had been wrong. He could not even think that he had been wrong as to the cause of the great quarrel. He was one so miserable and so unfortunate, – so he thought, – that even in doing right he had fallen into perdition !

He had had two enemies, and between them they had worked his ruin. These were Colonel Osborne and Bozzle. It may be doubted whether he did not hate the latter the more strongly of the two. He knew now that Bozzle had been untrue to him, but his disgust did not spring from that so much as from the feeling that he had defiled himself by dealing with the man. Though he was quite assured that he had been right in his first cause of offence, he knew that he had fallen from bad to worse in every step that he had taken since. Colonel Osborne had marred his happiness by vanity, by wicked intrigue, by a devilish delight in doing mischief; but he, he himself, had consummated the evil by his own folly. Why had he not taken Colonel Osborne by the throat, instead of going to a low-born, vile, mercenary spy for assistance ? He hated himself for what he had done; – and yet it was impossible that he should yield.

It was impossible that he should yield; – but it was yet open to him to sacrifice himself. He could not go back to his wife and say that he was wrong; but he could determine that the destruction should fall upon him and not upon her. If he gave up his child and then died, – died, alone, without any friend near him, with no word of love in his ears, in that solitary and miserable abode which he had found for himself, – then it would at least be acknowledged that he had expiated the injury that he had done. She would have his wealth, his name, his child to comfort her, – and would be troubled no longer by demands for that obedience which she had sworn at the altar to give him, and which she had since declined to render to him. Perhaps there was some feeling that the coals of fire would be hot upon her head when she should think how much she had received from him and how little she had done for him. And yet he loved her, with all his heart, and would even yet dream of bliss that might be possible with her, – had not the terrible hand of irresistible Fate come between them and marred it all. It was only a dream now. It could be no more than a dream. He put out his thin wasted hands and looked at them, and touched the hollowness of his own cheeks, and coughed that he might hear the hacking sound of his own infirmity, and almost took glory in his weakness. It could not be long before the coals of fire would be heaped upon her head.

'Louey,' he said at last, addressing the child who had sat for an hour gazing through the window without stirring a limb or uttering a sound; 'Louey, my boy, would you like to go back to mamma?' The child turned round on the floor, and fixed his eyes on his father's face, but made no immediate reply. 'Louey, dear, come to papa and tell him. Would it be nice to go back to mamma?' And he stretched out his hand to the boy. Louey got up, and approached slowly and stood between his father's knees. 'Tell me, darling; – you understand what papa says?'

'Altro!' said the boy, who had been long enough among Italian servants to pick up the common words of the language. Of course he would like to go back. How indeed could it be otherwise?

'Then you shall go to her, Louey.'

'To-day, papa?'

'Not to-day, nor to-morrow.'

'But the day after?'

'That is sufficient. You shall go. It is not so bad with you that one day more need be a sorrow to you. You shall go, – and then you will never see your father again!' Trevelyan as he said this drew his hands away so as not to touch the child. The little fellow had put out his arm, but seeing his father's angry gesture had made no further attempt at a caress. He feared his father from the bottom of his little heart, and yet was aware that it was his duty to try to love papa. He did not understand the meaning of that last threat, but slunk back, passing his untouched toys, to the window, and there seated himself again, filling his mind with the thought that when two more long long days should have crept by, he should once more go to his mother.

Trevelyan had tried his best to be soft and gentle to his child. All that he had said to his wife of his treatment of the boy had been true to the letter. He had spared no personal trouble, he had done all that he had known how to do, he had exercised all his intelligence to procure amusement for the boy; – but Louey had hardly smiled since he had been taken from his mother. And now that he was told that he was to go and never see his father again, the tidings were to him simply tidings of joy. 'There is a curse upon me,' said Trevelyan ; 'it is written down in the book of my destiny that nothing shall ever love me !'

He went out from the house, and made his way down by the narrow path through the olives and vines to the bottom of the hill in front of the villa. It was evening now, but the evening was very hot, and though the olive trees stood in long rows, there was no shade. Quite at the bottom of the hill there was a little sluggish muddy brook, along the sides of which the reeds grew thic¹ ¹⁻ and the dragon-flies were playing on the water. There was nothing attractive in the spot, but he was weary, and sat himself down on the dry hard bank which had been made by repeated clearing of mud from the bottom of the little rivulet. He sat watching the dragon-flies as they made their short flights in the warm air, and told himself that of all God's creatures there was not one to whom less power of disporting itself in God's sun was given than to him. Surely it would be better for him that he should die, than live as he was now living without any of the joys of life. The solitude of Casalunga was intolerable to him, and yet there was no whither that he could go and find society. He could travel if he pleased. He had money at command, and, at any rate as yet, there was no embargo on his personal liberty. But how could he travel alone, – even if his strength might suffice for the work ? There had been moments in which he had thought that he would be happy in the love of his child, – that the companionship of an infant would suffice for him if only the infant would love him. But all such dreams as that were over. To repay him for his tenderness his boy was always dumb before him. Louey would not prattle as he had used to do. He would not even smile, or give back the kisses with which his father had attempted to win him. In mercy to the boy he would send him back to his mother; – in mercy to the boy if not to the mother also. It was in vain that he should look for any joy in any quarter. Were he to return to England, they would say that he was mad !

He lay there by the brook-side till the evening was far advanced, and then he arose and slowly returned to the house. The labour of ascending the hill was so great to him that he was forced to pause and hold by the olive trees as he slowly performed his task. The perspiration came in profusion from his pores, and he found himself to be so weak that he must in future regard the brook as being beyond the tether of his daily exercise. Eighteen months ago he had been a strong walker, and the snow-bound paths of Swiss mountains had been a joy to him. He paused as he was slowly dragging himself on, and looked up at the wretched, desolate, comfortless abode which he called his home. Its dreariness was so odious to him that he was half-minded to lay himself down where he was, and let the night air come upon him and do its worst. In such case, however, some Italian doctor would be sent down who would say that he was mad. Above all things, and to the last, he must save himself from that degradation.

When he had crawled up to the house, he went to his child, and found that the woman had put the boy to bed. Then he was angry with himself in that he himself had not seen to this, and kept up his practice of attending the child to the last. He would, at least, be true to his resolution, and prepare for the boy's return to his mother. Not knowing how otherwise to manage it, he wrote that night the following note to Mr Glascock ;

Casalunga, Thursday night.

My dear Sir,
Since you last were considerate enough to call upon me I have resolved to take a step in my affairs which, though it will rob me of my only remaining gratification, will tend to lessen the troubles under which Mrs Trevelyan is labouring. If she desires it, as no doubt she does, I will consent to place our boy again in her custody, – trusting to her sense of honour to restore him to me should I demand it. In my present unfortunate position I cannot suggest that she should come for the boy. I am unable to support the excitement occasioned by her presence. I will, however, deliver up my darling either to you, or to any messenger sent by you whom I can trust. I beg heartily to apologise for the trouble I am giving you, and to subscribe myself yours very faithfully,
Louis Trevelyan.
The Hon. C. Glascock.

PS – It is as well, perhaps, that I should explain that I must decline to receive any visit from Sir Marmaduke Rowley. Sir Marmaduke has insulted me grossly on each occasion on which I have seen him since his return home.

85

The Baths of Lucca

June was now far advanced, and the Rowleys and the Spaldings had removed from Florence to the Baths of Lucca. Mr Glascock had followed in their wake, and the whole party were living at the Baths in one of those hotels in which so many English and

Americans are wont to congregate in the early weeks of the Italian summer. The marriage was to take place in the last week of the month; and all the party were to return to Florence for the occasion, – with the exception of Sir Marmaduke and Mrs Trevelyan. She was altogether unfitted for wedding joys, and her father had promised to bear her company when the others left her. Mr Glascock and Caroline Spalding were to be married in Florence, and were to depart immediately from thence for some of the cooler parts of Switzerland. After that Sir Marmaduke and Lady Rowley were return to London with their daughters, preparatory to that dreary journey back to the Mandarins; and they had not even yet resolved what they had better do respecting that unfortunate man who was living in seclusion on the hill-top near Siena. They had consulted lawyers and doctors in Florence, but it had seemed that everybody there was afraid of putting the law in force against an Englishman. Doubtless there was a law in respect to the custody of the insane; and it was admitted that if Trevelyan were dangerously mad something could be done; but it seemed that nobody was willing to stir in such a case as that which now existed. Something, it was said, might be done at some future time; but the difficulties were so great that nothing could be done now.

It was very sad, because it was necessary that some decision should be made as to the future residence of Mrs Trevelyan and of Nora. Emily had declared that nothing should induce her to go to the Islands with her father and mother unless her boy went with her. Since her journey to Casalunga she had also expressed her unwillingness to leave her husband. Her heart had been greatly softened towards him, and she had declared that where he remained, there would she remain, – as near to him as circumstances would admit. It might be that at last her care would be necessary for his comfort. He supplied her with means of living, and she would use these means as well as she might be able in his service.

Then there had arisen the question of Nora's future residence. And there had come troubles and storms in the family. Nora had said that she would not go back to the Mandarins, but had not at first been able to say where or how she would live. She had suggested that she might stay with her sister, but her father had insisted that she could not live on the income supplied by Trevelyan. Then, when pressed hard, she had declared that she intended to live on Hugh Stanbury's income. She would marry him at once, – with her father's leave, if she could get it, but without it if it needs must be so. Her mother told her that Hugh Stanbury was not himself ready for her; he had not even proposed so hasty a marriage, nor had he any home fitted for her. Lady Rowley, in arguing this, had expressed no assent to the marriage, even as a distant arrangement, but had thought thus to vanquish her daughter by suggesting small but insuperable difficulties. On a sudden, however, Lady Rowley found that all this was turned against her, by an offer that came direct from Mr Glascock. His Caroline, he said, was very anxious that Nora should come to them at Monkhams as soon as they had returned home from Switzerland. They intended to be there by the middle of August, and would hurry there sooner, if there was any intermediate difficulty about finding a home for Nora. Mr Glascock said nothing about Hugh Stanbury; but, of course, Lady Rowley understood that Nora had told all her troubles and hopes to Caroline, and that Caroline had told them to her future husband. Lady Rowley, in answer to this, could only say that she would consult her husband.

There was something very grievous in the proposition to Lady Rowley. If Nora had not been self-willed and stiff-necked beyond the usual self-willedness and stiff-neckedness of young women she might have been herself the mistress of Monkhams. It was proposed now that she should go there to wait till a poor man should have got together shillings enough to buy a few chairs and tables, and a bed to lie upon! The thought of this was very bitter. 'I cannot think, Nora, how you could have the heart to go there,' said Lady Rowley.

'I cannot understand why not, mamma. Caroline and I are friends, and surely he and I need not be enemies. He has never injured me; and if he does not take offence, why should I?'

'If you don't see it, I can't help it,' said Lady Rowley.

And then Mrs Spalding's triumph was terrible to Lady Rowley. Mrs Spalding knew nothing of her future son-in-law's former passion, and spoke of her Caroline as having achieved triumphs beyond the reach of other girls. Lady Rowley bore it, never abolutely telling the tale of her daughter's fruitless victory. She was too good at heart to utter the boast; – but it was very hard to repress it. Upon the whole she would have preferred that Mr Glascock and his bride should not have become the fast friends of herself and her family. There was more of pain than of pleasure in the alliance. But circumstances had been too strong for her. Mr Glascock had been of great use in reference to Trevelyan, and Caroline and Nora had become attached to each other almost on their first acquaintance. Here they were together at the Baths of Lucca, and Nora was to be one of the four bridesmaids. When Sir Marmaduke was consulted about this visit to Monkhams, he became fretful, and would give no answer. The marriage, he said, was impossible, and Nora was a fool. He could give her no allowance more than would suffice for her clothes, and it was madness for her to think of stopping in England. But he was so full of cares that he could come to no absolute decision on this matter. Nora, however, had come to a very absolute decision.

'Caroline,' she said, 'if you will have me, I will go to Monkhams.'

'Of course we will have you. Has not Charles said how delighted he would be ?'

'Oh yes, – your Charles,' said Nora, laughing.

'He is mine now, dear. You must not expect him to change his mind again. I gave him the chance, you know, and he would not take it. But, Nora, come to Monkhams, and stay as long as it suits. I have talked it all over with him, and we both agree that you shall have a home there. You shall be just like a sister. Olivia is coming too after a bit; but he says there is room for a dozen sisters. Of course it will be all right with Mr Stanbury after a while.' And so it was settled among them that Nora Rowley should find a home at Monkhams, if a home in England should be wanted for her.

It wanted but four days to that fixed for the marriage at Florence, and but six to that on which the Rowleys were to leave Italy for England, when Mr Glascock received Trevelyan's letter. It was brought to him as he was sitting at a late breakfast in the garden of the hotel; and there were present at the moment not only all the Spalding family, but the Rowleys also. Sir Marmaduke was there and Lady Rowley, and the three unmarried daughters; but Mrs Trevelyan, as was her wont, had remained alone in her own room. Mr Glascock read the letter, and read it again, without attracting much attention. Caroline, who was of course sitting next to him, had her eyes upon him, and could see that the letter moved him; but she was not curious, and at any rate asked no question. He himself understood fully how great was the offer made, – how all-important to the happiness of the poor mother, – and he was also aware, or thought that he was aware, how likely it might be that the offer would be retracted. As regarded himself, a journey from the Baths at Lucca to Casalunga and back before his marriage, would be a great infliction on his patience. It was his plan to stay where he was till the day before his marriage, and then to return to Florence with the rest of the party. All this must be altered, and sudden changes must be made, if he decided on going to Siena himself. The weather now was very hot, and such a journey would be most disagreeable to him. Of course he had little schemes in his head, little amatory schemes for prenuptial enjoyment, which, in spite of his mature years, were exceedingly agreeable to him. The chestnut woods round the Baths of Lucca are very pleasant in the early summer, and there were excursions planned in which Caroline would be close by his side, – almost already his wife. But, if he did not go, whom could he send? It would be necessary at least that he should consult her, the mother of the child, before any decision was formed.

At last he took Lady Rowley aside, and read to her the letter. She understood at once that it opened almost a heaven of bliss to her daughter; – and she understood also how probable it might be that that wretched man, with his shaken wits, should change his mind. 'I think I ought to go,' said Mr Glascock.

'But how can you go now?'

'I can go,' said he. 'There is time for it. It need not put off my marriage, – to which of course I could not consent. I do not know whom I could send.'

'Monnier could go,' said Lady Rowley, naming the courier.

'Yes; – he could go. But it might be that he would return without the child, and then we should not forgive ourselves. I will go, Lady Rowley. After all, what does it signify? I am a little old, I sometimes think, for this philandering. You shall take his letter to your daughter, and I will explain it all to Caroline.'

Caroline had not a word to say. She could only kiss him, and promise to make him what amends she could when he came back. 'Of course you are right,' she said. 'Do you think that I would say a word against it, even though the marriage were to be postponed?'

'I should; – a good many words. But I will be back in time for that, and will bring the boy with me.'

Mrs Trevelyan, when her husband's letter was read to her, was almost overcome by the feelings which it excited. In her first paroxysm of joy she declared that she would herself go to Siena, not for her child's sake, but for that of her husband. She felt at once that the boy was being given up because of the father's weakness, – because he felt himself to be unable to be a protector to his son, – and her woman's heart was melted with softness as she thought of the condition of the man to whom she had once given her whole heart. Since then, doubtless, her heart had revolted from him. Since that time there had come hours in which she had almost hated him for his cruelty to her. There had been moments in which she had almost cursed his name because of the aspersion which it had seemed that he had thrown upon her. But this was now forgotten, and she remembered only his weakness. 'Mamma,' she said, 'I will go. It is my duty to go to him.' But Lady Rowley withheld her, explaining that were she to go, the mission might probably fail in its express purpose. 'Let Louey be sent to us first,' said Lady Rowley, 'and then we will see what can be done afterwards.'

And so Mr Glascock started, taking with him a maid-servant who might help him with the charge of the child. It was certainly very hard upon him. In order to have time for his journey to Siena and back, and time also to go out to Casalunga, it was necessary that he should leave the Baths at five in the morning. 'If ever there was a hero of romance, you are he!' said Nora to him.

'The heroes of life are so much better than the heroes of romance,' said Caroline.

'That is a lesson from the lips of the American Browning,' said Mr Glascock. 'Nevertheless, I think I would rather ride a charge against a Paynim knight in Palestine than get up at half-past four in the morning.'

'We will get up too, and give the knight his coffee,' said Nora. They did get up, and saw him off; and when Mr Glascock and Caroline parted with a lover's embrace, Nora stood by as a sister might have done. Let us hope that she remembered that her own time was coming.

There had been a promise given by Nora, when she left London, that she would not correspond with Hugh Stanbury while she was in Italy, and this promise had been kept. It may be remembered that Hugh had made a proposition to his lady-love, that she should walk out of the house one fine morning, and get herself married without any reference to her father's or her mother's wishes. But she had not been willing to take upon herself as yet independence so complete as this would have required. She had assured her lover that she did mean to marry him some day, even though it should be in opposition to her father, but that she thought that the period for filial persuasion was not yet over; and then, in explaining all this to her mother, she had given a promise neither to write nor to receive letters during the short period of her sojourn in Italy. She would be an obedient child for so long; – but, after that, she must claim the right to fight her own battle. She had told her lover that he must not write; and, of course, she had not written a word herself. But now, when her mother threw it in her teeth that Stanbury would not be ready to marry her, she thought that an unfair advantage was being taken of her, – and of him. How could he be expected to say that he was ready, – deprived as he was of the power of saying anything at all?

'Mamma,' she said, the day before they went to Florence, 'has papa fixed about your leaving England yet? I suppose you'll go now on the last Saturday in July?'

'I suppose we shall, my dear.'

'Has not papa written about the berths?'

'I believe he has, my dear.'

'Because he ought to know who are going. I will not go.'

'You will not, Nora. Is that a proper way of speaking?'

'Dear mamma, I mean it to be proper. I hope it is proper. But is it not best that we should understand each other. All my life depends on my going or my staying now. I must decide.'

'After what has passed, you do not, I suppose, mean to live in Mr Glascock's house?'

'Certainly not. I mean to live with, – with, – with my husband. Mamma, I promised not to write, and I have not written. And he has not written, – because I told him not. Therefore, nothing is settled. But it is not fair to throw it in my teeth that nothing is settled.'

'I have thrown nothing in your teeth, Nora.'

'Papa talks sneeringly about chairs and tables. Of course, I know what he is thinking of. As I cannot go with him to the Mandarins, I think I ought to be allowed to look after the chairs and tables.'

'What do you mean, my dear?'

'That you should absolve me from my promise, and let me write to Mr Stanbury. I do not want to be left without a home.'

'You cannot wish to write to a gentleman and ask him to marry you!'

'Why not? We are engaged. I shall not ask him to marry me, – that is already settled; but I shall ask him to make arrangements.'

'You papa will be very angry if you break your word to him.'

'I will write, and show you the letter. Papa may see it, and if he will not let it go, it shall not go. He shall not say that I broke my word. But, mamma, I will not go out to the Islands. I should never get back again, and I should be broken-hearted.' Lady Rowley had nothing to say to this; and Nora went and wrote her letter. 'Dear Hugh,' the letter ran, 'Papa and mamma leave England on the last Saturday in July. I have told mamma that I cannot return with them. Of course, you know why I stay. Mr Glascock is to be married the day after to-morrow, and they have asked me to go with them to Monkhams some time in August. I think I shall do so, unless Emily wants me to remain with her. At any rate, I shall try to be with her till I go there. You will understand why I tell you all this. Papa and mamma know that I am writing. It is only a business letter, and, therefore, I shall say no more, except that I am ever and always yours, – Nora.' 'There,' she said, handing her letter to her mother, 'I think that that ought to be sent. If papa chooses to prevent its going, he can.'

Lady Rowley, when she handed the letter to her husband, recommended that it should be allowed to go to its destination. She admitted that, if they sent it, they would thereby signify their consent to her engagement; – and she alleged that Nora was so strong in her will, and that the circumstances of their journey out to the Antipodes were so peculiar, that it was of no avail for them any longer to oppose the match. They could not force their daughter to go with them. 'But I can cast her off from me, if she be disobedient,' said Sir Marmaduke. Lady Rowley, however, had no desire that her daughter should be cast off, and was aware that Sir Marmaduke, when it came to the point of casting off, would be as little inclined to be stern as she was herself. Sir Marmaduke, still hoping that firmness would carry the day, and believing that it behoved him to maintain his parental authority, ended the discussion by keeping possession of the letter, and saying that he would take time to consider the matter. 'What security have we that he will ever marry her, if she does stay ?' he asked the next morning. Lady Rowley had no doubt on this score, and protested that her opposition to Hugh Stanbury arose simply from his want of income. 'I should never be justified,' said Sir Marmaduke, 'if I were to go and leave my girl as it were in the hands of a penny-a-liner.' The letter, in the end, was not sent; and Nora and her father hardly spoke to each other as they made their journey back to Florence together.

Emily Trevelyan, before the arrival of that letter from her husband, had determined that she would not leave Italy. It had been her purpose to remain somewhere in the neighbourhood of her husband and child; and to overcome her difficulties, – or be overcome by them, as circumstances might direct. Now her plans were again changed, – or, rather, she was now without a plan. She could form no plan till she should again see Mr Glascock. Should her child be restored to her, would it not be her duty to remain near her husband ? All this made Nora's line of conduct the more difficult for her. It was acknowledged that she could not remain in Italy. Mrs Trevelyan's position would be most embarrassing; but as all her efforts were to be used towards a reconciliation with her husband, and as his state utterly precluded the idea of a mixed household, – of any such a family arrangement as that which had existed in Curzon Street, – Nora could not remain with her. Mrs Trevelyan herself had declared that she would not wish it. And, in that case, where was Nora to bestow herself when Sir Marmaduke and Lady Rowley had sailed? Caroline offered to curtail those honeymoon weeks in Switzerland, but it was impossible to listen to an offer so magnanimous and so unreasonable. Nora had a dim romantic idea of sharing Priscilla's bedroom in that small cottage near Nuncombe Putney, of which she had heard, and of there learning lessons in strict economy; – but of this she said nothing. The short journey from the Baths of Lucca to Florence was not a pleasant one, and the Rowley family were much disturbed as they looked into the future. Lodgings had now been taken for them, and there was the great additional doubt whether Mrs Trevelyan would find her child there on her arrival.

The Spaldings went one way from the Florence station, and the Rowleys another. The American Minister had returned to the city some days previously, – drawn there nominally by pleas of business, but, in truth, by the necessities of the wedding breakfast, – and he met them at the station. 'Has Mr Glascock come back?' Nora was the first to ask. Yes; – he had come. He had been in the city since two o'clock, and had been up at the American Minister's house for half a minute. 'And has he brought the child?' asked Caroline, relieved of doubt on her own account. Mr Spalding did not know; – indeed, he had not interested himself quite so intently about Mrs Trevelyan's little boy, as had all those who had just returned from the Baths. Mr Glascock had said nothing to him about the child, and he had not quite understood why such a man should have made a journey to Siena, leaving his sweetheart behind him, just on the eve of his marriage. He hurried his women-kind into their carriage, and they were driven away; and then Sir Marmaduke was driven away with his women-kind. Caroline Spalding had perhaps thought that Mr Glascock might have been there to meet her.

86

Mr Glascock as Nurse

A message had been sent by the wires to Trevelyan, to let him know that Mr Glascock was himself coming for the boy. Whether such message would or would not be sent out to Casalunga Mr Glascock had been quite ignorant; – but it could, at any rate, do no harm. He did feel it hard as in this hot weather he made the journey, first to Florence, and then on to Siena. What was he to the Rowleys, or to Trevelyan himself, that such a job of work should fall to his lot

at such a period of his life? He had been very much in love with
Nora, no doubt; but, luckily for him, as he thought, Nora had
refused him. As for Trevelyan, – Trevelyan had never been his
friend. As for Sir Marmaduke, – Sir Marmaduke was nothing to
him. He was almost angry even with Mrs Trevelyan as he arrived
tired, heated, and very dusty, at Siena. It was his purpose to sleep
at Siena that night, and to go out to Casalunga early the next
morning. If the telegram had not been forwarded, he would send a
message on that evening. On inquiry, however, he found that the
message had been sent, and that the paper had been put into the
Signore's own hand by the Sienese messenger. Then he got into
some discourse with the landlord about the strange gentleman at
Casalunga. Trevelyan was beginning to become the subject of gossip
in the town, and people were saying that the stranger was very
strange indeed. The landlord thought that if the Signore had any
friends at all, it would be well that such friends should come and
look after him. Mr Glascock asked if Mr Trevelyan was ill. It was
not only that the Signore was out of health, – so the landlord heard,
– but that he was also somewhat – And then the landlord touched
his head. He ate nothing, and went nowhere, and spoke to no one;
and the people at the hospital to which Casalunga belonged were
beginning to be uneasy about their tenant. Perhaps Mr Glascock
had come to take him away. Mr Glascock explained that he had
not come to take Mr Trevelyan away, – but only to take away a
little boy that was with him. For this reason he was travelling with
a maid-servant, – a fact for which Mr Glascock clearly thought it
necessary that he should give an intelligible and credible explanation. The landlord seemed to think that the people at the hospital
would have been much rejoiced had Mr Glascock intended to take
Mr Trevelyan away also.

He started after a very early breakfast, and found himself walking
up over the stone ridges to the house between nine and ten in the
morning. He himself had sat beside the driver and had put the maid
inside the carriage. He had not deemed it wise to take an undivided
charge of the boy even from Casalunga to Siena. At the door of the
house, as though waiting for him, he found Trevelyan, not dirty as
he had been before, but dressed with much appearance of smartness.
He had a brocaded cap on his head, and a shirt with a laced front,
and a worked waistcoat, and a frockcoat, and coloured bright
trowsers. Mr Glascock knew at once that all the clothes which he
saw before him had been made for Italian and not for English wear;
and could almost have said that they had been bought in Siena and

not in Florence. 'I had not intended to impose this labour on you, Mr Glascock,' Trevelyan said, raising his cap to salute his visitor.

'For fear there might be mistakes, I thought it better to come myself,' said Mr Glascock. 'You did not wish to see Sir Marmaduke?'

'Certainly not Sir Marmaduke,' said Trevelyan, with a look of anger that was almost grotesque.

'And you thought it better that Mrs Trevelyan should not come.'

'Yes; – I thought it better; – but not from any feeling of anger towards her. If I could welcome my wife here, Mr Glascock, without a risk of wrath on her part, I should be very happy to receive her. I love my wife, Mr Glascock. I love her dearly. But there have been misfortunes. Never mind. There is no reason why I should trouble you with them. Let us go in to breakfast. After your drive you will have an appetite.'

Poor Mr Glascock was afraid to decline to sit down to the meal which was prepared for him. He did mutter something about having already eaten, but Trevelyan put this aside with a wave of his hand as he led the way into a spacious room, in which had been set out a table with almost a sumptuous banquet. The room was very bare and comfortless, having neither curtains nor matting, and containing not above half a dozen chairs. But an effort had been made to give it an air of Italian luxury. The windows were thrown open, down to the ground, and the table was decorated with fruits and three or four long-necked bottles. Trevelyan waved with his hand towards an arm-chair, and Mr Glascock had no alternative but to seat himself. He felt that he was sitting down to breakfast with a madman; but if he did not sit down, the madman might perhaps break out into madness. Then Trevelyan went to the door and called aloud for Catarina. 'In these remote places,' said he, 'one has to do without the civilisation of a bell. Perhaps one gains as much in quiet as one loses in comfort.' Then Catarina came with hot meats and fried potatoes, and Mr Glascock was compelled to help himself.

'I am but a bad trencherman myself,' said Trevelyan, 'but I shall lament my misfortune doubly if that should interfere with your appetite.' Then he got up and poured out wine into Mr Glascock's glass. 'They tell me that it comes from the Baron's vineyard,' said Trevelyan, alluding to the wine-farm of Ricasoli,* 'and that there is none better in Tuscany. I never was myself a judge of the grape, but this to me is as palatable as any of the costlier French wines. How grand a thing would wine really be, if it could make glad the heart of man.* How truly would one worship Bacchus if he could make one's heart to rejoice. But if a man have a real sorrow, wine will not wash it away, – not though a man were drowned in it, as Clarence was.'*

Mr Glascock hitherto had spoken hardly a word. There was an attempt at joviality about this breakfast, – or, at any rate, of the usual comfortable luxury of hospitable entertainment, – which, coming as it did from Trevelyan, almost locked his lips. He had not come there to to be jovial or luxurious, but to perform a most melancholy mission; and he had brought with him his saddest looks, and was prepared for a few sad words. Trevelyan's speech, indeed, was sad enough, but Mr Glascock could not take up questions of the worship of Bacchus at half a minute's warning. He ate a morsel, and raised his glass to his lips, and felt himself to be very uncomfortable. It was necessary, however, that he should utter a word. 'Do you not let your little boy come in to breakfast?' he said.

'He is better away,' said Trevelyan gloomily.

'But as we are to travel together,' said Mr Glascock, 'we might as well make acquaintance.'

'You have been a little hurried with me on that score,' said Trevelyan. 'I wrote certainly with a determined mind, but things have changed somewhat since then.'

'You do not mean that you will not send him?'

'You have been somewhat hurried with me, I say. If I remember rightly, I named no time, but spoke of the future. Could I have answered the message which I received from you, I would have postponed your visit for a week or so.'

'Postponed it! Why, – I am to be married the day after to-morrow. It was just as much as I was able to do, to come here at all.' Mr Glascock now pushed his chair back from the table, and prepared himself to speak up. 'Your wife expects her child now, and you will never break her heart by refusing to send him.'

'Nobody thinks of my heart, Mr Glascock.'

'But this is your own offer.'

'Yes, it was my own offer, certainly. I am not going to deny my own words, which have no doubt been preserved in testimony against me.'

'Mr Trevelyan, what do you mean?' Then, when he was on the point of boiling over with passion, Mr Glascock remembered that his companion was not responsible for his expressions. 'I do hope you will let the child go away with me,' he said. 'You cannot conceive the state of his mother's anxiety, and she will send him back at once if you demand it.'

'Is that to be in good faith?'

'Certainly, in good faith. I would lend myself to nothing, Mr Trevelyan, that was not said and done in good faith.'

'She will not break her word, excusing herself, because I am – mad?'

'I am sure that there is nothing of the kind in her mind.'

'Perhaps not now; but such things grow. There is no iniquity, no breach of promise, no treason that a woman will not excuse to herself, – or a man either, – by the comfortable self-assurance that the person to be injured is – mad. A hound without a friend is not so cruelly treated. The outlaw, the murderer, the perjurer has surer privileges than the man who is in the way, and to whom his friends can point as being – mad!' Mr Glascock knew or thought that he knew that his host in truth was mad, and he could not, therefore, answer this tirade by an assurance that no such idea was likely to prevail. 'Have they told you, I wonder,' continued Trevelyan, 'how it was that, driven to force and an ambuscade for the recovery of my own child, I waylaid my wife and took him from her? I have done nothing to forfeit my right as a man to the control of my own family. I demanded that the boy should be sent to me, and she paid no attention to my words. I was compelled to vindicate my own authority; and then, because I claimed the right which belongs to a father, they said that I was – mad! Ay, and they would have proved it, too, had I not fled from my country and hidden myself in this desert. Think of that, Mr Glascock! Now they have followed me here, – not out of love for me; and that man whom they call a governor comes and insults me; and my wife promises to be good to me, and says that she will forgive and forget! Can she ever forgive herself her own folly, and the cruelty that has made shipwreck of my life? They can do nothing to me here; but they would entice me home because there they have friends, and can fee doctors, – with my own money, – and suborn lawyers, and put me away, – somewhere in the dark, where I shall be no more heard of among men! As you are a man of honour, Mr Glascock, – tell me; is it not so?'

'I know nothing of their plans, – beyond this, that you wrote me word that you would send them the boy.'

'But I know their plans. What you say is true. I did write you word, – and I meant it. Mr Glascock, sitting here alone from morning to night, and lying down from night till morning without companionship, without love, in utter misery, I taught myself to feel that I should think more of her than of myself.'

'If you are so unhappy here, come back yourself with the child. Your wife would desire nothing better.'

'Yes; – and submit to her, and her father, and her mother. No, – Mr Glascock; never, never. Let her come to me.'

'But you will not receive her.'

'Let her come in a proper spirit, and I will receive her. She is the wife of my bosom, and I will receive her with joy. But if she is to come to me and tell me that she forgives me, – forgives me for the evil that she has done, – then, sir, she had better stay away. Mr Glascock, you are going to be married. Believe me, – no man should submit to be forgiven by his wife. Everything must go astray if that be done. I would rather encounter their mad doctors, one of them after another till they had made me mad; – I would encounter anything rather than that. But, sir, you neither eat nor drink, and I fear that my speech disturbs you.'

It was like enough that it may have done so. Trevelyan, as he had been speaking, had walked about the room, going from one extremity to the other with hurried steps, gesticulating with his arms, and every now and then pushing back with his hands the long hair from off his forehead. Mr Glascock was in truth very much disturbed. He had come there with an express object; but, whenever he mentioned the child, the father became almost rabid in his wrath. 'I have done very well, thank you,' said Mr Glascock. 'I will not eat any more, and I believe I must be thinking of going back to Siena.'

'I had hoped yoy would spend the day with me, Mr Glascock.'

'I am to be married, you see, in two days; and I must be in Florence early to-morrow. I am to meet my – wife, as she will be, and the Rowleys, and your wife. Upon my word I can't stay. Won't you just say a word to the young woman and let the boy be got ready?'

'I think not; – no, I think not.'

'And am I to have had all this journey for nothing? You will have made a fool of me in writing to me.'

'I intended to be honest, Mr Glascock.'

'Stick to your honesty, and send the boy back to his mother. It will be better for you, Trevelyan.'

'Better for me! Nothing can be better for me. All must be worst. It will be better for me, you say; and you ask me to give up the last drop of cold water wherewith I can touch my parched lips. Even in my hell I had so much left to me of a limpid stream, and you tell me that it will be better for me to pour it away. You may take him, Mr Glascock. The woman will make him ready for you. What matters it whether the fiery furnace be heated seven times, or only six;* – in either degree the flames are enough! You may take him; – you may take him!' So saying, Trevelyan walked out of the window, leaving Mr Glascock seated in his chair. He walked out of the window and went down among the olive trees. He did not go far, however, but stood with his arm round the stem of one of them, playing with the shoots of a vine with his hand. Mr Glascock followed him to the window and stood looking at him for a few moments. But Trevelyan did not turn or move. There he stood gazing at the pale, cloudless, heat-laden, motionless sky, thinking of his own sorrows, and remembering too, doubtless, with the vanity of a madman, that he was probably being watched in his reverie.

Mr Glascock was too practical a man not to make the most of the offer that had been made to him, and he went back among the passages and called for Catarina. Before long he had two or three women with him, including her whom he had brought from Florence, and among them Louey was soon made to appear, dressed for his journey, together with a small trunk in which were his garments. It was clear that the order for his departure had been given before that scene at the breakfast-table, and that Trevelyan had not intended to go back from his promise. Nevertheless Mr Glascock thought it might be as well to hurry his departure, and he turned back to say the shortest possible word of farewell to Trevelyan in the garden. But when he got to the window, Trevelyan was not to be found among the olive trees. Mr Glascock walked a few steps down the hill, looking for him, but seeing nothing of him, returned to the house. The elder woman said that her master had not been there, and Mr Glascock started with his charge. Trevelyan was manifestly mad, and it was impossible to treat him as a sane man would have been treated. Nevertheless, Mr Glascock felt much compunction in carrying the child away without a final kiss or word of farewell from its father. But it was not to be so. He had got into the carriage with the child, having the servant seated opposite to him, – for he was moved by some undefinable fear which made him determine to keep the boy close to him, and he had not, therefore, returned to the driver's seat, – when Trevelyan appeared standing by the road-side at the bottom of the hill. 'Would you take him away from me without one word!' said Trevelyan bitterly.

'I went to look for you but you were gone,' said Mr Glascock.

'No sir, I was not gone. I am here. It is the last time that I shall ever gladden my eyes with his brightness. Louey, my love, will you

come to your father?' Louey did not seem to be particularly willing
to leave the carriage, but he made no loud objection when Mr
Glascock held him up to the open space above the door. The child
had realised the fact that he was to go, and did not believe that his
father would stop him now; but he was probably of opinion that
the sooner the carriage began to go on the better it would be for
him. Mr Glascock, thinking that his father intended to kiss him
over the door, held him by his frock; but the doing of this made
Trevelyan very angry. 'Am I not to be trusted with my own child in
my arms?' said he. 'Give him to me, sir. I begin to doubt now
whether I am right to deliver him to you.' Mr Glascock immediately
let go his hold of the boy's frock and leaned back in the carriage.
'Louey will tell papa that he loves him before he goes?' said
Trevelyan. The poor little fellow murmured something, but it did
not please his father, who had him in his arms. 'You are like the
rest of them, Louey,' he said; 'because I cannot laugh and be gay,
all my love for you is nothing; – nothing! You may take him. He is
all that I have; – all that I have; – and I shall never see him again!'
So saying he handed the child back into the carriage, and sat himself
down by the side of the road to watch till the vehicle should be out
of sight. As soon as the last speck of it had vanished from his sight,
he picked himself up, and dragged his slow footsteps back to the
house.

Mr Glascock made sundry atempts to amuse the child, with
whom he had to remain all that night at Siena; but his efforts in
that line were not very successful. The boy was brisk enough, and
happy, and social by nature; but the events, or rather the want of
events of the last few months, had so cowed him, that he could not
recover his spirits at the bidding of a stranger. 'If I have any of my
own,' said Mr Glascock to himself, 'I hope they will be of a more
cheerful disposition.'

As we have seen, he did not meet Caroline at the station, –
thereby incurring his lady-love's displeasure for the period of half-
a-minute; but he did meet Mrs Trevelyan almost at the door of Sir
Marmaduke's lodgings. 'Yes, Mrs Trevelyan; he is here.'

'How am I ever to thank you for such goodness?' said she. 'And
Mr Trevelyan; – you saw him?'

'Yes; – I saw him.'

Before he could answer her further she was up-stairs, and had
her child in her arms. It seemed to be an age since the boy had been
stolen from her in the early spring in that unknown, dingy street
near Tottenham Court Road. Twice she had seen her darling since
that, – twice during his captivity; but on each of these occasions

she had seen him as one not belonging to herself, and had seen him under circumstances which had robbed the greeting of almost all its pleasure. But now he was her own again, to take whither she would, to dress and to undress, to feed, to coax, to teach, and to caress. And the child lay up close to her as she hugged him, putting up his little cheek to her chin, and burying himself happily in her embrace. He had not much as yet to say, but she could feel that he was contented.

Mr Glascock had promised to wait for her a few minutes, – even at the risk of Caroline's displeasure, – and Mrs Trevelyan ran down to him as soon as the first craving of her mother's love was satisfied. Her boy would at any rate be safe with her now, and it was her duty to learn something of her husband. It was more than her duty; – if only her services might be of avail to him. 'And you say he was well?' she asked. She had taken Mr Glascock apart, and they were alone together, and he had determined that he would tell her the truth.

'I do not know that he is ill, – though he is pale and altered beyond belief.'

'Yes; – I saw that.'

'I never knew a man so thin and haggard.'

'My poor Louis !'

'But that is not the worst of it.'

'What do you mean, Mr Glascock ?'

'I mean that his mind is astray, and that he should not be left alone. There is no knowing what he might do. He is so much more alone there than he would be in England. There is not a soul who could interfere.'

'Do you mean that you think – that he is in danger – from himself ?'

'I would not say so, Mrs Trevelyan; but who can tell ? I am sure of this, – that he should not be left alone. If it were only because of the misery of his life, he should not be left alone.'

'But what can I do ? He would not even see papa.'

'He would see you.'

'But he would not let me guide him in anything. I have been to him twice, and he breaks out, – as if I were – a bad woman.'

'Let him break out. What does it matter ?'

'Am I to own to a falsehood, – and such a falsehood ?'

'Own to anything, and you will conquer him at once. That is what I think. You will excuse what I say, Mrs Trevelyan.'

'Oh, Mr Glascock, you have been such a friend ! What should we have done without you !'

'You cannot take to heart the words that come from a disordered reason. In truth, he believes no ill of you.'

'But he says so.'

'It is hard to know what he says. Declare that you will submit to him, and I think that he will be softened towards you. Try to bring him back to his own country. It may be that were he to – die there, alone, the memory of his loneliness would be heavy with you in after days.' Then, having so spoken, he rushed off, declaring, with a forced laugh, that Caroline Spalding would never forgive him.

The next day was the day of the wedding, and Emily Trevelyan was left all alone. It was of course out of the question that she should join any party the purport of which was to be festive. Sir Marmaduke went with some grumbling, declaring that wine and severe food in the morning were sins against the plainest rules of life. And the three Rowley girls went, Nora officiating as one of the bridesmaids. But Mrs Trevelyan was left with her boy, and during the day she was forced to resolve what should be the immediate course of her life. Two days after the wedding her family would return to England. It was open to her to go with them, and to take her boy with her. But a few days since how happy she would have been could she have been made to believe that such a mode of returning would be within her power! But now she felt that she might not return and leave that poor, suffering wretch behind her. As she thought of him she tried to interrogate herself in regard to her feelings. Was it love, or duty, or compassion which stirred her? She had loved him as fondly as any bright young woman loves the man who is to take her away from everything else, and make her a part of his house and of himself. She had loved him as Nora now loved the man whom she worshipped and thought to be a god, doing godlike work in the dingy recesses of the D. R. office. Emily Trevelyan was forced to tell herself that all that was over with her. Her husband had shown himself to be weak, suspicious, unmanly, – by no means like a god. She had learned to feel that she could not trust her comfort in his hands, – that she could never know what his thoughts of her might be. But still he was her husband, and the father of her child; and though she could not dare to look forward to happiness in living with him, she could understand that no comfort would be possible to her were she to return to England and to leave him to perish alone at Casalunga. Fate seemed to have intended that her life should be one of misery, and she must bear it as best she might.

The more she thought of it, however, the greater seemed to be her difficulties. What was she to do when her father and mother should have left her? She could not go to Casalunga if her husband would not give her entrance; and if she did go, would it be safe for her to take her boy with her? Were she to remain in Florence she would be hardly nearer to him for any useful purpose than in England; and even should she pitch her tent at Siena, occupying there some desolate set of huge apartments in a deserted palace, of what use could she be to him? Could she stay there if he desired her to go; and was it probable that he would be willing that she should be at Siena while he was living at Casalunga, – no more than two leagues distant? How should she begin her work; and if he repulsed her, how should she then continue it?

But during these wedding hours she did make up her mind as to what she would do for the present. She would certainly not leave Italy while her husband remained there. She would for a while keep her rooms in Florence, and there should her boy abide. But from time to time, – twice a week perhaps, – she would go down to Siena and Casalunga, and there form her plans in accordance with her husband's conduct. She was his wife, and nothing should entirely separate her from him, now that he so sorely wanted her aid.

87

Mr Glascock's Marriage Completed

The Glascock marriage was a great affair in Florence; – so much so, that there were not a few who regarded it as a strengthening of peaceful relations between the United States and the United Kingdom, and who thought that the Alabama claims and the question of naturalisation* might now be settled with comparative ease. An English lord was about to marry the niece of an American Minister to a foreign court. The bridegroom was not, indeed, quite a lord as yet, but it was known to all men that he must be a lord in a very short time, and the bride was treated with more than usual bridal honours because she belonged to a legation. She was not, indeed, an ambassador's daughter, but the niece of a daughterless ambassador, and therefore almost as good as a daughter. The wives and daughters of other ambassadors, and the other ambassadors themselves, of course, came to the wedding; and as the palace in which Mr Spalding had apartments stood alone, in a garden, with a separate carriage entrance, it seemed for all wedding purposes as though the whole palace were his own. The English Minister came, and his wife, – although she had never quite given over turning up her nose at the American bride whom Mr Glascock had chosen for himself. It was such a pity, she said, that such a man as Mr Glascock should marry a young woman from Providence, Rhode Island. Who in England would know anything of Providence, Rhode Island? And it was so expedient, in her estimation, that a man of family should strengthen himself by marrying a woman of family. It was so necessary, she declared, that a man when marrying should remember that his child would have two grandfathers, and would be called upon to account for four great-grandfathers. Nevertheless Mr Glascock was – Mr Glascock; and, let him marry whom he would, his wife would be the future Lady Peterborough. Remembering this, the English Minister's wife gave up the point when the thing was really settled, and benignly promised to come to the breakfast with all the secretaries and attachés belonging to the legation, and all the wives and daughters thereof. What may a man not do, and do with éclat, if he be heir to a peer and have plenty of money in his pocket?

Mr and Mrs Spalding were covered with glory on the occasion; and perhaps they did not bear their glory as meekly as they should have done. Mrs Spalding laid herself open to some ridicule from the British Minister's wife because of her inability to understand with absolute clearness the condition of her niece's husband in respect to his late and future seat in Parliament, to the fact of his being a commoner and a nobleman at the same time, and to certain information which was conveyed to her, surely in a most unnecessary manner, that if Mr Glascock were to die before his father her niece would never become Lady Peterborough, although her niece's son, if she had one, would be the future lord. No doubt she blundered, as was most natural; and then the British Minister's wife made the most of the blunders; and when once Mrs Spalding ventured to speak of Caroline as her ladyship, not to the British Minister's wife, but to the sister of one of the secretaries, a story was made out of it which was almost as false as it was ill-natured. Poor Caroline was spoken of as her ladyship backward and forwards among the ladies of the legation in a manner which might have vexed her had she known anything about it; but, nevertheless, all the ladies prepared their best flounces to go to the wedding. The time would soon come when she would in truth be a 'ladyship,' and she might be of social use to any one of the ladies in question.

But Mr Spalding was, for the time, the most disturbed of any of the party concerned. He was a tall, thin, clever Republican of the North, – very fond of hearing himself talk, and somewhat apt to take advantage of the courtesies of conversation for the purpose of making unpardonable speeches. As long as there was any give and take going on in the mêlée of words he would speak quickly and with energy, seizing his chances among others; but the moment he had established his right to the floor, – as soon as he had won for himself the position of having his turn at the argument, he would dole out his words with considerable slowness, raise his hand for oratorical effect, and proceed as though Time were annihilated. And he would go further even than this, for, – fearing by experience the escape of his victims, – he would catch a man by the button-hole of his coat, or back him ruthlessly into the corner of a room, and then lay on to him without quarter. Since the affair with Mr Glascock had been settled, he had talked an immensity about England, – not absolutely taking honour to himself because of his intended connection with a lord, but making so many references to the aristocratic side of the British constitution as to leave no doubt on the minds of his hearers as to the source of his arguments. In old days, before all this was happening, Mr Spalding, though a cour-teous man in his personal relations, had constantly spoken of England with the bitter indignation of the ordinary American politician. England must be made to disgorge. England must be made to do justice. England must be taught her place in the world. England must give up her claims. In hot moments he had gone further, and had declared that England must be – whipped. He had been specially loud against that aristocracy of England which, according to a figure of speech often used by him, was always feeding on the vitals of the people. But now all this was very much changed. He did not go the length of expressing an opinion that the House of Lords was a valuable institution; but he discussed questions of primogeniture and hereditary legislation, in reference to their fitness for countries which were gradually emerging from feudal systems, with an equanimity, an impartiality, and a persev-erance which soon convinced those who listened to him where he had learned his present lessons, and why. 'The conservative nature of your institutions, sir,' he said to poor Sir Marmaduke at the Baths of Lucca a very few days before the marriage, 'has to be studied with great care before its effects can be appreciated in reference to a people who, perhaps, I may be allowed to say, have more in their composition of constitutional reverence than of educated intelligence.' Sir Marmaduke, having suffered before, had endeavoured to bolt; but the American had caught him and pinned him, and the Governor of the Mandarins was impotent in his hands. 'The position of the great peer of Parliament is doubtless very splendid, and may be very useful,' continued Mr Spalding, who was intending to bring round his argument to the evil doings of certain scandalously extravagant young lords, and to offer a suggestion that in such cases a committee of aged and respected peers should sit and decide whether a second son, or some other heir should not be called to the inheritance both of the title and the property. But Mrs Spalding had seen the sufferings of Sir Marmaduke, and had rescued him. 'Mr Spalding,' she had said, 'it is too hot for politics, and Sir Marmaduke has come out here for a holiday.' Then she took her husband by the arm, and led him away helpless.

In spite of these drawbacks to the success, – if ought can be said to be a drawback on success of which the successful one is unconscious, – the marriage was prepared with great splendour, and everybody who was anybody in Florence was to be present. There were only to be four bridesmaids, Caroline herself having strongly objected to a greater number. As Wallachia Petrie had fled at the first note of preparation for these trivial and unpalatable festivities, another American young lady was found; and the sister of the English secretary of legation, who had so maliciously spread that report about her 'ladyship,' gladly agreed to be the fourth.

As the reader will remember, the whole party from the Baths of Lucca reached Florence only the day before the marriage, and Nora at the station promised to go up to Caroline that same evening. 'Mr Glascock will tell me about the little boy,' said Caroline; 'but I shall be so anxious to hear about your sister.' So Nora crossed the bridge after dinner, and went up to the American Minister's palatial residence. Caroline was then in the loggia, and Mr Glascock was with her; and for a while they talked about Emily Trevelyan and her misfortunes. Mr Glascock was clearly of opinion that Trevelyan would soon be either in an asylum or in his grave. 'I could not bring myself to tell your sister so,' he said; 'but I think your father should be told, – or you mother. Something should be done to put an end to that fearful residence at Casalunga.' Then by degrees the conversation changed itself to Nora's prospects; and Caroline, with her friend's hand in hers, asked after Hugh Stanbury.

'You will not mind speaking before him, – will you?' said Caroline, putting her hand on her own lover's arm.

'Not unless he should mind it,' said Nora, smiling. She had meant nothing beyond a simple reply to her friend's question, but he took her words in a different sense, and blushed as he remembered his visit to Nuncombe Putney.

'He thinks almost more of your happiness than he does of mine,' said Caroline; 'which isn't fair, as I am sure that Mr Stanbury will not reciprocate the attention. And now, dear, when are we to see you?'

'Who on earth can say?'

'I suppose Mr Stanbury would say something, – only he is not here.'

'And papa won't send my letter,' said Nora.

'You are sure that you will not go out to the Islands with him?'

'Quite sure,' said Nora. 'I have made up my mind so far as that.'

'And what will your sister do?'

'I think she will stay. I think she will say good-bye to papa and mamma here in Florence.'

'I am quite of opinion that she should not leave her husband alone in Italy,' said Mr Glascock.

'She has not told us with certainty,' said Nora; 'but I feel sure that she will stay. Papa thinks she ought to go with them to London.'

'Your papa seems to have two very intractable daughters,' said Caroline.

'As for me,' declared Nora, solemnly, 'nothing shall make me go back to the Islands, – unless Mr Stanbury should tell me to do so.'

'And they start at the end of July?'

'On the last Saturday.'

'And what will you do then, Nora?'

'I believe there are casual wards that people go to.'

'Casual wards!' said Caroline.

'Miss Rowley is condescending to poke her fun at you,' said Mr Glascock.

'She is quite welcome, and shall poke as much as she likes; only we must be serious now. If it be necessary, we will get back by the end of July; – won't we, Charles?'

'You will do nothing of the kind,' said Nora. 'What! – give up your honeymoon to provide me with board and lodgings! How can you suppose that I am so selfish or so helpless? I would go to my aunt, Mrs Outhouse.'

'We know that that wouldn't do,' said Caroline. 'You might as well be in Italy as far as Mr Stanbury is concerned.'

'If Miss Rowley would go to Monkhams, she might wait for us,' suggested Mr Glascock. 'Old Mrs Richards is there; and though of course she would be dull – '

'It is quite unnecessary,' said Nora. 'I shall take a two-pair back* in a respectable féminine quarter, like any other young woman who wants such accommodation, and shall wait there till my young man can come and give me his arm to church. That is about the way we shall do it. I am not going to give myself any airs, Mr Glascock, or make any difficulties. Papa is always talking to me about chairs and tables and frying-pans, and I shall practise to do with as few of them as possible. As I am headstrong about having my young man, – and I own that I am headstrong about that, – I guess I've got to fit myself for that sort of life.' And Nora, as she said this, pronounced her words with something of a nasal twang, imitating certain countrywomen of her friend's.

'I like to hear you joking about it, Nora ; because your voice is so cheery and you are so bright when you joke. But, nevertheless, one has to be reasonable, and to look the facts in the face. I don't see how you are to be left in London alone, and you know that your aunt Mrs Outhouse, – or at any rate your uncle, – would not receive you except on receiving some strong anti-Stanbury pledge.'

'I certainly shall not give an anti-Stanbury pledge.'

'And, therefore, that is out of the question. You will have a fortnight or three weeks in London, in all the bustle of their departure, and I declare I think that at the last moment you will go with them.'

'Never ! – unless he says so.'

'I don't see how you are even to meet – "him," and talk it over.'

'I'll manage that. My promise not to write lasts only while we are in Italy.'

'I think we had better get back to England, Charles, and take pity on this poor destitute one.'

'If you talk of such a thing I will swear that I will never go to Monkhams. You will find that I shall manage it. It may be that I shall do something very shocking, – so that all your patronage will hardly be able to bring me round afterwards; but I will do something that will serve my purpose. I have not gone so far as this to be turned back now.' Nora, as she spoke of having 'gone so far,' was looking at Mr Glascock, who was seated in an easy arm-chair close to the girl whom he was to make his wife on the morrow, and she was thinking, no doubt, of the visit which he had made to Nuncombe Putney, and of the first irretrievable step which she had taken when she told him that her love was given to another. That had been her Rubicon. And though there had been periods with her since the passing of it, in which she had felt that she had crossed it in vain, that she had thrown away the splendid security of the other bank without obtaining the perilous object of her ambition, – though there had been moments in which she had almost regretted her own courage and noble action, still, having passed the river, there was nothing for her but to go on to Rome. She was not going to be stopped now by the want of a house in which to hide herself for a few weeks. She was without money, except so much as her mother might be able, almost surrepitiously, to give her. She was without friends to help her, – except these who were now with her, whose friendship had come to her in so singular a manner, and whose power to aid her at the present moment was cruelly curtailed by their own circumstances. Nothing was settled as to her own marriage. In consequence of the promise that had been extorted from her that she should not correspond with Stanbury, she knew nothing of his present wishes or intention. Her father was so offended by her firmness that he would hardly speak to her. And it was evident to her that her mother, though disposed to yield, was still in hopes that her daughter, in the press and difficulty of the moment, would allow herself to be carried away with the rest of the family to the other side of the world. She knew all this, – but she had made up her mind that she would not be carried away. It was not very pleasant, the thought that she would be obliged at last to ask her young man, as she called him, to provide for her; but she would do that and trust herself altogether in his hands sooner than be taken to the Antipodes. 'I can be very resolute if I please, my dear,' she said, looking at Caroline. Mr Glascock almost thought that she must have intended to address him.

They sat there discussing the matter for some time through the long, cool, evening hours, but nothing could be settled further, – except that Nora would write to her friend as soon as her affairs had begun to shape themselves after her return to England. At last Caroline went into the house, and for a few minutes Mr Glascock was alone with Nora. He had remained, determining that the moment should come, but now that it was there he was for awhile unable to say the words that he wished to utter. At last he spoke. 'Miss Rowley, Caroline is so eager to be your friend.'

'I know she is, and I do love her so dearly. But, without joke, Mr Glascock, there will be as it were a great gulf* between us.'

'I do not know that there need be any gulf, great or little. But I did not mean to allude to that. What I want to say is this. My feelings are not a bit less warm or sincere than hers. You know of old that I am not very good at expressing myself.'

'I know nothing of the kind.'

'There is no such gulf as what you speak of. All that is mostly gone by, and a nobleman in England, though he has advantages as a gentleman, is no more than a gentleman. But that has nothing to do with what I am saying now. I shall never forget my journey to Devonshire. I won't pretend to say now that I regret its result.'

'I am quite sure you don't.'

'No; I do not; – though I thought then that I should regret it always. But remember this, Miss Rowley, – that you can never ask me to do anything that I will not, if possible, do for you. You are in some little difficulty now.'

'It will disappear, Mr Glascock. Difficulties always do.'

'But we will do anything that we are wanted to do; and should a certain event take place – '

'It will take place some day.'

'Then I hope that we may be able to make Mr Stanbury and his wife quite at home at Monkhams.' After that he took Nora's hand and kissed it, and at the moment Caroline came back to them.

'To-morrow, Mr Glascock,' she said, 'you will, I believe, be at liberty to kiss everybody; but to-day you should be more discreet.'

It was generally admitted among the various legations in Florence that there had not been such a wedding in the City of Flowers since it had become the capital of Italia. Mr Glascock and Miss Spalding were married in the chapel of the legation, – a legation chapel on the ground floor having been extemporised for the occasion. This greatly enhanced the pleasantness of the thing, and saved the necessity of matrons and bridesmaids packing themselves and their finery into close fusty carriages. A portion of the guests attended in the chapel, and the remainder, when the ceremony was over, were found strolling about the shady garden. The whole affair of the breakfast was very splendid and lasted some hours. In the midst of this the bride and bridegroom were whisked away with a pair of grey horses to the railway station, and before the last toast of the day had been proposed by the Belgian Councillor of Legation, they were half way up the Apennines on their road to Bologna. Mr Spalding behaved himself like a man on the occasion. Nothing was spared in the way of expense, and when he made that celebrated speech, in which he declared that the republican virtue of the New World had linked itself in a happy alliance with the aristocratic splendour of the Old, and went on with a simile about the lion and the lamb, everybody accepted it with good humour in spite of its being a little too long for the occasion.

'It has gone off very well, mamma; has it not?' said Nora, as she returned home with her mother to her lodgings.

'Yes, my dear; much, I fancy, as these things generally do.'

'I thought it was so nice. And she looked so very well. And he was so pleasant, and so much like a gentleman; – not noisy, you know, – and yet not too serious.'

'I dare say, my love.'

'It is easy enough, mamma, for a girl to be married, for she has nothing to do but to wear her clothes and look as pretty as she can. And if she cries and has a red nose it is forgiven her. But a man has so difficult a part to play! If he tries to carry himself as though it were not a special occasion, he looks like a fool that way; and if he is very special, he looks like a fool the other way. I thought Mr Glascock did it very well.'

'To tell you, the truth, my dear, I did not observe him.'

'I did, – narrowly. He hadn't tied his cravat at all nicely.'

'How you could think of his cravat, Nora, with such memories as you must have, and such regrets, I cannot understand.'

'Mamma, my memories of Mr Glascock are pleasant memories, and as for regrets, – I have not one. Can I regret, mamma, that I did not marry a man whom I did not love, – and that I rejected him when I knew that I loved another? You cannot mean that, mamma.'

'I know this; – that I was thinking all the time how proud I should have been, and how much more fortunate he would have been, had you been standing there instead of that American young woman.' As she said this Lady Rowley burst into tears, and Nora could only answer her mother by embracing her. They were alone together, their party having been too large for one carriage, and Sir Marmaduke having taken his two younger daughters. 'Of course, I feel it,' said Lady Rowley, through her tears. 'It would have been such a position for my child! And that young man, – without a shilling in the world; and writing in that way, just for bare bread!' Nora had nothing more to say. A feeling that in herself would have been base, was simply affectionate and maternal in her mother. It was impossible that she should make her mother see it as she saw it.

There was but one intervening day and then the Rowleys returned to England. There had been, as it were, a tacit agreement among them that, in spite of all their troubles, their holiday should be a holiday up to the time of the Glascock marriage. Then must commence at once the stern necessity of their return home, – home, not only to England, but to those antipodean islands from which it was too probable that some of them might never come back. And the difficulties in their way seemed to be almost insuperable. First of all there was to be the parting from Emily Trevelyan. She had determined to remain in Florence, and had written to her husband saying that she would do so, and declaring her willingness to go out to him, or to receive him in Florence at any time and in any manner that he might appoint. She had taken this as a first step, intending to go to Casalunga very shortly, even though she should receive no answer from him. The parting between her and her mother and father and sisters was very bitter. Sir Marmaduke, as he had become estranged from Nora, had grown to be more and more gentle and loving with his elder daughter, and was nearly overcome at the idea of leaving her in a strange land, with a husband near her, mad, and yet not within her custody. But he could do nothing, – could hardly say a word, – toward opposing her. Though her husband was mad, he supplied her with the means of living ; and when she said that it was her duty to be near him, her father could not deny it. The parting came. 'I will return to you the moment you send to me,' were Nora's last words to her sister. 'I don't suppose I shall send,' said Emily. 'I shall try to bear it without assistance.'

Then the journey from Italy to England was made without much gratification or excitement, and the Rowley family again found themselves at Gregg's Hotel.

88
Cropper and Burgess

We must now go back to Exeter and look after Mr Brooke Burgess and Miss Dorothy Stanbury. It is rather hard upon readers that they should be thus hurried from the completion of hymeneals at Florence, to the preparations for other hymeneals in Devonshire ; but it is the nature of a complex story to be entangled with many weddings towards its close. In this little history there are, we fear, three or four more to come. We will not anticipate by alluding prematurely to Hugh Stanbury's treachery, or death, – or the possibility that he after all may turn out to be the real descendant of the true Lord Peterborough and the actual inheritor of the title and estate of Monkhams, nor will we speak of Nora's certain fortitude under either of these emergencies. But the instructed reader must be aware that Camilla French ought to have a husband found for her ; that Colonel Osborne should be caught in some matrimonial trap, – as, how otherwise should he be fitly punished ? – and that something should be at least attempted for Priscilla Stanbury, who from the first has been intended to be the real heroine of these pages. That Martha should marry Giles Hickbody, and Barty Burgess run away with Mrs MacHugh, is of course evident to the meanest novel-expounding capacity ; but the fate of Brooke Burgess and of Dorothy will require to be evolved with some delicacy and much detail.

There was considerable difficulty in fixing the day. In the first place Miss Stanbury was not very well, – and then she was very fidgety. She must see Brooke again before the day was fixed, and after seeing Brooke she must see her lawyer. 'To have a lot of money to look after is more plague than profit, my dear,' she said to Dorothy one day; 'particularly when you don't quite know what you ought to do with it.' Dorothy had always avoided any conversation with her aunt about money since the first moment in which she had thought of accepting Brooke Burgess as her husband. She knew that her aunt had some feeling which made her averse to the idea that any portion of the property which she had inherited should be enjoyed by a Stanbury after her death, and Dorothy, guided by this knowledge, had almost convinced herself that her love for Brooke was treason either against him or against her aunt. If, by engaging herself to him, she should rob him of his inheritance, how bitter a burden to him would her love have been! If, on the other hand, she should reward her aunt for all that had been done for her by forcing herself, a Stanbury, into a position not intended for her, how base would be her ingratitude! These thoughts had troubled her much, and had always prevented her from answering any of her aunt's chance allusions to the property. For her, things had at last gone very right. She did not quite know how it had come about, but she was engaged to marry the man she loved. And her aunt was, at any rate, reconciled to the marriage. But when Miss Stanbury declared that she did not know what to do about the property, Dorothy could only hold her tongue. She had had plenty to say when it had been suggested to her that the marriage should be put off yet for a short while, and that, in the meantime, Brooke should come again to Exeter. She swore that she did not care for how long it was put off, – only that she hoped it might not be put off altogether. And as for Brooke's coming, that, for the present, would be very much nicer than being married out of hand at once. Dorothy, in truth, was not at all in a hurry to be married, but she would have liked to have had her lover always coming and going. Since the courtship had become a thing permitted, she had had the privilege of welcoming him twice at the house in the Close; and that running down to meet him in the little front parlour, and the getting up to make his breakfast for him as he started in the morning, were among the happiest epochs of her life. And then, as soon as ever the breakfast was eaten, and he was gone, she would sit down to write him a letter. Oh, those letters, so beautifully crossed, more than one of which was copied from beginning to end because some word in it was not thought to be sweet enough; –

what a heaven of happiness they were to her! The writing of the first had disturbed her greatly, and she had almost repented of the privilege before it was ended; but with the first and second the difficulties had disappeared; and, had she not felt somewhat ashamed of the occupation, she could have sat at her desk and written him letters all day. Brooke would answer them, with fair regularity, but in a most cursory manner, – sending seven or eight lines in return for two sheets fully crossed; but this did not discompose her in the least. He was worked hard at his office, and had hundreds of other things to do. He, too, could say, – so thought Dorothy, – more in eight lines than she could put into as many pages.

She was quite happy when she was told that the marriage could not take place till August, but that Brooke must come again in July. Brooke did come in the first week of July, and somewhat horrified Dorothy by declaring to her that Miss Stanbury was unreasonable. 'If I insist upon leaving London so often for a day or two,' said he, 'how am I to get anything like leave of absence when the time comes?' In answer to this Dorothy tried to make him understand that business should not be neglected, and that, as far as she was concerned, she could do very well without that trip abroad which he had proposed for her. 'I'm not going to be done in that way,' said Brooke. 'And now that I am here she has nothing to say to me. I've told her a dozen times that I don't want to know anything about her will, and that I'll take it all for granted. There is something to be settled on you, that she calls her own.'

'She is so generous, Brooke.'

'She is generous enough, but she is very whimsical. She is going to make her whole will over again, and now she wants to send some message to Uncle Barty. I don't know what it is yet, but I am to take it. As far as I can understand, she has sent all the way to London for me, in order that I may take a message across the Close.'

'You talk as though it were very disagreeable, coming to Exeter,' said Dorothy, with a little pout.

'So it is, – very disagreeable.'

'Oh, Brooke!'

'Very disagreeable if our marriage is to be put off by it. I think it will be so much nicer making love somewhere on the Rhine than having snatches of it here, and talking all the time about wills and tenements and settlements.' As he said this, with his arm round her waist and his face quite close to hers, – showing thereby that he was not altogether averse even to his present privileges, – she forgave him.

On that same afternoon, just before the banking hours were over, Brooke went across to the house of Cropper and Burgess, having first been closeted for nearly an hour with his aunt, – and, as he went, his step was sedate and his air was serious. He found his uncle Barty, and was not very long in delivering his message. It was to this effect, – that Miss Stanbury particularly wished to see Mr Bartholomew Burgess on business, at some hour on that afternoon or that evening. Brooke himself had been made acquainted with the subject in regard to which this singular interview was desired; but it was not a part of his duty to communicate any information respecting it. It had been necessary that his consent to certain arrangements should be asked before the invitation to Barty Burgess could be given; but his present mission was confined to an authority to give the invitation.

Old Mr Burgess was much surprised, and was at first disposed to decline the proposition made by the 'old harridan,' as he called her. He had never put any restraint on his language in talking of Miss Stanbury with his nephew, and was not disposed to do so now, because she had taken a new vagary into her head. But there was something in his nephew's manner which at last induced him to discuss the mater rationally.

'And you don't know what it's all about?' said Uncle Barty.

'I can't quite say that. I suppose I do know pretty well. At any rate, I know enough to think that you ought to come. But I must not say what it is.'

'Will it do me or anybody else any good?'

'It can't do you any harm. She won't eat you.'

'But she can abuse me like a pickpocket, and I should return it, and then there would be a scolding match. I always have kept out of her way, and I think I had better do so still.'

Nevertheless Brooke prevailed, – or rather the feeling of curiosity which was naturally engendered prevailed. For very, very many years Barty Burgess had never entered or left his own house of business without seeing the door of that in which Miss Stanbury lived, – and he had never seen that door without a feeling of detestation for the owner of it. It would, perhaps, have been a more rational feeling on his part had he confined his hatred to the memory of his brother, by whose will Miss Stanbury had been enriched, and he had been, as he thought, impoverished. But there had been a contest, and litigation, and disputes, and contradictions, and a long course of those incidents in life which lead to rancour and ill blood, after the death of the former Brooke Burgess; and, as the result of all this, Miss Stanbury held the property and Barty Burgess held his hatred. He had never been ashamed of it, and had spoken his mind out to all who would hear him. And, to give Miss Stanbury her due, it must be admitted that she had hardly been behind him in the warmth of her expression, – of which old Barty was well aware. He hated, and knew that he was hated in return. And he knew, or thought that he knew, that his enemy was not a woman to relent because old age and weakness and the fear of death were coming on her. His enemy, with all her faults, was no coward. It could not be that now at the eleventh hour she should desire to reconcile him by any act of tardy justice, – nor did he wish to be reconciled at this, the eleventh hour. His hatred was a pleasant excitement to him. His abuse of Miss Stanbury was a chosen recreation. His unuttered daily curse, as he looked over to her door, was a relief to him. Nevertheless he would go. As Brooke had said, – no harm could come of his going. He would go, and at least listen to her proposition.

About seven in the evening his knock was heard at the door. Miss Stanbury was sitting in the small up-stairs parlour, dressed in her second best gown, and was prepared with considerable stiffness and state for the occasion. Dorothy was with her, but was desired in a quick voice to hurry away the moment the knock was heard, as though old Barty would have jumped from the hall door into the room at a bound. Dorothy collected herself with a little start, and went without a word. She had heard much of Barty Burgess, but had never spoken to him, and was subject to a feeling of great awe when she would remember that the grim old man of whom she had heard so much evil would soon be her uncle. According to arrangement, Mr Burgess was shown up-stairs by his nephew. Barty Burgess had been born in this very house, but had not been inside the walls of it for more than thirty years. He also was somewhat awed by the occasion, and followed his nephew without a word. Brooke was to remain at hand, so that he might be summoned should he be wanted; but it had been decided by Miss Stanbury that he should not be present at the interview. As soon as her visitor entered the room she rose in a stately way, and curtseyed, propping herself with one hand upon the table as she did so. She looked him full in the face meanwhile, and curtseying a second time asked him to seat himself in a chair which had been prepared for him. She did it all very well, and it may be surmised that she had rehearsed the little scene, perhaps more than once, when nobody was looking at her. He bowed, and walked round to the chair and seated himself; but finding that he was so placed that he could not see his neighbour's face, he moved his chair. He was not going to fight such a duel as this with the disadvantage of the sun in his eyes.

Hitherto there had hardly been a word spoken. Miss Stanbury had muttered something as she was curtseying, and Barty Burgess had made some return. Then she began: 'Mr Burgess,' she said, 'I am indebted to you for your complaisance in coming here at my request.' To this he bowed again. 'I should not have ventured thus to trouble you were it not that years are dealing more hardly with me than they are with you, and that I could not have ventured to discuss a matter of deep interest otherwise than in my own room.' It was her room now, certainly, by law; but Barty Burgess remembered it when it was his mother's room, and when she used to give them all their meals there, – now so many, many years ago! He bowed again, and said not a word. He knew well that she could sooner be brought to her point by his silence than by his speech.

She was a long time coming to her point. Before she could do so she was forced to allude to times long past, and to subjects which she found it very difficult to touch without saying that which would either belie herself, or seem to be severe upon him. Though she had prepared herself, she could hardly get the words spoken, and she was greatly impeded by the obstinacy of his silence. But at last her proposition was made to him. She told him that his nephew, Brooke, was about to be married to her niece, Dorothy; and that it was her intention to make Brooke her heir in the bulk of the property which she had received under the will of the late Mr Brooke Burgess. 'Indeed,' she said, 'all that I received at your brother's hands shall go back to your brother's family unimpaired.' He only bowed, and would not say a word. Then she went on to say that it had at first been a matter to her of deep regret that Brooke should have set his affections upon her niece, as there had been in her mind a strong desire that none of her own people should enjoy the reversion of the wealth, which she had always regarded as being hers only for the term of her life; but that she had found that the young people had been so much in earnest, and that her own feeling had been so near akin to a prejudice, that she had yielded. When this was said Barty smiled instead of bowing, and Miss Stanbury felt that there might be something worse even than his silence. His smile told her that he believed her to be lying. Nevertheless she went on. She was not fool enough to suppose that the whole nature of the man was to be changed by a few words from her. So she went on. The marriage was a thing fixed, and she was thinking of settlements, and had been talking to lawyers about a new will.

'I do not know that I can help you,' said Barty, finding that a longer pause than usual made some word from him absolutely necessary.

'I am going on to that, and I regret that my story should detain you so long, Mr Burgess.' And she did go on. She had, she said, made some saving out of her income. She was not going to trouble Mr Burgess with this matter, – only that she might explain to him that what she would at once give to the young couple, and what she would settle on Dorothy after her own death, would all come from such savings, and that such gifts and bequests would not dminish the family property. Barty again smiled as he heard this, and Miss Stanbury in her heart likened him to the devil in person. But still she went on. She was very desirous that Brooke Burgess should come and live at Exeter. His property would be in the town and the neighbourhood. It would be a seemly thing, – such was her words, – that he should occupy the house that had belonged to his grandfather and his great-grandfather; and then, moreover, – she acknowledged that she spoke selfishly, – she dreaded the idea of being left alone for the remainder of her own years. Her proposition at last was uttered. It was simply this, that Barty Burgess should give to his nephew, Brooke, his share in the bank.

'I am damned, if I do!' said Barty Burgess, rising up from his chair.

But before he had left the room he had agreed to consider the proposition. Miss Stanbury had of course known that any such suggestion coming from her without an adequate reason assigned, would have been mere idle wind. She was prepared with such adequate reason. If Mr Burgess could see his way to make the proposed transfer of his share of the bank business, she, Miss Stanbury, would hand over to him, for his life, a certain proportion of the Burgess property which lay in the city, the income of which would exceed that drawn by him from the business. Would he, at his time of life, take that for doing nothing which he now got for working hard? That was the meaning of it. And then, too, as far as the portion of the property went, – and it extended to the houses owned by Miss Stanbury on the bank side of the Close, – it would belong altogether to Barty Burgess for his life. 'It will simply be this, Mr Burgess; – that Brooke will be your heir, – as would be natural.'

'I don't know that it would be at all natural,' said he. 'I should prefer to choose my own heir.'

'No doubt, Mr Burgess, – in respect to your own property,' said Miss Stanbury.

At last he said that he would think of it, and consult his partner; and then he got up to take his leave. 'For myself,' said Miss Stanbury, 'I would wish that all animosities might be buried.'

'We can say that they are buried,' said the grim old man, – 'but nobody will believe us.'

'What matters, – if we could believe it ourselves?'

'But suppose we didn't. I don't believe that much good can come from talking of such things, Miss Stanbury. You and I have grown too old to swear a friendship. I will think of this thing, and if I find that it can be made to suit without much difficulty, I will perhaps entertain it.' Then the interview was over, and old Barty made his way down-stairs, and out of the house. He looked over to the tenements in the Close which were offered to him, every circumstance of each one of which he knew, and felt that he might do worse. Were he to leave the bank, he could not take his entire income with him, and it had been long said of him that he ought to leave it. The Croppers, who were his partners, – and whom he had never loved, – would be glad to welcome in his place one of the old family who would have money; and then the name would be perpetuated in Exeter, which, even to Barty Burgess, was something.

On that night the scheme was divulged to Dorothy, and she was in ecstasies. London had always sounded bleak and distant and terrible to her; and her heart had misgiven her at the idea of leaving her aunt. If only this thing might be arranged! When Brooke spoke the next morning of returning at once to his office, he was rebuked by both the ladies. What was the Ecclesiastical Commission Office to any of them, when matters of such importance were concerned? But Brooke would not be talked out of his prudence. He was very willing to be made a banker at Exeter, and to go to school again and learn banking business; but he would not throw up his occupation in London till he knew that there was another ready for him in the country. One day longer he spent in Exeter, and during that day he was more than once with his uncle. He saw also the Messrs Cropper, and was considerably chilled by the manner in which they at first seemed to entertain the proposition. Indeed, for a couple of hours he thought that the scheme must be abandoned. It was pointed out to him that Mr Barty Burgess's life would probably be short, and that he – Barty – had but a small part of the business at his disposal. But gradually a way to terms was seen, – not quite so simple as that which Miss Stanbury had suggested; and Brooke, when he left Exeter, did believe it possible that he, after all, might become the family representative in the old banking-house of the Burgesses.

'And how long will it take, Aunt Stanbury?' Dorothy asked.

'Don't you be impatient, my dear.'

'I am not the least impatient; but of course I want to tell mamma and Priscilla. It will be so nice to live here and not go up to London. Are we to stay here, – in this very house?'

'Have you not found out yet that Brooke will be likely to have an opinion of his own on such things?'

'But would you wish us to live here, aunt?'

'I hardly know, dear. I am a foolish old woman, and cannot say what I would wish. I cannot bear to be alone.'

'Of course we will stay with you.'

'And yet I should be jealous if I were not mistress of my own house.'

'Of course you will be mistress.'

'I believe, Dolly, that it would be better that I should die. I have come to feel that I can do more good by going out of the world than by remaining in it.' Dorothy hardly answered this in words, but sat close by her aunt, holding the old woman's hand and caressing it, and administering that love of which Miss Stanbury had enjoyed so little during her life and which had become so necessary to her.

The news about the bank arrangements, though kept of course as a great secret, soon became common in Exeter. It was known to be a good thing for the firm in general that Barty Burgess should be removed from his share of the management. He was old-fashioned, unpopular, and very stubborn; and he and a certain Mr Julius Cropper, who was the leading man among the Croppers, had not always been comfortable together. It was at first hinted that old Miss Stanbury had been softened by sudden twinges of conscience, and that she had confessed to some terrible crime in the way of forgery, perjury, or perhaps worse, and had relieved herself at last by making full restitution. But such a rumour as this did not last long or receive wide credence. When it was hinted to such old friends as Sir Peter Mancrudy and Mrs MacHugh, they laughed it to scorn, – and it did not exist even in the vague form of an undivulged mystery for above three days. Then it was asserted that old Barty had been found to have no real claim to any share in the bank, and that he was to be turned out at Miss Stanbury's instance; – that he was to be turned out, and that Brooke had been acknowledged to be the owner of the Burgess share of her business. Then came the fact that old Barty had been bought out, and that the future husband of Miss Stanbury's niece was to be the junior partner. A general feeling prevailed at last that there had been another great battle between Miss Stanbury and old Barty, and that the old maid had prevailed now as she had done in former days.

Before the end of July the papers were in the lawyer's hands, and all the terms had been fixed. Brooke came down again and again, to Dorothy's great delight, and displayed considerable firmness in the management of his own interest. If Fate intended to make him a banker in Exeter instead of a clerk in the Ecclesiastical Commission Office, he would be a banker after a respectable fashion. There was more than one little struggle between him and Mr Julius Cropper, which ended in accession of respect on the part of Mr Cropper for his new partner. Mr Cropper had thought that the establishment might best be known to the commercial world of the West of England as 'Croppers' Bank;' but Brooke had been very firm in asserting that if he was to have anything to do with it the old name should be maintained.

'It's to be "Cropper and Burgess,"' he said to Dorothy one afternoon. 'They fought hard for "Cropper, Cropper, and Burgess;" – but I wouldn't stand more than one Cropper.'

'Of course not,' said Dorothy, with something almost of scorn in her voice. By this time Dorothy had gone very deeply into banking business.

89

I Wouldn't do it, if I was You

Miss Stanbury at this time was known all through Exeter to be very much altered from the Miss Stanbury of old; – or even from the Miss Stanbury of two years since. The Miss Stanbury of old was a stalwart lady who would play her rubber of whist five nights a week, and could hold her own in conversation against the best woman in Exeter, – not to speak of her acknowledged superiority over every man in that city. Now she cared little for the glories of debate; and though she still liked her rubber, and could wake herself up to the old fire in the detection of a revoke or the claim for a second trick, her rubbers were few and far between, and she would leave her own house on an evening only when all circumstances were favourable, and with many precautions against wind and water. Some said that she was becoming old, and that she was going out like the snuff of a candle. But Sir Peter Mancrudy declared that she might live for the next fifteen years, if she would only think so herself. 'It was true,' Sir Peter said, 'that in the winter she had been ill, and that there had been danger as to her throat during the east winds of the spring; — but those dangers had passed away, and, if she would only exert herself, she might be almost as good a woman as ever she had been.' Sir Peter was not a man of many words, or given to talk frequently of his patients; but it was clearly Sir Peter's opinion that Miss Stanbury's mind was ill at ease. She had become discontented with life, and therefore it was that she cared no longer for the combat of tongues, and had become cold even towards the card-table. It was so in truth; and yet perhaps the lives of few men or women had been more innocent, and few had struggled harder to be just in their dealings and generous in their thoughts.

There was ever present to her mind an idea of failure and a fear lest she had been mistaken in her views throughout her life. No one had ever been more devoted to peculiar opinions, or more strong in the use of language for their expression; and she was so far true to herself, that she would never seem to retreat from the position she had taken. She would still scorn the new fangles of the world around her, and speak of the changes which she saw as all tending to evil. But, through it all, there was an idea present to herself that it could not be God's intention that things should really change for the worse, and that the fault must be in her, because she had been unable to move as others had moved. She would sit thinking of the circumstances of her own life and tell herself that with her everything had failed. She had loved, but had quarrelled with her lover; and her love had come to nothing — but barren wealth. She had fought for her wealth and had conquered; — and had become hard in the fight, and was conscious of her own hardness. In the early days of her riches and power she had taken her nephew by the hand, — and had thrown him away from her because he would not dress himself in her mirror. She had believed herself to be right, and would not, even now, tell herself that she had been wrong; but there were doubts, and qualms of conscience, and an uneasiness, — because her life had been a failure. Now she was seeking to appease her self-accusations by sacrificing everything for the happiness of her niece and her chosen heir; but as she went on with the work she felt that all would be in vain, unless she could sweep herself altogether from off the scene. She had told herself that if she could bring Brooke to Exeter, his prospects would be made infinitely brighter than they would be in London, and that she in her last days would not be left utterly alone. But as the prospect of her future life came nearer to her, she saw, or thought that she saw, that there was still failure before her. Young people would not want an old woman in the house with them; – even though the old woman would declare that she would be no more in the house than a tame cat. And she knew herself also too well to believe that she could make herself a tame cat in the home that had so long been subject to her dominion. Would it not be better that she should go away somewhere, – and die?

'If Mr Brooke is to come here,' Martha said to her one day, 'we ought to begin and make the changes, ma'am.'

'What changes? You are always wanting to make changes.'

'If they was never made till I wanted them they'd never be made, ma'am. But if there is to be a married couple there should be things proper. Anyways, ma'am, we ought to know; – oughtn't we?'

The truth of this statement was so evident that Miss Stanbury could not contradict it. But she had not even yet made up her mind. Ideas were running through her head which she knew to be very wild, but of which she could not divest herself. 'Martha,' she said, after a while, 'I think I shall go away from this myself.'

'Leave the house, ma'am?' said Martha, awestruck.

'There are other houses in the world, I suppose, in which an old woman can live and die.'

'There is houses, ma'am, of course.'

'And what is the difference between one and another?'

'I wouldn't do it, ma'am, if I was you. I wouldn't do it if it was ever so. Sure the house is big enough for Mr Brooke and Miss Dorothy along with you. I wouldn't go and make such change as that; – I wouldn't indeed, ma'am.' Martha spoke out almost with eloquence, so much expression was there in her face. Miss Stanbury said nothing more at the moment, beyond signifying her indisposition to make up her mind to anything at the present moment. Yes; – the house was big enough as far as rooms were concerned; but how often had she heard that an old woman must always be in the way, if attempting to live with a newly-married couple? If a mother-in-law be unendurable, how much more so one whose connection would be less near? She could keep her own house no doubt, and let them go elsewhere; but what then would come of her old dream, that Burgess, the new banker in the city, should live in the very house that had been inhabited by the Burgesses, the bankers of old? There was certainly only one way out of all these troubles, and that way would be that she should – go from them and be at rest.

Her will had now been drawn out and completed for the third or fourth time, and she had made no secret of its contents either with

Brooke or Dorothy. The whole estate she left to Brooke, including the houses which were to become his after his uncle's death; and in regard to the property she had made no further stipulation. 'I might have settled it on your children,' she said to him, 'but in doing so I should have settled it on hers. I don't know why an old woman should try to interfere with things after she has gone. I hope you won't squander it, Brooke.'

'I shall be a steady old man by that time,' he said.

'I hope you'll be steady at any rate. But there it is, and God must direct you in the use of it, if He will. It has been a burthen to me; but then I have been a solitary old woman.' Half of what she had saved she proposed to give Dorothy on her marriage, and for doing this arrangements had already been made. There were various other legacies, and the last she announced was one to her nephew, Hugh. 'I have left him a thousand pounds,' she said to Dorothy, – 'so that he may remember me kindly at last.' As to this, however, she exacted a pledge that no intimation of the legacy was to be made to Hugh. Then it was that Dorothy told her aunt that Hugh intended to marry Nora Rowley, one of the ladies who had been at the Clock House during the days in which her mother had lived in grandeur; and then it was also that Dorothy obtained leave to invite Hugh to her own wedding. 'I hope she will be happier than her sister,' Miss Stanbury said, when she heard of the intended marriage.'

'It wasn't Mrs Trevelyan's fault, you know, aunt.'

'I say nothing about anybody's fault; but this I do say, that it was a very great misfortune. I fought all that battle with your sister Priscilla, and I don't mean to fight it again, my dear. If Hugh marries the young lady, I hope she will be more happy than her sister. There can be no harm in saying that.'

Dorothy's letter to her brother shall be given, because it will inform the reader of all the arrangements as they were made up to that time, and will convey the Exeter news respecting various persons with whom our story is concerned.

The Close, July 20, 186 –

Dear Hugh,

The day for my marriage is now fixed, and I wish with all my heart that it was the same with you. Pray give my love to Nora. It seems so odd that, though she was living for a while with mamma at Nuncombe Putney, I never should have seen her yet. I am very glad that Brooke has seen her, and he declares that she is quite *magnificently beautiful*. Those are his own words.

We are to be married on the 10th of August, a Wednesday, and now comes my great news. Aunt Stanbury says that you are to come and stay in the house. She bids me tell you so with her love; and that you can have a room as long as you like. *Of course, you must come.* In the first place, you must because you are to give me away, and Brooke wouldn't have me if I wasn't given away properly; and then it will make me so happy that you and Aunt Stanbury should be friends again. You can stay as long as you like, but, of course, you must come the day before the wedding. We are to be married in the Cathedral, and there are to be two clergymen, but I don't yet know who they will be; – not Mr Gibson, certainly, as you were good enough to suggest.

Mr Gibson is married to Arabella French, and they have gone away somewhere into Cornwall. Camilla has come back, and I have seen her once. She looked ever so fierce, as though she intended to declare that she didn't mind what anybody may think. They say that she still protests that she never will speak to her sister again.

I was introduced to Mr Barty Burgess the other day. Brooke was here, and we met him in the Close. I hardly knew what he said to me, I was so frightened; but Brooke said that he meant to be civil, and that he is going to send me a present. I have got a quantity of things already, and yesterday Mrs MacHugh sent me such a beautiful cream-jug. If you'll come in time on the 9th, you shall see them all before they are put away.

Mamma and Priscilla are to be here, and they will come on the 9th also. Poor, dear mamma is, I know, terribly flurried about it, and so is Aunt Stanbury. It is so long since they have seen each other. I don't think Priscilla feels it the same way, because she is so brave. Do you remember when it was first proposed that I should come here? I am so glad I came, – because of Brooke. He will come on the 9th, quite early, and I do so hope you will come with him.

Yours most affectionately,
Dorothy Stanbury.

Give my best, best love to Nora.

90

Lady Rowley Conquered

When the Rowleys were back in London, and began to employ themselves on the terrible work of making ready for their journey to the Islands, Lady Rowley gradually gave way about Hugh Stanbury. She had become aware that Nora would not go back with them, – unless under an amount of pressure which she would find it impossible to use. And if Nora did not go out to the Islands, what was to become of her unless she married this man? Sir

Marmaduke, when all was explained to him, declared that a girl must do what her parents ordered her to do. 'Other girls live with their fathers and mothers, and so must she.' Lady Rowley endeavoured to explain that other girls lived with their fathers and mothers, because they found themselves in established homes from which they are not disposed to run away; but Nora's position was, as she alleged, very different. Nora's home had latterly been with her sister, and it was hardly to be expected that the parental authority should not find itself impaired by the interregnum which had taken place. Sir Marmaduke would not see the thing in the same light, and was disposed to treat his daughter with a high hand. If she would not do as she was bidden, she should no longer be daughter of his. In answer to this Lady Rowley could only repeat her conviction that Nora would not go out to the Mandarins; and that as for disinheriting her, casting her off, cursing her, and the rest, – she had no belief in such doings at all. 'On the stage they do such things as that,' she said; 'and, perhaps, they used to do it once in reality. But you know that it's out of the question now. Fancy your standing up and cursing at the dear girl, just as we are all starting from Southampton!' Sir Marmaduke knew as well as his wife that it would be impossible, and only muttered something about the 'dear girl' behaving herself with great impropriety.

They were all aware that Nora was not going to leave England, because no berth had been taken for her on board the ship, and because, while the other girls were preparing for their long voyage, no preparations were made for her. Of course she was not going. Sir Marmaduke would probably have given way altogether immediately on his return to London, had he not discussed the matter with his friend Colonel Osborne. It became, of course, his duty to make some inquiry as to the Stanbury family, and he knew that Osborne had visited Mrs Stanbury when he made his unfortunate pilgrimage to the porch of Cockchaffington Church. He told Osborne the whole story of Nora's engagement, telling also that other most heart-breaking tale of her conduct in regard to Mr Glascock, and asked the Colonel what he thought about the Stanburys. Now the Colonel did not hold the Stanburys in high esteem. He had met Hugh, as the reader may perhaps remember, and had had some intercourse with the young man, which had not been quite agreeable to him, on the platform of the railway station at Exeter. And he had also heard something of the ladies at Nuncombe Putney during his short sojourn at the house of Mrs Crocket. 'My belief is, they are beggars,' said Colonel Osborne.

'I suppose so,' said Sir Marmaduke, shaking his head.

'When I went over to call on Emily, – that time I was at Cockchaffington, you know, when Trevelyan made himself such a d – fool, – I found the mother and sister living in a decentish house enough; but it wasn't their house.'

'Not their own, you mean?'

'It was a place that Trevelyan had got this young man to take for Emily, and they had merely gone there to be with her. They had been living in a little bit of a cottage; a sort of a place that any – any ploughman would live in. Just that kind of cottage.'

'Goodness gracious!'

'And they've gone to another just like it; – so I'm told.'

'And can't he do anything better for them than that?' asked Sir Marmaduke.

'I know nothing about him. I have met him, you know. He used to be with Trevelyan; – that was when Nora took a fancy for him, of course. And I saw him once down in Devonshire, when I must say he behaved uncommonly badly, – doing all he could to foster Trevelyan's stupid jealousy.'

'He has changed his mind about that, I think.'

'Perhaps he has; but he behaved very badly then. Let him show up his income; – that, I take it, is the question in such a case as this. His father was a clergyman, and therefore I suppose he must be considered to be a gentleman. But has he means to support a wife, and keep up a house in London? If he has not, that is an end to it, I should say.'

But Sir Marmaduke could not see his way to any such end, and, although he still looked black upon Nora, and talked to his wife of his determination to stand no contumacy, and hinted at cursing, disinheriting, and the like, he began to perceive that Nora would have her own way. In his unhappiness he regretted this visit to England, and almost thought that the Mandarins were a pleasanter residence than London. He could do pretty much as he pleased there, and could live quietly, without the trouble which encountered him now on every side.

Nora, immediately on her return to London, had written a note to Hugh, simply telling him of her arrival and begging him to come and see her. 'Mamma,' she said, 'I must see him, and it would be nonsense to say that he must not come here. I have done what I have said I would do, and you ought not to make difficulties.' Lady Rowley declared that Sir Marmaduke would be very angry if Hugh were admitted without his express permission. 'I don't want to do anything in the dark,' continued Nora, 'but of course I must see him. I suppose it will be better that he should come to me than that

I should go to him ?' Lady Rowley quite understood the threat that was conveyed in this. It would be much better that Hugh should come to the hotel, and that he should be treated then as an accepted lover. She had come to that conclusion. But she was obliged to vacillate for awhile between her husband and her daughter. Hugh came of course, and Sir Marmaduke, by his wife's advice, kept out of the way. Lady Rowley, though she was at home, kept herself also out of the way, remaining above with her two other daughters. Nora thus achieved the glory and happiness of receiving her lover alone.

'My own true girl !' he said, speaking with his arms still round her waist.

'I am true enough ; but whether I am your own, – that is another question.'

'You mean to be ?'

'But papa doesn't mean it. Papa says that you are nobody, and that you haven't got an income ; and thinks that I had better go back and be an old maid at the Mandarins.'

'And what do you think yourself, Nora ?'

'What do I think ? As far as I can understand, young ladies are not allowed to think at all. They have to do what their papas tell them. That will do, Hugh. You can talk without taking hold of me.'

'It is such a time since I have had a hold of you, – as you call it.'

'It will be much longer before you can do so again, if I go back to the Islands with papa. I shall expect you to be true, you know ; and it will be ten years at the least before I can hope to be home again.'

'I don't think you mean to go, Nora.'

'But what am I to do ? That idea of yours of walking out to the next church and getting ourselves married sounds very nice and independent, but you know that it is not practicable.'

'On the other hand, I know it is.'

'It is not practicable for me, Hugh. Of all things in the world I don't want to be a Lydia.* I won't do anything that anybody shall ever say that your wife ought not to have done. Young women when they are married ought to have their papas' and mammas' consent. I have been thinking about it a great deal for the last month or two, and I have made up my mind to that.'

'What is it all to come to, then ?'

'I mean to get papa's consent. That is what it is to come to.'

'And if he is obstinate ?'

'I shall coax him round at last. When the time for going comes, he'll yield then.'

'But you will not go with them?' As he asked this he came to her and tried again to take her by the waist; but she retreated from him, and got herself clear from his arm. 'If you are afraid of me, I shall know that you think if possible that we may be parted.'

'I am not a bit afraid of you, Hugh.'

'Nora, I think you ought to tell me something definitely.'

'I think I have been definite enough, sir. You may be sure of this, however; – I will not go back to the Islands.'

'Give me your hand on that.'

'There is my hand. But, remember; – I had told you just as much before. I don't mean to go back. I mean to stay here. I mean; – but I do not think I will tell you all the things I mean to do.'

'You mean to be my wife?'

'Certainly; – some day, when the difficulty about the chairs and tables can settle itself. The real question now is, – what am I to do with myself when papa and mamma are gone?'

'Become Mrs H. Stanbury at once. Chairs and tables! You shall have chairs and tables as many as you want. You won't be too proud to live in lodgings for a few months?'

'There must be preliminaries, Hugh, – even for lodgings, though they may be very slender. Papa goes in less than three weeks now, and mamma has got something else to think of than my marriage garments. And then there are all manner of difficulties, money difficulties and others, out of which I don't see my way yet.' Hugh began to asseverate that it was his business to help her through all money difficulties as well as others; but she soon stopped his eloquence. 'It will be by-and-by, Hugh, and I hope you'll support the burden like a man; but just at present there is a hitch. I shouldn't have come over at all; – I should have stayed with Emily in Italy, had I not thought that I was bound to see you.'

'My own darling!'

'When papa goes, I think that I had better go back to her.'

'I'll take you!' said Hugh, picturing to himself all the pleasures of such a tour together over the Alps.

'No you won't, because that would be improper. When we travel together we must go Darby and Joan fashion, as man and wife. I think I had better go back to Emily, because her position there is so terrible. There must come some end to it, I suppose soon. He will be better, or he will become so bad that, – that medical interference will be unavoidable. But I do not like that she should be alone. She gave me a home when she had one; – and I must always remember that I met you there.' After this there was of course another attempt with Hugh's right arm, which on this occasion was not altogether unsuccessful. And then she told him of her friendship for Mr Glascock's wife, and of her intention at some future time to visit them at Monkhams.

'And see all the glories that might have been your own,' he said.

'And think of the young man who has robbed me of them all! And you are to go there too, so that you may see what you have done. There was a time, Hugh, when I was very nearly pleasing all my friends and showing myself to be a young lady of high taste and noble fortune, – and an obedient, good girl.'

'And why didn't you?'

'I thought I would wait just a little longer. Because, – because, – because – . Oh, Hugh, how cross you were to me afterwards when you came down to Nuncombe and would hardly speak to me!'

'And why didn't I speak to you?'

'I don't know. Because you were cross, and surly, and thinking of nothing but your tobacco, I believe. Do you remember how we walked to Niddon, and you hadn't a word for anybody?'

'I remember I wanted you to go down to the river with me, and you wouldn't go.'

'You asked me only once, and I did so long to go with you. Do you remember the rocks in the river? I remember the place as though I saw it now; and how I longed to jump from one stone to another. Hugh, if we are ever married, you must take me there, and let me jump on those stones.'

'You pretended that you could not think of wetting your feet.'

'Of course I pretended, – because you were so cross, and so cold. Oh, dear! I wonder whether you will ever know it all.'

'Don't I know it all now?'

'I suppose you do, nearly. There is mighty little of a secret in it, and it is the same thing that is going on always. Only it seems so strange to me that I should ever have loved any one so dearly, – and that for next to no reason at all. You never made yourself very charming that I know of; – did you?'

'I did my best. It wasn't much, I dare say.'

'You did nothing, sir – except just let me fall in love with you. And you were not quite sure that you would let me do that.'

'Nora, I don't think you do understand.'

'I do; – perfectly. Why were you cross with me, instead of saying one nice word when you were down at Nuncombe? I do understand.'

'Why was it?'

'Because you did not think well enough of me to believe that I would give myself to a man who had no fortune of his own. I know it now, and I knew it then; and therefore I wouldn't dabble in the river with you. But it's all over now, and we'll go and get wet together like dear little children, and Priscilla shall scold us when we come back.'

They were alone in the sitting-room for more than an hour, and Lady Rowley was patient up-stairs as mothers will be patient in such emergencies. Sophie and Lucy had gone out and left her; and there she remained telling herself, as the weary minutes went by, that as the thing was to be, it was well that the young people should be together. Hugh Stanbury could never be to her what Mr Glascock would have been, – a son-in-law to sit and think about, and dream of, and be proud of, – whose existence as her son-in-law would in itself have been a happiness to her out in her banishment at the other side of the world; but nevertheless it was natural to her, as a soft-hearted loving mother with many daughters, that any son-in-law should be dear to her. Now that she had gradually brought herself round to believe in Nora's marriage, she was disposed to make the best of Hugh, to remember that he was certainly a clever man, that he was an honest fellow, and that she had heard of him as a good son and a kind brother, and that he had behaved well in reference to her Emily and Trevelyan. She was quite willing now that Hugh should be happy, and she sat there thinking that the time was very long, but still waiting patiently till she should be summoned. 'You must let me go for mamma for a moment,' Nora said. 'I want you to see her and make yourself a good boy before her. If you are ever to be her son-in-law, you ought to be in her good graces.' Hugh declared that he would do his best, and Nora fetched her mother.

Stanbury found some difficulty in making himself a 'good boy' in Lady Rowley's presence; and Lady Rowley herself, for some time, felt very strongly the awkwardness of the meeting. She had never formally recognised the young man as her daughter's accepted suitor, and was not yet justified in doing so by any permission from Sir Marmaduke; but, as the young people had been for the last hour or two alone together, with her connivance and sanction, it was indispensable that she should in some way signify her parental adherence to the arrangement. Nora began by talking about Emily, and Trevelyan's condition and mode of living were discussed. Then Lady Rowley said something about their coming journey, and Hugh, with a lucky blunder, spoke of Nora's intended return to Italy. 'We don't know how that may be,' said Lady Rowley. 'Her papa still wishes her to go back with us.'

'Mamma, you know that this is impossible,' said Nora.

'Not impossible, my love.'

'But she will not go back,' said Hugh. 'Lady Rowley, you would not propose to separate us by such a distance as that?'

'It is Sir Marmaduke that you must ask.'

'Mamma, mamma!' exclaimed Nora, rushing to her mother's side, 'it is not papa that we must ask, – not now. We want you to be our friend. Don't we, Hugh? And, mamma, if you will really be our friend, of course, papa will come round.'

'My dear Nora!'

'You know he will, mamma; and you know that you mean to be good and kind to us. Of course I can't go back to the Islands with you. How could I go so far and leave him behind? He might have half-a-dozen wives before I could get back to him –'

'If you have not more trust in him than that – !'

'Long engagements are awful bores,' said Hugh, finding it to be necessary that he also should press forward his argument.

'I can trust him as far as I can see him,' said Nora, 'and therefore I do not want to lose sight of him altogether.'

Lady Rowley of course gave way and embraced her accepted son-in-law. After all it might have been worse. He saw his way clearly, he said, to making six hundred a year, and did not at all doubt that before long he would do better than that. He proposed that they should be married some time in the autumn, but was willing to acknowledge that much must depend on the position of Trevelyan and his wife. He would hold himself ready at any moment, he said, to start to Italy, and would do all that could be done by a brother. Then Lady Rowley gave him her blessing, and kissed him again, – and Nora kissed him too, and hung upon him, and did not push him away at all when his arm crept round her waist. And that feeling came upon him which must surely be acknowledged by all engaged young men when they first find themselves encouraged by mammas in the taking of liberties which they have hitherto regarded as mysteries to be hidden, especially from maternal eyes, – that feeling of being a fine fat calf decked out with ribbons for a sacrifice.

91

Four O'Clock in the Morning

Another week went by and Sir Marmaduke had even yet not surrendered. He quite understood that Nora was not to go back to the Islands. And had visited Mr and Mrs Outhouse at St Diddulph's in order to secure a home for her there, if it might be possible. Mr Outhouse did not refuse, but gave the permission in such a fashion as to make it almost equal to a refusal. 'He was,' he said, 'much attached to his niece Nora, but he had heard that there was a love affair.' Sir Marmaduke, of course, could not deny the love affair. There was certainly a love affair of which he did not personally approve, as the gentleman had no fixed income and as far as he could understand no fixed profession. 'Such a love affair,' thought Mr Outhouse, 'was a sort of thing that he didn't know how to manage at all. If Nora came to him, was the young man to visit at the house, or was he not?' Then Mrs Outhouse said something as to the necessity of an anti-Stanbury pledge on Nora's part, and Sir Marmaduke found that that scheme must be abandoned. Mrs Trevelyan had written from Florence more than once or twice, and in her last letter had said that she would prefer not to have Nora with her. She was at that time living in lodgings at Siena and had her boy there also. She saw her husband every other day; but nevertheless, – according to her statements, – her visits to Casalunga were made in opposition to his wishes. He had even expressed a desire that she should leave Siena and return to England. He had once gone so far as to say that if she would do so, he would follow her. But she clearly did not believe him, and in all her letters spoke of him as one whom she could not regard as being under the guidance of reason. She had taken her child with her once or twice to the house, and on the first occasion Trevelyan had made much of his son, had wept over him, and professed that in losing him he had lost his only treasure; but after that he had not noticed the boy, and latterly she had gone alone. She thought that perhaps her visits cheered him, breaking the intensity of his solitude; but he never expressed himself gratified by them, never asked her to remain at the house, never returned with her into Siena, and continually spoke of her return to England as a step which must be taken soon, – and the sooner the better. He intended to follow her, he said; and she explained very fully how manifest was his wish that she should go, by the temptation to do so which he thought that he held out by this promise. He had spoken, on every occasion of her presence with him, of Sir Marmaduke's attempt to prove him to be a madman; but declared that he was afraid of no one in England, and would face all the lawyers in Chancery Lane and all the doctors in Savile Row. Nevertheless, so said Mrs Trevelyan, he would undoubtedly remain at Casalunga till after Sir Marmaduke should have sailed. He was not so mad but that he knew that no one else would be so keen to take steps against him as would Sir Marmaduke. As for his health, her account of him was very sad. He seemed, she said, to be withering away. His hand was mere skin and bone. His hair and beard so covered his thin long cheeks, that there was nothing left of his face but his bright, large, melancholy eyes. His legs had become so frail and weak that they would hardly bear his weight as he walked; and his clothes, though he had taken a fancy to throw aside all that he had brought with him from England, hung so loose about him that they seemed as though they would fall from him. Once she had ventured to send out to him from Siena a doctor to whom she had been recommended in Florence; but he had taken the visit in very bad part, had told the gentleman that he had no need for any medical services, and had been furious with her, because of her offence in having sent such a visitor. He had told her that if ever she ventured to take such a liberty again, he would demand the child back, and refuse her permission inside the gates of Casalunga. 'Don't come, at any rate, till I send for you,' Mrs Trevelyan said in her last letter to her sister. 'Your being here would do no good, and would, I think, make him feel that he was being watched. My hope is, at last, to get him to return with me. If you were here, I think this would be less likely. And then why should you be mixed up with such unutterable sadness and distress more than is essentially necessary? My health stands wonderfully well, though the heat here is very great. It is cooler at Casalunga than in the town, – of which I am glad for his sake. He perspires so profusely that it seems to me he cannot stand the waste much longer. I know he will not go to England as long as papa is there; – but I hope that he may be induced to do so by slow stages as soon as he knows that papa has gone. Mind you send me a newspaper, so that he may see it stated in print that papa has sailed.'

It followed as one consequence of these letters from Florence that Nora was debarred from the Italian scheme as a mode of passing her time till some house should be open for her reception. She had suggested to Hugh that she might go for a few weeks to Nuncombe Putney, but he had explained to her the nature of his mother's cottage, and had told her that there was no hole there in which she could lay her head. 'There never was such a forlorn young woman,' she said. 'When papa goes I shall literally be without shelter.' There had come a letter from Mrs Glascock, – at least it was signed Caroline Glascock, though another name might have been used, – dated from Milan, saying that they were hurrying back to Naples even at that season of the year, because Lord Peterborough was dead. 'And she is Lady Peterborough!' said Lady Rowley, unable to repress the expression of the old regrets. 'Of course she is Lady Peterborough, mamma; what else should she be? – though she does not so sign herself.' 'We think,' said the American peeress, 'that we shall be at Monkhams before the end of August, and Charles says that you are to come just the same. There will be nobody else there, of course, because of Lord Peterborough's death.' 'I saw it in the paper,' said Sir Marmaduke, 'and quite forgot to mention it.'

That same evening there was a long family discussion about Nora's prospects. They were all together in the gloomy sitting-room at Gregg's Hotel, and Sir Marmaduke had not yielded. The ladies had begun to feel that it would be well not to press him to yield. Practically he had yielded. There was now no question of cursing and of so-called disinheritance. Nora was to remain in England, of course with the intention of being married to Hugh Stanbury; and the difficulty consisted in the need of an immediate home for her. It wanted now but twelve days to that on which the family were to sail from Southampton, and nothing had been settled. 'If papa will allow me something ever so small, and will trust me, I will live alone in lodgings,' said Nora.

'It is the maddest thing I ever heard,' said Sir Marmaduke.

'Who would take care of you, Nora?' asked Lady Rowley.

'And who would walk about with you?' said Lucy.

'I don't see how it would be possible to live alone like that,' said Sophie.'

'Nobody would take care of me, and nobody would walk about with me, and I could live alone very well,' said Nora. 'I don't see why a young woman is to be supposed to be so absolutely helpless as all that comes to. Of course it won't be very nice, – but it need not be for long.'

'Why not for long?' asked Sir Marmaduke.

'Not for very long,' said Nora.

'It does not seem to me,' said Sir Marmaduke, after a considerable pause, 'that this gentleman himself is so particularly anxious for the match. I have heard no day named, and no rational proposition made.'

'Papa, that is unfair, most unfair, – and ungenerous.'

'Nora,' said her mother, 'do not speak in that way to your father.'

'Mamma, it is unfair. Papa accuses Mr Stanbury of being, – being lukewarm and untrue, – of not being in earnest.'

'I would rather that he were not in earnest,' said Sir Marmaduke.

'Mr Stanbury is ready at any time,' continued Nora. 'He would have the banns at once read, and marry me in three weeks, – if I would let him.'

'Good gracious, Nora !' exclaimed Lady Rowley.

'But I have refused to name any day, or to make any arrangement, because I did not wish to do so before papa had given his consent. That is why things are in this way. If papa will but let me take a room till I can go to Monkhams, I will have everything arranged from there. You can trust Mr Glascock for that, and you can trust her.'

'I suppose your papa will make you some allowance,' said Lady Rowley.

'She is entitled to nothing, as she has refused to go to her proper home,' said Sir Marmaduke.

The conversation, which had now become very disagreeable, was not allowed to go any further. And it was well that it should be interrupted. They all knew that Sir Marmaduke must be brought round by degrees, and that both Nora and Lady Rowley had gone as far as was prudent at present. But all trouble on this head was suddenly ended for this evening by the entrance of the waiter with a telegram. It was addressed to Lady Rowley, and she opened it with trembling hands, – as ladies always do open telegrams. It was from Emily Trevelyan. 'Louis is much worse. Let somebody come to me. Hugh Stanbury would be the best.'

In a few minutes they were so much disturbed that no one quite knew what should be done at once. Lady Rowley began by declaring that she would go herself. Sir Marmaduke of course pointed out that this was impossible, and suggested that he would send a lawyer. Nora professed herself ready to start immediately on the journey, but was stopped by a proposition from her sister Lucy that in that case Hugh Stanbury would of course go with her. Lady Rowley asked whether Hugh would go, and Nora asserted that he would go immediately as a matter of course. She was sure he would go, let the peopole at the D. R. say what they might. According to her there was always somebody at the call of the editor of the D. R. to do the work of anybody else, when anybody else wanted to go away. Sir Marmaduke shook his head, and was very uneasy. He still thought that a lawyer would be best, feeling, no doubt, that if Stanbury's services were used on such an occasion, there must be an end of all opposition to the marriage. But before half-an-hour was over Stanbury was sent for. The boots of the hotel went off in a cab to the office of the D. R. with a note from Lady Rowley. 'Dear Mr Stanbury, – We have had a telegram from Emily, and want to

see you, *at once*. Please come. We shall sit up and wait for you till
you do come. – E. R.'

It was very distressing to them because, let the result be what it
might, it was all but impossible that Mrs Trevelyan should be with
them before they had sailed, and it was quite out of the question
that they should now postpone their journey. Were Stanbury to
start by the morning train on the following day, he could not reach
Siena till the afternoon of the fourth day; and let the result be what
it might when he arrived there, it would be out of the question that
Emily Trevelyan should come back quite at once, or that she should
travel at the same speed. Of course they might hear again by
telegram, and also by letter; but they could not see her, or have any
hand in her plans. 'If anything were to happen, she might have
come with us,' said Lady Rowley.

. 'It is out of the question,' said Sir Marmaduke gloomily. 'I could
not give up the places I have taken.'

'A few days more would have done it.'

'I don't suppose she would wish to go,' said Nora. 'Of course she
would not take Louey there. Why should she? And then I don't
suppose he is so ill as that.

'There is no saying,' said Sir Marmaduke. It was very evident
that, whatever might be Sir Marmaduke's opinion, he had no
strongly-developed wish for his son-in-law's recovery.

They all sat up waiting for Hugh Stanbury till eleven, twelve,
one, and two o'clock at night. The 'boots' had returned saying that
Mr Stanbury had not been at the office of the newspaper, but that,
according to information received, he certainly would be there that
night. No other address had been given to the man, and the note
had therefore of necessity been left at the office. Sir Marmaduke
became very fretful, and was evidently desirous of being liberated
from his night watch. But he could not go himself, and showed his
impatience by endeavouring to send the others away. Lady Rowley
replied for herself that she should certainly remain in her corner on
the sofa all night, if it were necessary; and as she slept very soundly
in her corner, her comfort was not much impaired. Nora was
pertinacious in refusing to go to bed. 'I should only go to my own
room, papa, and remain there,' she said. 'Of course I must speak to
him before he goes.' Sophie and Lucy considered that they had as
much right to sit up as Nora, and submitted to be called geese and
idiots by their father.

Sir Marmaduke had arisen with a snort from a short slumber,
and had just sworn that he and everybody else should go to bed,
when there came a ring at the front-door bell. The trusty boots had

also remained up, and in two minutes Hugh Stanbury was in the room. He had to make his excuses before anything else could be said. When he reached the D. R. Office between ten and eleven, it was absolutely incumbent on him to write a leading article before he left it. He had been in the reporter's gallery of the House all the evening, and he had come away laden with his article. 'It was certainly better that we should remain up, than that the whole town should be disappointed,' said Sir Marmaduke, with something of a sneer.

'It is so very, very good of you to come,' said Nora.

'Indeed it is,' said Lady Rowley; 'but we were quite sure you would come.' Having kissed and blessed him as her son-in-law, Lady Rowley was now prepared to love him almost as well as though he had been Lord Peterborough.

'Perhaps, Mr Stanbury, we had better show you this telegram,' said Sir Marmaduke, who had been standing with the scrap of paper in his hand since the ring of the bell had been heard. Hugh took the message and read it. 'I do not know what should have made my daughter mention your name,' continued Sir Marmaduke; – 'but as she has done so, and as perhaps the unfortunate invalid himself may have alluded to you, we thought it best to send for you.'

'No doubt it was best, Sir Marmaduke.'

'We are so situated that I cannot go. It is absolutely necessary that we should leave town for Southampton on Friday week. The ship sails on Saturday.'

'I will go as a matter of course,' said Hugh. 'I will start at once, – at any time. To tell the truth, when I got Lady Rowley's note, I thought that it was to be so. Trevelyan and I were very intimate at one time, and it may be that he will receive me without displeasure.'

There was much to be discussed, and considerable difficulty in the discussion. This was enhanced, too, by the feeling in the minds of all of them that Hugh and Sir Marmaduke would not meet again, – probably for many years. Were they to part now on terms of close affection, or were they to part almost as strangers? Had Lucy and Sophie not persistently remained up, Nora would have faced the difficulty, and taken the bull by the horns, and asked her father to sanction her engagement in the presence of her lover. But she could not do it before so many persons, even though the persons were her own nearest relatives. And then there arose another embarrassment. Sir Marmaduke, who had taught himself to believe that Stanbury was so poor as hardly to have the price of a dinner in his pocket, – although, in fact, our friend Hugh was probably the richer man of the two, – said something about defraying the cost of the journey. 'It is taken altogether on our behalf,' said Sir Marmaduke. Hugh became red in the face, looked angry, and muttered a word or two about Trevelyan being the oldest friend he had in the world, – 'even if there were nothing else.' Sir Marmaduke felt ashamed of himself, – without cause, indeed, for the offer was natural, – said nothing further about it; but appeared to be more stiff and ungainly than ever.

The Bradshaw was had out and consulted, and nearly half an hour was spent in poring over that wondrous volume. It is the fashion to abuse Bradshaw, – we speak now especially of Bradshaw the Continental, – because all the minutest details of the autumn tour, just as the tourist thinks that it may be made, cannot be made patent to him at once without close research amidst crowded figures. After much experience we make bold to say that Bradshaw knows more, and will divulge more in a quarter of an hour, of the properest mode of getting from any city in Europe to any other city more than fifty miles distant, than can be learned in that first city in a single morning with the aid of a courier, a carriage, a pair of horses, and all the temper that any ordinary tourist possesses. The Bradshaw was had out, and it was at last discovered that nothing could be gained in the journey from London to Siena by starting in the morning. Intending as he did to travel through without sleeping on the road, Stanbury could not do better than leave London by the night mail train, and this he determined to do. But when that was arranged, then came the nature of his commission. What was he to do? No commission could be given to him. A telegram should be sent to Emily the next morning to say that he was coming; and then he would hurry on and take his orders from her.

They were all in doubt, terribly in doubt, whether the aggravated malady of which the telegram spoke was malady of the mind or of the body. If of the former nature then the difficulty might be very great indeed; and it would be highly expedient that Stanbury should have some one in Italy to assist him. It was Nora who suggested that he should carry a letter of introduction to Mr Spalding, and it was she who wrote it. Sir Marmaduke had not foregathered very closely with the English Minister, and nothing was said of assistance that should be peculiarly British. Then, at last, about three or four in the morning came the moment for parting. Sir Marmaduke had suggested that Stanbury should dine with them on the next day before he started, but Hugh had declined, alleging that as the day was at his command it must be devoted to the work of providing for his absence. In truth, Sir Marmaduke had given the invitation with a surly voice, and Hugh, though he was ready to go to the North Pole for any others of the family, was at the moment in an aggressive mood of mind towards Sir Marmaduke.

'I will send a message directly I get there,' he said, holding Lady Rowley by the hand, 'and will write fully, – to you, – immediately.'

'God bless you, my dear friend!' said Lady Rowley, crying.

'Good night, Sir Marmaduke,' said Hugh.

'Good night, Mr Stanbury.'

Then he gave a hand to the two girls, each of whom, as she took it, sobbed, and looked away from Nora. Nora was standing away from them, by herself, and away from the door, holding on to her chair, and with her hands clasped together. She had prepared nothing, – not a word, or an attitude, not a thought, for this farewell. But she had felt that it was coming, and had known that she must trust to him for a cue for her own demeanour. If he could say adieu with a quiet voice, and simply with a touch of the hand, then would she do the same, – and endeavour to think no worse of him. Nor had he prepared anything; but when the moment came he could not leave her after that fashion. He stood a moment hesitating, not approaching her, and merely called her by her name, – 'Nora!' For a moment she was still; for a moment she held by her chair; and then she rushed into his arms. He did not much care for her father now, but kissed her hair and her forehead, and held her closely to his bosom. 'My own, own Nora!'

It was necessary that Sir Marmaduke should say something. There was at first a little scene between all the women, during which he arranged his deportment. 'Mr Stanbury,' he said, 'let it be so. I could wish for my child's sake, and also for your own, that your means of living were less precarious.' Hugh accepted this simply as an authority for another embrace, and then he allowed them all to go to bed.

92

Trevelyan Discourses on Life

Stanbury made his journey without pause or hindrance till he reached Florence, and as the train for Siena made it necessary that he should remain there for four or five hours, he went to an inn, and dressed and washed himself, and had a meal, and was then driven to Mr Spalding's house. He found the American Minister at home, and was received with cordiality; but Mr Spalding could tell him little or nothing about Trevelyan. They went up to Mrs Spalding's room, and Hugh was told by her that she had seen Mrs Trevelyan once since her niece's marriage, and that then she had represented her husband as being very feeble. Hugh, in the midst of his troubles, was amused by a second and a third, perhaps by a fourth, reference to 'Lady Peterborough.' Mrs Spalding's latest tidings as to the Trevelyans had been received through 'Lady Peterborough' from Nora Rowley. 'Lady Peterborough' was at the present moment at Naples, but was expected to pass north through Florence in a day or two. They, the Spaldings themselves, were kept in Florence in this very hot weather by this circumstance. They were going up to the Tyrolese mountains for a few weeks as soon as 'Lady Peterborough' should have left them for England. 'Lady Peterborough' would have been so happy to make Mr Stanbury's acquaintance, and to have heard something direct from her friend Nora. Then Mrs Spalding smiled archly, showing thereby that she knew all about Hugh Stanbury and his relation to Nora Rowley. From all which, and in accordance with the teaching which we got, – alas, now many years ago, – from a great master on the subject,* we must conclude that poor, dear Mrs Spalding was a snob. Nevertheless, with all deference to the memory of that great master, we think that Mrs Spalding's allusions to the success in life achieved by her niece were natural and altogether pardonable; and that reticence on the subject, – a calculated determination to abstain from mentioning a triumph which must have been very dear to her, – would have betrayed on the whole a condition of mind lower than that which she exhibited. While rank, wealth, and money are held to be good things by all around us, let them be acknowledged as such. It is natural that a mother should be as proud when her daughter marries an Earl's heir as when her son becomes Senior Wrangler; and when we meet a lady in Mrs Spalding's condition who purposely abstains from mentioning the name of her titled daughter, we shall be disposed to judge harshly of the secret workings of that lady's thoughts on the subject. We prefer the exhibition, which we feel to be natural. Mr Spalding got our friend by the button-hole, and was making him a speech on the perilous condition in which Mrs Trevelyan was placed; but Stanbury, urged by the circumstances of his position, pulled out his watch, pleaded the hour, and escaped.

He found Mrs Trevelyan waiting for him at the station at Siena. He would hardly have known her, – not from any alteration that was physically personal to herself, not that she had become older in face, or thin, or grey, or sickly, – but that the trouble of her life had robbed her for the time of that brightness of apparel, of that pride of feminine gear, of that sheen of high-bred womanly bearing with which our wives and daughters are so careful to invest themselves. She knew herself to be a wretched woman, whose work in life now was to watch over a poor prostrate wretch, and who had thrown behind her all ideas of grace and beauty. It was not quickly that this condition had come upon her. She had been unhappy at Nuncombe Putney; but unhappiness had not then told upon the outward woman. She had been more wretched still at St Diddulph's, and all the outward circumstances of life in her uncle's parsonage had been very wearisome to her; but she had striven against it all, and the sheen and outward brightness had still been there. After that her child had been taken from her, and the days which she had passed in Manchester Street had been very grievous; – but even yet she had not given way. It was not till her child had been brought back to her, and she had seen the life which her husband was living, and that her anger, – hot anger, – had been changed to pity, and that with pity love had returned, it was not till this point had come in her sad life that her dress became always black and sombre, that a veil habitually covered her face, that a bonnet took the place of the jaunty hat that she had worn, and that the prettinesses of her life were lain aside. 'It is very good of you to come,' she said; 'very good. I hardly knew what to do. I was so wretched. On the day that I sent he was so bad that I was obliged to do something.' Stanbury, of course, inquired after Trevelyan's health, as they were being driven up to Mrs Trevelyan's lodgings. On the day on which she had sent the telegram her husband had again been furiously angry with her. She had interfered, or had endeavoured to interfere, in some arrangements as to his health and comfort, and he had turned upon her with an order that the child should be at once sent back to him, and that she should immediately quit Siena. 'When I said that Louey could not be sent, – and who could send a child into such keeping, – he told me that I was the basest liar that ever broke a promise, and the vilest traitor that had ever returned evil for good. I was never to come to him again, – never; and the gate of the house would be closed against me if I appeared there.'

On the next day she had gone again, however, and had seen him, and had visited him on every day since. Nothing further had been said about the child, and he had now become almost too weak for violent anger. 'I told him you were coming, and though he would not say so, I think he is glad of it. He expects you to-morrow.'

'I will go this evening, if he will let me.'

'Not to-night. I think he goes to bed almost as the sun sets. I am never there myself after four or five in the afternoon. I told him that you should be there to-morrow, – alone. I have hired a little carriage, and you can take it. He said specially that I was not to come with you. Papa goes certainly on next Saturday?' It was a Saturday now, – this day on which Stanbury had arrived at Siena.

'He leaves town on Friday.'

'You must make him believe that. Do not tell him suddenly, but bring it in by degrees. He thinks that I am deceiving him. He would go back if he knew that papa were gone.'

They spent a long evening together, and Stanbury learned all that Mrs Trevelyan could tell him of her husband's state. There was no doubt, she said, that his reason was affected; but she thought the state of him mind was diseased in a ratio the reverse of that of his body, and that when he was weakest in health, then were his ideas the most clear and rational. He never now mentioned Colonel Osborne's name, but would refer to the affairs of the last two years as though they had been governed by an inexorable Fate which had utterly destroyed his happiness without any fault on his part. 'You may be sure,' she said, 'that I never accuse him. Even when he says terrible things of me, – which he does, – I never excuse myself. I do not think I should answer a word, if he called me the vilest thing on earth.' Before they parted for the night many questions were of course asked about Nora, and Hugh described the condition in which he and she stood to each other. 'Papa has consented, then?'

'Yes, – at four o'clock in the morning, – just as I was leaving them.'

'And when is it to be?'

'Nothing has been settled, and I do not as yet know where she will go to when they leave London. I think she will visit Monkhams when the Glascock people return to England.'

'What an episode in life, – to go and see the place, when it might all now have been hers!'

'I suppose I ought to feel dreadfully ashamed of myself for having marred such promotion,' said Hugh.

'Nora is such a singular girl; – so firm, so headstrong, so good, and so self-reliant that she will do as well with a poor man as she would have done with a rich. Shall I confess to you that I did wish that she should accept Mr Glascock, and that I pressed it on her very strongly? You will not be angry with me?'

'I am only the more proud of her; – and of myself.'

'When she was told of all that he had to give in the way of wealth and rank, she took the bit between her teeth and would not be turned an inch. Of course she was in love.'

'I hope she may never regret it; – that is all.'

'She must change her nature first. Everything she sees at Monkhams will make her stronger in her choice. With all her girlish ways, she is like a rock; – nothing can move her.'

Early on the next morning Hugh started alone for Casalunga, having first, however, seen Mrs Trevelyan. He took out with him certain little things for the sick man's table; – as to which, however, he was cautioned to say not a word to the sick man himself. And it was arranged that he should endeavour to fix a day for Trevelyan's return to England. That was to be the one object in view. 'If we could get him to England,' she said, 'he and I would, at any rate, be together, and gradually he would be taught to submit himself to advice.' Before ten in the morning, Stanbury was walking up the hill to the house, and wondering at the dreary, hot, hopeless desolation of the spot. It seemed to him that no one could live alone in such a place, in such weather, without being driven to madness. The soil was parched and dusty, as though no drop of rain had fallen there for months. The lizards, glancing in and out of the broken walls, added to the appearance of heat. The vegetation itself was of a faded yellowish green, as though the glare of the sun had taken the fresh colour our of it. There was a noise of grasshoppers and a hum of flies in the air, hardly audible, but all giving evidence of the heat. Not a human voice was to be heard, nor the sound of a human foot, and there was no shelter; but the sun blazed down full upon everything. He took off his hat, and rubbed his head with his handkerchief as he struck the door with his stick. Oh God, to what misery had a little folly brought two human beings who had had every blessing that the world could give within their reach !

In a few minutes he was conducted through the house, and found Trevelyan seated in a chair under the verandah which looked down upon the olive trees. He did not even get up from his seat, but put out his left hand and welcomed his old friend. 'Stanbury,' he said, 'I am glad to see you, – for auld lang syne's sake. When I found out this retreat, I did not mean to have friends round me here. I wanted to try what solitude was; – and, by heaven, I've tried it !' He was dressed in a bright Italian dressing-gown, or woollen paletot, – Italian, as having been bought in Italy, though, doubtless, it had come from France, – and on his feet he had green worked slippers, and on his head a brocaded cap. He had made but little other preparation for his friend in the way of dressing. His long dishevelled hair came down over his neck, and his beard covered his face.

Beneath his dressing-gown he had on a night-shirt and drawers, and was as dirty in appearance as he was gaudy in colours. 'Sit down and let us two moralise,' he said. 'I spend my life here doing nothing, – nothing, – nothing; while you cudgel your brain from day to day to mislead the British public. Which of us two is taking the nearest road to the devil ?'

Stanbury seated himself in a second arm-chair, which there was there in the verandah, and looked as carefully as he dared to do at his friend. There could be no mistake as to the restless gleam of that eye. And then the affected air of ease, and the would-be cynicism, and the pretence of false motives, all told the same story. 'They used to tell us,' said Stanbury, 'that idleness is the root of all evil.'

'They have been telling us since the world began so many lies, that I for one have determined never to believe anything again. Labour leads to greed, and greed to selfishness, and selfishness to treachery, and treachery straight to the devil, – straight to the devil. Ha, my friend, all your leading articles won't lead you out of that. What's the news ? Who's alive ? Who dead ? Who in ? Who out ?* What think you of a man who has not seen a newspaper for two months; and who holds no conversation with the world further than is needed for the cooking of his polenta and the cooling of his modest wine-flask ?'

'You see your wife sometimes,' said Stanbury.

'My wife ! Now, my friend, let us drop that subject. Of all topics of talk it is the most distressing to man in general, and I own that I am no exception to the lot. Wives, Stanbury, are an evil, more or less necessary to humanity, and I own to being one who has not escaped. The world must be populated, though for what reason one does not see. I have helped, – to the extent of one male bantling; and if you are one who consider population desirable, I will express my regret that I should have done no more.'

It was very difficult to force Trevelyan out of this humour, and it was not till Stanbury had risen apparently to take his leave that he found it possible to say a word as to his mission there. 'Don't you think you would be happier at home ?' he asked.

'Where is my home, Sir Knight of the midnight pen ?'

'England is your home, Trevelyan.'

'No, sir; England was my home once; but I have taken the liberty accorded to me by my Creator of choosing a new country. Italy is now my nation, and Casalunga is my home.'

'Every tie you have in the world is in England.'

'I have no tie, sir; – no tie anywhere. It has been my study to untie all the ties; and, by Jove, I have succeeded. Look at me here.

I have got rid of the trammels pretty well, – haven't I? – have unshackled myself, and thrown off the paddings, and the wrappings, and the swaddling clothes. I have got rid of the conventionalities, and can look Nature straight in the face. I don't even want the Daily Record, Stanbury; – think of that!'

Stanbury paced the length of the terrace, and then stopped for a moment down under the blaze of the sun, in order that he might think how to address this philosopher. 'Have you heard,' he said at last, 'that I am going to marry your sister-in-law, Nora Rowley?'

'Then there will be two more full-grown fools in the world certainly, and probably an infinity of young fools coming afterwards. Excuse me, Stanbury, but this solitude is apt to make one plain-spoken.'

'I got Sir Marmaduke's sanction the day before I left.'

'Then you got the sanction of an illiterate, ignorant, self-sufficient, and most contemptible old man; and much good may it do you.'

'Let him be what he may, I was glad to have it. Most probably I shall never see him again. He sails from Southampton for the Mandarins on this day week.'

'He does, – does he? May the devil sail along with him! – that is all I say. And does my much respected and ever-to-be-beloved mother-in-law sail with him?'

'They all return together, – except Nora.'

'Who remains to comfort you? I hope you may be comforted; – that is all. Don't be too particular. Let her choose her own friends, and go her own gait, and have her own way, and do you be blind and deaf and dumb and properly submissive; and it may be that she'll give you your breakfast and dinner in your own house, – so long as your hours don't interfere with her pleasures. If she should even urge you beside yourself by her vanity, folly, and disobedience, – so that at last you are driven to express your feeling, – no doubt she will come to you after a while and tell you with the sweetest condescension that she forgives you. When she has been out of your house for a twelvemonth or more, she will offer to come back to you, and to forget everything, – on condition that you will do exactly as she bids you for the future.'

This attempt at satire, so fatuous, so plain, so false, together with the would-be jaunty manner of the speaker, who, however, failed repeatedly in his utterances from sheer physical exhaustion, was excessively painful to Stanbury. What can one do at any time with a madman? 'I mentioned my marriage,' said he, 'to prove my right to have an additional interest in your wife's happiness.'

'You are quite welcome, whether you marry the other one or not; – welcome to take any interest you please. I have got beyond all that, Stanbury; – yes, by Jove, a long way beyond all that.'

'You have not got beyond loving your wife, and your child, Trevelyan?'

'Upon my word, yes; – I think I have. There may be a grain of weakness left, you know. But what have you to do with my love for my wife?'

'I was thinking more just now of her love for you. There she is at Siena. You cannot mean that she should remain there?'

'Certainly not. What the deuce is there to keep her there?'

'Come with her then to England.'

'Why should I go to England with her? Because you bid me, or because she wishes it, – or simply because England is the most damnable, puritanical, God-forgotten, and stupid country on the face of the globe? I know no other reason for going to England. Will you take a glass of wine, Stanbury?' Hugh declined the offer. 'You will excuse me,' continued Trevelyan; 'I always take a glass of wine at this hour.' Then he rose from his chair, and helped himself from a cupboard that was near at hand. Stanbury, watching him as he filled his glass, could see that his legs were hardly strong enough to carry him. And Stanbury saw, moreover, that the unfortunate man took two glasses out of the bottle. 'Go to England indeed. I do not think much of this country; but it is, at any rate, better than England.'

Hugh perceived that he could do nothing more on the present occasion. Having heard so much of Trevelyan's debility, he had been astonished to hear the man speak with so much volubility and attempts at high-flown spirit. Before he had taken the wine he had almost sunk into his chair, but still he had continued to speak with the same fluent would-be cynicism. 'I will come and see you again,' said Hugh, getting up to take his departure.

'You might as well save your trouble, Stanbury; but you can come if you please, you know. If you should find yourself locked out, you won't be angry. A hermit such as I am must assume privileges.'

'I won't be angry,' said Hugh, good humouredly.

'I can smell what you are come about,' said Trevelyan. 'You and my wife want to take me away from here among you, and I think it best to stay here. I don't want much for myself, and why should I not live here? My wife can remain at Siena if she pleases, or she can go to England if she pleases. She must give me the same liberty; – the same liberty, – the same liberty.' After this he fell a-coughing violently, and Stanbury thought it better to leave him. He had been at Casalunga about two hours, and did not seem as yet to have done any good. He had been astonished both by Trevelyan's weakness, and by his strength; by his folly, and by his sharpness. Hitherto he could see no way for his future sister-in-law out of her troubles.

When he was with her at Siena, he described what had taken place with all the accuracy in his power. 'He has intermittent days,' said Emily. 'To-morrow he will be in quite another frame of mind, – melancholy, silent perhaps, and self-reproachful. We will both go to-morrow, and we shall find probably that he has forgotten altogether what has passed to day between you and him.'

So their plans for the morrow were formed.

93

Say that You Forgive Me

On the following day, again early in the morning, Mrs Trevelyan and Stanbury were driven out to Casalunga. The country people along the road knew the carriage well, and the lady who occupied it, and would say that the English wife was going to see her mad husband. Mrs Trevelyan knew that these words were common in the people's mouths, and explained to her companion how necessary it would be to use these rumours, to aid her in putting some restraint over her husband even in this country, should they fail in their effort to take him to England. She saw the doctor in Siena constantly, and had learned from him how such steps might be taken. The measure proposed would be slow, difficult, inefficient, and very hard to set aside, if once taken; – but still it might be indispensable that something should be done. 'He would be so much worse off here than he would be at home,' she said; – 'if we could only make him understand that it would be so.' Then Stanbury asked about the wine. It seemed that of late Trevelyan had taken to drink freely, but only of the wine of the country. But the wine of the country in these parts is sufficiently stimulating, and Mrs Trevelyan acknowledged that hence had arisen a further cause of fear.

They walked up the hill together, and Mrs Trevelyan, now well knowing the ways of the place, went round at once to the front terrace. There he was, seated in his arm-chair, dressed in the same way as yesterday, dirty, dishevelled, and gaudy with various colours; but Stanbury could see at once that his mood had greatly changed. He rose slowly, dragging himself up out of his chair, as they came up to him, but showing as he did so, – and perhaps somewhat assuming, – the impotency of querulous sickness. His wife went to him, and took him by the hand, and placed him back in his chair. He was weak, he said, and had not slept, and suffered from the heat; and then he begged her to give him wine. This she did, half filling for him a tumbler, of which he swallowed the contents greedily. 'You see me very poorly, Stanbury, – very poorly,' he said, seeming to ignore all that had taken place on the previous day.

'You want change of climate, old fellow,' said Stanbury.

'Change of everything; – I want change of everything,' he said. 'If I could have a new body and a new mind, and a new soul!'

'The mind and soul, dear, will do well enough, if you will let us look after the body,' said his wife, seating herself on a stool near his feet. Stanbury, who had settled beforehand how he would conduct himself, took out a cigar and lighted it; – and then they sat together silent, or nearly silent, for half an hour. She had said that if Hugh would do so, Trevelyan would soon become used to the presence of his old friend, and it seemed that he had already done so. More than once, when he coughed, his wife fetched him some drink in a cup, which he took from her without a word. And Stanbury the while went on smoking in silence.

'You have heard, Louis,' she said at last, 'that, after all, Nora and Mr Stanbury are going to be married?'

'Ah; – yes; I think I was told of it. I hope you may be happy, Stanbury; – happier than I have been.' This was unfortunate, but neither of the visitors winced, or said a word.

'It will be a pity that papa and mamma cannot be present at the wedding,' said Mrs Trevelyan.

'If I had to do it again, I should not regret your father's absence; I must say that. He has been my enemy. Yes, Stanbury, – my enemy. I don't care who hears me say so. I am obliged to stay here, because that man would swear every shilling I have away from me if I were in England. He would strive to do so, and the struggle in my state of health would be too much for me.'

'But Sir Marmaduke sails from Southampton this very week,' said Stanbury.

'I don't know. He is always sailing, and always coming back again. I never asked him for a shilling in my life, and yet he has treated me as though I were his bitterest enemy.'

'He will trouble you no more now, Louis,' said Mrs Trevelyan.

'He cannot trouble you again. He will have left England before you can possibly reach it.'

'He will have left other traitors behind him, – though none as bad as himself,' said Trevelyan.

Stanbury, when his cigar was finished, rose and left the husband and wife together on the terrace. There was little enough to be seen at Casalunga, but he strolled about looking at the place. He went into the huge granary, and then down among the olive trees, and up into the sheds which had been built for beasts. He stood and teased the lizards, and listened to the hum of the insects, and wiped away the perspiration which rose to his brow even as he was standing. And all the while he was thinking what he would do next, or what say next, with the view of getting Trevelyan away from the place. Hitherto he had been very tender with him, contradicting him in nothing, taking from him good humouredly any absurd insult which he chose to offer, pressing upon him none of the evil which he had himself occasioned, saying to him no word that could hurt either his pride or his comfort. But he could not see that this would be efficacious for the purpose desired. He had come thither to help Nora's sister in her terrible distress, and he must take upon himself to make some plan for giving this aid. When he had thought of all this and made his plan, he sauntered back round the house on to the terrace. She was still there, sitting at her husband's feet, and holding one of his hands in hers. It was well that the wife should be tender, but he doubted whether tenderness would suffice.

'Trevelyan,' he said, 'you know why I have come over here?'

'I suppose she told you to come,' said Trevelyan.

'Well; yes; she did tell me. I cam to try and get you back to England. If you remain here, the climate and solitude together will kill you.'

'As for the climate, I like it; – and as for solitude, I have got used even to that.'

'And then there is another thing,' said Stanbury.

'What is that?' asked Trevelyan, starting.

'You are not safe here.'

'How not safe?'

'She could not tell you, but I must.' His wife was still holding his hand, and he did not at once attempt to withdraw it; but he raised himself in his chair, and fixed his eyes fiercely on Stanbury. 'They will not let you remain here quietly,' said Stanbury.

'Who will not?'

'The Italians. They are already saying that you are not fit to be alone; and if once they get you into their hands, – under some

Italian medical board, perhaps into some Italian asylum, it might be years before you could get out, – if ever. I have come to tell you what the danger is. I do not know whether you will believe me.'

'Is it so ?' he said, turning to his wife.

'I believe it is, Louis.'

'And who has told them ? Who has been putting them up to it ?' Now his hand had been withdrawn. 'My God, am I to be followed here too with such persecution as this ?'

'Nobody has told them, – but people have eyes.'

'Liar, traitor, fiend ! – it is you !' he said, turning upon his wife.

'Louis, as I hope for mercy, I have said not a word to any one that could injure you.'

'Trevelyan, do not be so unjust, and so foolish,' said Stanbury. 'It is not her doing. Do you suppose that you can live here like this and give rise to no remarks ? Do you think that people's eyes are not open, and that their tongues will not speak ? I tell you, you are in danger here.'

'What am I to do ? Where am I to go ? Can not they let me stay till I die ? Whom am I hurting here ? She may have all my money, if she wants it. She has got my child.'

'I want nothing, Louis, but to take you where you may be safe and well.'

'Why are you afraid of going to England ?' Stanbury asked.

'Because they have threatened to put me – in a madhouse.'

'Nobody ever thought of so treating you,' said his wife.

'Your father did, – and your mother. They told me so.'

'Look here, Trevelyan. Sir Marmaduke and Lady Rowley are gone. They will have sailed, at least, before we can reach England. Whatever may have been either their wishes or their power, they can do nothing now. Here something would be done, – very soon; you may take my word for that. If you will return with me and your wife, you shall choose your own place of abode. Is not that so, Emily ?'

'He shall choose everything. His boy will be with him, and I will be with him, and he shall be contradicted in nothing. If he only knew my heart towards him !'

'You hear what she says, Trevelyan ?'

'Yes ; I hear her.'

'And you believe her ?'

'I'm not so sure of that. Stanbury, how should you like to be locked up in a madhouse and grin through the bars till your heart was broken. It would not take long with me, I know.'

'You shall never be locked up ; – never be touched,' said his wife.

'I am very harmless here,' he said, almost crying; 'very harmless. I do not think anybody here will touch me,' he added afterwards. 'And there are other places. There are other places. My God, that I should be driven about the world like this!' The conference was ended by his saying that he would take two days to think of it, and by his then desiring that they would both leave him. They did so, and descended the hill together, knowing that he was watching them, – that he would watch them till they were out of sight from the gate; – for, as Mrs Trevelyan said, he never came down the hill now, knowing that the labour of ascending it was too much for him. When they were at the carriage they were met by one of the women of the house, and strict injunctions were given to her by Mrs Trevelyan to send on word to Siena if the Signore should prepare to move. 'He cannot go far without my knowing it,' said she, 'because he draws his money in Siena, and lately I have taken to him what he wants. He has not enough with him for a long journey.' For Stanbury had suggested that he might be off to seek another residence in another country, and that they would find Casalunga vacant when they reached it on the following Tuesday. But he told himself almost immediately, – not caring to express such an opinion to Emily, – that Trevelyan would hardly have strength even to prepare for such a journey by himself.

On the intervening day, the Monday, Stanbury had no occupation whatever, and he thought that since he was born no day had ever been so long. Siena contains many monuments of interest, and much that is valuable in art, – having had a school of painting of its own, and still retaining in its public gallery specimens of its school, of which as a city it is justly proud. There are palaces there to be beaten for gloomy majesty by none in Italy. There is a cathedral which was to have been the largest in the world, and than which few are more worthy of prolonged inspection. The town is old, and quaint, and picturesque, and dirty, and attractive, – as it becomes a town in Italy to be. But in July all such charms are thrown away. In July Italy is not a land of charms to an Englishman. Poor Stanbury did wander into the cathedral, and finding it the coolest place in the town, went to sleep on a stone step. He was awoke by the voices of the priests as they began to chant the vespers. The good-natured Italians had let him sleep, and would have let him sleep till the doors were closed for the night. At five he dined with Mrs Trevelyan, and then endeavoured to while away the evening thinking of Nora with a pipe in his mouth. He was standing in this way at the hotel gateway, when, on a sudden, all Siena was made alive by the clatter of an open carriage and four on its way through the town to the railway. On looking up, Stanbury saw Lord Peterborough in the carriage, – with a lady whom he did not doubt to be Lord Peterborough's wife. He himself had not been recognised, but he slowly followed the carriage to the railway station. After the Italian fashion, the arrival was three-quarters of an hour before the proper time, and Stanbury had full opportunity of learning their news and telling his own. They were coming up from Rome, and had thought it preferable to take the route by Siena than to use the railway through the Maremma; and they intended to reach Florence that night.

'And do you think he is really mad?' asked Lady Peterborough.

'He is undoubtedly so mad as to be unfit to manage anything for himself, but he is not in such a condition that any one would wish to see him put into confinement. If he were raving mad there would be less difficulty, though there might be more distress.'

A great deal was said about Nora, and both Lord Peterborough and his wife insisted that the marriage should take place at Monkhams. 'We shall be home now in less than three weeks,' said Caroline, 'and she must come to us at once. But I will write to her from Florence, and tell her how we saw you smoking your pipe under the archway. Not that my husband knew you in the least.'

'Upon my word no,' said the husband, – 'one didn't expect to find you here. Good-bye. I hope you may succeed in getting him home. I went to him once, but could do very little.' Then the train started, and Stanbury went back to Mrs Trevelyan.

On the next day Stanbury went out to Casalunga alone. He had calculated, on leaving England, that if any good might be done at Siena it could be done in three days, and that he would have been able to start on his return on the Wednesday morning, – or on Wednesday evening at the latest. But now there did not seem to be any chance of that; – and he hardly knew how to guess when he might get away. He had sent a telegram to Lady Rowley after his first visit, in which he had simply said that things were not at all changed at Casalunga, and he had written to Nora each day since his arrival. His stay was prolonged at great expense and inconvenience to himself; and yet it was impossible that he should go and leave his work half finished. As he walked up the hill to the house he felt very angry with Trevelyan, and prepared himself to use hard words and dreadful threats. But at the very moment of his entrance on this terrace, Trevelyan professed himself ready to go to England. 'That's right, old fellow,' said Hugh. 'I am so glad.' But in expressing his joy he had hardly noticed Trevelyan's voice and appearance.

'I might as well go,' he said. 'It matters little where I am, or whether they say that I am mad or sane.'

'When we have you over there, nobody shall say a word that is disagreeable.'

'I only hope that you may not have the trouble of burying me on the road. You don't know, Stanbury, how ill I am. I cannot eat. If I were at the bottom of that hill, I could no more walk up it than I could fly. I cannot sleep, and at night my bed is wet through with perspiration. I can remember nothing, – nothing but what I ought to forget.'

'We'll put you on to your legs again when we get you to your own climate.'

'I shall be a poor traveller, – a poor traveller; but I will do my best.'

When would he start? That was the next question. Trevelyan asked for a week, and Stanbury brought him down at last to three days. They would go to Florence by the evening train on Friday, and sleep there. Emily should come out and assist him to arrange his things on the morrow. Having finished so much of his business, Stanbury returned to Siena.

They both feared that he might be found on the next day to have departed from his intention; but no such idea seemed to have occurred to him. He gave instructions as the notice to be served on the agent from the Hospital as to his house, and allowed Emily to go among his things and make preparations for the journey. He did not say much to her; and when she attempted, with a soft half-uttered word, to assure him that the threat of Italian interference, which had come from Stanbury, had not reached Stanbury from her, he simply shook his head sadly. She could not understand whether he did not believe her, or whether he simply wished that the subject should be dropped. She could elicit no sign of affection from him, nor would he willingly accept such from her; – but he allowed her to prepare for the journey, and never hinted that his purpose might again be liable to change. On the Friday, Emily with her child, and Hugh with all their baggage, travelled out on the road to Casalunga, thinking it better that there should be no halt in the town on their return. At Casalunga, Hugh went up the hill with the driver, leaving Mrs Trevelyan in the carriage. He had been out at the house before in the morning, and had given all necessary orders; – but still at the last moment he thought that there might be failure. But Trevelyan was ready, having dressed himself up with a laced shirt, and changed his dressing-gown for a blue frock-coat, and his brocaded cap for a Paris hat, very pointed before and

behind, and closely turned up at the sides. But Stanbury did not in
the least care for his friend's dress. 'Take my arm,' he said, 'and we
will go down, fair and easy. Emily would not come up because of
the heat.' He suffered himself to be led, or almost carried down the
hill; and three women, and the coachman, and an old countryman
who worked on the farm, followed with the luggage. It took about
an hour and a half to pack the things; but at last they were all
packed, and corded, and bound together with sticks, as though it
were intended that they should travel in that form to Moscow.
Trevelyan the meanwhile sat on a chair which had been brought
out for him from one of the cottages, and his wife stood beside him
with her boy. 'Now then we are ready,' said Stanbury. And in that
way they bade farewell to Casalunga. Trevelyan sat speechless in
the carriage, and would not even notice the child. He seemed to be
half dreaming and to fix his eyes on vacancy. 'He appears to think
of nothing now,' Emily said that evening to Stanbury. But who can
tell how busy and how troubled are the thoughts of a madman!

They had now succeeded in their object of inducing their patient
to return with them to England; but what were they to do with him
when they had reached home with him? They rested only a night at
Florence; but they found their fellow-traveller so weary, that they
were unable to get beyond Bologna on the second day. Many
questions were asked of him as to where he himself would wish to
take up his residence in England; but it was found almost impossible to get an answer. Once he suggested that he would like to go
back to Mrs Fuller's cottage at Willesden, from whence they
concluded that he would wish to live somewhere out of London.
On his first day's journey, he was moody and silent, – wilfully
assuming the airs of a much-injured person. He spoke hardly at all,
and would notice nothing that was said to him by his wife. He
declared once that he regarded Stanbury as his keeper, and endeavoured to be disagreeable and sullenly combative; but on the second
day, he was too weak for this, and accepted, without remonstrance,
the attentions that were paid to him. At Bologna they rested a day,
and from thence both Stanbury and Mrs Trevelyan wrote to Nora.
They did not know where she might be now staying, but the letters,
by agreement, were addressed to Gregg's Hotel. It was suggested
that lodgings, or, if possible, a small furnished house, should be
taken in the neighbourhood of Mortlake, Richmond, or Tedding-
ton, and that a telegram as well as letter should be sent to them at
the Paris hotel. As they could not travel quick, there might be time
enough for them in this way to know whither they should go on
their reaching London.

They stayed a day at Bologna, and then they went on again, – to Turin, over the mountains to Chambery, thence to Dijon, and on to Paris. At Chambery they remained a couple of days, fancying that the air there was cool, and that the delay would be salutary to the sick man. At Turin, finding that they wanted further assistance, they had hired a courier, and at last Trevelyan allowed himself to be carried in and out of the carriages and up and down the hotel stairs almost as though he were a child. The delay was terribly grievous to Stanbury, and Mrs Trevelyan, perceiving this more than once, begged him to leave them, and to allow her to finish the journey with the aid of the courier. But this he could not do. He wrote letters to his friends at the D. R. office, explaining his position as well as he could, and suggesting that this and that able assistant should enlighten the British people on this and that subject, which would, – in the course of nature, as arranged at the D. R. office, – have fallen into his hands. He and Mrs Trevelyan became as brother and sister to each other on their way home, – as, indeed, it was natural that they should do. Were they doing right or wrong in this journey that they were taking? They could not conceal from themselves that the labour was almost more than the poor wretch could endure; and that it might be, as he himself had suggested, that they would be called on to bury him on the road. But that residence at Casalunga had been so terrible, – the circumstances of it, including the solitude, sickness, madness, and habits of life of the wretched hermit, had been so dangerous, – the probability of interference on the part of some native authority so great, and the chance of the house being left in Trevelyan's possession so small, that it had seemed to them that they had no other alternative; and yet, how would it be if they were killing him by the toil of travelling? From Chambery, they made the journey to Paris in two days, and during that time Trevelyan hardly opened his mouth. He slept much, and ate better than he had done in the hotter climate on the other side of the Alps.

They found a telegram at Paris, which simply contained the promise of a letter for the next day. It had been sent by Nora, before she had gone out on her search. But it contained one morsel of strange information; 'Lady Milborough is going with me.' On the next day they got a letter, saying that a cottage had been taken, furnished, between Richmond and Twickenham. Lady Milborough had known of the cottage, and everything would be ready then. Nora would herself meet them at the station in London, if they would, as she proposed, stay a night at Dover. They were to address to her at Lady Milborough's house, in Eccleston Square. In that case, she would have a carriage for them at the Victoria Station, and would go down with them at once to the cottage.

There were to be two days more of weary travelling, and then they were to be at home again. She and he would have a house together as husband and wife, and the curse of their separation would, at any rate, be over. Her mind towards him had changed altogether since the days in which she had been so indignant, because he had set a policeman to watch over her. All feeling of anger was over with her now. There is nothing that a woman will not forgive a man, when he is weaker than she is herself.

The journey was made first to Dover, and then to London. Once, as they were making their way through the Kentish hop-fields, he put out his hand feebly, and touched hers. They had the carriage to themselves, and she was down on her knees before him instantly. 'Oh, Louis! Oh Louis! say that you forgive me!' What could a woman do more than that in her mercy to a man?

'Yes; – yes; yes,' he said; 'but do not talk now; I am so tired.'

94
A Real Christian

In the meantime the Rowleys were gone. On the Monday after the departure of Stanbury for Italy, Lady Rowley had begun to look the difficulty about Nora in the face, and to feel that she must do something towards providing the poor girl with a temporary home. Everybody had now agreed that she was to marry Hugh Stanbury as soon as Hugh Stanbury could be ready, and it was not to be thought of that she should be left out in the world as one in disgrace or under a cloud. But what was to be done? Sir Marmaduke was quite incapable of suggesting anything. He would make her an allowance, and leave her a small sum of ready money; – but as to residence, he could only suggest again and again that she should be sent to Mrs Outhouse. Now Lady Rowley was herself not very fond of Mrs Outhouse, and she was aware that Nora herself was almost as averse to St Diddulph's as she was to the Mandarins. Nora already knew that she had the game in her own hands. Once when in her presence her father suggested the near relationship and prudent character and intense respectability of Mrs Outhouse, Nora, who was sitting behind Sir Marmaduke, shook her head at her mother, and Lady Rowley knew that Nora would not go to St Diddulph's. This was the last occasion on which that proposition was discussed.

Throughout all the Trevelyan troubles Lady Milborough had continued to show a friendly anxiety on behalf of Emily Trevelyan. She had called once or twice on Lady Rowley, and Lady Rowley had of course returned the visits. She had been forward in expressing her belief that in truth the wife had been but little if at all to blame, and had won her way with Lady Rowley, though she had never been a favourite with either of Lady Rowley's daughters. Now, in her difficulty, Lady Rowley went to Lady Milborough, and returned with an invitation that Nora should come to Eccleston Square, either till such time as she might think fit to go to Monkhams, or till Mrs Trevelyan should have returned, and should be desirous of having her sister with her. When Nora first heard of this she almost screamed with surprise, and, if the truth must be told, with disappointment also.

'She never liked me, mamma.'

'Then she is so much more good-natured.'

'But I don't want to go to her merely because she is good-natured enough to receive a person she dislikes. I know she is very good. I know she would sacrifice herself for anything she thought right. But, mamma, she is such a bore!'

But Lady Rowley would not be talked down, even by Nora, in this fashion. Nora was somewhat touched with an idea that it would be a fine independent thing to live alone, if it were only for a week or two, just because other young ladies never lived alone. Perhaps there was some half-formed notion in her mind that permission to do so was part of the reward due to her for having refused to marry a lord. Stanbury was in some respects a Bohemian, and it would become her, she thought, to have a little practice herself in the Bohemian line. She had, indeed, declined a Bohemian marriage, feeling strongly averse to encounter the loud displeasure of her father and mother; — but as long as everything was quite proper, as long as there should be no running away, or subjection of her name to scandal, she considered that a little independence would be useful and agreeable. She had looked forward to sitting up at night alone by a single tallow candle, to stretching a beefsteak so as to last her for two days' dinners, and perhaps to making her own bed. Now, there would not be the slightest touch of romance in a visit to Lady Milborough's house in Eccleston Square, at the end of July. Lady Rowley, however, was of a different opinion, and spoke her mind plainly. 'Nora, my dear, don't be a fool. A young lady like you can't go and live in lodgings by herself. All manner of things would be said. And this is such a very kind offer! You must accept it, – for Hugh's sake. I have already said that you would accept it.'

'But she will be going out of town.'

'She will stay till you can go to Monkhams, – if Emily is not back before then. She knows all about Emily's affairs; and if she does come back, – which I doubt, poor thing, – Lady Milborough and you will be able to judge whether you should go to her.' So it was settled, and Nora's Bohemian Castle in the Air fell into shatters.

The few remaining days before the departure to Southampton passed quickly, but yet sadly. Sir Marmaduke had come to England expecting pleasure, – and with that undefined idea which men so employed always have on their return home that something will turn up which will make them going back to that same banishment unnecessary. What Governor of Hong-Kong, what Minister to Bogota, what General of the Forces at the Gold Coast, ever left the scene of his official or military labours without a hope, which was almost an expectation, that a grateful country would do something better for him before the period of his return should have arrived? But a grateful country was doing nothing better for Sir Marmaduke, and an ungrateful Secretary of State at the Colonial Office would not extend the term during which he could regard himself as absent on special service. How thankful he had been when first the tidings reached him that he was to come home at the expense of the Crown, and without diminution of his official income! He had now been in England for five months, with a per diem allowance, with his very cabs paid for him, and he was discontented, sullen, and with nothing to comfort him but his official grievance, because he could not be allowed to extend his period of special service more than two months beyond the time at which those special services were in truth ended! There had been a change of Ministry in the last month, and he had thought that a Conservative Secretary of State would have been kinder to him. 'The Duke says I can stay three months with leave of absence; – and have half my pay stopped. I wonder whether it ever enters into his august mind that even a Colonial Governor must eat and drink.' It was thus he expressed his great grievance to his wife. 'The Duke,' however, had been as inexorable as his predecessor, and Sir Rowley, with his large family, was too wise to remain to the detriment of his pocket. In the meantime the clerks in the office, who had groaned in spirit over the ignorance displayed in his evidence before the committee, were whispering among themselves that he ought not to be sent back to his seat of government at all.

Lady Rowley also was disappointed and unhappy. She had

expected so much pleasure from her visit to her daughters, and she had received so little! Emily's condition was very sad, but in her heart of hearts perhaps she groaned more bitterly over all that Nora had lost, than she did over the real sorrows of her elder child. To have had the cup at her lip, and then not to have tasted it! And she had the solace of no communion in this sorrow. She had accepted Hugh Stanbury as her son-in-law, and not for worlds would she now say a word against him to any one. She had already taken him to her heart, and she loved him. But to have had it almost within her grasp to have had a lord, the owner of Monkhams, for her son-in-law! Poor Lady Rowley!

Sophie and Lucy, too, were returning to their distant and dull banishment without any realisation of their probable but unexpressed ambition. They made no complaint, but yet it was hard on them that their sister's misfortune should have prevented them from going, — almost to a single dance. Poor Sophie and poor Lucy! They must go, and we shall hear no more about them. It was thought well that Nora should not go down with them to Southampton. What good would her going do? 'God bless you, my darling,' said the mother, as she held her child in her arms.

'Good-bye, dear mamma.'

'Give my best love to Hugh, and tell him that I pray him with my last word to be good to you.' Even then she was thinking of Lord Peterborough, but the memory of what might have been was buried deep in her mind.

'Nora, tell me all about it,' said Lucy.

'There will be nothing to tell,' said Nora.

'Tell it all the same,' said Lucy. 'And bring Hugh out to write a book of travels about the Mandarins. Nobody has ever written a book about the Mandarins.' So they parted; and when Sir Marmaduke and his party were taken off in two cabs to the Waterloo Station, Nora was taken in one cab to Eccleston Square.

It may be doubted whether any old lady since the world began ever did a more thoroughly Christian and friendly act than this which was now being done by Lady Milborough. It was the end of July, and she would already have been down in Dorsetshire, but for her devotion to this good dead. For, in truth, what she was doing was not occasioned by any express love for Nora Rowley. Nora Rowley was all very well, but Nora Rowley towards her had been flippant, impatient, and, indeed, not always so civil as a young lady should be to the elderly friends of her married sister. But to Lady Milborough it had seemed to be quite terrible that a young girl should be left alone in the world, without anybody to take care of her. Young ladies, according to her views of life, were fragile plants that wanted much nursing before they could be allowed to be planted out in the gardens of the world as married women. When she heard from Lady Rowley that Nora was engaged to marry Hugh Stanbury, – 'You know all about Lord Peterborough, Lady Milborough; but it is no use going back to that now, – is it? And Mr Stanbury has behaved so exceedingly well in regard to poor Louis,' – when Lady Milborough heard this, and heard also that Nora was talking of going to live by herself in – lodgings! – she swore to herself, like a goodly Christian woman, as she was, that such a thing must not be. Eccleston Square in July and August is not pleasant, unless it be to an inhabitant who is interested in the fag-end of the parliamentary session. Lady Milborough had no interest in politics, – had not much interest even in seeing the social season out to its dregs. She ordinarily remained in London till the beginning or middle of July; because the people with whom she lived were in the habit of doing so; – but as soon as ever she had fixed the date of her departure, that day to her was a day of release. On this occasion the day had been fixed, – and it was unfixed, and changed, and postponed, because it was manifest to Lady Milborough that she could do good by remaining for another fortnight. When she made the offer she said nothing of her previous arrangements. 'Lady Rowley, let her come to me. As soon as her friend Lady Peterborough is at Monkhams, she can go there.'

Thus it was that Nora found herself established in Eccleston Square. As she took her place in Lady Milborough's drawing-room, she remembered well a certain day, not two years ago, when she had first heard of the glories of Monkhams in that very house. Lady Milborough, as good-natured then as she was now, had brought Mr Glascock and Nora together, simply because she had heard that the gentleman admired the young lady. Nora, in her pride, had resented this as interference, – had felt that the thing had been done, and, though she had valued the admiration of the man, had ridiculed the action of the woman. As she thought of it now she was softened by gratitude. She had not on that occasion been suited with a husband, but she had gained a friend. 'My dear,' said Lady Milborough, as at her request Nora took off her hat, 'I am afraid that the parties are mostly over, – that is, those I go to; but we will drive out every day, and the time won't be so very long.'

'It won't be long for me, Lady Milborough; – but I cannot but know how terribly I am putting you out.'

'I am never put out, Miss Rowley,' said the old lady, 'as long as I am made to think that what I do is taken in good part.'

'Indeed, indeed it shall be taken in good part,' said Nora, – 'indeed it shall.' And she swore a solemn silent vow of friendship for the dear old woman.

Then there came letters and telegrams from Chambery, Dijon, and Paris, and the joint expedition in search of the cottage was made to Twickenham. It was astonishing how enthusiastic and how loving the elder and the younger lady were together before the party from Italy had arrived in England. Nora had explained everything about herself, – how impossible it had been for her not to love Hugh Stanbury; how essential it had been for her happiness and self-esteem that she should refuse Mr Glascock; how terrible had been the tragedy of her sister's marriage. Lady Milborough spoke of the former subject with none of Lady Rowley's enthusiasm, but still with an evident partiality for her own rank, which almost aroused Nora to indignant eloquence. Lady Milborough was contented to acknowledge that Nora might be right, seeing that her heart was so firmly fixed; but she was clearly of opinion that Mr Glascock, being Mr Glascock, had possessed a better right to the prize in question than could have belonged to any man who had no recognised position in the world. Seeing that her heart had been given away, Nora was no doubt right not to separate her hand from her heart; but Lady Milborough was of opinion that young ladies ought to have their hearts under better control, so that the men entitled to the prizes should get them. It was for the welfare of England at large that the eldest sons of good families should marry the sweetest, prettiest, brightest, and most lovable girls of their age. It is a doctrine on behalf of which very much may be said.

On that other matter, touching Emily Trevelyan, Lady Milborough frankly owned that she had seen early in the day that he was the one most in fault. 'I must say, my dear,' she said, 'that I very greatly dislike your friend, Colonel Osborne.'

'I am sure that he meant not the slightest harm, – no more than she did.'

'He was old enough, and ought to have known better. And when the first hint of an uneasiness in the mind of Louis was suggested to him, his feelings as a gentleman should have prompted him to remove himself. Let the suspicion have been ever so absurd, he should have removed himself. Instead of that, he went after her, – into Devonshire.'

'He went to see other friends, Lady Milborough.'

'I hope it may have been so; – I hope it may have been so. But he should have cut off his hand before he rang at the door of the house in which she was living. You will understand, my dear, that I acquit your sister altogether. I did so all through, and said the same to poor Louis when he came to me. But Colonel Osborne should have known better. Why did he write to her? Why did he go to St Diddulph's? Why did he let it be thought that, — that she was especially his friend. Oh dear; oh dear; oh dear! I am afraid he is a very bad man.'

'We had known him so long, Lady Milborough.'

'I wish you had never known him at all. Poor Louis! If he had only done what I told him at first, all might have been well. "Go to Naples, with your wife," I said. "Go to Naples." If he had gone to Naples, there would have been no journeys to Siena, no living at Casalunga, no separation. But he didn't seem to see it in the same light. Poor dear Louis. I wish he had gone to Naples when I told him.'

While they were going backwards and forwards, looking at the cottage at Twickenham and trying to make things comfortable there for the sick man, Lady Milborough hinted to Nora that it might be distasteful to Trevelyan, in his present condition, to have even a sister-in-law staying in the house with him. There was a little chamber which Nora had appropriated to herself, and at first it seemed to be taken for granted that she should remain there at least till the 10th of August, on which day Lady Peterborough had signified that she and her husband would be ready to receive their visitor. But Lady Milborough slept on the suggestion, and on the next morning hinted her disapprobation. 'You shall take them down in the carriage, and their luggage can follow in a cab; — but the carriage can bring you back. You will see how things are then.'

'Dear Lady Milborough, you would go out of town at once if I left you.'

'And I shall not go out of town if you don't leave me. What difference does it make to an old woman like me? I have got no lover coming to look for me, and all I have to do is to tell my daughter-in-law that I shall not be there for another week or so. Augusta is very glad to have me, but she is the wisest woman in the world, and can get on very well without me.'

'And as I am the silliest, I cannot.'

'You shall put it in that way if you like it, my dear. Girls in your position often do want assistance. I dare say you think me very straight-laced, but I am quite sure Mr Stanbury will be grateful to me. As you are to be married from Monkhams, it will be quite well that you should pass thither through my house as an intermediate resting-place, after leaving your father and mother.' By all which Lady Milborough intended to express an opinion that the value of the article which Hugh Stanbury would receive at the altar would be enhanced by the distinguished purity of the hands through which it had passed before it came into his possession; – in which opinion she was probably right as regarded the price put upon the article by the world at large, though it may perhaps be doubted whether the recipient himself would be of the same opinion.

'I hope you know that I am grateful, whatever he may be,' said Nora, after a pause.

'I think that you take it as it is meant, and that makes me quite comfortable.'

'Lady Milborough, I shall love you for ever and ever. I don't think I ever knew anybody so good as you are, – or so nice.'

'Then I shall be more than comfortable,' said Lady Milborough. After that there was an embrace, and the thing was settled.

95

Trevelyan Back in England

Nora, with Lady Milborough's carriage, and Lady Milborough's coach and footman, and with a cab ready for the luggage close behind the carriage, was waiting at the railway station when the party from Dover arrived. She soon saw Hugh upon the platform, and ran to him with her news. They had not a word to say to each other of themselves, so anxious were they both respecting Treve-lyan. 'We got a bed-carriage for him at Dover,' said Hugh; 'and I think he has borne the journey pretty well; – but he feels the heat almost as badly as in Italy. You will hardly know him when you see him.' Then, when the rush of passengers was gone, Trevelyan was brought out by Hugh and the courier, and placed in Lady Milbor-ough's carriage. Hugh just smiled as his eye fell upon Nora, but he did not even put out his hand to greet her.

'I am to go in the carriage with him,' said his wife.

'Of course you are, – and so will I and Louey. I think there will be room: it is so large. There is a cab for all the things. Dear Emily, I am glad to see you.'

'Dearest Nora! I shall be able to speak to you by-and-bye, but you must not be angry with me now. How good you have been.'

'Has not she been good? I don't understand about the cottage. It belongs to some friend of hers; and I have not been able to say a word about the rent. It is so nice; – and looks upon the river. I hope that he will like it.'

'You will be with us?'

'Not just at first. Lady Milborough thinks I had better not, – that he will like it better. I will come down almost every day, and will stay if you think he will like it.'

These few words were said while the men were putting Trevelyan into the carriage. And then another arrangement was made. Hugh hired a second cab, in which he and the courier made a part of the procession; and so they all went to Twickenham together. Hugh had not yet learned that he would be rewarded by coming back alone with Nora in the carriage.

The cottage by the River Thames, which, as far as the party knew, was nameless, was certainly very much better than the house on the top of the hill at Casalunga. And now, at last, the wife would sleep once more under the same roof with her husband, and the separation would be over. 'I suppose that is the Thames,' said Trevelyan; and they were nearly the only words he spoke in Nora's hearing that evening. Before she started on her return journey, the two sisters were together for a few minutes, and each told her own budget of news in short, broken fragments. There was not much to tell. 'He is so weak,' said Mrs Trevelyan, 'that he can do literally nothing. He can hardly speak. When we give him wine, he will say a few words, and his mind seems then to be less astray than it was. I have told him just simply that it was all my doing, – that I have been in fault all through, and every now and then he will say a word, to show me that he remembers that I have confessed.'

'My poor Emily!'

'It was better so. what does it all matter? He had suffered so, that I would have said worse than that to give him relief. The pride has gone out of me so, that I do not regard what anybody may say. Of course, it will be said that I – went astray, and that he forgave me.'

'Nobody will say that, dearest; nobody. Lady Milborough is quite aware how it all was.'

'What does it signify? There are things in life worse even than a bad name.'

'But he does not think it?'

'Nora, his mind is a mystery to me. I do not know what is in it. Sometimes I fancy that all facts have been forgotten, and that he merely wants the childish gratification of being assured that he is the master. Then, again, there come moments, in which I feel sure that suspicion is lurking within him, that he is remembering the past, and guarding against the future. When he came into this house, a quarter of an hour ago, he was fearful lest there was a mad doctor lurking about to pounce on him. I can see in his eye that he had some such idea. He hardly notices Louey, – though there was a time, even at Casalunga, when he would not let the child out of his sight.'

'What will you do now?'

'I will try to do my duty; – that is all.'

'But you will have a doctor?'

'Of course. He was content to see one in Paris, though he would not let me be present. Hugh saw the gentleman afterwards, and he seemed to think that the body was worse than the mind.' Then Nora told her the name of a doctor whom Lady Milborough had suggested, and took her departure along with Hugh in the carriage.

In spite of all the sorrow that they had witnessed and just left, their journey up to London was very pleasant. Perhaps there is no period so pleasant among all the pleasant periods of love-making as that in which the intimacy between the lovers is so assured, and the coming event so near, as to produce and to endear conversation about the ordinary little matters of life; – what can be done with the limited means at their mutual disposal; how that life shall be begun which they are to lead together; what idea each has of the other's duties; what each can do for the other; what each will renounce for the other. There was a true sense of the delight of intimacy in the girl who declared that she had never loved her lover so well as when she told him how many pairs of stockings she had got. It is very sweet to gaze at the stars together; and it is sweet to sit out among the haycocks. The reading of poetry together, out of the same book, with brows all close, and arms all mingled, is very sweet. The pouring out of the whole heart in written words, which the writer knows would be held to be ridiculous by any eyes, and any ears, and any sense, but the eyes and ears and sense of the dear one to whom they are sent, is very sweet; – but for the girl who has made a shirt for the man that she loves, there has come a moment in the last stitch of it, sweeter than any that stars, haycocks, poetry, or superlative epithets have produced. Nora Rowley had never as yet been thus useful on behalf of Hugh Stanbury. Had she done so, she might perhaps have been happier even than she was during this journey; – but, without the shirt, it was one of the happiest moments of her life. There was nothing now to separate them but their own prudential scruples; – and of them if must be acknowledged that Hugh Stanbury had very few. According to his showing, he was as well provided for matrimony as the gentleman in the song, who came out to woo his bride on a rainy night.* In live stock he was not so well provided as the Irish gentleman to whom we allude; but in regard to all other provisions for comfortable married life, he had, or at a moment's notice could have, all that was needed. Nora could live just where she pleased; – not exactly in Whitehall Gardens or Belgrave Square; but the New Road, Lupus Street, Montague Place, the North Bank, or Kennington Oval, with all their surrounding crescents, terraces, and rows, offered, according to him, a choice so wide, either for lodgings or small houses, that their only embarrassment was in their riches. He had already insured his life for a thousand pounds, and, after paying yearly for that, and providing a certain surplus for saving, five hundred a year was the income on which they were to commence the world. 'Of course, I wish it were five thousand for your sake,' he said; 'and I wish I were a Cabinet Minister, or a duke, or a brewer; but, even in heaven, you know all the angels can't be archangels.' Nora assured him that she would be quite content with virtues simply angelic. 'I hope you like mutton-chops and potatoes; I do,' he said. Then she told him of her ambition about the beef-steak, acknowledging that, as it must now be shared between two, the glorious idea of putting a part of it away in a cupboard must be abandoned. 'I don't believe in beef-steak,' he said. 'A beef-steak may mean anything. At our club, a beef-steak is a sumptuous and expensive luxury. Now, a mutton-chop means something definite, and must be economical.'

'Then we will have the mutton-chops at home,' said Nora, 'and you shall go to your club for the beef-steak.'

When they reached Eccleston Square, Nora insisted on taking Hugh Stanbury up to Lady Milborough. It was in vain that he pleaded that he had come all the way from Dover on a very dusty day, – all the way from Dover, including a journey in a Hansom cab to Twickenham and back, without washing his hands and face. Nora insisted that Lady Milborough was such a dear, good, considerate creature, that she would understand all that, and Hugh was taken into her presence. 'I am delighted to see you, Mr Stanbury,' said the old lady, 'and hope you will think that Nora is in good keeping.'

'She has been telling me how very kind you have been to her. I do not know where she could have bestowed herself if you had not received her.'

'There, Nora; – I told you he would say so. I won't tell tales, Mr Stanbury; but she had all manner of wild plans which I knew you wouldn't approve. But she is very amenable, and if she will only submit to you as well as she does to me – '

'I don't mean to submit to him at all, Lady Milborough; – of course not. I am going to marry for liberty.'

'My dear, what you say, you say in joke ; but a great many young women of the present day do, I really believe, go up to the altar and pronounce their marriage vows, with the simple idea that as soon as they have done so, they are to have their own way in everything. And then people complain that young men won't marry ! Who can wonder at it ?'

'I don't think the young men think much about the obedience,' said Nora. 'Some marry for money, and some for love. But I don't think they marry to get a slave.'

'What do you say, Mr Stanbury ?' asked the old lady.

'I can only assure you that I sha'n't marry for money,' said he.

Two or three days after this Nora left her friend in Eccleston Square, and domesticated herself for awhile with her sister. Mrs Trevelyan declared that such an arrangement would be comfortable for her, and that it was very desirable now, as Nora would so soon be beyond her reach. Then Lady Milborough was enabled to go to Dorsetshire, which she did not do, however, till she had presented Nora with the veil which she was to wear on the occasion of her wedding. 'Of course I cannot see it, my dear, as it is to take place at Monkhams ; but you must write and tell me the day ; – and I will think of you. And you, when you put on the veil, must think of me.' So they parted, and Nora knew that she had made a friend for life.

When she first took her place in the house at Twickenham as a resident, Trevelyan did not take much notice of her ; – but, after awhile, he would say a few words to her, especially when it might chance that she was with him in her sister's absence. He would speak of dear Emily, and poor Emily, and shake his head slowly, and talk of the pity of it. 'The pity of it, Iago ; oh, the pity of it,' he said once. The allusion to her was so terrible that she almost burst out in anger, as she would have done formerly. She almost told him that he had been as wrong throughout as was the jealous husband in the play whose words he quoted, and that his jealousy, if continued, was likely to be as tragical. But she restrained herself, and kept close to her needle, – making, let us hope, an auspicious garment for Hugh Stanbury. 'She has seen it now,' he continued ; 'she has seen it now.' Still she went on with her hemming in silence. It certainly could not be her duty to upset at a word all that her sister had achieved. 'You know that she has confessed ?' he asked.

'Pray, pray do not talk about it, Louis.'

'I think you ought to know,' he said. Then she rose from her seat and left the room. She could not stand it, even though he were mad, — even though he were dying!

She went to her sister and repeated what had been said. 'You had better not notice it,' said Emily. 'It is only a proof of what I told you. There are times in which his mind is as active as ever it was, but it is active in so terrible a direction!'

'I cannot sit and hear it. And what am I to say when he asks me a question as he did just now? He said that you had confessed.'

'So I have. Do none confess but the guilty? What is all that we have read about the Inquisition and the old tortures? I have had to learn that torturing has not gone out of the world; — that is all.'

'I must go away if he says the same thing to me so again.'

'That is nonsense, Nora. If I can bear it, cannot you? Would you have me drive him into violence again by disputing with him upon such a subject?'

'But he may recover; — and then he will remember what you have said.'

'If he recovers altogether he will suspect nothing. I must take my chance of that. You cannot suppose that I have not thought about it. I have often sworn to myself that though the world should fall around me, nothing should make me acknowledge that I had ever been untrue to my duty as a married woman, either in deed, or word, or thought. I have no doubt that the poor wretches who were tortured in their cells used to make the same resolutions as to their confessions. But yet, when their nails were dragged out of them, they would own to anything. My nails have been dragged out, and I have been willing to confess anything. When he talks of the pity of it, of course I know what he means. There has been something, some remainder of a feeling, which has still kept him from asking me that question. May God, in his mercy, continue to him that feeling!'

'But you would answer truly?'

'How can I say what I might answer when the torturer is at my nails? If you knew how great was the difficulty to get him away from that place in Italy and bring him here; and what it was to feel that one was bound to stay near him, and that yet one was impotent, — and to know that even that refuge must soon cease for him, and that he might have gone out and died on the road-side, or have done anything which the momentary strength of madness might have dictated, — if you could understand all this, you would not be surprised at my submitting to any degradation which would help to bring him here.'

Stanbury was often down at the cottage, and Nora could discuss the matter better with him than with her sister. And Stanbury could learn more thoroughly from the physician who was now attending Trevelyan what was the state of the sick man, than Emily could do. According to the doctor's idea there was more of ailment in the body than in the mind. He admitted that his patient's thoughts had been forced to dwell on one subject till they had become distorted, untrue, jaundiced, and perhaps monomaniacal; but he seemed to doubt whether there had ever been a time at which it could have been decided that Trevelyan was so mad as to make it necessary that the law should interfere to take care of him. A man, – so argued the doctor, – need not be mad because he is jealous, even though his jealousy be ever so absurd. And Trevelyan, in his jealousy, had done nothing cruel, nothing wasteful, nothing infamous. In all this Nora was very little inclined to agree with the doctor, and thought nothing could be more infamous than Trevelyan's conduct at the present moment, – unless, indeed, he could be screened from infamy by that plea of madness. But then there was more behind. Trevelyan had been so wasted by the kind of life which he had led, and possessed by nature stamina so insufficient to resist such debility, that it was very doubtful whether he would not sink altogether before he could be made to begin to rise. But one thing was clear. He should be contradicted in nothing. If he chose to say that the moon was made of green cheese, let it be conceded to him that the moon was made of green cheese. Should he make any other assertion equally removed from the truth, let it not be contradicted. Who would oppose a man with one foot in the grave ?

'Then, Hugh, the sooner I am at Monkhams the better,' said Nora, who had again been subjected to innuendoes which had been unendurable to her. This was on the 7th of August, and it still wanted three days to that on which the journey to Monkhams was to be made.

'He never says anything to me on the subject,' said Hugh.

'Because you have made him afraid of you. I almost think that Emily and the doctor are wrong in their treatment, and that it would be better to stand up to him and tell him the truth.' But the three days passed away, and Nora was not driven to any such vindication of her sister's character towards her sister's husband.

96

Monkhams

On the 10th of August Nora Rowley left the cottage by the river-side at Twickenham, and went down to Monkhams. The reader need hardly be told that Hugh brought her up from Twickenham and sent her off in the railway carriage. They agreed that no day could be fixed for their marriage till something further should be known of Trevelyan's state. While he was in his present condition such a marriage could not have been other than very sad. Nora, when she left the cottage, was still very bitter against her brother-in-law, quoting the doctor's opinion as to his sanity, and expressing her own as to his conduct under that supposition. She also believed that he would rally in health, and was therefore, on that account, less inclined to pity him than was his wife. Emily Trevelyan of course saw more of him than did her sister, and understood better how possible it was that a man might be in such a condition as to be neither mad nor sane; — not mad, so that all power over his own actions need be taken from him; nor sane, so that he must be held to be accountable for his words and thoughts. Trevelyan did nothing, and attempted to do nothing, that could injure his wife and child. He submitted himself to medical advice. He did not throw away his money. He had no Bozzle now waiting at his heels. He was generally passive in his wife's hands as to all outward things. He was not violent in rebuke, nor did he often allude to their past unhappiness. But he still maintained, by a word spoken every now and then, that he had been right throughout in his contest with his wife, — and that his wife had at last acknowl-edged that it was so. She never contradicted him, and he became bolder and bolder in his assertions, endeavouring on various occasions to obtain some expression of an assent from Nora. But Nora would not assent, and he would scowl at her, saying words, both in her presence and behind her back, which implied that she was his enemy. 'Why not yield to him?' her sister said the day before she went. 'I have yielded, and your doing so cannot make it worse.'

'I can't do it. It would be false. It is better that I should go away. I cannot pretend to agree with him, when I know that his mind is working altogether under a delusion.' When the hour for her departure came, and Hugh was waiting for her, she thought that it would be better that she should go, without seeing Trevelyan. 'There will only be more anger,' she pleaded. But her sister would not be contented that she should leave the house in this fashion, and urged at last, with tears running down her cheeks, that this might possibly be the last interview between them.

'Say a word to him in kindness before you leave us,' said Mrs Trevelyan. Then Nora went up to her brother-in-law's bed-side, and told him that she was going, and expressed a hope that he might be stronger when she returned. And as she did so she put her hand upon the bed-side, intending to press his in token of affection. But his face was turned from her, and he seemed to take no notice of her. 'Louis,' said his wife, 'Nora is going to Monkhams. You will say good-bye to her before she goes?'

'If she be not my enemy, I will,' said he.

'I have never been your enemy, Louis,' said Nora, 'and certainly I am not now.'

'She had better go,' he said. 'It is very little more that I expect of any one in this world; – but I will recognise no one as my friend who will not acknowledge that I have been sinned against during the last two years; – sinned against cruelly and utterly.' Emily, who was standing at the bed-head, shuddered as she heard this, but made no reply. Nor did Nora speak again, but crept silently out of the room; – and in half a minute her sister followed her.

'I feared how it would be,' said Nora.

'We can only do our best. God knows that I try to do mine.'

'I do not think you will ever see him again,' said Hugh to her in the train.

'Would you have had me act otherwise? It is not that it would have been a lie. I would not have minded that to ease the shattered feelings of one so infirm and suffering as he. In dealing with mad people I suppose one must be false. But I should have been accusing her; and it may be that he will get well, and it might be that he would then remember what I had said.'

At the station near Monkhams she was met by Lady Peterborough in the carriage. A tall footman in livery came on to the platform to show her the way and to look after her luggage, and she could not fail to remember that the man might have been her own servant, instead of being the servant of her who now sat in Lord Peterborough's carriage. And when she saw the carriage, and her ladyship's great bay horses, and the glittering harness, and the respectably responsible coachman, and the arms on the panel, she smiled to herself at the sight of these first outward manifestations of the rank and wealth of the man who had once been her lover. There are men who look as though they were the owners of bay horses and responsible coachmen and family blazons, – from whose outward personal appearance, demeanour, and tone of voice, one would expect a following of liveries and a magnificence of belongings; but Mr Glascock had by no means been such a man. It had suited his taste to keep these things in abeyance, and to place his pride in the oaks and elms of his park rather than in any of those appanages of grandeur which a man may carry about with him. He could talk of his breed of sheep on an occasion, but he never talked of his horses; and though he knew his position and all its glories as well as any nobleman in England, he was ever inclined to hang back a little in going out of a room,* and to bear himself as though he were a small personage in the world. Some perception of all this came across Nora's mind as she saw the equipage, and tried to reflect, at a moment's notice, whether the case might have been different with her, had Mr Glascock worn a little of his tinsel outside when she first met him. Of course she told herself that had he worn it all on the outside, and carried it ever so gracefully, it could have made no difference.

It was very plain, however, that, though Mr Glascock did not like bright feathers for himself, he chose that his wife should wear them. Nothing could be prettier than the way in which Caroline Spalding, whom we first saw as she was about to be stuck into the interior of the diligence, at Saint Michel, now filled her carriage as Lady Peterborough. The greeting between them was very affectionate, and there was a kiss in the carriage, even though the two pretty hats, perhaps, suffered something. 'We are so glad to have you at last,' said Lady Peterborough. 'Of course we are very quiet; but you won't mind that.' Nora declared that no house could be too quiet for her, and then said something of the melancholy scene which she had just left. 'And no time is fixed for your own marriage? But of course it has not been possible. And why should you be in a hurry? We quite understand that this is to be your home till everything has arranged itself.' There was a drive of four or five miles before they reached the park gates, and nothing could be kinder or more friendly than was the new peeress; but Nora told herself that there was no forgetting that her friend was a peeress. She would not be so ill-conditioned as to suggest to herself that her friend patronised her; – and, indeed, had she done so, the suggestion would have been false; – but she could not rid herself of a certain sensation of external inferiority, and of a feeling that the superiority ought to be on her side, as all this might have been hers, – only that she had not thought it worth her while to accept it. As these ideas came into her mind, she hated herself for entertaining them; and yet, come they would. While she was talking about her emblematic beef-steak with Hugh, she had no regret, no uneasiness, no conception that any state of life could be better for her than that state in which an emblematic beef-steak was of vital importance; but she could not bring her mind to the same condition of unalloyed purity while sitting with Lady Peterborough in Lord Peterborough's carriage. And for her default in this respect she hated herself.

'This is the beginning of the park,' said her friend.

'And where is the house?'

'You can't see the house for ever so far yet; it is two miles off. There is about a mile before you come to the gates, and over a mile afterwards. One has a sort of feeling when one is in that one can't get out, – it is so big.' In so speaking, it was Lady Peterborough's special endeavour to state without a boast facts which were indifferent, but which must be stated.

'It is very magnificent,' said Nora. There was in her voice the slightest touch of sarcasm, which she would have given the world not to have uttered; – but it had been irrepressible.

Lady Peterborough understood it instantly, and forgave it, not attributing to it more than its true meaning, acknowledging to herself that it was natural. 'Dear Nora,' she said, – not knowing what to say, blushing as she spoke, – 'the magnificence is nothing; but the man's love is everything.'

Nora shook herself, and determined that she would behave well. The effort should be made, and the required result should be produced by it. 'The magnificence, as an adjunct, is a great deal,' she said; 'and for his sake, I hope that you enjoy it.'

'Of course I enjoy it.'

'Wallachia's teachings and preachings have all been thrown to the wind, I hope.'

'Not quite all. Poor dear Wally! I got a letter from her the other day, which she began by saying that she would attune her correspondence to my changed condition in life. I understood the reproach so thoroughly! And, when she told me little details of individual men and women, and of things she had seen, and said not a word about the rights of women, or even of politics generally, I felt that I was a degraded creature in her sight. But, though you laugh at her, she did me good, – and will do good to others. Here we are inside Monkhams, and now you must look at the avenue.'

Nora was now rather proud of herself. She had made the effort, and it had been successful; and she felt that she could speak naturally, and express her thoughts honestly. 'I remember his telling me about the avenue the first time I ever saw him; – and here it is. I did not think then that I should ever live to see the glories of Monkhams. Does it go all the way like this to the house?'

'Not quite; – where you see the light at the end the road turns to the right, and the house is just before you. There are great iron gates, and terraces, and wondrous paraphernalia before you get up to the door. I can tell you Monkhams is quite a wonder. I have to shut myself up every Wednesday morning, and hand the house over to Mrs Crutch, the housekeeper, who comes out in a miraculous brown silk gown, to show it to visitors. On other days, you'll find Mrs Crutch quite civil and useful; – but on Wednesdays, she is majestic. Charles always goes off among his sheep on that day, and I shut myself up with a pile of books in a little room. You will have to be imprisoned with me. I do so long to peep at the visitors.'

'And I dare say they want to peep at you.'

'I proposed at first to show them round myself; – but Charles wouldn't let me.'

'It would have broken Mrs Crutch's heart.'

'That's what Charles said. He thinks that Mrs Crutch tells them that I'm locked up somewhere, and that that gives a zest to the search. Some people from Nottingham once did break into old Lady Peterborough's room, and the show was stopped for a year. There was such a row about it! It prevented Charles coming up for the county. But he wouldn't have got in; and therefore it was lucky, and saved money.'

By this time Nora was quite at her ease; but still there was before her the other difficulty, of meeting Lord Peterborough. They were driven out of the avenue, and round to the right, and through the iron gate, and up to the huge front door. There, upon the top step, was standing Lord Peterborough, with a billycock hat and a very old shooting coat, and nankeen trousers, which were considerably too short for him. It was one of the happinesses of his life to dress just as he pleased as he went about his own place; and it certainly was his pleasure to wear older clothes than any one else in his establishment. 'Miss Rowley,' he said, coming forward to give her a hand out of the carriage, 'I am delighted that you should see Monkhams at last.'

'You see I have kept you to your promise. Caroline has been telling me everything about it; but she is not quite a complete guide as yet. She does not know where the seven oaks are. Do you remember telling me of the seven oaks?'

'Of course I do. They are five miles off; – at Clatton farm, Carry. I don't think you have been near Clatton yet. We will ride there to-morrow.' And thus Nora Rowley was made at home at Monkhams.

She was made at home, and after a week or two she was very happy. She soon perceived that her host was a perfect gentleman, and as such, a man to be much loved. She had probably never questioned the fact, whether Mr Glascock was a gentleman or not, and now she did not analyse it. It probably never occurred to her, even at the present time, to say to herself that he was certainly that thing, so impossible of definition, and so capable of recognition; but she knew that she had to do with one whose presence was always pleasant to her, whose words and acts towards her extorted her approbation, whose thoughts seemed to her to be always good and manly. Of course she had not loved him, because she had previously known Hugh Stanbury. There could be no comparison between the two men. There was a brightness about Hugh which Lord Peterborough could not rival. Otherwise, – except for this reason, – it seemed to her to be impossible that any young woman should fail to love Lord Peterborough when asked to do so.

About the middle of September there came a very happy time for her, when Hugh was asked down to shoot partridges, – in the doing of which, however, all his brightness did not bring him near in excellence to his host. Lord Peterborough had been shooting partridges all his life, and shot them with a precision which excited Hugh's envy. To own the truth, Stanbury did not shoot well, and was treated rather with scorn by the gamekeeper; but in other respects he spent three or four of the happiest days of his life. He had his work to do, and after the second day over the stubbles, declared that the exigencies of the D. R. were too severe to enable him to go out with his gun again; but those rambles about the park with Nora, for which, among the exigencies of the D. R., he did find opportunity, were never to be forgotten.

'Of course I remember that it might have been mine,' she said, sitting with him under an old, hollow, withered sloping stump of an oak, which still, however, had sufficient of a head growing from one edge of the trunk to give them the shade they wanted; 'and if you wish me to own to regrets, – I will.'

'It would kill me, I think, if you did; and yet I cannot get it out of my head that if it had not been for me your rank and position in life might have been so – so suitable to you.'

'No, Hugh; there you're wrong. I have thought about it a good deal, too; and I know very well that the cold beef-steak in the cupboard is the thing for me. Caroline will do very well here. She looks like a peeress, and bears her honours grandly; but they will never harden her. I, too, could have been magnificent with fine feathers. Most birds are equal to so much as that. I fancy that I could have looked the part of the fine English lady, and could have patronised clergymen's wives in the country, could have held my own among my peers in London, and could have kept Mrs Crutch in order; but it would have hardened me, and I should have learned to think that to be a lady of fashion was everything.'

'I do not believe a bit of it.'

'It is better as it is, Hugh; – for me at least. I had always a sort of conviction that it would be better, though I had a longing to play the other part. Then you came, and you have saved me. Nevertheless, it is very nice, Hugh, to have the oaks to sit under.' Stanbury declared that it was very nice.

But still nothing was settled about the wedding. Trevelyan's condition was so uncertain that it was very difficult to settle anything. Though nothing was said on the subject between Stanbury and Mrs Trevelyan, and nothing written between Nora and her sister, it could not but be remembered that should Trevelyan die, his widow would require a home with them. They were deterred from choosing a house by this reflection, and were deterred from naming a day also by the consideration that were they to do so, Trevelyan's state might still probably prevent it. But this was arranged, that if Trevelyan lived through the winter, or even if he should not live, their marriage should not be postponed beyond the end of March. Till that time Lord Peterborough would remain at Monkhams, and it was understood that Nora's invitation extended to that period.

'If my wife does not get tired of you, I shall not,' Lord Peterborough said to Nora. 'The thing is that when you do go we shall miss you so terribly.' In September, too, there happened another event which took Stanbury to Exeter, and all needful particulars as to that event shall be narrated in the next chapter.

97

Mrs Brooke Burgess

It may be doubted whether there was a happier young woman in England than Dorothy Stanbury when that September came which was to make her the wife of Mr Brooke Burgess, the new partner in the firm of Cropper and Burgess. Her early aspirations in life had been so low, and of late there had come upon her such a succession of soft showers of success, – mingled now and then with slight threatenings of storms which had passed away, – that the Close at Exeter seemed to her to have become a very Paradise. Her aunt's temper had sometimes been to her as the threat of a storm, and there had been the Gibson marriage treaty, and the short-lived opposition to the other marriage treaty which had seemed to her to be so very preferable; but everything had gone at last as though she had been Fortune's favourite, – and now had come this beautiful arrangement about Cropper and Burgess, which would save her from being carried away to live among strangers in London! When she first became known to us on her coming to Exeter, in compliance with her aunt's suggestion, she was timid, silent, and altogether without self-reliance. Even they who knew her best had never guessed that she possessed a keen sense of humour, a nice appreciation of character, and a quiet reticent wit of her own, under that staid and frightened demeanour. Since her engagement with Brooke Burgess it seemed to those who watched her that her character had become changed, as does that of a flower when it opens itself in its growth. The sweet gifts of nature within became visible, the petals sprang to view, and the leaves spread themselves, and the sweet scent was felt upon the air. Had she remained at Nuncombe, it is probable that none would ever have known her but her sister. It was necessary to this flower that it should be warmed by the sun of life, and strengthened by the breezes of opposition, and filled by the showers of companionship, before it could become aware of its own loveliness. Dorothy was one who, had she remained ever unseen in the retirement of her mother's village cottage, would have lived and died ignorant of even her own capabilities for enjoyment. She had not dreamed that she could win a man's love, – had hardly dreamed till she had lived at Exeter that she had love of her own to give back in return. She had not known that she could be firm in her own opinion, that she could laugh herself and cause others to laugh, that she could be a lady and know that other women were not so, that she had good looks of her own and could be very happy when told of them by lips that she loved. The flower that blows the quickest is never the sweetest. The fruit that ripens tardily has ever the finest flavour. It is often the same with men and women. The lad who talks at twenty as men should talk at thirty, has seldom much to say worth the hearing when he is forty; and the girl who at eighteen can shine in society with composure, has generally given over shining before she is a full-grown woman. With Dorothy the scent and beauty of the flower, and the flavour of the fruit, had come late; but the fruit will keep, and the flower will not fall to pieces with the heat of an evening.

'How marvellously your bride has changed since she has been here,' said Mrs MacHugh to Miss Stanbury. 'We thought she couldn't say boo to a goose at first; but she holds her own now among the best of 'em.'

'Of course she does; – why shouldn't she? I never knew a Stanbury yet that was a fool.'

'They are a wonderful family, of course,' said Mrs MacHugh; 'but I think that of all of them she is the most wonderful. Old Barty said something to her at my house yesterday that wasn't intended to be kind.'

'When did he ever intend to be kind?'

'But he got no change out of her. "The Burgesses have been in Exeter a long time," she said, "and I don't see why we should not get on at any rate as well as those before us." Barty grunted and growled and slunk away. He thought she would shake in her shoes when he spoke to her.'

'He has never been able to make a Stanbury shake in her shoes yet,' said the old lady.

Early in September, Dorothy went to Nuncombe Putney to spend a week with her mother and sister at the cottage. She had insisted on this, though Priscilla had hinted, somewhat unnecessarily, that Dorothy, with her past comforts and her future prospects, would find the accommodation at the cottage very limited. 'I suppose you and I, Pris, can sleep in the same bed, as we always did,' she said, with a tear in each eye. Then Priscilla had felt ashamed of herself, and had bade her come.

'The truth is, Dolly,' said the elder sister, 'that we feel so unlike marrying and giving in marriage at Nuncombe, that I'm afraid you'll lose your brightness and become dowdy, and grim, and misanthropic, as we are. When mamma and I sit down to what we call dinner, I always feel that there is a grace hovering in the air different to that which she says.'

'And what is it, Pris?'

'Pray, God, don't quite starve us, and let everybody else have indigestion. We don't say it out loud, but there it is; and the spirit of it might damp the orange blossoms.'

She went of course, and the orange blossoms were not damped. She had long walks with her sister round by Niddon and Ridleigh, and even as far distant as Cockchaffington, where much was said about that wicked Colonel as they stood looking at the porch of the church. 'I shall be so happy,' said Dorothy, 'when you and mother come to us. It will be such a joy to me that you should be my guests.'

'But we shall not come.'

'Why not, Priscilla?'

'I know it will be so. Mamma will not care for going, if I do not go.'

'And why should you not come?'

'For a hundred reasons, all of which you know, Dolly. I am stiff, impracticable, ill-conditioned, and very bad at going about visiting. I am always thinking that other people ought to have indigestion, and perhaps I might come to have some such feeling about you and Brooke.'

'I should not be at all afraid of that.'

'I know that my place in the world is here, at Nuncombe Putney. I have a pride about myself, and think that I never did wrong but once, – when I let mamma go into that odious Clock House. It is a bad pride, and yet I'm proud of it. I hav'n't got a gown fit to go and stay with you, when you become a grand lady in Exeter. I don't doubt you'd give me any sort of gown I wanted.'

'Of course I would. Ain't we sisters, Pris?'

'I shall not be so much your sister as he will be your husband. Besides, I hate to take things. When Hugh sends money, and for mamma's sake it is accepted, I always feel uneasy while it lasts, and think that that plague of an indigestion ought to come upon me also. Do you remember the lamb that came when you went away? It made me so sick.'

'But, Priscilla; – isn't that morbid?'

'Of course it is. You don't suppose I really think it grand. I am morbid. But I am strong enough to live on, and not get killed by the morbidity. Heaven knows how much more there may be of it; – forty years, perhaps, and probably the greater portion of that absolutely alone; – '

'No; – you'll be with us then, – if it should come.'

'I think not, Dolly. Not to have a hole of my own would be intolerable to me. But, as I was saying, I shall not be unhappy. To enjoy life, as you do, is I suppose out of the question for me. But I have a satisfaction when I get to the end of the quarter and find that there is not half-a-crown due to any one. Things get dearer and dearer, but I have a comfort even in that. I have a feeling that I should like to bring myself to the straw a day.' Of course there were offers made of aid, – offers which were rather prayers, – and plans suggested of what might be done between Brooke and Hugh; but Priscilla declared that all such plans were odious to her. 'Why should you be unhappy about us?' she continued. 'We will come and see you, – at least I will, – perhaps once in six months, and you shall pay for the railway ticket; only I won't stay, because of the gown.'

'Is not that nonsense, Pris?'

'Just at present it is, because mamma and I have both got new gowns for the wedding. Hugh sent them, and ever so much money to buy bonnets and gloves.'

'He is to be married himself soon, – down at a place called Monkhams. Nora is staying there.'

'Yes; – with a lord,' said Priscilla. 'We sha'n't have to go there, at any rate.'

'You liked Nora when she was here?'

'Very much; – though I thought her self-willed. But she is not worldly, and she is conscientious. She might have married that lord herself if she would. I do like her. When she comes to you at Exeter, if the wedding gown isn't quite worn out, I shall come and see her. I knew she liked him when she was here, but she never said so.'

'She is very pretty, is she not? He sent me her photograph.'

'She is handsome rather than pretty. I wonder why it is that you two should be married, and so grandly married, and that I shall never, never have any one to love.'

'Oh, Priscilla, do not say that. If I have a child will you not love it?'

'It will be your child; – not mine. Do not suppose that I complain. I know that it is right. I know that you ought to be married and I ought not. I know that there is not a man in Devonshire who would take me, or a man in Devonshire whom I would accept. I know that I am quite unfit for any other kind of life than this. I should make any man wretched, and any man would make me wretched. But why is it so? I believe that you would make any man happy.'

'I hope to make Brooke happy.'

'Of course you will, and therefore you deserve it. We'll go home now, dear, and get mamma's things ready for the great day.'

On the afternoon before the great day all the visitors were to come, and during the forenoon old Miss Stanbury was in a great fidget. Luckily for Dorothy, her own preparations were already made, so that she could give her time to her aunt without injury to herself. Miss Stanbury had come to think of herself as though all the reality of her life had passed away from her. Every resolution that she had formed had been broken. She had had the great enemy of her life, Barty Burgess, in the house with her upon terms that were intended to be amicable, and had arranged with him a plan for the division of the family property. Her sister-in-law, whom in the heyday of her strength she had chosen to regard as her enemy, and with whom even as yet there had been no reconciliation, was about to become her guest, as was also Priscilla, – whom she had ever disliked almost as much as she had respected. She had quarrelled utterly with Hugh, – in such a manner as to leave no possible chance of a reconciliation, — and he also was about to be her guest. And then, as to her chosen heir, she was now assisting him in doing the only thing, as to which she had declared that if he did do it, he should not be her heir. As she went about the house, under an idea that such a multiplicity of persons could not be housed and fed without superhuman exertion, she thought of all this, and could not help confessing to herself that her life had been very vain. It was only when her eyes rested on Dorothy, and she saw how supremely happy was the one person whom she had taken most closely to her heart, that she could feel that she had done anything that should not have been left undone. 'I think I'll sit down now, Dorothy,' she said, 'or I sha'n't be able to be with you to-morrow.'

'Do, aunt. Everything is all ready, and nobody will be here for an hour yet. Nothing can be nicer than the rooms, and nothing ever was done so well before. I'm only thinking how lonely you'll be when we're gone.'

'It'll be only for six weeks.'

'But six weeks is such a long time.'

'What would it have been if he had taken you up to London, my pet? Are you sure your mother wouldn't like a fire in her room, Dorothy?'

'A fire in September, aunt?'

'People live so differently. One never knows.'

'They never have but one fire at Nuncombe, aunt, summer or winter.'

'That's no reason they shouldn't be comfortable here.' However, she did not insist on having the fire lighted.

Mrs Stanbury and Priscilla came first, and the meeting was certainly very uncomfortable. Poor Mrs Stanbury was shy, and could hardly speak a word. Miss Stanbury thought that her visitor was haughty, and, though she endeavoured to be gracious, did it with a struggle. They called each other ma'am, which made Dorothy uneasy. Each of them was so dear to her, that it was a pity that they should glower at each other like enemies. Priscilla was not at all shy; but she was combative, and, as her aunt said of her afterwards, would not keep her prickles in. 'I hope, Priscilla, you like weddings,' said Miss Stanbury to her, not knowing where to find a subject for conversation.

'In the abstract I like them,' said Priscilla. Miss Stanbury did not know what her niece meant by liking weddings in the abstract, and was angry.

'I suppose you do have weddings at Nuncombe Putney some-times,' she said.

'I hope they do,' said Priscilla, 'but I never saw one. To-morrow will be my first experience.'

'Your own will come next, my dear,' said Miss Stanbury.

'I think not,' said Priscilla. 'It is quite as likely to be yours, aunt.' This, Miss Stanbury thought, was almost an insult, and she said nothing more on the occasion.

Then came Hugh and the bridegroom. The bridegroom, as a matter of course, was not accommodated in the house, but he was allowed to come there for his tea. He and Hugh had come together; and for Hugh a bed-room had been provided. His aunt had not seen him since he had been turned out of the house, because of his bad practices, and Dorothy had anticipated the meeting between them with alarm. It was, however, much more pleasant than had been that between the ladies. 'Hugh,' she said stiffly, 'I am glad to see you on such an occasion as this.'

'Aunt,' he said, 'I am glad of any occasion that can get me an entrance once more into the dear old house. I am so pleased to see you.' She allowed her hand to remain in his a few moments, and murmured something which was intended to signify her satisfaction. 'I must tell you that I am going to be married myself, to one of the dearest, sweetest, and loveliest girls that ever were seen, and you must congratulate me.'

'I do, I do; and I hope you may be happy.'

'We mean to try to be; and some day you must let me bring her to you, and show her. I shall not be satisfied, if you do not know my wife.' She told Martha afterwards that she hoped that Mr Hugh had sown his wild oats, and that matrimony would sober him. When, however, Martha remarked that she believed Mr Hugh to be as hardworking a young man as any in London, Miss Stanbury shook her head sorrowfully. Things were being very much changed with her; but not even yet was she to be brought to approve of work done on behalf of a penny newspaper.

On the following morning, at ten o'clock, there was a procession from Miss Stanbury's house into the Cathedral, which was made entirely on foot; – indeed, no assistance could have been given by any carriage, for there is a back entrance to the Cathedral, near to the Lady Chapel, exactly opposite Miss Stanbury's house. There were many of the inhabitants of the Close there, to see the procession, and the cathedral bells rang out their peals very merrily. Brooke, the bridegroom, gave his arm to Miss Stanbury, which was, no doubt, very improper, – as he should have appeared in the church as coming from quite some different part of the world. Then came the bride, hanging on her brother, then two bridesmaids, – friends of Dorothy's, living in the town; and, lastly, Priscilla with her mother, for nothing would induce Priscilla to take the part of a bridesmaid. 'You might as well ask an owl to sing to you,' she said. 'And then all the frippery would be thrown away upon me.' But she stood close to Dorothy, and when the ceremony had been performed, was the first, after Brooke, to kiss her.

Everybody acknowledged that the bride was a winsome bride. Mrs MacHugh was at the breakfast, and declared afterwards that Dorothy Burgess, – as she then was pleased to call her, – was a girl very hard to be understood. 'She came here,' said Mrs MacHugh, 'two years ago, a plain, silent, shy, dowdy young woman, and we all said that Miss Stanbury would be tired of her in a week. There has never come a time in which there was any visible difference in her, and now she is one of our city beauties, with plenty to say to everybody, with a fortune in one pocket and her aunt in the other, and everybody is saying what a fortunate fellow Brooke Burgess is to get her. In a year or two she'll be at the top of everything in the city, and will make her way in the county too.'

The compiler of this history begs to add his opinion to that of 'everybody,' as quoted above by Mrs MacHugh. He thinks that Brooke Burgess was a very fortunate fellow to get his wife.

98

Acquitted

During this time, while Hugh was sitting with his love under the oak trees at Monkhams, and Dorothy was being converted into Mrs Brooke Burgess in Exeter Cathedral, Mrs Trevelyan was living with her husband in the cottage at Twickenham. Her life was dreary enough, and there was but very little of hope in it to make its dreariness supportable. As often happens in periods of sickness, the single friend who could now be of service to the one or to the other was the doctor. He came daily to them, and with that quick growth of confidence which medical kindness always inspires, Trevelyan told to this gentleman all the history of his married life, – and all that Trevelyan told to him he repeated to Trevelyan's wife. It may therefore be understood that Trevelyan, between them, was treated like a child.

Dr Nevill had soon been able to tell Mrs Trevelyan that her

husband's health had been so shattered as to make it improbable that he should ever again be strong either in body or in mind. He would not admit, even when treating his patient like a child, that he had ever been mad, and spoke of Sir Marmaduke's threat as unfortunate. 'But what could papa have done?' asked the wife.

'It is often, no doubt, difficult to know what to do; but threats are seldom of avail to bring a man back to reason. Your father was angry with him, and yet declared that he was mad. That in itself was hardly rational. One does not become angry with a madman.'

One does not become angry with a madman; but while a man has power in his hands over others, and when he misuses that power grossly and cruelly, who is there that will not be angry? The misery of the insane more thoroughly excites our pity than any other suffering to which humanity is subject; but it is necessary that the madness should be acknowledged to be madness before the pity can be felt. One can forgive, or, at any rate, make excuses for any injury when it is done; but it is almost beyond human nature to forgive an injury when it is a-doing, let the condition of the doer be what it may. Emily Trevelyan at this time suffered infinitely. She was still willing to yield in all things possible, because her husband was ill, – because perhaps he was dying; but she could no longer satisfy herself with thinking that all that she admitted, – all that she was still ready to admit, – had been conceded in order that her concessions might tend to soften the afflictions of one whose reason was gone. Dr Nevill said that her husband was not mad; – and indeed Trevelyan seemed now to be so clear in his mind that she could not doubt what the doctor said to her. She could not think that he was mad, – and yet he spoke of the last two years as though he had suffered from her almost all that a husband could suffer from a wife's misconduct. She was in doubt about his health. 'He may recover,' the doctor said; 'but he is so weak that the slightest additional ailment would take him off.' At this time Trevelyan could not raise himself from his bed, and was carried, like a child, from one room to another. He could eat nothing solid, and believed himself to be dying. In spite of his weakness, – and of his savage memories in regard to the past, – he treated his wife on all ordinary subjects with consideration. He spoke much of his money, telling her that he had not altered, and would not alter, the will that he had made immediately on his marriage. Under that will all his property would be hers for her life, and would go to their child when she was dead. To her this will was more than just, – it was generous in the confidence which it placed in her; and he told his lawyer, in her presence, that, to the best of his judgment, he need not change it. But still there passed hardly a day in which he did not make some allusion to the great wrong which he had endured, throwing in her teeth the confessions which she had made, – and almost accusing her of that which she certainly never had confessed, even when, in the extremity of her misery at Casalunga, she had thought that it little mattered what she said, so that for the moment he might be appeased. If he died, was he to die in this belief? If he lived, was he to live in this belief? And if he did so believe, was it possible that he should still trust her with his money and with his child?

'Emily,' he said one day, 'it has been a terrible tragedy, has it not?' She did not answer his question, sitting silent as it was her custom to do when he addressed her after such fashion as this. At such times she would not answer him; but she knew that he would press her for an answer. 'I blame him more than I do you,' continued Trevelyan, – 'infinitely more. He was a serpent intending to sting me from the first, – not knowing perhaps how deep the sting would go.' There was no question in this, and the assertion was one which had been made so often that she could let it pass. 'You are young, Emily, and it may be that you will marry again.'

'Never,' she said, with a shudder. It seemed to her then that marriage was so fearful a thing that certainly she could never venture upon it again.

'All I ask of you is, that should you do so, you will be more careful of your husband's honour.'

'Louis,' she said, getting up and standing close to him, 'tell me what it is that you mean.' It was now his turn to remain silent, and hers to demand an answer. 'I have borne much,' she continued, 'because I would not vex you in your illness.'

'You have borne much?'

'Indeed and indeed, yes. What woman has ever borne more!'

'And I?' said he.

'Dear Louis, let us understand each other at last. Of what do you accuse me? Let us, at any rate, know each other's thoughts on this matter, of which each of us is ever thinking.'

'I make no new accusation.'

'I must protest then against your using words which seem to convey accusation. Since marriages were first known upon earth, no woman has ever been truer to her husband than I have been to you.'

'Were you lying to me then at Casalunga when you acknowledged that you had been false to your duties?'

'If I acknowledged that, I did lie. I never said that; but yet I did lie, – believing it to be best for you that I should do so. For your honour's sake, for the child's sake, weak as you are, Louis, I must protest that it was so. I have never injured you by deed or thought.'

'And yet you have lied to me ! Is a lie no injury; – and such a lie ! Emily, why did you lie to me ? You will tell me to-morrow that you never lied, and never owned that you had lied.'

Though it should kill him, she must tell him the truth now. 'You were very ill at Casalunga,' she said, after a pause.

'But not so ill as I am now. I could breathe that air. I could live there. Had I remained I should have been well now, – but what of that ?'

'Louis, you were dying there. Pray, pray listen to me. We thought that you were dying; and we knew also that you would be taken from that house.'

'That was my affair. Do you mean that I could not keep a house over my head ?' At this moment he was half lying, half sitting, in a large easy chair in the little drawing-room of their cottage, to which he had been carried from the adjoining bed-room. When not excited, he would sit for hours without moving, gazing through the open window, sometimes with some pretext of a book lying within the reach of his hand; but almost without strength to lift it, and certainly without power to read it. But now he had worked himself up to so much energy that he almost raised himself up in his chair, as he turned towards his wife. 'Had I not the world before me, to choose a house in ?'

'They would have put you somewhere, and I could not have reached you.'

'In a madhouse, you mean. Yes; – if you had told them.'

'Will you listen, dear Louis ? We knew that it was our duty to bring you home; and as you would not let me come to you, and serve you, and assist you to come here where you are safe, – unless I owned that you had been right, I said that you had been right.'

'And it was a lie, – you say now ?'

'All that is nothing. I can not go through it; nor should you. There is only one question. You do not think that I have been – ? I need not say the thing. You do not think that ?' As she asked the question, she knelt beside him, and took his hand in hers, and kissed it. 'Say that you do not think that, and I will never trouble you further about the past.'

'Yes; – that is it. You will never trouble me !' She glanced up into his face and saw there the old look which he used to wear when he was at Willesden and at Casalunga ; and there had come again the old tone in which he had spoken to her in the bitterness of his wrath: the look and the tone, which had made her sure that he was a madman. 'The craft and subtlety of women passes everything!' he said. 'And so at last I am to tell you that from the beginning it has been my doing. I will never say so, though I should die in refusing to do it.'

After that there was no possibility of further conversation, for there came upon him a fit of coughing, and then he swooned; and in half-an-hour he was in bed, and Dr Nevill was by his side. 'You must not speak to him at all on this matter,' said the doctor. 'But if he speaks to me?' she asked. 'Let it pass,' said the doctor. 'Let the subject be got rid of with as much ease as you can. He is very ill now, and even this might have killed him.' Nevertheless, though this seemed to be stern, Dr Nevill was very kind to her, declaring that the hallucination in her husband's mind did not really consist of a belief in her infidelity, but arose from an obstinate determination to yield nothing. 'He does not believe it; but he feels that were he to say as much, his hands would be weakened and yours strengthened.'

'Can he then be in his sane mind?'

'In one sense all misconduct is proof of insanity,' said the doctor. 'In his case the weakness of the mind has been consequent upon the weakness of the body.'

Three days after that Nora visited Twickenham from Monkhams in obedience to a telegram from her sister. 'Louis,' she said, 'had become so much weaker, that she hardly dared to be alone with him. Would Nora come to her?' Nora came of course, and Hugh met her at the station, and brought her with him to the cottage. He asked whether he might see Trevelyan, but was told that it would be better that he should not. He had been almost continually silent since the last dispute which he had with his wife; but he had given little signs that he was always thinking of the manner in which he had been brought home by her from Italy, and of the story she had told him of her mode of inducing him to come. Hugh Stanbury had been her partner in that struggle, and would probably be received, if not with sullen silence, then with some attempt at rebuke. But Hugh did see Dr Nevill, and learned from him that it was hardly possible that Trevelyan should live many hours. 'He has worn himself out,' said the doctor, 'and there is nothing left in him by which he can lay hold of life again.' Of Nora her brother-in-law took but little notice, and never again referred in her hearing to the great trouble of his life. He said to her a word or two about Monkhams, and asked a question now and again as to Lord Peterborough, – whom, however, he always called Mr Glascock;

but Hugh Stanbury's name was never mentioned by him. There was a feeling in his mind that at the very last he had been duped in being brought to England, and that Stanbury had assisted in the deception. To his wife he would whisper little petulant regrets for the loss of the comforts of Casalunga, and would speak of the air of Italy and of Italian skies and of the Italian sun, as though he had enjoyed at his Sienese villa all the luxuries which climate can give, and would have enjoyed them still had he been allowed to remain there. To all this she would say nothing. She knew now that he was failing quickly, and there was only one subject on which she either feared or hoped to hear him speak. Before he left her for ever and ever would he tell her that he had not doubted her faith?

She had long discussions with Nora on the matter, as though all the future of her life depended on it. It was in vain that Nora tried to make her understand that if hereafter the spirit of her husband could know anything of the troubles of his mortal life, could ever look back to the things which he had done in the flesh, then would he certainly know the truth, and all suspicion would be at an end. And if not, if there was to be no such retrospect, what did it matter now, for these few last hours before the coil should be shaken off, and all doubt and all sorrow should be at an end? But the wife, who was soon to be a widow, yearned to be acquitted in this world by him to whom her guilt or her innocence had been matter of such vital importance. 'He has never thought it,' said Nora.

'But if he would say so! If he would only look it! It will be all in all to me as long as I live in this world.' And then, though they had determined between themselves in spoken words never to regard him again as one who had been mad, in all their thoughts and actions towards him they treated him as though he were less responsible than an infant. And he was mad; – mad though every doctor in England had called him sane. Had he not been mad he must have been a fiend, – or he could not have tortured, as he had done, the woman to whom he owed the closest protection which one human being can give to another.

During these last days and nights she never left him. She had done her duty to him well, at any rate since the time when she had been enabled to come near him in Italy. It may be that in the first days of their quarrel, she had not been regardful, as she should have been, of a husband's will, – that she might have escaped this tragedy by submitting herself to the man's wishes, as she had always been ready to submit herself to his words. Had she been able always to keep her neck in the dust under his foot, their married life might have been passed without outward calamity, and it is possible that he might still have lived. But if she erred, surely she had been scourged for her error with scorpions. As she sat at his bedside watching him, she thought of her wasted youth, of her faded beauty, of her shattered happiness, of her fallen hopes. She had still her child, – but she felt towards him that she herself was so sad a creature, so sombre, so dark, so necessarily wretched from this time forth till the day of her death, that it would be better for the boy that she should never be with him. There could be nothing left for her but garments dark with woe, eyes red with weeping, hours sad from solitude, thoughts weary with memory. And even yet, – if he would only now say that he did not believe her to have been guilty, how great would be the change in her future life !

Then came an evening in which he seemed to be somewhat stronger than he had been. He had taken some refreshment that had been prepared for him, and, stimulated by its strength, had spoken a word or two both to Nora and to his wife. His words had been of no special interest, – alluding to some small detail of his own condition, such as are generally the chosen topics of conversation with invalids. But he had been pronounced to be better, and Nora spoke to him cheerfully, when he was taken into the next room by the man who was always at hand to move him. His wife followed him, and soon afterwards returned, and bade Nora good night. She would sit by her husband, and Nora was to go to the room below, that she might receive her lover there. He was expected out that evening, but Mrs Trevelyan said that she would not see him. Hugh came and went, and Nora took herself to the chamber. The hours of the night went on, and Mrs Trevelyan was still sitting by her husband's bed. It was still September, and the weather was very warm. But the windows had been all closed since an hour before sunset. She was sitting there thinking, thinking, thinking. Dr Nevill had told her that the time now was very near. She was not thinking now how very near it might be, but whether there might yet be time for him to say that one word to her.

'Emily,' he said, in the lowest whisper.

'Darling !' she answered, turning round and touching him with her hand.

'My feet are cold. There are no clothes on them.'

She took a thick shawl and spread it double across the bottom of the bed, and put her hand upon his arm. Though it was clammy with perspiration, it was chill, and she brought the warm clothes up close round his shoulders. 'I can't sleep,' he said. 'If I could sleep, I shouldn't mind.' Then he was silent again, and her thoughts went harping on, still on the same subject. She told herself that if ever that act of justice were to be done for her, it must be done that night. After a while she turned round over him ever so gently, and saw that his large eyes were open and fixed upon the wall.

She was kneeling now on the chair close by the bed head, and her hand was on the rail of the bedstead supporting her. 'Louis,' she said, ever so softly.

'Well.'

'Can you say one word for your wife, dear, dear, dearest husband?'

'What word?'

'I have not been a harlot to you; – have I?'

'What name is that?'

'But what a thing, Louis! Kiss my hand, Louis, if you believe me.' And very gently she laid the tips of her fingers on his lips. For a moment or two she waited, and the kiss did not come. Would he spare her in this the last moment left to him either for justice or for mercy? For a moment or two the bitterness of her despair was almost unendurable. She had time to think that were she once to withdraw her hand, she would be condemned for ever; – and that it must be withdrawn. But at length the lips moved, and with struggling ear she could hear the sound of the tongue within, and the verdict of the dying man had been given in her favour. He never spoke a word more either to annul it or to enforce it.

Some time after that she crept into Nora's room. 'Nora,' she said, waking the sleeping girl, 'it is all over.'

'Is he – dead?'

'It is all over. Mrs Richards is there. It is better than an hour since now. Let me come in.' She got into her sister's bed, and there she told the tale of her tardy triumph. 'He declared to me at last that he trusted me,' she said, – almost believing that real words had come from his lips to that effect. Then she fell into a flood of tears, and after a while she also slept.

99

Conclusion

At last the maniac was dead, and in his last moments he had made such reparation as was in his power for the evil that he had done. With that slight touch of his dry fevered lips he had made the assertion on which was to depend the future peace and comfort of the woman whom he had so cruelly misused. To her mind the acquittal was perfect; but she never explained to human ears, – not even to those of her sister, – the manner in which it had been given. Her life, as far as we are concerned with it, has been told. For the rest, it cannot be but that it should be better than that which was passed. If there be any retribution for such sufferings in money, liberty, and outward comfort, such retribution she possessed; – for all that had been his, was now hers. He had once suggested what she should do, were she even to be married again; and she had felt that of such a career there could be no possibility. Anything but that! We all know that widows' practices in this matter do not always tally with wives' vows; but, as regards Mrs Trevelyan, we are disposed to think that the promise will be kept. She has her child, and he will give her sufficient interest to make life worth having.

Early in the following spring Hugh Stanbury was married to Nora Rowley in the parish church of Monkhams, – at which place by that time Nora found herself to be almost as much at home as she might have been under other circumstances. They had prayed that the marriage might be very private; – but when the day arrived there was no very close privacy. The parish church was quite full, there were half-a-dozen bridesmaids, there was a great breakfast, Mrs Crutch had a new brown silk gown given to her, there was a long article in the county gazette, and there were short paragraphs in various metropolitan newspapers. It was generally thought among his compeers that Hugh Stanbury had married into the aristocracy, and that the fact was a triumph for the profession to which he belonged. It showed what a Bohemian could do, and that men of the press in England might gradually hope to force their way almost anywhere. So great was the name of Monkhams! He and his wife took for themselves a very small house near the Regent's Park, at which they intend to remain until Hugh shall have enabled himself to earn an additional two hundred a-year. Mrs Trevelyan did not come to live with them, but kept the cottage near the river at Twickenham. Hugh Stanbury was very averse to any protracted connection with comforts to be obtained from poor Trevelyans's income, and told Nora that he must hold her to her promise about the beefsteak in the cupboard. It is our opinion that Mr and Mrs Hugh Stanbury will never want for a beefsteak and all comfortable additions until the inhabitants of London shall cease to require newspapers on their breakfast tables.

Brooke and Mrs Brooke established themselves in the house in the Close on their return from their wedding tour, and Brooke at once put himself into intimate relations with the Messrs Croppers, taking his fair share of the bank work. Dorothy was absolutely installed as mistress in her aunt's house with many wonderful ceremonies, with the unlocking of cupboards, the outpouring of stores, the giving up of keys, and with many speeches made to Martha. This was all very painful to Dorothy, who could not bring herself to suppose it possible that she should be the mistress of that house, during her aunt's life. Miss Stanbury, however, of course persevered, speaking of herself as a worn-out old woman, with one foot in the grave, who would soon be carried away and put out of sight. But in a very few days things got back into their places, and Aunt Stanbury had the keys again. 'I knew how it would be, miss,' said Martha to her young mistress, 'and I didn't say nothing, 'cause you understand her so well.'

Mrs Stanbury and Priscilla still live at the cottage, which, however, to Priscilla's great disgust, has been considerably improved and prettily furnished. This was done under the auspices of Hugh, but with funds chiefly supplied from the house of Brooke, Dorothy, and Co. Priscilla comes into Exeter to see her sister, perhaps, every other week; but will never sleep away from home, and very rarely will eat or drink at her sister's table. 'I don't know why, I don't,' she said to Dorothy, 'but somehow it puts me out. It delays me in my efforts to come to the straw a day.' Nevertheless, the sisters are dear friends.

I fear that in some previous number a half promise was made that a husband should be found for Camilla French. That half-promise cannot be treated in the manner in which any whole promise certainly would have been handled. There is no husband ready for Cammy French. The reader, however, will be delighted to know that she made up her quarrel with her sister and Mr Gibson, and is now rather fond of being a guest at Mr Gibson's house. On her first return to Exeter after the Gibsons had come back from their little Cornish rustication, Camilla declared that she could not and would not bring herself to endure a certain dress of which Bella was very fond; — and as this dress had been bought for Camilla with special reference to the glories of her own anticipated married life, this objection was almost natural. But Bella treated it as absurd, and Camilla at last gave way.

It need only further be said that though Giles Hickbody and Martha are not actually married as yet, — men and women in their class of life always moving towards marriage with great precaution, — it is quite understood that the young people are engaged, and are to be made happy together at some future time.

NOTES

All information on variants between the text of the first edition and the manuscript comes from P. D. Edwards's invaluable edition of the novel, published by the University of Queensland Press in 1974, in the series *Victorian Texts*.

p.5 All the world before him were to choose: Milton, *Paradise Lost* XII, 646–7: 'The world was all before them, where to choose/Their place of rest ...'

p.6 a man of whom all people said all good things: a translation of one of Trollope's favourite Latin quotations, from Terence, *Andria* 96–7: 'Omnes omnia bona dicere' ('All men began to say all good things').

p.21 Marshall and Snellgrove: the Oxford Street haberdashers, founded in 1837.

p.28 Oxford In Chapter One we are told that Trevelyan had been to Cambridge.

world as an oyster ... a sword with which to open it: 'the world's my oyster,/Which I with sword will open' – *Merry Wives of Windsor* II.ii.4.

the famous war between Great Britain and Patagonia: this Trollopian joke presumably relates to some minor incident of the 1860s, which I have not been able to trace. Two shiploads of Welsh-speakers left for Patagonia in 1862 and 1865 to found the Welsh-speaking settlement which still survives there. In 1866 it was thought that a treaty between the settlers and the government of Argentina for the supply of the settlement was not being honoured, but nothing seems to have occurred which could even jestingly be said to constitute a 'war'.

p. 37 King Cophetua ... his beggar maid: Cophetua was an imaginary African king who, having renounced women, saw a beggar-girl from his window, fell in love with her, and lived long and happily with her.

p.39 Let the heavens fall ... such injustice as that: a glance at 'Ruat coelum, fiat justitia' – 'Though the heavens fall, let justice be done' (Latin) – attributed to the Emperor Ferdinand I.

p. 44 a job: 'a transaction in which public interest is sacrificed to private advantage' (*Oxford English Dictionary*)

p. 47 the Ritualists: the High Church party which advocated what other members of the Church of England regarded as the excessive observance of religious rites.

the Commission: the Ecclesiastical Commission, which was founded in 1835 to manage the estates and revenues of the Church of England.

p. 50 literates: men admitted to holy orders without attending a university or theological college, and regarded as socially beneath graduate clergy.

ad eundem: 'to the same [degree]' (Latin). In certain graduation ceremonies, when numerous candidates are being admitted to a given degree, the name of the degree, once used, is not given again, further candidates being admitted 'to the same degree' ('ad eundem gradum'). Trollope is thus playing on the fact that the 'literates' did not hold degrees, and that Exeter society regarded social qualifications as at least as important as academic ones.

p. 50 saltzes: for the German 'Salze', 'salts' – i.e. the salts found in spa waters.

p. 54 the John Bull and the Herald: both the *Morning Herald* and the *John Bull*, a weekly devoted to the cause of High Church Toryism, were very old-fashioned papers which had flourished when Miss Stanbury was young.

Mr Disraeli and his bill: the Second Reform Bill, introduced not by the Liberals, but by a Conservative administration in which Disraeli was Chancellor of the Exchequer and Leader of the House of Commons.

Lord Derby: Conservative Prime Minister under whom Disraeli served.

Mr Lowe: Robert Lowe (1811–92, and later First Viscount Sherbrooke) a fierce Liberal opponent of the Second Reform Bill, and Chancellor of the Exchequer in Gladstone's first administration. Victoria Glendinning, *Trollope* (London: Hutchinson, 1992), records the tradition that at Winchester Trollope was violently beaten by the older Lowe.

three gentlemen who had dissevered themselves from Mr Disraeli when Mr Disraeli was passing his Reform bill General Jonathan Peel (1799–1879, and son of Sir Robert Peel), Henry Herbert, fourth Earl of Carnarvon (1831–90), and Viscount Cranborne (1830–1903, later 3rd Marquis of Salisbury and Prime Minister).

General Peel: see note above.

Lord Eldon John Scott, first Earl of Eldon (1751–1838), Tory Lord Chancellor 1801–29, and a vigorous opponent of all reforms.

p.55 chignon: a coil of hair, wound round a pad, and worn at the nape of the neck or at the back of the head.

rent charges: charges upon lands, granted to one who is not owner of those lands.

the commutation of clergyman's income: under the Commutation Act of 1836, tithes were replaced by fixed money payments.

Colenso   John Colenso (1814–83), Bishop of Natal, who had attacked the sacramental system in his *Commentary on the Epistle to the Romans* (1861) and whose *Critical Examination of the Pentateuch* (1862–79) denied the authenticity of the first five books of the Old Testament, had been excommunicated by the Bishop of Cape Town in 1863, but confirmed in possession of the see by the Law Courts in 1866.

p.58 iron Pillar boxes ... for the receipt of letters: Trollope himself is usually credited with effecting the erection of the first pillar boxes in St Hellier in 1852.

p.62 meetings in the parks: a reference to the meeting of the Reform League on 23rd July 1866. When the crowd was turned away from the park by the police, the park railings were pushed down, and in the ensuing disorder a policeman was killed and over a hundred people seriously injured.

p.73 a Captain bold of Halifax: see 'Unfortunate Miss Bailey', a ballad by George Colman the Younger (1762–1836), in which 'a captain bold of Halifax' says 'I am a handsome man, but I'm a gay deceiver.'

p. 77 Griselda: the model of a patient and submissive wife in medieval literature, in particular Boccaccio's *Decameron* and Chaucer's *Clerkes Tale*.

p.91 women are to vote, and become doctors: See note to p.416, for the campaign for votes for women, which was particularly topical during the writing and publication of this novel, as was the medical education of women also. Women had been excluded from the practice of medicine by the Medical Act of 1858, although Elizabeth Blackwell, who had qualified in the USA, had succeeded in registering as a medical practitioner in England, having been in practice before the Act. In 1874 Sophia Jex-Blake (1840–1912) founded the London School of Medicine, and in 1877 established the right of women to practise.

p.95 Tom-and-Jerry hats: soft hats, as worn by Pierce Egan's comic characters who explore high and low haunts of pleasure in *Life in London* (1821).

p.102 admirable Crichton: James Crichton (1560–85), a graduate of St Andrews who was a prodigy of learning, reputed to have defeated the foremost professors in Italy in disputations in science and philosophy conducted in a dozen languages.

p.102 outward sign of an inward gift of mind: compare 'An outward and visible sign of an inward and spiritual grace' – from the Catechism in the Book of Common Prayer.

p.107 Wives, obey your husbands: 'Wives, submit yourselves unto your own husbands, as unto the Lord', Ephesians 5:22.

p.120 drag: a device applied to a wheel or wheels of a horse-drawn vehicle to slow it on a downward gradient; a brake-shoe.

p.147 the Irish Church: disestablishment of the Irish Church was one of the great parliamentary issues of the period, having been rejected by the Commons in 1867, then passed by the Commons but thrown out by the Lords in 1868. It was finally passed in 1869, after the publication of *He Knew He Was Right*.

present state of society in Rome: as a response to Garibaldi's invasion of the Papal States, the French occupied Rome in October 1867, in the face of the general hostility of the people of Rome.

p.160 Apollyon: the angel of the bottomless pit, Revelation 9:11

p.163 the erotic manoeuvres of such a beast . . . the cooing of any turtle dove: first edition reads, 'the erratic manoeuvres of such a beast . . . the wooing of any turtle-dove'. The present edition follows the manuscript, since, unlike other changes made between MS and first edition, this emendment renders the sense obscure, and could well be an example of censorship.

p.166 Mr Beales: Edmond Beales (1803–81), barrister, and President of the Reform League at the time of the Hyde Park riots.

p.178 downy: (slang) wide-awake, knowing

p.191 vanity and vexation of spirit: Ecclesiastes 1:14.

p.209 Great Tribulation: see Revelation 7:14.

p.217 Non olet: 'It does not smell' (Latin). When Titus, the son of the Emperor Vespasian, objected to his father's drawing money from a tax on public urinals, the Emperor held a coin to his son's nose, and asked whether its smell was offensive to him. On Titus's reply of 'No', Vespasian said, 'Yet it comes from urine.' ('Atqui e lotio est.') The incident, recorded by Suetonius in his *Life of Vespasian* XXII.3, is traditionally summed up in the saying, 'Pecunia non olet': 'The money does not smell', or, 'Money does not smell'.

p.227 Burgess: P. D. Edwards conjectures that this should read 'Brooke', pointing out that Brooke Burgess was originally to have been called 'Burgess Burgess', and that although most occurrences of 'Burgess' as a first name were corrected in the manuscript, this one may have remained uncorrected through an oversight.

p. 237 the donkey between two bundles of hay: 'Buridan's ass', a commonplace illustration of a man who hesitates when appealed to from two sides. Buridan, the fourteenth-century scholastic philosopher, proposed the case of an ass equally motivated by hunger and thirst, and placed equidistant between a pail of water and a peck of oats

p.242 Waterloo Bridge Station: in the manuscript they arrive at Paddington Station. The change renders the cab-driver's estimate of the distance to St Diddulph's-in-the-East outrageous.

p.263 Beales and Bright ... Church ... Throne: Edmond Beales (see note to page 166) and John Bright (1811–89), the radical MP and orator, were strong advocates of reform and of the disestablishment of the Irish Church, but neither was a declared republican.

p.272 His lines had fallen to him in very pleasant places: Psalm 16:6, 'The lines are fallen unto me in pleasant places'.

p.273 I do not like thee, Dr Fell; – why I cannot tell:

> I do not like thee, Dr Fell,
> The reason why I cannot tell;
> but this I know, and I know full well,
> I do not like thee, Dr Fell.

– lines by Thomas Brown (1663–1704), said to be based on the 33rd Epigram of martial, and addressed to Dr John Fell (1625–86), Dean of Christ Church, Oxford.

p.277 Mr Fell's great project: Fell invented a three-rail system for the Mont Cenis Summit Railway from Saint Michel to Susa, built 1866–7 and inaugurated in August 1867.

p.281 the kingdom of Italy: Florence was the capital of Italy from 1864 to 1870.

p.284 mere leather and prunella: words of Alexander Pope, commonly interpreted to mean the material of shoes, and hence unimportant things; see *Essay on Man* IV.204–5:

'Worth makes the man, and want of it, the fellow:
    The rest is all but leather and prunella.'
In fact Pope uses 'leather and prunella' to designate the callings of cobbler and clergyman – prunella being the woollen stuff from which a cleric's gown was made.

p.287 Turin ... robbed of its life as a capital: Turin had been capital of Piedmont until 1860, when it became capital of the new Kingdom of Italy until succeeded by Florence in 1864.

p.306 fruges consumere nati: 'those born to consume the fruits [of the earth]', Horace, *Epistles* I.1.27.

p.309 It is easier ... for a camel to go through the eye of a needle, than for a rich to enter into the kingdom of God: Matthew 19:24.

p.313 The labour we delight in physics pain: *Macbeth* II.iii.48.

p.316 shook the dust off his feet: see Luke 9:5 'And whosoever will not receive you, when ye go out of that city, shake off the very dust from your feet for testimony against them.'

p.326 to take the goods the gods provided: 'Take the good the gods provide you', Dryden, *Alexander's Feast*, ll. 106.

p.333 Othello's demand of Iago: probably one of the following: 'Be sure of it; give me ocular proof'; 'so prove it/That the probation bear no hinge nor loop/To hang a doubt on'; or, 'Give me a living reason she's disloyal' – *Othello* III.iii.364, 368–70 and 413.

p.335 The pity of it, Iago: *Othello* IV.i.192.

p.337 There had been method in Trevelyan's madness: compare *Hamlet* II.ii.203–4: 'Though this be madness, yet there is method in't.'

p.341 if certain American claims were not satisfied: the claim for damages by the United States against Britain as a neutral nation in the recent Civil War (1861–65) for its failure to prevent the supply of a naval cruiser, the *Alabama*, to the Confederate navy. The claim for the loss of sixty-eight ships was finally settled by arbitration in 1872 at $15,500,000 in gold. This and a number of other disputes were put to arbitration following the Treaty of Washington of 1871, marking a new era in international law.

p.342 Story, Miss Hosmer, and Hiram Powers ... Greenough and Phidias: William Wetmore Story (1819–95), Harriet Goodhue Hosmer (1830–1908), Hiram Powers (1805–73) and Horatio Greenough (1805–52), were all well-known American sculptors and scarcely the equals of Phidias (born *c.* 490 b.c.), one of the most celebrated sculptors of the ancient world.

the victory gained by the gunboats at Vicksburg ... the battle of Actium: During the Civil War in 1862, Unionist gunboats attacked Vicksburg on the Mississippi, but achieved no notable success. The parallel with the great naval battle of Actium (31 b.c.), at which Octavius Caesar defeated Marc Antony, is extravagant.

p.347 could on a sudden have become so base a liar: a glance at one of Trollope's favourite Latin tags: 'Nemo repente fuit turpissimus', Juvenal, *Satires* II.83 ('No one on a sudden becomes most base').

p.350 Monstrum horrendum, informe, ingens: – 'a monster dreadful, shapeless, immense', Virgil, *Aeneid* III.658.

p.357 a Gallio: presumably Lucius Annaeus Gallio, who as proconsul of Acaea c. A.D. 52, refused to consider the case brought by the Jews against St Paul, and who was written of with great affection by Seneca.

Epicuri de grege porca: 'a pig from Epicurus's sty', Horace, *Epistles* I.iv.16.

leading politician ... her own political friends: Disraeli, whose Reform Bill was regarded by many as a betrayal of Conservative principles.

p.358 the way down Avernus: see Virgil, : 'facile descensus Averni', 'the descent of Avernus [i.e. the way down to hell] is easy'.

casus belli: 'a ground for war' (Latin).

p.364 Colenso: see note to p.55.

Old Proudie, from Barchester: Trollope's most famous bishop, who occurs in five of the *Chronicles of Barsetshire*. His earlier doings at the Ecclesiastical Commission are mentioned in *Barchester Towers*.

Jeremy Taylor ... the second sermon on the Marriage Ring: this sermon by Jeremy Taylor (1613–67) was popular with those who wished to maintain the supremacy of the husband in marriage.

p.395 a castle in the Apennines: the typical setting for a late-eighteenth-century gothic novel, such as Ann Radcliffe's *The Mysteries of Udolpho* (1794) or *The Italian* (1797).

p.405 Blessed are the peace-makers, for they shall be called the children of God: Matthew 5:9.

p.406 as grass of the field ... to be cut down and cast into the oven: see Matthew 6:30.

p.410 a tinkling cymbal: 1 Corinthians 13:1: 'I am become as sounding brass, or a tinkling cymbal'.

p.412 take the goods the gods provide you: see note to p.326.

p.415 euphonism: the manuscript reads 'euphuism'. Whichever reading Trollope finally preferred, a mistake for 'euphemism' is clearly intended.

p.416 John S. Mill: as a Member of Parliament, the philosopher J. S. Mill (1806–73) proposed an unsuccessful amendment to the Reform Bill of 1867 to extend the franchise to women. His book *The Subjection of Women* came out in 1869, the same year as *He Knew He Was Right*.

p.417 one, the same, and indivisible: the phrase 'one and indivisible' appears in the proclamation of the unity of the French Republic in the Revolutionary period, and is often used thereafter to convey the national unity of a republic, as it is in the American oath of Allegiance, which postdates Trollope's novel.

p.425 In spite of what the Scripture says ... he may call his brother a fool: 'whosoever shall say to his brother ... Thou fool, shall be in danger of hell fire', Matthew 5:22.

p.450 What I have done, that I should not have done; – what left undone ... that I should have done: 'We have left undone those things which we ought to have done; And we have done these things which we ought not to have done; And there is no health in us.' A General Confession, from the Book of Common Prayer.

p.459 the New Road: now Euston Road.

p.470 peccavi: 'I have sinned' (Latin).

p.483 he met Colonel Osborne: a mistake, since it is reported in Chapter 62 that Sir Marmaduke 'had constantly seen his old friend Osborne'.

p.404 Lady Glencora ... Lord Cantrip: a major and a minor character in Trollope's *Phineas Finn* (1867–69), which overlapped *He Knew He Was Right* in serialisation.

p.493 Creusa ... Jason ... Medea: in Euripides's *Medea*, Creusa, daughter of Creon, king of Corinth, is betrothed to Jason, whom Medea loves. Medea's vengeance is to kill her with a poisoned costume which catches fire when worn.

p.502 for many months: a mistake, since they met a month previously, on Trevelyan's return from Italy.

p.507 Sinned ... as the woman did, – in the Scripture: the woman taken in adultery in John 8:3–11.

p.513 Othello's occupation is gone: *Othello* III.iii.361.

p.519 Alan-a-Dale: see 'Allen-a-Dale', in Scott's *Rokeby*:

> Allen-a-Dale to his wooing is come;
> The mother, she asked of his household and home:
> 'Though the castle of Richmond stand fair on the hill,
> My hall,' quoth bold Allen, 'shows gallanter still;
> 'Tis the blue vault of heaven . . .'

p.520 honest laborious men were not to be seen begging their bread in the streets: see Palm 37:25: 'I have been young, and now I am old; yet have I not seen the righteous forsaken, nor his seed begging bread.'

p.521 heard nothing about Mr Glascock: a mistake. Sir Marmaduke heard of this in Chapter 64.

p.529 the 'Jupiter': Trollope's usual name for *The Times*, which was often called 'The Thunderer'.

p.532 Lydia: in Sheridan's play, *The Rivals* (1775), Lydia Languish is convinced that the only true fulfilment of love must be an elopement with a half-pay officer.

p.541 calf ... a returned prodigal: see Luke 15:23.

p.552 Those whom the God chooses to destroy, he first maddens: from a fragment of Euripides, best known in a Latin version: 'Quos deus vult perdere, prius dementat'.

p.574 when our war was raging all around me: the Civil War of 1861–65.

p.578 Xantippe: Socrates's wife, who was reputed to be a shrew.

p.583 Esill: vinegar; see Hamlet V.i.270: 'Woo't drink up eisel, eat a crocodile?'

p.590 Forgiveness may be spoken with the tongue: I cannot identify the poem from which this quotation is taken, and which has also eluded previous editors.

p.592 in want of a wife: a glance at the opening sentence of one of Trollope's favourite novels, Austen's *Pride and Prejudice*: 'It is a truth universally acknowledged, that a single man in possession of a good fortune, must be in want of a wife.'

p.593 the Cascine: a park in Florence, named after the dairy-farms on which it was laid out.

p.599 as the poet says to the king in the ode: Dryden to Alexander the Great; see note p.326

p.601 Saturday Review . . . English women: the *Saturday Review*, a lively weekly devoted to High Church, conservative views, ran a series of anonymous articles on the woman question, including one by Mrs Eliza Lynn Linton entitled 'The Girl of the Period' (14 March 1868), which among other things reproached fashionable women for not breast-feeding their children. Wallachia Petrie would otherwise be violently opposed to the views expressed in the paper.

p.607 stick . . . as big as your thumb . . . would not believe: Wallachia Petrie is right, and Mr Glascock is telling the truth, albeit in jest.

p.617 perturbed spirit: see *Hamlet* I.v.182.

p.620 I turn unto them the left: 'whosoever shall smite thee on they right cheek, turn to him the other also;, Matthew 5:39.

p.621 prurient, yet passionless, cold-studied lewdness: I am unable to identify the source of this quotation, which has also eluded previous editors

p.637 Ricasoli: Trevelyan's wine was probably Chianti, a wine newly developed in the 1850s by Bettino Ricasoli, the second Prime Minister of Italy, on his estates near Florence.

make glad the heart of man: see Psalm 104.15.

p.638 drowned in it, as Clarence was: George, Duke of Clarence is supposed to have been drowned in a butt of Malmsey in 1488. The incident is best known from Shakespeare's *Richard III*.

p.641 seven times, or only six: see Daniel 3.19: 'Then was Nebuchadnezzar full of fury . . . and commanded that they should heat the furnace one seven times more than it was wont to be heated.'

p.645 the Alabama claims and the question of naturalisation: for the Alabama claims see note to p. 341. The 'question of naturalization' concerns the arrest in Ireland of a number of members of the revolutionary Fenian Brotherhood who were naturalized citizens of the United States of America. The issue was resolved in 1868 when Britain granted the same rights to naturalized as native-born Americans.

p.649 a two-pair back: a back room up two pair (i.e. flights) of stairs.

p.561 a great gulf: Luke 16:26: 'between us and you there is a great gulf fixed'.

p.670 a Lydia: see note to page 2.168.

p.683 a great master on the subject: Thackeray, whose *The Snobs of England* was published in *Punch* from 1846–47, and republished in one volume as *The Book of Snobs* in 1848.

p.687 What's the news . . . Who out: see *Lear* V.iii.14–15: 'Talk of court news . . . /Who loses and who wins; who's in, who's out'.

p.708 The gentleman in the song, who came out to woo his bride on a rainy night: this song has not been traced.

p.715 hang back a little in going out of a room: i.e. he was prepared to forgo the precedence which was due to his rank.

TROLLOPE AND HIS CRITICS

The *Spectator* consistently printed the best reviews of Trollope's fiction, and he in turn called its literary editor, Richard Holt Hutton, 'of all the critics of my work . . . the most observant, and generally the most eulogistic'.[1] The authorship of the present review is not listed in the paper's editorial files, but it more resembles the reviews known to be by the political editor, Meredith Townsend, than those of Hutton. The review is a good example of the way in which a critic's moral judgments distort what otherwise seems to be a most perceptive account of the fiction.

Mr Trollope has chosen here a more than usually painful subject, and worked it out with a less than usually even hand. There are strokes of great power in the book; the history of the unhinging of Mr Trevelyan's mind under the influence of vanity, jealousy, and suspense, and the sense of degradation involved in using low means to guard himself against deception is really one of great power, furnished with a common-place but a very striking moral. There has been little in our recent literature so good or so painful as the account of the ex-policeman, Bozzle, whom Mr Trevelyan uses as a spy upon his wife's movements, and of the influence gained by the man's coarse assumptions over his employer's mind. In this part of the story, too, Mr Trollope shows his usual strenuous moderation, if we may be allowed the paradox. He takes great care to show that though Bozzle is an object of disgust to us, he is so almost wholly through the degrading *circumstances* of his profession; that Bozzle himself is no worse, and possibly even a little better, than we have a right to expect from a man under such circumstances, and that it is, on the whole, possible for an ex-policeman and spy, with the vulgarest of natures and the meanest of trades, to be at least as little unworthy of individual respect as many of the less degraded characters through whose faults he gains his bread. It is characteristic of Mr Trollope that he should write a tale about a truly tragic jealousy which has never even a reasonably adequate cause, the object of which jealousy is a man near sixty, old enough to be the heroine's father, too hollow as well as too old to do the sort of mischief attributed to him, and yet in a faint and unreal way

<hr />

[1] *An Autobiography*, (Oxford: Oxford University Press, 1950), p. 205.

hankering after mischief of that sort, and effectually doing a vast deal more mischief that he had ever contemplated, though after another sort. There is real genius in the conception of breaking a husband's hear and ruining his mind on so meagre a basis of fact as this, – using as the materials a proud, hard, wilful woman, with no trace of even the superficial flirt in her, and an elderly man of no real power of fascination, but a certain vanity which makes him feel pleasure in the reputation of wickedness. It is not only life, as Mr Trollope so well knows it, but it is true tragedy to ground such a 'wreck', as poor Mr Trevelyan in the sullen moods which precede his death himself calls it, on the absurd foundation of an old gentleman's foppish vanity, a young lady's bitter wilfulness, and a self-occupied husband's angry, suspicious, and brooding sense of indignity.

. . . So far we have found no fault either with the art or the morality of Mr Trollope's story. Indeed, throughout the first volume (except perhaps in relation to Nora Rowley, who is uniformly vulgar and uninteresting), Mr Trollope impresses us with a power of conception he has rarely equalled in any of his novels, and gives us quite his highest style of execution. In the second volume, however, as it seems to us, the truth and power of the drawing, no less than the realistic morality of the tale, fail very rapidly. The picture of Mr Trevelyan's breaking mind and overweening vanity, so powerfully commenced in the first volume, is spun out to wearisome length, and quite without any fresh artistic touches until the end is close at hand. The comedy touching Cammy French, with which Mr Trollope seeks to lighten the story, becomes exaggerated and coarse. And worst of all, the conception with which, as we believe, Mr Trollope clearly set out, of Mrs Trevelyan, – the conception of a self-willed, haughty, steely woman, whose little feeling for her husband and easily wounded self-love were even more the cause of the whole tragedy than her husband's conceit and weakness, melts away into something which it is almost impossible to define, – for nothing can exceed her real hardness and self-occupation on her husband's death-bed, and yet it seems the novelist's main effort to make you regard her as a deeply injured woman, who has been infinitely more sinned against than sinning. We entirely decline to take this view, and even assert that Mr Trollope in commencing his tale did not take it himself. We are both astonished and displeased at the sympathy which the novelist asks for on behalf of Mrs Trevelyan as the tale draws to its close, since he has drawn throughout a cold, self-willed, high-tempered woman, who, though doubtless entirely free from any imputation of the kind for which she suffers, never shows, till the end of the tale, a particle of sympathy for her husband's sufferings, does do a vast deal wilfully to provoke him, and is portrayed, even during his last illness, as without a shadow of self-reproach for the obstinate heartlessness of her own conduct in the beginning of the troubles, and solely occupied with the absorbing desire to extract her own complete exculpation from her husband's dying lips. Mrs Trevelyan is naturally enough drawn, if we were never called upon to pity her, and were permitted to condemn her as she deserves. But when Mr Trollope tries to lead us into wasting compassion upon her, and yet makes her so unlovely as he does, – so utterly without remorse for conduct which seems to us far worse than her husband's, though not in the way imputed to her, – so concentred in self even in the most solemn moments, – we not only rebel against the attempt, but have a right to say that the art of the story is thereby spoiled.

> Anonymous review, *Spectator* 42
> (12 June 1869), 706–8

Trollope paid a great deal of attention to his reviews, and he may have been swayed in his judgment by the moral attacks of the press on *He Knew He Was Right*. This is certainly a case in which his capitulation to philistine criticism can shock the modern reader.

In November 1867, I began a very long novel, which I called *He Knew He Was Right*, and which was brought out by Mr Virtue, the proprietor of the *St Paul's Magazine*, in sixpenny numbers, every week. I do not know that in any literary effort I ever fell more completely short of my own intention than in this story. It was my purpose to create sympathy for the unfortunate man who, while endeavouring to do his duty to all around him, should be led constantly astray by his unwillingness to submit his own judgement to the opinion of others. The man is made to be unfortunate enough, and the evil which he does is apparent. So far I did not fail, but the sympathy has not been created yet. I look upon the story as being nearly altogether bad. It is in part redeemed by certain scenes in the house and vicinity of an old maid in Exeter. But a novel which in its main parts is bad cannot, in truth, be redeemed by the vitality of subordinate characters

Trollope, *An Autobiography*, 1883; reprinted from the Oxford Trollope, ed. F. Page and M. Sadleir, 1950, pp. 321–2

Henry James warmly appreciated some of Trollope's characteristics, but his standards for the judgment of novels are to a large extent responsible for the disrepute into which the work of many mid-Victorian novelists fell. His insistence on formal considerations which were foreign to the genre as they practised it, and his belief that narrative self-consciousness was always an evil, told hard against Trollope. This is an extract from James's generous obituary of his older contemporary.

He often achieved a conspicuous intensity of the tragical. The long, slow process of the conjugal wreck of Louis Trevelyan and his wife (in *He Knew He Was Right*), with that rather lumbering movement which is often characteristic of Trollope, arrives at last at an impressive completeness of misery. It is the history of an accidental rupture between two

stiff-necked and ungracious people – 'the little rift within the lute' –
which widens at last into a gulf of anguish. Touch is added to touch, one
small, stupid, fatal aggravation to another; and as we gaze into the
widening breach we wonder at the vulgar materials of which tragedy
sometimes composes itself. I have always remembered the chapter called
'Casalunga,' toward the close of *He Knew He Was Right*, as a powerful
picture of the insanity of stiffneckedness. Louis Trevelyan, separated
from his wife, alone, haggard, suspicious, unshaven, undressed, living in
a desolate villa on a hill-top near Siena and returning doggedly to his
fancied wrong, which he has nursed until it becomes an hallucination, is
a picture worthy of Balzac. Here and in several other places Trollope has
dared to be thoroughly logical; he has not sacrificed to conventional
optimism; he has not been afraid of a misery which should be too much
like life.

Henry James, from 'Anthony Trollope', *Century Magazine* ns 4 (July 1883), 385–95.

Cockshut's book is one of the first to take Trollope's fiction
seriously. The intensity of the gloom in some of Trollope's novels
formed a major part of the critic's claim for them, and the pattern
he detected of a 'darkening' vision neatly resembled the diagnosis
he had recently made of Dickens's work, which preceded Trollope's
into critical esteem.

Trevelyan himself, along with Josiah Crawley, is Trollope's most careful
psychological portrait. He has the solidity which a character possesses
when he is seen in the author's mind as a whole, but revealed to the
reader by a long series of details. The method of the mystery story has
been applied to psychology. He has the philosopher's stone of madness,
the power of transmuting all new facts into evidence for his fixed idea.
But the frightening thing about his crazy mental processes is their
ordinariness. His vanity is ordinary; he can be proud in the midst of his
grief of his skill in writing long, affectionate, argumentative, and exhaustive letters. His jealousy is largely the consequence of a normal, if
exaggerated, self-pity. Having once made an accusation, even if he did
not fully mean it, he has to create imaginary facts to justify himself. He
can feel justified in making terrible charges, without believing that they
are true; words are for him the current coin of prestige and injury rather
than indications of objects and events. This aberration also is an extension
of something normal. Most people in their anger say things they do not
mean, and thoughtlessly answer one insult with another. But instead of
ceasing to do this when anger and the argument end, Trevelyan continues
it in long tedious dialogues inside his own mind. And self-pity makes him
proud of his misery. 'But Trevelyan did not turn or move. There he stood
gazing at the pale, cloudless, heat-laden, motionless sky, thinking of his
own sorrows, and remembering, too, doubtless, with the vanity of a

madman, that he was probably being watched in his reverie.' Towards
the end, this mood is varied by a fantastic levity and carelessness.

A. O. J. Cockshut, *Anthony Trollope* (1955, reprinted Methuen, 1968), pp. 175–6.

In the nineteen-fifties it was still necessary to be grateful for book-
length studies of Trollope, but Booth is largely to be read nowadays
for examples of old-fashioned judgments.

Trollope did not always have courage enough to let his tragic situation
stand alone. In fear of unrelieved blackness he often introduced romantic
plots and amusing social tableaux into sombre stories. A good illustration
of this is what he did with *He Knew He Was Right* (1869), one of his
most powerful stories. The main plot, involving Louis Trevelyan, a
jealous husband tormented by delusions of his wife's unfaithfulness, is
powerful but bleak and harsh. Trollope therefore balances what he
thought unpleasant with what he was certain would be welcome – three
or four love stories. If the Trevelyans' marriage was breaking up, there
would at any rate be many others to take its place. Indeed, Trollope must
break into one of the last chapters with a harried little note describing
the difficulties in which he has enmeshed himself. . . . To keep characters
and plots straight from beginning to end is no mean feat of memory. But
Trollope has thought it necessary to call to his aid this spreading social
panorama for lightly satiric purposes, weighting on the side of amusement
a story whose atmosphere threatened to become too dark and wintry.

Bradford A. Booth, *Anthony Trollope. Aspects of His Life and Art*, 1958.

This book is one of the first to apply up-to-date views of the nature
of narrative to Trollope's fiction.

The far more successful *He Knew He Was Right* also plays off death and
marriages against one another at the end. Even though the death is
much more explicitly present here, as are the madness and torture
preceding it, the novel's attempted balance of comedy and irony tips as
far into comedy as *The Claverings* sank into irony. Of the five love stories
presented in the novel, the one between Trevelyan and Emily ends
tragically, that between Arabella French and the Revd Mr Gibson ends
in pretty grim irony, but the other three are much more than just
successful; they are triumphs of pure romance, ending in marriages that
combine wit, spirit, love, and property. It is as if three Elizabeths married
three Darcys. With Raskolnikov and Mrs Willy Loman thrown in, one
might justly add. it is not an easy novel to sort out. Even if one sees
Trevelyan's madness and Emily's distress as the major subjects of the
novel, however, there is no denying the strong comic pressure that builds
up against that tragedy.
  Such a notion of Trevelyan's centrality is perhaps more vulnerable than
it at first appears. It is accurate, in a sense, to think of the treatment of
Trevelyan as 'psychological', but we generally mean more by that term

than just the extraordinarily acute analysis of motive and conscience we receive from the narrator. Such commentary does not, in itself, distance us, but the relentless social context into which the commentary places Trevelyan makes us think of him more as a case, less as a presence. He is always seen as part of a larger group and never really allowed to be alone. He extends the limits of the comic world, but he cannot leave it. We never, I submit, feel him to be existing solely as a being without context as we do somethings in the presence of Raskolnikov or Heathcliff or dozens of characters in Dickens, beginning with Fagin and Bill Sikes . . . Trollope later said that the novel failed dismally to realize his intentions, which were 'to create sympathy for the unfortunate man'. Looking back over the story, he realizes the strength of the comic scenes but can find no sympathy for Trevelyan (*Autobiography*, pp. 321–2). Whatever Trollope's intentions may have been, it is difficult to read the novel now and see in the treatment of Trevelyan any failure. The novel is not, of course, a successful tragedy, but it seems never to make that attempt. Trevelyan, however important in the novel's action, stands finally as a signal of the fierce dangers in the world, but not of the world itself. He severely limits the extent and power of comedy without counteracting it. He plays out a prominent but only cautionary plot to a dominant comedy.

James Kincaid, *The novels of Anthony Trollope*, 1977, pp. 149–50.

Jane Nardin's *He Knew He Was Right: The Independent Woman in the Novels of Anthony Trollope* (1989) is the first full-length study of Trollope's treatment of women and feminist issues, a subject which is open to considerably more work before the ideologies produced by his fiction have been fully explored.

In the novels that followed *Framley Parsonage* (1860), Trollope began to explore the tragedies of Victorian women, stressing their helplessness in a society that denies them power, the difficulty of successful rebellion, and the irreconcilable demands with which they must deal. The first rebel whose rebellion brings about her tragic destruction is Lady Mason; the first heroine who fails to find happiness because the code of feminine behavior makes impossible demands upon her is Lily Dale – quickly followed by Julia Ongar. The stories of Lily and Julia do not end comically, but neither are they tragic, for both women achieve a measure of contentment. Building on the foundations laid in *Orley Farm*, *The Small House at Allington*, and *The Claverings*, Trollope's novels of the 1870s and 1880s turn with increasing earnestness to the tragedies of women. But before he could return to the woman's tragedy, Trollope had to undertake a related project: debunking the notion of the male tragic hero that *The Bertrams* (1859) took so seriously. *He Knew He Was Right* (1868–9) clears the ground for the feminist tragedies of the later novels by suggesting that in a society where power is largely reserved for the male, men may wilfully seek tragedy, but are far less likely than women to have it thrust upon them.[1]

In *He Knew He Was Right* dissatisfaction with woman's social position has become so prevalent that, as P. D. Edwards remarks, 'all the novel's heroines either share or sympathize with the feminine grievances that Emily Trevelyan voices.'[2] but none of these heroins is by any means a radical feminist like the minor comic character, Wallachia Petrie. The heroines are willing to be mastered by men, but they do insist on being mastered through argument. They will not permit themselves to be treated as chattels. Yet this is precisely the way Louis, with his slightly outdated definition of his 'power as a man' (Chapter 79) tries to control Emily. 'He was her master and she must know he was her master' (chapter 5). Louis' initial tragic error results from a pathetic desire, born of insecurity, to destroy the autonomy of the only human being he loves.

When Louis delivers an ultimatum to Emily, the narrator comments that he does it with an air that is 'comic with its assumed magnificence' (Chapter 69). His indignant anger is described as 'almost grotesque' (Chapter 86), and he is mocked for referring, as a bona fide tragic hero might almost do, 'to the affairs of the last two years as though they had been governed by an inexorable fate which had utterly destroyed his happiness without any fault on his part' (chapter 92). By the close of the story, Louis has been unmasked as something very different from the tragic hero he pompously pretends to be – for the novel, as Andrew Wright notes, invites its reader 'to measure the distance between cosmic tragedy and domestic obsession.' But *He Knew He Was Right* does not lack real tragedy. Emily has her faults, but unlike her husband, she did not freely choose the deprivations of love, liberty, and reputation she undergoes. During most of the novel, she can end the conflict with Louis only by confessing – falsely – that she is an adulteress. Ostensibly a man's tragedy, the novel is in fact the tragedy of a woman. For in Victorian England, as a minor character remarks, 'it's two to one the young 'ooman has the worst of it' (Chapter 32), and those are not good odds. *The Bertrams* suggests that a powerful man can easily become the tragic victim of a powerless woman: *He Knew He Was Right* argues the opposite.

---

[1] Among the critics who argue that Trollope does not take *He Knew He Was Right*'s putatively tragic protagonist, Louis Trevelyan, seriously are Garrett, *The Victorian Multiplot Novel*, pp. 203–16; Edwards, *Anthony Trollope*, p. 114; and Kincaid, *The Novels of Anthony Trollope*, p. 150.

[2] Edwards, *Anthony Trollope*, pp. 116–17.

SUGGESTED FURTHER READING

Most major works on Trollope contain treatments of *He Knew He Was Right*, and it features most prominently in Jane Nardin's *He Knew She Was Right: The Independent Woman in the Novels of Anthony Trollope* (Carbondale and Edwardsville, 1989). Examples of other general works on Trollope are Bradford A. Booth, *Anthony Trollope: Aspects of His Life and Art* (London, 1958), A. O. J. Cockshut, *Anthony Trollope* (London, 1955), P. D. Edwards, *Anthony Trollope: His Art and Scope* (St Lucia, Queensland, 1977), John Halperin, *Trollope and Politics: A Study of the Pallisers and Others* (London, 1977), Geoffrey Harvey, *The Art of Anthony Trollope* (London, 1980), Walter M. Kendrick, *The Novel-Machine: The Theory and Fiction of Anthony Trollope* (Baltimore, 1980), James R. Kincaid, *The Novels of Anthony Trollope* (Oxford, 1977), Coral Lansbury, *The Reasonable Man: Trollope's Legal Fiction* (Princeton, 1981), Robert M. Polhemus, *The Changing World of Anthony Trollope* (Berkeley and Los Angeles, 1968), Arthur Pollard, *Anthony Trollope* (London, 1978), Michael Sadleir, *Trollope: A Commentary* (London, 1927), L. P. and R. P. Stebbins, *The Trollopes: The Chronicle of a Writing Family* (London, 1946), R. C. Terry, *Anthony Trollope: The Artist in Hiding* (London 1977), Robert Tracy, *Trollope's Later Novels* (Berkeley Ca., 1978), and Stephen Wall, *Trollope and Character* (London, 1988).

Despite a number of serious bibliographical errors, Donald Smalley (ed.), *Anthony Trollope: The Critical Heritage* (London, 1969), contains a useful collected of Victorian Criticism of Trollope's fiction. Trollope's contemporary reception is analysed in David Skilton, *Anthony Trollope and His Contemporaries: A Study in the Theory and Conventions of Mid-Victorian Fiction* (London, 1972). An annotated bibliography of later criticism is found in J. C. Olmsted and J. E. Welsh, *The Reputation of Trollope: An Annotated Bibliography 1925–1975* (New York, 1978), and a fuller listing of Trollope editions as well as selected secondary works is found in *Anthony Trollope: A Collector's Catalogue 1847–1990* (London: the Trollope Society, 1992). The standard descriptive bibliography of Trollope's works in their original editions is Michael Sadleir, *Trollope: A Bibliography* (London, 1928).

The most scholarly biographies are N. John Hall, *Trollope: A Biography* (Oxford, 1991), and R. H. Super, *The Chronicler of Barsetshire: A Life of Anthony Trollope* (Ann Arbor, 1988), while Richard Mullen, *Anthony*

Trollope: A Victorian in His World (London, 1990), gives a more opinionated account. Victoria Glendinning's *Anthony Trollope* (London, 1992) is fascinating and exceptionally readable, and contains very plausible speculations about unknown aspects of the author's life, including his marriage. Trollope's letters are admirably collected in N. John Hall (ed.), *The Letters of Anthony Trollope* (Stanford, Ca., 1983). Also useful in the study of Trollope as a public and private figure is R. C. Terry (ed.), *Trollope: Interviews and Recollections* (London, 1987).

TEXT SUMMARY

---

1. Showing how wrath began
... over the conflicting reactions of Trevelyan and Emily to the visits of Colonel Osborne.

2. Colonel Osborne
Osborne asks Emily to keep from Trevelyan news of her father's likely invitation to appear before the Parliamentary Committee.

3. Lady Milborough's dinner party
Discovering Emily's 'secret', combined with Lady Milborough's warning against Osborne, prompts Trevelyan to forbid Emily from receiving the Colonel. She refuses.

4. Hugh Stanbury
.. is introduced. The chapter details his love for Nora, and how his choice of career has angered his aunt in Exeter.

5. Showing how the quarrel progressed
Despite feeling 'a duty to be gentle', Trevelyan restates his orders to his unrepentant wife, this time by letter.

6. Showing how reconciliation was made
Emily becomes over-zealous in obeying Trevelyan, deliberately snubbing Osborne in public. Trevelyan's suspicions have 'made it impossible for ... [her] to behave with propriety'.

7. Miss Jemima Stanbury of Exeter
A thumbnail sketch of provincial *mores* is followed by a description of the reactionary Miss Stanbury, and her decision to take in her niece Dorothy.

8. 'I know it will do'
Dorothy accedes to her aunt's request, leaving her mother and sister at Nuncombe Putney.

9. Showing how the quarrel progressed again
Emily entreats Stanbury to intercede between herself and Trevelyan. He does so, but Trevelyan refuses to listen.

10. Hard words
Emily asserts her right to receive whomever she pleases. Trevelyan will not back down: 'I will refuse nothing and promise nothing.' 'Then we must part.'

11. Lady Milborough as ambassador
At Trevelyan's request, Lady Milborough urges Emily to be submissive. Again she refuses, vowing also that she will never relinquish her child.

12. Miss Stanbury's generosity
Miss Stanbury refuses both to meet Mrs Stanbury and Priscilla, and to forgive Stanbury his choice of occupation.

13. The Honourable Mr Glascock
. . proposes to Nora. She declines, telling herself that she loves Stanbury.

14. The Clock House at Nuncombe Putney
Emily and Nora move to Devonshire, joining Mrs Stanbury and Priscilla, who have taken the Clock House for the purpose of receiving them.

15. What they said about it in the Close
Miss Stanbury's circle of acquaintance discusses the Trevelyan affair.

16. Dartmoor
While Nora equivocates over the respective virtues of Stanbury and Glascock, Priscilla tells Emily to swallow her pride and return to Trevelyan.

17. A gentleman comes to Nuncombe Putney
Glascock arrives at the Clock House and again proposes to Nora, who again (categorically, this time) refuses.

18. The Stanbury correspondence
A frosty exchange of letters between Miss Stanbury and Priscilla is due to the former's automatic assumption that the gentleman caller at the Clock House must be Osborne.

19. Bozzle, the ex-policeman
Having established, through the services of Bozzle, Osborne's presence at Nuncombe Putney, Trevelyan sends a reluctant Stanbury to investigate.

20. Showing how Colonel Osborne went to Cockchaffington
. . having received Emily's written consent to his proposed visit to Nuncombe Putney.

21. Showing how Colonel Osborne went to Nuncombe Putney
Osborne's visit now means Priscilla is forced 'to eat humble pie' and write back to her aunt, admitting that the Colonel has been received at the Clock House.

22. Showing how Miss Stanbury behaved to her two nieces
Priscilla's honesty earns her the grudging respect of her aunt. Meanwhile, the latter now intends Dorothy to marry Mr Gibson.

23. Colonel Osborne and Mr Bozzle return to London
Observed by Bozzle, Stanbury and Osborne argue at Exeter Station. The detective reports back to Trevelyan.

24. Niddon Park
Stanbury and Nora separately reflect on their love for one another.

25. Hugh Stanbury smokes his pipe
Nora and Priscilla air conflicting views on the status and capabilities of women.

26. 'A third party is so objectionable'
Stanbury fails to convince Trevelyan of Emily's innocence. The latter feels doubly justified in his suspicions when Bozzle informs him that Emily has again written to Osborne.

27. Mr Trevelyan's letter to his wife
.. informs her of his plan to live abroad, and that she must vacate the Clock House.

28. Great tribulation
Emily writes back to Trevelyan, acquiescing with his demands. The Stanburys cannot persuade her and Nora to stay.

29. Mr and Mrs Osborne
Emily and Nora relocate to the East End of London, to live with their aunt and uncle.

30. Dorothy makes up her mind
.. that she will not accept Gibson. Miss Stanbury prepares for the arrival of Brooke Burgess.

31. Mr Brooke Burgess
Burgess arrives, and becomes the toast of the Close. Miss Stanbury advises Dorothy to reconsider her feelings towards Gibson.

32. The 'Full Moon' at St Diddulph's.
A short time spent with his son just serves to inflame Trevelyan's obsession. He quarrels with Stanbury, and retreats abroad.

33. Hugh Stanbury smokes another pipe
.. and determines to declare his love to Nora. Bozzle, meanwhile, has been given 'a roving commission' from Trevelyan, and continues to sniff around St Diddulph's

34. Priscilla's wisdom
Miss Stanbury fails to see Dorothy's reasoning over Gibson. Priscilla, however, urges her sister to be true to her own feelings.

35. Mr Gibson's good fortune
The internal politics of the marriage market come into their own; Gibson is forced to deceive Arabella French about his designs on Dorothy.

36. Miss Stanbury's wrath
Dorothy refuses even to see Gibson. Despite her aunt's scolding, she remains resolute.

37. Mont Cenis
Trevelyan and Glascock encounter each other, and the Spalding sisters, as they travel across Europe.

38. Verdict of the jury – 'Mad, my lord'
For the first time, the narrative openly treats of Trevelyan's insanity; he is, 'in truth, mad on the subject of his wife's alleged infidelity.'

39. Miss Nora Rowley is maltreated
Stanbury at last proposes to Nora. She refuses him, but he is convinced that his love is reciprocated.

40. 'C.G.'
The Spalding Sisters flippantly discuss the possibility of Carrie's marrying Glascock.

41. Showing what took place at St Diddulph's
To Mr Outhouse's displeasure, osborne appears at the rectory, enquiring after Emily.

42. Miss Stanbury and Mr Gibson become two
Dorothy again refuses Gibson. Her aunt blames Gibson so roundly for this that the two quarrel fiercely.

43. Laburnum Cottage
Against Stanbury's wishes, his mother and Priscilla move into the 'beastly hole', Laburnum Cottage.

44. *Brooke Burgess takes leave of Exeter*
. . and bids farewell to all the Exeter circle. He has become quite 'intimate' with Dorothy.

45. *Trevelyan at Venice*
Trevelyan, spurred on by Bozzle's correspondence, is convinced that Emily is still receiving the Colonel. He becomes determined to gain custody of his son.

46. *The American minister*
Glascock dines with the Spaldings. The narrative dwells on the pretensions and confusions of Americans in Europe.

47. *About fishing, and navigation, and head-dresses*
As his feud with Miss Stanbury progresses, Gibson now finds himself having to circumnavigate the attentions of Arabella French.

48. *Mr Gibson is punished*
The Frenches discover Gibson has already made two offers of marriage to Dorothy. In atonement, he proposes to Camilla.

49. *Mr Brooke Burgess after supper*
. . confides to Hugh Stanbury that he means to marry Dorothy.

50. *Camilla triumphant*
. . in ensuring that Gibson is finally committed to marriage.

51. *Showing what happened during Miss Stanbury's illness*
Burgess proposes to Dorothy. Despite her awareness that she now loves him, she refuses.

52. *Mr Outhouse complains that it's hard*
Bozzle, armed with a letter of authorization from Trevelyan, attempts to take the child from St Diddulph's, but is repulsed by Outhouse.

53. *Hugh Stanbury is shown to be no conjuror*
An exchange of letters between Stanbury and Nora finally confirms their mutual love.

54. *Mr Gibson's threat*
Gibson attempts a reconciliation with Miss Stanbury. Accused of treachery by the Frenches, he vows he will abandon Camilla if such accusations persist.

55. *The Republican Browning*
Glascock is assailed on all sides by the republican fervour of Spalding and Miss Petrie, while he would rather be talking to Caroline.

56. Withered grass

Despite severe doubts as to mutual compatibility, Glascock tells Caroline he has 'set . . . [his] heart fast on marrying an American wife.' She responds ambiguously.

57. Dorothy's fate

Dorothy tells her aunt of Burgess's proposal. The latter's disapproval causes Dorothy both to refuse Burgess, and to return to Nuncombe Putney.

58. Dorothy at home

. . receives a further love-letter from Burgess, accompanied by hints from her aunt of dire consequences should the courtship proceed. Again Dorothy refuses her lover.

59. Mr Bozzle at home

. . is paid a surprise visit by Trevelyan, still determined to gain custody of his son. Mrs Bozzle advises her husband to drop the case.

60. Another struggle.

Trevelyan visits Emily at the rectory. Caught irredeemably in the grip of his obsession, it is clear that reconciliation between him and Emily is now impossible.

61. Parker's Hotel, Mowbray Street

The night of Sir Marmaduke's arrival in London coincides with the kidnapping of the Trevelyan child.

62. Lady Rowley makes an attempt

Meeting Emily's mother, Trevelyan tells her he is adamant that his wife 'must be crushed in spirit . . . before she can again become a pure and happy woman.'

63. Sir Marmaduke at home

The Rowleys are displeased to discover Nora's love for Stanbury.

64. Sir Marmaduke at his club

. . encounters Osborne, who manages to convince Rowley that his motives in visiting Emily, his 'godchild', were entirely innocent.

65. Mysterious agencies

Gibson postpones the wedding, as his thoughts turn once again to Arabella.

66. Of a quarter of lamb

Miss Stanbury feels 'an almost uncontrollable longing to have her niece back again.'

67. *River's Cottage*
Trevelyan is traced to Willesden. He will not relinquish the child.

68. *Major Magruder's committee*
. . grills Sir Marmaduke thoroughly. However, it is implied that his
humiliation will have absolutely no practical consequences.

69. *Sir Marmaduke at Willesden*
. . confronts Trevelyan. His anger dissolves before the man's wretchedness.

70. *Showing what Nora Rowley thought about carriages*
Her father's disapproval notwithstanding, Nora insists she will marry
Stanbury.

71. *Showing what Hugh Stanbury thought about the duty of man*
Stanbury fails to talk Sir Marmaduke round. He proposes to marry Nora
clandestinely, or at any rate, present her parents with a *fait accompli*.

72. *The delivery of the lamb*
Martha arrives at Nuncombe Putney to find Dorothy engaged to Burgess.
Dorothy prepares to confront her aunt with the news.

73. *Dorothy returns to Exeter*
Miss Stanbury is at last reconciled to the prospect of Dorothy's marrying
Burgess.

74. *The lioness aroused*
Planning to transfer his allegiance back to Arabella, Gibson finally summons
up enough courage to jilt Camilla.

75. *The Rowleys go over the Alps*
. . to Florence, in pursuit of Trevelyan, and with hopes of forcing Nora
back with Glascock.

76. *'We Shall Be So Poor'*
Caroline confesses to Nora that she and Glascock are engaged.

77. *The future Lady Peterborough*
Lady Rowley mistakenly assumes the 'republican virago with a red nose' to
be Glascock's intended.

78. *Casalunga*
Glascock and Sir Marmaduke track down Trevelyan to an isolated hill-top
farm.

79. *'I can sleep on the boards'*
Emily visits Trevelyan; he has surrendered to his obsession completely.

80. 'Will they despise them?'
. . asks Caroline of Glascock, convinced that the sociocultural differences between them have predestined the marriage to failure.

81. Mr Glascock is master
. . and finally quells Caroline's republican misgivings.

82. Mrs French's carving knife
Gibson wallows in fear and self-pity, as Camilla threatens violence if he marries Arabella, while Mrs French hints at recourse to the law if he doesn't.

83. Bella victrix
To facilitate Arabella's wedding, Camilla is forcibly exiled to Gloucester.

84. Self-sacrifice
Trevelyan, in his despair, concedes that his son must be restored to Emily.

85. The baths of Lucca
Glascock sets out to retrieve the child.

86. Mr Glascock as nurse
Glascock, managing to negotiate Trevelyan's unpredictability, is successful in his mission.

87. Mr Glascock's marriage completed
Glascock and Caroline are married. The Rowleys return to England.

88. Cropper and Burgess
The Stanbury-Burgess feud is drawn to a close, as Miss Stanbury surrenders property to Barty in return for his share of the bank devolving to his nephew.

89. 'I wouldn't do it, if I was you'
Arrangements for Dorothy's approaching wedding prompt Miss Stanbury to reflect on the existence she proposes for the newlyweds.

90. Lady Rowley conquered
Nora and Stanbury finally gain Lady Rowley's blessing.

91. Four o'clock in the morning
Stanbury travels to Siena, as a telegram from Emily indicates a worsening of Trevelyan's condition.

92. Trevelyan discourses on life
Stanbury tries to persuade his old friend to return to England.

93. 'Say that you forgive me'

Trevelyan agrees to journey back with Emily and Stanbury. Emily is moved to indulge her husband's insanity by begging his forgiveness for the first time.

94. A real Christian

Nora goes to stay with Lady Milborough.

95. Trevelyan back in England

.. and Emily is resigned to bearing her husband's deranged belief in her past 'infidelity'.

96. Monkhams

Nora stays with the new Lord and Lady Peterborough.

97. Mrs Brooke Burgess

Dorothy and Burgess are married.

98. Acquitted.

Trevelyan dies. In his last moments, he finally acknowledges his fundamental belief in Emily's innocence.

99. Conclusion

Nora and Stanbury are married, while Emily inherits Trevelyan's property, and settles down to a life of widowhood.

ACKNOWLEDGEMENTS

The publishers are grateful for permission to reproduce extracts from the following works in the *Trollope and His Critics* section of this volume:

Bradford A. Booth, *Anthony Trollope: Aspects of His Life and Art (???)*
A. O. J. Cockshut, *Anthony Trollope* (Methuen)
James R. Kincaid, *The Novels of Anthony Trollope (???)*
Jane Nardin, *He Knew He Was Right: The Independent Woman in the Novels of Anthony Trollope* (Southern Illinois University Press, Carbondale and Edwardsville)